Tallyho – T[
Beauty, Truth and Goodness

Nine Dialogues by Plato:

Phaedrus, Lysis, Protagoras, Charmides, Parmenides, Gorgias, Theaetetus, Meno & Sophist

*A translation from F.D.E. Schleiermacher's
German translation of Plato
with an Introduction and Defense of Schleiermacher*

Zugleich eine Einführung in die Hermeneutik überhaupt

Phillip Lundberg

© Copyright 2005, by Phillip Lundberg,
All Rights Reserved.

No part of this book may be reproduced, stored in a retrieval system, or transmitted by any means - electronic, mechanical or photocopying, recording or otherwise, without written permission from the author, except in the case of brief quotations embodied in articles, books or reviews.

First published by AuthorHouse 03/09/05

ISBN: 1-4184-4976-8 (sc)
ISBN: 1-4184-4977-6 (dj)

Library of Congress Control Number: 2003099152

Printed in the United States of America
Bloomington, Indiana

This book is printed on acid free paper.

authorHOUSE™
1663 LIBERTY DRIVE, SUITE 200
BLOOMINGTON, INDIANA 47403
(800) 839-8640
WWW.AUTHORHOUSE.COM

Socr: The double love that you hedge within your soul, o Callicles, to the Athenians and to your beloved, stands in my way; but perhaps if we take this into consideration more often and if we manage to speak better, you shall become convinced. Thus, do remember we said that there would be two methods in the handling of each, the body and the soul, the first of which proceeds according to what is most pleasurable, but the other with a vision as to what is best and not merely pleasing, rather handling with steadfast determination. Was it not this by which we separated the one from the other?

Calli: Quite.

Socr: And the one that is only concerned with what is pleasurable, this was ignoble and essentially nothing other than sycophancy. Isn't it true?

Calli: So be it, however you want.

Socr: But the other, if we seek with all of our powers to do the best with what we touch and handle, be it now body or soul?

Calli: So it was.

Socr: Should we, then, make bold in our handling of the city and the citizens in order to make them better so much as is possible? For without this, as we found out earlier, it would be useless to bestow any other beneficial deeds – if the mindset of these is not directed to what is good and beauteous, neither for those who should succeed to great holdings in property, nor for those gaining lordship over others, or to any other capability whatsoever. Do we say that this is how it correlates?

Gorgias 513d–514a

Acknowledgements:

I would like to express my gratitude to Dr. Wolfgang Virmond at the Schleiermacher Institute in Berlin for his assistance in finding a copy of the now out-of-print *Akademie-Verlag* edition of Schleiermacher's *PLATON Werke* which was used for making this translation, as well as – and most especially – for his many helpful comments along the way.

Special thanks to my cousin, Dr. Lucy Kunz – for her willingness to proofread this book; she has corrected many errors and enhanced its readability considerably.

Finally, I should like to thank the people at 1st Books (now AuthorHouse) who have made *this* book a reality.

****   ****

Cover Artwork: *Beatrice Addressing Dante from the Carriage*
                William Blake Watercolour – Tate Gallery, London

- - - - - - -   - - - - - -

Questions and feedback regarding this book may be 'e-mailed' to:

philliplundberg@earthlink.net

Table of Contents:

I. General

It is not enough that one comes up with what one would like to assert as being a better translation into English of several of Plato's underpinning dialogues, rather one also must explain to the audience both why this was necessary and how it has been accomplished. Despite the added difficulty of this it is, nonetheless, a very understandable obligation – for then, admittedly, this truly is a most unusual undertaking: to be working on Greek texts from German sources. The truth of the matter, though, if I might be so brazen as to come right out and put it on the table, is that whether Plato be read in Greek, German, English or, whatever language, such details should really be quite irrelevant. For what is at issue is truly understanding the text that one has under one's purview and understanding – *don't you know* – is itself a universal, may I say, God given endowment, and one that is distributed amongst all of humanity without any regard to linguistic affiliation. All the same, on the other hand, with a translation of any text whatsoever it is apparent that the reader can only read what the translator himself has properly understood and, hence, been enabled to carry over – so that any and every translation is naturally burdened by the viewpoint of the individual who has accomplished this generally undervalued task, the task of translation. Now, in that Plato wrote his dialogues such a very long time ago, even in Greece there are no longer any people today who have a natural understanding of his language. Consider the problems faced by English speakers trying, say, to read Chaucer, texts that are a mere 700 years old! Now, a double translation would, seemingly, be doubly burdened. Still, some translations really are better than others, and there doesn't exist any doubt whatsoever that Schleiermacher's German translation of Plato has superbly stood the test of time and is generally recognized as being, if not the best, at least a very strong contender for this appellation. One also needs to seriously consider that the distance needing to be bridged was for me – in that, one could say: "I cheated" – much, much less. That is, the distance between Schleiermacher's early 19th century German and my idiosyncratic American-English. This shortcut made my work a great deal less difficult than would have been the case were I to be a Greek scholar attempting to grapple with Ancient Greek, although it also admittedly places a great deal of trust in Schleiermacher. Thus, if one stipulates that Schleiermacher was an exceptionally talented scholar, and I might add, a very exceptional human being, and that he was able to work through to an understanding of Plato in a deeper sense and, thus, also delivered a much better translation than one generally finds (at least in English), so then it is, I think, at least conceivable that pursuing a better translation of Plato into English is possible via this seemingly oblique route. An analogy will, perhaps, be helpful in clarifying this. Plato's philosophy may well be compared to gold that is buried deep in the fundament of mankind's history – that period of time in our evolution when history and thinking were *themselves* coming into being from out of the mythic era of human existence. (That not only our species has evolved, but that human consciousness itself is and has been evolving: this is a thought that places the idea of philosophy itself in a grander context, and likewise challenges us in the deepest manner, not to mention the relevance of this for our "God given endowments" mentioned just previously. Dare I call attention to *Isocrates*, Socrates' friend, who is mentioned very briefly at the end of Plato's dialogue, *Phaedrus*.) Scholars of Ancient Greek are like miners who labor very deep beneath the surface and attempt to bring the text, Plato's gold, up into the light of our modern times: not an easy task. Schleiermacher excelled in this work and his nuggets have a certain gleam[1] – my experience of which having led me to the making of this translation. Carrying these golden nuggets over from early nineteenth century German into English is, per my analogy, comparable to Christopher Columbus sailing West to go East, a possible shortcut that can only be proved by making the voyage. And so, the question must be left to the unbiased reader: Does the gleam of the sun delivered from these smuggled nuggets, does it bespeak your sensibilities better than other renditions?

Leaving what might be termed a merely formal issue behind us now and speaking of more material concerns – which, indeed, are of equal if not, perhaps, of even greater importance: the dialogues under discussion, particularly the *Parmenides* though also *Protagoras*, are rather too dialectical and seemingly laced with contradiction, not to mention obscurity (and/or downright nonsense) and this itself has been a major barrier and, indeed, not only to the understanding of the general public but likewise to the understanding of the experts. In this regard, too, it is my contention that the English reading public

---

[1] Not simply my opinion – "Im besonderen sei noch hingewiesen auf Fr. Schleiermachers Platonübersetzung die in gewissen Feinheiten unübertroffen ist." – Walther Kranz, *Die Griechische Philosophie* p. 334; Verlag Schibli-Doppler, Birsfelden-Basel, 1955; or –
Allan Bloom regarding his sources: "Schleiermacher's old German version was the most useful translation I found. Although his text [Greek sources] was inferior to ours, he seems to have had the best grasp of the character and meaning of the dialogues." *The Republic of Plato, Second Edition*; p. xxiii; Basic Books, 1968, 1991.

has been worse off than the German public and this should, in part, be understood in terms of the philosophic traditions at the turn into the nineteenth century, the time when it was no longer simply taken for granted that all truly well-educated people attempting to read Plato simply would know Greek. Just as Plato's masterpieces were produced at the end of a golden age that Plato shared with, amongst many others, the great dramatists Aeschylus, Sophocles and Euripides, so too Schleiermacher worked during a time of great spiritual ferment when Beethoven, Goethe, Victor Hugo and many other great men crossed onto the stage of human history. Whereas the German idealist philosophers – Fichte, Schelling and Hegel – were thriving at this time in Germany, it was quite a different story on the other side of the English Channel. Not long after Schleiermacher's death in 1834 the positivistic and rather materialistic world conception also took hold in Germany; but during the time that Schleiermacher did his translation this was not the case. Hence, even though, indeed, understanding is an universal endowment, history obviously plays a considerable role in predisposing one nation's peoples toward appreciating and harmonizing with what may be called an orientation toward the mind and spirit, that is, toward the enlightenment of philosophy so impassionedly championed by Plato. My own understanding of philosophy is one that, admittedly, has been substantially rooted in German Idealism – and it may be significant that my initial idea was to translate just the *Parmenides* along with Hegel's *Lectures on the Proofs of the Existence of God*; that, in short, I take the unity of thinking and being – both as grounded in soul and spirit – as a most serious matter. Fortunately or unfortunately, I jumped into *Gorgias* after the *Parmenides* and have, thus, been led from one Platonic dialogue always on to another. Thus, from multifarious reasons there may be some rhyme to my reasoning of challenging English translations from the Greek with my own from Schleiermacher's German, although my initial intent was much broader – albeit, I still think, in amazing conformity to what has come to be, for I do maintain with Hegel and Plato that all knowledge and, indeed, all of *Life*, essentially, should be bound together into one unified whole.

I also shall willingly admit, thirdly, that my translation work is a kind of personal therapy, although I don't think that this, necessarily, is so bad and would be something needing to be denied. That rather the aloof and hands-off professional manner that is so widespread today may be a mark of sophistry and nihilism that is quite incapable of relating to the text to the fullest extent possible. Let us not forget:

the experts tend to get paid for their teaching and are judged, promoted and tenured according to the perceptions of the academic market. As Socrates points out to Protagoras, engaging in dialogue is exposing oneself[2] – and in rising degrees dependent upon whether the dialogue is with oneself, with one's friends and collaborators, or with the general public.   However, one mustn't take oneself too seriously and I'd simply say that I felt a closer kinship to the style of prose and continuity of expression that I experienced in reading Schleiermacher's German over the various English renditions and, hence, set out on a more personal journey: whether Schleiermacher's insights might find an echo on this side of the Atlantic – and, then, matters progressed to what I think may be a fine introductory text for any individual wanting to gain in appreciation for Plato as seen through the eyes of an "idealist."

In any event, it is not my opinions that ultimately are to have any relevance, rather, as already stated, only the opinions of those who shall do me the favor of reading this 're-translation,' and I provide such readers with these thoughts and this introduction only because such is expected; nay, not just expected – but, indeed, required of me. All the same, in the final analysis things are pretty much as Schleiermacher contended in his own introduction/ *Vorerinnerung: "... als Übersetzer, der schlechthin für sein Bedürfnis Rat schaffen muß,"* that is – as a translator who invariably has to make his own way in creatively meeting the requirements, just as he perceives them. The purpose of this book is *not* to criticize anyone, rather that Plato be made more accessible for a wider audience; and I am happiest with those readers who, straight-away, are ready to turn to page 7 and "give it a go" without any pre-conditions or warming up exercises. Still, I have to do my best to indicate the "whence and whither" of this book for those who expect more – or, then too, for those who have already finished reading this, my Germanic Plato, from *Phaedrus* through *Sophist*, at least once.

In accord with my take on philosophy, the first matter that I would place before the reader is what I believe to be fundamental for truly understanding any philosophic text, which, to put it quite succinctly, is this: that one dwells within the wellspring of philosophy, giving oneself over to thought itself.   In connection to this it may prove fruitful to reflect upon the phrase: "beauty, truth and goodness" – a

---

[2] "Come here, Protagoras! Uncover yourself" – *Protagoras* 352ab (p. 156); or, likewise: *Phaedrus* 243b (p. 28) and *Theaetetus* 162b (p. 387) and *Sophist* 217e (p. 511).

phrase that, in various ways, recurs quite frequently in Plato's texts. Underlying this threesome is one most vital ingredient that is quite distinctly a human element – that, inDEED, which *makes us* human: the ego, the locus of thinking and of the being of our selves. Human beings, to the extent that we are most authentically human, are concerned with beauty, with truth, and with goodness. It may be worth noting that the Latin "homo sapiens" points to the oneness (*homo*) as well as to the truth (*sapiens* – wise) – that, in short, Greek and Latin are actually richer languages than are our modern, 'more developed' languages. That Plato seems to be quite difficult for us to comprehend, this is also due to the general unwillingness of modern consciousness[3] to face up to itself and to think seriously about thinking, or (excuse the redundancy) about beauty, truth and goodness. I would maintain that whether or not one knows Greek, it is *much* more important that whenever one reads any particular passage that one be able to stop and, so, be properly focused and, thus, attain a real understanding of that which underlies what is written on the page: that one relate in an inward manner and take on the text as – personal challenge. It is an essential part of Plato's artistry that he quite often puts things in such a way that the reader is challenged in the deepest sense, not only to dot the i's and cross the t's, but to read *through* the text to its underlying meaning, a meaning that often enough may be precisely the opposite to what seems, literally, to be said. An excellent example of this is the unspoken message[4] contained at the end of the *Meno* – that when one reads the *Meno* (or any other Platonic dialogue) properly one sees through a good deal of nonsense to the sense which is there, awaiting those who have gained the right perspective. This inner connection of "sense and nonsense" is remarked on in *Phaedrus {270a}* as, indeed, is this requirement for looking within: *Man, know thyself! {230a}* with which this paragraph begins. Such, I believe, is intrinsic to Plato's intent and to his message – that, namely, the human capacities and potentialities can only be developed by the reader's own efforts of will, that knowledge of "the Good" is itself good and, as such, cannot be taught by indoctrination or rote perusal of any text but is only possible of being learned by those who are most diligent in seeking and internalizing that which is put before them in such a puzzling way; and, in short, that he only might obliquely point out the way of self-discovery but that every individual must tread the path on his

[3] For greater depth on this issue of "modern consciousness," see: Owen Barfield's *Saving the Appearances, A Study in Idolatry*, Wesleyan University Press, 1965, 1988.
[4] Which I shall discuss later, at the end of the third section of this introduction.

own. In relation to the state of learning as it exists in our own time, I might remark that this path of meditation upon a hidden meaning is entirely contrary to the general approach – that one's training in whatever field is generally taken as being supplied to one from *without* and, so, the idea of reading and re-reading a text multiple times is not generally advanced in most academies; that, indeed, "they" seem to want that one should read a great deal and supply a bibliography of pages and pages, but not that you should ever think that just a small bit of the most precious insight is priceless. For it is one thing to conquer and appear to control the world around one, that one's seeming success in doing this then precludes any deeper questioning; it is another thing just to let all things be and to focus oneself on the meaning of meaning, or upon the meaning of beauty, truth and goodness.

Beauty is a word that expresses the fact that there exists in the world around us much that is grounded in something divine, spiritual or beyond: whatever it may be that really enthuses, animates and gives fulfillment to our existence. To take the biggest image, when one looks up into a clear night sky and sees the heavens above one – I believe the awe thus engendered is a common experience – this is a sight that has immense beauty. And a beauty that is in no way contradicted or confounded by the scientific fact, as I learned at the Rose Center for Space in NYC, that we view with the naked eye only a small portion (<10%) of our own galaxy, the Milky Way. The beauty of man's knowledge of astronomy and of all of the other sciences is also undeniably something worthy of marvel. But, nonetheless, the experience of beauty per se, be it in the night sky or in a flower, a nest of bees – or even in a work of poetry or free verse – all of these things are given to us (provided we manage to cast our gaze in the appropriate direction) and the first three examples underlie what has come down to us in philosophic parlance as the cosmological argument. That *"the all"* displays in manifold ways a mesmerizing majesty that man need not understand in order to appreciate, this is captured in the one word, beauty. Indeed, the experience of beauty is something that is, as it were, a health inducing requirement of the human soul. That many appear as blind to this requirement is a bad sign of the times. Beauty is ready and waiting for those who are desirous of it, be it in a primal form as mother nature, or in art, music and literature, pursuits upon which countless numbers of people expend their lives without worrying at all as to the meaning of their endeavors – except, of course, to the extent that we are all philosophers; the reward is provided in the experience of beauty itself – "Art for art's sake" – as this idea is unequivocally expressed today.

Truth is a concept that, most obviously, is central not only to philosophy but also to all human knowledge and, indeed, any human aspiration. Who would want anything at all if one understood that what was desired was fake, phony and a lie? Nobody in his or her right mind. And yet there is to this very day (June 2nd, 2001) no clear and undisputed knowledge regarding what truth itself is! That is to say, unless one not only has read but that one also has worked through to some comprehension, be it of Plato or of any other philosopher who is worthy of the name. This is due to the fact that no matter how many times and how many philosophers and enlightened persons have pointed out what and where the source of truth is, every person who is to know the truth regarding truth has to experience this truth in him or herself. Truth, being a spiritual reality, is an experience of the ego, a truth that is manifestly evident, for example, in Socrates' many admonitions to Callicles in Plato's dialogue, *Gorgias*. This is no minor accomplishment in the history of philosophy, that Plato has clearly and unequivocally professed his allegiance to this thought of pure ego, thinking all alone being sufficient unto itself. Indeed, this is the very fundament of philosophy as understood by Plato – and philosophy is fundamental to living in the fullest sense. But, even yet, I can still make out the groans of the vast majority, those who, above all things, don't want to venture down this road of solipsism. This is a battle regarding the *desire* for where truth would have to be sought after, for the very idea of truth is experienced by very many people as being practically nauseating for, indeed, as Plato himself says: "it goes against the grain." {*Gorgias* – *513c*} People insist that all truth should be objective, or, as we rejoice in saying nowadays: scientific; and that it certainly should never be a subjective or – heavens forbid! – an esoteric or supersensible matter. And in their insisting upon this it is they themselves who are being utterly subjective and contradicting the matter itself. Truth exists within the human being's ego experience and nowhere else, or, I should say: everywhere else only insofar as it has radiated out from this spiritual point to encompass '*the all*' (of which Plato speaks). E.g.: does the earth revolve around the sun? – or vice-versa?: this is a pointed question that may help to illustrate my point. This truth, that truth is grounded within, this points toward man's essential relationship to spirit. For when fully experiencing this truth within, man rises above the subjective /objective *antithesis* (assuming one has progressed through the hard work) and this, in turn, is one way in which one may be led into dialectics, another of the most fundamental keys to an enlightened understanding, be it of Plato, of Schleiermacher, or of Hegel: three great beacons of idealism (read humanism) in humanity's past.

I make no bones about the circumstance that whereas I fully support Schleiermacher's contention that Plato's *Phaedrus* must be viewed as *the foundation text* for working through to a firm understanding of Plato's philosophy – of which a most essential component is an appreciation of dialectics – it is the *Parmenides* that is most crucial for approaching the core of Plato's idealism: an exercise in pure thinking that, in itself, is the only proof possible of man's inter-relatedness to and with the divine *Logos*.   What is *the one* to which so many contradicting assertions are predicated? – and what is *other* than the one? Is God the one and are we other? Is the one spirit and are the others matter? Is pure thought an absurd impossibility, that rather all thinking is somehow merely grounded in language? (where the accent falls hard on "merely") – a thought that is so tempting to the current age. I certainly do not want to give a simple answer to these dilemmas of thought but wish simply to point out that dwelling within this vast sea of quandaries is paramount for the ego's initiation into philosophy, and that this is true despite most people's common belief that such questions are totally worthless and, as Callicles states in *Gorgias*: fine issues for adolescents to discuss but an unwarranted and ridiculous waste of a *real man's* time. Plato's dialogues are guaranteed of immortality because he deals head-on with the very capacities of what I would now term the intellectual soul. The characters of Platonic dialogues are living representations of attitudes and soul types that point toward man's inner development. And, on the other side, the thoughts that are presented and elucidated in these dialogues may become living thoughts which, then, may *take wing* – and that they then have the power to unfold man's latent potentialities and capacities for spiritual growth that, particularly for our current age, need to be rooted in clear conceptual thinking. That, moreover, such an orientation toward philosophy and toward humanism is the burning issue that will point mankind in the right way in our times of decadence – if I might be allowed to pull a word from Jacques Barzun's tome of our times, *From Dawn to Decadence*.[5] If one is truthful to one's own thinking then there is no getting around the vast difficulties that await one in the admittedly slippery domain

---

[5] *From Dawn to Decadence 1500 To The Present 500 Years of Western Cultural Life*, Jacques Barzun, HarperCollins*Publishers*, 2000.

of pure thought. Whereas beauty is given to man from many sides, truth is a product of man's own will-imbued thinking that has stepped back from its natural relatedness to the world and – in this barren realm – has been man enough to dare to begin work on the difficult and downright arduous tasks brought about through the soul's honest admission of its state of need. (I may note, parenthetically, that the issue of manliness as well as the constant attention that, seemingly, is bestowed upon adolescent boys, these themselves are symbols for the ego's attention upon the soul; at least this is my reading of this, see, e.g. – *Phaedrus 234d* or *Sophist 227a–230b*.)

My understanding of Plato may appear to run somewhat contrary to the general viewpoint one often finds as is exemplified in what I'd warrant as being Plato's most quoted phrase, namely, Socrates' avowal that: "The only thing that he knows is that he knows nothing." If one took this on face value as also applying to Plato then one could simply ignore all of Plato's writings. The truth of the quote, however, becomes more and more apparent as one experiences the inward art of pursuing a higher standpoint of truth, that this is a quest of self-authentication and a grappling with the void. I would say that far too much has been made of this quote from the *Apology* (a dialogue that Schleiermacher places in an appendix as not being an actual part of Plato's philosophy, that rather it is a remarkably accurate historical testimony: Plato's recollection of Socrates' actual speech!) and far too little to contrary statements as, e.g. – in *Theaetetus, 145d:*

"*Socr:* So tell me, then: have you learned something of geometry from Theodorus?
Theae: Oh, sure.
Socr: And also regarding astronomy and 'harmonics' and mathematics?
Theae: At least, I've been making efforts to do so.
Socr: I too, o youth, have been taking pains to learn from this teacher and from others as well – those in whom I have trust that they have some understanding. But, all the same, despite that for the rest I'm quite up in my knowledge regarding these things, still, I have doubts regarding a small matter regarding which I'd like to investigate together with you and these others."

The philosopher isn't at all cut off from interest in and knowledge of those matters that are generally spoken of as knowledge, but his focus has changed from all of these different sciences to what Socrates calls "a small matter." This small matter is, of course, a matter the knowing of which is of the utmost relevance and, as I would like to assert, one that is as crucial for mankind living in the 21st century as it was for the generations of people who have come before us, many of whom, I would like to think, understood Plato as well if not, in certain essential aspects, better than the greater portion of our modern scholars. The crucial moment of the *negation* in the dialectical explication of being, this itself is, I think, what challenges man in the deepest sense. Parmenides instructs the novice Socrates that he not only has to postulate being, but likewise non-being,[6] if he wishes to know truth in its fullest sense. It is, certainly, very natural that the reader may desire to be informed about being; but very few are those who have the inclination to follow the ways of non-being: how, for instance, false notions come to be – or, in a more existential domain, what are we to say about death? Yet, if Plato is to be believed, then it's only through this, the most arduous exercises in mental gymnastics and a life that is lived in full consciousness of death, only so is it that man's understanding is going to be led from out of the shadows of opinion and political expediency into the bright sunshine of authentic knowing and an initiation into the deeper mysteries that lurk behind human existence.

The final member of the threesome: "the Good," this word, in that I'm only seeking a quick overview of the threesome, can be pointed to as the transcendent unity of beauty and truth. It should already be quite apparent from the above that my understanding of Plato and the importance that I place on his works is one that seriously contends that man has a relation through spirit to the divine. Man's relatedness to God has become one that *must* include knowing – and, of course, historically philosophy has (until very recently) very much bordered upon theology. Now that, as Nietzsche most aptly pointed out, "God is dead,"[7] philosophy too seems to have become a rather dry and moribund anachronism. But if the liberal arts become revitalized as the shallowness of the scientific/technological paradigm proves untenable – having no true understanding of morality, or of history, or particularly of itself for that matter – so too may the *divine word* as humanity's deep-seated rootedness in its heritage may become an ever more respected matter. Schleiermacher was imbued with strong Christian faith, as were all of the German idealist philosophers, e.g. – from Fr. Schelling's *Philosophy of Revelation*:

---

[6] *Parmenides* 136a (p. 218).
[7] *Also Sprach Zarathustra* – Zarathustra's Prologue – section 2.

"... mein Standpunkt ist überhaupt das Christenthum in der Totalität seiner geschichtlichen Entwicklungen, mein Ziel jene erst wahrhaft *allgemeine* Kirche (wenn Kirche hier noch das rechte Wort ist), die allein im Geist zu erbauen ist, und nur im vollkommenen *Verständnis* des Christenthums, seiner wirklichen Verschmelzung mit der allgemeinen Wissenschaft und Erkenntnis bestehen kann." [8]

"... I have oriented myself from the absolute perspective that encompasses Christianity in the entirety of its historical evolution; my goal being the truly *Universal Church* – if, indeed, "Church" is still the right word to use in such a context – which may only be constructed upon a spiritual basis, and only then when one's understanding of Christianity has become consummate, having been fully integrated within the entirety of human knowledge within which alone it is able to stand erect in a manner truly appropriate."

(Transl. mine)

Thus, it should come as no great surprise that goodness and God are intertwined and that our efforts in understanding Plato aright are, as it were, an initiation into truths that point toward unity with a transcendent purpose, a unity, need I add, that includes all of philosophy, all religions, and – as Plato makes evident in his inspiring digression to Theodorus in *Theaetetus {175a}* – all of mankind. In this short introduction I do not at all wish to go into how one is to understand the word transcendent, or the *word* "God"; suffice it to say that one shouldn't totally misunderstand these words by pretending that one understands them straight-away. Nor too, on the other hand, should one allow oneself to become scared off by the very idea of reflecting upon these words. Such timidity, though quite common, is ultimately an insult to one's own self and authentic well-being, not to mention again the terrible dangers of imagining oneself and one's age as being somehow far superior to one's neglected heritage! In relation to this timidity in respect to divine matters, consider Socrates' mock defense of Protagoras in *Theaetetus {162d}*:

"You all are really outstanding, children and old men alike, that you sit here together and lead one another about and are beguiled and ensnared by these speeches in that you bring the gods into matters from which I entirely exclude them, both in my speech and my writings – *whether they are or are not* – and all of the rest of it

---

[8] p. 110 – *Schelling Künder Einer Neuen Epoche des Chistentums, – 37. Vorlesung;* Robert Goebel, Urachhaus.

which, indeed, would make such an impression upon the great multitudes if they should hear it; and so on matters like these you converse as if it would be something so utterly horrendous if each and every person wouldn't be any better off in respect to wisdom than any animal. Proofs, however, and the rules and necessity of logic, of these there isn't even a single solitary example!"

II. Schleiermacher's Ordering of the Dialogues

As may be apparent in the above remarks, my take on Plato is one that combines intellectual curiosity with existential and moral implications. I have been very much drawn to Schleiermacher's translation as, for me, Plato best *comes to life* through his re-creation of these masterworks. Schleiermacher's stature is beyond doubt: as *the translator* of Plato into German, and as a major theologian and, not to be overlooked, as the father of hermeneutics: the philosophical science of understanding, named after *Hermes*, the messenger of Zeus. The reader should be aware that Schleiermacher was acclaimed in his time as someone who finally had succeeded in explaining the ordering of Plato's works. Indeed, this latter fame was taken away later as others stepped up to prove that *Phaedrus* belonged to the late period of Plato's writings. It is, I think, quite incumbent upon us that we take a good look at what this "proving" is really all about. To begin with I shall admit, again, that I only have an opinion to offer and that, certainly, I am no Greek scholar. All the same, Schleiermacher's Greek seems to have been adequate for his undertaking; and he is a person whose stature would only be doubted by those who have neglected to study his writings and his influence; plus he translated almost the entire corpus of Plato's dialogues – hence, what I say is said in defense of Schleiermacher's findings, findings that were at one time universally accepted, and with great applause. Basically my position is one of marvelling how odd all of this really is! The modern ordering is one that very proudly announces itself as being based primarily upon "philological" considerations of the Greek text. Not the meaning contained in the dialogues, but the external use of language: which words occur how often, the avoidance of hiatus (vowels both ending one word and beginning the next), sentence rhythm – a myriad of external clues all tabulated together, perhaps even using computers. This is anathema to Schleiermacher's fundamental principle that the ordering must be interwoven intrinsically within the development of the philosophic content that is to be found in the dialogues. The original editions of Plato's texts translated by Schleiermacher came with introductions[9] by Schleiermacher to each of these dialogues, as well as notes within the translation.   How odd it is and, at least as I see it, what a lamentable disservice to Schleiermacher, that when one buys Plato in Germany today one is given a book[10] which states: "Nach der Übersetzung von Friedrich Schleiermacher," and yet, if one is diligent and studies the fine print a little further one also reads: "nicht dem Buchstaben Schleiermachers" – that is: "Schleiermacher's translation *but not* necessarily Schleiermacher's words"![11]   And, of course, the ordering that Schleiermacher regarded as so critical to one's being able to grasp the meaning of the dialogues is – in the *Rowohlts Klassiker* edition – also not even close to being Schleiermacher's! One doesn't have to be a great scholar to find all of this terribly disconcerting.   One hears a great deal about the dead "rolling over in their graves"; well, Schleiermacher has very good reasons to perform somersaults.   As I am translating Schleiermacher's translations into English, I am sticking to and defending not only Schleiermacher's order, but likewise the meaning that he proclaimed, for the two are one, and it is an *unconscionable* undersight to be unaware of the depth of Schleiermacher's contention of the same.

Before stating this order in detail it is helpful, first, that we consider Schleiermacher's grouping of the dialogues. The first group (Roman numeral I on p. xxii) may be called the elementary group. It provides the *foundation for everything* that follows. The last group (III) is the constructive group that contains the *Republic, Critias, Timaeus and Laws;* although Schleiermacher never completed his translation which ends, most unfortunately, with the *Republic*.   The middle

---

[9] An English translation of these introductions was published in 1936 by William Dobson, Cambridge; a German edition is available *Über die Philosophie Platons*, Felix Meiner Verlag, Philos. Bibliothek Band 486, Hamburg 1996.

[10] I'm referring to the most popular edition: *Rowohlts Klassiker*, herausgegeben von Ernesto Grassi, Walter F. Otto, Gert Plamböck, Hamburg, 1958. The *Akademie-Verlag* edition, Berlin, 1984 – is both accurate and ordered properly (not to mention out-of-print) and it is the one upon which this translation is based, although the third edition – *Verlag Georg Reimer*, Berlin, 1856 – was also used as a touchstone.

[11] The full quote to which I am referring is found in Band 4: "Um dem Leser die Gewähr zu geben, daß er in diesen dialektisch schwierigsten Dialogen Platons einen nach Ansicht der Herausgeber vertretbaren Text liest, wurde die Übersetzung einer Durchsicht unterzogen. Besonders im <Parmenides> erwiesen sich an zahlreichen Stellen Änderungen als notwendig. Nicht dem Buchstaben Schleiermachers, wohl aber seinem rastlos forschenden Sinn zu dienen und Platons Text so getreu wie möglich wiederzugeben, war das Ziel dieser Durchsicht." (p. 6, right before *Phaidros*.)

group is transitional between these two poles having similarities to both.   There is likewise a grouping of the dialogues into three classes whereby the division between first and second class is most pronounced only in the first group, the one that I have called the elementary group.   Moreover, one also needs to point out that some of the dialogues are grouped into related families.   I indicate these families by placing single quotes around them; there are four families evident in the chart (see page xxii).   Returning briefly to the classes, dialogues of the first class are defined by Schleiermacher as Plato's most important works that were recognized by Aristotle.   These he calls the "trunk" around which all of the other dialogues are to be organized.   This trunk is composed of the following dialogues: *Phaedrus, Protagoras, Parmenides, Theaetetus, Sophist, Statesman, Phaedo, Philebus, Republic, Critias* and *Timaeus*. The *Parmenides* makes the turn from the first group which is concerned with the working out of the elementary, fundamental teachings to the stage where ethics and physics may be developed side by side in a more constructive manner. The culminating dialogues in the second group are the two dialogues, *Phaedo* and *Philebus,* that belong together as a family.   For Schleiermacher, the *Republic* has to be preceded by all of the dialogues of the second group just as the upper story of a house can only be built when the lower story is complete; just like the lower story can only be done properly if there exists a solid foundation, what I have called the elementary group – which, as I (following Schleiermacher) would stress, culminates in *Parmenides* – a rock solid fundament upon which many heads have been smashed and, as it were, become bloody.   Finally, the third and lowest class of dialogues exists amongst the first two groups.   These are inconsequential dialogues amongst which, indeed, are more than a few that Schleiermacher contends are wrongly attributed to Plato, and then others that were written for some specific purpose *{Gelegenheitsschriften}*, e.g. the *Apology* being a true historical rendering of Socrates' actual speech. These inconsequential dialogues were put into appendices and were not considered of *any* relevance to Plato's philosophy. I shall list them below in my chart within brackets [and with a smaller font]. Thus, Schleiermacher's order which appeared in two editions between 1804 and 1828 is listed on page xxii right next to the modern order as presented by R.E. Allen. As one picture should be worth a thousand words, I have attempted to place the maximum content into this comparison chart. The last three dialogues that Schleiermacher never managed to find the time to translate are: *Timaeus, Critias*, and – Plato's last dialogue: *The Laws* (& *Epinomis*) – as well as Plato's letters. All of these latter dialogues belong after the Republic; regarding this there is no controversy.   However, 18 primary and 13 "inconsequential" dialogues is a translation feat of considerable proportions, and one that spanned 25 years of Schleiermacher's otherwise very productive life. What is likewise of great relevance, as already noted once, is that this translation, though watered down, has remained the undisputed "King James" version, as it were, in Germany. Now, the situation in English is remarkably different.   English speakers who are looking for a *complete edition* historically have had the choice of Jowett or Cornford, to which now a complete translation by R.E. Allen[12] is in the works. Alongside of these complete translations there exists what can only be called a *plethora* of translations of individual dialogues and subsets of selected dialogues – as well as, interestingly enough, a "Revised" version of "Selected Dialogues" from Jowett's translation by Hayden Pelliccia.[13]   That so very many different attempts even exist, this itself should serve as an indicator that, perhaps, something is "fishy" here. Schleiermacher was quite adamant in stating his view that a faithful translator of Plato has to work with the internal meaning and its development, that is that the interrelationships between the various dialogues are absolutely critical to properly understanding Plato's philosophy and, in short, that one cannot hope to fully grasp Plato's philosophy without seeing it unfold in the proper order.   Thus, Schleiermacher contends to have traced this development of philosophic content within Plato's dialogues, that this content is initially expressed as an embryonic whole in *Phaedrus*, and then is deepened and broadened in the following dialogues. That, moreover, ethics and physics are the two areas that develop together, one alongside of the other, and that Plato's myths are precursors to his more mature thought – that, namely, the myths foreshadow the mature dialectic which unfolds later on, in his mature philosophy and, finally, in his constructive dialogues.

Having now given a very broad outline of Schleiermacher's viewpoint and contrasted the situation in Germany to the one that exists here, I think it a good idea to place the orderings themselves into contrast

---

[12] That Allen offers anything substantially more than Cornford, at least in relation to the *Parmenides* (which Allen also admits is of critical significance) is called into question by Allen himself in his Preface to Volume 4, *Plato's Parmenides* – in that he says: "Very little in the book is new: almost everything has been said before, except that it needed to be connected a little differently. F.M. Cornford is the foundation of it all." Page xiii; Revised Edition, 1997 – Yale University.

[13] *Selected Dialogues of Plato   (Ion, Protagoras, Phaedrus, Symposium, Apology)* The Modern Library, Random House, 2000.

by exploring Dr. Allen's thinking regarding this which is given in his introduction to *Volume I*[14] of his translation – as his views should be seen as representative of the currently accepted standpoint. On page 15 of this introduction one finds the dialogues ordered so:

*************** ***R.E. Allen*** ******* *"a likely story"* ***********
I. *[in any order]:*   Apology, Crito, *Laches*, Ion, Hippias Major,
  Hippias Minor, *Charmides*, Alcibiades Major, Lysis, Euthyphro,
  Euthydemus, *Protagoras*   {399–387BC}
II. *Meno, Gorgias*, Menexenus, Cratylus, *Symposium, Phaedo,*
  Republic, **Phaedrus**
>> transition from II. >> III. ***Parmenides****, Theaetetus*   {367 BC}
III. *Sophist, Statesman* (Politicus), Timaeus, Critias   {361 BC}
  Philebus, The Laws   {352BC..348BC}

************ ***Schleiermacher*** **** *see footnote #27, p. xxx* ****
I. ***Phaedrus****, Lysis, '*Protagoras*, Laches, Charmides,'* Euthyphro,
  {Socrates' Execution – 399BC}   ***Parmenides***
      [Apology, Crito, Ion, Hippias Minor, Hipparchos, Minos, Alciabides II]
II. '*Gorgias, *Theaetetus*, Meno*'; Euthydemus, Cratylus;
  '*Sophist, Statesman, Symposium (Philosopher)*';
  '*Phaedo, Philebus*';   [Theages, Erastae/Rival Lovers, Alciabides I,
                          Menexenus, Hippias (Major), Cleitophon]
· III. *Republic*, << Critias, Timaeus, The Laws >>
****

This ordering, outwardly, is similar to Schleiermacher's; for one Allen separates Plato's dialogues into three periods: early, middle and late. What should be apparent even to a cursory review is that there is extensive congruity between Schleiermacher and Allen as they both divide Plato's writings into three groups and the dialogues that fall into each group are the same more than they differ.   But Allen's groupings of early, middle and late are simply based on Plato's relative age and his trips first to Italy and Syracuse – 388 BC; his second trip to Syracuse – 367 BC; and his last visit there in 361 BC. That is to say that there is absolutely *no specific philosophic* rationale given for these major divisions! Allen states of the first group that: "It is difficult to assign even a probable order to them."[15] Of equal importance, there is no separation of the dialogues into "classes"

---

[14] *Euthyphro, Apology, Crito, Meno, Gorgias, Menexenus – The Dialogues of Plato, Volume I,* by R.E. Allen; Yale University Press, 1984.
[15] Ibid. – p.13.

per se – what is indicated by Schleiermacher (above) either by being underlined or, more importantly, by being placed within [brackets]. Not to diminish the immense significance of these two points, the most important disparity, I believe, and what has really determined scholarly opinion is the disparity found with just two dialogues: *Phaedrus* and *Parmenides*; though there is also very significant disparity with the *Republic, Phaedo,* and indeed – the obliteration of all of Schleiermacher's *"families."* I have highlighted and italicized these dialogues in the chart comparison as these disparities are quite critical and define, I think, the dispute – although, I guess, I'm the only one so brazen as to reopen the controversy and make it into a big deal. Whereas Schleiermacher goes into quite considerable detail on the precise ordering of each and every dialogue of consequence, Allen is, may I say, generally lackadaisical on detail except for a few significant determinations; indeed, he finishes his brief discussion stating that "we must sometimes rest content with 'a likely story.'"[16] This needs to be considered in view of the vast difference between the methods used to arrive at the ordering. This is made most apparent by quoting Allen:

"But the evidence of doctrinal development must be used with care lest it *degenerate* into arguments over what is 'mature' and 'immature' in Plato's thought. Estimates of philosophical maturity tend rather to reflect the interpreter's own philosophical predilections than to constitute hard evidence. *Speculative guesswork* has been a main motive for attempting to determine the order of the dialogues on other grounds. In matters of scholarship, the patience of philology precedes philosophy." [17]   (Italics mine)

Again, I really marvel at the view expressed. It should be immediately apparent to everyone that the entire question regarding the ordering of the dialogues is only relevant insofar as the ordering might itself become the hinge upon which the door to our fuller understanding of Plato is opened: what his philosophy actually is! Are we to totally give up on philosophical speculation and find a shared consolation in having "a likely story" based upon the "hard evidence" of philology – that now, like Socrates, we all know that we don't really know? And, on another level, is this whole carping on "hard evidence" not, in its own way, itself a materialistic predilection against philosophy, at least philosophy in the manner that Plato understood it! Thus, with

---

[16] Ibid. – p. 16.
[17] Ibid. – p. 17.

Schleiermacher, it is his avowed understanding of Plato upon which he bases his ordering – an ordering that includes all of the important dialogues; with Allen, it is his avoidance of "doctrinal predilections" that guide his non-speculative assurances! If my opinion should have any relevance in the determination of such subtle issues, I would have to say that I'd put my money on those philosophers who dare to philosophize regarding philosophy and not on those who are so intent upon studying the so-called "hard evidence" provided by the stylometry of philology. I would even go so far as to submit that if philosophy should be incapable of having the final word in the understanding even of itself, and no matter which language it is in which the words and thoughts are expressed: Greek, English or Swahili (actually Bantu), well then, what's the point of it at all! Moreover, on the other hand, hard evidence can very easily be softened up, assuming that one is somewhat brazen and dares to go so far as to think seriously about it. For instance, it doesn't require much effort to consider the very real possibility that Plato himself may well have reworked and revised a few (and very probably more than a few) of his dialogues.[18] What would such rework do to the hard results provided by philology! – and, as I shall focus my attention on later, particularly with rework of what Schleiermacher so strongly contends as being the foundation dialogue, *Phaedrus*, which, if it is indeed the foundation text, might well be the prime candidate for substantial editing and revising, as is perhaps some-what alluded to in a playful manner by Plato himself, *Phaedr. {278d}*:

"*Socr:* Hence, he who has nothing better than that which results after tedious turnings this way and that, the mere augmentation of one thing on top of another, and a great deal of scratchings-out, those who write and compose in such a manner as this shall, wouldn't you agree, be rightly named poets, or speechwriters or law-givers?
Phae: How else?"

That near the conclusion of *Phaedrus* Plato quite playfully divides the lovers-of-wisdom from the law-givers and asks us to believe that the lowly law-givers might well find occasion to rework their papers, but we philosophers always say what we mean the first time! I'd certainly

---

[18] In his article– *Stylometry and Chronology*, Leonard Brandwood states [p102]: "Lastly he [Janell] remarked on the frequency of hiatus in the *Phaedrus* as being somewhat lower than the rest of the earlier dialogues. To explain this he accepted Blass's view – that Plato later revised it, and ..." – *The Cambridge Companion to Plato*, Cambridge Univ. Press, 1992. Note too that *Theaetetus* has been viewed by many as a dialogue that underwent extensive revision by Plato.

have to remark that this introduction has gone through numerous revisions and is, possibly, due a few more. And Plato's dialogues seem to me, as a whole, to be the work done by a genius and redone, moreover, over the course of a lifetime. How could he *not* have had occasion to improve upon them? – this is the better question that one might ask oneself. Let us not fail to note that the ancients considered *Phaedrus* the first Platonic dialogue; and, then, per the historical tradition that has come down to us from Dionysius:

"Secondly, there is some slight evidence that Plato was all his life an assiduous polisher and reviser of his own works. Dionysisus of Halicarnassus, in a rather unhappy metaphor, says that 'up to his eightieth year Plato never ceased combing and curling and every way braiding his own dialogues' ..." [19]

This really is not some minor issue, rather standing at the Cross Roads the civilized world[20] must either learn to embrace Plato with an impassioned and thorough-going understanding, or else slip ever further into barbarism – having no real foundation upon which we might rest our laurels. As one studies Plato's dialogues over time one really cannot help but notice how all of his texts are constantly referring back and forth upon one another, that Plato must intentionally be approaching his central concerns (education of the youth toward virtue, politics, epistemology, ontology) from various sides that need to be balanced, one with the other. I have made extensive footnotes within my translations so that the reader may jump back and forth for common expressions, themes and allusions; that in all of these it was *very* evident to me that Schleiermacher was on to something the significance of which is most fundamental,

---

[19] Page 51 – *A History of Greek Philosophy, Vol. Four* – W.K.C. Guthrie, Cambridge Univ. Press, 1975. Guthrie goes on to quote Field who "scorned" this historical tidbit saying that "this idea is in every case a purely gratuitous invention, introduced to bolster up the pet theory of some particular scholar..." Well, nobody likes it when a monkey wrench is thrown into the works – and this certainly begs the question: Whose pet theory is being propped up by whom? Ultimately, I concur with Schleiermacher that in the last instance one needs to look to Plato's dialogues themselves and the meaning contained therein – that each and every one of us may decide from him or herself.

[20] It would be a grave misunderstanding if one read into this mention of the "civilized world" any sort of prejudice. Rather, I believe that any person who gives himself up to philosophy in a platonic fashion will understand what is meant – and, as is obvious from world history, the greatest evils often come from those nations that, supposedly, are "foremost." One wonders what the impact of global warming will be upon our planet, whilst so many Americans race about mindlessly in their gas-guzzling SUVs, not to mention potential epidemics caused by strains of disease that, perhaps, result from human "science."

something that, indeed, he was able to carry over from the Greek, and I have taken my cue accordingly.

Is it, perhaps, overly construed by me that even in *The Laws of Plato* I see on the very first page a hint by Plato to the shady "resting spot" under the *flowering* plane [sycamore/cypruss] tree of *Phaedrus*? Allow me to quote extensively from Thomas Prangles' excellent translation, right from the beginning of Plato's last dialogue – as there is much here worthy of reflection *{Laws 624a–625c}:*

"*Athenian Strng:* Is it a god or some human being, *strangers*, who is given the credit for laying down your laws?
Kleinias: A god, *stranger*, a god – to say what is at any rate the most just thing. Among us Zeus, and among the Lacedaimonians, from whence this man comes, I think they declare that it's Apollo. Isn't that so?
Megillus: Yes.
Ath-Str: Don't you people follow Homer, and say that Minos got together with his father *every ninth year* and was guided by his oracles in establishing the laws for your cities?
Kleinias: So it is said amongst us.   And also that his brother *Rhadamanthus*, at least – you've both heard the name – *became very just*. We Cretans, at any rate, would assert that he won this praise because he regulated judicial affairs correctly *in those times.*
Ath-Str: His fame is splendid at least, and very appropriate for a *son of Zeus*. But since you and this man here were reared in such conventions and habits, I expect it would not be unpleasant for you *to pass the present time* discussing the political regime and laws, *talking and listening as we go on our way.* The road from Knossos *to the cave* and temple of Zeus is altogether long enough, as we hear, and there are resting places along the way, appropriate for this *stifling heat; there are shady spots under tall trees,* where it would be fitting for men of our age *to pause* often. Encouraging one another with speeches, we would thus complete the whole journey in ease.
Kleinias: And as one goes along this route, stranger, there are groves with *cypresses of amazing height and beauty,* and *meadows* in which we could rest and pass the time.
Ath-Str: What you say is correct.
Kleinias: Yes indeed.   *And when we see them we'll assert it even more emphatically.*" [21]   (Italics mine)

---

[21] *The Laws of Plato* – Translation with an introduction by Thomas Prangle – 1980 Basic Books, Inc.; 1988 Chicago Univ. Press.

There is so very much here that is tied to the whole of Plato's writings; so much, indeed, that I recoil from expounding upon it all. Let my italics work as pointers toward 'things' that the reader may desire to reflect upon as he or she reads the nine dialogues contained in this book – and allow me, simply, that I return to the very general point that I was making: that the first and the last dialogue of Plato are intimately tied, one to the other, as it is so, too, that right at the beginning of *Phaedrus* Plato has Phaedrus refer to Socrates as a *"stranger."* From my translation: *Phaedrus {230b}*:

"Socr: By Hera! – this is indeed a beauteous resting spot. For the sycamore is itself magnificently attired and of a great height, one offering copious amounts of shade and, now, as it stands here in full bloom, so the very air is quite full of its glorious scent. Then too, underneath the sycamore there flows the loveliest little spring of water, most deliciously chilled, that is – if one is to trust one's feet. Also it seems, to judge by the statues and figurines, that these grounds are inhabited by a consecrated host of nymphs, and Achelous is here too. But should you be looking for a light breeze that sweetly wafts about in a most welcoming manner, gently lolling one in its summertime fashion, and yet with a choir of crickets chirping so merrily in the background – well, this is the spot. But amongst all of this what is yet most enticing is the lusciously soft green grass that grows here in such abundance that one cannot help but stretch oneself out, laying one's head gently upon the warm folds of verdure. In short, my dear Phaedrus, you have led us most admirably and proven yourself a first-rate guide.
Phae: But –you amazing man!– you display yourself most unusually. For, in all actuality, just as you say: you are *like a stranger* who lets himself be led about and not at all one native to this place ..."

Is this an instance of Plato's editing capabilities: that he ties together Socrates with the final *character* of "the Athenian Stranger"[22] in the *Laws*? And moreover, in a more essential sense: Is the quality or characteristic of experiencing oneself as a stranger an immanent signifier that man's ego is experiencing its birth within humanity? Indeed, is Plato the first fully conscious teacher of man's new orientation[23] toward the divine? – from which, now, we have become

---

[22] One also should note that Diotima, Socrates' *teacher* introduced in the *Symposium*, is likewise referred to as the "Mantinean Stranger" at 211d. Of course, the "Eleatic Stranger" is Socrates' replacement in the two dialogues: *Sophist* and *Statesman*.

[23] I say "fully conscious" as one must not overlook the mythic prescience of this matter – to take the most obvious example, Odysseus; and a more striking one yet, Oedipus who killed

quite estranged. And is it possible that not only here but, as I shall go into greater detail later on, is it possible that Plato has tied not only his first dialogue to his last, but all of his early and middle dialogues together in a playful manner?   This is quite conceivable to me: that earnestness and play co-exist in Plato's philosophy in a most intriguing mixture; that Plato revised his early dialogues so that they would be in accord, both aesthetically and doctrinally, with his late ones and, most importantly, that Plato had his middle dialogues all pointing back and forth in and through one another in a most creative and astonishing manner. In that this is so fundamental to the thesis that I am developing, in my small way, that Plato/Socrates is the founder of understanding for "what morality is" for humanity (not that this is a new thesis at all, just one that is under-appreciated nowadays) – as humankind has evolved in accordance with divine guidance, and that education toward the full understanding of moral doctrine is truly essential for humanity's health and well-being. Allow me to quote even more from *The Laws of Plato*, as this is most pertinent {Prangles' Transl. – *Laws: 642c*}:

"*Meg:* Athenian stranger, you probably are not aware of the fact that our *hearth* happens to be the consulate[24] for your city. And in *all us children* who hear that we are the "consuls" for some city there probably sinks in, from the time we are young, a friendly disposition toward that city, *as if it were a second fatherland* after one's own city. Now, this is just what happened to me. For whenever the Lacedaimonians were blaming or praising the Athenians for something, I would immediately hear the children crying, "*That's your city*, Megillus, that's dealing with us ignobly or nobly."   Hearing these things, and always fighting over them on your behalf against those who blamed your city, I became entirely well disposed; even now your dialect is a friendly sound to me, and I believe that what is said by many is very true,[25] namely, *that those Athenians who are good are good in a different way. They alone are good by their own nature without compulsion, by a divine dispensation: they are truly, and not artificially, good.* So with regard to me at any rate, you should take heart and talk as long as you like.

---

his father at the *intersection of the three paths* {Gorgias 524a} and then had an incestuous marriage to his mother.

[24] Prangle's footnote #51: The word is *proxenus*; this was a local person or family who looked after the interests of a foreign city and aided its citizens when they visited.

[25] This may be read in juxtaposition to Plato's more general extreme satire as regards the views of *the many* and, as Plato loves to do, here he boldly goes forth and argues out both sides of his mouth, as it were.

Kl: Once you've heard and accepted what I too have to say, stranger, you may surely take heart and talk as much as you wish ...
Ath: It's likely, then, that you're ready to take your part and listen. I'm willing to take my part, but it's not a part that's very easy to carry out.   Still, it must be tried.   First, for the purposes of the argument, *let's define education* – saying *what it is* and what *power* it has. That's the way we assert the argument we have now taken in hand should go, *until it arrives at god.*" [26]

Again, all of the italics are mine – and the point I wish to be placing such a great deal of stress upon is that the moral education of all us children since the advent of the ego is that we become good in a different way – through the knowledge of our deeper selves; that the divine is no longer given to us from without as it was during mankind's mythic era, but that now our second fatherland is one that must be found (and strengthened) within – if, indeed, we don't "dose off and are caught napping by the crickets during the heat at midday."

- - - - - - -

Returning for now to less speculative matters, another most curious item regarding the ordering that Allen advocates is that he does not himself follow the order which he asserts in his publication.   The dialogues in his Volume 1 are: *Euthyphro, Apology, Crito, Meno, Gorgias and Menexenus*; Volume 2 is the *Symposium*; Volume 3: *Ion, Hippias Minor, Laches* and *Protagoras*; and Volume 4 is the *Parmenides.*   This seems to say, rather heavy-handedly, that although current scholarly research now assuredly knows better in what order Plato's dialogues were written (more or less) – still, it doesn't care that students who are reading and trying to grasp Plato's thinking have any need to follow *this* order – somehow the order has become somewhat irrelevant as our understanding of Plato has matured! Or, is it so that students of Plato should jump around between the various volumes published by Allen?   This would certainly be a boon for the publishers.   My continual stressing of all of this should be viewed in perspective to what Schleiermacher stated on numerous occasions, for instance, right from the beginning of his introduction to *Gorgias*:

---

[26] Ibid. – pp. 22–23.

"Wie alle bisher vorgelegten größeren Gespräche des Platon, so ist auch dieses in Absicht auf seine Hauptbedeutung fast überall mißverstanden worden. Denn auch das ist, beim Platon zumal, für ein gänzliches Mißverstehen zu rechnen, wenn etwas nur halb verstanden wird, weil die Verbindung der Teile unter einander und ihr Verhältnis zum Ganzen verfehlt wird, auch jede richtige Einsicht in das Einzelne und jedes gründliche Verstehen unmöglich wird." [27]

It should be obvious from the above that the differences that exist between Schleiermacher's view of Plato and the current opinion (at least as presented by Allen) are like night and day. Even though I realize that this, my defense of Schleiermacher, challenges the consensus of scholarly opinion and authority and that many may dismiss this as quite farfetched, still I think an informed reader needs some acquaintance as regards to what Schleiermacher's standpoint really was and how he arrived at it so that, perchance, scholarly opinion may flip-flop yet again. In this regard I am quite happy that I too may flip-flop by quoting Dr. Allen in support of this:

"It is curious but true: Parmenides in this dialogue implicitly rejects his own hypothesis that the sum of things is one, accepts in its place the theory of Ideas, and levels against that theory a series of objections he knows are not cogent. If Plato ever abandoned the theory of Ideas, he did not announce his intention in this part of the *Parmenides*, and it is a remarkable testimony to the *vagaries of scholarship* that anyone ever thought he did." [28]   (Italics mine)

There are, finally, a few more items that relate directly to *Phaedrus* that I do consider extremely relevant. My own experience as a translator (and I freely admit that my own understanding of Plato has continually matured as I worked through these translations) – my experience, I say, was that the first two-thirds of *Phaedrus* felt very different from the translation work that I had done earlier: *Parmenides, Gorgias, Protagoras, Meno*. That, indeed, this felt like

---

[27] "Just as it is with all of the previously considered major dialogues of Plato, so too with *Gorgias* – the general tendency has been a total absence of any real understanding. For this itself, and particularly in relation to Plato, must be reckoned as a total failure of understanding when things are only halfway understood. That, in short, whenever the connection of the parts amongst one another and their relationship to the whole is lacking, so too every possibility of right insight into the parts as well as into the whole becomes fundamentally impossible." (My translation); *Über die Philosophie Platons* – p. 177, Felix Meiner Verlag, Philos. Bibliothek Band 486, 1996.
[28] p. 111; *PLATO'S Parmenides, The Dialogues of Plato Volume 4*, Yale University, 1997.

a youthful, exuberant Plato; but, then, that the last one-third seemed suddenly quite mature, as obviously added on (or substantially revised) later. This, perhaps entirely subjective experience that I share with Schleiermacher would not be particularly worthy of mention except that having the above indicated controversy regarding *Phaedrus* in mind, I was quite enthused when I reached the translation at 275c–277a (pp. 71–73). The reader may wish to review what Socrates tells Phaedrus in these sections as the quote seems a little unwieldy for placing it here. For me what appeared to be stated with amazing wit "as time is brought forward" was that Plato himself was reviewing his own works from *Phaedrus* through the *Symposium* and comparing all of these shorter dialogues to an "Adonis garden" – that, in short, Plato was playing with us in a very serious manner indeed, and clueing us in to his shorter dialogues and their ordering between these erotic dialogues. And, so, as the whipped cream on top of this, my speculation, one may read – *Phaedrus {277d}*:

"*Socr:* That whenever, be it now with Lysias or with anyone else, something has been written or will yet be written and be it in relation to some particular area of concern or in regards to the public weal as a whole – in that, perhaps, advice regarding the Laws might be brought forward, that, thus, legislative bills for a Republic are being drawn up in the opinion that there would be great thoroughness regarding fundamental issues and that also there would be great clarity in the document, all of this exposes the author to excoriation – whether or not, now, anyone actually comes forward with such. For not to be capable of differentiating between day and night in relation to righteousness and injustice, evil and good, that is – in all actuality and undeniably – most execrable, and no matter if all the people praise it.
Phae: Certainly."

If the reader takes the full import of this sentence seriously, then it is – I think – very necessary that *Phaedrus* be placed in contrast to all of the many dialogues that have seemingly negative outcomes, particularly the threesome, '*Gorgias, Theaetetus and Meno*'; though also to the other dialogues that Schleiermacher places in the foundation category: *Lysis* through *Charmides*. Thus, *Phaedrus* clearly stands out as a dialogue that promises the most positive of outcomes, that one is able to know in an essential sense *what righteousness is* and that anything short of this is simply execrable. Likewise, it should be readily obvious to a discerning reader that the treatment of love in Plato's *Phaedrus* may be likened to black and white, whereas in the *Symposium* the treatment displays all of the colors in the rainbow and, hence, these two dialogues really should not be from the same time. In light of all of this, it is evident that *Phaedrus* should not be placed into the midst of all of these earlier dialogues, dialogues that are all indirect in their conclusions, nor after them in proximity to *Symposium* – a dialogue that fits in remarkably well into the triad: *'Sophist, Statesman, Philosopher.'* I believe that the many arguments brought forward by Schleiermacher in his introduction to *Phaedrus* more than suffice to warrant that it be placed at the head, with the proviso that Plato reworked the ending of this most relevant dialogue so that, then, it did indeed encompass *his own* "Adonis garden" of dialogues, just as the opening section of a book might give an index of whither it intends to go: namely toward the dialogues that do deliver the positive results promised, most particularly, the *Republic* and the *Laws* (which, interestingly enough, may be compared to Kant's *Critiques of Pure and Practical Reason.*) And, moreover, that the Roman numeral III dialogues are 'prefaced' by *Phaedo* just as the entirety of Plato's dialogues are 'prefaced' by *Phaedrus* (see footnote #50, p. 26). Finally, how has everyone managed to overlook the significance of the twice repeated declaration which comes near the end of *Phaedrus {271a–274b}* that "it is absolutely requisite that the types of souls and the types of speeches be thoroughly investigated" and that this is precisely what Plato does in his following dialogues, specifically in Roman numeral I and II dialogues, and what an amazing array of characters and fantastic kaleidoscope of speeches ensue! – the entirety of which, thus, clearly needing to be preceded by *Phaedrus*, the dialogue in which Plato announces his full program, his "Whence and whither."

In this manner, the entire corpus of Plato's works is brought into an order that contains beauty and truth; an order, moreover, that is grounded in divine love, this fount of goodness being the essential basis for all human society and for the providential unfolding of humanity's full potential.

III. A Few Examples

It is certainly lamentable but nonetheless in keeping to the need of explaining to the reader why I have translated these *Nine Dialogues by Plato* from Schleiermacher's German translations that I not only question the big picture but likewise show in a few concrete examples specific passages where Schleiermacher's Plato differs substantially from what one finds in English. These examples will also demonstrate concretely why it is that someone who freely admits to no understanding of Greek can, nonetheless, raise fundamental issues with those who are quite fluent. Were I to place all of the passages before the reader in which I perceive some deficiency in English compared to Schleiermacher's German then this part of my introduction would have to go on for dozens upon dozens of pages. Indeed, the curious are very much encouraged to compare my translation word for word with any other English translations – that, in doing so, they might reflect inwardly on this hidden discourse that is always present beneath the surface of the text and which is addressed to that portion of their souls where understanding itself is rooted. They might also marvel at how through minor changes – who, for instance, actually says which words in the dialogues (e.g. *Gorgias 503d; Theaetetus 189e*) major differences arise! The following examples are only meant as elucidations of what I perceive as quite typical shortcomings. Even should my contentions be laughed out of the scholarly courtroom, it is still a very worthwhile endeavor that a very different view of Plato be made available to the general English readership. Ultimately these translations, through their reflection of the clarity and depth pervasive in Schleiermacher, must in themselves defend themselves and Schleiermacher. And I might also note, parenthetically, for those wondering how, indeed, such criticism is even possible – that, the whole needs to relate appropriately to the parts and that, moreover, there is a third interlocutor to the conversation who hears, perchance, may only recognize two.

One needs to be quite conscious in reading Plato that he understands himself very well as a writer: Plato is attempting to put down in a dramatic setting *teachings* that others – by reading, diligent study, and prolonged reflection – may experience as true. Let it be clearly and unequivocally stated that I am seconding what I see as being Schleiermacher's most basic contention: that Plato is indeed a philosopher of the highest rank and one of mankind's greatest teachers. Returning, now, to this matter of writing – as a written text it should be inherently obvious that there is no reason for one of the interlocutors to repeat himself. We repeat ourselves when actually speaking to one another because the other person didn't hear us properly. Contrarily, in a written dialogue the only reason to have one interlocutor ask the other to repeat his lines and verify what he said is to make some type of point, and this is quite a different matter. In this first example I will be comparing my English with that of R.E. Allen from his first Volume which has been footnoted extensively above (footnote #14 – p. xxii).

Gorgias [473c] – My translation of Schleiermacher (p. 289):
"*Polus:* How do you mean? If an unrighteous man is captured, that perhaps counter to the laws he has attempted to grab power, and then he undergoes torture and his tongue is *cut* out and his eyes are *burnt* out and not just he himself undergoes such great and manifold tortures, rather also he sees his wife and children likewise being punished, and at last he shall be nailed to the cross, or tarred and lit ablaze – he should then be happier than if he had remained undiscovered and had become installed as the tyrant, living on and ruling over the state and accomplishing whatever works he wants, an enviable person and joyously praised by the citizens and all others? This, you opine, should be impossible to disprove?
Socr: Now you're frightening me, brave Polus, and again are not disproving me; before you called up witnesses. But just the same help me a little to remember whether you said, if unrighteously striving after power."

Gorgias [473c] – Allen's translation (pp. 258/259):
"POL. What do you mean? Suppose a man is caught wrongfully plotting to make himself a tyrant. He is caught, racked, castrated, has his eyes burnt out. Horribly mutilated in all sorts of ways, he is made to watch his wife and children subjected to every kind of torment, and at the end he is crucified or burnt in a coat of pitch. That man will be happier than if he had escaped, established himself as tyrant, lived out his life ruling his city and doing whatever he wished, envied and felicitated by citizens and foreigners alike? You mean it is impossible to refute *that*?
SOC. This time you make my flesh creep, noble Polus, and yet you do not refute. And just now you were summoning witnesses. Nevertheless, please do refresh my memory a little: wrongfully plotting to become tyrant, you said?"

The underlying fundamental question, as I see it, is this: Is one always necessarily unrighteous just because one acts contrary to the laws? Whereas, indeed, this is left totally unresolved in Schleiermacher – as Socrates' misquote of what Polus actually said is allowed to stand. Allen doesn't intuit any need to "misquote," that there might be a very slight but fundamental alteration in what Polus actually said as compared to what Socrates misquotes him as having said, i.e. with Allen in both cases it is wrongfully plotting, whereas, I would warrant – and without having any recourse to "the Greek" – that Polus left a little room open in his original statement so that one might question: What if these laws themselves are not truly in accord with the good? The whole issue of overcoming tyranny, wars – be they civil or regular, and the matter of civil disobedience – all of this, thus, is covered over. And, sure enough, if one is awake to the question, then too, the answer may be more easily apprehended when it appears:

Gorgias [507d] – My translation of Schleiermacher (p. 330):
"But if it is true, so it is necessary, as it seems, that he who wants to be happy will seek and practice mindfulness but flee from dissipation, distancing himself from the latter so far and so rapidly as is possible and so seek before all other things to achieve that he does not require to be disciplined; but if either he requires it himself or one of his friends or relatives requires it, be it an individual or the state, then lay down the punishment and discipline, if he is to be happy."

There is yet a second and, I might say, a more cutting issue, namely the matter that is intimately bound up with the above, this being the oft-repeated mention of "cutting and burning" themselves – which the attentive reader has noticed popping up throughout the text of *Gorgias*.[29] Gorgias first mentioned these drastic curative procedures as he is touting his abilities in rhetoric:

---

[29] Not to mention *Protagoras* 354a! "Good people, you that also say that many things which are painful are yet good – don't you mean by this such things as vigorous exercise, field maneuvers, *being treated by doctors with cutting and burning*, medicine and fasts – that such things as these are good, though painful?" – just one of very many examples that could be sited to support the claim of Dionysius quoted earlier: that Plato tweaked his dialogues to no end. Likewise: *Lysis* 210a (p. 87); *Charmides* 173e (p. 196); *Cratylus* 387; *Statesman* 293; and *The Republic* 406d & 426b. In a more philosophical sense: cutting and burning are the two modes of 'becoming': change where the parts remain basically the same, and 'true' or total transformation.

Gorgias [456b] – My translation of Schleiermacher (p. 270):
"Namely, quite often have I gone with my brother or some other doctor to an ill patient who either refused his medicine or wouldn't allow the doctor to cut or burn and, as the doctor wasn't able to persuade him, so I spoke up and simply by my art of speechcraft I was able actually to persuade him."

It is a task for the reader to set these passages together, that what the doctor may do for the better health of his patient may, perchance, need to be done as well to a state in some analogous manner! What I should like, however, to point to here is simply that one needs to see these repetitions of cutting and burning; that, namely, the reader might very easily miss these analogies altogether when other words are used; such as with Allen:

Gorgias [456b] – Allen's translation (p. 241):
"I often go with my brother and other doctors to visit patients who are unwilling to take medicine or submit to surgery or cautery, and when the doctor cannot persuade him, I do, by no other art than rhetoric."

Again, with no recourse to the Greek, I would warrant that the repeated refrains of cutting and burning are likewise to be found in the original.[30] This word "cautery" doesn't fit in at all with the way medicine must have been practiced in Greece circa 400 BC, before the discovery of electricity and, my goodness, before the use of anesthesia! It is not surgery and cautery that the Greek patients experienced but "cutting and burning," these curative procedures are what the unfortunate patients had to suffer through (not to mention all of the other horrors of early medicine) – all of which, certainly, would best be described as torture, thus completing the analogy and making Plato's *Gorgias* a dialogue with greater resonance.

- - - - - - - -

---

[30] Indeed, the "cutting and burning" may well originate with Agamemnon's speech in Aeschylus' *Agamemnon*, upon his return from sacking Troy: "For affairs of State, and this feared disaffection [of the citizens of his own State, Argos], we will set a day; For assembly and debate among our citizens, and take wise counsel; where disease wants remedy; Fire or the knife shall purge this body for its good." – p. 71: *AECHYLUS The Orestian Trilogy*, translated by Philip Vellacot, Penguin Books, 1956.

For my second example, let us consider the translation[31] by Mary Louise Gill and Paul Ryan of Plato's *Parmenides*, the most difficult of all of Plato's dialogues excepting, perhaps, *Timeaus* and *Cratylus*. My first point – which is a major criticism and one that can and should be levelled against any book (except, of course, *The Republic* and *The Laws)* containing just one dialogue – is simply that the *Parmenides* stands quite naked, being all alone[32] in this book. All the same, I do consider this translation as being head and shoulders above the translations of Jowett and Cornford, though not superior to that of Th. Taylor, 1793, which translation, however uses English in an outmoded style. Indeed, a few translators have gone so far as to question the dialogue, that the whole of it might be some elaborate joke! – the joke, though, is on them; and I might ask why they even bother at all if this is all they can see in this dialogue. It is also a practically universal shortcoming (in English) that the narrated *Gestalt* of this dialogue is destroyed, and at least Gill and Ryan make significant strides in basically maintaining the literary structure of the dialogue. I think that Schleiermacher, however, preserved the peculiar Gestalt of this dialogue in the most consummate fashion, and my structure follows Schleiermacher's exactly – as it does, too, with *Protagoras*, a dialogue which has a somewhat similar Gestalt. Do note that the accepted practice of modernizing the style may do a great deal in hiding the essential characteristics of the dialogues, characteristics that otherwise would be much more apparent, as this translation, hopefully, will make most evident. Now, let us to turn to a specific example: consider the opening discussion, that part of Zeno's speech to Socrates when Zeno is explaining how and when his treatise "on the many" was written:

Parmenides [128e] – My translation (pp. 209–210):
"Hence, in that respect you deceive yourself, o Socrates, insofar as you believe that this manuscript was not written out of youthful contention but think it a veneration *{Ehrliebe}* that becomes a more ripened age."

---

[31] *PLATO Parmenides*, Translated by Mary Louise Gill and Paul Ryan, Hackett Publishing Company, Inc., 1996.
[32] The flip side to the problem of books containing only a single dialogue are those weighty *Collections* containing ALL the dialogues – by more translators than octopuses have tenacles! – monstrosities of gargantuan proportions… but I said I wouldn't be critical.

Parmenides [128e] – Gill/Ryan's translation (p. 128):
"So in this respect you missed the point, Socrates: you think it was written not out of a young man's competitiveness, but out of a mature man's vainglory."

I hope that the reader might notice that vainglory is a negative trait and a defect, whereas veneration is one of the most positive of human feelings and a trait of soul conducive to enlightenment. Here the very issue of Parmenides and Zeno being most respected personages – as is so essential to their characters and not only in this dialogue but as this is essentially related to Plato's entire philosophical orientation (see *Theaetetus*, 183e) – this, I say, is turned upside down and the full intent of this passage is obfuscated. It doesn't matter to me that all the other English translations make the exact same mistake;[33] at least for me Schleiermacher got it right and, as always, I make this assertion without any reference to the Greek.[34] A very crucial point should be inserted here regarding what even I have been referring to as "*the* Greek." There is absolutely no such a thing! Rather there are, this is indisputable, multiple sources – both in Greek and in Latin (and, who knows, perhaps Arabic, Hebrew, etc.?) – and most all of these sources are in various states of disrepair, not even to mention the vast hoards of scholarly papers that exist, so that anyone attempting to come to grips with "*the Greek*" has a great deal of work and numerous judgment calls before him. One not only needs an advanced command of Ancient Greek and Latin, et cetera, one also needs access to all of these old manuscripts that exist in various institutions and, I would presume, in private collections. Not even to mention having ample leisure time and the means to pursue such research. I, by taking the aforementioned shortcut, have allowed Schleiermacher to perform all of this requisite labor and, hence, the reader is once again cautioned against recoiling too quickly from this notion that I criticize without having a foot to stand upon. My touchstone, on the one hand, is Schleiermacher *and his milieu* – a time when Greek was far more popular amongst the educated class.

---

[33] Except for Thomas Taylor's translation of 1793 which is neutral: "You are ignorant, therefore, Socrates, that this discourse, which was composed by me when a youth, through the love of contention, and which was privately taken from me, so that I was not able to consult whether or not it should be issued into the light – you are ignorant, I say, that it was not written through that desire of renown which belongs to a more advanced period of life, but through a juvenile desire of contention: though ..." *The CRATYLUS, PHAEDO, PARMENIDES, TIMAEUS and CRITIAS of PLATO.* WIZARDS BOOKSHELF, Minneapolis, 1976.

[34] Indeed, for the best clarification of Plato's dismissal of vanity, *Gorgias* 457d (p. 271).

On the other hand, it's ultimately my own making sense of the whole. And the whole includes all of my 'book learning,' as well as, of equal importance, my life – which tells me that vainglory, though not necessarily limited to one's younger period, should be overcome as one matures. And, since I'm digressing, a very Platonic thing to do (if done well) and something which may bring one more readily to the heart of the matter, let me state how difficult it has been just to arrive at: the German, namely, *the German* that Schleiermacher actually wrote! Consider a most relevant passage:

Parmenides [156d] – Current *Akademie Verlag* translation (p. 240): "When, then, does it transition? – for neither at rest nor in motion can it transition? nor being in time. ~ No, indeed not. ~ Is this, then, perhaps, what is amazing – where it is as it transitions? ~ What's this? ~ The moment."

Parmenides [156d] – Initial *Rowohlts Klassiker* translation [1999]: "When, then, does it transition? For neither at rest nor in motion can it transition, nor being in time. – No, Indeed. – Is this then perhaps inconceivable, where it is as it transitions. – What's this? – The moment."

To make things more interesting yet, we can add another version of the same:

Parmenides [156d] – Gill/Ryan's translation (p. 163): ' "So when does it change? For it does not change while it is at rest or in motion, or while it is in time." – "Yes, you're quite right."
    "Is there, then, this queer thing in which it might be, just when it changes?" – "What queer thing?" – "The instant." '

This is, without a doubt, one of the most central (or should I say essential) passages in the whole of Plato's *Parmenides*. Just as the *Parmenides* is the one most essential dialogue for understanding the foundation upon which Plato's philosophy is based. And yet, here we have three words that are very different: amazing {*wunderbar*}, inconceivable {*unfaßbar* [ungraspable]} and queer. Then, there are yet other translations that have yet other words, e.g.: John Warrington's translation[35] has "paradoxical," Allen's has "strange thing," and Th. Taylor has "wonderful thing." With difficulties of this

---

[35] *Plato Parmenides and other Dialogues*, Everyman's Library 456, J.M. Dent & Sons LTD, NY E.P. Dutton & Co., Inc., 1961

magnitude – and here we are only talking about one word! – I can only maintain that what I think essential is simply that whoever it may be that is translating Plato, let him or her translate *the whole* as best as he or she can, and keep all the others away, that those who cannot work with some whole and offer a translation with clarification as an entirety, these shouldn't be allowed to fuss around with the parts. For myself and for Schleiermacher, the most essential quality to *this moment* – this moment being being itself (as it both is and is not) – is wonder or amazement. That some, I would presume Kantian scholars, should come along and make "the thing in itself" "inconceivable," this tells more of their own preconceptions than it does of Plato. That, then, these editors should feel so privileged that they can make such a change to Schleiermacher's translation and don't even bother to add a footnote for this. Well, I'm still somewhat in shock. Do note the difficulty of digging back just 200 years to Schleiermacher's German before skewering me for not knowing Greek – *as if* there would be some hermetically sealed *bona fide* copy of Plato's writings that has come down to us and is accessible to all at the local bookstore, and *as if* Ancient Greek would be a language that wasn't shrouded in a great deal of rather dense fog. If this is what the German scholars are capable of changing in their very own German (the Germans being notorious sticklers for detail), that we have a *"vertretbaren Text"* (footnote #11), what, one may well wonder: what are the British and Americans capable of altering (consciously or unconsciously) in order to bring matters into accord with their sensibilities? Let there be no unclarity regarding this, the best one can hope for when "reading Plato" in English is the reflection of a reflection of a reflection, and even this is being overly optimistic: there is no authentic physical text that has survived and what has been pieced together is third-hand at best. Hence, we need to think long and hard about Plato's injunction given near the end of his *Phaedrus* regarding this very same theme! – and note as well the implications for yet other texts that date from this same era; texts, perhaps, of the greatest relevance of all.

And now, what are we to say about "this queer thing" – doesn't this somehow fit in rather nicely with modern man's alienation and being out of *touch* with the tradition and the true depths of the thought and spiritual heritage that actually undergird our civil society? –

I merely wish to pose this question.

- - - - - - -

For my third comparison set, I will use the revision of Jowett by Hayden Pelliciccia.[36]

Phaedrus [261a] – My translation (pp. 51–52):
"*Socr:* Do come hither, ye beauteous toddlers, and persuade this father of beautiful children, Phaedrus, that if he abstains from philosophizing right down to the fundamental core, then, so too, he shall never speak regarding anything at all in a fundamentally[37] sound manner."

Phaedrus [261a] – Pelliccia's revised translation of Jowett (p. 166):
"*SOCRATES:* Come out, fair children, and convince Phaedrus, who is the father of similar beauties, that unless he becomes a good philosopher, he will not ever be a good speaker, either – on any subject."

Phaedrus [266b] – My translation (p. 58):
"*Socr:* It is of this, Phaedrus, that I myself am a great friend: of these divisions into parts and grasping together into one, in that, indeed, I am capable of speaking and thinking;"

Phaedrus [266b] – Pelliccia's Revised Jowett (p. 175):
"*SOCRATES:* I am myself a great lover of these processes of division and generalization, Phaedrus; they help me to speak and to think."

Phaedrus [267c] – My translation (p. 60):
"*Socr:* And how might we ever do justice to Polus' grand collection of words – like doubletalk and speaking-in-riddles and speaking-in-pictures; not to mention the conquest of melodiousness using the words of Licymnius which, then, he was able to attach onto the former inventions?"

Phaedrus [267c] – Pelliccia's Revised Jowett (p. 177):
"*SOCRATES:* And there is also Polus, who has treasuries of tropes, such as 'diplasiology' and 'gnomology' and 'iconology' and words of which Licymnius made him a present; they were to give a polish."

---

[36] *Selected Dialogues of Plato – The Benjamin Jowett Translation (Revised)*, The Modern Library, New York, 2001 Modern Library Paperback Edition.
[37] "wenn er nicht gründlich philosophiert, er auch niemals gründlich über irgend etwas reden wird."

I believe that the reader can easily see for him or herself how a few minor alterations in text can, like the "small matter" referred to much earlier in the quote from *Theaetetus,* make a major difference in enabling the reader to better comprehend the full depth of Plato's thought.   I maintain that Plato delivers to the serious student a roadmap to the foundation of knowing, which is a lot more than just "a good read"; and that his works do more than just "help," they are intended to bring the capabilities of the human soul to life as the *an sich* and *für sich* are melded into one and man realizes his place in being as one experiences awe and veneration for the powers and wisdom that pervade the universe.

If one is following Allen, then *Phaedrus* will not even have been read, as it's not in any of the first four volumes! If one is reading Pelliccia, then *Phaedrus* will come after *Protagoras,* which, according to Schleiermacher, is a reversal of their proper sequencing and, thus, one will have a much harder time trying to discover and understand Plato's philosophy as it unfolds better and is comprehended much more easily, I do maintain, when read in the proper sequence, the sequence championed by Schleiermacher. At the same time, one's understanding of any given passage is immanently dependent upon seeing through the apparent words to the connections that are, as it were, alluded to. It is much easier to see through words such as "doubletalk" rather than "diplasiology," that one actually may get much closer to the Greek by getting further away from it! Doubletalk is one of Plato's fundamental tools and works well with his irony. Speaking in riddles and speaking in pictures are also fundamental tools that recur time and again throughout Plato's dialogues. It seems to me to be exceedingly natural and practically a matter of common sense that Plato's *Phaedrus* would, as Schleiermacher maintained, have to be an early dialogue. Phaedrus as a character is the beginner; he has, indeed, a vital thirst for speeches and knowledge, but he is consistently unable to remember what was just said, and this is the novice *par excellence.*   Naturally, his speech comes first in the *Symposium* – and what a lackluster speech it is! That a philosopher of Plato's stature would 'write about writing' and describe the tools of his trade in this early work, what could be more natural. That he should come back to the *Phaedrus* many years later and update it with more 'goodies' and that such revision misleads the modern philologists – well, I certainly don't mind speculating that this, too, is quite natural.

Finally, it was mentioned at the start of this introduction that the end of Plato's *Meno* had a message that is somewhat hidden. One has to develop a sense for reading through nonsense in Plato if one is to appreciate his depth. Plato seems to be saying at the end of *Meno* that virtue is *not* taught – for there are not any teachers; and so one can only acquire virtue by being fortunate enough that the gods bestow it upon one. This would be the ultimate nonsense – for if this were the case and if this were taken alone (undialectically!): well, why read Plato (or the *Bhagavad Gita, Talmud,* the Christian *Bible, Koran,* etc.) or do anything else other than wait around for the gods, willy-nilly, to bestow their graces upon one? – But if *Meno* is read along after *Gorgias and with Theaetetus,* as Schleiermacher contends that these three dialogues belong together as a family, then one might still have in mind what Socrates has said in *Gorgias, 522d*:

"Callicles: Can you then believe it, that this be good for a person that he finds himself in such a pickle within his own state and is incapable of helping himself?
Socr: If only the following be not missing, which you have often enough admitted: that he has succored himself never to have spoken or done injustice, neither against men nor against the gods. For this is, as we ourselves often have been one in admitting, the most important help that each of us can only himself accomplish."

Having this fresh in one's mind is quite helpful when Plato teases one, as he does at the end of *Meno*, with lines such as these at *98cd*:

"Socr: If, then, it's not only by and through their knowledge that men are virtuous and useful for the *polis*, they who are such, but rather also through their having the right notions, and if neither of these subsists in man by nature, neither knowledge nor right notions, and also if neither of these is something which one might earn through effort – or, do you think that either of these two would come to be through nature?"

Socrates leaves the "through effort" clause hanging (a beautiful instance of the way that Plato is constantly speaking to those who listen between the lines) and turns back to the dilemma that there are not any discernable teachers of virtue... Except that, Socrates' own teaching may be quite apparent to those 'students' or adherents who are reading *through* the text and are able to see it properly in its contextual relationship with other dialogues, which, again, I shall never tire of saying, need to be read in the most meaningful sequence.

Thus too, the absolute centrality of Plato's *theory of remembrance* as presented in the *Meno* can only be fully grasped if it is read in intimate conjunction with the *Theaetetus* – as Socrates quite pointedly states in *Theaetetus {188a}* that he wishes to set the issues of "learning and forgetting" off to the side and simply wishes to explore knowing strictly in terms of whether someone "knows" something or if he "doesn't know." With such posturing, it is no great wonder that the dialogue repeatedly runs into *aporia*. And, to return once more and demonstrate the critical nature of Schleiermacher's ordering, consider Dr. Allen's commentary on this dialogue,[38] the *Meno*. Allen states practically right off from the outset of his commentary two things which I, most respectfully, would dispute:

"The question [as to whether virtue can be taught] is pursued through the rest of the *Meno*, and in the end *it remains unanswered*. Meno and Socrates cannot determine whether virtue is taught because they do not know what virtue is." (p. 134)

"Socrates' insistence on the distinction between the essence of a thing and its characteristics, his insistence on the priority of the "What is it?" question over others, *is the major theme* of the *Meno* and the key to its interpretation."   (Italics mine)   (p. 135)

Of all of Plato's dialogues that I have studied, there is none that for me is so *beauteous* and – may I say, profound – as is the *Theaetetus*. As Shakespeare is famous for *Hamlet* and Beethoven for his quartets, exactly so should Plato be famed for *Theaetetus*. Let us hear how Plato himself places his own admiration right into the words uttered by Socrates in this dialogue. (In both of these instances one needs to make allowance for Plato's great love of saying things indirectly):

"Or, shall it be so that you two comedians are going to say to me that there exist cognitions both of cognition and of fatuousness that the possessor is going to trap into some other ludicrous birdcage or upon some wax tablet, and that he knows them if and for as long as he possesses them – even if he isn't thinking about the matter and doesn't have it at hand?"   (*200b* – p. 442)

"*Socr:* Thus today, in such a manner we have attained what many wise men from time immemorial have grown old in their searching after it, and they have done so without their ever having found it?"
(*202d* – p. 446)

---

[38]   *Euthyphro, Apology, Crito, Meno, Gorgias, Menexenus – The Dialogues of Plato, Volume 1*, Translated with Comment by R.E. Allen, Yale Univ. Press, 1984.

– Except that Shakespeare's *Hamlet* stands basically alone, whereas Plato's *Theaetetus* belongs together within Plato's overall scheme, with the *Meno* just after it, and, then too: *Parmenides* before and *Sophist* being after the *Meno*. And all of these dialogues need to be tied together in the right way for the full revelation of Plato's thought to ring out clearly. Ontology and epistemology are two philosophical terms for which Western society owes much to Plato; and two other terms are – ethics and theology. These are all wrapped up in *one* and the "What is it?" question is *not* privileged over the "How do you know that!" exclamation; nor the most fundamental issue as to "the whence and whither" of the human species. We do, indeed, know to a certain extent what virtue is – we just have a very hard time coming out and putting our implicit knowledge into words; how otherwise could human existence be bearable were we to be so dumb as Socrates has us appear. Somewhere, it seems to me, I have heard lines something like these:

> "O man, empty is the place of your heart;
> You have lost your connection to the heavenly spheres;
> Living in the cold, spirit-forsaken house of earth."

Plato's own immense and unquestioned stature in the history of philosophy is only explicable by the historical recognition of his actually having taught virtue – insofar, namely, as virtue can be taught.[39] The fact that Plato has Socrates demonstrate his central tenet of remembrance upon a slave boy, this – in itself – should open one's eyes to Plato's sublimity; the flip side being his oft-repeated exhortations that the Great King himself may well be living in misery! Just as the results at the end of *Meno* are generally underappreciated, so too with *Theaetetus* the positive results of the investigation into how "false notions" are possible are generally undervalued and most experts rest content with the paltry adage that

---

[39] As Plato himself has Alciabides declare in the *Symposium* – beginning at 215b: "You are a flute player." – which calls *Protagoras* to mind, that virtue may be likened to flute playing, and then at 216a: "... it was not worth living in the way I am" and, in conclusion at 222a: "For he talks of packasses, blacksmiths, shoemakers and tanners, and it looks as if he is always saying the same things through the same things; and hence every inexperienced and foolish human being would laugh at his speeches. But if one sees them opened up and gets oneself inside of them, one will find, first, that they alone of speeches have sense inside; and, second, that they are most divine and have the largest number of images of virtue in them; and that they apply to the largest area, indeed to the whole area that is proper to examine for one who is going to be beautiful and good." – Quoted from: *Plato's Symposium*, translated by Seth Benardete, The University of Chicago Press, 1993 & 2001.

first we need to understand knowing before approaching the problems of not-knowing. The precise corollary that this has to the *Meno* – that we need to know "what virtue is" before we might know "how it's to be sought after," this beautiful symmetry of these two dialogues, one to the other, seems to have eluded the experts. And, in the deepest sense, the correlation between knowing and death (or being and non-being) – as Theaetetus is assuredly on the path to his grave as the dialogue *Theaetetus* begins – this, likewise, needs to be stressed. One might likewise mention Socrates' recommendation that Meno not rush off, but stick around for the "initiation" {*76e–77a*}; and, if more examples are desired: Midas' tomb {*Denkmal*} from the *Phaedrus* {*264d*}, or the quote from Euripides in *Gorgias* {*493a*}. But – there always appears a major stumbling block when issues of the soul are addressed – *Sophist* {*224a*}. Isn't it time for mankind to awaken from out of our slumbers and take ourselves and our heritage as seriously as we and it deserve to be taken?

Typical classes on Plato, if I might use my own experience as a guide, classes typically concern themselves with just one or, at the most, two dialogues, and strive to dig as deeply as possible into the content of whichever dialogue has been selected. Indeed, sometimes only a small portion of a dialogue will be studied. This, without a doubt, is one approach that is entirely necessary, but I would hope that this book will be an impetus toward balancing this overly strong tendency toward specialization with a different modus. That all of the dialogues in this book be read together as a whole, and that by such holistic reading and, indeed, in the proper order that Schleiermacher champions, I would assert that a deeper and more lively understanding of Plato's philosophy may well be obtained. Specialization itself is a phenomenon that threatens mankind in a fundamental way. My father told me the truism: that now, assuredly, modern man knows more and more about less and less – and soon, we shall know absolutely everything about nothing at all!

My most fundamental criticism against the Greek scholars – and I'm aware that this is an oversimplification and certainly is not true in all cases, but still worth saying: that in their burrowing into the depths of Plato's thought they tend to bring a great deal of coal to the surface, rather than diamonds; that they have missed the forest in their extreme penchant to analyze the trees and, what is most unfortunate, the great majority of well-educated people in our times couldn't care *in the least* as regards the relevance of philosophy, particularly as they find it paraphrased in the dry and lifeless journals of academia.

I'm also quite conscious of the fault which inevitably is coming my way: that I've allowed my personal, idiosyncratic conceptions bordering on religion and spirituality to get all mixed up in my work and also have put myself way out on a limb. Well, I'm quite fond of this limb and the beauty of the view it affords, this is my reply, and I have attempted my best to remain honest to myself in working from Schleiermacher's translation – and so I, just as he did earlier, desire that these nine, interrelated dialogues should find an ever larger audience of readers who may find solace in and a better understanding of Plato's thought, which, as I expect is quite clear by now, has a great deal more to it than the issues that tend to be microscopically examined in academia, that rather, as Plato says in his most curious manner, that philosophy deals with: "the most important things."

IV. *The Pudding*

All of the remarks and perspectives given above are provided contrary to my better opinion – that, namely, as a translator it is much more my proper stance to act as a silent messenger, that Plato is well able to speak directly to the reader himself (or should I say indirectly) – and that the value of this or any translation should stand or fall dependent upon the text's ability to enthuse the reader, that, as I found with Schleiermacher, so the English audience might likewise find with what I lay before it. There is, indeed, a great deal of mystery behind what some may call the "progress" of human knowledge; others, indeed, may well call it something else. For myself, I should like to take a middle stance and wholeheartedly enjoin the reader to study Plato's *Protagoras* well (a dialogue that has not received the attention that it, I think, is due) – as this dialogue, amongst many other things, deals with this whole matter of textual exegesis. And it is certainly worthy of note that after Plato writes about speaking, thinking and writing in *Phaedrus*, *Protagoras* then is the next major dialogue that comes along and it contains a critique of textual critique'ing! Then too, Schleiermacher himself may very profitably be studied. Schleiermacher's introduction to the dialogue *Phaedrus* is chock full of sound reasoning as to why *Phaedrus* is an early dialogue – and I have yet to find any book that even attempts to counter his arguments, rather, as noted earlier, his arguments are simply ignored as the modern linguists pursue their penchant for "hard evidence." It's as if the classicist scholars haven't a clue about the fundamental tenets of hermeneutics. However, quoting or reproducing all of these arguments seems to me to be an unnecessary labor for his eloquence is not to be improved upon and the interested scholar is better off going to the primary source. What is, however, much more vital to me is delivering to the unprejudiced reader this translation of Schleiermacher's translation of Plato: this is the pudding (as the true Englishman would state it) – or, as it's spoken on this of the Atlantic: "Here's the beef." Schleiermacher, too, viewed his own introductions only as a clearing up of misconceptions rather than as an explanation of Plato's philosophy. Plato speaks most eloquently for himself – if only the reader knows where to begin and how to listen. So, begin with the *Phaedrus* and let Plato instruct you as to how one should listen in to his speech and his thought. And allow me that I finally bring these rather contradictory reflections to a close with a quote from Schleiermacher's introduction, a quote that I find very poignant:

"Von der Philosphie des Platon selbst soll aber absichtlich, wäre es auch noch so leicht und mit wenigem abgetan, hier vorläufig nichts gesagt werden, indem der ganze Endzweck dieser neuen Darlegung seiner Werke dahin geht, durch die unmittelbare genauere Kenntnis derselben allein jedem eine eigne, sei es nun ganz neue oder wenigstens vollständigere, Ansicht von des Mannes Geist und Lehre möglich zu machen. Welchem Endzweck ja nichts so sehr entgegenarbeiten würde, als ein Bestreben, dem Leser schon im Voraus irgend eine Vorstellung einzuflößen. Wer also mit diesen Werken bisher noch nicht unmittelbar bekannt gewesen, der lasse, was ihn fremde Berichte über ihren Inhalt und die daraus zu ziehenden Folgerungen gelehrt haben, unterdessen auf seinem Werte beruhen, und suche es zu vergessen; wer aber aus eigner Kenntnis derselben sich bereits ein Urteil gebildet hat, wird bald inne werden, in wiefern durch den Zusammenhang, in welchem er diese Schriften hier dargelegt findet, auch seine Ansichten eine Abänderung erleiden, oder wenigstens sich besser verknüpfen und mehr Umfang und Einheit gewinnen, dadurch, daß er den Platon auch als philosophisher Künstler genauer, als wohl bisher geschehen ist, kennenlernt. Denn in vielfacher Hinsicht hat wohl unter allen, die es von jeher gegeben, kein Philosoph ein solches Recht gehabt, jene nur zu allgemeine Klage anzustimmen über das falsch oder gar nicht verstanden werden als eben der unsrige." [40]

---

[40] *Über die Philosophie Platons, Die Einleitungen zur Übersetzung des Platon,* Felix Meiner Verlag, Hamburg, Meiner 1996 (Philos. Bibliothek Band 486) – page 28; or *PLATON Werke Band I.1,* Akademie-Verlag, Berlin, 1984 – page 7.

"I purposefully abstain from saying anything at all regarding the tenets of Plato's philosophy – no matter how easy it may or may not be to make such assertions. For it is entirely my intent that this translation of his works should speak for itself and this simply by placing it immediately before the reader – that he, alone in his study, may himself gain an acquaintance *{Kenntnis* [knowledge]*}* of Plato that, even if it's not entirely new, is at least richer than what he may previously have experienced and, thus, this may enable a deeper insight into Plato's spirit and teachings. Nothing would run so counter to this my intent than making any representations as regards Plato's thought. He, then, who is as yet unacquainted with Plato's writings, may he place in abeyance and forget about any assumptions and reports of what Plato's philosophy might be. Whoever, on the other hand, should have already formed an opinion of his own [from perusal of other translations], such a person might take note in his own reflections regarding the interrelationships which come to light in this edition, how greatly his own insights may undergo some catharsis – that, perchance, the ideas and the dialogues may be connected somewhat tighter together, and also that they may gain something in their reach and *unity* in that Plato's philosophical artistry has gained in precision in this edition over what previously has been offered. For it is, I think, a sad truth that no philosopher has suffered so greatly by either being misunderstood or by not being understood at all, as has Plato – albeit misunderstanding seems to be rather the rule than the exception when one enters into the domain of philosophy."

(Translation mine)

V. Explanation of brackets, text highlighting and Tallyho

In that some words and, indeed, certain key terms are better rendered in German than English, e.g. *Vermögen, einstimmen, sich verhalten* – I have provided the reader with the German *{deutsch}* in curly brackets and italicized when I thought it particularly helpful. Moreover, in that in a few instances there were two English words which could equally well be used, I also sometimes include the other possible English translation in square brackets, and sometimes I even combine both of these crutches – e.g. with certain *{gewisse* [known]*}* words. Moreover, there are numerous occasions when it appeared necessary to 'fill in' words that implicitly were there – and, finally, [not to forget] a few instances when the inspiration of the translator's moment was given free reign; an event that, when it comes to the insertion of whole sentences or sentence fragments, is pretty much limited to *Phaedrus* – a dialogue that itself, so is the belief of this translator, calls for and grants some license for such free play: to beautify the verse, as it were. In all [obvious] cases, such English is bracketed. But actually, and this issue gets right to the heart of what a good translator has to do, all of the words of a translation are bracketed for the mere words on the page being translated have to be imbued with a new life and breath from the insights that the translator brings with him or herself. Thus too, each and every word is a candidate for a certain amount of wiggling, and each must be weighed and balanced within the overall context – and, now, this context has two sides: the side of what I might term the pure meaning that, I say, is totally non-dependent upon the language being used; and the side of the concrete instantiation of this meaning, which side has everything to do with which language is being used and which period of humanity's evolving consciousness is being addressed. And here the totally amazing matter of fact is manifest: that, at least as I see it, Plato's dialogues still are overbrimming with the most profound wisdom – of which I shall be very happy if I, resting so squarely upon Schleiermacher's shoulders, have managed to carry over just a few more bits.

Since the modern audience expects a little sugar coating, I have generally followed the *Rowohlts Klassiker* edition in dividing the dialogues up into sections. However, as these sections are neither in Schleiermacher himself (and certainly not in Plato), I simply point at the Section numbers in the Margins "<##~Steph_No" alongside with the Stephanus numbers.

Although I was particularly warned by an editor that one shouldn't, as it were, insult the reader by abusing italics and that one should never embolden text, well – I've now advanced to the stage about which Fichte had occasion to remark: from his *Vorrede* to *Anweisung zum seligen Leben:*

"Denn ich für meine Person bin durch den Anblick der unendlichen Verwirrungen, welche jede kräftigere Anregung nach sich zieht, auch des Dankes, der jedem, der das Rechte will, unausbleiblich zu Teile wird, an dem größern Publikum also irre geworden, daß ich mir in Dingen dieser Art nicht selber zu raten vermag und nicht mehr weiß, wie man mit diesem Publikum redden solle, noch ob es überhaupt der Mühe wert sei, daß man durch die Druckpresse mit ihm rede." [41]

I would note that the more discerning reader might excuse me for this, my proclivity to leave no stones unturned in attempting *to help* the reader to understand Plato as I think he meant that he should be understood. I also think that it may be allowed for someone writing in the modern age of computers and self-publishing to use the pallet available a little more creatively than is the norm, if one can even speak of norms in this day and age. Schleiermacher translated various Greek phrases of encouragement with the one German word, *"Wohlan."* In that such encouragement to seek the truth is absolutely paramount to Plato's philosophy, and in that hunting analogies recur throughout the dialogues, and in that mounting a horse is a frequent analogy to man's soul capacities and, finally, in that counting or tallying is an oft-used image of the power of intellection – I have taken the liberty of always translating *"Wohlan"* with the English foxhunting cry: *Tallyho.* I may be allowed to prop up this admittedly idiosyncratic rendering with a quote from the late Allan Bloom: "If ever there was a perfect description of Socrates, this is it, the man of the great hunt."[42] And so: Tallyho, aspiring Platonists – and may you capture that elusive prey whom so many have tracked, following in the footsteps of one of mankind's greatest teachers, a teacher whose primary dialogues are all essentially related and interwoven, one into the other, as is only natural for one for whom, indeed, the foundation is the One.

---

[41] J.G. Fichte – *Die Anweisung zum seligen Leben,* Verlag Freies Geistesleben, Stuttgart, 1962, pages 5–6.

[42] *The Ladder of Love* – Originally published in *Love and Friendship* by Allan Bloom; my quote is taken from *Plato's Symposium,* a translation by Seth Bernardete, The University of Chicago Press, 1993 & 2000, page 133.

Phaedrus

dedicated to

Friedrich Daniel Ernst Schleiermacher

for inspiring me

And even for this reason, now, you should take another good look turning the matter all different ways – whether, perhaps, an easier or shorter path than this one shows itself – so that you don't go down a long and difficult road if, then, one which is shorter and more level stands open before you.

Phaedrus – 272c

Phaedrus – Sections:

Phaedrus

****

SOCRATES, PHAEDRUS

Socr: My dear Phaedrus, whither and whence?

Phae: From Lysias, the son of Cephalus, o Socrates; and I'm off for a refreshing hike outside the city for I spent a great deal of time sitting, having risen early this morning, and so – in accord, namely, with the views of Acumenus who is both my friend and yours: I have taken up the habit of wandering upon the open roads as this, says he, is less tiring than walking upon the footpaths [in the city].

Socr: And in this he's totally right, dear friend. Hence Lysias was, as it appears, present in the city.

Phae: Yes, at Epicrates' – whose house lies close by the Olympieum temple, the [house known as] Morychia.

Socr: And what, then, were you all up to? Or, it's quite self-evident that Lysias was serving up choice speeches for you from out of his collection?

Phae: You should experience it yourself, Socrates, if you are at leisure and have the time to come with me and hear it.

Socr: How now? Don't you believe that, as Pindaros has it – *this too is urgent business*[43] *for me* – to listen to this conversation that you had with Lysias?

Phae: So, come along then.

Socr: And you – *speak.* [c]

Phae: It is certain, Socrates, that this is right appropriate for your ears. For the speech upon which we conversed was, I don't quite know exactly how – a speech on love.[44] Namely, Lysias composed it as if a beauteous youth should be won over; however, *not* by a lover. Rather, and even this is the subtlety in the speech: he claims that it is preferable and one would have to gratify a 'non-lover' rather than someone who is in love.

Socr: Oh! – what a marksman! If *only* he'd also write: preferably a poor man over a rich man, and preferably an older man over one younger, and whatever else would prove useful for me and for most all the rest of us. And truly, such nifty speeches would be quite useful

---

[43] It seems that having ample amounts of leisure time is "urgent business" for Socrates. Compare with *Theaetetus* 172cd (p. 402) and the calling of philosophy.

[44] *Symposium* 177e: Socrates claims to have "expert knowledge" on nothing other than erotics; *Lysis* 204c (p. 79) Socrates is "capable of knowing who is in love"; *Parmenides* 137b (p. 219) "to ride upon the track of love"; *Theaetetus* 169c (p. 398).

for us common folk. I for my part now desire so greatly that I might hear this speech that even then, if it should it be your pleasure to wander forth like Herodicus and only turn back when you come up hard upon the walls of Megara, still, I would never slacken my pace but would stick close to you.

Phae: How do you mean this, most worthy *{bester}* Socrates? Do you believe that that which Lysias has worked out by expending so much of his time and effort, he who is now the greatest master of all in the art of crafting speeches, do you believe that I – being so totally uninstructed – that I should be able to worthily recall what he has delivered simply from out of my own memory? For this a great deal is wanting, although I should prefer having such an ability over piles of money.   *<2.~228ab]*

Socr: O Phaedrus, if I shouldn't know you any better than this then I also should have to have forgotten my very own self. But the one so little as the other. I know it quite well that if *he* would hear the speech once, so that would never suffice, rather he would request to hear it over and over, and from beginning to end, and Lysias would be most happy to comply. And even yet, he still isn't satisfied and so at last he's off and taken the manuscript with him – that he may look it over by himself, studying those parts that he finds most pleasing. And so, sitting from early in the morning onward he at last has grown weary and goes off for a refreshing hike in the countryside, and yet – *by the dog!* – at least as I believe, already knowing the speech through and through, assuming that it's not overly long. Thus, taking the road leaving the city he's off on his way in order that he might properly learn it by heart. But, as then, he meets up with someone who is sick due to his quest of hearing speeches, so he's overjoyed to have met up with such a one, that he'll have a companion with whom he might share his elation, and so he calls out that he should "come along with." As now, this lover of speeches requests of him that he "go to and speak," so he makes a big fuss and pretends as if somehow this wouldn't be pleasant – though in the end he would force the speech on the other and do this even if his companion hadn't the good will to hear it. Thus, Phaedrus, dear friend, request it of him: what he'd do soon enough by all means and of his own accord, rather might he prefer to do so straight-away.

Phae: Truly, by far the best thing for me to do is just tell you the speech so well as I am able. For it seems that you don't want to let up from badgering me unless somehow I manage to speak.

Socr: You're totally right in this, your belief as regards me.

Phae: Very well then, I shall make an attempt. For in all <3.~228d]
actuality, Socrates, although I can't possibly remember the speech
word for word, still the main contents of it all, those parts wherein
Lysias sets apart the differences betwixt the matter of the lover as
opposed to the non-lover, this I will repeat for you point for point and
in the proper order starting from the beginning.

Socr: But only first after you've shown me, my dear man, what that
is that you're holding in your left hand[45] – there, under your cloak.
For I have a suspicion that you have the very manuscript itself and if
that should be the case so take my word for it that, indeed, though I
am dearly fond of you myself, still, if Lysias is here as well – well, you
should give up on your designs of using me as a sounding board for
your own practice for, you see, I'm of a different mind. Come now,
show it to me!

Phae: Oh, do calm down! Now that you've foiled me and my vain
hope of practicing this speech upon you. So, where would you like
that we go so that we might sit down together and read it?   *[229a]*

Socr: Let's branch off here, this way down toward Ilissus, and see if
we can't find a pleasant spot where we might rest ourselves, all alone.

Phae: At an opportune moment, as it seems, am I myself going
barefoot – for then, you're always barefoot.[46] And it's so delightful
splashing along through this little brook and not in the least bit
unpleasant when the water dances over our feet, particularly at this
time of the year and at this hour of the day.

Socr: So you lead on and take a look around: where may it well be
that we might best seat ourselves.

Phae: Do you see the tallest sycamore tree, there, over yonder?

Socr: 'Twould be hard to miss it.

Phae: There we'll have a shady spot, a comforting breeze and lots of
green grass to sit upon – or, if we should prefer, lay ourselves.

Socr: Lead on.

Phae: Tell me, Socrates, shouldn't it be right in this vicinity that
Boreas carried off fair Oreithyia?

Socr: That's how the story goes.

Phae: Perhaps, even right here? At least, this is a most pleasant spot
with a clear, cool pool of water, just right for a young maid to play
about in.

---

[45] Later – 266a (p. 58) – Socrates speaks of a "lefty-love" and a right-handed love; see also
Sophist 264e (p. 577) – classifying the sophist "always upon the right side."

[46] Except in *Symposium* – the companion late dialogue in which Socrates is elegantly dressed
and wearing sandals. According to Schleiermacher, *Lysis* is the companion early dialogue.

Socr: No, rather it's yet another half-mile or so further down where there's also an entrance for the temple of Artemis.   There too, somewhere abouts, is an altar for Boreas.   *<4.~229cd]*
Phae: I didn't quite know the specifics. But tell me – for the sake of Zeus! – Socrates, do *you* also believe it, that this story is true?
Socr: If it were to be that I, being like those clever people, if I didn't believe in the story, then too I would be ready with an explanation. And so, persisting in being clever I would clarify things in a clever fashion saying that the wind Boreas had thrown her down from off the cliffs where she had been playing with her friend, Pharmacia, and that it was simply due to such an accidental death that the people say the wind-god, Boreas, had carried her off; or it may also have been off the Areopagos – for that story, too, is in circulation. But, o Phaedrus, for the rest I find that such stories are all too picturesque and, besides, only a most accomplished artisan, a man who labors hard and long, only such a person would have the requisite time to dig to the bottom of all of this, though such a one is not to be envied – and all the more so as not only would he have to dig down to the underlying cause of the problems posed in the above but, moreover, he would by necessity also have to progress to an explanation of the centaurs and, after them, also the chimeras – and yet on their heels there streams in a whole swarm of living beings *{Wesen}* like the gorgons, pegasuses and many other endless multitudes of inconceivably wondrous creatures; and whoever attempts to explain this unbelievable manifold of particulars and explain it all down to something that is plausible,[47] such a person would have to expend a fairly prodigious amount of time upon this overly ornate wisdom, and then, all of his time would be spoiled. But for all of this I don't have a bit of free time – and the reason for this, my dear Phaedrus, is quite simple: I still have not yet been able to do as bidden by   *[e4]* the Delphic oracle: *Man, know thyself.* And it would be downright ludicrous, so it seems to me, until I first attain knowledge regarding myself that I might expend any time at all thinking about other things like these. For this reason I just let all of this be as it may be and accepting whatever the general beliefs are as regards these things, as I even just stated, I don't think about it at all – but, rather, only about my own self: whether I may be some monstrosity of a build yet more convoluted and more destructive than that monster, Typho; or perhaps, whether I'm essentially a gentler and more simple being, one that takes delight in partaking naturally of godlike and noble

---

[47] "und wer die ungläubig einzeln auf etwas Wahrscheinliches bringen will" – bringing a multitude of things underneath one concept is the task of dialectics – 266bc (p. 58).

qualities. But, my friend, let's not forget: isn't this the tree toward which you were directing me?

Phae: Yes, the very one.   *<5.~230b]*

Socr: By Hera! – this is indeed a beauteous resting spot. For the sycamore is itself magnificently attired and of a great height, one offering copious amounts of shade and, now, as it stands here in full bloom, so the very air is quite full of its glorious scent. Then too, underneath the sycamore there flows the loveliest little spring of water, most deliciously chilled, that is – if one is to trust one's feet. Also it seems, to judge by the statues and figurines, that these grounds are inhabited by a consecrated host of nymphs, and Achelous is here too. But should you be looking for a light breeze that sweetly wafts about in a most welcoming manner, gently lolling one in its summertime fashion, and yet with a choir of crickets chirping so merrily in the background – well, this is the spot. But amongst all of this what is yet most enticing is the lusciously soft green grass that grows here in such an abundance that one cannot help but stretch oneself out, laying one's head gently upon the warm folds of verdure. In short, my dear Phaedrus, you have led us most admirably and proven yourself a first-rate guide.

Phae: But – you amazing man! – you display yourself most unusually. For, in all actuality, just as you say: you are like a   *[d]* stranger who lets himself be led about and not at all one native to this place, so little have I ever seen you wandering about out in the countryside, nor even, as it seems to me, as far as the city gates.

Socr: Do pardon me this, most worthy Phaedrus. For I am one who thirsts after knowledge and the fields and trees don't want to teach me anything at all but, then again, the people in the city do. But you, I'd fancy that you've discovered the right bait to lure me out and, so, to deliver me. For just as the farmers will lead their hungry livestock about by holding out a morsel of corn or wheat, so too you're quite able – when you place before my eyes such rolled up manuscripts – to lead me throughout the whole of Attica and, for that matter, wherever else you may desire. But now, as we have arrived at our destination and resting spot, so I shall most probably recline myself here; but you, take up whichever position you believe best so that you might read me this speech: choose it and, as I've said – *go to.*

Phae: Then, listen up.   *<6.~231a]*

Regarding that which touches upon me you have been instructed and, as I believe, we shall carry on if this should come to pass – as you have heard it. But I should not wish to fail in what I ask merely for this reason, that I am not amongst your lovers, as it is even these who tend to rue whatever good they might do for you just as soon as their appetites have been satisfied; but then, for others there seems to be no time in which they might raise themselves to a different state of mind. For not driven by any urgency, rather of a free will, this is the way in which everyone best consults with themselves as regards whatever goodness of which they are capable. Moreover, the lovers tend to weigh those matters that they have neglected and, thus, have performed badly due to their preoccupation of being in love, they put these losses on the scale along with whatever good they have done for you and, so, when they add on to this all of their anguish as well as their business losses, so they believe that they have done much more than their fair share and that you, the beloved, are more than recompensed. But those who are not all wrapped up in such temperamental sufferings, these would never blame you – neither for any shortcomings in their own affairs, nor would they bring into the equation the difficulties and anguished moments that have been overcome, nor too is there any issue as regards the hostilities and wranglings that your presence causes these lovers to have with their other friends and relations – so that, being elevated above so many awful circumstances they have nothing else to do other than being best able and at the ready to do everything that they believe will make you happy. Furthermore, should it be that the lovers earn their   *[c]* high status, as they claim, due to their *total* devotion and due to their willingness to do anything at all for you, whether or not their words and deeds are hateful to others who may be effected just so long as they might be pleasing to you, so, it's an easy matter to see through this, to what extent they speak truly – because things will fall out in a similar fashion later on when their affections have shifted to someone else whom they then will revere higher than their earlier *amour* and, obviously, if this latter beloved so wishes it, then they stand ready to be nasty and do evil against their former *beau*. In view of all of this, how could it ever be acceptable that one grants such great favors to a person who suffers under such a regrettable condition, a condition that, even for someone who has an understanding of it, such a person still would know better than to even attempt to help out. For even the lovers themselves are more than willing to admit that they are lovesick and are not in their right minds and that, indeed, they know how poorly their understanding is functioning but, nonetheless, they are incapable of overcoming[48] themselves and their calamity. Thus, how could it well be possible that they might consider that what they

---

[48] See *Protagoras* 352c–353a (p. 156).

have desired from out of their being in such a condition to be for the best once they return to their right minds? Beyond all of this consider that if you choose from amongst all of those who have fallen in love with you then you choose from a small number of persons, whereas if from amongst the non-lovers then your chances of finding someone who is best suited to you are so much the greater. And so, there is a much better hope from amongst the many to actually meet up with *that someone* who best deserves your friendship. But   <7.~231e] should you also, perhaps, be fearful of the rumor mill and of public opinion, that, namely, when everyone hears tales of what's been going on that a scandal could well arise, so too it's most probable that, indeed, it's the lovers who labor under the assumption that all the others are envious of them, just as, on the other hand, they are themselves most envious amongst one another; and so it is that they brag about their conquests with their tales of seduction and each one strives to outdo the other in congratulating themselves on their exploits, that they haven't been busy for nothing; but then, from the side of those who are not head-over-heels in love, as these are much more in control of themselves and don't go off blabbing, so too these are the ones who'll do you the better favor by remaining mum on the issue and withholding from the public any *bravado* regarding their affairs. And apart from this it's likewise the case that many people will also be taking note and observing how it is that the lover pursues his beloved and how he has become quite preoccupied with this and, indeed, even if it should be that the lover and beloved are seen simply having a routine conversation with one another, then, nonetheless, such people will presume that the *amours* have either just come from satisfying their desires, or else that they are now on the path of   [b] having a private *tête-à-tête*. But, with those who are not in love – nobody at all would ever happen upon such a thought simply due to having seen them conversing with each other in that it's only part of life's natural course that one speaks together with one's fellow human beings, be it due to some mutual interest or simply for some other enjoyment. And really, if you should consider it and become fearful of the possible consequences when you think about how difficult it is that a mere friendship should remain constant over time and how in those cases where a breakup does occur and disharmony arises, how such a misfortune takes its toll on both sides; but here where you will have granted the greatest favors, so too even more dire consequences may well be in store for you; thus, it is from the lovers that you have the most of all to fear. For then, there are many things that throw them into turmoil and they are always ready to believe that whatever happens happens to their disadvantage. And it is for this reason that they try to cut off their beloved's commerce with other people, out of their fear that those who have more riches will be preferred over them due to their wealth and that those who are better educated may be preferred due their insights, and so on, whatever else it may be wherein someone may be better off than they are themselves; and so it is that they stand in dread fear of being outdone and they   *[232d]* strive to seclude you – so as to protect themselves from these others possibly exerting their charms. Now, if they talk you into turning against all of your other acquaintances, so they strip away from you all of your friends; however, if your more rational judgment of what is in your best interests should prevail, so you come to be at odds with your lovers. But those whom you've acquired not as lovers but those who have earned your affections through their own virtues, these shall have no need to selfishly deprive you of your other friends and acquaintances, rather, quite to the contrary they will hate those who want that this be so – in the opinion, namely, that thus they shall most easily be overlooked as being insignificant and, likewise, as they also shall be supported by your other acquaintances, and so this is the way by which you shall have the best expectations that friendships will be in store for you rather than rivalry, hate and discord. It's also the case that from amongst the lovers many more tend to be seeking after satisfying their physical desires rather than getting to know you in your own unique characteristics and personality so that it's uncertain as to whether they'll still desire to be friends with you once their desires have been satisfied – but, quite to the contrary, those who are not in love will hold back from such pursuits until much later when they shall have become better acquainted and your friendship will have had more time to develop, and so it's not at all to be expected that when in the course of time you are so good as to gratify them, it's not at all to be expected, I say, that thereby their friendship with you should be by any means lessened, rather much more will this become a memorable signifier for all of that which may yet unfold in the future. And indeed, your outlook in respect to   *<8.~233ab]* your future development toward the good also is improved if you grant me and not your lovers your attentiveness. For the lovers praise matters contrary to what is best, both in regard as to what you might say as well as what you do, and this due in part to their fear that such would turn out to be unpleasant for themselves, in part too as their desires tend to align them with that which is ignoble and malefic. For things such as these are the fruits of love: love reverses matters so that these unfortunate ones are tormented by situations in which normal people encounter no unpleasantness at all and, then, when they are beyond themselves in feeling fortunate, so too this is due to love's excessive praise of that which is in itself of no particular value. And so, these lovers should much rather be pitied and not be envied. But if you are attentive to my speech then you may be assured that first off I shall take care not merely for the momentary pleasures but, rather, for those future advantages which may be expected to accrue to you due to my companionship – as I do not stand conquered beneath the yoke of my *Leidenschaften*, rather I am standing fully in control of myself and being master of my soul – thus, in no way letting small matters erupt into major calamities but, as I say, first taking careful review of the most important things and calmly seeing the big picture, hence, excusing all of the minor irrelevancies and attempting to squarely face up to those matters that really are of the utmost relevance. For then, these are the characteristics of a friendship that is destined to persevere over the long haul. But if, perchance, if you should worry yourself that such a friendship would be incapable of being strong when there is no great suffering from such *being in love*, so you need only consider that if such were to be the case then we also wouldn't place such particular value in our own children, nor in our parents, nor yet could we be capable of being true to our friends whose friendship doesn't spring out of any such   *[d]* compulsions and drives but springs, rather, from other desires. Moreover, if one should be most endearing to the ones who have the greatest needs, so too it would be requisite that good rewards be bestowed not upon those who are most accomplished but, rather, on these who are the most helpless – for being freed from the greatest evils, so too they would have to be the most grateful. Indeed, were this to be so then one would no longer invite one's friends to the special festivities celebrated in one's life, rather one would have to invite these others who are begging for alms from off the streets as these are the ones who are most in need of being fed. And these also are the ones who will stick by him and who will wait patiently for him to return home and it is these who will be most delighted to see him around town and not at all question that they might know anything more but, simply, will wish him well in all ways. So, if you will follow my advice then it's not to these who are in the greatest need to whom you shall display your charms, rather it's to those of us who are ready and able to give proof of their knowledge and, thus, not just   *[234a]* these who suffer, rather, those who prove to be worthy of the matter; nor too all of these who take their delight in your youth but rather those who will share their goodness with you likewise throughout your life; and certainly not these who will go forth and brag about their conquest of your modesty but rather those of us who persevere in their shame and know how to remain silent to one and all; not these whose strong urgings are directed at you for a short while, rather those whose manner remains constant and whose friendship perseveres throughout the whole of your life; nor yet these who once having satiated their desires shall seek out some excuse whereby they might be at odds and enter into a fray with you, rather those who shall give proof of their virtuousness long after your youth has passed by. Thus, dear friend, consider well what I have spoken and weigh this also in your considerations: that the lovers are commonly scolded even by their friends for having fallen into such an awful enterprise, but that never once has anyone ever berated those who do not suffer from such pangs, as if somehow their counsel thereby would be worsened. But, perhaps you should like to   <9.~234bc] question me as to whether I'm suggesting that you grant favors to all of the non-lovers? – however, I wouldn't think that even a lover would dare suggest that you be of such a mind to all of your lovers! For if this were to be the case then for him who achieved success it would not entail the same degree of thanks, nor too would it be the same for you – as you do want that this remains hidden from all the others and only by discretion is this easily done. Hence, harm should be avoided by all means and, rather, it is advantage for both, this is what is to come into fruition. Now, I hold the aforesaid as being sufficient, but should it be that you find anything to be lacking, that something was overlooked, well, just ask me.

– Now, Socrates, what do you fancy about this speech? Isn't it wonderfully beautiful, not only for the rest but particularly as its eloquence is so well constructed?   [d]
Socr: Totally divine, indeed, friend – so that I'm beside myself in my elation! And this is what *you* have done to me, o Phaedrus, in that I watched you as you were reading to me: how your face seemed to glow for joy as you progressed through the speech. For in regards to the thoughts, which you no doubt understand far better than I, I followed along with you and, thus, in your wake I became wholly entranced by you: o majestic soul.
Phae: Well! So this is how you want to poke at me, by making fun of me!
Socr: Do you think that I'm playing around with you and that I don't mean what I say in total seriousness?
Phae: Indeed, Socrates, I do not. But tell me, truly – by Zeus, the god of friendship: do you believe that any other Hellene would be able to say anything other that would be greater or more extensive regarding this very same subject?   <10.~234e]

Socr: How's that? In this too the speech is to be praised by me and by you: that the author has said *what is right* and not simply due the fact that the words are so well rounded and precisely set upon the paper, and with a firm hand? If I needs must, so as to please you, then I'll have to concede it. For then, I've totally missed it due to my being incapacitated, because, namely, I was placing all of my *[235a]* attention on the rhetorical aspects and, moreover, I tend to doubt that even Lysias himself would consider this speech as being sufficient. Indeed, and may this not contradict your better opinion, Phaedrus – it seems to me that he repeats himself two and three times over as if it wouldn't be quite an easy matter for him to come up with something else that he might say regarding the same topic, or perhaps for him this wasn't in the least bit important. And, thus, to me it has the appearance of being like those adolescent term papers where one has joy in saying the same thing first using these words and, then again, using some other ones and, thus, speaks quite admirably in both cases.

Phae: You can't mean that, Socrates. For even this too is what is so remarkably apt about the speech. Nothing at all that would be pertinent to the matter has been overlooked – so that nobody could ever bring anything forward that would be greater or better in any way than what Lysias has brought up.

Socr: Now, Phaedrus, I'm no longer in a position that I can believe what you say. For there are wise men and women of bygone times who have spoken and written regarding these matters and, were I to grant to you what you are claiming, then they would indict me for speaking falsely.

Phae: Who are these people? And where have you heard something that is yet better than this?   *<11.~235c]*

Socr: So now, right off, I'm not able to say... but, obviously, I have heard the like from somebody – whether it was from the beautiful Sappho or the wise Anacreon or, then again, from some other author who wrote in free verse. And how is it that I draw this conclusion? My heart is fully laden, most precious Phaedrus, so that I feel to be overbrimming in that I have totally other things to say than that which previously was spoken, and these things are by no means worse. That none of these thoughts is a product of my own indagations – this I know of a certainty – as I am conscious of my own deficiency regarding such understanding. Hence, I think, there only remains the other possibility: that I have become filled up by hearing such from foreign sources, like a barrel filled in distant lands;[49] but

---

[49] See *Gorgias* 493a–494a (pp. 312–313).

then, due to my own daffiness now I've already forgotten exactly how and from whom it was that I heard such things.

Phae: That's just great! – you artful dodger – how admirably spoken! Thus, you shan't be able to tell me from whom or how it is that you've heard it, and this despite all of my entreaties. But, just this – what you say – now it's my turn: *go to*! Promise me that going beyond what stands written here in my book you overflow with something other, something that is better, and that you speak not one whit the less. In return I give you my promise, just as it is with the nine archons, that I shall [build and] worship a fully life size statue made of gold and, indeed, not just my own, rather yours as well.   *[235e]*

Socr: What a loving and, in all actuality, golden person art thou, Phaedrus, if you opine that I am claiming that Lysias has failed totally and completely and that it would be possible to say things radically other than what he has said. However this, I think, this doesn't even happen to the worst of authors. And even here as regards this speech, a speech which sets out to prove that a non-lover is to be preferred over someone who is in love, who, would you well opine – who would overlook praising the rationality of the one and criticizing the total lack of understanding of the other, isn't this totally necessary and how could anyone be in a position to say anything other than this? Much rather, I believe, one has to leave this be and accept it; and in things such as these it is not the discovery but rather the organization that is to be studied and praised; but for those matters which are not necessarily so and that are hard to discover, on these besides the organization also the discovery is to be praised.   *<12.~236ab]*

Phae: I can accept that, just as you say; for I'd fancy that what you've said is most obvious. Hence, I'll follow your lead and that the lover more than the non-lover would be sick – I allow that you use this as a premise and, so, if only as regards the rest you expound upon something other that is better and more extensive than what Lysias has brought forward, then you still shall stand beside the Cypselidian incense burners, a hammered work of art in Olympia.

Socr: You're quite serious about this, Phaedrus, that I assault your darling for your own edification... and it's your opinion, perhaps, that I really shall 'give it a go' in an attempt to outdo him by saying something other, something that is more richly embellished.

Phae: As to how this relates, friend, so now it's you who's been caught with your pants down. For now you'll have to speak and no matter what, and just as well as you are able. That it's not necessary for us that once again we go through the whole of those arduous antics and complete the comedy in that one of us returns the favor done him by the other, so look to it and don't force me to start off by saying: *If I, o Socrates, don't know Socrates any better than this then I should also have to have forgotten my very own self*, and *so he pretends that somehow this wouldn't be pleasant and makes a big fuss*; rather, bethink yourself that we're not going anywhere at all until you speak out what you claim to be carrying within your bosom. We're all alone here, there's just the two of us, and I'm both younger and stronger than you. From all of this *"pick up on my meaning"* and make it your preference that, rather, you go to – and that you *[d]* do so of your own free will rather than by force.

Socr: But you, heavenly Phaedrus, I should make myself ludicrous if after this marksman in speechcrafting I, uneducated and unprepared, if I would speak regarding the same subject matter.

Phae: Don't you know how things stand? *Basta*, that's quite enough with your coy masquerades; or else I know just what to say that straight-away you will be forced into speaking.

Socr: Then – just don't say it!

Phae: No way, rather I'll say it right now and what I say shall be an oath. I swear to you... but then, to which god? – or would you like by the spirits of this sycamore tree? – that truly, if you don't go to with your speech right here and now beneath this tree then nevermore shall I share with you in any other speeches by anyone at all, neither written nor spoken!

Socr: O woe! – you're really bad! How well you've managed to find the compulsion for a man who is in love with speeches, that he will do whatever it may be that you desire.

Phae: So then, what gives, are you still dickering with me?

Socr: No no, not in the least – not since you've made such an oath. For how could I ever possibly get out of such a trap?

Phae: Speak then.

Socr: Do you well know how it is that I intend to go about it?

Phae: How's that?

Socr: With my face covered over; for in this way I'll make the hunt most expeditiously and I won't become ashamed and get all befuddled by looking at you.   *<13.~237a]*

Phae: Just so long as you speak, for the rest you may do as you like.

Socr: Then tallyho, o ye muse! – may your art of song be named after the upper voice registers or be it due to the long-necked swans whose voices are so rich in their tonalities: Lend me your aid in grappling with this work of speech that this marksman has foisted upon me, so that his friend who always has seemed to be rich in his artistry, may these seemings even now seem – most seemly.   *[b]*

There once was a boy or, more precisely, a half-grown youth who was quite striking in his beauty, and he had ever so many lovers. Amongst all of these there was one whose cunning was excessive and, so, this one convinced the boy – with whom, nonetheless, he had fallen in love just as much as any of the others – he convinced him that he was *not* in love; and it came to the juncture as he was overwhelming him and forcing his views upon him that he persuaded him even to the point that the boy would have to give precedence to the non-lover over those who were in love. And this is how he spoke:

In all things, my child, there is but one starting point for those who want to arrive at the right counsel: they needs must know what it is about which they are tendering their advice; for if not, then, by   *[c]* necessity, they shall end up by going astray. The great majority have never even noticed that they remain unacquainted with the essence of any given thing. As if they had such an acquaintance they proceed along with their investigation and don't even bother to ask themselves that first they come to an understanding about this right from the start – and so, as a consequence they end up eventually having to pay the piper; they are, namely, neither with their own selves nor amongst one another as one. But may this not become our lot, that which we accuse of all the others, rather, as the question stands before us as to whether it would be better to establish friendship with a lover or with a non-lover so let us first take into consideration what this is – love, and what power belongs to her, and then, only after we're first of one mind and speak in one voice and, thus, having achieved clarity regarding this, then only, I say, and in hindsight and correlation to this shall we proceed along with our investigation as to whether love brings forth advantages or harm. That love *<14.~237d]* is a craving, to this everyone agrees; and, then again, we know that even those who are not in love have a strong desire for the beautiful. Upon what, then, do we want to differentiate between those who are in love and those who are not? We need to become cognizant of the fact that there are in each one of us two ruling and directing drives that we follow wherever it may be that they lead us, one of them being already present at birth which strives for whatever is pleasurable, and the other being a matter of character, something that is acquired – and this is the one that always strives for what is best. Now, both of these are sometimes working together in unison and, then again, sometimes working contrary to each other; and in the latter case now the one and, then again, the other conquers. If, now, our intentions are ruled by reason and this is what is guiding us toward what is best, so this governance is called mindfulness [prudence]; but if the

drive toward pleasure irrespective of reason takes over and   *[238a]*
rules our behavior, so this governance is named wantonness. But
wantonness goes by many names for it is composed of many parts
and has many types. And so, whichever of these types has chanced
to win and dominates, this type then determines the name given to
whomsoever it may be that is so dominated – and these names
neither have anything of beauty nor are they worth being wished
for. If, for example, if the type be one that is directed toward the
culinary delights of various foodstuffs and this drive has overruled
and taken conquest of reason and of the other passions, so this is
called gluttony – and whoever has fallen underneath this passion will
be named accordingly. Then, those who are focused on drink, if this
has conquered whomsoever and if this passion is the one in control,
well, it's quite clear what name goes to this type; and so too with all of
the other names that are related to all the other passions which may
govern, and all of these are well known. Now, why it is that all of
the previous has been stated, this is illuminated all on its own;
nonetheless, it may become clearer still if it shall be stated expressly
rather than being left unspoken. Namely, the unreasonable and, just
as with the previous, overruling what is better and being passionately
driven upon the pleasurable and so pursuing beauty – in this instance
the beauty of the body – if this power has grown and so triumphed *[c]*
to become the dominating and ruling force, so it likewise acquires its
name from it's object, namely the *lust for the body*, and this is called
love. – All the same, my dear Phaedrus, does it not seem to you also
as it appears to me: that something divine has taken hold of me and
is inspiring my speech?
Phae: Indeed, o Socrates, a torrent of words is flowing forth and
something seems to have taken possession of you.
Socr: Quiet, then, and listen in to the rest. For in truth, this spot
seems to be holy so that if a troupe of nymphs should come and carry
me off, well, you shouldn't have any cause for wonder. Indeed, I'm
already practically speaking in dithyramb.
Phae: Very rightly observed.
Socr: And you, my friend, *you* are the cause of it all. But, keep still as
you hear the rest – for otherwise they might, perhaps, be frightened
off. But this is best left in the care of God and we need to turn our
speech back to the boy.   *<15.~238e]*

Well then, my precious, what it is, that about which we were taking
counsel, this has now been spoken out and has been determined. In
relation to this, therefore, let us elaborate: what are the advantages
and what are the 'harms' which most likely await the beloved – be it,

now, if he gratifies someone who is in love, or if it be the non-lover. It is necessary, now, that he who stands conquered underneath this craving and he who has become a servant for such pleasures, he shall seek to arrange that the beloved be most pleasurably disposed for himself. For the sick, though, everything that doesn't struggle against them is pleasant, but what is of equal or greater strength is hated. Hence, neither better nor equal to himself would the lover like   [a] to suffer that his beloved might ever be, rather weaker and less fully developed he shall always strive to make him. But the less educated is weaker than the wise and the coward weaker than the courageous, the tongue-tied is weaker than the loquacious and the dullard weaker than the quick-witted. Such as these, then, and yet other evils as well – if they can be elicited out from within the character of the beloved or if they inhabit it through nature – such would bring joy to the lover and, in part, he himself would encourage them or else see himself robbed of his momentary pleasures. Hence, he would have to be of an envious disposition and already in that he holds him back and deprives him of others and derails him from all of the advantageous connections through which and to the highest degree he might unfold in his becoming a man, so he shall be the cause of great harm and the greatest of all in that he is deprived of access to those who, and in a real, authentic sense, would make him wise. This, now, is the divine love of wisdom from which, indeed, the lover most certainly shall strive to hold him back, due to his fear that such would make the lover contemptible; and so for the rest the lover shall do everything so that the beloved remains ignorant of all things and that he be dependent upon the lover and be needful of looking just to him, that he should be such as best befits his lover's lusty desires and, thus, for himself even so is delivered over to such grievous harms. Hence, for the soul of the beloved the man who is driven by love is in no respect whatsoever a healthy or beneficial companion. But how   <16.~239c] about the body of which he has become master, how shall he take care of it as regards its training and nurturing and whatever else, how shall this be handled by this lover who is driven by his striving for that which he finds most pleasurable rather than that which is most good? – this is what we need to consider next. It becomes most apparent, though, that he will be seeking out a body which will be soft and not one which is hard; and likewise one which has not grown up in the pure sunshine, rather one raised in tenebrous shadows; and not one that is accustomed to the hard labors of men and arduous gymnastic exercise, rather one grown fond of delicate and effeminate modes of living, one which paints on imported rouge, is adorned with frills and bedizened by frippery – and all of this due to the deficiencies of his own physique, and everything else which relates to this, these are the areas where the beloved's attentions are focused. But all of this is well known and so it's not at all necessary that we elaborate any further regarding this, rather having once touched upon this in all generality let's now turn ourselves to other matters. Having such a physique such a beloved will – in times of war and during other urgent calamities – inspire the enemy with courage, but his friends and even the lover himself will suddenly experience an influx of concern. But this too, we need not dwell upon any of this, rather we're all very well acquainted with this and we need to move on and consider as well what follows, namely, what are the advantages and what are the harms that may well be expected in reference to the beloved's erstwhile possessions? – what results are to be expected due *[e]* to this lover's influence and his stewardship? It should be totally apparent to everyone and most of all to the lover that even as regards the most lovely, most advantageous and most revered of all the beloved's possessions he wishes that the beloved shall be made destitute. Gladly he stands by and watches as father and mother, friends and relatives, they all disown him – as, then, these are the ones who interrupt their being together and these the ones who seek to criticize him and deprive him of his most pleasurable moments, the time he seeks to enjoy himself alone with his beloved. But, then too, a beloved who stands in possession of vast sums of wealth, gold or other possessions, such a one is not deemed as being so easily won over, nor too once won so easily kept in bounds. And for this reason it is quite necessary that the lover is most distraught due to all of his beloved's resources and capacities, all the goods that he possesses; but then, if they should be lost, then the lover is overjoyed. And, yet more, he desires of him that he be unwed, without children, and absolutely deprived of human society altogether! – such is his ardent wish so that he might alone and so long as ever is possible take delight in this, his tender pomegranate. There are, indeed, yet many other things by which lovers bring about ruination, *<17.~240b]* but then, some daemon has mixed in with most of them an element of pleasure; so, for instance, as it is with the sycophant – who is himself a terrible beast and the cause of untold evils – still and all the same there is yet a certain satisfaction partaking in some degree of education that belongs to such natures. Likewise, it is easy enough to find fault with the prostitutes and all other such creatures, and all that tends to go along with such pursuits; though, yet again, it is not to be denied that at least as regards the momentary pleasures all of this can be quite pleasant. But with the lover besides the ruination elaborated above it is for the beloved also the case that even one's everyday social interaction becomes a continual source of torment. For *like and like in age*, as the old proverb has it, *is most pleasing for one another* – because, I believe, this equality in age tends to lead toward like tastes in one's enjoyments and, thus, through this similarity one strengthens one's friendships. But nonetheless, there can be surfeit as well even in such companionship. Then again, that which is forced, it is said, such certainly becomes a burden on one and all, and in all things – and this added on, on top of their dissimilarity in age, all of this is found quite particularly to be the case in the companionship of the lover and the beloved. For the elder one is loathe ever to leave the younger alone and, be it day or night, so powerfully is he driven by his inner torments and the thorns   *[240d]* that prick him which, indeed, assuming that the beloved be present, all of this is subdued and in this there may be a continual cause for contentment for the lover in that he might see, hear, touch and enjoy his beloved through all of his senses and, so, clinging to him it is his pleasure to wait upon him at all times; but what consolations and what pleasures await the beloved, that somehow it may not come to pass that in having his lover about him for such great stretches of time he doesn't develop the greatest aversion and antipathy toward him in that he begins to see him for what he is: an aging figure, someone well past the bloom, who is standing there before him and, thus, everything else as well, all of which is interrelated to this – and even the telling of it is not in the least bit pleasant for the ears to experience, and so much the less when it has to be experienced in all actuality and when one is continuously being forced to deal with the situation and come to grips with it all, and all the while, moreover, being watched attentively by this lover who has the one eye chock full of suspicions and the other one overbrimming with arguments; and this goes on everywhere and no matter who else may be present and to be at all times forced into hearing the same old overly excessive fawning, and likewise always the same carping, the various arguments and the constant berating, all of this would be quite unbearable even were it to be coming from someone who is in his right mind – but then, it's so much the worse when the source is someone who's still head over heels, drunk in his infatuation: this overstuffed, insatiable, uncompromising and brazen old oaf. In that he is in love, hence, he is ruinous as well as repugnant;   *<18.~241a]* but then, if the love should come to an end, well then, from this time forward he becomes false, and this despite all of the many oaths and all of his previous begging and pleading whereby, indeed, his promises just barely sufficed to reassure the beloved and he only put up with all of this unpleasantness in his hopes for some future advantage.   And just then, however, when the payoff is expected due, then the aforementioned lover is suddenly of a different mind and has taken on some other lord and leader – namely that of rationality and of mindfulness instead of this insanity of love – and so he's become a totally different person unbeknownst to his beloved. The latter, then, is expecting his thanks for all that he has done and sacrificed for him and he reminds him of all of his previous words and deeds, *as if* he were to be speaking with the same man. The former, however, due to his own shame doesn't even want to admit that he's become a different person, nor too does he have any idea as to how he'll be able to fulfill all of his earlier vows and promises, all of which were made during a time that he himself no longer even understands – now that his rationality is once again in command and he's come back to his senses; that is, unless he should once more revert to being the infatuated lover that he once was.   Hence, suddenly he's overcome with an urgent desire to *move on*, and as he's forced by necessity to renege on everything that previously was promised, so now as the winds blow from the other side and fate has fallen out differently, so he suddenly takes wing and flies off.   But now it's the beloved who finds himself chasing after, and this against his own will and all the while cursing vehemently [though not too loudly] because even from the start he hasn't had a clue in understanding this entire affair; that, namely, he never should have been so foolish as to gratify the lover, he who quite necessarily is not in his right mind, rather, far better is it to share one's companionship with the non-lover, he who   *[c]* at least is sensible; for, if not, then every time one shall suffer the consequences of giving in to someone who cannot possibly remain true, someone who is ever so difficult, envious, repugnant, ruinous for your ever attaining all of your potential, ruinous also for the health, strength and beauty of your body, most ruinous of all, however, for the progress and development of your soul – regarding which, in all truth, there neither is nor will there ever be anything which might possibly be more precious, and be it for man or for the gods. Regarding all of this you needs must bethink yourself, o child, and you need to become knowledgeable regarding the friendship of lovers, that their nature does not in any way promote your developing toward the good but, rather, is related in type as food is to the appetite and becoming satiated, and you are as the lamb to the wolf: so is the lover's infatuation with lambkins.

– There you have it, Phaedrus!   Not one word more shall you hear out of me, rather, may this be the end of my speech.   *<19.~241d]*

Phae: But I was thinking that you were only at the halfway point and would now go on to expound in a similar way on the non-lover, that one would have to give precedence in gratifying the non-lover and place before us all the good that belongs to him. Why then, o Socrates, why do you insist upon stopping already?   *[e]*

Socr: Haven't you noticed it yet, you blessed one, that already I've started speaking in verses and no longer merely in dithyramb – and that yet in that I'm still admonishing the boy. If, then, if I were to start up again and speaking this time around in praise of the non-lover, what, can you well opine, what might well happen then! You do know quite well that these nymphs, regarding whom you did very well before in that you forewarned me, that then they should take full possession of my spirit. Hence, I'll say it simply with one word: that for the same reasons as we have reviled the one, so too to the other belongs all the good that stands diametrically opposed to the former. What's the need for long speeches? For even as regards the both of them quite sufficient has already been spoken; and so this fairy tale may be left to meet up with whatever fate may decree as right; but I, I'm going back upstream before you force something upon me which is yet more exasperating.   *<20.~242a]*

Phae: Just not quite so fast, Socrates, as the heat of day is still too intense. Or, haven't you noticed that the sun is now directly overhead? Rather, why don't we remain here and chat with one another regarding these speeches until things start to cool off, and then we can go back.

Socr: You are as a god, Phaedrus, in respect to your proclivity for speeches, and right worthy of wonder! For I would warrant that of all the speeches that have been composed during your lifetime there is no one who has brought more into the light of day than you have; in part narrating them yourself, in part by one means or another that you necessitate that someone else speaks. To this I would make just one exception, that of the Theban, Simmias[50] – but as regards all others you are by far the foremost. And so, then, even now too it seems that you are the cause that yet another speech has to be made.

Phae: Well, Socrates, it's not as if you were making a declaration of war. But, how so, and what sort do you have in mind?

---

[50] This may be an allusion to the *Phaedo* and its critical importance in Plato's overall scheme and, indeed: *Why else* would someone of Plato's genius insert this reference to Simmias right here?! – and, should this be the case, consider the repercussions to the *"Ordering of the Dialogues"* as presented on p. xxii: how this absolutely is in one accord with Schleiermacher's ordering but wouldn't make a bit of sense within the ordering of the "current scholarly consensus."

Socr: As I was preparing to go, good friend, and just as I was about to step into this stream, the daemonic – that omen which notifies me from time to time – it presented itself as it tends to do and holds *[c]* me back from some action which I otherwise would take, and I believe that I could make out a voice calling to me from out yonder and it held me back, that I might not leave this spot until I purify myself, as if somehow I had sinned against the divine powers. Now, it's also the case that I am an augur, indeed, not much of one but just in my small way, rather as one whose handwriting is terribly hard to read and only so much as I myself require. Therefore it is that I'm already precisely aware of what the transgression was. As an entity through which wisdom speaks, friend, this too is an imminent quality of the soul. Indeed, already for quite some time I have been on edge and somewhat ill at ease as I spoke my oration, and I experienced some trepidation like Ibycus – whether or not I might be speaking contrary to the gods and, thus: *"committing an outrage in substituting the vain glorifications of the all-too-human."* But now, as I say, I know the outrage and my transgression. *[242d2]*

Phae: And what, pray tell, what might that be?

Socr: A malefic speech, Phaedrus, and one truly abominable have you carried to this place and, then, forced this upon me, that I might outdo it.

Phae: But, how so?

Socr: A naïve and rather dastardly heinous one – and what, then, what might be more malefic than this?

Phae: Certainly nothing at all, if what you say is right.

Socr: How now? Don't you maintain that Eros, being the son of Aphrodite, is a god?

Phae: So I have heard; that's how the story goes.

Socr: But this is not at all what Lysias has said, nor what stands written, nor yet that which you bewitched my tongue into speaking. But if, as indeed is true, if Eros is a god and love something divine, so then it's not possible that love is something malefic. But this is how both of the former speeches spoke regarding love. And, thus, in this they committed sacrilege against Eros, as if love would be such. And so, they did sin against Eros; but then right along with this they displayed a naïveté which came with a great deal of artifice:[51] that both of these speeches without ever speaking out something wholesome or true give themselves the appearance *as if* they were on to something – and perhaps there may be a few saps who might stand to

---

[51] Deceitful images are the stock trade of sophists as shown in the *Sophist* where, likewise, the purification of the soul is pointed to 227c (p. 525); also *Protagoras* 313a–314b (p. 113).

profit by such deceptions. Hence, as for me, I need to purify *[243a]*
myself. But for the poets who commit sacrilege against the gods
there's an old remedy and way for atonement regarding which Homer
was oblivious, but Stesichorus well knew it. For as he lost his vision
due to the defamation of Helen, so unlike Homer he knew right away
what the cause for this was and rather as one who is intimate with the
muses he recognized his mistake immediately and, so, composed the
following verse straight-away: *"Untrue is this speech; for never didst*
thou climb aboard the bespangled ships; nor camest thee ye to the
Trojan feasts." And just as soon as he composed this, his so-called
recantation, just as quickly his eyesight was again restored. Now, I
intend to do him one better. For even before something awful should
happen to me due to my defamation against Eros I shall make the
attempt that I disavow the previous speeches and I shall do this not
speaking from beneath a veil and covered in my shame, but rather
now with my head upright, fully exposed.

Phae: Something yet more pleasurable than this, Socrates, 'tis not
possible for you to say to me.   *<21.~243c]*

Socr: And you, my virtuous Phaedrus, you likewise share in this
insight: how shameless both of the foregoing speeches were in that
which they spoke – the latter as well as the first that was read from
the book? For if a noble person of refined character, a gentleman who
either now or at some previous time was in love with someone who
possessed similar qualities, if such a person would have listened in
and heard us as we said that lovers might quarrel vehemently with
one another and this over small, insignificant matters, and also that a
lover would act disfavorably toward the beloved and be the cause of
his ruination: wouldn't you be of the opinion that he might well come
to the belief that he was hearing people speaking who were the dregs
of society, some helots who load the merchant ships and whose whole
life has passed on the docks amongst ignoramuses, people who have
never even seen a respectable, loving relationship? – and that there
would be a great deal lacking that he might ever voice his agreement
in that regarding which we deprecated love?   *[d]*

Phae: Well, perhaps – by Zeus – o Socrates.

Socr: Out of shame before the gentleman and out of my trepidation
before Eros himself I would like to propose a speech of a much finer
vintage, that we rinse the saltwater taste from out of our mouths.
And I also would advise Lysias that he make all haste to rewrite his
manuscript, that namely it's far preferable and one would have to
gratify a lover over a non-lover, assuming that all the rest is equal.

Phae: Rest assured, it is certain that what you say shall happen. For once you have spoken out in praise of the lover so too and necessarily I shall require the same from Lysias, that he also rewrite his paper and from this vantage.

Socr: And I am glad and do believe it: so long as you remain true to your self.   [e]

Phae: Summon up your courage, then, and speak.

Socr: But where is that boy with whom I was speaking? – that he too may listen in on this and doesn't hurry off untaught, that he might precipitously give himself over to the non-lover.

Phae: The lad is always quite close to your side, Socrates, and receptive to you – as often as you like.   <22.~244a]

Socr: So know it, then, beauteous boy, that the former speech has as its origin Phaedrus of Myrrhinous, son of Pythocles; but the one that I am to speak is from Stesichorus of Himera, son of Euphemus. And this is how it has to be spoken:

Untrue is the former speech that maintains that although a lover be present one nonetheless must give precedence in gratifying the non-lover because the former would be crazy, the latter in his right mind. For, indeed, if it were totally valid and there weren't any exceptions to the rule that insanity is an evil, then and then only would this be well spoken; but now the greatest goods of all come to be for us due to insanity – an insanity, however, which is bestowed upon us out of divine favor. For the prophetesses at Delphi and the priestesses at Dodona – it is through madness that these have brought about much which is good for Hellas, in respect both to the public affairs as well as private concerns, but through their understanding they have accomplished the most meager trivialities or nothing whatsoever. And if we wanted to go on and expostulate on this, bringing in the sibyl and everything else of this sort, all the examples of how by inspired augury so many have been helped so much, well, all of this would become tedious and a bore to go through it all – and, besides, it already is common knowledge. But then, it is worthwhile that I mention that amongst the men of yore, those who were in on the exercise of philological matters and who set down which names were the right and proper ones, these ancients did not at all look down on the idea of being possessed by the truth *if* this should happen by divine dispatch, as if this were to be something that one had to be ashamed about and keep covered up and hidden, because how   [c] otherwise can it be explained that they inserted this right into the name of the most noble of the arts, the art through which the future is assessed, and due to the divinity of such possession they named it

divination. But now that the modern interpretations have caught on
and displaying their complete ineptitude to get clarity right down to
the bottom of this matter, the deconstructionists have added in an "r"
and changed the "ss" to be an "f" – and so it is that instead of being
possessed by the truth as a divine matter they claim to *profess* the
truth [what with all the professors in academia, you know what I'm
talking about: how they don't even bother to put brackets around the
additions in their editions of sacred text but brutally manhandle the
noblest conceptions of their progenitors, ad-libbing wherever it just
seems to them as being necessary and, what is much worse, simply
deleting those *sections* that they can't comprehend or think to be
irrelevant, like the Areopagos which is flown away, though this is an
odd way of moving mountains] and so this is how one studies the
past and attempts to come to grips with the future! And even in this
same way they have re-interpreted that which in bygone times was
researched by those who really were enlightened – and be it through
the agency of natural portents or by other such omens and signs like
those having to do with the flights of birds, these ways by which the
future may be foretold. And as these ways brought about insight and
wisdom and as the revelations lit up human consciousness, so this
higher vision was spoken of as a "ray-of-sun"; but now the moderns
have altered this as well and have come up with their supreme
attachment to reason.   Now, just as the possession mentioned
formerly is so much more holy and noble than this professing, and
not only linguistically but also as regards the facts of the matter, so
too and in full accord with the evidence of these ancients divine
inspiration and initiation into the sun mysteries is likewise so
much greater in worthiness than the mere reasonings of human
understanding.   And in much the same manner these ancients'
approach toward disease and the most dreadful plagues that
periodically decimate mankind are superior, as these afflictions were
attributed to the [divine] wrath that had accumulated upon earlier
generations and which, then, falls hard upon successive generations;
and so too, verily, there is a madness that steps forward and
prophesizes for those who are suffering under such awful duress, that
these too might find their way back to salvation; and so it was that
they set down which prayers were required and how the gods   *[e]*
were to be revered, that by such means as these acts of purification
and through the attainment of the wisdom of the mysteries everyone
might secure consolation, and not only for the current time but for
all times to come as well – that, thus, those who in the right manner
were possessed of madness could find the solution to the riddle of
sufferings that hold sway.   The third sort of influx of spirit and

madness catches hold of a sensitive and divinely favored soul through the muses and such a soul becomes excited and inflamed and, thus, breaks forth in celebratory songs and other creative works of art and poesie – and, so, in thousands of acts of ornamentation dedicated to the primal father-gods such a soul prepares the way for future generations. But whoever should find himself or herself in the preparatory stages of these poetic arts and opines that alone through the practice of such crafts, that hereby he or she might become a real artist or poet, such a one is not a true initiate – and also the works that such people bring forth, those flowing from mere understanding, such works will be left in darkness behind those that are inspired by a divine madness. To this extent and even further am I ready *[b]* and able to sing praise of the madness that is divinely inspired and that comes to us from the gods, such heavenly works. And so it is that we don't want to shy away from this, nor allow ourselves that we be misled into error and confusion, that we might be frightened into believing that the mindful are to be preferred as friends over those who are ecstatic and in transport, but rather only then shall they take the prize if first they are able to prove to us as well that love is not bestowed upon both lover and beloved as a divine grace given them for their salvation and sent to them by the gods. But now, it's up to us to prove the opposite, that it is for our greatest bliss and happiness that the gods bestow such favors upon us. And those who consider themselves reasonable will not deem this proof believable, but it will be believed by those who are wise. But first of all it is requisite that we acquire right insight into the nature of soul, both divine as well as human; and we'll do so by taking into consideration what it does and what it suffers.[52] The beginning of this proof *<23.~245cd]* is as follows. Every soul is immortal. For that which subsists as constantly in motion cannot die, but that which is moved by others and which is the cause that others move, insofar as such motion is sectioned, so too such as this gets only a section of life. Thus, only that which moves itself is, as such, never abandoned by itself, and such never comes to an end of its activity, rather everything else that comes into movement has this as its source and as its beginning. But the beginning is uncreated. For it is only from the beginning that all of creation has come-into-being, but it itself from naught. For then, if the beginning itself were to come to be from something [other] then naught would come to be from the beginning. But since the beginning itself is not created, so too it needs must be eternal.

---

[52] Wirken und Leiden: *Theaeteus* 156a (p. 378); *Sophist* 247e–249e (p. 553); *Parmenides* 138b (p. 220); *Phaedrus* 270d ; *Gorgias* 476d (p. 293); and *Charmides* 165c (pp. 186–187).

For if, then, the beginning should cease-to-be, so then neither could it come-into-being out of something other nor could something other come to be through it, as then, everything should come to be from out of the beginning. Hence and in full accord with the foregoing, the source of all movement is that which moves itself; but it is not possible that this should itself ever be created or cease-to-be, or else the entire heavens and all of creation would have to succumb into a state of being-at-rest and would have nothing through which   *[e]* they might be moved and by which it would be possible for them to come back into being. Consequent to this, that which has shown itself as that which moves itself is eternal – and so it is that one needn't be ashamed when clarifying that it's even this which is the essence and concept of the soul. For each body that is set into motion from something external to it is called inanimate, but those that have this activity in themselves are called ensouled as this is the nature of soul. But if this is how it correlates, that nothing other than soul is that which moves itself, so too, then, soul is neither created nor is it susceptible to death. Regarding the immortality of the soul, now, this is sufficient; but as regards the essence of soul we have to admit that in respect to whatever its qualities are in themselves, this is utterly and in every regard a divine matter and, accordingly, one that requires the most elaborate and, indeed, superhuman investigation; but saying that to which the soul might be compared, this is an easier investigation and one more befitting to human conceptions. Thus, it needs to be spoken of in such a wise. Accordingly,   *<24.~246b]* the soul can be *likened* to the amalgamated power of a winged chariot and its guide. The divine steeds and the charioteers are all them-selves good and are of noble lineage, but the others are mixed. And next, it's now so that the guide holds the reins of the chariot and, further, one of the steeds is both good and noble having such as its origin, but the other has the exact opposite qualities and lineage. For this reason the steerage for us is necessarily hard and tiresome. Wherefore, furthermore, that the naming originates of mortal and immortal animals – this too we have to attempt to bring into clarity. Everything that is soul reigns over everything inanimate and soul subsists throughout the entirety of the heavens; it shows itself, however, differently in different formations. Those which are fully developed and consummate, now, and being in full plumage, these glide about in the upper regions and exercise their dominion over the whole world, but those lacking in plumage glide down into our locale until they strike upon something rigid, where it is, then, that they take up residence – and this taking on of an earthly body which, now, due to the power of the soul the body seems to be moving on its own,

and so this whole, the composite of soul with body, gets the name
animal and it is qualified as being mortal; an immortal composite,
however, has never been adequately proven, rather we only imagine
such a being without ever having seen God, nor are we sufficiently
cognizant of Him: an immortal animal composed of both body and
soul and yet both unified as one throughout all eternity. All the same,
may the latter correlate as God pleases and this, accordingly, has only
been spoken in passing. But now let us consider what the cause is
for the loss of plumage, why it is that the soul's plumage falls out.
This is as follows: the power of the plumage is   <25.~246de]
expressed in this – to lift up that which is weighed down and lead
it upward toward the dwelling place of the race of the gods. It is
also the case that the plumage partakes to the greatest extent in that
which stands in contra-relation to the body, that is, in that which is
godlike. But the divine is beautiful, wise, good and everything else
that is similar to this. It is, thus, above all from things such as these
that the soul's plumage receives nourishment and grows, but it is
due to all those things that are misshapen, malefic, evil and all that
stands in opposition to the former that the plumage withers and dies.
Now, the great leader in the heavens, Zeus, guiding his amply plumed
carriage, he pulls out first and ordering and taking care of everything
he is followed, then, by the regiments of gods and spirits who follow
him ordered in eleven trains. For Hestia, she remains alone within
the home of the gods. But all of these others who as ruling   [247a]
gods are ordered to the number twelve, all of these issue forth and are
led onward according to the order that has been ordained for each
of them. There is now much magnificence that is to be viewed and
much that transpires within the spheres of the heavens, and it is with
such matters as these that the gods concern themselves, each doing
his or her own appointed tasks. But now they follow Zeus, each [god
or daemon] as well as he can and will, for all rancor and envy are
forbidden within the ranks of the heavenly choir. But as now they
proceed to the great banquet and their meal and as they climb upward
along the steep ascent toward the outermost vaulted arch of the
heavens, lo, then it is true that, indeed, the chariots of the gods all
proceed apace with their well-bred steeds making an easy go of it, but
all of the others only by the most strenuous of efforts. For the steed
that has of yet something of the malefic, if its upbringing and training
have not been accomplished exceptionally well by its guide and
leader, well, this steed leans heavily downward toward the ground
and pressing downward with all its weight and, thus, herewith there
is much difficulty and the greatest combat occurs within the soul.
For these who are named immortal, as they approach upon the

outermost border of the heavens and turn themselves looking out and thus, standing upon the hindermost part, so they are caught up and ripped along by the *transformation* and they view that which is outside of heaven. But as regards the region beyond the heavens, never once has a single poet sung adequate praise of this place, nor shall it ever be worthily described. But it is so created and such are its qualities – for I needs must take the plunge that I speak the truth and particularly so as I have yet to speak of truth herself.   <26.~247cd] Without color, form or matter, essential being which truly is [53] – capable of being viewed by the soul's guide alone, reason, about which here abouts the noble house and genealogy of true knowledge subsists – it is namely this which contains the former region as-one. As now God's Understanding nourishes itself from pure, unqualified reason and knowledge, as too does every soul that concerns itself to take up that which is meet and proper: so it is that they experience joy that once more they have had a glimpse of Being, and so they take nourishment into themselves by contemplating that which is true and they bask themselves in this until once more the transformation comes about full circle and brings them back to their former positions. In this circumnavigation, now, they have a vision of right-eousness herself, and likewise mindfulness and knowledge; but not of instantiations of these which come to be, nor too of these insofar as they exist in an other form in some other thing, those things, namely, that we name as real; but rather such as that which truly is which is found in true knowledge – and so it is also that the soul gazes upon true Being apart from the others and, thus, after the soul is revitalized so she dives back into the center of the heavens and returns to her abode. Once she arrives back home, so she places the steeds before the feeding troth and throws in ambrosia and gives them nectar to drink withal. This, now, is the gods' way of life. From   <27.~248a] amongst the other souls, however, a few of them – namely those who are most adept at following the gods – these few are able to stretch out their guides' heads into this external region and so participate in the consummation of the revolution, still and yet, however, with great anxiety due to the need to control the steeds and being, thus, barely able to get a good glimpse of Being; and then there are others who do manage to raise themselves sporadically, but then plunge back

---

[53] Cf: *Being and Logos, The Way of Platonic Dialogue* – John Sallis; Humanities Press International, Inc.; 1975. page 144, footnote #27: "It is virtually impossible to translate the [Greek] phrase "…" with any suitability from the point of view of philosophical interpretation. The difficulty stems from the fact all three words are derivatives of the same word (I am), so that, most literally (and awkwardly) the phrase says something like: (the) beingly being being."

down again so that with all of their intense struggles with the horses
they manage just to catch sight of a bit but, then again, miss other
parts. All of the rest, now, all of these are indeed striving so that they
might follow along to these heights but, then, they are incapable and
are driven about this way and that in the lower regions, and they are
limited to knocking into one another and pushing and shoving one
another in that each attempts to get ahead of all the others. A great
tumult arises, thus, and combat and anxious sweat whereby due to
the fault of incompetent leaders a great many become all tangled up
and mutilated, what with the soul's plumage being torn out and
damaged in every manner; and then after all this suffering of so many
travails all of these go away without having been able to partake in
the contemplation of Being and, so, having missed their opportunity
they support themselves on semblances and illusory nourishment.
And it is for this reason that there is so much enthusiasm that   *[c]*
the field of truth be purveyed, there where it is – namely these are the
appropriate pastures for the most noble of souls and it is in these
meadowlands that the soul finds the nourishment she needs that
empowers the plumage by which the soul is born upwards and,
indeed, the *Law of Adrasteia* is this: that whichever soul hath
accompanied the gods in their ascent and, thus, caught view of that
which truly is, so this soul shall be spared from all harm until the next
exodus takes place, and if the soul is always able to accomplish this
great feat so it shall always remain undamaged. But, should it be
incapable of attaining these heights and so it sees naught, that rather
it meets up with some accident and thereby falls into forgetfulness
and becomes weighed down and filled with torpor, and so pressed
downwards it loses its plumage and falling hard upon the earth, so in
this case the law states that in the first instance such a soul shall not
be implanted in any brutish creature, that rather those who have
glimpsed the most shall find themselves in the seed of a man who is
destined to be a friend of wisdom or someone who is devoted to
beauty, be it a servant of the muses or some other servant to love; the
second shall become king and law-giver, or else a great warrior and
conqueror; the third shall become a statesman or someone ruling
over a household and leading the life of a businessman or merchant;
the fourth becomes a friend of the exercises which strengthen *[248e]*
the body, an athlete – or else someone who is occupied in the health
professions as a physician or healer; the fifth shall be an augur and
shall lead a life devoted to the mysteries; the sixth shall be a poet or
else someone who occupies himself with imitation; the seventh shall
live upon the land as a farmer or else pursue some trade of handwork;
the eighth shall be a sophist or some sycophant exciting the populace;

and the ninth shall become a tyrant. Amongst all of these, now, he who lives life righteously advances up to a better position; but he who lives unjustly, his lot worsens. For thither, there where every soul arrives, it doesn't return for a span of ten-thousand years, for it takes so much time that the soul might renew its plumage excepting, that is, those who have philosophized without falsehood, those who have loved youths in a way not unphilosophical. For these it <28.~249a] is possible that in their third period of one thousand years, if for three times running they have chosen the same *modus vivendi*, then it is possible that these return home after just three thousand years. But all of the rest, once they have brought their first life to a conclusion, so these come to stand before judgment. And after receiving judgment some are sent to the place of punishment which lies underneath the earth where it is that they must atone for their transgressions; but then there are others who are raised up into the heavens by the exercise of justice and there they live a life that is commensurate with the one that they led whilst in human form. After the passage of one thousand years, however, both sorts of souls are released and they have to choose which sort of life they desire for their next incarnation, and each soul chooses as it wills. At this time it is possible for a human soul to go over into that of an animal and also for that of an animal that, note it, earlier was human to return and incarnate as a human once more. Because, then, for one that never has had a glimpse at truth, such as these may never take on human form – for it is requisite that humanity grasps whatever may be expressed in generic terms in that human beings proceed from the many impressions to arrive at one that is brought together in   *[c]* their understanding. And this is remembrance of the former, that which our souls at one time perceived when we followed along in the train of the gods and looked up into that which lies beyond and at that which now we refer to as Being, namely that which truly is Being and to which our guides raised up their heads. And it is for this reason also that it is rightful that only the souls of philosophers attain such plumage – for these are the ones who by their remembrance strive to remain as much as possible amongst those former things, those things, namely, through the partaking in which the gods are given their divinity. In righteous service of such remembrance, thus, and always consecrating themselves to the holy, thus alone is it possible for humans to reach their full potential, their consummation. And in that such a person holds himself aloof from human strivings and traffics with the divine, so it is that such individuals are severely berated by the people: that they are all confused; but that such individuals are inspired, this escapes the people's notice. <29.~249d]

Here, now, the entire speech has arrived at [it's aim] – the fourth sort of madness: in hindsight to which whoever gazes upon beauty as it exists here abouts is reminded of its true Being and, as the plumage becomes active and as this growth continues, indeed, the soul attempts to take flight but isn't yet capable, like a bird looking heavenwards and taking little heed of what lies beneath itself – and so such a person is criticized and spoken of as being heartsick; that, namely, this amongst all of the forms of inspiration is the most noble and proves itself of having the noblest source, and both on him who is thus inspired as well as on whomever the inspiration falls, and that whoever partakes in loving a beauty, such a person is called – lover. Namely, as has already been explained, the soul of every person must necessarily have had a glimpse of Being, or else the soul would never attain human form; but then it's no easy matter to be reminded by what exists here abouts of the former, neither for those who   *[250a]* had only a meager glimpse nor for those who have fallen so low and have met with unfortunate accidents so that they have gone astray, what with their commerce in unrighteousness and, thus, the former holy vision has been misplaced due to their forgetfulness; and so it is that few remain with an abiding memory, one having a sufficiency in strength. Now these, when they see a mirror image *{Ebenbild}* of that which truly is, so they become enraptured and are no longer in control of themselves; but what it is that really has transpired, this they themselves don't even know because they aren't sufficiently capable of seeing through it. For the representations *{Abbilder}* of righteousness, mindfulness and whatever else is so precious for the soul, these have lost their shine here abouts; rather with gross implements and with a prodigious amount of effort only a few are able to render something that somewhat approximates the genealogy of that which is being imitated. But beauty as it subsists there shone forth and was perceived in all its brilliancy as we followed along in Jupiter's train, but then others followed after the other gods, and thus we delighted in the divine vision and in this sublime spectacle and, so, became initiated into the mystery which, indeed, one would have to name the holiest; and all of this was celebrated by us when we   *[c]* ourselves were without blemish and hadn't as of yet been struck by the evils that yet awaited us in future times to come; and so, as I said, without blemish, without falsehood, unchanging, in anticipation of the most blessed countenance and consecrated in the pure brilliance, pure and totally unencumbered by the coarseness of our body, as such have we named it, and into which we now have been imprisoned and caged like the turtle within his shell, this body that now we carry about with us. May this be as a gift given unto our remembrance that the aspiration toward the beyond be presented, and it is due to the very same that this has been presented at such length and with so much detail. And how all of this relates to beauty, so her radiance sparkles, as was said, sufficiently before us just as she   <30.~250d] subsists amongst the former things and now that we too have arrived at this juncture, so we have grasped hold of her essence through the clarity of the clearest of our senses and her radiance shines upon us. For sight is the sharpest of all of our corporeal senses and though it is so that through sight's agency we do not, indeed, perceive wisdom – for then how great would the pangs of love be should this be the case that a mirror image of such would be presented before us – nor too do we perceive all the others that are so worthy of love, rather only with beauty has this become so: that she in part shines out to us with her great splendor and her effects extend even unto the delight of our bodies, that she pricks us with her arrows of love. Now, it also is true that he who is lacking in the contemplation of the eternal verities or for someone who otherwise has fallen into corruption, such a person does not, indeed, feel drawn from here thither where beauty itself subsists in that he catches sight of that which bears beauty's name; and so it is true that such a person doesn't revere her appearance but, rather, right away gives himself over to lust and immediately sets himself to considering how he might go about satisfying his base desires like an animal and, so, such a one approaches beauty in a manner most uncouth having neither the proper fear nor having any shame but totally contrary to his higher nature such a person allows his lust to guide him. But he, on the other hand, he who has   [251a] recently participated in the mysteries and who has contemplated the beyond from multifarious perspectives, if such a person as this should encounter a heavenly beauty – and be it just in a face or an entire body filled with grace and, thus, beauty finds her full expression – so, first off, a shiver will run up his spine and then he becomes altered as his memory of the beyond begins to awaken within; and so too his anxiousness re-awakens as he has an inkling of the transformation and, so, consequent to this he begins to worship this visage of beauty as something divine, and at the same time he has no fear regarding what other people say about him, that they think that he's taken things far too far with such madness, this is his repute; and so it is that he sacrifices himself, bowing down as if to a sacred image or to a God: to this person – his beloved. And when he meets up with his *amour*, so he is transformed in a similar fashion as one might experience a transformation due to illness, like a high fever which causes the shivers and cold sweats, though, indeed, the body feels all ablaze. And thus, too, is his experience, namely, he feels permeated by a warmth in that he has succumbed to this effluence of beauty that streams forth from his *amour*, that which his very eyes present to him and due to which, then, the roots of his soul's plumage begin to bestir themselves, like flowers after a spring rain. And now, as this warmth permeates him, so the hardening suffered by his soul melts away and his plumage that has been dormant for such a long while due to this rigidity, his plumage begins sprouting out all over. Thus, receiving its nourishment from this beauty, so the feathers are popping out and the quills break through all over his soul for, verily, once his soul was fully covered in plumage. Thus, everything has come   *<31.~251c]* alive within the soul and there is a seething and a spuding, the fomentations of a riotous growth, and so, in a similar fashion as with a small child whose teeth are first breaking through – the pain, irritation and prickling sensations, just such an experience awaits those whose souls are brought into uproar as the plumage begins popping out, the tumultuous ferment, the tickling and lacerations that are experienced as the quills break forth all over the soul. When it comes to pass, now, that the soul in her perception of beauty that is granted her due to the presence of her beloved, when she is – as it were – showered by that which streams forth and which, therefore, is called the titillations of love, and she takes this up and becomes consumed by her passion, thus, she is fructified and is all aglow in warmth and this, then, brings about a lessening of her pains and she experiences joy. But then, when she becomes separated from her beloved, so it is that she dries up and all the apertures close up where the plumage had been breaking through, the soul is all scrunched and, hence, the irritation becomes intolerable as the soul's impulse toward growth is hemmed in. Thus, this drive that has been titillated into life – it pulsates in a similar fashion as the blood pounds in the arteries – and so these quills cut into and make lacerations throughout the soul and attempt to break through the apertures so that the entire soul is set into a frenzy due to these intolerable pricklings, though, all the same, the soul is yet in possession of its memory of the beautiful and due to this still retains its joyous transport. In that both the pain and the joy are all mixed up with one another, so the soul is driven to the utmost extremity due to this vexatious contradiction and this tempest that is raging within, and so it is that the soul becomes totally disoriented and it is due to this madness that it neither is able to sleep during the night nor   *[e]* can it retain any composure or concentration during the day, rather it's always ready to rush off to wherever it may be that there's the least bit of hope that it may catch a glimpse of the beloved. And then, when at long last the soul does finally catch sight of this beauty and once more receives all the titillations thus engendered: so the *spring showers* perform their feat once more and all of the quills become unstuck, the soul recovers her composure and well-being in that all the lacerations are brought to a stop and now she savors, at least for the moment, the sweetest bliss given unto man. And this, then, is the reason why it is that she never wishes to take leave from her beloved, nor is there anyone at all whom she might respect to the same degree, rather she forgets her mother, brothers and friends entirely, she thinks nothing at all of the fact that all her business affairs, all of her possessions and even her good name and high moral standing, all of these are tottering on the brink of ruin – *what does it matter!* – all of this which formerly, indeed, she may well have handled with the greatest astuteness, all of this is thrown to the winds and now she is fully ready just to remain right here attending upon her beloved, that ever more she might rest in his embrace. For besides her reverence for her beloved it is only here with this possessor of beauty that she has found the right physician for the most intolerable pains and lacerations. This state of being, o beauteous youth to whom I'm now speaking, this is what humanity calls love, but the way that the gods name it, this, when you hear it, may well make you laugh due to the newness [of these ideas]. Namely, there are a few Homeric bards, as I believe, who have in two of their obscure poems a couple of stanzas in which hidden meaning upon the subject of love may be found, one of which being quite whimsical and, indeed, lacking even in proper rhyme and rhythm. This, then, is how it is sung: *"The mortals call this now the God of wing'd love; Gods of flight that from time to time the mighty plumage breaketh through."* It's totally up to you, now, whether or not you choose to put your faith in all this but, all the same, the former account is in truth the state of those in love and this is its underlying cause. He who follows along in the <32.~252c] train of Zeus, now, if he should become smitten and falls underneath love's grasp, such a person is better able to tolerate the pains due to what was called the *wings of love*. But if it should be a servant of the god Ares, someone who is following along this path, and such a person gets caught up and believes himself to have been injured by the beloved, such people as these are quick to seek bloody retribution and think nothing of sacrificing themselves and their loved ones. And it's quite the same thing with all of the other gods, to whichever train it may be to which one belongs; thus, each and every lives in imitation and honors the god each follows to the full extent of his capabilities and for as long as he still remains unspoiled and is yet pursuing his first existence, living his life here abouts; and it is in this manner that he interacts with his lovers and with all of the rest; this is how things correlate betwixt him and them. And so it is that everyone picks out a lover in accordance to his character of soul and each perceives beauty just as if this were to be his god itself, and so it is that he decks him out and decorates his *amour* like a holy image so that he might worship him and celebrate his festivities duly inspired. Thus, those who belong to Zeus strive that their lovers may have   [e] souls that are similar to that of Zeus. Accordingly, they seek about for someone of a philosophical nature, someone who is a leader – and if they find such a person and win him over in love, so they do everything possible that he actually becomes such. And even if it should be so that they have no experience at all in such matters and have never labored at this before, still they learn as they work and struggle and exert themselves with all their power, and however it may be that they happen upon it – and, so, they also investigate into themselves. And in that they follow the leads that are present within, so they have success discovering the nature of their god because they are driven unceasingly that they look upon their lord and that they come to grasp him in their memory, and so they become enthused and take up his ethics and his challenges, everything for which he strives; and they do all of this to the full extent possible that a human being might share in what is divine; and so it is that they ascribe all of this to their beloved and become even more attached to him. And if it should be that their creative energy is derived from Zeus, as it is with the bacchantes, so they lift up their cups in honor and homage to this soul in whom they have found love and they make their beloved that he be so much as ever possible similar to this, their god.   [b] But those who follow along in Hera's train, so these seek after someone of the most royal of natures and if they find him, so they likewise proceed in all details – just so. And so too with those who worship Apollo and all of the other gods, they all seek out a young lad who resembles their god, someone of a similar type, and once they have found him so they lead him on to the way of life that is practiced by this god, that his character be just the same in that they themselves imitate this god and, so too, they convince their *amour* that he be conjoined with them and to the fullest extent possible and they do this without a bit of envy and without leaving any room open to ignoble desires or unfavorable wishes against their beloved – that, rather, it all be for the best and in every wise attempting to lead onward toward the goal of similarity to themselves and to the god; thus is it done. In eager pursuit, he who loves truly, and seeking consecration, if they attain that which so eagerly is being pursued, as I have described it, thus much beauty and happiness falls upon the beloved who is being pursued by this friend who is madly in love, once the conquest has been made. But the conquest shall be made if the beauty is found and he is found in even this manner. Just as at the beginning of this narrative the soul was divided   <*33.~253d]* up into three parts, two of which were compared in form to steeds and the third being similar to the charioteer, so this analogy remains likewise our presumption. Of the two steeds, we went on to say, one would be good but the other isn't. But wherein the excellence of the one consists and the malfeasance of the other, this we didn't clarify and now we need to do so. Of the both of them, then, the one that takes on the better position, this one has grown straight and tall, stands lightly on his legs, holds his head high with an upturned nose, his coat is all white, eyes black, of a nature full of respect and loving honor, a nature that is rooted in mindfulness and shame and having a strong proclivity toward truthfulness – and so it is that he becomes a friend without any need for the whip, rather he's led onward simply through command and by the word; but then, the other droops, he's plump and of a poor build, obstinate, short-necked, pug-nosed, having a black hide with glassy eyes shot through with red, full of wildness, stubborn, obtuse, raw about the ears, deaf and barely heeding – and to neither the spurs nor the whip. If, now, the charioteer should catch sight of a titillating beauty and the whole soul starts to melt due to this lovely sight and, soon enough, the prickling sensations occur and the impulse becomes manifest: <*34.~254a]* so the steed who is easily led holds himself back – as this one always tends toward bashfulness due to his shame and so there's no danger of him leaping forward; but then, the other now is totally oblivious, neither to spurs nor to the whip does he pay any heed, rather springing forward he strives to force his way onward and likewise is urging both charioteer and wagon-mate: that they take a good look; and so he forces them to make haste that they pursue this beauty and, then too, he begins considering the favors that might be bestowed, all of the pleasures of love. Now, both of his companions are initially most unwilling and they strive against the banter of this vexatious and quite unprincipled wagon-mate, but finally, as there's no end to his troublesome agitation, so they finally give in and promise to do as he asks and so they are dragged along and, hence, now they arrive in full view of the beloved's shining figure *{Gestalt}*. In that, now, the charioteer finds himself face to face with such a radiant form, so his remembrance is carried back to the essence of beauty and now once more he is viewing beauty with mindfulness as she stands there upon sacred ground. With this vision he is overcome by trepidation as he becomes filled by this awesome reverence – and so he stoops down and pulls back hard on the reins, indeed, he's incapable of doing *[c]* otherwise, and he pulls back with such force on the reins that both steeds are immediately brought down on their haunches, the one most willingly as he never contradicts, but the wild steed is terribly upset. In that, now, they are beating their retreat, so the first one breaks out in a full sweat due to his shame and wonderment, but the other, just as soon as he's recovered from the awful pain consequent to the bit being jerked in and his fall, though practically with his first breath, he, on the other hand, breaks out in a most righteous indignation and angrily heaps invectives upon his companions, cursing them vehemently: that they've proven themselves to be cowards, not real men, and that they would be guilty of having broken their promises and, then too, demanding once again that they move forward and approach this beauty despite their wills to the contrary and, so, he's loathe to give in even a little and hardly appeased as these two plead their case: that it would be better to put things off for a little while. And so, when the wait that finally was agreed upon is over, so now he reminds them about that which they are quite intent upon forgetting, and he takes violent measures, wailing and whinnying and dragging them forward, and so once more he forces them on, that they approach the beloved again and with the same intent as previously. And as they draw nigh upon their destination, so impetuously he redoubles his efforts, his tail shoots up in the air and he takes the bit firmly between his teeth, clamping down on it, and so he pulls his companions onward in a shameless fashion. *[e]* But now the charioteer experiences exactly the same thing as before, indeed, this time even more so, it's as if his main sail has been thrown about by the wind, and so it is that he pulls back even more violently on the reins, wrenching the bit out from the wild steed's teeth and thus ripping it into his tongue and cheeks, bloodying up the hardware on this horse that's seemingly dead set on abuse and now is being held firmly, down low, close to the ground – and not on his haunches as before but now down on his knees and, thus, he lets him do penance. Finally, after suffering from similar occurrences on multiple occasions this steed does lay his wildness aside and is humbled and, thus, now follows his leader's well-considered directives; and so it is that he is out-manned during their future encounters with the afore-mentioned sight, that of the titillating beauty. And so, at last it comes about that the lover's soul pursues the beloved in a manner that is both bashful and conscientious. As, now, the beloved   *<35.~255a]* is respected with all the deference befitting a god and, moreover, from someone who not only pretends that he is in love, rather someone who truly finds himself to be in this state, and as the beloved himself is also naturally disposed toward such a reverential attitude, and even if it may also be the case that earlier on he may have been misled by his playmates or by whomever else it may have been and falsely persuaded by those who maintain that it would be a scandal were he to approach someone in love and, thus, he may well have avoided such people – so, nonetheless, in the course of time both his youth and the inevitability of it conspired against this and finally it does occur; thus, he makes acquaintance with someone who is in love. For never shall this be allowed to happen: that he who is malefic shall be a true friend to someone else who also is malefic; nor that he who is good shall not be friend to someone else who also is good. But once he allows himself to be approached by such a person and once he starts talking to him and having commerce with him, so the true goodwill of the lover becomes immediately apparent and the beloved is thrilled as now it dawns upon him that all of his other friends and relations taken in their entirety amount to as much as nothing in comparison with this impassionedly devoted friend. Hence, once he has allowed him access for a meaningful span of time and has been in close vicinity to this well-wisher's presence, so the effluence pours forth – perhaps as they come into contact when wrestling in the gymnasium or wherever else it may be that they come together – the source of that mighty river which Zeus named the titillations of love when he was infatuated with Ganymede: so this pours forth in all [c] of its richness upon the lover, and in part it streams into him and in part too it pours forth from him as he is overfull – and just as it is that the wind or a sound wave when meeting up against a flat, hard body bounces back and reverberates once more thither whence it came, so too this effluence of beauty is driven back toward the *beaut* and entering through his eyes and through all of the other passages by which the soul receives her nourishment and once arrived thither, so the spring showers do their work once more and the apertures become moistened and the plumage begins to sprout as this impulse toward growth becomes manifest – and, so too, the soul of the beloved is filled with love. Thus, the beloved loves – but whom? This he doesn't know, indeed, he has no idea at all as regards to what has happened, at least he doesn't have a clue as to what he might say, but rather, like someone who has caught an affliction such as an inflammation of the eyes from someone else, so he doesn't know what has caused it, for that it should be that he has been struck by his very own beauty that is reflected back upon him by his lover acting like a mirror, this he doesn't know. And when it happens that the other is present, so too just like the lover he is set free from the pain, but then when his lover is absent, so too he experiences the longings and lacerations just as the lover experiences these longings for him and, thus, he is afflicted with the shadow image of love and love reciprocates. But, all the same, he doesn't name it as such and does not even know that he's in love, rather he thinks that this is   *[e]* merely friendship – and yet he longs for the other, just not quite to the same pitch and fervor: that he might see him, touch him, put his arms around him and, indeed, lay on the couch next to him, and – as is only to be expected – soon he does all of these things. And now that they find themselves on the same couch, well, the lover's wild steed doesn't waste any time proposing to the charioteer that as recompense for all of the past travails, the numerous bloody scenes and tribulations, all of that which has been suffered through, well, a small reward certainly wouldn't be too much to ask for – and, it is true, the wild steed on the beloved's side withholds from making any such requests, perhaps due to its being so fully aroused   *[256a]* by this previously unknown longing that he has become quite pre-occupied, what with all of the kissing and hugging, all of the loving endearments that are duly given to one's best friend; and in that they are lying now so sweetly together, so there wouldn't be any hesitation from his quarter that the beloved should do everything to gratify this lover, whatever it may be that he wishes and desires. But then, the other two wagon-mates and the charioteers are wrestling against such ideas due to their bashfulness and due also to the dictates of reason. If it should be that the better parts of the soul, those   *<36.~256b]* parts that direct one to a well-ordered life and toward the love of wisdom, if these parts succeed and are victorious, so they lead the soul on toward a life that is blessed, a life focused on integrity and the one: being lord over oneself and having made the conquest in one's soul over that which tends toward the malefic and, thus, being set free and abiding in what is most admirable; but if they should die, so it shall have transpired that already they are in full plumage and have become lighter, that of the three Olympian contests they already have proven victorious in this one, and a greater good is not to be brought into being, neither through human mindfulness nor through divine madness. But if it should be that they have chosen a path that is less noble and not philosophical but, still, that they lead a life devoted to honor, so it easily may happen that the occasion arises – perhaps one evening after enjoying a fine *Gewürztraminer* or at some other careless moment – it may happen that the two wanton steeds conspire together and, thus, do deliver the soul over when the charioteers aren't paying any heed and, so, the two are brought together in that manner which the multitudes hold as being most blessed, and so they choose this and fulfill their desires and, thus, if they have done so once, so too they're quite likely to do so again, that they share in this pleasure, but seldom, because not the whole of their soul is in favor and voices approval for what they do. Thus, such as these also shall be friends, although not quite to the same extent *[d]* as the former ones, each with the other, and both during the time of their love as well as afterwards when they have gone beyond it, that they live together with the firm conviction that they have each given pledges to the other and each has accepted the other's testimonials – and it would be a crime and an outrage if this ever should be invalidated and these should find themselves as enemies. Thus, at the end of their lives they go forth, indeed, without plumage but still with this impulse that they desire as much, they go forth, as I say, from their corporeal bodies with this impulse and, so, they too carry off more than a little recompense due to this madness of love. For then, in the darkness and upon the underworldly paths, these ways definitely are *not* in their agenda, that they should find themselves there, as then they already are on the way toward the heavenly path and, so, they proceed upon this radiant path of life and wander forth together sharing in all their happiness, and thus it is that when finally they do attain plumage, so due to their love for one another this happens to both simultaneously. These advantages, so *<37.~256e]* great and so godly, o boy, these are the bounty earned as the fruits of the lover's friendship. But intimacy with the non-lover which is a diluted affair and the meager result of a death oriented mindfulness which, likewise, only generates mortal and scanty rewards, this promotes a vulgarity in the soul of the beloved that, indeed, may be praised as virtue by the common sort and by the masses – and such is also the cause that such a soul be driven about hither and yon for nine thousand years both here upon the earth as well as upon the paths underneath the earth, those ways that are bereft of reason. *[a]* May this speech be delivered as recompense unto thee, dear Eros, as the best and most beauteous recantation that lies in our power – and, indeed, for the rest and particularly due to Phaedrus it necessarily was composed in a somewhat poetic vein. And may it find your favor, Eros, that you might forgive us for our earlier speeches and grant to us your approbation, and may your beneficence and mercy fall upon me and my art of love, that which thou hast given unto me, that you neither take back nor diminish the same due to your wrath. Rather, do bestow thy graces upon me that I might find even greater praise before the beauties. But if it should be that our earlier speeches contained something odious and irreverent, Phaedrus' and mine: so put the blame for this onto Lysias' account – as he is the father *[b]* of these speeches – and may it be that he desists in writing such speeches, that rather he might give precedence to philosophy to which, indeed, already his brother, Polemarchus, has turned; that he also might direct his attentions thither so that his disciple no longer carries such speeches about as now upon both shoulders, that rather he also devotes himself to the love of philosophical discourse.   <38.]

Phae: I share in your prayer, Socrates, that insofar as this is better for us may it come to pass. But for quite some time now, Socrates, I have been in wonder, awed by how much your second speech surpasses your first in its beauty, how you have managed to work this through. Thus, I have my doubts as to whether Lysias, even if he were to make the attempt, I doubt that it should amount to much at all in comparison to your speech. It's also so that quite recently one of our statesmen made disparaging remarks and heaped scorn on Lysias due to his speech, and so he named the entire diatribe as speechifying, through and through. Perhaps, then, it might be better if he withdrew himself entirely from writing speeches, due, namely, to the delicacy of such matters.   *[257d]*

Socr: That's a really ludicrous opinion, young man, that you now are proposing; and you are failing your friend ever so much by allowing that he might agree that speechwriting itself should be so shocking. Perhaps, indeed, you might even believe that the person who heaped such scorn upon him meant that this was to be taken even so, just as he said it?

Phae: That was sufficiently apparent, indeed, Socrates. And you know it just as well as I, that it's the same everywhere: that those who are most able and the most respected people in the state, these would shame themselves if ever they should write speeches and leave such writing behind – due to their fear that later on they might be taken as having been sophists.

Socr: Only you don't at all know, dear Phaedrus, how all of this is interrelated and, moreover, you also don't know that precisely those who consider themselves the greatest statesmen are likewise precisely the ones who are most enamored in writing speeches and leaving such writings for posterity; and that it is affirmatively so that whenever they write a speech they are also quite concerned about their admirers and so right off at the beginning they put down their names, who it is that shall praise them.

Phae: How do you mean this? – for I don't understand it.   *[258a]*

Socr: You don't understand that at the beginning of their speeches the statesman starts off by naming his admirers?

Phae: How's that?

Socr: "It hath pleased the parliament," he says, or "We the people" or "Being advised and in accordance to this or with that," etc. – whereby, then, the author dutifully places his "I" and thus gives self-reference in a noble and salutary fashion. And only now does he continue on with his speech and present his wisdom to his admirers and, from time to time, he produces a document of quite some length. Or, does it seem to you that composing a speech should be anything other than this?

Phae: No, not to me.   *[b]*

Socr: Isn't it true – if such a beginning is allowed to remain standing, so the poet jumps merrily out of the drama; but then, if this beginning should be extinguished like a taper and the poet has to go forth *empty* by his speechwriting and if it should be that he is not considered respectable enough to be leaving speeches for posterity, well, then he and his friends shall all pine together?

Phae: Very much so, that's the way it goes.

Socr: Obviously then, indeed they're not despisers of this profession but are its great admirers.

Phae: Most certainly.

Socr: But, how now?   If an orator or king has brought things so far that he comes out wearing the noble armor and has the reputation of Lycurgus, or Solon or Darius – that he's become an immortal speechwriter of his state, does he not hold himself up as being like a god and don't the ensuing generations also think this of him as they study and admire his speeches?

Phae: Very much so.

Socr: Then, do you believe that one of these detractors – and no matter how much it may be that he despises Lysias' speech – do you believe that he also reckons *this* in with his scorn, namely *that* he composes speeches?

Phae: It's not at all possible to believe this and yet remain in accord with that which you have just said, or else he would have to despise his own inclination.   *<39.~258d]*

Socr: This is entirely apparent to everyone: that speechwriting is not in itself something that is evil.

Phae: How could it be?

Socr: But this, I believe, this shall be malefic – if someone speaks and writes in an ugly manner, one that is in bad taste or that is nasty.

Phae: Well, obviously.

Socr: But what, then, are the ways and means by which one does and does not write well?   Should we take this into consideration and put Lysias to the test on this – and also whosoever else either has or shall compose something in writing, and be it either an official paper of the state or a paper of any other sort, either in verse, as the poets write, or lacking verse and meter, and unpoetic?   *[e]*

Phae: You ask me, whether we should? What, if I may express myself so, what is the point of living, o Socrates, if it be not for such pleasures? Not, indeed, merely for doing those things regarding which one also first feels displeasure, or, then too, those things in which the pleasure abates afterwards, all of the things, in short, that almost all of the corporeal delights have in themselves and are therefore named the lower desires.

Socr: Leisure time for such discourse, indeed, it seems that we have this. And I also would fancy that the cicadas, as is their tendency in such heat, that they are carrying on with their songs above our heads and talking to one another about us as they observe what we're up to. If, now, they should observe that we are no better than the others and that we weren't discoursing with one another, that rather due to the heaviness of our souls we were to be charmed into sleep by their incessant music: so then, quite rightfully they would make fun of us and think to themselves that a pair of lowly helots had been caught here in their shady spot, just like the sheep that tend to nap beside the wellsprings during the heat of midday. But then, if it should be that they see us held firmly in the grasp of our conversation, that we slide by them like Odysseus in our boat of discourse and that we are not mesmerized by their tune, then it would be allowable that they bestow upon us that gift which the gods have given unto their keeping, this they might share with us as proof of their satisfaction.

Phae: And what gift might this be? For I have never heard any tales regarding this. <40.~259b2]

Socr: 'Tis not a fine matter when a connoisseur of the muses hasn't heard this one. Namely, the tale is told that the cicadas once were human, that is, in the age before the muse. As, however, this our time was raised into being and as song, thus, was first making its appearance, so a few of the people at that time would have been so enthralled by the pleasures of song that they totally forgot all about eating and drinking, and so it came to pass that they all died unnoticed. And it is from these, then, that the race of cicadas has sprung into being; and it's also said that this race comes equipped by the muses with a gift, namely, that from birth onward the cicadas don't require a bit of sustenance, that rather without food or drink they start off singing at birth and continue on unabated until they die; but then it is that they come before the muses and inform them as regards who here amongst us reveres them. And, thus, they announce and recommend to Terpsichore those of us who have displayed reverence to the choral events of song and dance; but it's to Erato that they report those of us who have enjoyed in the [d] festivities of love; and so too with all the rest, each in accordance with his or her own songs of reverence. But, now, the oldest of the muses, Calliope, and also her younger sister, Urania – these two who excel all the others and are so greatly admired, they who rule the heavens and preside over mortal and immortal speech and whose intonations are the most beauteous of all – so the cicadas inform these regarding those of us who have lived a life philosophically and have shown reverence toward their type of music. Thus, there are many reasons why it is that we really do have to converse about these matters and that we don't let sleep overpower us at midday.

Phae: Very well then, let's converse.   <41.~259e]

Socr: Do we want, now, that we investigate into that which we placed before ourselves just a moment ago: how, namely, a person writes well and rightly, and how not; shall we converse on this?

Phae: Certainly.

Socr: And isn't it necessary that wherever something is to be spoken of well and beauteously, doesn't the understanding that is speaking have to have recognized and doesn't it need to know the true nature and qualities of that regarding which it speaks?

Phae: Much rather is it the case, as I have always heard it, my dear Socrates, that whoever wants to become an orator need not bother with learning about what is truly right, rather only just about what the populace who are making this determination holds as being such; and it seems even so, also not what truly is good or beauteous but, rather, only what shall seem to be so: for it is based solely upon this that one persuades others and not at all upon the true nature and qualities of the matter under discussion.

Socr: Not a word is to be stricken from the record, o Phaedrus, from that, namely, which the wise have spoken; rather that we investigate whether or not something true was said. So too, we don't want to let anything go from that which you have just spoken.

Phae: Totally right.

Socr: Let's have a good look and observe it, so.

Phae: How then?   [260b]

Socr: If I were to convince you that in order to advance upon the enemy you should procure a horse – but then, neither one of us would be acquainted with what a horse is, however I knew this about you, that Phaedrus believed that horses belong to the group of tame animals and was the one having the longest ears.

Phae: But that's ridiculous – Socrates!

Socr: Now *hold on*; but if I really belabored myself upon convincing you and composed my speech to do so, and I spelled it all out: how valuable such an animal would be both at home and in the field of battle, advantageous that one is able to fight one's foes from a high perch, most adept in porting the supplies, and useful for many other things.

Phae: Ridiculous beyond all limits, that's what this would be.

Socr: But isn't it better that one is ridiculous and a friend rather than ferocious and an enemy?

Phae: Well, obviously.

Socr: If, then, the orator who doesn't know the difference between good and evil undertakes to influence a state that likewise shares in this disposition, and he sets out to convince others – but not that he's praising an insignificant ass, that such would be a horse, rather that he praises an evil as something good, and after having become acquainted with the opinions of the populace so now he does convince them that they do evil rather than good – what, then, what shall be the fruits and what do you believe will be the harvest gained from the planting of such seeds?

Phae: Nothing particularly remarkable.   <42.~260d]

Socr: And is it not so, my good man, that we have been overly malicious and rather coarse by the manner in which we dealt with the art of oratory? For then, she might perhaps say to us: "What's all this idle-gossip[54] that you amazing people toss about like spaghetti? For I don't force – neither truth nor ignorance – upon anyone in that they learn the art of speaking, rather, as my advice is valid, so may each take truth or ignorance as he has earned it, but, all the same, don't neglect me. For this I do assert: that without me even he who knows what is true, even he shall not understand how to artfully persuade others." Now, wouldn't she be speaking entirely what is right if she were to say this to us?

Phae: I admit as much.   *[e]*

Socr: If only those speeches that I see rising up against her allow that this be valid: that she is an art. For I believe that I'm beginning to hear a few speeches marching this way asserting that: "She lies" and that "She isn't an art at all but, rather, a totally artless handicraft."

Phae: O Socrates, we're in need of these speeches. Bring them up into the dock and perform your cross-examination: what, indeed – what is it that they say, and how do they mean it.

Socr: Do come hither, ye beauteous toddlers, and persuade this father of beautiful children, Phaedrus, that if he abstains from philosophizing right down to the fundamental core, then, so too, he

---

[54] See *Parmenides* 135de regarding the need for "twaddle" (p. 217); and *Theaetetus* 195c (p. 435); *Geschwätz* also reoccurs at 270a where it's translated as "blather" and, as regards Anaxagoras, "sense and nonsense"; likewise *Lysis* 221d (p. 101) where it is translated as idle chit-chat; *Charmides* "hot air" 176a (p. 199) and the *Sophist* 225b–226a (pp. 522–523).

shall never speak regarding anything at all in a fundamentally sound manner. Thus, Phaedrus should answer.

Phae: Just ask me.

Socr: Is it not, then, entirely the case that speechcraft – this art of oratory – is it not a guiding of the soul through speeches, and this not only in legal proceedings and in other places where matters of public concern are determined, rather also in one's everyday life as well and in regards to matters both large and small, and nothing is more esteemed than what is right whether or not it touches upon   *[261b]* major concerns or just with trivial things? Or, what have you heard tell regarding all of this?

Phae: By Zeus, nothing at all like this; rather, it's actually so that only in respect to the functioning of the judicial process is there anything that is said or written in respect to oratory being an art – and, then too, in public oration; but beyond these I haven't heard tell.

Socr: Is it, then, so: that you've only heard about the dictates given by Nestor and Odysseus regarding speechcraft, that which they worked out in their leisure during the time of their encampment before Troy, but of those from Palamides you haven't heard a thing?

Phae: Indeed, by Zeus, I've not even heard of any such   *<43.~261c]* as regards Nestor, unless it should be that you're setting up Gorgias for punishment – as if he were to be Nestor; or it might be for Thrasymachus... and Theodorus, then, would be Odysseus.

Socr: Perhaps,[55] but let's just leave them be. But you tell me, then: what is it that the parties do in the places where justice is meted out and determined? Don't they speak in opposition to one another? – or, how should we give this a name?

Phae: Precisely so.

Socr: And regarding what is just and unjust?

Phae: Yes.

Socr: Now, he who does this with artistry, shall he not make the same matter appear to the same people that now it seems just and, if he wants, then again as unjust?

Phae: How else?

Socr: And so too in the public assemblies – that the same matter is now fancied by the state as being good and, then again, as the opposite?   *[d]*

Phae: So it is, quite.

---

[55] Theodorus, a famous mathematician, takes part in the dialogues *Theaetetus* and *Sophist* – where he introduces the Eleatic stranger; Thrasymachus is one of the interlocutors in *The Republic*. This jab at Gorgias could be taken as "proving" that *Phaedrus* was written after *Gorgias*, it could just as well demonstrate Plato's fine penchant for reworking his earlier dialogues as outlined in my introduction.

Socr: And don't we know this about the Eleatic Palamides – that he had an art of speaking such that for those listening the same appeared as similar and as dissimilar, as one and many, and as at rest and in motion?

Phae: Indeed.

Socr: Not only, then, in the courts of law and by political orations before the populace does the art of speaking for and against extend its reach, rather – as it seems – for everything spoken there would be, if it should be that one exists at all, just this one art through which a person is enabled to display as similar each and every thing as being all kinds of things, whatever may be possible; and likewise what another conceals as being dissimilar, to bring this to light.

Phae: Just how do you mean this, actually?

Socr: For him who digs deep into this investigation, I believe, it shall become apparent. Is it more likely that error and deception arise between matters that differ greatly, or with those things having only a small amount of difference?

Phae: In those in which the difference is small.   *[262a]*

Socr: But still, you shall most easily lead others on to the opposite of truth without their ever noticing it if you take them with small steps rather than with large ones?

Phae: How else!

Socr: It has to be, thus, that indeed, whoever wants to deceive others but also doesn't want that he himself should be deceived, such a person must know precisely the similarity and dissimilarity of the things?

Phae: Necessarily.

Socr: But shall he be capable and in a position to do this if he isn't acquainted with the true nature and qualities of each and every thing? – for how, otherwise, how could he differentiate between the greater and the lesser similarities of that with which he is not acquainted in the other things?

Phae: Impossible.   *[b]*

Socr: And, isn't it true? – for those who have notions and represent something as being different than it actually is, in short, those who are in error and deceive themselves, isn't this obviously due to some sort of similarity having slipped itself in?

Phae: That's the way it happens.

Socr: Is it, then, well possible that this art which always leads one on, bit by bit, through similarity with that which in every instance is true – is it possible for her to do so and, thus, lead one to that which is the opposite or possible for her to protect herself from being thus led astray, in short, can this art be possessed by someone who is not acquainted with that which in every given instance is true?

Phae: Never.

Socr: Whoever, then, doesn't know the truth and he who has only gone hunting after opinions – such a person, dear friend, as it seems, shall only patch together a quite ludicrous and inartistic art of speech.

Phae: Well, that's about it.   <44.~262cd]

Socr: Would you like that we take up Lysias' speech that you have in front of you and, likewise, those which we spoke – and see if there's not something in them that we might ascertain as being artless, and also something that stands in one accord to artistry?

Phae: Most happily, and particularly so because as of yet we've spoken in a rather dry fashion without any substantiating examples.

Socr: And just as luck would have it, as it seems, both of these speeches that we have before us contain an example of how he who knows what is right is able to playfully[56] lead others astray. And I, o Phaedrus, I'd ascribe this to the gods that reside here abouts. And perhaps as well that these servants of the muse, the cicadas who sing so incessantly above our heads, that they have infused us with this as their gift. For, indeed, I don't partake in any school of oratory.

Phae: That may well be as you say; only make it clear to me what you mean.

Socr: So, come now – and read me the beginning of Lysias' speech.

Phae: "Regarding that which touches upon me you have been   *[e]* instructed and, as I believe, we shall carry on if this should come to pass – as you have heard it. But I should not wish to fail in what I ask merely for this reason, that I am not amongst your lovers, as it is even these who tend to rue ..."

Socr: Hold it right there! Where it is that Lysias fails and proceeds inartistically? – this is what we should say, is it not so?

Phae: Yes.   <45.~263a]

Socr: Now, isn't it apparent to everyone that regarding some words we all speak with one meaning but regarding others this is not so?

Phae: I believe that I understand what it is that you opine, but can you say it yet more clearly.

Socr: If someone speaks out the word iron or silver, don't we all think of the same?

Phae: Certainly.

Socr: But how about righteous or good. Doesn't the one of us turn this way, another that way, and aren't we at odds with one another and even with ourselves?

---

[56] Plato is rather earnest in his play, see *Parmenides* 137ab (p. 219), or Plotinus – *Ennead 30*.

Phae: Indeed.

Socr: In some we agree as one, but not in others. *[b]*

Phae: So it is.

Socr: But in which of the two shall it be more likely that we shall be deceived and, thus, in which of them will speechcraft be most capable of leading us astray?

Phae: Obviously, in those in which we vary.

Socr: He who wants to discover the art of speech, firstly he has to separate both of these – where each of them belongs – and do this in a pure fashion and, thus, he becomes empowered by the recognition of both species: the one in which the populace is unsteady and the other in which they're not. *[c]*

Phae: A beauteous concept, o Socrates, would be in the grasp of him, he who has become empowered by his comprehension of this matter.

Socr: Then, I believe, for any particular case he must not go astray and be led into error, rather that he recognizes precisely that regarding which he wants to speak and to which of the two species this belongs.

Phae: How else [could it be]?

Socr: And what about love? Do we want to say that it belongs to the ambiguous, or is it one of the others?

Phae: To the ambiguous, without further ado. Or how otherwise could it be that love has allowed you to say, as you even just did say, first, that love would be a ruination of the lover and the beloved and, then again, that love would be the greatest of all possible goods? *[d]*

Socr: Very rightly spoken. But tell me this as well – as due to my being so inspired I'm unable to remember this properly – whether or not I clarified what love is at the start of my speech?

Phae: By Zeus! – without even mentioning how well.

Socr: Do you see! – how much greater is the artistry in accordance with, as you say: when the nymphs of Achelous and Pan himself, son of Hermes, are inspiring one than is the case with Lysias, son of Cephalus! Or, am I saying nothing, rather did Lysias begin his speech by compelling us to take on that love be one determinate [*Gestalt*], whatever he himself wanted, and then afterwards ordered the whole development of his speech upon this? Do you want that we read his beginning once more?

Phae: As you like. Yet what you're looking for isn't there.

Socr: Just read it so that I might hear him myself. <46.~263e2]

Phae: "Regarding that which touches upon me you have been instructed and, as I believe, we shall carry on if this should come to pass – as you have heard it. But I should not wish to fail in what I ask merely for this reason, that I am not amongst your lovers, as it is even

these who tend to rue whatever good they might do for you just as
soon as their appetites have been satisfied."

Socr: Yes, there is much, indeed, much that is lacking that this
should do what we are calling for; this speech which doesn't even
begin at the beginning but rather wants to start at the end and then
swims backward and, so, it starts up at a point where the lover might
just as well have already stopped speaking to the beloved. Or, am I
saying nothing again, my dear Phaedrus, most noble friend?   *[b]*

Phae: Indeed, this well is the end, Socrates, where he starts up his
speech.

Socr: And how now? – everything else in the speech, doesn't it seem
disorganized and all thrown together in a mish mash? – or, is it clear
why it is that that which comes second would have to be second? –
or anything else from amongst the following sections? At least it
seems to me as if the author, in that he would be totally lacking in
knowledge as regards how to proceed, has quite admirably said just
whatever happens to come into his mind. Would you, perhaps, be
able to show any rhetorical necessity to point to, why it is that this
man places things in the order in which he puts them, one after the
other?

Phae: It's very good of you that you show such trust in me, that I
should judge this work so precisely.   *[264c]*

Socr: But this, I believe, you also indeed shall assert: that a speech is
just like a living entity *{Wesen}* and must be built as such and each
speech needs to have its own unique body so that it neither is missing
its head, nor lacking feet – rather it has both middle and ends which
relate one to the other and each part is related to the whole having
been worked into a purposeful interdependence.

Phae: Well, of course, how else?

Socr: Examine, thus, your friend's speech: whether or not it has such
a correlation, and certainly you shall find that it's no different than
that aphorism which is attributed to Midas of Phrygia.

Phae: And what aphorism is that to which you allude? – and to what
is it in particular that you are referring?

Socr: It is this:

Honorable virgin am I, lying upon Midas' grave;
Until the waters cease to flow, nor plume the high stemmed trees;
Always pining, rooted here upon this tear bestained tomb;
That the wanderer knows as well, where Midas is laid to rest. [57]

---

[57] "Eherne Jungfrau bin ich und lieg an dem Grabe des Midas;
   Bis nicht Wasser mehr fließt, noch erblühn hochstämmige Bäume;

That, now, it makes no difference with this – which verse is read first and which last – you have noted this, I would warrant.   <*47.~264e]*

Phae: But you're making fun of our speech, Socrates!

Socr: So we want, that you don't become too annoyed by this, that we just leave this be – despite that it seems there's yet many sorts of things contained herein which, if one takes a look at it, might well be useful, though if one were to undertake to imitate it, this wouldn't be particularly helpful; and so let's just continue on to the other speeches. For there was something in them and it behooves those to pay attention to it, those, namely, who want to reflect and think hard about speechcraft.

Phae: And what is it that you're meaning?   *[265a]*

Socr: That, indeed, they stand in opposition, one to the other. For the one asserted that you would have to gratify the lover, and the other, that it would be the non-lover.

Phae: And both of them were entirely stalwart.

Socr: I thought you would have said, in accordance with truth, entirely insane. Nevertheless, that toward which they were seeking is even this. As, indeed, we did assert that love would be a type of insanity, didn't we?

Phae: Yes.

Socr: And that as regards insanity there are two sorts: the one due to human illness and the other due to divine intervention that turns matters inside out from their normal, orderly state.

Phae: So it was.   *[b]*

Socr: But we divided the god inspired state again into four parts in accordance to the four gods – in that we ascribed the augury of providential insight to the breath or infusion of spirit by Apollo; to Dionysus went initiation; to the muses the poetic; but to the fourth, namely that of Aphrodite and Eros, went this insanity of love which we then clarified as being the best; and I don't know anymore quite how it was that we painted a picture of this state of being-in-love whereby, perhaps, we hit upon something that was right and also, perhaps, digressed a good deal into other domains; and so we mixed a speech which wasn't through and through beyond belief with a mythic hymn and sang our praises rather earnestly and piously to your lord and mine, to Eros, the protector of beauteous lads.

Phae: Yes, and how! – for it wasn't in the least bit unpleasant to my ears.

Immer verweilend allhier an dem vielbeträneten Denkmal;
Daß auch der Wanderer wisse, wo Midas liege begraben."

Socr: Let's see if this may be salvaged from out of all of this: how the speech progressed from deprecation of the lover to praise.

Phae: How do you mean this?   <48.~265cd]

Socr: It seems to me that everything else was only spoken in jest, but just both of these two matters that the earlier speeches had in themselves, as our lucky stars had it, if one would be fundamentally capable of appropriating this power into one's own being, that this would be a beautiful affair.

Phae: To what, indeed, are you referring?

Socr: That which is multifariously scattered about, to review all of this together and lead it over into one *Gestalt* in order that it be precisely determined and made crystal clear, such is the manner that teachings are imparted; even so as we just have clarified in regards to love – that, first, what she is, perhaps speaking well and also, perhaps, speaking rather poorly, but at least going about it in a clear and in itself non-contradicting manner, this came into our speech from such [a methodology].

Phae: And what, then, do you mean as the second, Socrates?   [e]

Socr: In even the same manner, that one is capable of dividing the concepts structurally and showing how each has its genesis; and doing this without – to take an approximate analogy from cooking class: that one doesn't proceed like an inept chef and break the egg yolks when separating out the whites. That rather, it be so: just as in our preceding speeches the irrational part of the soul was conceived and grasped as one concept in the entirety of its aspects and, thus, just as it comes to be with our own bodies – that as a one we develop on both sides and like-named parts issue forth which may be designated as our right and left halves[58] – and even so the mania of love which grows in us as one Gestalt: this our speech took up and made it believable, separating it out on the left side and pursuing matters to the extreme form and whittling away at this non-stop until, that I might express myself so, a lefty-love was uncovered, which sort of love you might quite rightly revile; the other approach led us to the mania on the right and one that would be like-named, but finding a divine love on this side and displaying it, so this was praised as the underlying cause of our greatest well-being.

Phae: Totally right.   <49.~266b]

Socr: It is of this, Phaedrus, that I myself am a great friend: of these divisions into parts and grasping together into one, in that, indeed, I am capable of speaking and thinking; and if I judge someone other as capable of seeing what metamorphoses into one or into many –

---

[58] Compare with *Parmenides*: 129b−e (p. 210).

him I follow *"as in the footsteps of an immortal."* Whether it be that I name these rightly or improperly, God may be the judge of this, but up until the present moment I have named them dialecticians. But now, why don't you also tell me how one should name those who are taught by you and by Lysias? Or, would this be the speechcraft that Thrasymachus and the others put into service in that they themselves are artists in speech and, likewise, capable of making others that they be such, those, namely, who want to bring gift offerings unto them as if they were kings?

Phae: Royal men they are, indeed, but not informed in regards to that about which you question. From this circumstance I fancy that you've named the former totally right in that you call it dialectics; but rhetoric, I fancy, this has escaped us for the time being.   *[d]*

Socr: How was that? This must be something of beauty, which though bereft of the former should still and yet be achieved through art. All the same, we don't want to spurn it, you and I, that rather we might just say what, then, it may well be, that which still remains as being the left-over part of speechcraft.

Phae: All sorts of things, Socrates, and you'll find them all catalogued in the books that have been written upon rhetoric.   *<50.~266]*

Socr: It's so good of you to remind me of this. The introduction first off, how it is that the beginning of any speech would have to be spoken, this is what you mean? Isn't it true, these majesties of artistry?

Phae: Yes.   *[e]*

Socr: Then, secondly, there comes the narration – as they have named it – and don't forget the evidence which enters in here; and third is the proof; fourth come the probabilities; and then there's yet the convictions and the secondary convictions. I think that it was the most admirable Byzantine, Daidalus, who spoke of these matters in his orations.

Phae: That's the valiant Theodorus whom you'd be meaning? *[267a]*

Socr: Who else? And then, that one has to bring forth a rebuttal and a backup-rebuttal, and both for the prosecution as well as for the defense. And let's not overlook that most beauteous parry which comes to us from the illustrious Parain himself, even Evenus, *touché*, he who was the first to discover the opening allusion or premonition, and, not to forget, the coincident panagyric {*Nebenlob* 59}. Indeed, a

---

59 *Neben~*, unfortunately, has been variously translated as *secondary, backup* and *coincident* though the idea of throwing in an *extra~* which is nothing more than the first is, among other things, what Socrates is satirizing. His own incidental abuse of Evenus is remarkably witty and reminiscent of the parody found in *Protagoras*.

few people have remarked that he's brought all sorts of incidental abuse into his verses due to his love of remembrance. For then, he is a clever fellow. But of Teisias and Gorgias, we'll just let them be and not stir up anything: these who first made the discovery of that-which-seems-to-be and that this is elevated above truth and would be more noble; these who make the small great and that the great seem small due to the immense power of their speech and who speak of the latest events in an old-fashioned way but speak most beauteously as well of the ancients, rendering their hieroglyphics into the most modern parlance, and not to forget the conciseness of speech, nor the never-ending verbosity with which they can discourse regarding each and every object, such are their great discoveries. As Prodicus heard tell of this latter invention, so he chuckled and spoke: that he alone has discovered what sort of sentences the art was most in need of, namely, neither short ones nor long ones, but sentences that are moderate.

Phae: Very wise, o Prodicus!

Socr: And of Hippias too, don't we want to speak of him? I believe that this foreigner from Elis stands by him with his approval.

Phae: But, why not?   *[~c]*

Socr: And how might we ever do justice to Polus' grand collection of words, like doubletalk and speaking-in-riddles and speaking-in-pictures; not to mention the conquest of melodiousness using the words of Licymnius, which, then, he was able to attach onto the former inventions?

Phae: And doesn't Protagoras, too, doesn't he likewise boast of such devices?

Socr: A certain straight-talk, my son, and then there's yet a great deal more, and all most beauteous. But it's with his yammerings and tonal undulations, that which he's gleaned from the poor and the aged – such artistries as these have assured the mighty power of this Chalcedonian and made him quite invincible. Then too, this man is a titan whenever it comes to stirring up the masses, and also most adept when it comes to placating an enraged mob – *"like a magician"* as he says; and then when it comes to libel and slander or the matter of dancing out of the way of such; and no matter whither the latest trends are going you can be sure that he shall be the first to arrive. But finally, to return to speechcraft, as regards the end of any speech, everyone is of the opinion that this is where the recapitulation belongs, though some have given it a different name.

Phae: That at the end of one's speech one should give a short review reminding the audience of everything that was said, is this what you're meaning?

Socr: Precisely; and what else remains that you have yet to say as regards speechcraft?

Phae: Trivialities and nothing worth the mention. [268a]

Socr: Let's leave the trivialities well enough alone; but let's take a good look at these other things and view them under a stronger light: *what* is the power of their artistry and *when* is it really effective?

Phae: A power, indeed, which is very strong, o Socrates, in the public assemblies.

Socr: Indeed, as you say. But, you marvel, take another look and see if the whole fabric doesn't seem as poorly knit together to you as it does to me.

Phae: Just show me. <51.~268ab]

Socr: Tell me, then, if someone were to approach your friend Eriximachus or his father, Acumenus, saying: "I understand such things in respect to the body, that I'm able to raise its temperature if I want to, or, then again, to lower its temperature; and if I should fancy that such would be good I'm able to make it urinate or force an evacuation of the bowels, and many other sorts of things similar to these, and because I understand all of these matters I claim to be a physician and, moreover, I can make others that they too are able to do all of these things by sharing my techniques with them" – what, do you opine, what shall be their response after they have heard such a statement?

Phae: What else other than questioning him as to whether or not he also understands to whom and when he should do all of these things, and also to what degree.

Socr: And if, now, he says, "No, not at all" and that he rather expects that whoever learns all these matters from him would have to already understand this on his own,[60] that about which you're asking. [c]

Phae: Then I believe that he would say: this man is a crackpot that he believes simply because he's found out a few methods, be it from reading or from wherever else it may be, he now believes that he's become a physician although he understands nothing at all of our professional art.

Socr: And how about this: if someone were to present himself before Sophocles or Euripides saying that he understands the composition of long speeches regarding trivial matters and really short and concise ones about the most important matters, that he's also able to write in a plaintive vein if he wants and, then again, frighten the audience or compose speeches that disturb the audience in all sorts of ways – and

---

[60] See *Gorgias* 459d–461b (pp. 273–275).

now he imagines, as he also can teach these matters to others, that he's a teacher of tragic poetry?

Phae: This also, o Socrates, would be, I think, a cause for great peals of laughter by these who believe that tragic poetry would be something other than a placing together of the various parts as these are proportioned to one another and to the whole.

Socr: But not without civility, I believe, would they proceed to knock him off of his high horse, rather, that it would be more like the case of a musician, an artist of tones, if he were to meet up with someone who imagined that he understands harmony due simply to the circumstance that he has acquired understanding of how to sound the strings on a lute – that, namely, he is capable of striking both the highest and the lowest notes possible – so the true musician wouldn't say in his gentle voice: "You poor imp, you're insane," rather   *[e]* as befits an artist he'd speak softly and in such a manner: "Most worthy man, indeed, one who would become a musician also needs to know these things but this in itself doesn't preclude that someone, even though familiar with this, still may not have even the slightest understanding of harmony, for he possesses only the prerequisites which necessarily belong to harmony, but they are no guarantee of knowledge of harmony itself."

Phae: Quite right.

Socr: And so too, Sophocles would say to that person who was boasting of his understanding that he has the prerequisites to tragic poetry but not this artistry itself; and likewise Acumenus would say that the pretender has the prerequisites to the art of healing but not the healing art itself.

Phae: Quite, indeed.   *<52.~269a]*

Socr: But, how now? Should we believe that Adrastus whose sweet orations are so admired, or Pericles, if they were to catch wind of these beauteous pieces of artistry upon which we were just expounding, speaking concisely and speaking-in-pictures and everything else that we wanted to hold up closer under the light – would they, perhaps, also become indignant like you and me, and lacking in proper civility would they blurt out an unrefined word against these, that namely they have written and taught the former things *as if* such were to be speechcraft; or would they, in that they are so much wiser than we are, would they put us in our proper places by saying: "O Phaedrus and Socrates, one need not become indignant, rather that one has forbearance and a more inclusive view – if, then, such people who are utterly without any understanding of how one is to proceed with concepts, if such people also prove themselves incapable of determining what speechcraft actually is, and this due to the circumstance that they are only in possession of the prerequisites *[c]* to this art and yet they believe to have discovered the art itself; and, so too, if they should teach others these matters as if they were consummate instructors of the art and yet, to the contrary, they make use of all of this in their compelling manner: that a whole shall be brought together from out of these pieces" – and yet, the bringing of this consummation into their speeches, don't they leave this as a task for their pupils, as if such were a mere triviality?

Phae: Indeed, o Socrates, there seems approximately to be such a posturing in the artistry that these men teach as rhetoric, and that about which they lecture in their writings; and it seems to me that what you've said is totally true. But now, this art of the truth and compelling oratory, how and where is it that someone is enabled to make this their own?   *[d]*

Socr: As regards to anyone's being able – that you or someone else becomes a consummate fighter – this seems in truth and, indeed, perhaps by necessity so: that it works out about the same here as it does in everything else. Namely, if you have the predisposition toward oratory then you shall become a renowned orator insofar as you add on to this both knowledge and practice; but to the extent that either of these is neglected, from this side you shall fall short of being consummate. But as regards the art of the matter, it seems to me that the proper leads toward this are not to be found upon the path on which Lysias and Thrasymachus are going.

Phae: But, then – which path?

Socr: Pericles, most worthy Phaedrus, may well have been the greatest initiate as regards the crafting of speeches.

Phae: How so?   *<53.~270a]*

Socr: All of the greater arts require something, indeed, of super-cilious and high-flying blather upon nature. For it is only possible through this that the aforementioned excellence and reliability come to be, namely, when such meets up with success; and it's this which Pericles, on top of his natural talents, attained to such a high degree. These, at least, are my thoughts on this matter: it is because of Pericles' attachment to Anaxagoras, who blathered a great deal, that Pericles became filled up with these high-flying scraps of knowledge, and so he attained an acquaintance of the nature of understanding and 'non-understanding' about which, you know, Anaxagoras was always making speeches. Thus, it was from this source that he was able to bring over into speechcraft what was useful.

Phae: How do you mean?

Socr: The case is the same with speechcraft as it is with the art of healing.   *[b]*

Phae: How's that?

Socr: In both of these you have to dissect and do a thorough analysis on nature, be it the nature of the body for the one or the nature of the soul for the other – if, then, you are to go beyond what is passed on by tradition or that which experience has to tell you, that rather you proceed in accordance with art in that in the one case you foster health and strength through the application of different medicines and by the proper nutrition, and in the other case it's by structured teachings and by fostering morality that you bring about whichever convictions and virtue you may want, just as you desire.

Phae: That's just the way things look, Socrates, just as you say.   *[c]*

Socr: And do you believe to be able to properly grasp the nature of soul without also grasping the entirety of nature?

Phae: If one is to believe Hippocrates the Asclepiad, then one's not even able to understand the body without venturing down this road.

Socr: 'Tis very beauteous, my friend, that he has said this. But then, besides Hippocrates we also have to investigate the matter by asking reason and see if she also voices her approval.

Phae: Admittedly.   *<54.~270d]*

Socr: So, take a good look – what is it that Hippocrates and right reason say about nature? Is it not necessary to reflect upon each and every thing in nature in this manner: firstly, whether or not it is unitary or if it comes in various forms – that, namely, which we ourselves treat as artists, and also that regarding which we want to make others capable. Then, if it is unitary, that one investigates into its power, what its essential nature would be, and upon what things it expresses this power, that is, how it works; and also, not to forget, how other things essentially work upon it and how it takes up the workings of these things, whatever they happen to be; but if it should have various forms then these are to be counted up, and from each one of these you then proceed as earlier – and so, you look at each one: what effects each produces due to its nature and what each suffers from any of the others.

Phae: That's the way it would have to be done.

Socr: Any other way of proceeding except for this would be like wandering about blind. But in no way is it permissible for anyone who strives toward any matter at all in an artistic manner, in no way is it permissible that he might be compared to a blind man or to someone who is deaf, rather, it is obvious that whoever is to share in that oratory which is in accord with art, he also has to be able to display exactly what the essential nature is to whomever it is that he wants to deliver up these speeches; but then this would, indeed, this would have to be the soul.

Phae: What else? [271a]

Socr: Thus, his entire struggle is focused on the soul, for it is in the soul that the convictions are to be brought forth. Isn't it true?

Phae: Quite.

Socr: It is, then, quite obvious that Thrasymachus and whoever else it may be who desires to struggle through the labor of presenting teachings regarding the art of rhetoric – firstly, and with all due precision, he would teach and bring this into view: whether the soul is one and similar in all domains, or whether it's like the body and of many different types. For it is this, as we asserted, that is called – displaying the nature of any given thing.

Phae: Indeed.

Socr: Secondly, where it is that its nature expresses itself and upon what, and from where and from what does it experience effects.

Phae: Indeed, this too. [b]

Socr: Thirdly, after a thorough and orderly dissection and analysis of the types of speeches as well as the types of souls and of their different relationships, so he shall go through all of the different causes holding up each together with every other and teaching: essentially which souls shall be persuaded by which speeches and what are the underlying causes that either they are persuaded or why they remain unconvinced.

Phae: Most superb, as it seems, thus indeed – thus it would have to be done.

Socr: Until this at least, o friend, is accomplished: never shall that which is spoken or taught in some other manner, never shall such be written or spoken in accordance with art, and neither in regard to any other subject matter nor as regards this one. But those whom you have heard and those who even now are busy writing their technical manuals upon the art of oratory, these people are tricky and use subterfuge to conceal the matter that, indeed, they do understand the soul most admirably. However, not until they begin to speak and write in this manner, not until then do we want to believe them, that they are writing in accordance with art.

Phae: But then, which is the right manner?

Socr: To really lead one through all of this using determinate words, this is not easily done; nonetheless I want to clarify how one would have to write if one's writings should be of this quality – what art requires.

Phae: So then, clarify this. <55.~271d]

Socr: As the power of speech is that which guides the soul, so it is necessary that whoever wants to become an orator, he must know how many types of souls there are. These, then, are so and so many and thus and such are their qualities – whereby, then, a few people become this type and other people, again, some other type. Once this is all laid out and categorized, so, then too there are so and so many types of speeches, and thus and such are their qualities. Now, such people as these are easy to persuade by such speeches as these regarding such things due to this cause and that, but then others are difficult to persuade due to the same cause. Once, now, he has comprehended all of this properly, so furthermore he has to be able to pursue all of this precisely as it unfolds in his field of vision and as he begins to see the matter itself in life and he treats things accordingly – for otherwise he won't know anything more than the rules about which he has heard. But if he knows to properly identify what sort of person shall be persuaded by which sort of speech and if he likewise is in a position to recognize this sort when he meets up with him and he displays these things to himself: here comes such a one who has such a nature about which we conversed earlier on, and now in all actuality he's standing here right in front of me *[272a]* – and so now I have to put this type of speech to use in order to persuade him regarding such a matter – if, then, he has absorbed all of this internally and yet he still has the time and knows how to judge when he should speak and when he's to remain silent, and likewise as regards the compressed passages and the places for working upon the sympathies and passions and, then, all the rest of the available sorts and ways of strengthening the speech, all of which he has learned, and from all these things he knows where they belong in his speech and where they are out of place: then it is that his art is beauteous and wholly consummate, but not before this, rather, whichever of these pieces has been neglected, that such was allowed to be deficient – and whether it be in speaking or teaching or writing – and yet he asserts that he is speaking artfully, well, whoever withholds his belief, he is the one who is more clever. "How now?" – perhaps our speechwriter now shall come forward and say to us: "O Phaedrus and Socrates, does it now seem to both of you that speechcraft when it is treated in such a way or when it is treated in some other wise, which would be worthy that one takes it up?"

Phae: Impossible, o Socrates, in any other way, although when taken in this manner it seems that this is no small task.

Socr: That's probably true. And even for this reason, now, you should take another good look turning the matter all different ways – whether, perhaps, an easier or shorter path than this one shows itself – so that you don't go down a long and difficult road if, then, one *[c]* which is shorter and more level stands open before you. Have you then heard anything from Lysias or from anyone else that may prove helpful? – so call it back into your memory and make an attempt that you expound upon it.

Phae: If it should only depend upon my making the effort, then for sure I'd have something to say, but now I don't have anything ready at hand.

Socr: Would you like, then, that I tell you what I have heard from a few who give themselves up to such matters?

Phae: Sure, why not?

Socr: It is indeed said, o Phaedrus, that it would be right that one also defends the wolf's standpoint.

Phae: So do this, then, Socrates.   <56.~272d]

Socr: They assert, then, that one isn't allowed to treat this so earnestly, nor does one have to lead up to the answer from such a great distance – for in no way whatsoever, as we also said right at the start of our speech, in no way is it necessary that *he* needs to partake in truth or any portion thereof, neither regarding what is right nor what is good as these relate to any undertakings, nor too regarding who would be so amongst mankind, be it from natural disposition or due to education and upbringing – *he*, namely, who strives to become an accomplished orator. For it is wholly and utterly of no concern in the places where justice is meted out and nobody has the smallest degree of interest in the truth about these things, rather, only upon that which is believable, and this is that-which-seems-to-be and, so, it's upon this that he has to turn all of his attention, he who wants to speak right artfully. For then, from time to time he's not even allowed to say what it is that has actually transpired – if, then, this doesn't itself have an appearance [of being true] on its own; rather it's only about *that-which-seems-to-be* and both in the accusation as well as for the defendant, and in all ways one needs only to hunt after the appearance and say *adios* to the truth and *lebe wohl;* for if one has this for oneself everywhere in one's speech, just this makes up the whole art.   *[273a]*

Phae: That's it exactly, o Socrates, just as you have expounded it: *this* is what they say – those, namely, who proffer themselves as having understanding of the art of speaking. And I well remember that we touched upon this matter quite briefly earlier on; but those who give themselves over to these matters, they fancy this as being very grand.

Socr: You yourself were an ardent follower of Teisias; so mayn't Teisias also now tell us as to whether he means something other with that-which-seems-to-be other than this: that which the populace easily believe?   *[b]*

Phae: What else could he possibly mean?

Socr: Thus, this is, as it seems, thought out very wisely and is richly
endowed with art, what he writes: that if, namely, a weak but
courageous individual should overcome someone who is strong but a
coward, and if he steals his coat or whatever else it might be and then
they should be brought before the judicial authority, then neither of
them would have to speak out the truth, rather the coward would
have to take care not to admit that this brave weakling was able to
force him down all alone; but then the other would indeed assert that
they were all alone and then make use of this to his own advantage
saying: how should I being such as I am dare to enter into a fray with
such a strong person as this?   Then the other would be loathe to
admit his cowardice and, in that he should think up a new lie, so,
perhaps, he would put some other proof in the hands of his opponent.
And just so, with even such qualities as these are all of the other
instances according to this art that was spoken of above.   Isn't it so,
Phaedrus?

Phae: How else?

Socr: Ouch!   – an utterly obscure art[61] is this which Teisias has
discovered; or whoever else it actually would be and from wherever
this comes from and is cherished.   But, friend, do we want to speak to
him in this manner or not?

Phae: How's that?   <57.~273d]

Socr: Something along these lines: O Teisias, already for quite
awhile before your arrival here we have been saying that that-which-
seems-to-be seems to people so only due to a similarity to truth that
accompanies it; but similarities, we also have shown, shall best be
discovered by that person who knows in all instances the truth of the
matter in that he has an acquaintance with truth.   So that, if you have
anything else to say regarding the art of oratory we would be very glad
to hear it, but if not then we'll have to put our belief in that which was
just treated above: that if someone isn't in a position that he can
count up the different natures of listeners as well as categorize the
types of subject matters, that he grasps the pieces and binds them
together underneath one concept – so he shall never be as rich in the
art of oratory as it is possible for a human being to be; and that,
furthermore, one shall never be able to achieve this without
multifarious struggles that every reasonable person should undertake,
not that he might speak and have dealings with the rest of humanity
but, rather, only because he then shall become enabled to speak what
is pleasing to the gods, and that he accomplishes everything to the

---

[61] The art of sophistry and the immense difficulties of understanding non-being and its
relation to the images of deceit; see – *Sophist* 236e (p. 537), etc.

best of his abilities. For it's not his fellow vassals, o Teisias, thus say those who are wiser than we, whom one would have to please, this is not the endeavor of the man of reason – or, if so, then only as an aside – rather [to please] his good and elevated master. Therefore, if the path be long, so be not in wonder, for the charms of grander things are bestowed upon us, not merely that about which you are thinking. But it shall be, as the speech has shown, that this too awaits you, if only your will is there, and it's through the former path that this is best achieved.

Phae: Totally on the mark, I fancy, is that which you've just said, o Socrates, if only one were in a position and capable of doing this.

Socr: But, when striving after beauty, so too it is beauteous that one accepts whatever it may be that fate decrees. *[274b]*

Phae: Very true.

Socr: Regarding this, now, what the art is and what is lacking in art, in regards to speech – this may well suffice.

Phae: Totally.

Socr: But regarding the decency and indecency of writing, where its utility is beneficial and where writing proves to be inept, this would yet remain for us to converse about. Isn't this true?

Phae: Yep.

Socr: Would you know, perhaps, how – in order to please God most authentically – how you should treat speeches and how you would have to speak of them?

Phae: No, not at all; but you, would you? *<58.~274c]*

Socr: At least I have an anecdote that I might tell you about, one which comes down to us from the men of yore; but the truth of the matter, they alone know this. But then, if we were able to find this out, would we be at all concerned regarding the judgments of men?

Phae: That's a ridiculous question! But, tell me the story – what you assert to have heard.

Socr: This is what I've heard. In the city of Naucratis in Egypt there would have been one amongst the older gods – amongst whom also Ibis the bird-god was worshipped – there was, as I was saying, this one god whose name was Theuth. It is from him that originally numbers and calculation were invented, then also the measuring arts [geometry] and starlore, furthermore board games and dice throwing,[62] and then, the letters of the alphabet. At that time Thamus ruled over the whole of Egypt and resided in the great city in the upper region, the region that the Greeks call Egyptian Thebes, but

---

[62] Same arts as in *Gorgias* 450e–451d (pp. 263–264) and *Theaetetus* 145d (p. 363).

this god was called Ammon.[63] It was to this great King, Thamus, that the god went and he displayed his arts and spoke his desire that these should be divvied out and shared with all of the Egyptians. The King inquired of him as regards the utility that each of them would confer upon the people and, as he fancied that which Theuth brought forward in each instance as being right or not right, so it was that he praised or reviled each of these arts. There was a great deal that Thamus related to Theuth, speaking both for and against each of *[e]* his inventions, and it would take us way out of our way if we were to get into all of this. But then, as he finally arrived at the alphabet, then Theuth spoke thusly: "This art, o King, shall make the wisdom of the Egyptians grow and likewise enriches their memory – for it has been invented as a means of remembrance and wisdom." But then, the King replied: "O Theuth, thou who art so rich in the arts, one of us knows how to bring forth into the light what belongs to each of the arts, another how to judge how much is the damage and how much the benefit that each will bring to those who make use of it. So too now, as you are the father of the alphabet, so out of your love for it you have spoken out the opposite of what its effects shall be. For out of this invention forgetfulness shall much rather stream into the souls of those who learn it due to their neglect of remembrance – as they shall put their trust in the external markings, this writing that comes to them from outside and is expressed in foreign ciphers and, thus, not trusting in that which itself lies within themselves and is imminently contained as memory. Not, then, for memory have you invented the alphabet, rather only for remembering is it a tool, and of wisdom you are bringing for your students only what would be a seeming and not the matter itself. For now, in that they will have heard much without having been instructed, so it is that they'll fancy to have become knowledgeable regarding much, although of the greater portion, indeed, they won't know a thing – and, so, they will be difficult to deal with in that they seem to have become wise but are not."
                                                                [275b3]

Phae: O Socrates, it seems a very easy matter for you to poeticize Egyptian anecdotes and whatever scripts you want, if only they might be from some foreign land.

Socr: Shouldn't this, my friend, be the case: that in Zeus's temple at Dodona the source of the first great prophecies was an oak tree. The Hellenes during that period, now, as they weren't so wise as you our youths are nowadays, this sufficed for them due to their simple-

---

[63] Classical name of Egyptian deity – *Amen*, the personification of air or breathe represented either as a ram or a goose; later part of *Amen-Ra*, the supreme god of the universe.

mindedness and they would listen to rocks as well as to trees, if only these spoke truly. But to you it seems, perhaps, to make a difference: who is speaking and where it is that he may come from. For your attention is not alone focused on this, whether or not the matter bespoken correlates so or otherwise. <59.~275c]

Phae: You are right in that you scold me. I'd fancy that the alphabet correlates just so as the Theban spoke.

Socr: He, then, who leaves an art behind in written treatises and he also who takes them up in the opinion that something clear and certain might possibly be transmitted through these dead letters that are on the page – such people are simpletons indeed and in truth they know nothing of this wise anecdote of Ammon – if, then, they believe that written scripts would be anything other than tools for remembrance for that person who already knows that about which they are written.[64] *[d]*

Phae: You are quite right.

Socr: For this is what is bad about writing, Phaedrus, and in this writing is really quite similar to painting – for this art also gives birth to its works as if they were alive, but then, if someone should pose a question to these paintings, so they remain silent and are quite noble in their stillness. And so too with writings. You might, perhaps, believe that they would have spoken up as if they had understood something, but then, if in your appetite for learning you ask them regarding what they've said, so indeed: they steadily describe just one and the same. But once a script is written, so she traipses about everywhere and it's no more likely that she will end up with people who understand her than with those with whom she doesn't at all belong, for she doesn't have any understanding about this issue as to whom she should and should not speak. And if she is injured or rudely castigated and cursed due to no fault of her own, so then she is always in need of her father's help, for then, she is in no position either that she might shield herself or do anything in her own defense.

Phae: Here too, what you say is said totally right. <60.~276a]

Socr: How now? – do we want that we take a look at some other script, the legitimate *{ächte}* sister of this one: how it is that she comes to be and how much better she is and more powerful than the former, so is her constitution, the way she grows?

Phae: And which script might this be that you'd be meaning, and how does she come to be?

---

[64] Note that the *Meno* demonstrates (through geometry) that even a common slave boy has knowledge regarding everything in his soul, waiting to be remembered (pp. 478–482).

Socr: The one that is written within the soul of him, he who learns –
and this script is well positioned, that she is able to help herself and
well knows to whom she should speak and when it's better to remain
silent.

Phae: You'd be meaning the living and ensouled script of the man
who truly knows as opposed to which the written version could
rightfully be seen as a shadow image.   [b]

Socr: Indeed, even she. But tell me this, would a landsman who
understands what he's about, would he take the seeds for whose
tending he is responsible, that others might partake in the fruit that
he nurtures, and would he construct a small Adonis garden in the
very imminence of the mid-Summer heat, and will he experience joy
if already on the eighth day he sees the plants shooting up into the
heights? – or shall it be so that he'd only do this out of playfulness
and on festive occasions if, then, he does it at all; but these seeds, if
he is really to be serious about his business, then he shall sow them
in accordance to the prescripts of the art of horticulture and in the
proper ground where they belong, and he shall be satisfied if what
he has sown reaches its consummation after eight months?   [c]

Phae: It is certainly so, o Socrates, the latter would be done in all
earnestness but the former only for some other purpose.

Socr: And shall we say that he who possesses knowledge of
righteousness, beauty and the good – that he shall proceed with less
understanding than this landsman?

Phae: In no way, that couldn't well be.

Socr: Thus, it shall not be with all earnestness that he writes them in
water, sowing these seeds with ink and an instrument made of reed,
with words that, indeed, are incapable of helping themselves through
speech and also incapable of adequately teaching about truth?

Phae: Well no, I wouldn't suppose so.   [d]

Socr: Indeed not, rather this garden of dialogues shall only be done
in play, as it seems, so it's sown and so described. But if he writes for
his very own intent, that he have a stockpile of remembrances
collected in anticipation of the forgetfulness of old-age when he shall
be in need – and, then too, for everyone who is following along in
his tracks: so he shall be overjoyed if he sees them sprouting about,
all so tender and full of beauty; and then, if others are enthralled in
other games, besprinkling one another at their symposiums and
whatever else is related to this, then it shall be that the former plays

with this whilst the latter is playing with that and, thus, time is brought forward.[65]   *[e]*

Phae: Indeed, as a master, o Socrates, do you name amongst these lesser games the play of that person who knows how to make a game from out of the poetry of speech, and this regarding justice and whatever else it was that you just mentioned.

Socr: So it is, quite, Phaedrus. But far more masterful, I think, is the earnestness with these things: that if someone in accordance to the prescripts of the art of dialectics chooses the proper soul and then with insight he sows the speeches and the plants shoot forth and are in a position to help themselves as well as receive help from the one who planted them, and that they bear fruit issuing forth with new seeds, some of which grow in a few people here, others in other souls there and so are capable of supporting themselves and continuing on, immortal, and for whomever it may be that possesses them, to make him so blessed as it is possible that a human being may be.

Phae: This, indeed, is something yet far more masterful than what you said earlier on.   *<61.~277ab]*

Socr: But only now, Phaedrus, are we capable of making that decision about which we spoke formerly, after having seen eye to eye and having become as one in regards to this.

Phae: But, what decision was that?

Socr: That which we really wanted to take a good look at before we digressed and, so, ended up here. Whether, namely, we wouldn't be capable of discovering how appropriate it was that Lysias was chastised due to his composition, and also in regards to the composition of speeches itself: which would be composed in accordance with art and which would be totally lacking in artistry. Now, that which accords with art and that which doesn't – this, I'd fancy, this has now been made rather clear.

Phae: I'd fancy so as well... but remind me about this one more time, if you don't mind.

Socr: Namely, not until someone is acquainted with the true nature and qualities of each and every thing regarding which he speaks and writes, and not until he is in a position to fully clarify it and, once clarified, also able to dissect it down into its subtypes and, thus, categorize it right down into the elemental particles that no longer admit of division – and, likewise, he's acquainted with the nature of soul and he understands how to go about discovering the fitting type

---

[65] This sentence is key to my interpretation of Plato's playfulness in describing all of his shorter dialogues (*Phaedrus* through the *Symposium*) here at the end of his first dialogue, the revised *Phaedrus*, as detailed in my introduction.

of persuasive argument for each soul type; and then he orders all of this and decks it out with the proper ornamentation, that for motley souls he's able to come up with motley arguments, and simple speeches for simple souls, etc.; until and unless this be so he won't be deemed capable of treating the genealogy of speeches to the highest degree of artistry that is allowed, and neither for teaching nor for persuasion, just as the whole of our previous discussion has demonstrated most amply.

Phae: Quite, this is approximately how it all seemed to be to us.

Socr: But, how about this earlier question – whether   *<62.~277d]* or not it would be beauteous or despicable that speeches be written and presented, and how one should go about this that it would rightly be reviled or not? Has that which was just spoken of above also made this clear?

Phae: Say what?

Socr: That whenever, be it now with Lysias or with anyone else, something has been written or will yet be written and be it in relation to some particular area of concern or in regards to the public weal as a whole – in that, perhaps, advice regarding the Laws might be brought forward, that, thus, legislative bills for a Republic are being drawn up in the opinion that there would be great thoroughness regarding fundamental issues and that also there would be great clarity in the document, all of this exposes the author to excoriation – whether or not, now, anyone actually comes forward with such. For not to be capable of differentiating between day and night in relation to righteousness and injustice, evil and good, that is – in all actuality and undeniably – most execrable, and no matter if all the people praise it.   *[e3]*

Phae: Certainly.

Socr: But he who knows that in any written speech and in regards to every subject matter there is, necessarily, much that has to be mere play, and that there's no writing at all, neither in verse nor in prose, that is particularly worth the effort of writing or speaking – insofar, namely, as it's done only as a matter of persuasion without any deeper investigations or teachings within; that, rather, even the best from amongst all of the literary masterworks, these are there only as a service for remembrance for those who already have been instructed; but in these, on the other hand, these that truly are taught and spoken for the sake of that learning which actually is inscribed within the soul as regards what is righteous, beautiful and good – in these alone, know it – that here there is something that is real and consummate and well worth the effort; and it is for this reason that only these deserve, likewise, that they shall be named legitimate children, these that firstly are discovered abiding within one's own self and, after these, those which may be taken as being children or as brothers and sisters and which have grown up in other souls and express other relationships; but all the rest, one lets these others go; and may this speech be such a one, Phaedrus, as you and I would wish that you and I might be.

Phae: In every wise, I also want and wish with you that which you say. <63.~278bc]

Socr: Thus, we have joked sufficiently amongst ourselves regarding this subject of speeches; and you should now go thither and inform Lysias that the two of us took a pleasant hike down into this peaceful arbor by the wellspring of the nymphs and we have heard speeches that command us, firstly, that Lysias and all of the others who busy themselves with the compositions of speeches and, then too, Homer and all of those who compose poetry – and be it for recitation alone or accompanied by music – and then, not to forget, thirdly, Solon and all of the rest of these who meet together in various conventions of the citizenry to draw up legislative bills that they call the laws: to say to all of these that if each composes things such as these and well knows how it is that the subject matter truly correlates and likewise is in a position to go into and elaborate on the particulars of what was written and to succeed in helping the speech out when necessary and, moreover, when in one's speaking one can outdo even that which was written down and demonstrate that it's only something bad, then he would not have to be named with those names that are derived only from here, that rather he be named with one which is connected to that which was spoken of above and in respect to those matters with which he is working so seriously. [d]

Phae: What sort of name do you want him to share?

Socr: That someone is named wise, o Phaedrus, this I'd fancy as being something grand, and fit and proper only for God alone; but a lover of wisdom or something along these lines, this might well be more appropriate for him as well as being, in itself, more poignant.

Phae: And not at all farfetched.

Socr: Hence, he who has nothing better than that which results after tedious turnings this way and that, the mere augmentation of one thing on top of another, and a great deal of scratchings-out, those who write and compose in such a manner as this shall – wouldn't you agree? – be rightly named poets, or speechwriters or law-givers?

Phae: How else?

Socr: So then, you carry this news to your dear friend, Lysias.

Phae: But you? what shall you do? For, indeed, we shouldn't allow ourselves that we overlook your friend.

Socr: But, which friend?

Phae: Isocrates, that *beaut* – what news will you deliver to him, Socrates? What should we say that he shall be?

Socr: Isocrates is still young; but my inkling about him, this I might tell you.   *[279a]*

Phae: And what, pray tell, what would that be?

Socr: I'd fancy that, as regards his natural talents, he's too good that we should place him in the same class – that his work be compared with this speech by Lysias; that, moreover, his character seems to be of a more noble blend so that it wouldn't, indeed, be a cause for wonder if as he ripens in age, if his efforts shouldn't surpass by far the speeches upon which he currently is expending so much labor and that he may well leave them behind as child's play; and, then too, if all of this erudition no longer should satisfy him, then a divine inspiration might lead him on to something that is grander still. For already as a matter of natural disposition there is something philosophical in the soul of this man. Thus, this is the news that   *[b]* I will give to my beloved in the name of these gods who have inspired us here; but you, do inform Lysias about what we spoke earlier.

Phae: Indeed, that shouldn't be overlooked. But, let's be on our way now as the midday heat has abated.

Socr: Is it not better that first we give thanks to these gods, and then we'll go?

Phae: Sure, why not?

Socr: O lovely Pan and all of the other gods who are present here:

Grant me that I may have beauty within, and that my external trappings be in friendly rapport with what lies within. As rich I should like to proclaim the wise, and for myself I'd want a purse of gold that no other than a man of moderation might bear and manage.

Would there yet be anything else, o Phaedrus, that we might require? as I, for myself, have finished my prayer.

Phae: Include me in your prayer as well, for amongst friends everything is shared in common.[66]

Socr: Well then, so let's be on our way.

****

---

[66] Compare with *Lysis* 207cd (p. 83).

Lysis

for Eleanor Hale

"If someone is going to think these things through in a correct manner, he must necessarily examine the nature of friendship, of desire, and of what are called 'the erotic desires.' For there are two entities here, and from their combination comes yet a third form, but because they are all given just one name, total confusion and obscurity is created."

The Laws of Plato [67] *– 837a*

Lysis – Sections:

---

[67] *The Laws of Plato*, translated by Thomas Prangle, University of Chicago Press, 1988 – Copyright 1980 by Basic Books, Inc.

Lysis

SOCRATES NARRATES

<1.~203a]

I was going from the academy straight on my way to the Lyceum, on the path that skirts along outside of the city walls, right underneath them. But as I came upon the small gateway which is there at the source of the Panops [river], this is where I met up with Hippothales, the son of Hieronymus, as well as Ctesippus, the Pæanian – and there were many others there, beautiful lads who were congregating about them, and all these youngsters stood tightly pressed up amongst one another. And as Hippothales caught sight of me approaching, so he called out: Whither, Socrates, whither are you going, and whence? ~ From the academy, I replied, and I'm directly on my way to the Lyceum. ~ Thus, you're not coming here to join us? Indeed, it would well be worth your while. ~ Really, how's that, and what might you be meaning? – and who else is part of this gathering? ~ Right here, said he, we're not the only ones who have come together here, rather there's quite a few other *beauts*; and as he said this he pointed toward an enclosed space which was there across from the wall with the doorway standing open. ~ But, what's that over there? – *[204a]* and what is it that all of you are up to? ~ That there, said he, is a newly constructed Palaestra – and then, for the most part we're engaged in discourse in which we would be very happy that we share it with you. ~ It's very good of you, said I, that you do so. But who is it that's teaching here? ~ One of your good friends and someone who holds you in high esteem, Miccus. ~ By Zeus, said I, not a bad man, rather a most capable sophist. ~ Would you like to come along and follow us, said he, that you also might see who is inside? ~ Rather, most gladly would I first hear from you what it is that shall transpire with me should I accompany you within... and then, who is this *beaut*, actually? ~ The one of us, said he, places the one up upon a pedestal; another, someone else. ~ But what about you, o Hippothales, who do you hold up? Do tell me. – When asked this question he blushed, and so, I spoke further: O son of Hieronymus, you need not tell me anything more in regards as to whether you are in love or not: for not only can I already see that you are in love, rather too that you are far advanced in this, your being in love. For the rest I may be quite *[c]* incompetent and rather a useless fellow, but then this has been bequeathed to me by God, that right off I'm quite capable of knowing who is in love, as well as who the beloved is. ~ As he heard me say this, he became redder still. But Ctesippus remarked: That's really exquisite, Hippothales, that now you're all flushed and that you have

such qualms about telling Socrates the name – since, really, if only he spends a short amount of time in your company so then he'll be tired to death of having to hear you speak about him, so constantly do you always harp back upon him, always bringing up his name! At least with us, o Socrates, he has quite filled our ears and deafened us with the name, Lysis. And then, if he's had a bit to drink, so we've become totally used to this, that when we wake up out of our sleep we believe to hear this name, *Lysis*, still echoing in our heads. But, all the same, that which is so annoying to hear over and over again in his conversation, this isn't nearly so vexing as when he starts off drenching us with his love sonnets and all of his speeches! And really, what's the worst of all is when he goes so far as to sing about his love in that most amazing voice of his! – and we don't have any choice but that we must patiently listen and hear all of this. *But now*, when you ask him about it, he only turns red. ~ This Lysis, said I, he's one of these lads who's just now coming into bloom, as it seems. I've drawn this *[e]* conclusion, namely, only because his name is one with which I'm as of yet unacquainted, since now you've just told it to me. ~ They don't generally call him by his name, he answered me, rather he's still referred to by his father's name, and this is because his father is so well known. And, then too, I'm certain that you'd recognize the lad just by his figure *{Gestalt}* for by this all alone everyone is capable of recognizing him with ease. ~ So tell me then, said I, to whom does he belong. ~ He is the eldest son of Democrates from Aexone. ~ A *beaut*, said I, o Hippothales! – what a noble and in every manner majestic love it is that you've managed to track down! So come on now and do let me hear it all, that which you give these others to hear, so that I might see whether you also know what's proper for the lover to say in his speeches, and both to the beloved himself as well as to all the others. ~ And to this he said: Aren't you getting a little carried away, o Socrates, by what Ctesippus has said about me? ~ Perhaps, said I, you might want to deny it and that you wouldn't be in love with him, he who was named? ~ No, not that, said he; but I'm neither composing verse nor any speeches upon my beloved. ~ He's not really in his right mind, Ctesippus spoke up, rather now he's talking nonsense and has quite lost his bearings. ~ To this   *<2.~205b]*
I said: I'm not asking you, o Hippothales, and I have no desire to hear any such verses nor the manner in which you recite them, if it really should be that you have composed such for the boy. Rather, just tell me the sense of these so that I might experience in which manner it is that you are treating your beloved. ~ Well, let *him* tell you everything then, since *he* knows it all so precisely and has everything in his memory – as then, he says he's heard it all from me, and to excess. ~

By the gods, said Ctesippus, very well do I know it, Socrates! – it is, after all, ludicrous enough. For then that a lover, he who more than anyone else is always thinking about his beloved, that he himself shouldn't know anything more to say about him than each and every child wouldn't also be quite capable of saying, how might it be that this isn't ludicrous? But that about which the whole city is speaking in regards to Democrates and Lysis, the lad's grandfather – and then, about their entire hereditary line: all of their riches, their horse breeding and their victories in the Pythian, Isthmian, and Nemean games, what with their chariots and race horses – all of this he transposes into poems and speeches. And then too, he takes things to even greater extremes in matters pertaining to Lysis' ancestry. For then, of late it's the feasts of Heracles that he depicts for us in I don't know what for an ode – how namely due to some common relation whom he traces back to their distant forefathers... and so it is *[205d]* that he takes up the descendents of Heracles, that, thus, Lysis too is a descendent of Zeus who had offspring with the daughter of some remote ancestor of his district; in short, the same stuff that all the old women sing to their grandchildren, and lots more of a similar mold. Such as this is it, that about which he lectures us in his speeches, and he forces all of this upon us, that we hear it all recited – *and in epic verse!* ~ As I heard this, so I said: You ludicrous man, Hippothales! – even before you have proven victorious in your quest, already you are composing verses and singing songs for yourself in that you compose such poetic adulations? ~ Upon *myself*, o Socrates, said he, never yet have I done so, neither in song nor in verse, indeed! ~ At least, you don't mean to have done so. ~ But how would you be meaning this? he asked me. ~ In every respect, said I, these songs have this as their goal. For if it should come to pass that you do indeed win your beloved over in such a manner as this, so these adulations will then serve you as your very own ornamentation, all of these things that you have spoken and have sung and, so, they will be a true hymn of adulation for yourself because you are the one who has attained this prize. But if he should escape you, so then, ever the greater the praise that you have spoken for your beloved, and so too in relation to his beauty and his virtues, thus too, ever the more *[a]* shall you have failed and ever the more shall you be made into a laughingstock. He then, o friend, who is to be a master in the art of love, he saves his adulation for that day when he proves victorious, and he does so out of fear: how shall the whole affair play out at the end. And beyond this it's also the case that the beauties, if it should be that one praises them and places them up upon majestic pedestals, so they become filled with their vain imaginations of high stature; or wouldn't you agree? ~ That's rather probable, said he. ~ And isn't it also the case that ever the higher one's praise is, even so much more difficult shall it be to make the conquest?   ~   That seems most probable. ~ What sort of a hunter then, essentially, do you take *him* to be, he who in his hunt upon the wild game startles them so that they become ever the more difficult to capture? ~ Obviously, a bad one. ~ And so too, that one through one's speeches and songs makes the prey wilder rather than quiescent, this is manifest ignorance, isn't it? ~ I'd fancy it so. ~ Do take heed, Hippothales, that you don't bring harm upon yourself by all of your poetry. For then, I do believe it, he who harms himself through his own poeticizing, you wouldn't want to admit this of such a poet, that he be a good poet, since he is the cause of his own misfortune. ~ No, by Zeus, said he, verily, that would indeed show the greatest deficiency in reason. But it's even due to this, o Socrates, that I place my trust in you, and if you might have something other, so do advise me: about what should one speak and what is it that one would have to do in order that one shall be pleasing to the beloved. ~ This is no easy matter, said I,   <*3.~206c]* to say what this would be; but then, if you might want to bring matters about so that Lysis himself would come to speak with me, so then perhaps I might be able to put on display an attempt as regards what one might speak about with him instead of that, what these have said of you, all of that about which you speak and sing. ~ That, said he, is not hard at all. For then, if only you go in with Ctesippus here and take a seat and partake in the discourse, so I believe that this shall happen all on its own – for then, above all other things Lysis has a desire and a fondness for listening. And beyond this, in that now's the time that the festival to Hermes is being celebrated, so young and old are to be found together without any prejudices against this. So he'll most certainly come join the circle with you. And even if he shouldn't, then, nonetheless, he is very well acquainted with Ctesippus because of the latter's cousin, Menexenus, who amongst all of them is Lysis' most trusted friend. So that Ctesippus only needs to call his cousin over – if, then, they don't simply come over of their own accord. ~ So, said I, this is how we'll have to make do; and right away I took Ctesippus along with me and made my way into the Palaestra, and the others came along behind us.   *[206e]*

As now we entered inside, so we discovered the boys – in that already they had finished in making the offerings and most all of the religious ceremonies had reached their conclusion – and so, as I say, we found them all playing a game of bones. Now, most of them were playing outside in the forecourt but then a few were playing in one corner of an alcove which served as a changing room; and they played "Even and Odd" with quite a good number of bones that they had picked out from the baskets. Around these still other boys were standing about as observers and one of these was Lysis who was standing there amongst these boys and teenagers – and he wore a garland and stood out from amongst them all due to his strikingly handsome appearance, not only that he'd deserve to be called beautiful, rather beautiful and noble. So now, the two of us bent down and seated ourselves across from one another, for it was peaceful inside, and so we spoke something over amongst ourselves.[68] But Lysis was constantly looking over our way and it was obvious that he would very much have liked it that he might come over to join us. So now, for awhile he was thoughtful and quite at a loss, how he might come join us all alone by himself, but after awhile Menexenus left the game that was going on out in the forecourt and, as he noticed that Ctesippus and I were there, so he came right up to us and took a seat.   *[207b]* As Lysis saw this, so he followed Menexenus' lead and sat down too, right next to him. Thereupon now all of the others also gathered around us, and Hippothales too, since he saw a good many standing about, so he hid himself behind these others, placing himself where he believed that he wouldn't be noticed by Lysis due to his fear that this might go against him – and so, being quite close to all of us he too listened in on the conversation. But now I turned myself toward Menexenus and spoke: Which of the two of you, o son of Demophon, may well be the elder? ~ We argue about this with one another – this was his answer. ~ And about this as well, said I, are you also able to argue about this: who of the two of you would be more distinguished? ~ Indeed. ~ And certainly too, who would be more beautiful, isn't this even so? At this they both cracked up in laughter. But by no means shall I ask you who would be the wealthiest of you two, for then you are good friends, isn't this true? ~ Indeed, very much so. ~ And amongst friends everything is shared in common, as they say. So that in this no differences should be capable of having any particular significance, if then you've spoken to me truly in regards to your friendship. ~ They admitted as much. ~ And at this moment I was just about to inquire who of the two of them would be more righteous and who would be wiser. But someone came up to Menexenus with the news that the master of ceremonies had just

---

[68] Compare with the opening scene at Callias' estate in *Protagoras* 314c (p. 114) and following; and likewise, the opening scenes in *Charmides* 153e–154c (pp. 173–174) and *Parmenides* 127d (p. 208) – Parmenides, Pythodorus and Aristotle "tarried outside."

called for him; it seemed to me as if it would have been his turn to
watch over the sacrificial offerings.   <4.~207d2]

So this one took his leave but I turned myself to Lysis and asked him
further, saying: Certainly, o Lysis, your mother and father love you
very much indeed? ~ Quite, said he. ~ Hence, they also would want
this to be so, that you might be so happy as is at all possible? ~ How
else? ~ But does *he* seem to you to be happy, said I, he who serves[69]
and isn't allowed to do whatever it may be that he wants and whatever he considers pleasurable? ~ By Zeus, not to me, said he. ~
Hence, as it is so that your parents love you and wish you well in all
ways, so, certainly, they do indeed take care that you are totally
satisfied? ~ How mightn't they not do so? said he. ~ Then, they let
you do whatever it may be that you want to do and never scold you
about anything at all; nor do they disallow that you might not do
something or other, whatever you think pleasant? ~ But indeed they
do, by Zeus, they disallow me a great deal, o Socrates. ~ How? you
don't say, said I, they want that you should be happy and find *[208a]*
satisfaction and yet they disallow you from doing whatever it might
be that you please? But tell me this. If you should want to drive one
of your father's chariots and if you yourself wanted to hold the reins
and lead the team whenever the races were being run, wouldn't they
let you do as you liked? – or rather, wouldn't they forbid you from
doing this? ~ By Zeus, said he, they wouldn't let me do so, not at all.
~ But then, who would they allow? ~ That would be the charioteer,
he receives his wages from father. ~ How? you don't say? – a paid
lackey is allowed to do this which is forbidden of you, that he may do
whatever he wants with the horses, and on top of all this they pay
him? ~ But how else? said he. ~ But all the same, they do allow you
that you might drive the mules and take the mule cart out for a spin,
and that you command it; and this even if you should want to take the
whip and give the mules a few good strokes, this would be granted to
you, that you might do so? ~ How do you mean, said he, that they
would allow me so much? ~ But is no one allowed to strike them? ~
Yes indeed, said he, the mule driver. ~ And is he a freeman or a
slave? ~ A slave. ~ A slave, then, as it seems, they respect a slave to
a higher degree than they respect you, their own son; and they put
things in his hands and show him preference over you, and they let
him do whatever he wants but they disallow you that you might do
the same? But then, do tell me this at least, they do allow of you that
you might rule over yourself, or do they forbid you this as well, *[c]*

---

[69] Compare with *Gorgias* 491e–492c (p. 311).

that you might not take care of yourself? ~ How might it be, indeed, that they would allow me this! – said he. ~ Rather, someone rules over you? ~ Right here, said he, my governor. ~ And he too, isn't he a slave? ~ What else? – one of our own in any event. ~ Certainly that must be really vexatious, that you a free person should be governed over and led about by a slave! But then, what is it that your governor does, really, in that he governs you? ~ He takes me to my teachers. ~ And perhaps these teachers also tell you what it is that you have to do? ~ Indeed they do. ~ Thus, there's quite a number of taskmasters that your father places before you in that he's given this matter considerable thought. But, still and yet, when you finally return home to your mother, well, at least she allows you that you might do just as you please so that you may be totally happy with her and enjoy all the pleasures of life – whether now, this might mean that you play around with her spools of wool or mess about with her loom, assuming that she's set it out in the room for weaving? For certainly, she wouldn't forbid you anything and lets you play catch with the shuttle or do whatever with the boom and, then too, with everything else that belongs together with the weaving art? ~ As I asked him this, Lysis just had to laugh and he said: By Zeus, Socrates, not only does she forbid me to play with any of these things, rather too it is quite certain that I would get a good beating if I were so much as to touch any of them. ~ Heracles! – said I – have you, perhaps, done some harm to your mother or your father? ~ By Zeus, said he, not I. ~ But then, why is it that they disallow you that <5.~208e] you might be happy, and that they do so with threats of beatings, and why don't they let you do just as you please; and then for the whole day you're constantly being led about and commanded by someone else, that you do whatever, so that, as it seems, neither are all of your vast riches of any particular benefit to you, for all of the others and even the slaves have more authority to do as they will than you, nor too even with your striking good looks, for here as well there's always someone else who looks after you and takes good care of you. But you, o Lysis, you don't appear to have any authority at all and aren't allowed to do anything of significance, whatever it might be that you would like to do. ~ I'm not yet old enough, said he, o Socrates. ~ But that can't well be the reason, o son of Democrates, said I, this isn't what it is that's hindering you! For with things such as these, I do believe, these things both your mother and your father do give over to you and they don't wait around until you shall have come of age: for instance, if they need something to be read to them or written [b] down for them, so I'd bet that they'd sooner allow that you fulfill this task for them than anyone else in the house. Isn't it so? ~ You may rely on it, said he. ~ And isn't it true, here you have total freedom: which letter you might write first and which one comes second,[70] and isn't it even the same with reading. And then if you pick up your lyre, I do believe it, neither your father nor your mother will forbid you that you shouldn't tune the strings lower or higher, nor do they stop you from plucking at the strings, whichever ones you choose, nor even from beating out some accompaniment on the sounding board. Or do they forbid you from doing these things? ~ Utterly not, not at all. ~ Well, what might the root cause of all of this be, that they don't disallow you from doing any of these things, but then, in the former matters they do, just as we were saying? ~ I believe, said he, it's because I understand these matters but not the former ones. ~ Well spoken, I answered him, most virtuous Lysis. Hence, it's not your age that your father is waiting on, in that he'll give over to you the authority in all of these matters, rather it's the day when he shall believe that you'd be more clever than he is; and on that day he'll pass even himself on over into your authority as well as everything else that he owns. ~ I myself do believe this to be so, said he. ~ Very good, said I, and what about your neighbor? – doesn't he have the same rule as your father does? Wouldn't you be meaning this too, that he'd just assume give over to you the maintenance of the *[209d]* affairs of his household if he were to believe that you would be better at it than he is? or is it so that even then he'd want to leave all this in his own hands? ~ He'd place all of this into my hands, I think. ~ And what about the people of Athens? – do you believe that they wouldn't hand over to you their authority over the city if they were to take notice of this, that you have sufficient cleverness to run all the affairs of state? ~ I do believe it. ~ And, by Zeus, I continued on: what about the Great King of Persia? whether it would well be his own eldest son, he to whom the regency over all of Asia is to fall, if it were to be so that a meat stew is being prepared, would he let his son spice up this stew with whatever his son would like to throw into it, or – if we were to come to him and showed him that we know better than his own son does, how a good stew is to be made – wouldn't he prefer us over his son? ~ Obviously, said he, it would be us. ~ And the former wouldn't be allowed to contribute a single thing, not even the smallest bit; but for us, and even if we took both hands full of salt and threw it into the pot, still, he would allow us that we do so. ~ How mightn't he not allow this? ~ But how about this? what if his son were to be suffering from an affliction of the eyes, would he let his

---

[70] Compare with *Theaetetus* 207d–208a (p. 454). Since everyone agrees that *Lysis* is an early dialogue and *Theaetetus* a late one, it seems quite obvious that Plato tweaked his works.

son do whatever it may be to his own eyes – if now, he didn't hold him up as being a doctor, or wouldn't he forbid him that he do anything? ~ He'd certainly forbid him. ~ But in regards to us, *[a]* if he were to hold us as being informed in medicine, and even if we wanted to cut open the lids of his son's eyes and sprinkle ashes into them, nevertheless he wouldn't, as I opine it, he wouldn't stop us or defend his son if he were to believe that we would understand the matter in a fundamental way. ~ What you say is very right. ~ And wouldn't he much rather allow us to do whatever it might be, more so than he either allows himself or his son – in those matters, namely, in which we seem to be wiser than both he and his son are? ~ It's necessarily so, Socrates. ~ Thus, this is the way the matter correlates, dear Lysis, said I. Regarding such matters in which we have attained for ourselves right insight, everyone will *<6.~210b]* leave decisions on these matters in our hands, whether they be Hellenes or foreigners, men or women – in matters such as these we may do just as we want and no one would gladly step up in our stead and hinder us, that rather in these things we're able to handle matters with total freedom, and we'd also command the others and this would be our privilege, for we would get satisfaction from handling these matters. But regarding those things in which our understanding is deficient, that we haven't achieved such understanding, in these nobody at all would allow us to do whatever it may be that we might fancy as good, rather everyone would hinder us from doing anything at all and they would do so by all means available to them, and not just the foreigners, rather father and mother and whoever – if even it were possible that someone would be yet more closely related to us than our mothers and fathers are. Much rather shall we ourselves have to follow the lead of others in whatever pertains to things like this, and all of these things will seem to us as being strange [foreign] – for then, we wouldn't have any satisfaction in partaking in them. Do you give in and make allowance that this is how it correlates? ~ I do. ~ Now, shall we be loved by anyone and shall anyone be fond of us in relation to matters in which we are useless? ~ That doesn't follow, said he. ~ So then, now, neither your father loves you nor does anyone else love anybody insofar as he is incompetent. ~ One couldn't believe this possible, said he. ~ But then, if you *[d]* should become a person having understanding, o son, then everyone shall be your friend and all people will be drawn toward you: for then you will be competent and will be good. But if not, so then, neither your own father nor mother, nor anyone else from amongst your relatives, no one will be your friend. Is it then well-nigh possible, o Lysis, that one knows a great deal about those matters regarding which one doesn't as of yet have *any* knowledge? ~ And how could one do so, said he. ~ And if it be so that you still require teachers, so you don't as of yet know? ~ Right. ~ Hence, you also don't know much yourself, if you are as of yet without knowledge? ~ Truly, Socrates, said he, I also don't believe to.　　　　　*<7.~210e]*

As I heard him say this, so I was turning myself about to catch sight of Hippothales and, indeed, I practically blushed myself. For then I was just about to say: So, o Hippothales, this is the way one has to speak to the beloved – that one humbles him and sets him to rights, not that one blows him up, placing him upon some pedestal and spoiling him. But then, as I did catch sight of him, how he was utterly in fright and totally at a loss in respect to what had just been said, so I remembered that he didn't want that Lysis should notice his being there, lurking behind these others. And so I took a firm hand upon myself and held back from speaking out a word; and then Menexenus returned and took his seat next to Lysis, the same one that he had just recently vacated. Now, Lysis had become like a child and a friend, and he spoke to me very softly so that Menexenus wouldn't hear:　　*[a]* What you just told me, Socrates, so tell the same thing to Menexenus. ~ I answered: You, assuredly, can tell him all of this yourself, o Lysis, for then you did take pains to pay precise attention. ~ Indeed I did, said he. ~ Thus, do make the attempt that you retain it all in your memory so that you will be able to tell him the whole of it, precisely as I spoke. But should it be that you come to realize that you've forgotten some part of it, so just ask me about it later on, whenever you meet me on the street.[71] Very well, said he, this is what I will do, Socrates, and with the utmost in exactitude, you can count on me. But then, tell him something else, so that I might listen in as well until the time comes when I have to go home. ~ Yes, I'll have to do this, particularly as it's your wish that I do so. But do watch closely so that you might come to my aid if Menexenus starts off by contradicting me. Or don't you know that he is very argumentative? ~ Yes, by Zeus, said he, and mighty powerful. It's for this very reason that I want you to converse with him. ~ So, said I, that I might　*[c]* make myself ludicrous? ~ No, by Zeus, rather that you might tame him a bit. ~ How's that? said I, this won't be that easy. For then he's become a person mighty in rhetoric since he is, you know, one of Ctesippus' students – and, speaking of him, there he is too, don't you

---

[71] Compare with *Theaetetus* 143a (p. 360) – Euclid's mastery of the dialogue; and similarly: Apollodorus' learning of the dialogue *Symposium* which he heard second-hand from Aristodemus, checking some points with Socrates at 173b.

see him, Ctesippus himself! ~ Don't you worry yourself about anyone, Socrates, said Lysis, rather just go right ahead and speak with him. ~ Well then, I'll have to begin, said I. ~ Now, in that we were speaking all of this softly to one another, so Ctesippus spoke up and asked us: Hey, you two, what are you both whispering about so nicely alone to one another that you don't want us to hear and partake in it? ~ Indeed, said I, we do want to share in it with all of you. Lysis, namely, doesn't understand something, something that I said, but he opines that Menexenus shall understand it and so he calls upon me that I ask him. ~ Then why don't you ask him? said Ctesippus. ~ That's just what I shall do, said I.   <*8.~211d]*

So tell me then, o Menexenus, that which I'm going to ask you. From my childhood onward I've always had a great yearning for a particular matter, just as everybody has something about which they are especially keen. For then, the one has an especial joy in horses, another likes dogs, another money, and someone else goes for honor. But none of these things means much to me at all – but, on the other hand, I do quite passionately want to acquire friends and having a good friend would be far dearer to me than having any prize quails or even the most prized chicken in all the world, indeed, by Zeus, dearer than any horse or dog and, I do believe it – *by the dog* – I'd sooner have a good friend than all of the gold of Darius [King of the Persians], even more than if I were to be Darius himself, so greatly do I have this passion for having a friend. In that now I see you two, you and Lysis, so I am struck and utterly amazed and I prize you two as being blessed, that still so young you've quickly achieved possession of this and earned each other's affections so easily, that, namely, you have earned his affections as your friend and, inversely, he your friendship and affections in your being his friend. But I am still such a laggard in this matter that I don't even once know this: upon what manner it is that one becomes someone else's friend. Rather, this is what I wanted to ask you about, since, obviously, you   <*9.~212b]* are informed about this. So do tell me, if someone should be in love with someone else, who is it that is a friend to the other: is it the lover to the beloved, or the beloved to the lover? – or doesn't this make any difference? ~ At least to me, said he, it doesn't seem to make any difference. ~ How's that? – said I! – both of them shall be friends to one another even if only the one of them loves the other? ~ At least, said he, I'd fancy this to be so. ~ But indeed, how so? – doesn't it happen that the lover likewise becomes an object of love for the beloved, the one whom he loves? ~ This happens. ~ But how now, doesn't it also happen that the lover might be hated? – and this

despite the lover's firm belief in his own love of the beloved? For in
that some say that they love the other to the fullest extent possible, so
too a few of them also believe that they aren't loved in return and,
indeed, a few that they even are hated! Or would you fancy that this
isn't true? ~ Very true, said he. ~ And in such an instance as this,
said I, the one of them is indeed in love and the other one is loved? ~
Yes. ~ And which of them is the other's friend? Is the lover the
friend of the beloved whether or not his love may be reciprocated, or
even if he were to be hated? Or is the beloved the friend of the lover?
Or, quite to the contrary, are neither of these in such an instance a
friend to the other – if then, they don't both love each other? Well, it
certainly has the appearance that it would correlate in the latter
manner. ~ Thus, it now appears to us differently than it did before.
Earlier, namely, it was so that even if only the one of them would be
the lover, still both would be friends. But now if not both of them are
lovers then neither of them is a friend to the other. ~ That's the way
things have fallen out. ~ The lover, thus, isn't a friend to anyone who
wouldn't also reciprocate and also be in love with him? ~ It seems
not. ~ Thus, he too isn't a friend of horses, if these horses don't love
him in return; nor does anyone love quail or dogs or wine or wisdom
– if then, wisdom doesn't return the favor? Or is it so that each is in
love with these objects but, still, he isn't a friend to him [or it]; that
rather the poet has spoken falsely, that poet, namely, who said:

*"Most fortunate is he, he who is a friend to many: children and
valiant steeds, dogs for the hunt and the gracious hospitality of
foreign acquaintances who live the world round."*

[212e]

~ At least, it doesn't appear to me that this is the case. ~ That rather,
it seems to you that the poet who spoke these lines spoke what is
right? ~ Yes. ~ The lover, then, is indeed a friend to those whom he
loves, as it seems, o Menexenus, and whether now the latter love him
or hate him. And so it is as well with the children, the one part being
likewise the infants, they who are yet too young to love, and then the
other part being the children who are full of hate in that they've just
been punished by their mother or by their father – and yet, all the
same, even during this time in which they hate them, still they're
more friends to their parents than to anyone else in the entire world.
~ To me, said he, it does appear to be just as you say. ~ Not the one
who is loved, then, is the friend in accordance to this speech, but
rather the lover. ~ That's clear. ~ Thus too, the one who hates is
the enemy, and not the one hated? ~ So it seems. ~ There are many
who love those who are their enemies and, on the other hand, many

who hate those who are their friends – and thus, they are friends *[b]*
to their enemies and, inversely, enemies to their friends – if, namely,
the lover is the friend and not the beloved? But then, indeed, this is
the pinnacle of absurdity, dear friend, or much rather – I believe –
quite impossible that one might be a friend to one's enemies and an
enemy to one's friends? ~ Obviously, Socrates, said he, you're very
right about this. ~ Hence, if this is impossible, so then it would be
the one whom is loved who is the friend of the lover? ~ Apparently.
~ And then too, the one whom is hated is the enemy to the hater? ~
That's necessary. ~ But shall it not likewise fall out the same from
out of this, that once more we necessarily shall have to admit the
same as we did earlier, that quite often one is a friend to someone
who is not on friendly terms with oneself and often enough even with
someone who is one's enemy – if someone who loves isn't loved in
return, and that he might even be hated; and also that someone is an
enemy to someone who himself doesn't hold the former in bad esteem
nor take the other as being his enemy, that rather he might even be on
friendly terms with him – if someone should be hated and yet he
doesn't hate back... or, indeed, that he might even reciprocate with
love? ~ It is so, it does seem that all of this might happen, said he. ~
What then, what are we to make out of all of this, said I, if neither the
lovers should be friends nor those whom are loved, nor too if it only
should be when lovers and those loved simultaneously reciprocate,
that rather we should have to assert of some others as being friends
outside of these? ~ By Zeus, said he, o Socrates, I haven't got a clue.
~ Haven't we perhaps, said I, o Menexenus, haven't we proceeded
along with our investigation utterly in an ungrounded and improper
manner? ~ So do I well fancy it, Socrates – Lysis interrupted us –
and right as he said this he became all red, that his words seemed to
have slipped out from him against his better judgment because he
was totally caught up in the conversation with his entire soul, just as
it was being spoken. And, as was evident, this was what he constantly
had been doing.   *<10.~213de]*

Thus I – in part as I wanted to give Menexenus a little while to
recover himself and in part due to my joy over Lysis' thoughtfulness –
so I changed [interlocutors] and directing my speech upon Lysis I
said: O Lysis, it seems to me that you speak rightly, for then if we
would have grounded our investigation rightly, well then, we wouldn't
have strayed off course so easily and been thrown into such a state
of total confusion. Let's not tread along this path any further for,
obviously, this is a bad way to conduct the investigation; that rather
we go back to where we lost our bearings, that's the point, I believe,

which we have to revisit and, as the poets put it – investigate. For these poets, indeed, are likewise our fathers and our leaders into the realm of wisdom.[72] But they speak so that they themselves haven't done at all badly with their clarification of friendship, who the friends are; that rather God himself – so they say – God directs friends to one another and makes them to be friends. The lines, if I haven't confused myself in this, are these: *"As indeed constantly God is bringing like together with like, and He maketh them acquainted."* Or, haven't you ever heard these verses? ~ I have, very well, *[214b]* said he. ~ And then too, there are the writings of men who are held to be wise which you have seen and they say even the same thing, that the similar by necessity is always a friend to that which is similar. And these are those books which speak and are written about nature and which describe *the all.* ~ That's right, said he. ~ And do they speak truly? ~ Perhaps, said he. ~ Perhaps, said I, half of what they say is true and perhaps the whole of it, and we just don't understand it. For it seems to us that when evil approaches evil, and ever the more so the closer they encroach upon one another and ever the more each one has dealings with the other, so too do they have to become ever the more enemies, the one to the other. For evil does damage, and that which damages and that which is damaged cannot possibly be friends. Isn't it so? ~ Certainly, said he. ~ And in this manner the half of what the poets said wouldn't be true – if, indeed, it is so that the evils also are similar one to the other. ~ You're right. ~ But I would fancy it so, that they only want to be speaking about those who are good, that these are similar one to the other and are friends; but those things that are evil, and no matter what else might be said about them, these wouldn't even once be similar to themselves, that rather evil things are changeable and can't even be reckoned on one way or the other. But that which is dissimilar even to itself and comes to be in contradiction internally with itself, such as this has a *[d]* good way to go before it should ever become similar and a friend to some other. Or, don't you also opine this? ~ Quite, indeed I do, said he. ~ It is this, o friend, that these wise men and poets were alluding to, as I fancy it, these who say that the similar is a friend to the similar – that namely only the good is a friend and is always only a friend to the good, but that which is evil never achieves friendship, neither with the good nor with something else which is evil. Are you 'as one' with me on this, that you assert the same? ~ He answered, yes. ~ That, then, would be settled now – which people are friends –

---

[72] Cf: *Protagoras* 326a (p. 127) – and, indeed, the whole thrust of Simonides' poem and the "thwack" of the arrow, right in the bull's-eye ... (or is it Ulysses taking aim at the suitors?)

for this speech has displayed it to us with total clarity: it would be those who are good. ~ It does, said he, indeed have the appearance of doing so. ~ And to me also, said I, though there is yet one thing that I find vexing. Come now and for the sake of Zeus, let's examine this, that which I believe to see. The similar is to be a   <11.~214e] friend to that which is similar and this insofar as it is similar; but, is such to such also useful? Or isn't it much rather so: each and every similar – what advantage might a similar bring to some other similar or what harm would be added to it that it itself wouldn't also do? – or, utterly, what could be done with the friend that couldn't just as well be done without him? Such things as these, thus, how might they be capable of having any attraction for one another since, then, they don't offer the least bit of help, one to the other? How might this be possible at all? ~ It cannot possibly be, not at all. ~ And without there being attraction, how is friendship possible for any something? ~ There's no way, none at all. ~ Singularly, this being so, then indeed the similar is not a friend to the similar, but it may well be that the good is a friend to the good, not insofar as they are similar but insofar as they are good? ~ Perhaps. ~ But, how so? Shall not the good, insofar as it is good, thus too shall it not be sufficient itself unto itself? ~ Yes. ~ But that which is sufficient unto itself, such is not in need of anything or anyone other, at least insofar as this sufficiency extends? ~ Indeed, how might it? ~ But that which doesn't have any need for anything, such also shall not have any dependency or attachment to anything? ~ No, indeed not. ~ But that which isn't attached to anything else, such also won't be in love with anything? ~ No, that wouldn't follow. ~ And what isn't in love, such also wouldn't be a friend? ~ No, obviously not. ~ Thus, how shall it ever be at all possible that a good becomes a friend to a good – if, then, neither has any longing for the other when this other is absent, for then, each is sufficient unto itself all alone; nor, moreover, even when brought together as one neither has any sort of utility for the other. How are we to work this out, that such as these may have any value one to the other? ~ In no manner at all, said he. ~ But indeed, they can't well be friends one to the other if, then, neither of them has any particular worthiness for the other. ~ You're quite right. ~ Do take a look at this, o Lysis, how badly things have fallen out for us! May it well be, perhaps, that we've been totally deceived? ~ But, how's that? – said he. ~ Sometime or other I heard someone say,   <12.~215c] though at the moment I don't recall the circumstance, that the similar would be the greatest enemy to the similar, and so the good would be the greatest enemy to some other good. And affirmatively, Hesiod also delivers evidence to this effect in that he says that the one potter is an enemy to the other, the one singer to the other singers and even the one beggar to all the other beggars – and from all of these he displayed in the same manner that it is necessarily so, that the most similar has the utmost in jealousy, strife and enmity, that each must be full of such, one against the other; but then, that the most dissimilar is full of friendship. For then, the rich would have to be friends to the poor and the strong to the weak, that they might each abet the other and offer assistance, just as the physician is a friend to the sick and each and every person who is deficient in understanding is dependent upon the one who is informed, and that he loves him. And indeed, he goes even further in what he deduces from this proposition in that he asserts that in an even higher sense the previous proposition is far from being on target, namely that proposition which states that the similar would be a friend to the similar, and that much rather the opposite to this is shown to be true, that the opposites would be the greatest friends to their opposites. For it is for such that each has the strongest desires and urgings, but not for what is similar, namely – the dry attracts the moist, cold warmth, the bitter for the sweet, the sharp for the dull, that which is empty is seeking to be filled and that which is full is seeking release – and so it is with everything else too, in just this same manner. For every opposite would be nourishment for its contrary and the similar wouldn't offer any satisfaction at all for what is similar. And indeed, o friend, he fancied himself as right in this matter of great   *[216a]* importance – since he did say all of this – for then, he spoke most excellently. But for you, said I, are you pleased by this speech of his? ~ Very well, said Menexenus, so much of it as we've heard. ~ Do we want that we accept this and take it up, that each would to the fullest extent be a friend to that which is its opposite? ~ We want to. ~ Very well, said I, and is this also not something that is lacking in rhyme and reason, Menexenus? – and shall not those most highly esteemed for their wisdom come jumping upon us full of joy, and won't they ask us about this, whether the greatest contradiction to enmity wouldn't be friendship? What now, what should we give as our answer to these? Or wouldn't we have to admit this, that it is necessarily so, that what they say would be true? ~ That's necessary. ~ Thus is it so, this is what they shall say: that enmity is a friend to friendship or that friendship is a friend of enmity? ~ Neither one of these, said he. ~ But still, righteousness to injustice, or mindfulness to wantonness, or the good to the bad? ~ It doesn't seem to me to correlate in such a manner as this. ~ But, all the same, said I, if it is due to contrariness that the one shall be a friend to that which is its opposite, so these too would have to be friends. ~ That's necessary.

~ Neither, then, is the similar a friend to the similar, nor too are opposites friends one to the other. ~ No, these don't allow that such might be. ~ But let's also take a look at this too: doesn't <13.~216c] friendship promise us yet more and, as it's not possible from all of the foregoing, shall it not rather only be some such as this, that what is neither good nor evil shall be a friend to the good. ~ How do you mean this? said he. ~ Really, by Zeus, said I, I don't know myself, rather in all actuality everything is spinning around me too, and makes me dizzy from all of this confusion regarding the matter and, so, things shall probably fall out at the end in accordance with the old proverb: that love is of the beautiful. At least, this is most readily accepted as something that is soft, smooth and slippery. And it's most probably for this very reason that it manages to get away from us so easily, since this is its nature and modus. I mean, namely, that the good would be beautiful. Wouldn't you mean this as well? ~ I, likewise. ~ Thus, I mean this in a similar wise, that I simply have an intimation of the same, that what is neither good nor evil is a friend to that which is beautiful and good. But do listen to my premonition about this. I myself think this, namely, as being three different categories: firstly the good, next that which is evil, and finally that which is neither good nor evil. But, how about you? ~ I do too, said he. ~ And that neither is the good a friend to the good, nor too is that which is evil a friend to the evil, nor yet is the good a friend of that which is evil – just as our previous conversation wouldn't allow any of these. Hence there remains, if indeed anything is to be a friend to something else, there only remains that what is neither good nor evil shall be a friend either to the good or to such as it itself is. For then the evil, indeed, cannot possibly be a friend to anything. ~ That's right. ~ But, then too, nor can the similar be a friend to the similar, as we said this earlier, isn't it true? ~ Yes. ~ Hence, it isn't possible that what is neither good nor evil might be a friend to something else that is even such? ~ No, as one sees. ~ Thus, it follows all alone that what is neither good nor evil is able to become a friend of the good alone. ~ Necessarily, as this has the best look about it. ~ But shall this also, said I, o my   <14.~217a] children, what was said just now, shall this lead us aright? If, for instance, if we might want to examine this in relation to a healthy body: such a body is neither in need of medicine nor of any help, for it is sufficient unto itself and no one who is healthy has any need of friendship with a doctor due to his state of health. Isn't this true? ~ Indeed, no one. ~ But he who is sick, I believe, and due to sickness? ~ How shouldn't he be in need. ~ And sickness, indeed, is some-thing bad, but medicine is something that helps and it is good?

~ Yes. ~ But the body, insofar as it is a body, it is neither good nor evil? ~ So it is. ~ But the body is required to have dependency upon medicine due to sickness and loves medicine because of this? ~ It does seem to me to be so. ~ That which is neither good nor evil shall be a friend to the good due to an evil affliction? ~ This follows. ~ But obviously, then, before this evil affliction that is attached to it transforms it so that it too has become evil. For once it became evil, indeed, it couldn't long for that which is good and be a friend to what is good; for it is impossible, this is what we asserted, that what is *[c]* evil might possibly be a friend to the good. ~ And it is impossible, too. ~ So do weigh and consider this, what I shall say. Namely I say that, indeed, a few things do become just like that which is attached to them, but then others don't. Just as it is if someone paints something with whatever color it may be, so this color is attached to whatever it was that became colored. ~ Indeed. ~ But is, then, that which has been painted the same color as the paint with which it is afflicted? ~ I don't understand you, said he. ~ But this is how I mean it, said I. If someone were to paint your blond hair with white paint, would your hair then be white, or would it only seem to be so? ~ It would only seem so. ~ But all the same, this whiteness would be attached to your hair. ~ Yes. ~ But nonetheless, it still wouldn't be white, rather despite this affliction of whiteness it would be neither white nor black. ~ That's right. ~ But if, o friend, your age should bestow upon you this same color then it is so that your hair has become just so as this, that which was painted upon it – white, namely due to this affliction of whiteness. ~ How else? ~ It was regarding this that I was asking you, whether that which has something that is attached to it, whether this is always so as that which is afflicting it? – or whether it would only be so if it were attached in a certain manner that it would have become so, but otherwise it wouldn't be? ~ The latter, then, said he. ~ Then too, what is neither good nor evil would, from time to time, when it becomes afflicted with evil nevertheless not yet be evil, but then in other instances it shall already have become so. ~ Quite. ~ Hence, if it hasn't as of yet become evil despite this attachment to evil, so then, this affliction with evil stirs up a desire for what is good; but an affliction that has made one become evil, such an affliction robs one of this desire as well as robbing one of any friendship toward the good. For now,   *[218a]* in this latter case it no longer is something neither good nor evil, rather it has become evil; and what is evil is no friend of the good. ~ No, indeed not. ~ In accordance to all of this we then would be able to say that those who already are wise are no longer friends of wisdom, whether they be gods or men, nor too would those be friends of wisdom who are so afflicted by a lack of understanding that they have become evil – for then, no evil person nor someone incapable of being taught loves wisdom. There only remains, thus, those who do indeed have such an affliction of evil, this lack of understanding, but still they haven't as of yet become so that they lack all understanding through this, or that they have become erudite... but rather they still are of the opinion that they don't know it, what they actually do not know. And it's for this reason that only these are the philosophers, those who are neither good nor evil; but all the evil ones have no cause to pursue studies in philosophy, nor too do those who are good. For it was so that neither the contrary was a friend to that which was contrary to it, nor the similar to the similar – just as this was shown in our earlier conversation. Or, don't you two remember this? ~ Very well do we remember it, this is what they said. ~   *<15.~218c]*

Now then we have, said I, o Lysis and Menexenus – and with total certainty – we have discovered what a friend is and what he isn't, haven't we? Namely, we assert that in relation to the soul just as with the body and everywhere else: that which is neither good nor evil would be a friend of the good due to some affliction with that which is evil. ~ In every wise they wanted to assert this and give in to this, that this is the way it correlates. And I too was very self-satisfied and I enjoyed the moment: that like a hunter I now had made hunt upon this, and had done so to sufficiency. But after awhile something came to me, don't ask me whence it came, the most peculiar doubt – that not everything might well be true, all of this which together we had discovered. And so, in that I was very vexed at this, I said: O woe, Lysis and Menexenus, it seems that only in our dreams have we raised the prize up above our heads. ~ Now, what's this again? Menexenus asked me. ~ I fear this, said I, that we have behaved like braggarts, that it may well be so that just like these we have arrived upon false thoughts in regard to friendship. ~ Now what's wrong? – he asked me. ~ Let's examine this so, said I. He who is a friend, is he a friend to someone, or not? ~ That's necessary, said he. ~ And isn't it for the sake of some goal or purpose and not simply without cause? – or is it due to something and for the sake of something? ~ For something and due to some cause. ~ Now, is he likewise a friend to this matter, for the sake of which he's a friend to the other, or is he neither a friend nor a foe toward it? ~ I'm not following you *[218e]* aright, said he. ~ That doesn't amaze me, said I. But if I state it so, thus perhaps you shall better be able to follow and, I think, I shall better know what it is that I mean to say. He who is sick, this is even what we said, he is a friend to the doctor. Isn't this true? ~ Yes. ~

And indeed, due to the illness and for the sake of health, it is for these reasons that he is a friend to the doctor. ~ Yes. ~ Sickness, though, is something that is evil? ~ How shouldn't it be? ~ But health, is this good or evil, or neither of both of these? ~ Good, said he. ~ Hence we say, as it seems, the body which is neither good nor evil would be a friend of the art of medicine due to sickness, that is due to something that is evil. But the art of medicine is something that is good, and for the sake of health the art of medicine is receptive to this friendship; but health itself is good. Isn't it so? ~ Yes. ~ Now, is health a friend or not a friend? ~ A friend. ~ But sickness is the foe? ~ Indeed. ~ That which is neither good nor evil is a friend of the good due to the evil and due to that which is hated, and is so for the sake of the good, that to which it is a friend? ~ This is the way that the matter was shown. ~ One is a friend to that to which one is a friend for the sake of something to which one is a friend because of something else that is one's enemy. ~ That's how it looks. ~

<16.~219bc]

Good, said I. Since now we've gotten this far along, children, so let's be sure that we pay close attention so that we shan't be deceived. For that a friend has become a friend to that which is one's friend, I'll leave this off to one side although, even so, the similar has become a friend to what is similar which is something that we have clarified as being impossible. But let's at least weigh and consider this other matter so that what we have taken up doesn't deceive us. The art of medicine, this is what we said, this shall be one's friend for the sake of one's good health? ~ Yes. ~ Hence, one is also a friend of good health? ~ Quite. ~ If so, then, this too is for the sake of something else? ~ Yes. ~ And, indeed, once again so for the sake of something else to which one also is a friend – if, then, this should proceed along following the same route as the former [examples]. ~ Quite. ~ Hence, this too shall be a friend for the sake of something other, that to which one also is a friend? ~ Yes. ~ Don't we have to become tired of this always going about in circles and don't we have to finally come upon some beginning that doesn't itself once more lead back to some other friendship, that rather it goes right to the heart of the matter, that to which we are friends first and that we admit that we are friends to all of these others only due to our friendship to this [root] friendship? ~ That's necessary. ~ Now, even this is what I am meaning in that everything to which we confess that we are friends, all of these shan't always simply deceive us as being mere shadow images, but that really it's only this first to which we truly are friends. Namely, we want to reflect upon this in the following manner. If someone is making a really big deal out of something, just as the father tends to place the welfare of his son before all other things, *[e]* isn't it possible that for a father such as this – and even for this reason, because he values his son above everything else – can't he also make a big deal out of something other? That perhaps he's noticed that the former is particularly fond of *Gewürztraminer*, wouldn't he then make a big deal out of collecting wine in that he then believes that this might be key to his son's salvation? ~ For him, the sky's the limit *{Was wird er nicht?}*, said he. ~ Yes, and also the cup into which the wine was poured? ~ Sure, that's quite possible. ~ But because of this does he respect neither of them any higher than the other, the glass that rings true or his own son? the three bottles of wine or his son? Or much rather, doesn't the following correlation hold: all such attentions and all of his care isn't lavished upon that which is brought into being for the sake of something other, but rather upon the former for whose sake all of these other things are brought into existence. Just like when we're constantly saying that we make a big deal out of gold and silver, so nonetheless this may not really be the truth of the matter, that rather that regarding which we're making such a big deal, this would be something that is prior, namely that which becomes apparent [as we enjoy our wealth] and for the sake of which we've earned all this gold and everything else that we've attained. Do we want to assert this? ~ Indeed. ~ And also in regards to the friend, the same is valid? For then, that about which we say that we are his friend for the sake of some other to whom we are friend, obviously we name this just with a strange name, friend, but we'd like in all actuality only to be referencing the former, that in which all of these so-called friendships find their end. ~ That's the way all this shall well correlate, said he. ~ Hence, that to which we are in all truth a friend, we are not friends with this for the sake of something other to which we also would be friends? ~ *<17.~220b]* That's right. ~ We're quite finished with all of this, then, with whom we'd be friends, this shan't be something for the sake of something other to which we're likewise friends. – But, aren't we friends to that which is good? ~ I'd fancy that we are. ~ Thus, shall we love the good because of that which is evil and does it correlate so: if of these three categories that we mentioned earlier: the good, the evil and that which is neither good nor evil, if the two of them should be stipulated but the evil might be taken out of the mix entirely and it no longer should be possible that evil might touch us, neither our body nor our soul, nor anything else of which we say that it, in and of itself, is neither good nor evil – would it then be the case that the good wouldn't any longer have any usefulness, that rather it would have become useless? For then, if nothing would do us any harm, so too

we wouldn't require any more help. And so it would then be   *[d]*
obvious that it was only due to the evil that we were dependent upon
the good and loved it – because, namely, the good would be the
medicine that counteracts what is evil, but the evil is a disease. And
so if there aren't any diseases any longer, so too we don't have any
need for medicine. Is this how matters are constituted in respect with
the good, and shall it be so that it is loved by us due to what is evil in
that, indeed, we do subsist right in the middle betwixt the two of
these, the good and the evil – and is it so that the good doesn't have
any benefit in and of itself? ~ It does have this look about it, said he,
that this is how it correlates. ~ The former, then, that which comes
first of all and in which all of the other things find their end, all these
others to which we are friends for the sake of something other,
this has no similarity with all of these others at all. For all of these
others we called friend for the sake of something else to which we
also were friends, but this former most authentic friend seems to
be wholly of an opposite nature in that it has been shown that we
are friends with him due to something that is our enemy. But if this
latter were to be gotten rid of, so, as it seems, we wouldn't any longer
be friends with the former. ~ I'd fancy not, said he, at least in
accordance to all of that which was spoken previously. ~ Whether it
might well be so, said I – for the sake of Zeus – that if all of the evil
were to be annihilated, whether then we might still have hunger and
thirst, and everything else like this? Or shall there yet,   *[221a]*
indeed, be hunger – if, then, men and animals should yet exist, but it
just wouldn't be pernicious, and so too with thirst and all of the other
appetites, only they wouldn't any longer be evil since the evil shall
have been annihilated. Or isn't this quite a ludicrous question – what
then might be and might not be? For who knows the answer to this?
But this is what we do know, that even already now, he who has
hunger may well be damaged due to it; but, then too, he also might
derive some benefit from it – isn't this true? ~ Quite. ~ And isn't
it also so that he who experiences thirst or whatever else is like this,
those things that we desire – sometimes we desire things to our
detriment and other times they are beneficial, and sometimes, again,
they are neither the one nor the other? ~ Certainly. ~ Hence, even if
it were so that evil should be annihilated, how might it be so that
what isn't necessarily bad would also be annihilated along with it? ~
There's no such possibility. ~ Those desires, then, that are neither
good nor bad shall remain with us even if it should be that evil were
annihilated? ~ Apparently. ~ But, is it well possible that one desires
something or has love for something without being a friend to that
which one loves and desires? ~ No, I'd fancy not. ~ Hence, even

then if evil were to be annihilated, as it seems, we few shall still remain friends? ~ Yes. ~ But, indeed not – not if evil were to be the cause of friendship, then one couldn't possibly remain friends *[c]* with anyone else after evil had been destroyed. For if the cause were to be taken away, so it cannot still be possible that that would still take place, that for which this was the cause. ~ You're right. ~ But regarding this we were 'as one': that whoever would be a friend, he also would love this and, indeed, due to some cause; and back then, at least, we believed that what was neither good nor evil loved what is good due to what is evil? ~ Right. ~ But now, as it seems, there's another cause of love and of being loved that has appeared? ~ It seems so. ~ Is it now in all actuality so, just as we now are saying it, is desire the cause of friendship and that which desires a friend of that which is desired? and this even at that time when it occurs? But then, everything else that we said earlier regarding friendship, all of this was just a lot of idle chit-chat, a rather grand and imposing house of cards? ~ That's most probably the case, said he. ~ But, said I, that which desires, indeed, such desires what it is lacking. Isn't this true? ~ Yes. ~ He who lacks something, he would be friendly *[e]* toward this, whatever it might be that he lacks? ~ I'd fancy as much. ~ But everyone is missing what has gotten away from him? ~ How else? ~ Thus, upon that which belongs to him, as it seems, this is the object toward which love and friendship and desire are directed; this has become apparent, o Lysis and Menexenus? ~ They agreed with this. ~ Then you two, if you are both mutual friends one to the other, so you'd have to somehow belong to one another from out of your natures. ~ Obviously – this is what they said. ~ And likewise elsewhere, my children, said I, wherever someone desires and has love for another, he wouldn't desire him or love him, nor would he be a friend of his if it wouldn't be the case that the beloved utterly didn't belong to him either in relation to his soul, or due to some other sensibility, nature or quality. ~ Certainly, said Menexenus; but Lysis didn't say a word. ~ Very well, I said. That which belongs to us by our very natures, this – as it presents itself – we would have to love by necessity? ~ That follows, said he. ~ Thus it is necessary that the genuine lover, that is he who doesn't merely put on a show of loving, he would have to be loved in return by the beloved? To this neither Lysis nor Menexenus hardly wanted to give a nod of agreement. But Hippothales, meanwhile, was turning all different shades of color on account of his joy. So then, I said, in that I wanted *<18.~222b]* to bring this proposition underneath greater scrutiny: and really, if that which belonged would somehow be different from that which is similar, o Menexenus and Lysis, then we really would have something of significance to say about friendship – what it is. But if the similar and that which belongs are the same, well then, indeed, our previous proposition isn't so easily cast aside, that namely the similar to that which is similar and insofar as it is similar would be useless. But to confess of oneself that one is a friend to that which is useless, this is outrageous. Do you want, now, since we're practically in a drunken stupor due to all the ins and outs of our speech, do you want that we let up a bit and so make the assertion that that which belongs would be something that is different from that which is similar? ~ Quite. ~ Do we want, furthermore, that we say that the good would belong with the former and that the evil is of a foreign disposition to the former? – or that what is evil belongs to evil and what is good belongs to the good, and finally – that what is neither good nor evil belongs together with such as itself? ~ They were of the opinion that in this last manner each and every seemed to belong to each and every. With this, then, o children, said I, we've stumbled right back into *[d]* those earlier thoughts that we had regarding friendship, thoughts that we had thrown aside. For if this is so then the unrighteous shall not be any less a friend to the unrighteous, nor the evil to the evil, than the good shall be a friend to the good. ~ So it seems, said he. ~ But how about this, if we say that the good and that which belongs would be 'one and the same' *{einerlei}* – shall not, then, the good be a friend alone to that which is good? ~ Certainly. ~ But then, this too is something that we ourselves believed to have disproved. Or, don't you two remember this? ~ Very well, we do we remember it. ~ Well, what now do we have left remaining with this proposition? – well, obviously nothing. I plead with you, therefore, just as the lawyers tend to plead before the jury: that once again you call back everything into your memory. If, namely, neither the lovers nor those loved, neither the similar nor the dissimilar, neither the good nor those who belong, nor any other of all the possibilities through which we have run – for then due to the great multitude I can't myself remember it all properly – if, then, nothing from all of these is the object sought after for clarifying what friendship is, so I myself for my part don't have a clue as to what I should say. *[223a]*

As then, I spoke this, I was just about to turn myself to one of the elder persons and stir up the conversation. But just then, like evil spirits, up came the governors, those of Lysis and Menexenus, and they were leading their brothers along by the hand and, so, they called out to us: It's time to go home; for then, it had already gotten rather late. At first we all wanted to drive them off, but since it became quite apparent that they weren't in the least concerned about us, rather they continued to roar out in their hideous Greek and, indeed, they were on the point of swearing and wouldn't let up from their yelling, well, we quickly came to see that there wasn't anything to be done with them, in part too as it seems they had been tippling *[b]* a bit due to the festivities in honor of Hermes; so, as I say, being forced into this by them we decided upon breaking up our gathering. But still, I called out to them as they were taking their leave: This time, o Lysis and Menexenus, we have made ourselves ludicrous, I an old man and you boys. For all of these others when they are leaving here, they all will say that we have imagined that we are friends of one another, namely I count myself together with you two – but what it is that a friend is, this is something that we wouldn't have been able to discover.

****

Protagoras

in memory of mother

Ann Pamela Lundberg
(1925–1984)

For then, he added – if only you want to observe these things aright, namely what courage and mindfulness are for the others, so this shall appear to you to be totally amazing. ~ But how's that, Socrates? ~ Well, you do know, don't you, said he, that all the others count death amongst the gravest of all evils. ~ Quite. ~ And isn't it due to fear of yet greater evils that the bravest amongst them become reconciled with death – if, then, they do become reconciled? ~ That's true. ~ Hence, because they are afraid and due to their fear all of these are brave, except for those who love wisdom, although this is without rhyme – that someone would be brave due to fear and cowardice. ~ Well, indeed. ~

Phaedo – 68c

OVERVIEW:

Protagoras – Sections:

PROTAGORAS
****
A FRIEND, SOCRATES

<1.~309a]

Friend: Whither, Socrates, that you appear here amongst us? – or isn't it self-evident: you're on the hunt for that beauty, Alcibiades? And truly, I too had the impression having just recently met him that *he* really is a *beaut*; but still, Socrates, just between you and me, he is already a man whose beard bristles.

Socr: Now, and what's that got to do with it? Don't you praise   *[b]* Homer who names this to be a sign that youth has reached the peak of comeliness,[73] the fuzz on a ripening peach? And even now Alcibiades is delighting himself in this, his coming of age.

Friend: But what else? Have you just seen him? – and how did he behave toward you?

Socr: Very well, as I fancy, and especially so today. For he spoke up and said many things in my defense, and I even just left him. But still, there's something wondrous that I haven't said to you as of yet, namely, that although he too was one of those present, I didn't really pay much attention to him, indeed, often enough I forgot about him entirely.

Friend: And how is it possible that such a great change has come   *[c]* over you two? There can't well be someone other who is yet more beauteous whom you've met in our city?

Socr: But indeed there is, someone *far* more beauteous.

Friend: Say what! – one of our own, or a foreigner?

Socr: A foreigner.

Friend: But, from where?

Socr: From Abdera.

Friend: And this foreigner is such a beauty that you'd fancy him yet more beautiful than the son of Cleinias?

Socr: How could it be otherwise, my clever friend – than that the wiser would appear more beauteous?

Friend: Thus, you've been fraternizing with the wise and now have come directly hither to us?

Socr: Yes indeed, and with the wisest of all, at least of those currently living, that is – if you hold Protagoras as being the wisest.   *[d]*

Friend: Zounds – what you say! Protagoras has wandered in amongst us?

Socr: Already three days.

---

[73] "die holdesten Reize" – *Reize* was translated in *Phaedrus* as titillation, what one experiences when encountering beauty 251cd (p. 39) and 255c (p. 44).

109

Friend: And you were just in his company?   [a]
Socr: And we spoke quite a while together; and I heard him out.
Friend: Well then, why don't we let the boy stand over there and you
come sit down with us here and tell us about your meeting – if there's
nothing preventing you?
Socr: Most gladly, straight-away; and I shall very much appreciate
your attentiveness.
Friend: But truly, we too shall appreciate your telling us, if you will.
Socr: Hence, both of us happen upon our wishes – so, *listen up.*

<2.~310b]

Just last night, at the first signs of the gray morning, Hippocrates, son
of Apollodorus and brother to Phason, rapped mightily on the door
with his staff and, as someone opened the door for him, he stormed
directly into the house calling out in a loud voice: Socrates, are you
awake or still sleeping? ~ I, recognizing him by his voice, replied:
That would be Hippocrates! Do you bring news? ~ Nothing but good
[news]. ~ May that be the truth, said I, but what is it? and why have
you come so early? ~ Protagoras is here, said he, as he approached
me. ~ Since the day before yesterday, said I, you've only just heard?
~ By the gods, said he, only last night. At the same time he found
his way to the bed and sat down at my feet, continuing on. Yesterday
evening quite late when I returned home from my trip to Oinoae.
Satyros, that young rascal, has run away from me again and, I wanted
to say to you, I was going to 'put on the chase' but something else
made me forget about him. As now I was back at home, but only after
having eaten dinner and just as we were going to bed, quite late in the
evening – that's when my brother told me that Protagoras had come.
At first I wanted to come immediately to see you, but then it seemed
to me that it was already far too late. But now here I am, as prompt
as I could be after being so worn down by the journey: just as   [d]
soon as my sleep has allowed me I sprang up and so I have come here
to you. ~ Now I, being well acquainted with his strong-willed and
impetuous nature, I asked him: So, what's the big hurry? – has
Protagoras done you some wrong? ~ To this he replied, with a good
laugh: Yes, *by the gods*, Socrates, that he alone is wise and hasn't
made me to be so as well. ~ Now, by Zeus, said I, if only you pay him
in gold and persuade him to do so, then he'll be well able to make you
wise also. ~ If only Zeus and all of the gods want, he shouted out,
that it only should depend upon this, so neither would I prove to be
deficient in my part nor should my friends who underwrite and stand
by me! But – it's even for this reason that I've come here to you, that
you might speak with him on my behalf. For not only am I myself
too young, but I also have never even met Protagoras nor spoken

with him, for I was but a child the first time that he came here. But
everyone, o Socrates, everyone is most adamant in their praise   *[a]*
of this man and they say that he stands at the pinnacle in the richness
of his rhetorical art, speechcraft. But why don't we go at once to him
so that we might still catch him at home? He's living now, as I have
heard it, by Callias, son of Hipponicus. Do let's go! ~ To this I said:
Right now, my good man, let's not go thither just yet, for it's still too
early; rather shall we not get up ourselves and go walk a bit out in
the courtyard – and thus we'll spend some time walking together,
to and fro, until day has broken properly, and then we'll go. Besides,
Protagoras stays mainly at home so be of a good spirit, we'll catch up
with him yet. And so we rose and went out into the courtyard.

<3.~311b]

I wanted to test Hippocrates in his determination and so I took
careful measure of the youth and asked him: Tell me, Hippocrates,
you want now that we go off to see Protagoras in order that we
arrange payment, but *to whom* are you going and *what is it* that you
desire to become? For instance, if you were to be going to that
person whose name you share, Hippocrates of Cos, the Asclepidian,
and were to be arranging payment for his lessons and someone were
to ask you: Tell me, Hippocrates, you go to arrange for your tuition
payments by Hippocrates, and who is he? – what would you answer?
~ I would answer, said he, that he's a doctor. ~ And what shall you
become? ~ A doctor, said he. ~ Or if you had made up your mind to
go to see Polycleitus of Argos or to see Phidias who lives here in
Athens, if you were going to come to terms with one of these for
payment and someone were to ask you: To what sort of a person are
you off to see that you are desiring to establish the fee? – what would
you answer? ~ I would say, to a sculptor. ~ And what is it that   *[d]*
you want to become? ~ A sculptor as well, that's obvious. ~ Good,
said I. But now we are going off to see Protagoras, you and I, and we
are ready to hand over the tuition for you, if the money that we have
suffices and if we can convince him to take you on at this price, but if
not, we shall turn to our friends. Now, if someone were to see us
making haste and quite set upon this matter and he were to question
us: Do tell me, Socrates and Hippocrates, as *to whom* are you so
intent upon giving to Protagoras this money? What would be the
answer? What is the name that we hear spoken as regards
Protagoras, just as Phidias is a sculptor and Homer a poet? – do we
hear Protagoras spoken of in a similar way? ~ A sophist, o Socrates,
said he, this is what they call the man. ~ Thus, we are going to
arrange payment for lessons from a sophist? ~ Indeed. ~ And if
someone were to ask you further: And what, then, do you want   *[a]*

to become that you are going to see Protagoras? ~ In answer to this
he said, *blushing* – for the day was itself already dawned somewhat
so that I could see him clearly: If this correlates as do the previous
examples then it is obvious, in order to become a sophist. ~ And you,
said I, for the sake of the gods, wouldn't you be ashamed of yourself
to set yourself up before the Hellenes as a sophist? ~ By Zeus,
Socrates, said he, if I should speak as I think, yes. ~ But perhaps,
Hippocrates, your opinion is not at all that your lessons by Protagoras
should be such, rather that they might be like those given by your
speech teachers or your music teachers or by the teachers of
gymnastics. For in all of these one takes lessons *not* in order that one
might become a professional and pursue a living doing such, rather
only for one's liberal education, as befits someone raised a free man
who wants to experience life fully. ~ Quite right, said he, I fancy that
the lessons from Protagoras are more of the latter sort. ~ Do you
well know, then, what you have set your mind upon doing, or haven't
you noticed it? – said I. ~ What do you mean? ~ That   <4.~312c]
you are about to go and deliver up your soul to a sophist, as you say,
that he may work his talents upon it, but what a sophist actually is,
I should be amazed if you were to know this. And yet, if you aren't
acquainted with this then you also don't know to whom you are
delivering up your soul, whether this would be something good or
something bad. ~ I believe at least, said he, to know it. ~ So tell me
then, what you believe a sophist would be? ~ I for my part, said he,
it's even as the name bespeaks: someone who is wise, someone quite
clever in their understanding. ~ But, said I, one could say the same
also as regards painters or carpenters, that they be those who are
quite clever in their understanding. But if someone were to question
us further: Upon what, then, are these painters so clever? – then
we would say to him: Upon that which belongs to the making and
the composition of paintings; and so too for all the remaining
professionals. But if someone were to ask us: And the sophist,
wherein lies his cleverness? what would we answer him as regards
what the accomplishment is, that for which he strives? – and what
would we say that he himself would be? ~ O Socrates, said he, the
sophist understands how to make one mighty in speech. ~ Perhaps,
said I, we would speak rightly in saying this, but still it is not
sufficient. For this answer requires yet another question, namely:
Upon what does the sophist make one to be mighty in speech? Just
as the master musician would make his students to be mighty   *[e]*
in speech, namely over the material in which he teaches proficiency,
music. Isn't it so? ~ Yes. ~ Good, thus the sophist, upon what
does he make one mighty? Obviously, regarding that which he

understands. ~ One would think so. ~ What, then, is this: that in which he is proficient and which he delivers up for his students? ~ By Zeus, Socrates, said he, I don't know anything more that I might tell you. ~ To this I said: How now? do you know, then,   <5.~313a] what the risks are that you intend to run, what it is, that to which you would expose your soul? Or if you were to be running such risks with your body by entrusting it to someone, that either it would be strengthened or would be corrupted, then wouldn't you consider this first from various angles, whether you'd want to entrust him with this or not; and wouldn't you call upon your friends and relatives to advise you in the matter and give it a few days of serious consideration; but that which you regard as far superior than your body and in relation to which all of your undertakings must fare well or poorly depending upon its having been strengthened or corrupted, the soul, regarding this you haven't shared or communicated, neither to your father or brothers, nor to any one of us, your friends – whether or not you should entrust your soul to this foreigner who has just happened upon us; rather, having only just heard late last night of his arrival, as you say, you have come here today at morning's first glimmerings, but not that you'd care to discuss it or receive some advice as to whether or not you should go thither to him – *No* – rather you're already all ready to go and ready to spend your own and your friends' equity as if this were already a done deal and a closed case, that in every respect you just have to be taken in by Protagoras, he with whom you   [c] have never been acquainted, as you say, nor with whom you've even spoken; rather, you call him a sophist, but what a sophist really is, to whom you want so much to deliver yourself up, in this you show yourself as being totally ignorant. ~ Having listened to what I was saying, he replied: Indeed, it does have that appearance, o Socrates, and is in accord with what you say. ~ Perhaps, Hippocrates, the sophist is a merchant or cost monger of those goods that nourish the soul? At least, he seems to me to be such a one. ~ But what is this, Socrates, what is it that nourishes the soul? ~ *Bites of knowledge,* it must well be, said I. That only the sophist doesn't deceive us, my friend, in that in his praise of what he's marketing he might be following the practice of other salesmen and hawkers who push their wares for the nourishment of the body. For these also do not themselves understand which amongst the goods that they are hawking are healthy and which are damaging, rather, they praise everything if it just happens to be in season; nor too do those understand this, those who purchase such goods – unless, perchance, it be a doctor or someone who understands the training of the body. And even so, these who move about from city to city with their know-how, offering it up to anyone who has a taste for it, that they might make a sale, and they praise everything that they just happen to have for sale; but perhaps, my good man, it may well be that they too know even so little as regards what is healthy and what damages the soul, and those who buy also have just as little knowledge to go on, unless, perchance, amongst them is someone who is informed as regards the health of the soul. If, now, you understand this: what is healthy and what damaging, then, without having any second thoughts about it you are able to go and purchase knowledge from Protagoras   *[314a]* or from any of the others; but if not, my good man, you'd best pay heed that you're not throwing dice with that which is most dear and laying a wager in a risky game of chance. For in regards to this, the nourishment of the soul, the risks are yet far greater than they are when going shopping at the green grocers. Because when you buy groceries at the vegetable stand or beverages from the merchant you carry these home in bags or some other container and before you ingest or drink the goods and take them into your body you first have to bring them home and can then call someone over who has an understanding of the matter and you can take his counsel, what you should eat and drink and what not, and also how much and how often – so that by grocery shopping the risk doesn't really mean all that much. But knowledge is not something that you are able to carry off in some other container, rather, once you have paid the price you have to take it up into your soul through learning and so right away you've gotten either your advantage or your damage, even before you walk away. So it would be best if we would consider this thoroughly and, indeed, let us do so with people who are themselves our elders: for we are yet too young that we might make such an important determination as this business is. All the same, in that we've set our minds upon going, let's go and hear what this man has to say and once we've heard him, then we'll talk this over with others. For Protagoras is not all alone there, rather, Hippias of Elis and, I believe, also Prodicus of Ceos and many other men who are quite wise are there too. – This being decided we set off. And as we   *<6.~314c]* came into the forecourt we stood still and continued speaking about a matter that had occurred to us as we were on our way. In order that we not break off our discussion but bring it to a conclusion before we ventured inside, we remained standing before the entrance and spoke until we were of one mind with one another. This, I would fancy, the man who stands watch by the door, a eunuch, may well have heard, and it seemed that due to the crowd of sophists being around all visiting the house he was quite out of temper. As, then, we rapped upon the door he opened it up and gave us a good look, then called out: *Ha*, yet more sophists! – having no time to spare he took the door in both hands and without any explanation slammed it back into place with a mighty bang; and so we had to rap again a second time. Upon this he replied to us through the closed door: Brothers, didn't you hear, he doesn't have any time to spare? ~ But, good man, I replied, we are neither coming in order to see Callias, nor are we sophists. Be at peace, we have only come to pay a visit upon Protagoras and so please announce us. ~ Upon this the man finally opened up the door, but with the utmost circumspection. <*7.~314e3]*

As now we entered inside we found Protagoras making a procession through the halls, these being all decorated with tapestries. Promenading along to the one side of him was Callias, the son of Hipponicus, and behind him his half-brother on his mother's side, Paralus, the son of Pericles, and also Charmides, the son of Glaucon; and upon the other side was Pericle's other son, Xanthippus, and also Philippedes, the son of Philomelus, as well as Antimoerus of Menda – the most highly praised of all of Protagoras' pupils who was rigorously applying himself to the study of his art, that he himself might also become a sophist. The rest, following after these, were all ears for what was spoken and were for the most part foreigners, people whom Protagoras had picked up in all of the cities through which he traveled and whom he brought along as they were entranced by the power of his intonations, like those following Orpheus, *[315b]* and they followed mesmerized by the tone, his devotees; all the same, there were a few Athenians who also found themselves amongst this choir. As now I studied the choir I was held in awe, and in particular by the artful manner in which they always took care that they shouldn't get in Protagoras' way, that rather whenever Protagoras and his entourage should come about, how orderly and tactfully they spread themselves out to either side and then, in a circular motion they swung themselves around in such a fine, graceful manner and, so, they managed always to be bringing up the rear. And *after this the sight next to appear* – as Homer says – this would be Hippias of Elis who sat across from the tapestried corridor upon a great chair. And all about him on benches were seated: Eryximachus, son of Acumenus; and Phaedrus of Myrrhinous; and Andron, son of Androtion; and yet some strangers, in part countrymen from Elis and in part some others. It seemed that they were laying all sorts of questions about nature and the appearances of the heavens, all kinds of astronomical queries, they were laying these down for Hippias to consider and he, sitting upon his throne, he would go through the particulars of each question and then pronounce his judgment. And,

then too, *my eyes fell upon Tantalus* – namely Prodicus of Ceos   *[d]*
who also had come here and who was to be found tucked away in an
alcove which Hipponicus had previously put to use as a storeroom
but that now, due to the hoards of people pilgrimaging here, he
had ordered that it be cleared out and turned into a guest room.
Prodicus lay there now, all covered up beneath a great mound of
quilts and animal hides and, indeed, there were a gracious plenty as
one could well see. And on the cushion next to him sat Pausanias, the
Ceramean; and next to him a youth, barely seventeen [of age], and of
a beauteous and noble nature, as I believe, but certainly very beautiful
in appearance[74] – I fancy to have heard that his name was Agathon
and I wouldn't be at all surprised if he wouldn't be Pausanias' lover.
This youth, thus, and the two Adeimantuses – the son of Cepis and
that of Leucolophidas – these along with a few others were all there to
be seen. But that about which they were speaking – I, being outside
the room, I wasn't at all able to pick up on, and this despite my real
desire to hear Prodicus, for I fancy that this man, indeed, is wise and
godlike. Singularly, due to the enclosed space the deepness of his
voice caused a dull, muffled roar that made it all but impossible to
pick up anything of the conversation.   And then, just as we ourselves
had stepped into the room, Alcibiades entered in directly behind us,
"that *beaut*" as you say, and as I would agree, and along with him
came Critias, the son of Callaeschrus. We, now, had taken pause after
our entrance for a bit in order that we might have a good look at all of
this; then we approached Protagoras and I said: Protagoras, there's
something that we've come to you about, myself and   *<8.~316b]*
Hippocrates here. ~ Would you like, he asked, to speak to me about
this alone, or here with all the rest? ~ For us, said I, it doesn't make
any difference; but listen as to why we have come here and then you
consider it yourself. ~ Then what is it, he asked, why is it that you
have come here? ~ This Hippocrates lives here in Athens, said I, the
son of Apollodorus – a great family lineage and one with a sparkling
reputation – and he himself, as I fancy, both in respect to his
disposition and his natural talents promises to be high amongst those
of his generation who are most capable and who have the pleasure of
becoming outstanding and distinguished individuals in our city, and
it's even for this purpose that he believes it to be in his best interests
if he could be with you. Whether, now, you opine that you would

---

[74] Compare with the description of Lysis in *Lysis* 207a (p. 83). *Lysis and Protagoras* also are
marked as being close to one another by 'blushing.' Finally, the seven speeches 'unto Eros'
that are in the *Symposium* are spoken by: Phaedrus, Pausanius, Erixymachus, Aristophanes,
Agathon, Socrates and – finally: the "drunk" Alciabides, on his own love for Socrates.

need to speak with us alone regarding this or before the others, you consider this yourself. ~ You are very right, Socrates, said he, in being concerned about my welfare. For a stranger who travels through all the great cities and withal persuades the most promising young men that they give up in their being together with their family, friends and compatriots, old and young alike, and that   *[316d]* henceforth they hold out alone with him, and that by doing this they would become better – such a one must well be on his guard. For more than a little enmity arises from this, and evil wishings and underhanded pursuits of every variety. And it is just for this reason that I would assert that – although the art of sophistry is indeed quite old as arts go – still, those who have practiced it throughout the ages have hidden it beneath a veneer, out of fear of those who hate their profession; and some hid it by pretending to be poets, like Homer, Hesiod and Simonides; others hid it beneath the mysteries and the oracular teachings, like Orpheus and Musaeus; and indeed a few – I have noticed – used gymnastics as a cover, like Iccus of Tarentum, and now there's yet another seeming gymnast who is as much a sophist as any, Herodicus of Selymbria, originally though of Megara. It is music which Agathocles, one of your own countrymen, hides behind – and he is a great sophist – and so also Pythoclides from Ceos and yet many others as well. All of these, as I said, make use of the formerly mentioned arts as covers and cloaks behind which they might hide due to their fear of envious reprisals. But I, I refuse to follow their example; moreover I don't believe that they actually accomplished what they wanted; namely, their subterfuge didn't fool those who hold the power in the cities – and it is for the sake of this that such pretexts were sought after, for the great throng,   *[317b]* I may as well speak the plain truth: the great throng doesn't take any notice of anything at all but simply prattles back whatever it is told. If, now, someone wants to steal away and is not able to do so, that rather he is discovered, so already the attempt itself is extremely foolish and this simply embroils the people even more for amongst everything else they then hold such a one as being a troublemaker. For this reason I've beaten out a path which is exactly the opposite, that I tell everyone straight-out that *I am a sophist* and that I want to educate all people, and I maintain that my cautious approach is better than the one mentioned formerly, that it is much better to acknowledge such things rather than to deny everything and to dissemble. And there are yet a few others whom I have observed who do likewise, so that for me – and may it be spoken with God – as of yet there haven't been any bad consequences to my openly pro-claiming that I am a sophist; and I have been pursuing this vocation now for many years and it is evident that I'm no spring chicken, indeed, there is no one now present here whose father I wouldn't be at least equal to in age! Hence, it is far preferable to me that when you wish something of me that you bring the matter up openly before everyone here present. ~ To this I said – for I had taken care to notice that he wanted that Prodicus and Hippias should be let in on this and thereby make a big deal out of the situation, that we had come here honoring him: Why don't we invite Prodicus and Hippias over right away, as well as all of those with them, so that they too may hear us? ~ Oh sure, said Protagoras. ~ If you all would like, Callias spoke up, why don't we convene a sitting so that you might make yourselves comfortable and, thus, all assembled together we may proceed. ~ With this we were all content and extremely pleased: that now we should be able to listen to these wise men speak – and so everyone took part in putting the chairs and benches to rights and we did so over next to Hippias as the benches were there already. And we were joined by Callias and Alcibiades, and also by Prodicus whom they stirred up from out of his liar along with his entourage.

<9.~317e]

As, now, we had all taken our places Protagoras commenced: Now then, Socrates, as all of these men are present here, so repeat again what you mentioned to me earlier in regards to this young man. ~ Thus I said: My beginning, o Protagoras, is the same as before, why it is that I have come here. This Hippocrates here, namely, hedges a great desire to be accepted into your circle, but what shall actually accrue to him if he joins in as your pupil, this he should like, as he says, to hear first from you. This is what we have to say. ~ To this Protagoras took up the word and spoke: Young man, this is what shall happen if you come and join in to my circle. Already on your first day that you spend here with me you shall return home having become a better person, and the same shall occur on the next day, and so too on all of the following days you shall make progress in being ever better. ~ As I heard what was spoken, I said: There is [318b] nothing so amazing in this, Protagoras, rather it is only natural. For you too, despite that you are so old and so wise, if someone were to teach you what you don't as of yet know, you too would become better. But not thus, rather so – as if Hippocrates suddenly changes in his desires and now yearns to apprentice beneath that young man who recently arrived here, Zeuxippus of Heraclea, and if he were to approach him and heard the same thing that you now say, that he would with each passing day become better and that he would make progress, and he questioned further: How so is it that you mean this? – and: In what shall I make progress? – then Zeuxippus would certainly answer him: In painting; or if he were to give himself over to Orthagoras of Thebes and were to hear the same from him as from you and he inquired further – In what would he become better due to the association? then this one would certainly respond to him: *[d]* In playing the flute.   Even so, you tell the young man and me, as I am questioning you in his stead: Hippocrates should, if he holds himself in association with Protagoras – and already on the first day that he has accompanied him when he returns home and so too on all of the successive days – make progress; but how so, Protagoras, and in what? ~ And Protagoras, after having listened to me as I stated my case, he said: You question very well, Socrates, and it gives me joy to give answers to those who so question. If, then, Hippocrates should thus come and apprentice by me, then it would *not* occur to him as it would had he have gone to a different sophist.   For the others obviously mistreat their pupils.   For just when these young men are extremely happy with their good fortune, that finally they are done with their school work, these lead them right back against their wills to the same old same old.   And so they teach them the arts of calculation and astronomy, and also the art of measuring[75] and music – whilst stating this he turned his eyes on Hippias.   But with me he shan't learn anything other than that for the sake of which he actually has come.   But this knowledge consists in cleverness in his very own affairs: how he best would administer his household and, then too, the affairs of state: how he shall become most capable in leading and speaking about these matters. ~ Am I well following you, said I to this, is this your speech?   It seems to me, namely, that you are pointing to the art of politics and that you are promising that you want to educate these to be *men*, indeed, most capable men in the realm of politics? ~ Even this, said he, is what I am offering, and that for which I proffer myself. ~ It is certainly a beautiful   *<10.~319b]* art [profession] that you possess, if you do possess it, for what I say to you should be nothing other than what I think.[76]   I was of the opinion, namely, Protagoras, that such would not be teachable; but now as you say that it is, I don't know how I am not to believe you. But why it is that I think that this is not teachable nor that it is possible that any person brings it into being for another, this I must say to you in all simplicity.   I hold, namely, the Athenians as being wise, as do also all the Hellenes, and now I see how it is that when the

---

[75] The last sections of *Protagoras*, sections 36–39, consider the art of measuring in respect to pleasure and pain to be essential to virtue as it is defined there.
[76] Hippocrates says the same at 312a5. See the *Gorgias* footnote #146 (p. 314) for global references to the fundamental importance of speaking what one actually thinks.

community is gathered together in session and there is a matter up for discussion regarding a construction project for the city, then they send for the building engineers, that they may hear their advice as regards the project; but if it has to do with the design of ships,[77] then they call for the shipwrights; and so too for all of the other things that they hold to be capable of being taught and of being learned. But if somebody else should start off in an attempt to give them his advice and if they believe that he doesn't have any expertise in the matter – and no matter how beautiful and rich and distinguished he otherwise may be – so, nonetheless, they don't take him up for the discussion,[78] rather they laugh him down and make a lot of noise until either the noise drives him to step back of his own accord or else the deputies of the court drag him down and set him on his way by the authority of the Prytany. And in everything of which they believe that the matter is grounded on art and technical expertise, this is how they   *[d]* proceed. But when it comes to getting advice on the administration of the *polis*, then anyone at all may stand up and give them his counsel: carpenters, blacksmiths, shoemakers, fishmongers, sea-captains, the rich, the poor, distinguished or non-distinguished – one just as well as the other – and no one brings up a complaint as was done in the previous examples, that someone without the credentials of having studied and learned the matter and without having had any teachers still wants to take it upon himself, that he give advice. Obviously then, they believe that it isn't teachable. And not only is it that the assemblies of the populace think this, rather too our most educated and most admired citizens are not in a position that they could share these virtues that they possess with others. Pericles, for instance, who is the father of these two young men, he has let them be instructed in everything that is dependent upon teachers, but *[320a]* in this matter in which he himself is so wise he has neither instructed them himself, nor has he given them over to anyone else, rather they run freely around as it suits them and so find their own pasture alone by themselves, whether they might happen to meet up with something of this virtue all on their own. And if you want still more, the same Pericles is also the guardian of Cleinias, the younger brother of Alcibiades here, and due to his worry that Cleinias might be corrupted

---

[77] The reader should be aware that the rise to power of the Greek city-states, of which Athens and Sparta were the leaders, was due in great measure to the superior design of the Athenian warships and, thus, it was supremacy at sea which kept the Persians from taking advantage of their overwhelming numerical advantage.

[78] Note: the claim here stands diametrically opposed to what is more of less agreed on in *Gorgias*, viz. that the orators do indeed have a great influence on the building of the walls, the ships, et cetera: 455b–456a (p. 269).

by Alcibiades he separated them and delivered Cleinias over to Ariphron's house so that he might get his upbringing there; but it all ended up by his being sent back before even six months had passed because Ariphron had no idea as to what he should do with him. And so, I could name you very many others, people who were themselves most admirable men but, nonetheless, all incapable of making anyone else to be better, neither anyone from their own families nor otherwise. I for my part, Protagoras, taking my cue from hindsight of this, I hold that virtue would not be teachable. But now that I hear you make such a claim, I change my gait and think: You shall well be in the right about this – because I do hold to you as someone who has experienced much in the world, having both learned a great deal from others and also found much out all by yourself. Are you able, then, to clearly show us that virtue is teachable, so please don't keep this to yourself but do show us. ~ Good, Socrates, said he, I also don't want to just keep it to myself. But how am I to show you? Shall I present you with a mythic tale just as the elders tend to take care of the younger generation in this manner, or shall I deliver up a lecture? ~ Many of those present sitting all around encouraged him that he might deliver up and present whatever he wanted, whichever way he found most appealing. ~ So I would fancy it to be more becoming, said he, if I might tell you all a mythic tale.   <11.~320d]

Once, long long ago, there were, indeed, yet gods, but not yet any mortal species; but after the predetermined time had elapsed and the time arrived for the creation of such species, so the gods built them up within the earth from earth and fire, and also from a mixture that was composed out of earth and fire. And as the gods were to bring them forth into the light they delegated to Prometheus and Epimetheus the responsibility of decking them out and distributing amongst them the powers, dividing these up amongst the species, giving to each just as it should be. But Epimetheus requested of Prometheus that he wanted to make these divisions and, said he, once this is all done then do come and look it all over in review. And so, after convincing him, he made the divisions. And in giving out the parts Epimetheus bestowed upon some strength but not speed, but to the weaker species he bestowed speed; a few were given weapons and for others that had no weapons he thought up some other means by which they might save themselves. Those, for instance, that were enshrouded in small bodies, upon these were bestowed wings [321a] for flying or the homes given to them were underground; others that received very large bodies were protected simply by their great size; and so too he divvied things up amongst all of the rest taking similar precautions to equalize things. But all of this was conceived due to his concern that no species should totally disappear. As, now, he gave them ways of escaping from the ravages of mutual destruction, so he also began to consider their housing needs and their outer garments – as the time of Zeus was approaching – and so to some he gave for clothing thick coats of hair or strong hides that sufficed not only in keeping out the cold but also were good when it was hot outside; and thus at the same time he gave to each species a suitable outfit for its habitation and, depending upon its place of taking rest, its own night-dress. And in regards to the feet, some were equipped with hooves and claws and others were given hairy feet or strong, bloodless appendages. Next, he indicated that some should eat of one variety, others of another – thus, those underground should partake of the roots and others should eat the fruit from the trees, and then for a few it was established that they might feast upon the meat of the other animals. For this last sort he established that procreation should be limited and, in contrast to these, for those who were the prey he gave strong powers of procreation so that these species had yet another means for survival. As, however, Epimetheus was not fully wise so it came out that he had dispersed all of the powers and capacities without holding back anything to give to the human species – *[321c]* and he was totally stumped as regards what he should do for them. And such was his state when Prometheus now arrived in order to look over and review the divisions and so he saw that the rest of the animals, indeed, were in all particulars wisely considered, but that humanity remained naked, without shoes, without coverings, without weapons – and already the appointed day was at hand, the day in which humanity should venture out of the earth into the light. And so, being likewise in great perplexity as to what means could yet be found to save mankind, Prometheus steals from Hephaestus and Athena the riches of artful wisdom, and he also steals fire – for it would be impossible that any of the arts could belong to man or be useful without fire – and so he bestowed these gifts upon mankind. And so man received the store of knowledge that was necessary for his life, but still he didn't have that knowledge which enables a society to flourish. For this knowledge was kept by Zeus and Prometheus had been forbidden free entry into Zeus' fortress – and, moreover, the home of Zeus was well protected by guards and these were fearsome indeed. But into the dwelling of Hephaestus and Athena, there where they practiced their arts, he snuck in secretly and once, thus, he had stolen the fire of Hephaestus and the other arts that belonged to Athena, he was able to give these over to mankind. And from this point onward humanity has enjoyed the better things of life; but for

Prometheus, as the tale goes, went the punishment for this thievery to which he had grasped out of his desperation for Epimetheus' sake. As now humanity had become so that mankind possessed   <12.~322a] godlike advantages, so too men alone of all creatures believed in the gods due to man's relatedness to God, and so also men attempted to erect altars and set up images of the gods, to which soon thereafter were added intonations and words that were ordered together by art, and then dwelling places and clothing and footwear and places for resting and ways of gaining sustenance were also discovered upon the earth. And so strengthened, humanity lived at first scattered all around, for of cities there were yet none. Therefore the wild animals made savage hunt upon mankind as men were yet weaker than were the beasts and though the works that the arts accomplished, indeed, were sufficient help for obtaining sustenance, still they didn't work nearly so well when it came to the battle for survival against the other animals – for mankind didn't yet possess the civic arts and the art of warfare is one part of this. So they attempted to save themselves through gathering together and by construction of cities; but once they got together they provoked one another and suffered damage from themselves – for they hadn't yet the civic arts – and so, once more they were driven apart and then once again decimated by the wild beasts. Thus, Zeus, in his concern for our race, that it wouldn't succumb and, indeed, be totally obliterated, Zeus took care   *[322c]* and dispatched Hermes down that he might bring to us shame and righteousness, that these might give order to our cities and bind us together as instruments and enablers of affection. Now Hermes questioned Zeus: In what manner should he bestow shame and righteousness upon mankind? Should I distribute these just as the other arts are distributed? These, namely, are so distributed that one person who is accomplished and understands the healing arts suffices for many who are not trained as physicians, and so too with all of the other arts. Should shame and righteousness also be established in a like manner amongst mankind, or should they be distributed to everyone? To everyone, said Zeus, and all should partake in them because no society could endure if only a few were to partake in these things as it is with the other arts. And give them also a law based solely on my authority: that whosoever is incapable of making shame and righteousness his own, he should be killed as an evil menace and as a destroyer of society. Thus, Socrates, in this manner and from this root cause all of the others and also the Athenians believe that if the virtue of a master builder or some other artisan is up for discussion, then to only a few belongs the privilege of submitting their advice, and if anyone else should stand up to offer advice so they have no patience for it, as you say; and indeed this is totally justified, as I too have said. But if they are taking counsel regarding the civic virtue upon which society rests and upon those matters in which everything is based upon righteousness and mindfulness, so they do indeed [a] listen patiently to each and every because it is meet and proper that everyone has a share in this or else there wouldn't be any society at all. This, Socrates, is the root cause regarding the matter. But take also this as yet a further proof, so that you don't perhaps simply believe to have been tricked and outsmarted by my tale and that all of mankind really does subscribe hereto, that everyone has a part in righteousness and the rest of civic virtue. In the other things, as you yourself say, if someone claims to be an outstanding flutist or to be outstanding in any other artistry in which, actually, he isn't – either the people dismiss this with their laughter or they become disgruntled and his compatriots approach him and talk to him, that he is quite confused. But in matters of righteousness and the rest of the virtue that undergirds society, if they know very well that someone is unrighteous but he himself wants to speak the truth – which goes against himself – and he does so before many people, so in this instance that which earlier they would hold as being reasonable, namely to speak the truth, in this instance they would explain this as insanity and would assert that everyone should at least make the claim that he desires to be righteous, whether he is actually righteous or not, otherwise he would be crazy if he were not to subscribe to the principles of justice, as if it were necessary that every person would have to have a part in this or simply not live within human society. That they are justified in their supposition that each   <13.~323c2] and every may give advice in matters concerning this virtue because they believe, namely, that everyone shares a part of it, this I have amply demonstrated. But that, nonetheless, they don't believe that one has this virtue from nature nor that it comes to be simply from itself, rather that it is indeed something which is learned and that everyone acquires it through diligent effort – everyone, that is, who does acquire it – this is what I shall now seek to prove. Namely, in regards to some malignancy which everyone believes that whoever has it, he has gotten it from birth or through some misfortune, nobody gets upset or berates another, nor do they punish or admonish those who are blemished in this wise – as if, somehow, they might be able to put a stop to being this way; rather one has pity for these individuals like one does for those who are ugly or puny or weaklings; who could be so lacking in understanding that he could do any of these things to someone so unfortunate? – because one knows, namely, I believe, that in these things the good and that which is contrary come to man through nature or by chance. But of the good things that they believe are acquired by man through his own effort, practice and studies – if someone doesn't have these but has those evils that are contrary to these – then there does arise angry discord and punishments and admonishments. And of these one also is unrighteousness and impiety and, in general, everything that *[324a]* is in opposition to civic virtue. In all of this one scolds and berates the other, obviously as if, indeed, these were to be attained through respectful attention and having lessons. For if you would bethink yourself as regards punishing those who act improperly – what this might well imply – so this itself would teach you that all men believe that virtue would be something that is attainable when diligently sought. For nobody punishes those whose behavior is wrong *[b]* simply with the mindset and just for this reason that one has done something wrong, outside of those who are totally lacking in reason and who actually only want to get revenge like an animal. But he who consults reason in his response and punishes someone, he punishes not because of the past misdeed, for there is no way that the past might thereby be altered and the done be undone, rather because of what may happen in the future, so that this will not happen any more, and neither with this same person nor with anyone else who has witnessed the punishment, that otherwise they might repeat the same unrighteous deed. And insofar as he is viewing the matter in this wise he indeed thinks that virtue is something that can be taught – for he punishes, indeed, to discourage such behavior. And in that he has set his sights upon this he must well be thinking that virtue is capable of being inculcated by one's upbringing and education, for he punishes to straighten out those who go astray. Thus, this is the opinion of all of those who impose punishment, and be it in the public domain or at home. But all of humanity punish and inflict their strictures upon those who are believed to have acted improperly – and so is the case just as well with the Athenians, your fellow citizens; so that one may conclude from this that the Athenians also belong to those who take the position that virtue is something that one is able to learn and that it is brought forth by the means of all sorts of institutions. That, therefore, your compatriots are totally justified in their assumption, as also a blacksmith and a shoemaker do take part in giving their advice on civic matters, and that, all the same, they do believe that virtue is something which is capable of being taught and of being learned, this, o Socrates, has been sufficiently demonstrated, as it seems to me. Now, there yet remains the dubious matter *<14.~324d]* that you brought up earlier regarding the outstanding individuals: why, namely, they see to it that their sons are instructed and made to be wise in everything that is dependent upon teachers but that in the virtue in which they themselves are so proficient, somehow they are incapable of making them to be any better than anyone else. Regarding this, Socrates, I won't just present you with a story, rather the underlying reasons. Weigh and consider the matter thus: Is there or is there not some certain thing *{etwas Gewißes}* that all citizens have to possess in themselves if there should be a state? For it is through this that those doubts that so trouble you are to be resolved, and through nothing other than this. For if there is such a thing, and if this something is not the art of carpentry and not the art practiced by blacksmiths, nor is it to be found in the potting crafts; if, rather, it is righteousness and mindfulness and piety and everything all together which – to bring these together into one I would like to call it: the virtue of being human – if this is so and if this is what everyone has to have in themselves and it is with this that each and every person who wants to learn or wants to accomplish anything at all in a proper manner, this is how he does it, and without this nothing is done properly; and if someone would be lacking in this, and be it man, woman or child, he or she shall be taught or disciplined   *[b]* until he or she has become better by such disciplining, and whoever takes no notice of the teaching and disciplining, such a person is driven into exile or, indeed, is killed as someone who is incurable; if this is how it correlates and if in such interrelated matters these outstanding individuals should have their sons educated in everything else but not in this, so take a good look – how amazing these outstanding individuals would have to be! For that they hold it to be something that may be learned both at home and within the public realm, this we have demonstrated. And although it is taught and can be inculcated through a person's upbringing should it still be possible that they allow that their sons are instructed in everything else, things that do not entail the possibility of a death sentence or some other harsh punishment if they don't know these things, but for those who have failed to learn and become educated in virtue there is this possibility of death or exile and also the possible confiscation of all of one's goods and properties and, that I say it in one breath, the ruination of one's entire family and estate! – this, then, should somehow be withheld from their upbringing and no care should be lavished and directed toward learning this? One must at least rather believe, Socrates, that they do do so. Already beginning   *<15.~325d]* during one's most tender childhood and continuing on throughout one's entire life children are taught and encouraged just as soon as they might understand what is spoken, as well by the nursemaid as by the mother, as well by those who lead the children in their activities

as also by the father – all are earnestly concerned that the child
unfolds and grows up in the best manner possible and so they all
teach and demonstrate to him in every action and in their speech:
this is right, this wrong; this is good, this bad; this is pious, this
irreverent; do this but *do not* do that. And if he is good-natured and
behaves, this is praised as good, but if not then they seek to do to him
as one also handles young saplings that are leaning the wrong way or
bent and askew and he is straightened out once more by threats and
by beatings. And after this, when it's time to be sent off to school,
so they encourage that the teachers be particularly sharp in their
attentions to their children's moral upbringing, that this task is yet
more urgent than the care lavished on the reading skills and how well
one plays the lyre. The teachers, thus, respect this desire and once
the children have learned how to read and are able to understand the
written word as well as music, which is taught first, then they are
given at their desks the poetry of the very best poets,   *[326a]*
that these poems be read and learnt by heart – and in these poems
there are contained not only many lessons in righteousness and much
clarification but also high praise and great admiration for the ablest
men of yesteryear, so that the adolescent's sense of wonder is
awakened and that they might strive to imitate these and become
such themselves. The music teachers are also conscious of morality
and they do their utmost to ensure that their pupils don't get into
any mischief-making. Moreover, once they have learned how to play
the lyre then they also teach them other admirable poets, those
namely who composed songs of poetry – and these poems are based
on the ways of song and so they work with this, rhythmic timing and
vocal harmony, that the souls of the children experience this beauty
so that they might be made milder; and in that they hold to the
proper pitch and timing, so they become more accomplished also
in both their speaking as well as in all of their other activities.
For in everything in man's life proper harmony and good timing are
essential. And, beyond all of this, they are sent to the masters of
gymnastics so that their bodies may be strengthened and that also
they may have instilled the proper attitude and develop   *[c]*
fortitude, in that without this and due to the weakness of their bodies
they otherwise would have to act cowardly, be it now in battle or in
any other pursuit. And the best leaders in this are those who are the
most able, but the most able are those who have the greatest wealth
and it is their children who begin earliest in their childhood to seek
for teachers and, likewise, they also are the ones who persevere the
longest in their studies. But when the time comes that they leave
their teachers, so now it is the state that requires of them that they

learn its laws and that they live in accordance with these as by
a prescript – so that they don't go wandering off in their own feelings
of what's right and thereby start off doing something inept, rather
that just like it is with one's speech teacher who shows to those who
don't yet know how to write how it is that one must hold the pencil
and then demonstrates how all of the letters should be properly
written upon the paper – and then, taking another sheet of paper,
commands: these strokes, just as I have written them, you make a
copy. Even thus is it that the state prescribes the laws that have been
thought out by the most outstanding elder statesmen of times past –
the law-givers, and they are commanded: it is by these laws that we
rule and allow of ourselves that we be ruled. But whosoever strays
from the law, he is disciplined[79] by them and this disciplining is
given the name, not only here but in many other places as well due to
the circumstance that the punishment makes one wise, a correction.
As now, as well in the home as also in the state, so much care and
attention is spent upon instilling this virtue, how is it, Socrates, how
is it that *you* are yet in wonder! and how can you hedge any doubt as
to whether it is something that is capable of being learnt? Regarding
this there is nothing to wonder about, rather, much more would it be
a wonder if this were not to be so. But why is it that the sons of many
outstanding individuals go astray? The reason for this   *<16.~327a]*
you also may experience. Namely, this too is nothing to cause you to
wonder – if, then, I have spoken aright that in this matter, namely as
regards virtue, that if states are to exist then nobody is allowed to be
lacking in such knowledge. If this correlates so as I say that it does
correlate, then indeed, it is in every manner even thus: just consider
the matter in respect to any other art or skill, whichever one you want
and find most appealing. If no state would be able to exist unless
everyone were to play the flute and, indeed, be just as competent in
flute playing as is at all possible, and if everyone gave lessons to
everyone else both at home and in the public sphere, and if bad
flutists were to be scolded and no one would ever enviously hold back
what he knows, just as now nobody refrains or covers up their
knowledge of what is right and what lawful, though this does occur in
the other arts – for every one of us, I believe, is abetted by all the rest
of us in that we all are virtuous and act righteously and it is for this
reason that we are eager to teach one another what is right and

---

[79] "zuechtigen" – to punish, castigate or train as animals are trained; note as well that the
narrator of *Parmenides*, Antiphon – is engaged in "Pferdezucht"; if we desire to move
beyond such training that is related to animals, then dialectics is the other path, the inner way
of purification, as pointed out in the *Sophist* 230a–e (pp. 528–529).

lawful. If now, in just this manner we all were to display an equal ardor and willingness to be of service in teaching one another how to play the flute, that each should play just as well as is at all possible: do you believe, Socrates, said he, that the sons of good flute players would then be more likely to become good flute players than those who played poorly? I don't believe it, rather whichever son would have the best predisposition for flute playing, he would unfold to become an exceptional flutist, and whoever lacked in such a pre-disposition, he would remain without fame; and often it would *[c]* be the son of a good flutist who would turn out to be bad and the son of a bad one good, but they all would indeed become adept flutists in comparison to those who hadn't had any instruction, those who understand nothing at all about how one plays the flute. So do believe it, that also now even he who displays the greatest amount of unrighteousness and whose behavior is worse than all of the others who have been raised in a civil society where laws do exist, his behavior, nonetheless, is still righteous and he is actually a well-practiced artist in this matter – should you compare him to those who haven't been brought up at all, those who have no halls of justice, no laws and, indeed, no compulsion that would force them to belabor themselves with all of the interrelated parts of virtue, those, rather, who would yet be savages just as such were portrayed for us last year by the poet Pherecrates at the festival in honor of Bacchus. Truly, if you were to find yourself surrounded by such men as those inhuman fiends were who composed the choir, then you would be most relieved if the worst you had to meet up with should be just an Eurybatos or Phrynondas, and then even you would yammer in your desire for the maleficence of just these men who exist here amongst us. But now, Socrates, you have grown used to this and have become spoiled in your expectations of a civilized existence – as everyone here is a teacher in virtue and each and every does as well as he is able and, thus, you never see a real savage. It's just as if you were to *[328a]* question where there might well be a teacher in the Greek language and you wouldn't be able to find a single one. Indeed, I believe that not even then if you were to inquire as to who would be the instructors of our handworkers, who teaches the art of pottery and weaving, you would be hard-pressed to find anyone other than the fathers who teach their sons whatever they might know and a few relatives who likewise are engaged in similar livelihoods. Who would be an especial expert in these matters? I believe you would have great difficulty in finding such an expert but, on the other hand, it would be a simple matter to find people who know nothing at all. This is how it is as regards virtue and all the other things. Thus, if there be one whose understanding surpasses our own, and be it by just a small amount – how to advance along the path of virtue – this would have to be taken up and happily accepted. And of this sort I believe to qualify as being one; there are many sorts in which my understanding is better, the means by which someone advances toward the good and how one becomes more adept; all well worth the tuition that I expect and, indeed, worth far more than my fees; and this is the opinion of those who have themselves learned from me. And it is for this reason that I have arrived at the manner in which I levy my charges. If, namely, someone has received instruction from me and he so wants, he may pay me the price that I expect; but if not, he simply goes to the temple and makes a solemn oath there as to how high a valuation he places on the knowledge that he has acquired and this, then, is what he pays. With this, Socrates, said he, I have demonstrated to you through history and also by providing the underlying reasons that, indeed, virtue is teachable and that also the Athenians hold this to be true and that, nonetheless, it is not to be marvelled over when the sons of good parents turn out bad or when the sons of bad parents become good. For also the sons of Polyclitus, who are of the same age as Paralus and Xanthippus here, these sons are nothing in comparison to their father, and so it is as well with many others, sons of other artists. But just for this reason one is not allowed to be critical toward them, rather one must hope for the best, for they are young. ~   <17.~328d]

– Now Protagoras, after having displayed this for us to such a remarkable extent and with such detail, he now came to an end with his speech; but I, having already been entranced for quite some time, I continued gazing upon him as if he might start up and speak again, and I yearned for the pleasure of yet hearing more. But, as finally it did become apparent to me that he really had finished, so I collected myself and, as it were, with some difficulty I turned myself toward Hippocrates and said to him: How thankful I am to you, son of Apollodorus, that you came to me and urged me to accompany you here! For it is worth quite a lot to me to have heard from Protagoras that which I have heard. Until now, namely, I was of the opinion that it wasn't through human efforts that those who are good become good, but now I am convinced of this. Except that there is still a small matter which stands in the way – regarding which, obviously, Protagoras will easily be able to teach me, as already he has taught me so many things. For if someone were to speak about such matters with one of our great orators he might well hear such speeches   [a] also from Pericles or from some other master in speechcrafting, but then if one were to question a bit further, so they are just like the books and don't know how either they might answer one nor how to lead in the questioning, rather, when one questions over some minor issue, then, like the striking of a metal gong, the same tone rings out for a long while provided that one doesn't disturb it. So also is the case with these orators when asked about small matters, namely, out comes a speech ten miles long. But our Protagoras understands equally well both the long and beauteous speeches, as his deed has just demonstrated, but also he understands how to give short answers to questions as well as how to wait and take up the answers given to him when he questions, and only a few are qualified in doing this. Now then, Protagoras, I am missing still a small bit that I might have everything, if you would like to answer me this. You say that virtue would be teachable, and I, if I am to believe anyone at all – I certainly do believe you. But what occurred to me as you were speaking, please make whole that which is lacking in my soul. Namely, you said: Zeus delivered righteousness to mankind, and shame also; and then again there are many instances in your speech where you make mention of righteousness and mindfulness and piety, and all of these as if they all together would be one, virtue. Even this is what I would like for you to establish more precisely: how these all relate one to the other; whether, indeed, virtue is one and yet the parts of it are righteousness and mindfulness and piety; or whether everything that I have just named are only different names for one and the same matter. This is what I am yet missing. ~ It is very easy, said he, <18.~329d] to answer this, Socrates; that of virtue, which is one, these are the parts about which you are questioning. ~ Whether they are well parts in the manner, said I, as the parts of the face are parts: mouth, nose, eyes and ears? Or is it so, as the parts of gold are not at all any different from one another and from the whole other than through their being larger and smaller? ~ In the former manner, it seems to me, Socrates, just as the parts of the face correlate to the whole face. ~ Then amongst mankind, I questioned, are they possessed in differing amounts – that one has this, another that; or is it necessary that he who has one part also has them all? ~ In no way, said he, for there are many who are indeed courageous, but not righteous; others who are righteous but not wise. ~ Thus, these too are parts of virtue, I questioned, wisdom and courage? ~ Indeed, before all [330a] other things, said he, and the greatest of them all is wisdom amongst these parts. ~ And each of them, I said, is something other than the others? ~ Yes. ~ Does each also have its own operation, just as the eye is not the same as the ear nor does it operate in the same manner and, in general, no part is like any other, neither in its operation nor in any other manner; is now in just this way each of the parts of virtue none like the others, neither in itself nor in its operations? Or wouldn't it be obvious that this has to be the correlation if our example should indeed be similar? ~ It correlates just so, Socrates, said he. ~ Thereupon I said: Thus, there is no other part of virtue which is like knowledge, and none that is like righteousness, and none like mindfulness [prudence], and none like piety? ~ No, said he. ~ Then tallyho, said I, let's together take a look and see of what sort each of them is. Firstly then: Is righteousness something definite? or is it not something definite? It seems to me that it *[c]* would be such, but how about you? ~ To me also, said he. ~ How now? If someone were to ask us, you and me: But do tell me, Protagoras and Socrates – this, that which you have just named, righteousness, is this itself righteous or unrighteous? Then I would certainly answer him, righteous; but you, how would you voice your opinion? – the same as I did or something different? ~ The same, said he. ~ Thus, righteousness is even such as being righteous, this is what I would say in answer to him who so questions. And you too? ~ Yes, said he. ~ If hereafter he yet should question us: Don't you also say that there should yet be piety? Then I believe we would indeed say "yes" to this? ~ Indeed, said he. ~ And do you two also say that this is something definite? Should we give our assent to this also, or not? ~ This too, he affirmed. ~ Now do you two also say that even this itself is so from its nature as being impious, or [is it itself] pious? I, said I, would become indignant with this question and I would say: Hold your tongue – man! How might anything else be pious if piety itself were not to be so! And what about you? Wouldn't you answer so? ~ Quite, said he. ~ If, now, he would yet question *<19.~330e2]* us about this and he would say: What did you two even say just a little while ago? Did I, perhaps, not rightly pick up on what you said? I fancy that you said that the parts of virtue correlated one to the other so that none of them would be like the others? Then I would say to him: You have heard right well except for this, that you believe that I also had said this, in this you misheard. For it is Protagoras here that so answered, I was only questioning. If, now, he questions: Is Socrates speaking the truth, Protagoras? Is it you who says that no part of virtue would be like the others? Is this your speech? What would you answer him? ~ Naturally, said he, I confess as much. ~ What then, Protagoras, shall we, if we are eye to eye in our understanding of this, what shall we answer him if he should yet question us: Thus, piety would not be the same as being righteous and righteousness not the same as being pious, rather as not pious and piety as not righteous, hence unjust – and wouldn't the former [righteousness] be impious? What would we answer him now? *[b]* I for my part at least would say that righteousness would indeed be pious and piety righteous; and I'd answer the same for you too, if you were to allow me to do so then I would say the same thing: that righteousness either is the same as piety or at least so similar to it as is at all possible; and thus in all ways righteousness would be like piety and piety like righteousness. Look to yourself – whether you forbid me that I answer so, or if you also fancy that it be so? ~ In no way, said he, do I fancy that this be so without qualification, that one would have to admit as much: that righteousness would be pious and piety righteous, rather I fancy that there is probably yet something different in how they are. But, indeed, what does it matter? – said he. If you want then righteousness should be pious and also piety righteous. ~ Hold it right there! – said I. I don't at all desire that such an "if you want" or "as you like" shall be investigated; rather, I and you. But this "I and you" I say in the opinion that the proposition shall best be tested and proven if we leave this "if" out of it altogether. ~ But, indeed, said he: Is righteousness *[331d]* similar to piety, so too everything is to a certain extent similar to everything else. Indeed, in one manner white is similar to black, and hard to soft, and whatever else seems, one to the other, to be most contradictory; and that too of which we were speaking earlier, that each would have its own operation and the one wouldn't be like the others – the parts of the face are indeed similar to one another to a certain extent and one *'is'* as well as the other – so that in this way you would also be able to prove, if you should want to, that everything is similar to everything else. But it's not right that straight-away you name things as similar that have some similarity, and those that have some dissimilarity as dissimilar, also if they only have a little similarity or dissimilarity. ~ I now was amazed about what he had just said and I said to him: Do then righteousness and piety correlate for you one to the other that each has a small amount of similarity one with the other? ~ Not wholly so, said he, but also not quite so as it seems that you believe. ~ Hey now, said I, as this seems to be rather awkward for you, what do you say, shall we leave this be and place our attention upon this other matter that you have said.

<20.~332a]

You do name something foolishness? ~ He said, yes. ~ Is not the exact opposite of this wisdom? ~ I fancy it so, said he. ~ And when people do things properly and in a healthy manner, do they seem to you *then* to be mindful, when they act so, or when they act in the opposite manner? ~ That is when they are mindful, said he. ~ Isn't it true that it is through mindfulness that they are mindful?

~ Naturally. ~ And isn't it also true: those who act and do things improperly do so foolishly and are not mindful in that they so act? ~ I fancy that too, said he. ~ The opposite from mindful, then, is acting foolishly? ~ He agreed. ~ And isn't it true that what is done foolishly is done through foolishness, and what is done mindfully, this is done through mindfulness? ~ He concurred with this. ~ And isn't it true, if something is done with strength, such is done 'strongly,' and if it is done with weakness, then weakly? ~ It seemed so to him. ~ And that which is done quick, quickly; and with *[332c]* slowness, slowly? ~ He assented. ~ And if something, then, is done in such a manner, so it becomes done from the same; and if in the opposite manner, then also from that which is the opposite? ~ He agreed with this. ~ Well, now then, said I, is there something beauteous? ~ He concurred with this. ~ And is there anything other than the ugly which is the opposite of this? ~ Nothing other.[80] ~ And how? Is there something that is good? ~ There is. ~ Is there anything outside of evil that would be the opposite of this? ~ No, nothing other. ~ And how? Is there such a thing as a high voice? ~ He assented. ~ Is there nothing other that is the opposite of this outside of a low voice? ~ No, said he. ~ Thus, said I, each of these singularities of opposite pairs has only one that is the opposite of it and not many? ~ To this he knowingly agreed. ~ Come then, *[d]* said I, let's add it up all together, that to which we are *'as one'* in our understanding. We do agree that to each one only one is the opposite, but more than one are not? ~ We are one in our understanding as regards this, said he. ~ And also that that which is done in an opposite manner is done through opposites? ~ He assented. ~ And we are also one in our understanding that that which is done in a foolish manner is done in an opposite manner to that which is done mindfully? ~ He assented to this. ~ And that which is done mindfully is accomplished with mindfulness, but what is done foolishly through foolishness? ~ He concurred with this. ~ Hence, *[e]* as it is done in an opposite manner, then it must be accomplished through the opposite? ~ Yes. ~ But, then, the one is accomplished through mindfulness and the other is accomplished by foolishness? ~ Yes. ~ In opposite manners? ~ Indeed. ~ Hence, through opposites? ~ Yes. ~ Hence, foolishness is the opposite of mindfulness? ~ That's quite clear. ~ Do you well remember that earlier on we saw eye to eye on this – that foolishness was the opposite of wisdom? ~ He admitted it. ~ And that to one only one is the opposite? ~ I assert this. ~ Which of our two assertions *[333a]*

---

[80] Cf: *Sophist* 257b–258a (pp. 567–568).

do we want, now, to give up, Protagoras? The one, that each one has only one opposite, or our earlier assertion when we said that mindfulness would be something other than wisdom? And that both would be parts of virtue? And outside of this, that each would be something other – as they were to be dissimilar to one another both in themselves and in their operations, just as the parts of the face are? Which of the two of these do we want to sacrifice? For at the same time we are not able to carry on harmoniously with both assertions, for they neither agree nor ring out well together. And how could they possibly ring harmoniously if it is necessary that only one is the opposite to the other one, more than one aren't, but foolishness, *[b]* which is one, has shown itself as being the opposite both to wisdom as also to mindfulness? Is it so, Protagoras, I asked him, or is it somehow otherwise? ~ He admitted it, but quite reluctantly and obviously with displeasure. ~ So then, these would well be one: mindfulness and wisdom? But earlier on righteousness and piety also were practically shown as being the same. Come now, said I, Protagoras, let's not allow ourselves that we become tired, rather let's still go through the rest. Does it seem to you that a person who does something that is improper, does he seem to you to be mindful that he is doing something wrong? ~ I would shame myself, o Socrates, said he, to make this admission, although the great majority of people would well say that this is so. ~ Should I deliver my speech upon these, the great majority, or upon you? ~ If you want, said he, do deliver it first against the former, the proposition of the majority. ~ Good, said I, it doesn't confound me whether these answers be your own or not, if only you answer the questions. For indeed, I really only want to test the proposition, though well, it does also occur by itself, as it were, that in this process I, the questioner, and also the respondent likewise, we both undergo scrutiny and testing. ~ At the start, now, Protagoras made a big fuss and complained: that this would be a most difficult and arduous proposition; but finally he relaxed himself and agreed to answer. ~ Come now,   *<21.~333d]* said I, answer me starting at the beginning. Do you fancy that there are some people who in that they do unrighteousness are mindful? ~ It should be so, said he. ~ But by this "being mindful" – do you opine that they have well bethought themselves? ~ He assented to this. ~ And to rightly bethink oneself means that they are well counseled in that which they are wrongfully doing? ~ That should be valid, said he. ~ Whether it may well be, I questioned, if they should feel good about what they are doing, or if they don't feel good at all but have awful feelings? ~ If they should feel good about it. ~ Do you agree that a few things are good? ~ I say so. ~ Is perhaps, said

I, that good which is useful for man? ~ Yes, and also, by Zeus, there is much that is not useful for man that I at least name good all the same. ~ And I fancied that Protagoras was already becoming extremely annoyed and that he was starting to have feelings of *Angst*, that he was fighting against giving me any answers, and as I saw that he was in such a condition I took counsel with myself and I questioned further in a measured and thoughtful manner: [334a] Is it just your opinion, said I, what isn't useful for any human being? or do you also mean that which is wholly and utterly useless, and do you call such things good? ~ In no way, said he, but I know of lots and lots of things that are utterly useless for people – foods, drinks, various medicines and, besides these, tons and tons of other things; then there are others that are useful for man; then again others which, indeed, are neither of the two but are maybe useful for horses, and others again for oxen and yet others for dogs; and then there are yet others that aren't useful for any of these at all, but are, perhaps, for trees; indeed, a few things are good for the roots of the trees but are bad for the branches as, for instance, manure,[81] which if it is spread on the ground then it promotes health for all of the plants, but if you were to place manure on the shoots or the young stems, this would ruin everything. So too, oil is extremely bad and does damage to all of the plants and it also does damage to the coats of the animals, only for man's hair is this not the case as it promotes growth and, beyond this, it also is good for man's skin. And so, the good shifts and shimmers, transforming and metamorphosing itself continuously – that even this which is so good for our external body is yet most evil if taken internally. It is for this reason that the physicians forbid the sick that they use any oil internally, except for the very minor amount that they too do allow them to enjoy, just the right amount, for the purpose of smoothing-out the adverse characteristics of various food-stuffs and to lessen the sensibility from which otherwise they might suffer, particularly the sensibility in relation to the nasal passages and the olfactory interworkings. ~   *<22.~334d]*

As he finished saying this those present indicated their approval of his beautiful speaking style with a murmur of bravos and other signs of encouragement. But I said: O Protagoras, my memory is not at all as good as it might be and so when people speak in such lengthy

---

[81] It is right curious how Plato, when expounding upon the "being of ideas" shifts from the grandest to the lowest: compare to *Parmenides* 130cd (p. 211). Oil is mentioned at the start of *Theaetetus* 144bc (p. 362) which I would speculate has something to do with "just the right amount"; likewise, *Charmides* 162a (p. 182).

sentences I totally forget what the conversation is really about. So now – it's as if I were to be somewhat deaf and you would then believe, if you were indeed to want to speak to me, that you would have to speak up louder to me than you would with others, so too now, as you have to make allowance for someone with a short memory span, please cut down on the length of your answers and make them nice and short – if, then, I am to be able to follow you. ~ How do mean this? said he, that I somehow answer you shorter than is necessary? ~ In no way, said I. ~ Hence, as much as is necessary. ~ Oh sure, said I. ~ Should I speak as much as I hold to be necessary or as much as you hold to be necessary? ~ Indeed, said I, I have heard that you would be one who has the skill – a skill that   *[335a]* you parcel out to others – that you might either be able, if you so desire, to speak so long regarding the same matter that nobody is able to grapple the speech away from you, or again, on the other hand, with such brevity that nobody could say the same thing as you with fewer words. If you want, then, to conduct a conversation with me, so please make use of the latter mode of speaking, speech with brevity. ~ O Socrates, said he, I have conquered already many people in the battle of words but if I were to do as you bid me to do, namely to always conduct my speech in the art and manner that my opponent requests of me, then it is certain that I never would have overcome anyone at all and then Protagoras would be a nobody amongst all the Hellenic peoples. ~ But I, as I had taken careful notice of it, that he was not at all happy with his earlier answers and that he no longer wanted to be a voluntary interlocutor in the conversation, I believed that for me there was nothing I might yet do for the continuation of our speech and so I said: But Protagoras, I too am not keen on the idea that our conversation should be conducted other than as you consider to be right, rather if it shall be convenient for you to conduct the conversation in such a manner that I shall be able to follow you, then I want to converse with you. For you, as you are famed and as you yourself have said, understand both – to conduct the speech in long as well as in short formats – for then, you are even a man   *[c]* of wisdom; but I don't at all know how to make do with these long speeches, although I do wish very much that I might also understand this. Thus, you would have to be the one to give in, as you are quite adept in both modes, if this conversation is yet to come to be. Now, if you don't want to do so and as I too don't have any more time and I can't just wait around for this to change, and as you insist upon dragging out your speeches indefinitely, well, I have other things to do and so I must be going, although I should have liked to have continued on with our conversation. ~ And with these words I stood up in order to take my leave, but just as I got up Callias took hold of me with one hand on the right and with his other hand he took hold of my coat and said: We're not going to let you go, Socrates, for if you take your leave from us then our speeches will not be the same at all. Thus, please do stay here with us for I don't know of anyone whom I might prefer to hear rather than you and Protagoras speaking with one another. Be so kind for the sake of us all. ~ I replied, although I was already standing in order that I might go: Always, Callias, have I had my joy on your love of the treasures of knowledge and so also *[e]* now I do praise and love this – so that I would most gladly do as you request, if then you requested something that would be at all possible. But now it's as if you were to ask of me that I might run a race with Crison of Himera, our fastest champion in running, or to run with some other champion or messenger, and that I should keep up with him step for step; I would have to say to you regarding this that it would be far more pleasing for me than for you if I were to be capable of keeping up with these in the race, but still, I am not able to do so. Thus, if it's your ardent desire that I should run together with Crison and you'd love to see this, then request it of him, that he let up in his long strides, for I am unable to run like the wind but he is quite able to go slowly. If, then, it's your wish that you hear Protagoras and me speaking together then make your plea to him that he answer me as he did previously with short words and [just] regarding that about which I questioned him, that he might now answer me even so; but if not, what then is our mode of speech going to be? For I at least have always believed that these would be two wholly different things: to carry on a mutual conversation and to hold a lecture. ~ But look now, Socrates, said he, Protagoras seems to be in the right when he contends that he should be allowed to speak as he wants and that you too may speak as you want. ~ To this Alcibiades took up *<23.~336b]* the word and said: You're wrong, Callias! – for Socrates has indeed admitted that he's no expert in knowing how to conduct long lectures and in this he gives in that Protagoras has the advantage; but to carry on an orderly conversation and conduct this aright – that each is interrogated by the other and each interrogates – in this I would be astounded if Socrates would ever concur that someone else might be more adept. If, then, Protagoras on his side would concur that he is worse in leading such conversations than Socrates, then Socrates would be satisfied; but if he wants to place himself in opposition to Socrates, well, then he might also speak with him in an orderly manner with questions and answers but not simply spin out after each question some lengthy speech and thereby evade answering and, rather than letting the other person take his turn in the conversation, keep on talking and talking until the greater portion of the audience has forgotten what the question really was about. As for Socrates, you can take my assurance that he wouldn't ever forget, despite the fact that he's joking with us when he says that his memory would be failing. Thus, to me it seems that what Socrates says is the better argument, for each [of us] has to speak his mind. ~ And after Alcibiades it was, I believe, Critias who said: O Prodicus and Hippias, I fancy that, indeed, Callias is always on Protagoras' side; but Alcibiades, once he sets his mind to something, he always wants to claim to be in the right with that, whatever he thinks. But for us it is not becoming that we take sides with either of the two parties, neither with the one rooting for Socrates nor the one rooting for Protagoras, but that we rather only plead in common with both of them that they not break off this conversation in the middle. ~ After he said this Prodicus spoke: Quite right, I fancy that you have spoken   [337a] well, Critias. For by such a conversation those who are present must indeed listen in to the whole of what is said, though not giving equal weight to both – as these are not one and the same. Namely, we have to listen to the whole but not sanction both to the same extent, rather, to him who is wiser, more, to him who is not so wise, less. I too, o Protagoras and Socrates, plead with both of you, that you both relent; that you should, indeed, argue about your propositions, but you need not have a row with one another; for friends too may be at odds and argue with good will but only those are capable of having a row who are disunified and who are adversaries, each to the other. And it is in this manner that our conversation shall continue on most beauteously. For thus you two, the speakers, shall get the greatest respect from us, the listeners; respect I say, not praise; namely, one earns respect in the souls of those who are listening with no need for deceit but praise in the words of such people who often speak falsely, contrary to their own convictions; but we, those who hear, shall have the most satisfaction from this; satisfaction I say, not pleasure, for everyone has satisfaction who learns something and is able to take something up with the soul itself, but it is only pleasure that is provided for those who eat something or otherwise receive a pleasant sensation through the mediation of their bodies. ~ With this speech Prodicus found great applause from the larger portion of those present. After Prodicus, next to speak was Hippias, the wise. I think, said he, that you men gathered together here, we are all   <24.~337d] of us relatives and friends and compatriots from nature, but not so through law. For the similar is related to the similar by nature but law is tyrannical over men and compels many to act contrary to their nature. Thus, for us it would be a travesty that we, we who do have

knowledge of the nature of the matter, if nonetheless and despite that we are the wisest of all the Hellenes and even for this reason find ourselves in this city that is the capital of Hellenic wisdom and also even in this house which is most admired and has the most sparkling of reputations, that we be gathered together and yet display ourselves as undignified of all this dignity, that rather we disagree and break up the unity as if we should be the most common sort of men. For this reason I plead with you, and also advise you, o Protagoras and Socrates, that you be led back together into the middle of this circle by us, your referees, and that you come together as one so that neither you, Socrates, demand this most stringent manner of speaking, that the answers be crammed into the briefest sentences possible and rob Protagoras of his pleasure, that rather you might allow him a little more play in the reins so that his speeches might display greater comeliness and a more beauteous flow; nor too, though, should Protagoras put out all his sails that he might capture the full brunt of the wind and thus lose sight of land, embarked, as it were, out upon the high seas of rhetoric and thus flown off; rather that you both hold yourselves to a middle course and compromise. Do follow me, then, and take up my suggestion – that you elect a referee and overseer and presiding judge, someone who holds you accountable that each of you observes the proper proportions in his speeches. ~   <25.~338b]
This pleased all present and everyone praised him and Callias assured everyone that he wouldn't let go of me and they implored that an overseer be elected. Thus, I said that this would be an abomination if a referee would be set up to oversee our conversation – for if the overseer were to be worse than us then it wouldn't be right that the worse should have oversight over the better. But if he should be similar to us then that too wouldn't be right as then the similar would do similarly to what we ourselves would do and, thus, he would be totally superfluous. But then, you all would surely elect someone who would be better than we are. In all actuality, though, someone wiser than our Protagoras it is not, I believe, possible for you to elect. But if you do elect someone who wouldn't be any better but of whom you would claim this to be so, so this too would be an abomination for him, that you should thereby treat him like a common person and set up a referee – though as for me, it's all the same. But this is what I shall do so that, as you all wish it, the conversation between us may yet come to be. If Protagoras doesn't want to answer then he may ask the questions and I will answer him and at the same time make the attempt to show him how I mean it that the respondent would have to respond. But after I have answered his questions, just as many as he wants to ask me, then he also should once more stand up to my

questions – and if he shows himself as being adverse to answering the questions that I put to him, then I along with all of you will plead with him that he do so, just as you all now are doing to me, that the conversation not be dashed. And so there doesn't need to be any one overseer, rather all of you together shall lead with common oversight. All were of the opinion that this is how it would have to be done. And Protagoras, indeed, he didn't really want to make this promise, but he was forced to do so nonetheless – that he would now ask the questions and once he had questioned enough then he too would be questioned in turn and [that he might] want to answer in the short mode. Thus, he started off with his questioning something like this. ~

<26.~339a]

I believe, he said, o Socrates, that it is a critical part of man's apprenticeship in becoming wise that he be particularly strong in his reading of the classics.   But this only exists if he is in the position that he understands what the poets have said: namely, what was well composed and what was not, and also be able to clarify – and if he should be questioned then he should be able to give an accounting. So too, even now the question should still be about the same matter regarding which we even were speaking, you and I, namely about virtue, just that now this will be brought into relation with a poem, this is the whole difference.[82] Simonides says somewhere or other to Scopas, the son of the Thessalian Creon:

To become an outstanding man already truly – this is hard – stalwart to the core, with hand and foot and meaning, one's build unassailable.

Are you acquainted with this poem or shall I recite for you the whole of it? ~ That's not necessary, said I, I am acquainted with it and I have spent much effort, indeed, over this poem. ~ That's nice, said he. Do you then believe that this is done well and rightly composed, or not? ~ Very much so, said I, well composed and also right. ~ Do you fancy that it be well composed if the poet also should contradict himself? ~ No, that's not good, I said. ~ Take better consideration of it, said he. ~ But, my good man, I have already bethought myself sufficiently. ~ Do you then know, said he, that somewhere later on in the poem he says:

---

[82] Identity in difference – such dialectic repeats itself in many ways and on many levels throughout the dialogue, *Protagoras*; here the play between studying classical poetry and one's own thinking is particularly beautiful; as is also the play between – you and I – sophistry and philosophy.

[339c]

*Distanced enough I shall never be from the Pittacian word, tho'
spoken by a man most wise: It is hard, said he, to be virtuous.*

Have you well bethought yourself that this is spoken by the very same
man as was the former quote? ~ I know it well, said I. ~ You fancy,
then, said he, that this would be in harmony with the former quote?
~ It seems so to me, said I. But at the same time I experienced
trepidation, that what he was saying might well be something; and so
I asked: But you, it doesn't seem so to you? ~ How should it not
appear to be a contradiction when the same person who says both of
these at first is himself taking the position that it would be hard to
truly become an outstanding man and then, after he's gone on a little
further in the same poem, he forgets about this and to Pittacus who
says something that's entirely the same, that it would be hard to be
virtuous, he scolds him over this and withholds any assent – and,
indeed, he has asserted just the same thing himself a little earlier. If,
now, he scolds someone who says exactly the same thing that he
himself has said, then it's quite obvious that he also is scolding
himself. So that either the first lines or the other lines are not right.
As he said this he once more excited many of those who were
listening to express their agreement with applause. But, at first I felt
as if I had just received a knockout blow from someone who fights
well with his fists, everything became dark and I was reeling as he
said this and the others who were listening broke in with their
applause. But now I turned myself – in that I want at least that I tell
you the truth of the matter, that thereby I might win a little time for
thinking the matter over: what, pray tell, might the poet well mean –
so I turned myself to Prodicus, called out to him and said: Prodicus,
Simonides is your fellow countryman and, thus, you too owe him the
favor of standing by him. I shall call you thus, so I fancy,   [340a]
to bring succor – just as Homer has it that Scamandros whilst being
assailed by Achilles had called out for help from Simoeis and had
said: *"Brother, tallyho! – the power of this man requires the both of
us, that he be put in bonds."*   In this wise I call to you also for
assistance, that Protagoras doesn't throw Simonides and us with him
into the dust. Moreover, Simonides also requires the defense of your
art by which you differentiate between wanting and desiring, that
these are not one and the same and what, furthermore, you have laid
out in much detail and with beauty. So examine this here with me,
whether you and I are of like opinion. To me, namely, it seems that
Simonides is not contradicting himself. But you, Prodicus, you take

the first crack on this nut by stating your opinion. Would you fancy that becoming and being are 'one and the same,' or that they are of two different sorts? ~ Different, by Zeus, said Prodicus. ~ And isn't it so that in the first quote Simonides was expressing his own opinion, that it is hard for one, in all truth, to become an outstanding man? ~ You are totally in the right, said Prodicus. ~ And Pittacus, I continued on, he whom he was scolding, didn't at all say, as Protagoras believes him to have said, the same thing, rather he said something different. Because Pittacus didn't clarify at all that it would be hard to become virtuous, as Simonides did, rather, to be so. And as our Prodicus says, o Protagoras, becoming and being are not names for the same, but since they are not the same thing, so too Simonides didn't contradict himself. Perhaps also Prodicus and many others would say, as it stands in Hesiod – that it would indeed be difficult to become good, because the gods have decided that mankind shall only achicvc virtue through his sweat, but once one has attained this peak then it becomes easy despite how arduous the ascent itself may have been. ~ As Prodicus heard me   *<27~340d]* say this, he praised me. But Protagoras spoke up saying: Your defense commits yet more grievous transgressions than that which you defend. ~ Then, said I, I have made a bad job of it and am most probably a comical physician – if, then, through my treatment the disease has been made all the worse. ~ But this is how it correlates, said he. ~ And how's that? – said I. ~ It would show a great lack in understanding, said he, if the poet were to hold it to be such a minor accomplishment that one possesses virtue, this which amongst all things is the hardest of all, as all men believe. ~ To this I spoke: By Zeus, just at the right time Prodicus stands ready in our midst at this gathering. For it may well be, o Protagoras, that the wisdom which Prodicus possesses has a long history, whether it begins   *[341a]* with Simonides or yet even earlier. But you, although you are so well informed regarding so many things, regarding this you are uninformed – though I am informed because I am Prodicus' pupil. Now too, I fancy that you have not taken notice that this "hard" of which Simonides speaks, he didn't mean it in the sense in which you take him to have meant it, rather it's like the word "dreadful" regarding which Prodicus has scolded me on numerous occasions – if I should say in praise of you or in praise of someone other: "Protagoras is truly a wise and dreadful man," so he questions me as to whether I'm not ashamed to be calling something that is good to be dreadful; for that which is dreadful, says he, is evil, nobody ever speaks of dreadful riches or dreadful peace or dreadful health; rather of dreadful diseases or dreadful wars or dreadful poverty – so that

that which is dreadful is evil. Perhaps, now, the Ceans and with them Simonides understand this word "hard" in even this sense, either as evil or as something other, which you don't know. Thus, let's just ask Prodicus, for it's quite apparent that he's the one to question regarding Simonides' use of speech: What then, o Prodicus, does Simonides mean with his use of "hard"? ~ Evil, said he. ~   [c] And it's for this reason also, Prodicus, said I, that he scolded Pittacus who said: *"It is hard to be virtuous"* – as if he would have heard him say that it would be evil to be virtuous. ~ What else, said Prodicus, would you believe that Simonides wanted to say other than even this, and that he would censure Pittacus that he doesn't understand to differentiate the meaning of words as he was from Lesbos and, thus, someone raised in a barbaric mode of speaking. ~ You have heard it, Protagoras, said I, that which Prodicus has said; do you have anything to say to the contrary? ~ To this Protagoras said: Not by a long shot! – Prodicus, that this should be how it correlates. Rather, I know it with complete certainty that Simonides with "hard"   [d] understood even that which we others also understand, namely, not what is evil but, rather, that which isn't easy and what can only be achieved through strenuous effort. ~ I too believe, said I, that this is what Simonides meant, and that Prodicus knows this right well, but he's joking with you and seems to want to put you to the test, whether or not you shall be able to stand by your proposition. For that it is not what is evil that Simonides understands when he speaks of what is hard, for this the following is ample proof, where he says: *"Only God alone may possess this dignity."* For then, if he had said, it is evil to be virtuous, so then he wouldn't possibly be able to say right after this that this belongs to God alone and that only to God is this advantage to be attributed. Or else Prodicus would have to mean that Simonides was wholly despicable and not at all one who is from Ceos. But what it seems to me that Simonides meant with this ode, this I will tell you – if, then, you even want to see me make a stab at it: whether I might be, as you say: powerful in my understanding of the classics; but if you prefer, then I'd also be happy to hear it from you. ~ Now Protagoras, when he heard me say this, responded: If you want to, Socrates. ~ But Prodicus and Hippias were very adamant about this, and so too were the others.   <28.~342a]

So then, I will attempt, said I, what I fancy the meaning of this ode is, I will attempt to lay it out for you. Namely, the oldest and the greatest amount of philosophy of the Hellenic peoples is in Crete and Sparta. And also the greatest number of sophists call this area home; but they deny it and pretend to be bereft of wisdom so that they won't be recognized in this, that they are far advanced above the rest of the Hellenes in wisdom – just like the former sophists upon whom Protagoras just recently touched; rather they prefer to give the appearance as if they might only supercede all others in armored combat or in their courageousness, because they believe that if ever this should become known, that the former is where their true strength lies, then everyone else by becoming more diligent would catch up with them. But now, in that they keep the truth hidden from all the others, they have pulled a fast one on all of these who desire to keep up with them through Lacedaimonization – and these do so through imitation, but imitate only what they know, and so it is that these let their ears be punched and keep to the company of the   [c] toughies, they give themselves over to the body-builders and to the masters in gymnastics and they wear short tunics – *as if* it were only through such things as these that the Lacedaimonians rule over all the rest of Hellas. The Lacedaimonians, however, when they resolve that enough is enough and wanting to hear their sophists in peace – and being quite fed up with always having to meet with them in secret gatherings – so they organize a policy of expulsion of all of these copycats, as well as the other foreigners who are staying by them, and, thus, they visit with their sophists unobserved by the preying eyes of foreigners. But they also never allow their own youths   [d] that these might travel to the other cities in Hellas – just as the Cretans also do not allow this – and this is so that they don't have their teachings corrupted by others. And in both of these city-states there not only are men but women too who are famed for their knowledge. But that I am speaking the truth in what I say and that the Lacedaimonians, both in philosophy as well as in speaking, are the best instructed of all Hellenes, this is apparent if you consider the following. Even if you should meet up with the least educated and most rustic Spartan you shall discover that, although he may show himself for a very long while to be poor in speech, then, all of a sudden, and just at the most opportune moment of your conversation – he shoots out with an effectual, utterly short and remarkably concise word, like the 'thwack' delivered by an arrow dispatched by a most powerful sharpshooter, right in the bull's-eye, so that, and no matter to whom he might be speaking, this person suddenly appears as being no better than a mere child in comparison with him. And even this has been noticed by a few, both by our contemporaries as well as in the past – that, namely, Lacedaimonization entails love of wisdom to a much greater extent than the love of body building; and these have known that the ability to come up with such pithy aphorisms is only possible to those whose instruction has   *[343a]* been consummate. And amongst these were Thales of Miletus, Bias from Priene, our own Solon, Cleobulus from Lindus, Myson of Chenai and, as the seventh should be counted the Spartan, Chilon. All of these were enthusiasts and devoted students to the classic arts of the Lacediamonians. And it's apparent to everyone that this is the source of their wisdom, this wisdom that typically is expressed in such a style of a short, thought-provoking and noble aphorism, which all of them have uttered. They also have dedicated together their masterpieces of wisdom and offered these up at the temples of Apollo and Delphi, writing upon the stone, as we all have heard: *Know thyself*, and *Moderation in all things*. And, why am I now saying this? – because this is the manner of the philosophy of the ancients, such laconic pithiness. And so too was the case with this aphorism of Pittacus that was highly prized by the ancients: *"It is hard to be virtuous."* Now Simonides, who also was striving for fame upon this path of wisdom, he thought to himself: if he might be able to overthrow this aphorism like a mighty knight and conqueror, then he too would insure his notoriety and become famed amongst his contemporaries. And so in opposition to this saying and out of this cause he made hunt upon this aphorism, and in order to overcome it he composed the entire lyrical poem. This is how it seems to me. Let's all take   <29.~343c] a good look at this together, whether or not I may be right about this. For already right at the start of the poem it would have to have appeared as pure foolishness if he only had wanted to say that it would be hard to become an outstanding man and would have brought in this word "already."   For this would have to be seen as being thrown in for no reason at all, unless it were to be the case that Simonides said it in his battle against the aphorism of Pittacus. What Pittacus, namely, was saying was – It is hard to be virtuous – and fighting against this Simonides is saying: No, rather *already* becoming an outstanding man is hard, o Pittacus, truly. Not – "a truly outstanding"; for with this "truly" he didn't say in such a relation as if there might be a few who are truly outstanding and then again some others who, indeed, are outstanding but are not truly outstanding – for this would only be simple-mindedness and is not possibly from Simonides; rather, one would have to accept that this "truly" would be a word-transference and, as it were, counterpoint in the ode – and so one would have to add on Pittacus with one's thinking, approximately so: as if it were to be the case that Pittacus himself were speaking and then Simonides answered him – O ye peoples, it is hard to be virtuous; and then the answer: O Pittacus, you are not speaking aright, for not being – rather *already* becoming an outstanding man, stalwart in hand and foot and meaning, one's build unassailable, *this* is truly hard. In this manner the word "already" is reasonably brought into context and the "hard" stays at the end, as is only meet and proper; and also everything that follows this confirms that this is what was meant. For one would be able to demonstrate in multifarious ways and by each singularity of what is said in this ode: how beauteously it is composed – for all of it is very becoming and full of meaning; alone, this would carry us far afield that we should go through it all; but the entire outline and sketch allows us that we see through it, that it has this intent, that in every way and throughout the entire ode it stands as proof contrary to Pittacus' aphorism. For hereafter, after he has added   <30.~344b] on a few other deft touches, he says, as if he were carrying through [with his proposition] that already it is truly hard to become an outstanding man, but yet it is possible, at least for a few moments of time; but once man has become so, that one also remains in this condition *{Verfassung[83]}* and that one is an outstanding man over some length of time, this is, as you say, Pittacus, impossible – and such is not befitting for human beings, rather God alone is allowed to possess such dignity. *"For mankind, alas, it is not possible not to be malefic for ever-present misfortune throws us into travails."* Now, who is thrown down by ever-present misfortune in the command of a ship? Obviously, it wouldn't be a know-nothing, for he is already always in such a state of being thrown down. Just as no one can hurl onto the ground someone who is lying there already, rather, indeed, only he who is standing can be hurled down so that he too becomes one who also is lying; this doesn't happen, though, to those already prostrate; and so too it's only possible for him – he who otherwise well knows the right counsel – only he is hurled from his upright position by merciless fate against which one looks in vain for advice. And it is quite possible for the best helmsman to be utterly without recourse when in the teeth of a mighty gale that overtakes him; or even the agronomist who remains on land might be so overcome by malefic weather phenomena; and so too the doctor doesn't cure every disease. For just those who stand out due to their excellence, just for these is it possible that they may be brought low – as also another poet attests – who says: *" 'Tis well – now the admirable does poorly but, then again, 'tis fame."* – but for him who is malefic this never occurs that he might at one time be brought low, rather it is necessary that he always be such, so that the man who is well counseled, *[344e]* wise and adept – if, then, he be hurled down by fickle fortune, so

---

[83] "Verfassung" – The German "Fass" – reminds us of the binding of Barrels: *Gorgias* 493b; (p. 312) as well as the binding of Daedalus's works of art in the *Meno* 98a (p. 498).

then, "*he too is incapable of being other than bad.*" But you, Pittacus, you say: '*Tis hard to be virtuous.* But it is already hard to become virtuous, but still possible; yet impossible to be so. "*For every man whose actions are good is good, but malefic if bad.*" What action, then, is good whilst reading? And what is it that makes a man a good reader? Obviously, if he learns from it. And which good deeds make the physician good? Obviously, that he has learned the proper actions for treating those who are ill. "*But those malefic who do bad.*" So who might possibly become a bad physician? Obviously, only he about whom one firstly might say that he is a physician, and then, that he's a good physician. For he too is able to become a bad one. But for us, we who are not at all informed regarding the art of medicine, we by our inept actions are incapable of ever becoming physicians, nor carpenters, nor anything else at all; and he who is incapable of becoming a physician in that he misdiagnoses   *[b]* whomever, so too, he is incapable of becoming a bad physician. So it is also possible that an admirable man might well – in the course of time – become malefic, simply through the fault of aging, from being overly tired, through sickness or by some other chance event; for this, then, is the only malpractice: being robbed of one's knowledge; but it is never possible that a bad man might become bad as he is always so, rather, if he will become bad he must first have become good. So, then too, this portion of the ode is intent upon showing us that to be an admirable man and to remain forever so without travail, this wouldn't be possible; but one would be able to become good and the same one might also become malefic; but those that thrive most of all and are most outstanding are they – those, namely, who partake in divine love. All of this is said   *<31.~345d]* contrary to Pittacus and also the following in the ode makes this clearer still. Namely he says: "*Therefore also I shan't by searching for that which never may be so throw away a part of time in useless, unfulfillable hope – seeking a man without blemish amongst all who break bread upon this widely peopled earth. Should I find him, then you will know of it.*" With such vehemence and throughout the whole of this ode does he quarrel with Pittacus. "*Thus I praise and love them all, they who commit no wrong, and by free choice; against necessity, nonetheless, not even the gods take issue.*" And this too is likewise said in opposition to the same. For Pittacus wasn't so utterly uninstructed that he might possibly have meant that he would praise those who do wrong with free choice – as if there might be some who choose evil freely. I, at least, believe this: that there is no wise person who is of the opinion that any person at all fails due to his free choice or accomplishes anything that is malefic or evil from free choice;

rather, these well know it that everyone who does something badly or something evil does so without freedom of will. And so Simonides is not claiming to be praising those who do evil out of their lack of free will; rather this *"by free choice"* he is predicating *of himself.* He believes, namely, that a good, noble man often compels himself to become someone's friend and eulogist – as it does happen to many that they have a father who doesn't deserve love or praise, or such for a mother, or such for one's fatherland or anything else of this sort. Now, for men who are bad, when this occurs, they take it practically with glee and so they scold and condemn the maleficence of their parents or of their fatherland and they do so before one and all, and this is so that they themselves might be excused by all the others regarding their own shortcomings and that these might be reckoned on the tab of this prior ignominy, namely that they themselves were short-changed. Wherefore it also occurs that they take things *[346b]* too far with their criticisms and add in their own obscure intimations that they have made up and then blended these in together with everything else, matters that are unavoidable in life. But good men seek to conceal such things and force themselves that they find praise – and this despite the fact that they may have been aggravated by their parents or their fatherland due to their having suffered unrighteously – and so they admonish themselves and reconcile themselves and, with this, they do force it upon themselves that they love and praise their own. And it also occurred quite often, I opine, that Simonides himself believed it to be necessary that he praise and eulogize some tyrant or some such fact of life such as this, and not from his own free will but through compulsion. And for this reason he also said to Pittacus: I, o Pittacus, don't scold and berate thee simply, perhaps, as if I were to be one who likes to cast aspersions. *"For I am quite satisfied and content with those who are not malefic nor wholly devoid of accomplishment – being informed of the Rights which undergird the civil state and make man healthy. I shan't scold such as he,"* for I'm not given to berating others with glee, *"the multitudes of fools are assuredly beyond human reckoning"* so that if anyone should enjoy the sport, he, then, is able to exercise it sufficiently that he cast his aspersions on these. *"Everything is beauteous which has not become mixed with the malefic."* He didn't mean to say this so as if he were to say: everything is white that *[d]* hasn't been mixed with black, for this, indeed, would be comical in every way; rather he wants to say that he lets himself be quite satisfied with the middling, the run of the mill, that he doesn't find fault with this. And he is not searching, says he, an unassailable man amongst all of us who break bread upon this widely peopled earth.

If I find him, then you will know of it. So that I don't want to praise anyone, rather I'm quite content if everyone just holds himself or herself to a middle course and doesn't do anything bad. Therefore I shall praise and love them all – and here he actually goes way out of his way, so far as to bring it to a T in that, using the slang of Mytilene, he says, looking right at Pittacus: *I praise and love them one and all, they who bring no maleficence to consummation,* and here one needs to hold on inwardly with these words: *sans peur et sans reproche* – and I do so out of my own free choice, for there are also others whom I praise and love against my will. You, now, if only you would have said something that's true on the average and something that is comprehensible,[84] o Pittacus, I never would have scolded you then, but now you're fooling yourself all too much and this regarding the most important matters, and yet you believe that you've said something that is true, therefore I scold and berate you. With such an opinion, o Prodicus and Protagoras, said I, I fancy that Simonides composed this poem. ~   *<32.~347b]*

Hereupon Hippias said: Well done! – Socrates, I fancy that you have also clarified the meaning of this ode and, in like fashion, I too have something I might say on it, something that is quite beauteous, and I would like to address all of you with it, if you don't mind. ~ Oh sure, said Alcibiades, namely, afterwards. But now Protagoras and Socrates need to keep to their agreement that either, if Protagoras still wants to question Socrates regarding anything, Socrates shall answer him; or, if not, he then shall answer Socrates' questions.   *[c]* ~ To this I said: I for my part leave this up to Protagoras, whether he prefers to question or to answer; but whichever it may be let's leave all the poetic allusions and such impossible classical studies out of it; but that, Protagoras, regarding which I first questioned you, this is what I should find most pleasing – if you and I brought our investigation to a conclusion regarding this. For I fancy that holding discourse regarding the classics, be they song or poetry, this has too great a similarity to the banquets that one finds by the uneducated and commoner sort of men. For these too are incapable of making conversation with one another whilst imbibing and due to their lack of cultivation their own voices are left mute and they, speechless; and so they put their trust in the flutists and hire out these and others for

---

[84] This harangue of Socrates is truly hard to make sense of, though easier once one sees that he's intent upon breaking every rule of interpretation and swing outrageously from one extreme to the next (saying much that is true and a good bit of seeming nonsense) – and note that his reply could hardly be seen as being a good example for Protagoras to follow in giving "short answers"! As a whole, I would venture to say that it all makes perfect sense.

a pretty penny, that their entertainment and intercourse consists in listening to these foreign voices[85] as they themselves have nothing that they might articulate. But where there are good, noble and well-educated tipplers coming together – you won't find any flutists there, nor dancers, nor those who beat on chimes; rather these you find discoursing together with one another and possessing a sufficiency unto themselves without any need of such clowns and amusing entertainers, rather by exercising their own voices and each one taking his turn, now to speak, now to listen to the others – and doing both with a most respectful demeanor – and this *no matter* how   *[e]* many bottles of wine there are which stand open! So that there's no need at all for foreign voices nor for the poets, rather, just as here with us, that the majority of us do profess our renown and fame, that we are men who know how to hold our own in discourse and we don't require any foreign voices nor poets, people whom one is incapable of cross-examining regarding what they say, as those who bring their speeches up for discussion waver to and fro, some saying that they meant things this way, others maintaining that, no, they meant it some other way – and so they are incapable of laying out the matter at hand; but such a discussion we turn away from, that rather we ourselves prefer that we make our own speeches and allow each in turn to probe them and to be probed. Such, I fancy, is the preferable *modus* that we might imitate and, thus, leaving the poets aside, we speak our own minds with one another and so investigate into truth, and also into ourselves. If you want, then, that you question me yet further – so, I am ready to place myself before you and answer; or if you prefer to stand before me, so the object of our prior conversation, the conversation having been broken off, might now be brought to its conclusion. ~ To this and to similar entreaties that I made   *[348b]* Protagoras refused to clarify which of the two roles he wanted to take up. Therefore Alcibiades turned to Callias and said: How is this, Callias? Do you fancy that Protagoras is behaving properly in that he won't give Socrates any clear answer as to whether he is ready to take his turn and stand up before Socrates and answer his questions? I fancy that he's not, he either should continue on with the conversation or he should say that he doesn't want to continue it so that we might know what we shall do next, and if not with him then perhaps Socrates might continue on with someone else, or whoever else it

---

[85] Note the irony: not only is Protagoras spoken of at the start as a *foreigner*, but the conversation has *already* gotten rather out of hand; as regards becoming speechless, this is the fate of Protagoras toward the end of this dialogue, just as Callicles will experience the same in *Gorgias*. Note as well the relation to the opening of the *Symposium*.

may be who might find pleasure in continuing to converse with any one of us. And now, as he was shamed, as it seemed to me, that Alcibiades had said this, and Alcibiades along with most everyone else pleaded with him that he answer, so, finally he made himself comfortable with continuing the conversation and he specified that I might question him and now he wanted to answer me.   *<33.~348c3]*

I started off, then, by saying: But just don't believe, Protagoras, that I have any other purpose to my questioning other than that we investigate thoroughly into that regarding which I am in such a quandary. For I believe that Homer was quite right in his assertion when he said: *"Where two wander forth together, there the one notices something, and the other, something else"* – for in this way all of us are better provisioned for every undertaking, speech and investigation. That, indeed, the individual, if he notices something, so he goes about seeking all around until he happens upon someone to whom he shows what he has discovered so that with him he may establish a solid foundation. And, so too, it pleases me exceedingly that I discuss this with you, that you are the one whom I prefer over all others as I believe that you not only are best in everything else which well becomes a righteous man to reflect upon – that you are best able to place these very things in their proper relationships – but most particularly this matter that touches upon virtue itself. For who else other than you? As not only do you yourself believe that you are good and noble – just as others do, others who, indeed, are themselves totally righteous individuals; but these others are incapable of making anyone else to be so. But you are not only a person of consequence who's made his mark on the world, but rather, moreover, you make others that they too be such; and you have such an assurance in your own abilities that whereas the other sophists all cover up and hide their profession, you call out publicly proclaiming yourself before all Hellenes and so name yourself as being a sophist, that you are *[349a]* a teacher in virtue and you profess to share in this consummation and are, indeed, the first that expects monetary recompense[86] for your services. How should one possibly do otherwise than call upon you to investigate such things, to question and examine these matters and to receive your advice. Certainly, there is no way around it. And so even now I still wish that that regarding which I questioned you earlier, that in part you start at the beginning and refresh my memory and in part bring this conversation further along, that we might investigate this matter together. But I believe that this was the question:

---

[86] Note: *Gorgias* 520e (p. 345): The abomination of taking money for lessons in virtue!

whether wisdom and mindfulness and courage and righteousness and piety, whether these are only five different names for one matter, or whether each of these names points at a particular concept that underlies it and is its own matter – and, then, each has its own special operation so that each one is not like the others. Now, you had said that these would not be different names of a one, rather each of these names would have its own particular matter that underlies it – and all of these would be parts of virtue, not as the parts of gold are similar one to another and all are similar to the whole of which they are the parts but, rather, as the parts of the face are dissimilar to the whole face of which they are the parts, and also are dissimilar one to the other and that each one has its own particular operation. Do you still fancy this to be even so as before, so say it; but if it's otherwise, so clarify this for me. For I won't make you responsible now if you maintain something other than before in that I wouldn't be amazed that you were only probing me earlier and putting me to the test and, so, would have only said what you then said for this reason. ~ I say to you, Socrates, said he, that all of these are indeed   *<34.~349d]* parts of virtue and the four others are quite close to one another, but courage is very much different from all the rest. But that I am speaking aright, you are able to recognize this from the following. Namely, you will find many individuals who are very unrighteous and infamous, quite unrestrained and lacking in all understanding, but yet they are still worthy of admiration for their courageousness. ~ Hold it right there, said I, for what you have said, it is well worthwhile that we examine it. Do you call those who are courageous daring or something other? ~ And also brazen in that they go boldly forward where no man has gone before. ~ So come now! do you say that virtue would be something beauteous? and that you proffer yourself to be a teacher in that which is beauteous? ~ And, indeed, said he, in that which is most beautiful of all, if then, I haven't lost my mind. ~ Whether perhaps, then, said I, that a few things are bad regarding virtue and the rest are beauteous? or everything is beauteous? ~ Everything is beauteous through and through, as much as ever is possible. ~ Do you also know who they would be, those who dare to jump into the ocean? ~ Oh sure, those who can swim. ~ *[350a]* Because they understand it, or due to some other cause? ~ Because they understand it. ~ And who are they, those who dare to fight riding upon the horses into battle? the horsemen or those who have never ridden? ~ The horsemen. ~ And who fights most daringly with the short shields? the light infantry or some others? ~ The former, said he, and in general in all of the other things, if this is what you are leading up to, those who are informed and understand the matter are more daring than those who are not so informed and lack such understanding, and once they have learned the matter they become more daring than they were before they had learnt it. ~ And have you also seen such as these, people who are uninformed in all of these things but are ready and daring to do anything? ~ Oh sure, said he, and very daring. ~ And are these daredevils also courageous? ~ Then it would well be, said he, that courage would be something very bad, for these people are nuts. ~ What, then, was it that you said regarding those who are courageous, said I, wasn't it that they have daring? ~ And I also say that now as well. ~ *[350c]* But these, said I, these who are daring in this manner, these don't seem to be courageous, rather they are nuts? And earlier, there the wisest were also the most daring, and if they were the most daring, then too, they were the most courageous? And so, in accord with this speech, wisdom would be courage? ~ That's not right, said he; you've distorted what I said in answer to your questions. When you asked me if the courageous would be daring, this I answered in the affirmative; whether or not the daring are also courageous, this you haven't yet asked me. For if you would have asked me this, then I would have answered you: not all of them. But that the courageous wouldn't also be daring and that I would have made this assertion in error, this you haven't proven to be the case anywhere at all. Accordingly you have only shown that those who are informed regarding some matter are more daring in its pursuit than they themselves were earlier and, so too, more daring than others who are not informed, and therefore you opine: wisdom would now be the same as courage. But if you're going to turn everything around in this manner then you would also be capable of believing that strength would be wisdom. For, firstly, if you were to ask me and set me *[e]* up for your tricky maneuver – whether those who are strong would be powerful, so I would say "yes"; and then you'd ask whether those who are informed as regards fighting are more powerful than those who are not so informed and also, once these have learned it whether they are not more powerful than before they had learnt it – and to these questions I likewise would answer affirmatively. And after I had admitted all of this you would then be able to turn around with even this same proof and say that according to my admissions wisdom would be strength. But I don't at all agree that those who are powerful are necessarily strong, rather that the strong are powerful – for power and strength are not one and the same, for the former, power, may also come to be through knowledge, but also equally well due to insanity or because of the passions of the soul, but strength arises from the natural well-being and from the proper nutrition of the body. So too with our earlier case it is not so that daring and courage are one and the same – so that, indeed, it does follow that the courageous are daring; but it's not necessarily so that the daring are always courageous. For daring also comes to be in people through art or from insanity or from some passion of the soul, just as it was with power; but courageousness arises from the well-being and the proper nurturing of the soul. ~ Do you say, then, Protagoras,   <35.~351b] said I, that some people live well but others live poorly? ~ He answered affirmatively. ~ Do you now fancy, perhaps, that someone lives well if he suffers and is living in pain? ~ No. ~ But how about this? – if he comes to the end of his life having lived through nothing but pleasure? Do you fancy one such as this to have lived well? ~ Yes, this is living well. ~ Hence, living in pleasure is good but living in displeasure is bad? ~ Namely, said he, if one lives by finding pleasure in the beautiful. ~ How's that, Protagoras? Don't you like most everyone else call a few things that are pleasurable to be bad and a few things that are painful to be good? I mean, namely, insofar as it is pleasurable whether it wouldn't be to that extent good and not that something else arises from it? – and, on the other side, as regards the painful, whether it is bad insofar as it is painful? ~ I don't know, Socrates, said he, whether I should answer you in the unqualified *[d]* way in which you have posed your question – that everything that is pleasurable is good and everything painful bad. Rather, I'd fancy it to be a much surer answer not only in relation to the present question but likewise in reference to the rest of my life as a whole that I say that there are a few things amongst the pleasurable that are not good and, on the other side, a few things amongst the painful that are not bad, others that are and, thirdly, some things that are neither of both, neither good nor bad.[87] ~ But you call that pleasurable, said I, that which generates a pleasing sensation or wherein one finds enjoyment. ~ Indeed, said he. ~ This, then, is what I'm getting at, said I, whether or not it is good insofar as it is pleasurable and whether this "being pleased" is itself something that is good? ~ To this he said: Let's examine this and take a good look, as you yourself always say, and if the investigation seems to befit the matter and if it shows itself that the good and the pleasurable are one and the same, then we want to be unified in maintaining this, but if not, then we shall dispute it. ~ Would you like, now, said I, that you lead the discussion onward? –

---

[87] Cf. *Lysis* 216d (p. 95). Note as well the four sweeping generalizations: *Lysis* – that love is of the beautiful; *Protagoras* – that living in pleasure is good; *Charmides* – that doing good is mindfulness, 164a (p. 185); and *Meno* – that virtue is to delight oneself in beauty and being capable of it, 77b (p. 471).

or shall I? ~ It goes without saying, said he, that you are the one leading it, for you are the one directing this speech. ~ Perhaps then, said I, it shall become obvious to us in the following manner. *[352a]* Just as it is, namely, if someone should examine a person in respect to his health or some other physical attribute and so he investigates by observing his features, and if at first he only would see his face and his hands, then he certainly would say to him: Come over here and expose your chest, that I might examine your chest and your back, show me these that I shall be able to examine you even more precisely; and this is approximately what I find lacking in our investigation and I would like – now that I have observed how you think in regards to the beautiful and the good – I would like to say to you even as it was above: Come here, Protagoras! Uncover for me as well your convictions regarding the following: where do you place knowledge, do you think about knowledge in a similar fashion as do the majority of mankind, or differently? The majority, namely, think about knowledge approximately so: that it is not something that is strong, nor is it something which leads and directs man, much less does it rule man; and so they respect it accordingly and are of the opinion that more often than not, even though human beings have "some" knowledge, still, it does not rule, rather something else – sometimes anger, sometimes pleasure, sometimes displeasure, and on occasion also love, often enough, though, it is fear – so that, *[c]* obviously, they think about knowledge as if it were to be some miserable weakling that lets itself be dragged about by all of these others. Do you also fancy that it be something like this, or is it much more the case that knowledge is something beauteous which does well rule human beings? – and once man has recognized what is good and what bad then he isn't compelled by anything else that he would do something other than that, what his knowledge commands him to do, rather right insight would be sufficiently strong that it helps man overcome all of the rest? ~ So I fancy it, was his answer, just as you say, Socrates; and moreover it would be for me, if for anyone at all, quite unbecoming to maintain anything else other than that wisdom and knowledge would be the mightiest of all that is human. ~ Very well spoken, said I, and very true. But then, you also know that most people don't believe this, what you and I have said, rather they say that there are many who despite that they recognize very well what the better thing to do is, yet they don't want to do it despite that they are perfectly able to do so, rather they do something else. And I have asked many such people: What, then, might well be the cause for this? – and all of them have told me that they were *overcome* by pleasure or by displeasure or from one of the others that I just enumerated, and that, thus, they were compelled to do just as they did. ~ Well, people say all kinds of things, Socrates, which things are not necessarily right. ~ So come now and make *[353a]* the attempt with me to persuade these people and to teach them – what, then, is this, what they call being overcome by pleasure, and wherefore is it that they do not do what would be better – for, indeed, they have recognized that it would be better. Perhaps, if we just were to say to them: You people are wrong and you have lost your bearings, then they might question us: O Socrates and Protagoras, if it should be that our situation is other than as we say that it is and that we are not overcome by [our desires for] pleasure, well, what is it then, and how do you explain this? But do tell us! ~ But, o Socrates, said Protagoras, why should we even bring the opinions of such people into our considerations at all, these people who say whatever comes into their minds? ~ I simply believe, said I, that this shall help us somewhat so that we discover how courage actually correlates to the other parts of virtue. Do you keep to that upon which we just agreed, that I should lead the conversation, so follow me thither where I believe that the matter shall present itself most clearly. But if you don't want to do this then I also want that we just let things be, if this is your preference. ~ No, said he, you are quite right; just bring this to a conclusion as you have started off in this direction. *<36.~c]* ~ Once more then, if they question us: How do you two clarify this, what we call being too weak to resist and giving in to pleasure? – so I would say to them: Listen up! – Protagoras and I, we want to make an attempt to clarify this for you. You all do mean by this nothing other than what happens to you with such things as, for instance, when you are compelled by the pleasures of food or drink or whatever else you particularly enjoy – and this despite that you know quite well that to do so is bad for you – that you do it all the same? ~ They would answer affirmatively to this. ~ And isn't it true, we would then question them yet further, you and I: But why is it that you say that such things are bad? – perhaps it's for this reason, because these things promise momentary pleasure and each of them is pleasant in itself, or is it because they lead to sickness or some deficiency in the future and because they are the causes of many other things of this sort? Or, should it also be so even if there were not to be any such consequences – if, rather, they only brought you pleasure and enjoyment, should they still be bad nonetheless just because these things give pleasure, and no matter what it might be that one desires? Should we believe, Protagoras, that they would answer us with anything else other than that it would *not* be because of the pleasures that these things promise, rather, indeed, only due to the diseases and other such things which arise later? ~ I believe, said Protagoras, that this is how these people would answer. ~ And that which brings disease, this brings displeasure; and what brings poverty, this too brings displeasure? I think that they would admit as much. ~ Protagoras also had such an opinion. ~ Hence it seems to you, *ye people* who so answer, just as Protagoras and I maintain: *[354a]* that these things have no other cause in being bad other than that they eventually lead you into pain and rob you of other pleasures? – wouldn't they admit as much? ~ It seemed to the both of us to be so. ~ And if, now, we were to ask them about that which stands in contradistinction to this: Good people, you that also say that many things that are painful are yet good, don't you mean by this such things as vigorous exercise, field maneuvers, being treated by doctors with cutting and burning, medicine and fasts, that such things as these are good, though painful? – wouldn't they say "yes" to this? ~ It seemed to him also to be so. ~ Whether now, that they would call this good for this reason, because for the moment they cause the most intolerable sufferings and great pain and torment? – or is it because they have the eventual result of bringing about health and feelings of well-being for the body, not to mention the salvation of city-states, and conquest, and riches? They would certainly agree to the last of these, as I see it. ~ He also believed that they would agree. ~ Are, then, these things good for any other reason other than that they eventually lead to pleasure and drive away displeasure? – or would they have any other aim that they might put forward in relation to which they would call these things good, something other than pleasure or displeasure? I don't believe that they would have *[354c]* anything else that they might put forward. ~ I also don't believe that they would, said Protagoras. ~ Hence, you all make hunt upon that which brings you pleasure as that which is good, and you all flee from displeasure as from evil? Wouldn't they admit as much? ~ It seemed to him also to be like this. ~ This, then, is what you actually consider to be bad, displeasure; and pleasure is good – if, then, you people do indeed maintain that feeling-good would be bad in that instance if it should rob one of greater pleasures than those which it provides or if it should lead to greater displeasure than the pleasure that it brings. For if there were to be some other standpoint by which you might maintain that feeling-good would be bad and in relationship to some other goal, so then, you would be able to tell us what this would be, but you are unable to say anything other than this. ~ I too don't believe that they might tell us anything else other than this, said Protagoras. ~ And is it not also exactly the same way with what makes one feel awful? For, then too, they call feeling awful to be good if either it should prevent yet greater displeasure than it itself is or if it is preparatory to yet greater pleasures than the displeasure that it brings. For if, then, there were to be anything else that they might have in view – why it is that they call feeling awful to be good other than what I have stated, then they should be able to say what this is, but they are not able to say anything else. ~ You're totally right, said Protagoras. ~ And further, said I, if you people should yet question me, my curious cross-examiners: And why is it that you berate us to such an extent and from all different angles? – so then, I would answer them: Do have forbearance with me for firstly it is not at all easy to show you what, then, it actually would be, that which you call being overcome by pleasure – and, then too, the entire proof rests entirely upon understanding this. And moreover, you people still and yet have the freedom that you may call out and deny that   *[355a]* the good would be something other than that which consists in promoting pleasure, that is, if you all know of anything else that you might bring forward; and also that evil would be something other than that which brings displeasure. Or is it so that this is sufficient for all of you, that you spend your life in a pleasant manner and always avoid displeasure? If, now, this should suffice for you and you don't know of anything else that you might say, what else would be good and what evil – something that wouldn't simply reduce to these terms – well then, listen up to what follows. I say to all of you, namely, if this is how things correlate then that becomes a comical speech, what you all say: that a human being despite that he is cognizant of evil, that it truly is evil, nonetheless he does it and this totally irrespective that he stands free and that he need not do so, because you say he is driven by pleasure and is benumbed; and then you also say that a human being, though he has recognized what is good, still he tends to avoid doing it due to being caught up in momentary pleasures and overpowered by these. That   *<37.~355b]* this is comical, this shall become clear to you as soon as we leave off using this multiplicity of names: the pleasant and painful, and the good and evil; rather, as it has been shown that these may all be reduced to just two terms we now want to restate the situation using only two words: firstly, consistently saying good and evil and, then again, consistently saying pleasurable and painful. Laying this down as our foundation we now say that a person who has recognized evil, that it is evil, nonetheless he does it. If, now, someone were to question us: Why is this? – then we shall say: Because he is over-come. But what is it that overcame him? – so the former questioner asks; but now we aren't allowed anymore that we say: By pleasure, for this has received a different name and instead of pleasure we call it the good. So we answer this questioner and we say: Because he has become overcome. But by what? – he asks. By the good, by Zeus, this is what we have to say. Now, if he who is questioning us should enjoy making fun of us, well then, he would laugh and say: Truly *[d]* this is quite a comical matter, what you have told me, that a person who does evil and does so having recognized that it really is evil and despite the fact that he doesn't have to do it, still he does it – but why? – because he has been overcome by the good! By a good, he shall ask us, that is worthy or that is not worthy that it overcame the former evil? Obviously we would have to reply to him: From one that is not worthy; for otherwise he wouldn't have failed, he of whom we say that he was too weak to hold out against pleasure. And how is this, he might perhaps query us: Is then the maleficence of goodness or the goodness of maleficence unworthy? – is there, perhaps, any other reason other than this, because one should be greater and the other lesser? or that one would be more, the other less? We wouldn't be able to provide any other answer. Obviously, then, he shall say to us: Do you mean to say regarding this person who is overcome that someone has received a greater amount of evil for a lesser amount of good. So this would proceed, in such a manner. But now let us call back and review the same situation using the other two names, the pleasant and the unpleasant, and let's say – before we said that which was evil but now we shall say that which is unpleasant and, as before, recognizing that it isn't pleasant and being overcome by that which is pleasant; obviously again a pleasantness that is not worthy that it conquer. And what other valuation might one give in   *[356a]* comparing pleasure against displeasure other than the excess or deficiency of the one against the other, that is to say whichever is to be greater or smaller than the other, more or less, stronger or weaker? For if someone were yet to say to me: But, Socrates, there is really a great difference between the immediate momentary pleasure and that pleasure or displeasure which is only to occur in the future, so I would ask him: Does this difference consist in something other than pleasure or displeasure? – in no way does it consist in something other than these. Rather, as one who is informed as regards how to measure such things, lay out all of that which belongs together with the pleasant and all of that which belongs together with the unpleasant and taking into consideration what is distant and what close-by, lay all these together on the scales and then speak out the result, how do the scales tip? For if you are measuring pleasures against pleasures, then you always have to decide for that which is more and the larger, but if displeasures against displeasures then you take the smaller, what is less; but if you are measuring the pleasant against the unpleasant then you have to – should it be that the pleasant is greater than that which is unpleasant and no matter whether it be that what is closer is in opposition to what is further away or that what is further away is in opposition to what is closer – this, all the same, this is the activity that you have to choose, that by which the pleasant tips the scales; but if it should be that the unpleasant has the greater weight in the balance, this, then, is what you have to avoid doing. Is this how things correlate, o ye people? this is what I would say; and I know that they wouldn't know what else might be said. ~ Protagoras fancied this also. ~ If this, *[c]* now, is the way that things correlate, then supply me with answers to the following – this is what I shall say next. Does the same face appear to you when it is close-by[88] to be larger, and when you see it from far away to be smaller, or not? ~ They would answer in the affirmative, said Protagoras. ~ And that which is thick and the numerous, are they not even so? And the same tone, is it not louder when closer but weaker when further away? ~ They would answer "Yes." ~ If now, our happiness should be based upon this – that we would draw large lines and seek to accomplish such, but that we should avoid the smaller ones and not draw things diminutively: what, then, would show itself as being the salvation of our lives? – the art of measuring or the power of mere semblance? Or wouldn't it be so that the latter of these would certainly lead us into errors and would make us such that quite often we would have to turn things topsy-turvy, that the lower would necessarily reverse itself and go up and become the highest in regards to the same matter and that, again, we would grasp other resolutions in our choices regarding what is greater and what smaller? – but, quite to the contrary of this, the art of measuring would make it so that the deceptive appearances would no longer work upon us, rather this art would make precise *[e]* measurements regarding the truth of the soul which then would abide in truth, creating tranquility and, thus, in this manner this art brings salvation into our lives. Wouldn't the people have to recognize this, that in such a case the measuring arts would have to bring salvation into our lives, or would they name something else? ~ The art of measuring, Protagoras admitted it. ~ But how about if our lives' salvation were to be dependent upon the choice between even or odd numbers – from one of the two of these, whichever one would be right, to choose betwixt them which of them is either larger or which smaller in comparisons of every variety both with themselves and with the other, and no matter whether or not they be nearer to us or

---

[88] See *Parmenides* – footnote #108, 130d (p. 211).

further away – what, then, would be the salvation of our lives? Wouldn't it also be some sort of knowing? – and wouldn't it also be, since here we also are dealing with magnitude and diminutiveness, wouldn't it also be some sort of measuring art? And as it would have to do with the even and the odd, could it well be possible that it would be any other than the art of calculation? Wouldn't the people have to be one in admitting this, or not? ~ Protagoras was also of the belief that they would have to admit as much. ~ Good, o ye people, as it has now been sufficiently demonstrated that the salvation of our lives is dependent upon making the right choice between that which brings pleasure and that which brings displeasure, which is more and which less, which is larger and which smaller, whether they be close-by or far-off in the distance – and doesn't this also show itself as being a sort of measuring as it does have to investigate into magnitude, diminutiveness and equality, the one against the other.   *[357b]* ~ Yes, necessarily. ~ And if it should be a measuring, then too, necessarily, it is an art and is knowledge? ~ They would agree to this. ~ What type of an art and what sort of knowledge it shall need to be, this we want to look into a bit later; but that it is indeed some sort of knowing, this has been sufficiently demonstrated by what Protagoras and I have brought forward regarding that about which you had questioned us. You people questioned us, namely, as you may have forgotten how it was that we got off onto this tangent back then when Protagoras and I had reached a mutual understanding and were one in agreeing to the fact that there would be nothing that is stronger than knowledge and that wherever knowledge exists it would rule over the passions and over everything else; but you wanted to maintain that often the passions would rule and that they even rule over a person who knows better; but we didn't want to give in to this opinion of yours; and then you questioned us: O Protagoras and Socrates, if this shouldn't be the case that one becomes overcome by pleasure, well, so tell us then what this may well be and how   *[357d]* do you clarify this? If, then, we had said to you straight-away that such would be nothing else other than a lack in understanding, well, you would then have had a good laugh; but now, if you still want to have a good laugh on us, so you'll also have to have a good laugh on yourselves – for you too have been one in affirming that whoever might fail by the choice between pleasure and displeasure, that is to say between the choice of good and evil, he fails due to a deficiency in knowing – and not just in knowing, rather you also have admitted that it would have to be with some sort of measuring knowledge. But any deeds which fail and go astray due to a lack of knowledge, these, you yourselves do know, these are those that are accomplished with a lack of understanding, so that saying that these fail due to a weakness and that one was overcome by passion, this would be the greatest misunderstanding; and it is just for such people that Protagoras here claims to be a physician, and Prodicus and Hippias as well. But as you people opine that such failures result from something other than from a lack in understanding, so neither do you yourselves go and learn from these teachers, the sophists, nor do you send your sons to them, as if such a thing wouldn't be teachable; rather you keep your purse strings firmly knotted and are tight-fisted with your capital, not wanting to deliver it over to these, and in this you show yourselves as being awful parents and a disgrace to your homeland, that you don't subscribe for lessons from these leaders in civic virtue. This, then, is what we would have given in answer to these people.   *<38.~358a]*

But now I should like to ask the both of you, Hippias and Prodicus, whether you also agree with Protagoras and me, for you too share in this community and in our conversation, whether or not you also agree with what I have said, whether it might be that I have spoken truly or without truth. ~ Everyone held that what had been spoken was right in excess to all measuring. ~ You concur, then, with the postulate that what is pleasurable is good and what is painful is evil? But in this regard I won't tolerate that Prodicus' differentiation of words has any relevance. That is, what I mean you may call it whatever you like: pleasurable or enjoyable or satisfying or whatever and however you might prefer to designate it; most worthy Prodicus, answer my question in relation to what I want. ~ Laughing, Prodicus admitted now that he was in agreement, and the others did also. ~ But how now, comrades! said I, what's next? – are not those deeds that relate to this, the life of pleasure that entails no pain, are they not also themselves beauteous? – and isn't every deed that is beautiful also good and useful? ~ This seemed to them to be so as well. ~ If now, that which is pleasurable is good, then it is affirmatively so that nobody, be it that he knows better or whether he only believes to know better – that nobody, if there would be something better than what he is doing and that it also would be possible that he   *[358c]* might do this other, nobody would remain content with his former actions if he might do something that is better; and this being 'too weak' against one's very self is, thus, nothing other than a deficiency in understanding, and being in command of one's self is nothing other than wisdom. ~ To this, everyone gave applause. ~ How now? – don't you name this as a deficiency in understanding that one has false opinions and that one fools oneself regarding important things? ~ To this, too, they all were in agreement. ~ And isn't it also true that nobody pursues an evil course out of his own free choice, nor too does one do anything that he holds as being evil? and that this, as it seems, doesn't at all lie in man's nature that he should want to pursue anything that he holds as being evil rather than pursue what is good; but if he shall be compelled to choose between two evils nobody would choose the greater if he might also choose the lesser? ~ All of this was apparent to all of them, one as well as the next. ~ How now? – said I, do you call something dread and fear? and indeed, just the same as I do? It is for your sake, Prodicus, that I say this – namely I understand with this the expectation of some evil, you may like to call this dread or fear. ~ Protagoras and Hippias said that such would be dread or fear; but Prodicus maintained to the contrary that it would only be dread and would not be fear. ~ It doesn't have anything to do with such distinctions, Prodicus, said I, rather it only has to *[358e]* do with this: if, then, what I have said heretofore is right, whether then any human being wants to pursue something if he is in dread of it and if, then, he also is able to choose to do something other, or whether this is impossible in consequence to that upon which we all are in agreement. For that in regards to which someone experiences dread, that, so we have been one in admitting, he holds as being evil, and nobody wants either to pursue such, nor do they want with good will that such be allowed to happen to them. ~   This, too, was affirmed by everyone. ~ If all of this, now, has been   *<39.~359a]* established, said I, o Prodicus and Hippias, so our Protagoras, indeed, may want to defend himself regarding what he said earlier in answer to my question. Not what he said at the very beginning, for then he maintained that of the five parts of virtue that exist, that none would be like the other and each would have its own operation – this is not what I am referring to, rather what he maintained afterwards. For later on he said something else in answer to the same query, namely, that four of them would indeed be quite close, one to the other, but that the one, courage, would be very different from all of the rest. And I would be able to recognize this, said he, from the following: You shall find, namely, Socrates, many individuals who are very unrighteous and infamous, quite unrestrained and lacking in all understanding, but yet they are still most worthy of admiration for their courageousness, and from this you may easily conclude that courage is very much different from the rest of the parts of virtue. And even then I was quite amazed and in wonder regarding this answer, but now I am even more amazed by it, after having established with all of you what we have just established. And so I asked him as to whether he says that the courageous would also be daring and he replied, not only this but brazen as well.   *[359c]*

Do you remember saying this, Protagoras, said I, that this is what you answered. ~ He concurred. ~ So come now, said I, and tell us what it is — that regarding which you opine that these courageous individuals are so daring in their behavior? — perhaps, namely, the same as the cowards? ~ No, said he. ~ Hence, upon something different? ~ Yes, said he. ~ And are the cowards running toward what is harmless and the courageous running toward the fearful? ~ This is what the people say, Socrates, such was his answer. ~ That may well be, said I, but that's not what I was asking; rather you, what is it that you say that the courageous are pursuing so brazenly — whether they are head to head with the dreadful in that they venture forth into what they hold as being dreadful, or upon that which is not dreadful? ~ But this, said he, has been proven to be quite impossible in accordance with what was said earlier. ~ In this too, said I, you are totally right, so that if this is rightly proven then nobody pursues something that he holds as being fearful as, indeed, this "being incapable of ruling oneself" was found to be a lack of understanding. ~ He admitted as much. ~ But that toward which one's temperament is well disposed, each and every person goes forth, cowards as well as the courageous, and in this manner both of them are pursuing the same, both cowards and heroes. But nonetheless, said he, these are totally opposite things, Socrates, that toward which the   *[e]* courageous are running and that toward which the cowards run. Right away, for instance, when the army marches off into war, the brave ones go forth quite readily but the others don't want to go at all. ~ In that it is beautiful, said I, that they venture forth, or that it would be bad? ~ Beautiful, said he. ~ And if it should be beautiful, said I, then it also would be good — this is what we agreed to earlier, for we agreed and were one in maintaining that all beautiful actions would be good. ~ That's right; and I myself have always thought that this would be so. ~ Very well, said I. But which of the two of them do you maintain would be the ones who do not want to go off *[360a]* into the battlefield? — if, then, the going is to be beautiful and good? ~ The cowards, said he. ~ And, said I, if it is to be good and beautiful shall it not also be pleasurable? ~ That, at least, said he, fits in well here also. ~ Hence, knowing full well that doing so is more beauteous, better and more pleasurable than not doing so, the cowards still don't want to do it? ~ But this too, if we were to admit this, said he, this would destroy what we agreed upon above. ~ And how is it with the courageous, I questioned him, don't they pursue what is more beauteous, better and more pleasurable? ~ It is necessary, said he, that we carry through with this [proposition]. ~ Thus altogether, if the courageous have any trepidation, this isn't any

malefic fear; and if they are daring, this isn't a malefic brazenness? ~
Totally right, said he. ~ And, if not malefic, then both would be
beauteous? ~ He admitted it. ~ And, if beauteous, then good also?
~ Yes. ~ And shall not, to the contrary, the cowards and the
audacious and the crazy daredevils, shall these not have trepidation
with a malefic fearfulness and a daring with an awful daringness? ~
He admitted as much. ~ And could they possibly be so daring from
any cause other than their lack of knowledge and understanding? ~
This is how it would have to correlate, said he. ~ And how? – that
through which cowards act cowardly, do you name this cowardice or
courage? ~ Cowardice, that goes without saying, said he. ~ And
haven't we seen that they are cowards due to their lack of knowledge
regarding what is fearful? ~ Indeed, said he. ~ Hence, due to this
lack of knowledge they are cowards? ~ He admitted as much. ~ And
that through which they act cowardly, that, you do concur, is
cowardice? ~ He said "Yes." ~ Hence, it is indeed the lack of
knowledge regarding what is fearful and what is not fearful, *[360d]*
this is cowardice? ~ He nodded his consent. ~ But then cowardice,
said I, is indeed the opposite of courage? ~ He answered in the
affirmative. ~ And is it not so that being acquainted with what is
fearful and what is not fearful, that being unacquainted with these
things is the opposite? ~ To this also, his consent was given by a nod.
~ And not being acquainted with such things was cowardice? ~ At
this point it was only with great effort that he managed to supply a
nod. ~ So, in accordance to all of this, it is wisdom of what is fearful
and not fearful that is courage – as this is the opposite from being
uninformed regarding these things. ~ To this he no longer wanted
to respond at all, not even by nodding, rather he was speechless and
was stock still. ~ So, Protagoras, said I, you neither say yea nor nay
to what I have asked you? ~ If only you might just bring this to a
conclusion alone, said he. ~ Only one thing more, said I, do I have
to question you about: Whether now it also seems to you that there
are some individuals who are quite lacking in understanding and yet
admirably courageous? ~ You seem to be especially interested,
Socrates, that I should answer this question. So then, I want to be
courteous and so I say that in accordance to what we have established
with one another earlier, this seems to be impossible. ~ *<40.~361a]*
In no way, said I, do I question about all of this with any other intent
other than *laying a foundation* in regards to how it all actually
correlates with virtue, and what virtue itself may well be. For so
much I do know: if this, what virtue itself is, if first we only could
make this out, so then everything else would quickly be determined,
all of those things that you and I have been discussing to such great

lengths: my contention that virtue would not be teachable and yours that it would be teachable. And now, it seems to me that the result of our conversation is doing a proper "about-face," as if it were to be a human being and it wants to deride us and have a great laugh at our expense – and if it were able to speak it would say to us: You most amazing people, Socrates and Protagoras! – you, Socrates, you who maintained previously that virtue would not be teachable, now you're pressing the point that itself goes contrary to what you maintained in that you are seeking to show that everything having to do with virtue is knowledge: righteousness, mindfulness and courage – and in this manner virtue would seem to get the most reliable foundation that it is teachable. For if virtue were to be something other than knowledge, that which Protagoras had undertaken as his claim, so it is most certain that it would not be teachable. But now, if it shall be revealed that virtue is knowledge – that upon which you are so *[c]* insistent – well, it would be totally amazing, then, if it should not be teachable. And again from the other side, Protagoras, he who previously maintained that it would be teachable, seems now to be doing everything possible to maintain to the contrary that virtue should be most anything else at all, just not knowledge, and in this wise it would be least likely that virtue is teachable. Now I, Protagoras, in that I see how horribly all of this has become jumbled together and that the lowest is up on top, I am more eager than ever that we bring clarity to this matter and I should very much wish, now that we have taken the trouble of going through all of this, if we might be able to return again to our central question as regards what virtue is itself – and then we could start afresh on our discussion as to whether or not it would be teachable – so that it wouldn't happen to us again as it did with Epimetheus, he who only after the fact thought about our predicament, that he also is cheating us in our present indagations with his sly cunning and getting the last laugh at our expense, just as he did by his earlier distribution, as you said. And then too, in respect to your historical myth it was Prometheus, he who thinks first, who pleased me the best; and this may be because I even find myself to be like him in that I too would like to reflect on the whole of life first – and so I concern myself with these things – and if you only should be willing, then, as I already said earlier on, I would love to continue to investigate these things together with you. ~ To this Protagoras said: I for my part, Socrates, have nothing but the highest praise for your zeal and for the manner in which you carry through the discussion – for, then too, for the rest I think to be no evil person and the least envious of all of mankind. And as I also have said of you already before many others, that amongst all of those with whom I have been acquainted I treasure you most highly and especially so of those your age – and I would append onto this that I should not at all be amazed if sooner or later your name shall be inscribed amongst those most famed for wisdom. Regarding all the rest we want, if you like, to continue with our discussion at a later juncture, for now it is time that I move on to something else. *[362a]* ~ Good, said I, we want to hold to this, as you opine. For I too have been detained here already a long while and, as I already said, it's time I was going and only for the sake of Callias the fair, as an especial favor to this beauty, for him I have tarried here so long. These speeches were traded and, so, we all went on our way.

****

Charmides

for Anupam.

"O Weib, vertraue auf mein Wort: Es kommt die Zeit, da ihr weder auf diesem Berge noch in Jerusalem dem Vater euren Dienst verrichten werdet. Eure Anbetung gilt einem Wesen, das sich eurem Bewußtsein entzieht.   Unser gottesdienstliches Leben geht mit dem erkennenden Bewußtsein Hand in Hand. Deshalb mußte sich unter den Juden das wahre Heil der Menscheit vorbereiten. Einmal kommt eine Zeit, und die ist schon da, dann werden die wahren Gottesverehrer dem Vater mit der Kraft des Geistes und in der Erkenntnis der Wahrheit dienen. Und der Vater verlangt nach den Menschen, die ihm auf diese Weise dienen. Gott ist Geist, und die ihn anbeten, müssen es mit der Kraft des Geistes und in der Erkenntns der Wahrheit tun."

John IV – Emil Bock's translation

O woman, have faith in my word.   There will come a time when neither upon this mountain, nor in Jerusalem – in no such a place shall your worship service for the Father be celebrated. Your prayers belong to an Essence that is withdrawing from your consciousness. Our life service to the divine Will, this goes hand in hand with ego-consciousness that is cognizant of what it does. It is for this reason that the true salvation of mankind was prepared within the Jewish nation. There will come a time, and already it is at hand – then shall those who truly honor and serve the Father do so in the full power of the spirit, and in knowledge of the truth. And the Father is longing for such people, those who serve Him in this manner. God is spirit and those who offer up prayers unto Him have to do so in the spirit's power and with the recognition of truth.

Charmides – Sections:

Charmides

****

SOCRATES NARRATES

<1.~153a]

I had only just returned on the previous evening from the army encamped before Potidaea and, after having been away for such a long span of time, I was feeling really good now to be out walking and *en route* to one of the gymnasiums, my old hunting grounds. So it was that I arrived at the palaestra of Taureaus which stands across from the temple, Basile; and arriving there I met up with a gracious many – some, indeed, whom I didn't at all recognize, but being well-acquainted with the majority. And as, then, they saw me walking in quite unexpectedly, so right off they called out their greetings to me from a distance: the one from here, another from over there. But Chaerephon, who's always so abrupt, he sprang up from his *[b3]* companions and ran right over to me, taking me by the hand and spoke: O Socrates, how is it that you have come back from the battle? Shortly before we rode off from there the fight began to rage, about which everyone here has only just begun to hear tell. ~ I answered him: So, as you see. ~ At least, said he, a report has it that this battle would have been very fierce, and that many notable men were left in the midst. ~ And very accurate, said I, is this report. ~ You too were there, weren't you? – he asked. ~ I was there. ~ But do come hither and take a seat here with us, that you tell us all about it as we've only heard rumors and nothing at all precise. ~ And with this he led me over to sit next to Critias, son of Callaeschrus. In taking my seat I gave greetings to Critias and to all of the others, and then I told them all about my stint in the army, answering whatever anyone asked me: the one would ask regarding this, another about something else. *[d]* As we finally had our fill of such topics, so I for my part inquired as to how matters might stand hereabouts in regards to *philosophia*, and also as regards the younger generation – whether there might be any who stand out in their understanding or in beauty or both, whether any excelled since my lengthy absence. Critias, whose eyes had been directed at the door through which a troupe of intrepid youngsters came, driving one another inside, and with yet an even larger *[154a]* group venturing in behind them – he spoke up: In regards to our newly hatched beauties, o Socrates, you shall, as it seems to me: you shall see for yourself soon enough. For even these who are entering in are his harbingers and, indeed, they all are enthralled in him – he who is held up as being the most beauteous of all, at least for now, and, certainly, he too must be nearby, on his way hither. ~ Who, I asked: who is he then? and of what family? It's almost a certitude

173

that you're already acquainted, said he; but he wasn't yet amongst the youngsters before your departure – *Charmides*, my cousin, the son of my uncle, Glaucon. ~ Indeed, I do know him, by Zeus, said I.   *[b]* Already back then he wasn't bad at all, although yet a child; but by now, I'd say, he must be a fully-grown young man. ~ Right away, said he – you shall see how big he's grown and how beautiful he's become. And just as he said this, Charmides also entered into the room. Now, as regards myself, friend, indeed it doesn't take a whole lot, for I am, when it comes to differentiating in beauty, like white chalk upon a white board: to me they all appear beauteous, anyone of this age. It follows: he also appeared to me as being totally worthy of wonder, both in his stature as well as for his beauty. But, then too, all of the others – it seemed to me that everyone had fallen for him, we all were taken aback by him and utterly befuddled as he entered. Likewise, he had many admirers amongst those following in after him. And that he should have made such an effect upon all of us older men, well *this* wasn't anything so astounding; singularly, though, I noted also the exact same thing amongst the other youngsters – that not a one of them was looking anywhere else! – not even the youngest amongst them, rather they all stared upon him as if he were a divine image. Then Chaerephon called out to me, saying: Now, Socrates, what's your impression of this youngster? *[154d]* Have you *ever* seen a prettier face? ~ Beyond all expectations, said I. ~ And yet, said he, if he were to remove his clothes, then you'd say that his face is nothing – so through and through beauteous is his *Gestalt*. And the others, too, they all said the same thing as Chaerephon. ~ Heracles, I cried out, how irresistible is your description of this person – if only there be added a small bit. ~ And what's that? asked Critias. ~ If he, said I, also in his soul, that it also would be so well formed. And such wouldn't be in the least bit out of place, Critias, since he has been brought up in your home. ~ Also in this respect, said he, is he very beauteous and good. ~ But now, said I, why don't we disrobe him even in this: that we place his soul up for viewing rather than his body. For then, since he's come of age, so there's no reason to exclude him from our conversation. ~ *[155a]* Most happily, said Critias. For then, he is very thoughtful and, then too, as some others and he too fancies it, quite the poet. ~ This fine trait, my dear Critias, said I, comes quite naturally into your family from long ago due to your ancestor, Solon. But what's holding you back from calling the young man over, that he might display himself? For even were it not the case that he's now full-grown, nonetheless there'd be nothing wrong in him partaking in our conversation in your presence as then, you are his guardian as well as being cousins.

~ Very well spoken, said he, and that's just what we want to do – and at once he commanded his servant: Go, call for Charmides and tell him that I'd like to introduce him to a physician on account of his ailment {*Übels*}, that about which he recently spoke to me, that he was suffering. He complained to me just recently, Critias explained to us, that his head would be pounding terribly when he arose in the morning. And then, where's the harm in your pretending as if you might know some remedy that's good for headaches? ~ Nothing at all, said I, if only he comes. ~ He won't disappoint us, said Critias. And indeed, he came rather promptly. But his arrival was a   *[155c]* scene of great comedy. For then each one of us, as we were all sitting together along a bench, each shoved the next one over to make room for Charmides so that he might take his seat next to him, and thus the two poor souls sitting on the ends, well – the first one had to stand up *pronto*, but the other fell plump upon the floor. As now he had arrived, so he took his seat between Critias and me. And already right from the start, friend, I became totally disoriented and my former pluck disserted me – *as if I* should be immune to him and able to speak lightly about this or that. But after this initial shock, as Critias explained to him that I would be the one who would know the cure, and then he turned toward me – I can't at all describe his expression and his eyes, and how he began to ask me, and all the while everyone in the Palaestra was converging around us, then, o dear God, somehow I caught a glimpse beneath his loose garments and I became enflamed, decimated and drawn out of myself – rather reflecting on Kydias, he who is so wise in respect to love and who painted poetic pictures regarding the lure of youth's beauty: *May some god help the fawn who wanders beneath the lion's gaze, that she not be devoured forthwith and rent asunder!* For I myself fancied to be torn into shreds, captured in the jaws of such a beast. All the same, as it was me whom he was questioning: Whether I might know of some remedy against headache? – so I, but only by the greatest exertion possible, I just managed in such an extremity to supply the answer: I know it. ~ What, then, he inquired of me, what is it? ~ To this I replied: Actually, it would be a leaf – but then there's also a word charm that belongs together with it: if one speaks the charm simultaneously with the application of the leaf, so this cure makes one totally healthy, through and through. But without the charm the leaf does nothing at all. ~ So then I shall, spoke   *[156a]* he, write down this charm of yours. ~ Even though I haven't been persuaded to tell it to you? – I asked him; or only if I have. ~ Laughing at my question he replied: Indeed, Socrates, only once you've been persuaded. ~ How nice, said I: you also know my name?

~ That would be really bad, said he, not to know your name since we youngsters are always talking about you; and I also still remember you from when I was yet a child and you came to pay a visit with Critias here. ~ It's very good of you, said I, that you do so. This also sparks my courage, that I am able to speak openly to you about this *mantra* – how it is constituted. For earlier on I admit, I was *[b]* somewhat at a loss, in what manner should I clarify its power. It is, namely, o Charmides, of this sort: that not only does it promote health for one's head, rather too – as you perhaps have already heard from good physicians: if, say, someone comes to them complaining of some malaise with his eyes, that they might say: It wouldn't be possible to undertake a cure merely for the eyes alone, rather they also would have to undertake measures for one's head too, if the proper functioning of the eyes is to be restored. And, then too, to believe that one might undertake to cure the head without simultaneously curing the entire body, this would be the greatest of follies. Accordingly, they now turn themselves and write up their prescriptions for the entire body, thus, both handling and healing the part right along with the whole. Or, haven't you taken any notice that this is how any decent physician speaks: that just this is the proper correlation. ~ Indeed, said he. ~ And would you fancy this as being well spoken and right? and do you accept this speech as stated? ~ Above everything else, said he. ~ Now I, since I heard him agreeing so readily to everything that I had said, so my courage was gaining ground and, little by little, my audacity returned as my powers grew. And so, I spoke: Even in this manner, now, o Charmides: the *[156d]* same thing applies with this maxim. But I've learned this out in the field from one of the physicians working amongst the Thracians from Zalmoxis – about whom, incidentally, it has also been said that they bestow immortality. Now, this Thracian spoke thus regarding what I said previously, that *in this* the Hellenic physicians are entirely right; but Zalmoxis our King, said he, He who is a God says: Just so as one wouldn't undertake healing the eyes unless the head also would be included, nor the head apart from the entire body, so too: not the body in exclusion from the soul; rather even this is the root cause why the Hellenic physicians are yet primitives in respect to their handling of the larger number of diseases, because, namely, they misconstrue the whole toward which their care should be directed and, then, due to this greater evil it's not possible that any of the other parts might truly be healthy. For then everything, said he, would spring forth from out of the soul – goodness and malignancy into the body and the entirety of man: it streams into him from out of the soul regions just as the eyes appear from out of the head. The former, then, would *[a]* have to be attended to first of all and, indeed, with the utmost care if one should expect any improvement in relation to the head, or to the body in its entirety. But the soul, my good man, said he, is to be taken care of by means of certain incantations, and these incantations would be the beautiful speeches. For it is through such speeches that mindfulness comes to be within the soul; and once this has been implanted and exists within, then matters become easy that one brings about health within the head and all of the rest of the body. As, thus, he was teaching me about his methods and the various incantations, he said that nobody should ever talk me into treating them – neither head nor toe – with his sort of medicine unless first off they have allowed an examination of their soul and only then, after the application of incantations for their soul, then only would I be allowed to proceed to heal with the other incantations. For even now, said he, this is the mistake which mankind tends to fall for, that they take on only one of these two sorts of doctoring totally cut off from the other. And with great severity did he command me forthwith that nobody at all, no matter how rich or admirable or beautiful he might be, from no one should I allow myself to be persuaded that I might do any other. Now, I gave him my oath, and, necessarily, I have to keep it, no matter what. And as for you – if you'd want that first off you deliver over to me your soul in accordance to this stranger's principles, that his incantations might be applied to it, so too, then, I shall also apply his methods upon your head. But if not, my dear Charmides, I really don't have a clue as to what I might do for you. ~

<2.~157d]

As now Critias heard me say this, so he spoke up saying: A good find, o Socrates, that's what these headaches would be for the young man if thereby it would be required that he improve his soul so that the state of his head might likewise be improved. Howsoever, I assure you that it's not only through his *Gestalt* that Charmides appears to stand out from all his schoolmates, rather too in even that element for which you claim the first incantation applies; but you claimed that it's for mindfulness? – isn't this true? ~ Just so, said I. ~ Well then you should know, said he, that he's considered as being the most prudent person by far amongst all of our youngsters – just as in regards to everything else, in as much as his age allows it, he doesn't play second fiddle to anyone! ~ *Indeed*, said I; and such is only to be expected, o Charmides, that you would stand out above all the rest in such things as these. For I don't believe that anyone here amongst us would easily be able to come up with an intersection in two family lines that would be the equal in it's sparkling reputation and out of which a better and more noble offspring would be expected – as the two are from which you draw your heritage. For the nobility on your father's side which, indeed, overlaps with that of Critias here, son of Dropidies, is praised as being particularly elevated containing, as it does, the *odes* composed by Anakreon as well as being directly related to Solon and his works, and many other fine poets and authors – due, I say, to the beauty and virtuousness found here, not to mention *[a]* everything else which tends to be calculated into one's happiness and well-being {*Glückseligkeit*}; and your mother's side is quite the same. For there's none who surpasses your Uncle Pyrilampes in beauty and noble stateliness – at least none whose feet tread upon *terra firma* – so that it's no surprise that he's been sent out as our Ambassador to the Great King, or to wherever else royal matters are discussed. And so, the whole estate doesn't show any deficiencies, nowhere at all, and stands out above all others. Now, having sprung up out of such stock, well it's no surprise that you rank as first in everything. What strikes one right off in seeing your *Gestalt*, from this aspect there's obviously no possibility that you might bring shame upon any of your ancestors, but if it should also be so in relation to mindfulness and all of the rest of it about which Critias here just spoke, praising your upbringing and education – so then, it must be said, dear Charmides, said I, that your mother was blessed, indeed, on the day that she delivered you. So, this being how matters stand – if mindfulness, as Critias says, suits your character so well and you are fully adept in your prudence, well then you are no longer in need of such incantations, whether they might stem from Zalmoxis or from Abaris, the hyperborean; rather already right from the start the prescriptions for headache themselves might be delivered over to you. If you would fancy, though, that there still may be something lacking in this, so you would have to allow that the former incantations be given first, before using the cure given for headache. So – tell me yourself whether you are in agreement with Critias' assertions and you make the claim to have a sufficiency in mindfulness, or whether there still may be some deficiency. ～ At this point Charmides blushed – and therewith our eyes beheld a beauty even more resplendent than previously! for shame at this age in life wears well. But hereafter he answered my question in a way lacking nothing in nobility. He said, namely: It wouldn't be an easy thing, so at the moment, that he might either deny or affirm what was being asked of him. For then, said he, if he would deny it, to be *[158d]* mindful, so in part this goes against one's own sensibilities[89] and, in part too, doing so would drag Critias into [a state of] untruthfulness –

---

[89] Cf: *Protagoras* 323bc (p. 124) – "otherwise he would be crazy not to subscribe to the principles of justice.."

and yet others as well who likewise vouchsafe me that I am prudent, just as Critias said. But then, should I make such a claim and, thus, bestow such praise upon myself, so doing this is a very good way to make the others all hate me. So that, I don't at all know what I should say in answer to your query. ~ To this I responded: It seems to me that your point is well taken, Charmides, and therefore I'd fancy that we might conduct an investigation together: whether or not you possess that about which I inquired so that neither will you be forced into saying what you don't want to say, nor will I proceed to make you healthy without the considerations which are due. If this is all right by you, so let's proceed on to the investigation; if not so let's just leave things be. ~ By all means, said he, this is all right by me – therefore do proceed with the investigation however you opine to be able to get the firmest grasp upon it. ~ In the following manner, said I, thus I fancy will we best be enabled to make rapid progress with our investigation.   *<3.~159a]*

It is obvious, namely, that if mindfulness subsists within you, so too you'd have to know something to speak out about it. For it is necessary that its subsistence – if it does subsist within you – this brings forth a sensation upon the grounds of which, then, some notions of mindfulness arise: what it is and in what substantiated.[90] Or, do you opine it's not so? ~ No, the former is what I opine, said he. ~ And it's this, I continued on, that which you opine – since you are able to speak fluently in Hellenic – indeed: you have to know to speak it. ~ Perhaps, said he. ~ So that, now, we shall be able to make a judgment, whether or not mindfulness does subsist within you. And so tell me, said I: What do you maintain that mindfulness is in accord to your notions? ~ At the beginning, now, he appeared to be lost in thought and he didn't want to answer this question properly; but after awhile he did, indeed, provide me with an answer: he fancied that mindfulness is this: If one does everything ethically and with forethought, whether it be walking along the street or talking, and everything else, just so. And I fancy it so, said he, principally it's a certain thoughtfulness: such is *the being* of that about which you asked. ~ Is that also, said I, a good clarification? Indeed, Charmides, they say this about those having forethought: that they are mindful. Thus, let's look into this, whether they are *[c]* saying something with this. Tell me, then, doesn't mindfulness belong amongst the beautiful? ~ Aye, indeed, said he. ~ Which of

---

[90] "*worin sie besteht*" – *bestehen* is generally translated as "to endure" (as opposed to things that change) – see e.g.: *Parmenides* 139b (p. 221).

these now is more beauteous when your language teacher gives you lessons – to write out the letters quickly or self-consciously, assuming they come out just as well? ~ Quickly. ~ And in reading – quickly or slowly? ~ Quickly. ~ And playing on the lyre, quick is good too; and thus also when ringing the bells – doing so with alacrity is much better than thoughtfully and slowly? ~ Yes. ~ And how about in boxing and wrestling, isn't it even so? ~ Quite. ~ And in running and jumping and all of the other activities of the body, isn't quickness and alacrity also more beauteous, but that which happens slowly and arduously and self-consciously, wouldn't these be worse? ~ *[d]* That's how it looks. ~ It has been shown, then, said I, that as far as the body is concerned, it's not what is done with the greatest amount of forethought, rather that which is done the fastest and with great alacrity, this is the most beauteous. Isn't it true? ~ Indeed. ~ But mindfulness was to be something of beauty? ~ Yes. ~ Thus it would be, at least in respect to the body, not self-conscious behavior that's mindful, rather what's fast – if, indeed, mindfulness is something beautiful. ~ That's how it looks, said he. ~ But how now,   *[159e]* I continued right along, is erudition or illiteracy more beautiful? ~ Erudition. ~ But this is substantiated, said I, such intelligence, in that one reads and learns things quickly; but then, the illiterate are slow learners and tend to be rather self-conscious. ~ Yes. ~ And teaching someone else, isn't this more beauteous if it's done quickly and powerfully rather than self-consciously and at a slow pace? ~ Indeed, very much so. ~ And how? – grasping something in your mind and facility in remembering whatever it may be, would this be more beautiful with forethought and slowly, or rapidly and with ease? ~ Rapidly and easily. ~ And presence of mind, isn't this an alacrity in the soul, but not a slowness? ~ Right. ~ But also grasping what your language teachers or your music teachers teach, and everything else, 'what and where ever it ever may be' *{überhaupt}*, all of this doesn't happen most beauteously if it's done with the greatest self-consciousness, rather when it's done as quickly as possible? ~ Yes. ~ But certainly too, if you're focused upon an investigation regarding the soul or getting serious advice about this or that, then too it's not the most self-conscious, I think, and he who only with exertion in giving his council and finding out something or other – it's *[160b]* not, I say, this one who is most respected and worthy of praise, but rather the one who does this easily and quickly. ~ So it is, said he. ~ In all things, thus, said I, Charmides, as well as that which effects the body as also the soul, it appears to us that that which shows itself with power and speed – *this* would be the more beauteous. ~ That's the way things have turned out, said he. ~ Therefore mindfulness would

not be self-consciousness, and the mindful life not overly pensive –
in accord, namely, with this speech, since the mindful should be the
more beautiful. For one out of these two, either not at all or else only
in a very few instances, have we found that self-conscious activities in
life would be more beauteous than those which are done quickly and
with alacrity and power. And now, if also – my dear Charmides – to
sum up: not less thoughtful activities are the more beautiful than
fast, spirited and plucky ones, so too it wouldn't be, indeed, that self-
conscious activities are more mindful than those that are quick and
rapid: neither in walking, nor reading, and, likewise, everywhere else:
nowhere would the self-conscious life somehow be more mindful than
the un-self-conscious one, since we made it our stipulation for this
clarification that mindfulness belongs to the beautiful, and now the
fast has shown itself as not being any less beauteous as that which is
done slowly and self-consciously. ~ That's right, Socrates, said he, I
fancy that your point is well taken. ~   *<4.~160d2]*

Thus, once again, Charmides, said I, and with greater precision take
note as you look within yourself and observe to what end does the
mindfulness subsisting *{einwohnende}* within you direct you, and
what must it well be that it makes you to that, that toward which it is
directing. – And taking all of this together tell us straight-out and
boldly: what does mindfulness appear to you to be. ~ At this he
collected himself, and after valiant *{wacker}* considerations he said:
Well, I'd fancy that mindfulness makes for shame, and that it bestows
shame upon mankind – and that, therefore, mindfulness is what
shame is. ~ Very well, said I. Didn't you admit awhile back that
mindfulness would be something beauteous? ~ Indeed, said he. ~
Thus, mindful people are also good? ~ Yes. ~ Is it possible for
something to be good that wouldn't promote goodness? ~ No, that's
not well probable. ~ Not only, then, is mindfulness something
beauteous, rather also something good? ~ So I'd fancy it. ~ How
now, said I, don't you believe that Homer was right when he said:
For a man with dire needs, shame is not good –? ~ Well yes, I do,
said he. ~ Thus, as it seems: shame is good and also not good? ~ It
appears so. ~ But mindfulness is good since it makes those who
subsist within it become good, not bad. ~ That's totally certain, I'd
fancy that it would be just as you now say. ~ Thus, mindfulness
wouldn't be shame if everyone has a propensity toward goodness;
but shame tends no more to goodness than it does toward badness. ~
It seems to me, Socrates, that what you say is totally right. But take a
look at the following, how you'd fancy this about mindfulness.
                                                                [161b]

Namely, I'm just remembering what I've already heard someone say: Mindfulness would be if each does his own *{das Seinige tue}*. Reflect upon this and whether for you he's to be fancied as having clarified it properly, he who said this. ~ My, aren't you the sly one – you've heard this from Critias or from some other sage. ~ It would well have to be from someone other, said Critias – for, at least, it's not from me. ~ But Socrates, Charmides spoke up again: What   *[c2]* difference does it make from whom it may be that I heard it? ~ None at all, said I. For whatever the goal it's never that pertinent to know who said what, rather *only* whether if what was said is right or not right. ~ Now you're speaking fittingly, said he, putting things just where they belong. ~ By Zeus, said I, but whether also we only shall find out what it is that actually was meant – I should be amazed – for it has every appearance of being a riddle. ~ But indeed, how so? he asked. ~ Because, indeed, he who said it certainly didn't mean it so, just as the words ring out: Mindfulness would be this, that each does his own. Or do you believe that your language teacher wouldn't be doing anything if he should be reading or writing? ~ I, said he, do believe that he is. ~ Now, do you opine that this language teacher is always only reading and writing his own name, and that this would be how he goes about teaching all you children? Or wouldn't you read and write about the names of your enemies not any less than you do of your own and of those who are your friends? ~ None the less. ~ Yet, you wouldn't be "doing your own" – if, then, reading and writing are what you are doing. ~ That's certainly true. ~ And healing, dear friend, and building and weaving and whatever profession it ever may be – that you'd want to accomplish this or that artistically[91], all of this, indeed, would be a "doing"? ~ Quite. ~ But how now, said I, do you think that any law such as this that commands: Each and every should weave his or her own clothes, and do their own laundry and washing, and cobble their own shoes, *und mit ölschläuchen und Kratzeisen*[92] and everything else having the same correlation, *[162a]* namely having *nothing to do with what's foreign*, never touching it; rather each makes his own and accomplishes things only for himself? ~ I wouldn't fancy that, no, not at all. ~ But still, such regulations are mindful, and ruling mindfully is good? ~ How else? said he. ~ Thus, it cannot be that things performed in this manner, that each does his own, this isn't the mindfulness that he had in mind? ~

---

[91] See *Gorgias* – footnote #132 (p. 259).
[92] "and slathering on the oil and, then, scraping it off ..." – cf: *Protagoras*, footnote #81 (p. 136); another example of the interconnectedness of Plato's dialogues.

Obviously not. ~ Hence, he was speaking in riddles, as it seems, and as I already said this once, he who says: doing one's own would be mindfulness? For so naïve, indeed, no one is so simple-minded? Or, was the person you heard saying this so asinine, Charmides? ~ *That* in no way, said he. Much more I'd fancy him as being exceptionally wise. Then it's totally certain, as I'd fancy it, that he just threw this out like a riddle – since, namely, it is so difficult to know what this should be called: to do one's own. Are you able to tell me? ~ By Zeus, said he, I don't know. But what's stopping us, then, from assuming that he himself, he who said this, also didn't know what he was thinking? And as he was saying this, so he broke out in a smile and looked toward Critias. But already it was plainly obvious *[162c]* to see by Critias' expression how painful the foregoing had been for him and how glad he would have been to display himself before Charmides and all of those who were present *{den Anwesenden}*, and how before it had only been through forceful effort that he had held himself high and dry from the fray – but now, he couldn't keep it up any longer. For this reason I believe that it actually was so, as I had suspected at first, that Charmides had heard this answer regarding mindfulness from Critias. Now Charmides, it was obvious that he wasn't particularly thrilled about defending this answer, but rather that Critias should do so and he indicated as much and provoked him: that otherwise this, *his* answer, would be considered refuted. But Critias, now, couldn't remain aloof any longer, rather he seemed quite upset at Charmides, just like the poet can't stand by and see his poem poorly enunciated, massacred in its presentation; and so he looked right back at him and said: *So do you mean this*, Charmides – just because *you* don't know what this person was thinking, he who said: Mindfulness would be if everyone does his own, that therefore he himself also wouldn't know? ~   <5.]

But I spoke up, best of men, that is nothing to marvel over, that Charmides doesn't know this, seeing how young he is; but one might well believe that you, at your age and having pondered over matters like these in your indagations, you do know. Thus, if you are   *[e]* going to accept this, that this would be mindfulness, what he (our unnamed author) says, and you want to take over the defense of this proposition – so it's only so much the more in accord with my passion that I investigate into this together with you: whether what was said is true or not true. ~ Indeed, said he, I accept that and take this on. ~ Admirably done, said I. And so tell me whether that, what I even was asking earlier, whether you also admit as much, that all of the craftsmen, those who work with their hands, are they making some-

thing? ~ I do, certainly. ~ And do you opine that they are only
making their own, or likewise that they are making things for others?
~ Also for their others. ~ Thus, people are mindful who, indeed, are
not only making their own? ~ What's there to hinder it? – said he. ~
Nothing for me, said I; but take a look as to whether there may be
a hindrance for him, he who has taken on the proposition:
Mindfulness is to do your own – if hereafter he also says that there'd
be no hindrance that also these who do for their others, these also are
quite able to be mindful. ~ Have I, then, said he, admitted as much,
that those who are doing something for others are mindful? or
haven't I only given in that they make things? ~ But do tell   *[163b]*
me, said I, isn't this for you the same: to do and to make? ~ In no
manner, indeed, nor also to execute and to make. This, namely, I
have learned from Hesiod, he who said: *No execution is shameful.*
Do you then believe he would have made this assertion if he would
have named *these* as being executions? and that to execute and to do
were to be what you have put forth – that it wouldn't be shameful to
be a mere shoemaker, or to be out on the street peddling one's wares
and haggling about the price and, indeed, for those prostituting
themselves, the price of themselves! One's not at all permitted to
believe this! – Socrates; rather he too, I believe, holds making to be
something other than executing and doing – and that from time to
time making something might well be shameful, if the beautiful is not
contained within, but no execution would ever be shameful. For only
that which in its making is beautiful and useful – only such did he
name works; and only such making executions and acts. And one
would have to assert, only the like as these would he have held as
being fitting for each one of us, that such belongs here; but everything
that does damage wouldn't belong. So that one would have to believe
that Hesiod and everyone else who only is reasonable considers him,
he who does his own, as being mindful. ~ O Critias, said I, right   *[d]*
off from the start of your clarification I understood pretty much
whither you were headed: what it is that you would understand
beneath the words of "belonging for each of us" and "his good"; and
then underneath the activities, what those who are good would make.
For I have heard the likes a thousand times from Prodicus, how he
differentiates amongst words. And I am nothing but glad to allow you
all of this, to take each word as you want – if only you tell me that to
which each word is connected, that is, for the words doing you
service. Thus, determine now once again from the beginning onward
more clearly whether it's to be the act or the execution, or what have
you, however you'd want to name it in respect to the good: whether
this is that which you are naming mindfulness? ~ I'll do so, said he.

~ Hence, he is not mindful, he who does evil; rather [only] he who does good? ~ And you, best of men, said he, wouldn't fancy it so? ~ Indeed I may, I answered. For then, we're not investigating what it is that I think, rather just what you, now, have said. ~ I for my part, ever constant, said he, would deny that he who doesn't make good but evil – that he is mindful. For then, that doing good is mindfulness, this is a determination for you that is totally clear. ~ Perhaps *[164a]* there's no hindrance that you are in the right about this, said I; at the same time, though, this causes me to wonder: if you believe that it is possible for mindful people also not to know that they are mindful. ~ But I don't believe that either, said he. ~ Didn't you say a bit earlier, said I, that there wouldn't be anything standing in the way that artists and professionals, also when they are making things for others, they still are capable of being mindful? ~ That was said, said he; but what's the problem with this? ~ Nothing. But tell me this, would you fancy that a physician, in that he is making someone to be healthy – that he'd be making something useful for himself as well as for the other, the one whom he is healing? ~ I'd fancy that he is. ~ And he does, indeed, do what belongs to him and to his profession, he who does this? ~ Yes. ~ And he who does what is fitting, isn't he mindful? ~ You're not just whistling Dixie, he is mindful. ~ But does every physician necessarily have to know when his actions shall be useful in his work and when not? ~ Well, perhaps not. ~ Hence, from time to time, said I, in that he is acting usefully or with harm, so the doctor himself doesn't know how he is acting; but, all the *[c]* same if he acts in a useful way – in accord with your speech – so he has acted in a mindful manner. Or, would you say it's not so? ~ Quite. ~ Hence, from time to time he indeed acts mindfully, in that his actions are useful, and so he is mindful – but doesn't even know it himself, that he is acting mindfully. ~ But this, o Socrates, said he, indeed this cannot be, there's no way at all; rather if you opine that something from that which I asserted earlier necessarily leads one to this, well then, I'd rather take something back from what I said earlier and I'll not be ashamed about admitting it, that I expressed myself a bit shy of what's right rather than that I should have to admit this, that anyone at all would be incapable of knowing it himself, that he is mindful.[93] Much more I would like to move in the direction of saying that even this would be what mindfulness is: that one is cognizant of oneself {*das Sich selbst kennen*}, and that I whole-heartedly voice my approval for him, he who placed this aphorism up in Delphi. For this is the sense that it seems to me that this dictum has been put there –

---

[93] Note – this is where things began with Charmides hedging on saying the same.

as an address of the God upon anyone entering – instead of the *[e]*
Be glad – as if, namely, this wish to be glad wouldn't be quite right
and that we wouldn't have to somehow find the courage to this, rather
that we be mindful. In this manner, thus, god greets those who are
entering into his temple entirely different than mankind – in accord
with the opinion of those who sanctified this tablet, at least as I'd
fancy it, and speaks to each and every who enters in nothing other
than *Be mindful* bespeaks, so he addresses one. Somewhat, indeed,
as a riddle uttered by a soothsayer does he express himself. Thus the
oracle – *Man, know thyself,* and *Be mindful* – these are quite the *[a]*
same, as the former aphorism asserts and I also assert this; but it may
easily be believed by many that the two would be different, and I'd
fancy that this is what has occurred to those, the ones who have
placed the following dictums there: *Everything in moderation* and
He who offers a pledge, he's halfway to perdition. For then, these
were of the belief that the *Know thyself* also would be good council,
a piece of advice, but not the greeting of the god for those entering in
– and, so, that they too might set up healing councils that wouldn't be
any less beneficial, that's why these were written down and placed
alongside the others. But why it is, now, that I have said all of this,
o Socrates, I shall tell you.   *<6.~165b]*

All of the above you may consider a present, from me to you. For
perhaps you said a few things above that were more right, perhaps
too, I did; but nothing at all was precisely determined as being right
in all of it, what was spoken above. But now I am willing to stand up
for my speech – if it should be that you don't accept this: that mindfulness would be self-recognition, *das sich selbst kennen.* But Critias,
said I, you are dealing with me now as if it were I who had asserted to
know it, that about which I am questioning, and as if I would be able,
if only I wanted, to determine this like you have. But that's not the
proper correlation, rather I'm only just entering into the search for it
with you – that which we have taken on – because even I myself do
not know. Thus, once I've investigated into this, then and then only
do I well want to say as to whether I accept your answer or not. But
please have some patience with me until I have investigated. ~ *[c]*
So, said he, then make your investigation. ~ I'm already underway,
said I. If, then, mindfulness consists in and is substantiated in this,
that one recognizes something, so, obviously, it is a cognition? and a
cognition of something. Or, not? ~ Indeed, mindfulness is this as
well, said he, namely, of itself. ~ And isn't medicine or the art of
healing, said I, isn't it cognizant of something? namely of that which
is healthy? ~ Quite. ~ If, now, you were to question me, said I, the

art of healing as the recognition of all of that which is healthy, to what purpose is this useful and how does it achieve its effect[94] upon us, so I would answer you: It's no small advantage, health namely – an utterly beauteous work is the effect she has upon us – if, then, *[165d]* you are willing to accept this answer. ~ I do accept it. ~ And if you were to question me further as regards the art of construction, as the cognitions needed to make buildings: Essentially what do I assert that it is? and what effects does construction have? – so I would say: Dwellings, places to live. And so too with all of the other arts and professions. And, even so, something like this, now, you also have to know about mindfulness, since you have asserted that it would be a knowledge of itself. If you shall be queried: Critias, mindfulness as self-recognition – essentially what, then, is the beautiful and, in accord with its name, worthy effect which it produces as its work for us? So come now and tell me. ~ But Socrates, said he, you are not investigating this in the right manner. For this knowledge, in accordance with its nature, is dissimilar to all of the others; as also the others, too, show differences amongst themselves. But then, you are conducting your investigation as if they would all be similar, each one to the others. For you tell me, said he, with mathematics or geometry, the art of measuring distances – where is there such a work just as the house is the end product of construction, or a dress being the work completed as a result of the art of weaving, or other works that are like these of which there is no end to the examples which *[a]* could be given. Do you have, perhaps, also from these such a work, that you might show it to me? Certainly, you don't. ~ To this I responded, you are quite right. But I am able to show you "of what" each of these cognitions is cognitive – something that, again, is different from the cognition itself. So mathematics is the cognition of the even and the odd, how these relate amongst themselves and one to the other, in every collection, big or small. Isn't it true? ~ Indeed. ~ And are not the even and the odd themselves something different from mathematics itself? ~ How else? how shouldn't they be different? ~ And physics has to do with the heavy and the light in terms of weight and mass; but heavy and light are themselves different from physics itself? Do you admit as much? ~ Oh, yes. ~ Thus tell me also: of what, then, is mindfulness the cognition – something that is other than mindfulness itself. ~ But that's even the crux of this matter, Socrates, said he; now you are right on the trail and have the spoor of that wherein mindfulness itself differs from all of the other cognitions; but you are searching for some similarity *[c]*

---

[94] *"was bewirkt sie uns" – wirken und leiden,* cf: footnote #52, (p. 31).

to all of the others. But that's not the way it is, rather all of the others are cognitions of an other; but only mindfulness, it alone is as well the cognition of the other cognitions as also that of itself. Also there is a good deal lacking that this should have escaped you. But I'm beginning to believe, that which earlier on you denied, that you would do such a thing, indeed, *this is* what you are doing – namely your prime interest is in contradicting me and you are not particularly concerned about that about which we are speaking. ~ Don't make a stew, said I, that you'd think, even if I actually do refute you,   *[166d]* that I'd do so for the sake of some other cause than the one for which I'd also cross-examine myself, just the same – whether I'd well be saying something that's right – out of my earnest concern, namely, that unawares I might imagine to know something that, indeed, I do not know. And now too I do assert that this is all that I am doing, namely investigating for clarification and, indeed, primarily for myself, though perhaps also for the sake of other good friends. Or don't you share in this opinion, that this is a common good and, indeed, for practically all mankind – if each and every thing shall be made apparent, how all of this correlates? ~ Certainly, said he, I do believe this, Socrates. ~ Thus, be consoled, intimate friend, said I; and now answer my questions just as matters appear to you and letting it all be the same, whether it may be Critias or Socrates who shall be refuted, that rather your attentions are simply focused on the clarification, how it may be that the investigation shall run its course right to the end. Very well, said he, I will do so; for I fancy what you have said is totally acceptable. ~ So tell me then, said I, how do you actually mean this with mindfulness? ~   *<7.~166e4]*

Well then, I say, spoke he, that it alone underneath all cognitions[95] *{Erkennissen}* is the cognition of itself as well as of all the rest. ~ And wouldn't it also, said I, recognize non-cognizance if it recognizes cognizance? ~ Indeed, said he. ~ Only someone who is mindful, he alone shall achieve self-recognition and, so, be in a position to lay the groundwork for that which he really knows and what he doesn't – and even so too, be enabled to make judgments of others: what someone else knows and likewise believes that he knows, since he does know it; and also, again, what someone merely believes to know but doesn't really know; but aside from him, no one at all. And, thus, this is being mindful and mindfulness and knowledge of one's self – to know what one knows and what one doesn't know. Is it this? that which you opine? ~ That it is, said he. ~ Hence, once more, said I, the third of

---

[95] Cf: *Theaetetus*, footnote #155 (p. 364).

these three good things, let's weigh this in our considerations again, and beginning at the beginning: firstly, whether this is possible   *[b]* or not – what one knows and doesn't know, to know that he knows it and that he doesn't know it; and after this, if this is possible, also this: essentially what advantage it would well be and what usefulness would it have, that we know all of this.   ~   Indeed, said he, all of this needs to be considered.   ~   So come now, Critias, said I, take a look and see whether you might have better council regarding all of this than I do – for I don't have any, none at all. But how it is that I'm so totally in the dark, should I tell you?   ~   Yes, please do.   ~   Isn't it so, said I, all of this takes place if – as you even said – there exists[96] *{es gibt}* a certain cognition which is a cognition of nothing other than of itself and of the other cognitions and, simultaneously, the same also as regards that of which we are not cognizant, the non-cognitions.   ~   Quite.   ~   But do look at this, friend, what marvelous assertions we have taken upon ourselves! For if you were to search amongst all of the other things looking for the same, you would have to fancy that it's quite impossible.   ~   But, how's that and *where*?   ~   This is how I mean it. Just reflect on this, whether you are capable of believing that that there might be a seeing which, utterly, is not a seeing of things, that which other seeing sees, rather only a seeing of itself and of the other seeings, and likewise of not-seeing; but then it does see itself and the other seeings. Do you believe it, that such exists?   ~   By Zeus, not I.   ~   And how about this, a hearing that doesn't hear any voices, but hears itself and, then too, other hearings and silence?   ~   No, not that either.   ~   And so, go on to weigh and consider utterly all the sorts of perceptions and sensations – whether you fancy that there exists any one from amongst them that senses its own sensing and other sensings, but that senses nothing of that which the other senses sense?   ~   I'd fancy not.   ~   But perhaps you believe that there exists a longing, but not a longing for any sort of pleasure, rather just a longing for itself and for other longings?   ~   No, not probable.   ~   Nor probably not too, I think, a willing that doesn't will any particular good, that rather it only wills itself and the willings of other willings. ~   No, indeed not.   ~   Or would you like to assert that there exists a love which is not a love of some beauty, rather only of its self and of other loves.   ~   I, said he, no.   ~   Or have you taken notice of a fear that only fears itself and other fears but doesn't fear anything   *[168a]* that's fearful?   ~   Nothing of the like, said he.   ~   But a notion of notionality itself and of other notions which, however, of that of which the other notions are notions, of this it hasn't the slightest

---

[96] Cf: *Parmenides* footnote #109 (p. 212).

notion. ~ Never. ~ But such a cognition, as it seems, we do want
to assert that this does exist, this which isn't the cognition of any
cognitive object, rather only of itself and of the cognitions of other
cognitions. ~ Indeed, this is what we assert. ~ Isn't this uniquely
rare – if it is at all? For let's not yet assert that it isn't, rather only
investigate into whether it is. ~ Rightly stated. ~ Then tallyho, this
cognition is, indeed, a cognition of something, and it has such a
unique quality {*Eigenschaft*} by the power or capacity of which it is
connected to something. Isn't it true? ~ Quite. ~ For also "bigness,"
we assert, has such a unique quality, namely, that it is bigger than
something? ~ It has such. ~ Isn't it true, from something that is
smaller if, indeed, it should be bigger. ~ That's necessary. ~ If only,
now, we might find a [sort of] bigness that would be bigger than other
bignesses and of itself, but utterly not from something lying beneath
it, that in respect to which the other bignesses are big – wouldn't it, in
every manner, have to be an attribute of this, if it is bigger   *[168c]*
than itself, that it also would be smaller than itself? – or not?   ~
That's entirely necessary, Socrates, said he. ~ Not also, if something
is double to all of the other doubles, as well as the double of itself – so
it can do so only if it's also half of itself and of the others, only so can
it simultaneously be double? For there isn't anything else of which a
double is double other than of a half. ~ Right. ~ And that which is
more than itself, shall not this, likewise, be less; and what's heavier,
also lighter; what is older, also younger – and even so in all of the
other things, that which has its quality in relation to its own self, shall
this not also have to have that upon which this quality is related?
Namely, this is what I'm meaning: hearing, namely, we did indeed
say that it's solely of that which is voiced and of nothing other? – isn't
this true? ~ Yes. ~ Hence, if it should hear itself, so, likewise, it
would have to hear its own voice – for otherwise it cannot hear. ~
There's no way around that, it's entirely so. ~ And also with sight,
best of men, if it itself should see itself – so it has to have some
coloration, for sight is incapable of seeing that which lacks coloration.
~ Yes, no. ~ You see it, thus, o Critias, from the little that we've gone
through, just from this: so it has been shown in part that it's wholly
impossible and in part as highly improbable and very hard to believe
that something might ever be able to have its own unique quality in
reference upon itself. For with that which is big or many, and the
like, it was totally and utterly impossible, wasn't it? ~ Quite. ~ And
of hearing and seeing and, further, as regards movement, that
something moves itself, and of warmth, that something might warm
itself, and from everything of this type it may appear to a few   *[169a]*
as very unbelievable but to others not possibly. No small personality,

indeed, friend, would have the sufficiency that belongs here: that this be decided in all generality whether utterly nothing is of this type, that its own unique quality of relating itself upon itself, rather that everything relates only upon an other; or whether a few would be so-qualified and others aren't; and, then again, if a few do relate so to themselves, and whether also cognition and knowledge belong underneath these – from which, then, we asserted that it [such self-reference] would be mindfulness. Now, I don't trust myself to this, that I am in a position to make a decision on this, wherefore I also am not able to assert with certainty that this is possible, that something such as this exists [call it what you will]: a cognition of cognition or knowledge of knowledge; nor also – if such as this would exist – am I able to accept that this is mindfulness, at least not until I have investigated when it should be possible that it would be as stated and whether this would be something that would be useful or not. For that mindfulness would have to be something good and useful, this is my intimation, that of which I have a premonition. So you, dear son of Callaeschrus, for you do affirm it, that this is what mindfulness would be: the knowledge of knowledge and, hence, also of ignorance – so show me this firstly, that this is possible and all that I've even said just now; and then after it being possible that such also is useful – and so you might perhaps satisfy me that you have clarified mindfulness correctly and spoken what's right: what it is.   *<7.~169c]* As, now, Critias heard me out and saw how I was clueless and in the dark, it seemed to me that exactly as this tends to happen – if someone observes another yawning, so he too might start yawning – so he too was overpowered by the futility of the wild-goose chase and he too became ensnared by my helplessness. Now, since he always tended to harvest praise, so he now was shamed before all who were present, and neither did he want to admit to me that he would be incapable of delivering that which I had urged of him, nor too would he say anything definite – rather he only attempted to hide his perplexity. But so that, indeed, we might yet make some progress in this matter, so I spoke up: Good, Critias, if this is all right with you, so for now anyway we want to make room for this conjecture, that it may actually be possible that knowledge of knowledge exists, and that we leave this for some other time to investigate into whether or not it correlates so. But do come now and tell me if, indeed, this also is possible – what therefore is easier to know, what one knows and what one doesn't know? For we asserted that this, affirmatively, would really have been the *Know thyself* and such is being mindful? Isn't it true? ~ Quite, said he; and this does follow, too, Socrates. For if one has the knowledge that self-recognition provides, so he also has to be just as that is which he has – just as one who is quick has quickness, and is beautiful if one possesses beauty – and so too if cognizing knowledge, that anyone having the knowledge of himself [or herself], so one would have to have self-knowledge. ~ Upon this, said I, I too don't have any doubts, that whoever has self-knowledge shall not also be cognizant of themselves, rather only whether he who has this necessarily would have to know what he knows and what he doesn't know. ~ Because that is one and the same, Socrates, the   *[170a]* latter and the former. ~ Perhaps, said I. But, unfortunately, I'm always the laggard. For already once again I don't understand how this can be one and the same: to know what one knows or doesn't know and whether one knows [himself]. ~ How do you mean this? said he. ~ So, said I. There exists a knowledge of knowledge. Now, shall this be able to differentiate anything more than this, that of two 'knowledges' the one is knowledge but the other is not? ~ No, rather precisely so much. ~ Is it with this the same as with knowledge or ignorance of what's healthy, or knowledge or the lack thereof in regards to what's just? ~ No, not at all. ~ Rather these latter would be, I believe, for the first, medical lore, and, for the second, jurisprudence. But the former which is something other is nothing more or less than [pure] knowledge? ~ How else? ~ Hence, if someone isn't also informed as regards to health and justice, that rather he'd only be cognizant regarding knowledge itself – in that it is this alone of which he has cognizance – so shall he, indeed, that he does know something and does have some sort of cognition, he shall know, presumably, about his own self and of others – isn't this true? ~ Yes. ~ But what he recognizes, how should he know it through the power of such cognition? For that which is healthy he recognizes   *[c]* through the faculty of the healing arts and not through the power of mindfulness; and what rings out harmonically, this is recognized through the faculty acquired by musicians and, again, not through mindfulness; and what belongs to *building* through the various construction arts and, again, not through mindfulness; and, so too with all of the rest. Or not? ~ Obviously. ~ But through the power of mindfulness, if this is only the knowledge of knowledge, how should he ever know that he's cognizant of that which is healthy? or that he'd be cognizant of that which essentially belongs to builders? ~ There's no way. ~ And he who doesn't know this, indeed: he won't know what he knows, rather only *that* he knows? ~ So it seems.   *[e]* ~ Hence, that wouldn't be mindfulness and being mindful – to know what one knows and doesn't know; rather, as it now seems, only *that* one knows and *that* one doesn't know. ~ That's how it looks. ~ Nor too shall such a one be in a position to test anyone other, whoever asserts that he knows something, whether he actually knows it, that which he pretends to know, or whether he doesn't know it; rather, as it seems, only this much shall he recognize: that someone has some sort of cognition – but that of which the cognition is cognizant, this he won't be enabled to know. ~ Obviously not. ~ And, thus too, whoever gives himself out as being a physician but who isn't one, so he shall not be in a position to differentiate him from someone who actually is one, nor too shall he be positioned to differentiate in all of the other things – between those who are informed and those who aren't. Let's visualize this for ourselves to make it crystal clear. If an enlightened person, or whoever else it might be, wants to recognize the true physician and also the pretender, shall he not proceed as follows? He won't speak to him about medicine. For the doctor, as we said, understands nothing more than what is healthy and what isn't. Or, isn't this what we said? ~ Yes, quite so. ~ But about cognition itself, he doesn't know anything about this, rather this *[a]* knowledge has been ascribed to mindfulness. ~ Yes. ~ Hence, even the astute doctor doesn't know anything about the healing lore *qua* knowledge, since medicine is made up of cognitions? ~ Right. ~ That, now, the doctor has some sort of cognition, this is something, indeed, into which an enlightened individual would have insight; but if he undertakes to probe more deeply into essentially which sort – so, necessarily, he doesn't see "of what" the cognition would be. Or, isn't it precisely through this that each and every cognition is a determinate cognition – not merely that it is a cognition but essentially such a one, that it would be a cognition *of something*? ~ Precisely. ~ Thus, also the healing lore is determined as being different from all of the other cognitions through this, that it is of what is healthy and not healthy. ~ Yes. ~ And, thus, it's even in this – if somebody wants to make a study into medicine, this is what would be studied, that in which it consists and is substantiated. And, indeed, certainly not into something outside of this in which it wouldn't consist? ~ No, indeed not. ~ Thus, in that which is healthy and unhealthy, it has to be in this that the physician would be tested, if he is to be tested in the right way – to what extent he's informed as regards healing. ~ So it has shown itself. ~ Namely, to be sure, in this: in everything that he says or does, this is tested – whether what was spoken by him is true, and whether what he has done was done properly, the right way? ~ That's necessary. ~ Now, would someone be able to follow the ins and outs of all that belongs to this without also being informed as regards medicine? ~ Certainly not. ~ *[171c]* Hence, no one else other than a physician, not even the Buddha himself? Unless, of course, the Buddha had graduated from medical school. ~ That's the way it is. ~ Thus, from every vantage, if mindfulness is only the knowledge of knowledge and of ignorance, so it also is not in a position to differentiate between the physician who has understanding of this art and the charlatan, the one who only makes out as if he'd know and who has phantasies – nor also anyone else, whether whoever it may be really knows his profession whatever it ever may be – outside, of course, of another who shares in the profession, his colleague, just as it is with all of the arts and crafts. ~ That's obvious, said he. ~ So where's the usefulness, Critias, said I, that we would gain from mindfulness so construed? For if then, as we had assumed at the start, if a mindful person would know what he knows and also know what he doesn't know – of the first, that he knows it, and of the second that he doesn't know it – and thus too with the others, to be in a position to judge them just like he judges himself, then it would be for us – we are able to assert this – highly useful and advantageous to be mindful. For then we might press on with our lives without falling into error and being mistaken in anything, possessing such mindfulness, and so too with all of the others who would be ruled by us. For neither would we undertake to do something that we didn't understand, rather we'd locate those having the understanding and then we'd leave this in their capable hands; and so too with all of the others, those over whom we ruled, that we wouldn't allow them to do anything other than that which, if they would do it, they'd do it properly. But this would be that of which they have the knowledge. And, thus, a household that is administered through mindfulness would be well governed, and so too with a city or a state – and everything else over which   *[172a]* mindfulness might rule. For when an end is made to falling into error and when everything is done in the right way with righteousness prevailing in all things, so those who exist underneath such a state of affairs and being a part of such a constitution, these, by necessity, would have to lead a beauteous and a good life; and such who live so well would have to be blessed. Isn't it this, said I, isn't this what we would say of mindfulness, o Critias, if we wanted to describe how great a good it would be to know what you know and what you don't know? ~ Quite, this. ~ But now you do see, don't you, said I, that such knowledge hasn't been demonstrated by us anywhere at all? ~ I see it, said he. ~ Does perhaps, said I, mindfulness as we now have discovered it – namely [only] *that* one recognizes knowledge and is cognizant of ignorance – doesn't it have this bonus *{Gute}*: that   *[b]* whoever possesses it shall learn whatever he learns more easily, and that everything shall gain somewhat in clarity – because aside from what he learns he also sees his knowledge of it? and, then too, that he shall be better in his judgments of others, namely in that which he also has learned; but those who want to pass judgment upon others without mindfulness, so these would be worse as they do so in an ungrounded manner? Is it, perhaps, in something like this, friend, that we yet shall give preference to those having mindfulness? and that we had something more in mind in our earlier search for it than it truly would be? ~ Perhaps, said he, perhaps this is how it correlates. ~ But perhaps, said I, we have only been searching after something that's utterly useless. I'm only thinking this because all sorts of wonderful things come to me as regards mindfulness if it would be something along the lines of what we were saying.

<8.~172cd]

Indeed, if you want, let's take a look and see. Under the presumption that it would be possible to recognize knowledge – and let's no longer make a fuss about the other proposition but give in and admit this as well, that which was proposed as the being of mindfulness: the knowledge of what one knows and of what one doesn't know; and having supposed all of this, let's reflect upon this even better than we did previously – whether it shall be some help for us, now, if its reach extends as circumscribed. For what we were saying a bit earlier, that mindfulness would be such a great good if it would be this and that it had such pre-eminence in the administration of the home and of the state, I'd fancy that all of this, Critias, wasn't so praiseworthy. ~ *What?* – how's that, said he. ~ Because we, said I, like those climbing up high upon the mountains, we were terribly dizzy when we said that it would be such a great good for mankind if everyone would do what he knows and, then, what he doesn't know, this he'd leave for the others to do, others who would know. ~ And this, he asked me, wasn't declared by us as being praiseworthy? ~ No, not as I fancy it. ~ Wonderful things, in all actuality, said he, do you speak, Socrates. ~ By the dog, said I, and I'm fancying it even so myself. For this is just what I was meaning earlier on when I said that wonderful things were coming to me and that I was fearful that our investigation wasn't being conducted in the right manner. For, in all actuality, if *[173a]* mindfulness really is everything that we said, so I fancy that it's not in the least bit clear that its effect is in any way salutary, that any good comes to us. ~ But, how so? said he – do tell us so that we might know what you are meaning. ~ I'm ready to believe, said I, that I'm beginning to rave; but still, all the same, one has to speak one's mind whatever dances into view, that one pulls this into consideration and not act absent-mindedly by passing by unawares if, then, one should only be in the least bit considerate of oneself. ~ Well said. ~ So then hear it, my dream, whether it be the delusions of a raving maniac or a bit of the whitest ivory. If mindfulness, namely, in so far as it is this, that which we have firmly set down – also still should rule over us so verily, wouldn't we guide our behavior everywhere and in every manner in accordance to the dictates of knowledge? and no one would assert to be a helmsman if he wouldn't be one, and nobody else would make any claims about this or that which wouldn't be substantiated, and all of this would be obvious and nothing would remain in doubt or undiscovered? But, even if it does correlate so, would anything else arise from out of this other than that we would be healthier in our bodies than we are currently, and better able to be rescued whether dashing off upon the high seas or into some battle in war; and that all of our household utensils and our clothing and shoes and everything that belongs together here with this, all of these *[173c]* would be artfully constructed because in all cases the true artist would be in our service? And, yes, if you'd like we also want to give in as regards the fortune tellers and inspired prophets, that here we'd have knowledge of what shall come, all of the future; and this too should be at the disposal of mindfulness so that false prophets would easily be swept aside and that the true ones would be installed as diviners and interpreters of the future. That, now, the human race would act and be tended to in accords with understanding, and so live out our lives – this is something upon which I have a firm grasp. For mindfulness, ever diligent, wouldn't allow that those lacking understanding might ever be able to sneak in. But that living so, in accordance with understanding and knowledge, that this also would be living well and blessedness – this still is something into which we don't have any insight, my dear Critias. ~ But, said he, indeed you won't very easily find some other goal of what "living well" would be if living in one accord with knowledge isn't good enough for you. ~ Teach me only yet this small bit, said I: according to which piece of knowledge would you be meaning? Perhaps, in accordance to that knowledge the shoemaker uses when he cuts leather for shoes? ~ *[e]* By Zeus, said he, that's not what I mean. ~ Or from the skills of the metallurgic arts? ~ In no way. ~ Or spinning wool or woodworking or anything like this? ~ No, not that either. ~ Hence, said I, let's not remain stuck any longer on this clarification, that he lives a blessed life, he who lives in accordance to knowledge – for these, although they live with all of the fruits that such knowledge provides, you don't want to admit it, that they are living happily and are blessed; rather you seem to me to ascribe a blessed existence only to those who in one certain respect live in accordance with knowledge – and perhaps you'd be meaning the one whom I brought up previously, he who has foreknowledge of everything that's in the future, the soothsayer. *[a]*

Is he the one whom you mean or some other? ~ Him too, but others as well. ~ But, which ones? I questioned. Is it not perhaps him, he who not only would know the future but likewise everything from the past as well as the present – he to whom utterly nothing at all would remain unknown? For let us assume that such a person might exist. And I do think that you shall not assert that anyone would live in better accord to knowledge than he. ~ No, indeed not. ~ But, even now – I'm still missing which of his insights into all of this knowledge, which would make him blessed, or would it be all of them in the same manner? ~ That's easy, all in the same way. ~ But which takes precedence? Indeed, what from everything in the past, present and future, what does he know from knowing all of this? Perhaps something belonging to the recreation found in board games? ~ Say what! – boardgames? ~ Or from calculating? ~ No, not by any means. ~ Or, something pertaining to health? ~ Now you're getting warm. ~ But, of what I'm looking for, which goes deepest? – said I, this is what I'm meaning – and what does he know through it? ~ The good, said he, and the evil. ~ Oh you devil, you! said I, for so long you have pulled me about in circles and all the while hiding this from me: that it's not living in accordance to knowledge that makes one live well and find blessedness, and not even if you take all the other sorts of knowledge and add them all up together, rather only this one alone which is related to good and evil! *[174c]* For Critias, when you take this knowledge away from all of the others – shall the healing arts be any less healthful, the art of cobbling shoes make fewer shoes, the art of weaving produce fewer garments, the art of navigation protect us one whit the less when we're out on the high seas – just like the insights of the major general wouldn't protect us any the less when in war – that we shouldn't all perish? ~ Not one whit the less. ~ But, my dear Critias, that all of this would be good and that it happens to our benefit, this is something that we shall have sacrificed if the former knowledge is taken away. ~ That's right. ~ But, indeed, *this* knowledge isn't mindfulness, as it seems, rather it's the knowledge whose business it is to look out for our benefit. For then, it's not the knowledge of knowledge and ignorance, rather the knowledge of what's good and what's evil – so that if this is the knowledge that benefits us, mindfulness must be something other than what is beneficial. ~ How's that? – said he; mindfulness shouldn't be beneficial? For if, indeed, mindfulness is the knowledge of knowledge and, so, takes precedence above all other *[174e]* knowledge, so it also has to take precedence over the knowledge that is related to good and evil and, thus, does indeed benefit us. ~ And is it, perhaps, mindfulness that makes us healthy and not the healing lore? – and so too with all of the other arts and professions; does mindfulness accomplish the business that these do accomplish – or isn't it much more the case that each accomplishes their own? Or haven't we already admitted as much long ago, that it would only be the knowledge of knowledge and of ignorance, that such alone is its subject matter? Isn't it so? ~ Well, indeed. ~ Thus, it doesn't bring about good health? ~ No, I wouldn't say that it does. ~ Because health, namely, belongs to some other profession. Not so? ~ *[175a]* Yes, to an other. ~ Thus too, nothing pertaining to what's beneficial for us, it wouldn't bring about any such effects. For we have attributed this business to a different "art." Isn't this true? ~ Indeed. ~ How can mindfulness be useful for us if, utterly, it doesn't have any beneficial use? ~ In no manner, Socrates, as it seems. ~ Thus you do see, Critias, don't you – how very much I was right to be harboring such concerns, and most probably had sound grounds for accusing myself: that I wouldn't have anything useful that I might bring forth in respect to mindfulness. For certainly it would never come out so that that which everyone is unified in agreeing to – that   *[b]* mindfulness shall be the most admirable of all – for such to appear to us as being useless, this should never have happened if I were the least bit useful in guiding the investigation through in a good manner. But now we've been clobbered from every side and we don't have a thing to show as regards what, then, this is: that which the genius of language has placed inside of this name. And this despite the fact that we've given in and admitted a great deal that was never substantiated in our speech. For first off we made room for the supposition that there is such a thing as knowledge of knowledge, and this contrary to everything that came out from our earlier   *[c2]* investigation which neither asserted this, or even allowed for such a supposition, that such exists; and then even further in respect to this knowledge we supposed that it should be cognizant of the works that the other knowledges accomplish – since our speech also didn't allow us this either – and all of this was admitted so as to bring the mindful person to the point that he would be cognizant of what he knows and that he knows it, and also what he doesn't know and that he doesn't know it. And, in all actuality, all of this was liberally agreed to and without even looking into how impossible it is, what somebody wholly and utterly doesn't know, nonetheless to know it to a certain extent. For what he did not know we still, indeed, admitted of him that he does know – although, as I believe, this is obviously more unrational than anything else. And, all the same, despite our liberal generosity and willingness not to be in the least bit strict with our admissions, still our investigation came to naught and we were quite incapable of discovering the truth, rather it all turned back upon us in the form of jeering satire: that that which by endless supposition and poetic fancy we had set up as being the essence of mindfulness, so this itself displayed itself as being something totally useless despite all the extremity of our zeal. Admittedly, in regards to myself I am not so much irked by this – not so much as I am for your sake, o Charmides, as indeed I am distressed very much for you, what with your having so fine a *Gestalt* and, beyond this, possessing a disposition that is so mindful; and yet that you shouldn't have any benefits from this and that it won't be any help for you in your life – none at all! And even more irksome is this in relation to the incantations which I have learned from the Thracians, that I exerted so much time and effort in learning something that turns out as having utterly no value at all. But, then too, I don't really believe it, that this is how it all correlates, rather only that I'm a devilishly bad investigator and that, indeed, mindfulness is certainly a great good – and that you, if you   *[176a]* do possess it, are very much blessed. Hence, do look within – whether somehow it does subsist within you and that you're not really in need of these incantations. For if you do possess it, so I'd rather advise you that you simply count me amongst the windbags, someone overly full of hot air who is quite incapable of searching for anything whatever in an orderly manner in my speech[97]; but, as for you, the ever more mindful, so the ever more blessed. ~

<9.~176]

To this Charmides replied: But by Zeus, Socrates, I don't really know as to whether I have it or not. And how mightn't I well know this since you two aren't even in a position that you might find out what it is – just as you've said. But, all the same, for myself I don't actually believe you all that much, Socrates, but I do believe myself to be in need of these incantations, very much so. And from my side there is nothing that would hinder it, that I am willing to listen to you each and every day until you would say that it would be enough. ~ Good, said Critias, and if you do do this, Charmides, so this shall be a proof for me that you are mindful, that you should give yourself over to Socrates and let him perform all of his mantras with you, and that you'd never let up from him, neither in matters big nor small. Certainly, said he, I shall follow him and remain always by him. It would indeed be falsehearted of me if I didn't obey you, you who   *[c]* are my guardian, and that I wouldn't do just as you command. ~ And very firmly, said he, do I command this. ~ So – I shall do it, Charmides answered, from this day onward. ~ Hey there, said I,

---

[97] Cf: *Theaetetus* – Socrates' art of midwifery 150c (pp. 371–372) and 161b (p. 386).

what are you two counseling one another about doing? ~ Nothing,
said Charmides; we're all done in our deliberations. ~ Force, then,
said I – this is what you intend to use upon me and not even once
offer me any choice in this matter? ~ Yes, force, said he – should I
need it, particularly as this is what my guardian has commanded. So,
now you take council with yourself, what you think that you are going
to do about it. ~ Against such advice, indeed, there's nothing that
might be done. For you, if you take this on, following through with
such a plan and, indeed, even to the point of using force if needs be[98],
so there is no person who might ever stand in your way and   *[176d]*
prevent it. ~ So, don't you attempt to prevent this either, said he. ~
I won't, said I, not at all.

                                    ****

---

[98] ' Socrates: I went down to the Piraeus yesterday with Glaucon, son of Ariston, to pray to
the goddess; and, at the same time, I wanted to observe how they would put on the festival,
since they were now holding it for the first time. Now, in my opinion, the procession of the
native inhabitants was fine; but the one the Thracians conducted was no less fitting a show.
After we had prayed and looked on, we went off toward town.

   Catching sight of us from afar as we were pressing homewards, Polemarchus, son of
Cephalus, ordered his slaveboy to run after us and order us to wait for him. The boy took
hold of my cloak from behind and said, "Polemarchus orders you to wait." ~ And I turned
around and asked him where his master was. ~ "He is coming up behind," he said, "just
wait." ~ "Of course we'll wait," said Glaucon. ~ A moment later Polemarchus came along
with Adeimantus, Glaucon's brother, Niceratus, son of Nicias, and some others – apparently
from the procession. Polemarchus said, "Socrates, I guess you two are hurrying to get to
town." ~ "That's not a bad guess," I said. ~ "Well," he said, "do you see how many of us
there are?" ~ "Of course." ~ "Well then," he said, "either prove stronger than these men or
stay here." ~ "Isn't there still one other possibility . . . . ," I said, "our persuading you that
you must let us go?" ~ "Could you really persuade," he said, "if we don't listen?" ~
"There's no way," said Glaucon. ~ "Well, then, think it over, bearing in mind that we won't
listen." ~ Then Adeimantus said, "Is it possible you don't know that at sunset there will be a
torch race on horseback for the Goddess?" ~ "On horseback?" I said. "That is novel." '

                   (Note: spacing altered by using tilde ~ rather than line-feed.)

The opening of Book I: *The Republic of Plato, Second Edition*, Allan Bloom –
Basic Books, pages 3–4; Copyright 1968, 1991.

Parmenides

dedicated to

Usha

OVERVIEW:

A. Introduction:
   Antiphon's transmittal of the dialogue.   *Section 1.*

B. Main:

   I.   The problem brought up by Socrates:
        The being of the concepts in themselves.

                                            Sections 2 – 9.

   II. Parmenides' exemplary lecture:
        Practice in dialectics: The being of the one:
        (a) If one is.   *Sections: 10 – 23.*
        (b) If one is not.   *Sections: 24 – 27.*

C. Conclusion: Final Synopsis.   *Section 28.*

- -

The Eight Hypotheses {Propositions/*Sätze}:*

I.	If one is – *exclusive* thinking.	10 – 12	137c
II.	If one is – *inclusive* thinking.	13 – 20	142b
II(a).	The transition in the *moment.*	– 21 –	155e
III.	If one is: both inclusive and exclusive – positive.	– 22–	157b
IV.	If one is: both inclusive and exclusive – negative.	– 23 –	159b
V.	If one is not – positive.	– 24 –	160b
VI.	If one is not – negative.	– 25 –	163c
VII.	If one is not – both, positive.	– 26 –	164b
VIII.	If one is not – both, negative.	– 27 –	165e

Parmenides – Sections:

Parmenides
****
CEPHALUS NARRATES

<1.~126a]

Having left our homeland, Clazomenae, and arriving in Athens we met Adeimantus and Glaucon in the marketplace. And Adeimantus reached his hand out to me and spoke: Welcome, Cephalus – and should you be in need of anything here that lies within our power,[99] so tell us. ~ For just this purpose, I replied, that I might request something of you, this is why I am here. ~ Only say what it is that you wish, said he. ~ To this I replied: What is the name of your stepbrother on your mother's side? – for right now I cannot remember it, he was but a small child the first time I came here from Clazomenae and that, already, is long ago. His father, I believe, was named Pyrilampes. ~ Quite right, was his answer, and he himself, Antiphon. But tell me: why, actually, are you inquiring about him? ~ With me here, I replied, are fellow citizens, very philosophically inclined men, and we have heard that this Antiphon would have lived a long while with a certain Pythodorus who, in turn, was a friend of Zeno and, thus, that he was privy to the discourses in which at one time Socrates, Zeno and Parmenides had engaged themselves; that, in short, he had memorized these discourses by having heard them repeatedly through Pythodorus. ~ Totally right, Adeimantus responded. ~ Well, these discourses, I continued on, these are what we were wishing to hear. ~ There's nothing so hard about that, he answered. For even as a maturing youth Antiphon had made them his own; but now, on the contrary, just as his like-named grandfather before him, he occupies himself pre-eminently in the breeding and training of horses *{Pferdezucht}*. So, whenever you please, let's go and see him for he has only just left from here to go home and lives very close-by, in Melite. ~ Having said this we left together and met up with Antiphon at his home just as he was giving a bridle[100] over to the blacksmith for some improvements. As he finished up with him and his brothers explained to him why we had come, he recognized me from my first trip to Athens and welcomed me. And when we requested that he might tell us the discourse, well, at first he made

---

[99] "Vermögen" – also translated as capability, potency and as capacity; defined by the Eleatic Stranger in *Sophist* 247e (p. 553) as the foundation of Being or of "that which is."

[100] Including the bit upon which the linkage of the horses depends. Note Plato's recurrent analogies to horses as similes to man's soul, particularly the soul's capacity for intellection and as the wellspring of virtue. In that the *Parmenides* is a meditation on the being of the concepts, this reference to improving *{Verbesserung}* the bridle is worth special mention.

objections because, said he, that would be an arduous matter indeed; howsoever, in the end he spoke.   *[127b]*

Thus Antiphon said that Pythodorus had spoken to him: Once[101] Zeno and Parmenides had come to the Great Panathenaea. At this time Parmenides would already have been quite advanced in age, his hair totally white, but bearing a noble countenance, a good sixty-five years old. Zeno, however, would have been around forty, of a tall build with fair features and reputed as having been Parmenides' lover. They were living at that time at Pythodorus' – beyond the city walls in the Ceramicus [potter's quarter] – whither also came Socrates with a few others, and all of them were eager to hear Zeno's speech for at this time he finally had 'published' it. Now, Socrates then would still have been very young. Zeno himself gave the reading whilst Parmenides tarried outside and only a little of the reading was left when he himself, Pythodorus, as he said, came in from outside together with Parmenides and also Aristotle, who later belonged to the group of thirty [tyrants], and so they only would have heard a very little at the end of the book. Besides, he himself would already have heard the whole of it earlier from Zeno.   *<2.~127de]*

Now, after Socrates had listened through to the end he requested that the first proposition of the first book be read once more and, as that was done, he said: How, o Zeno, do you mean this? If *that which is* were to be plural *{Wenn das Seiende vieles wäre}*, so this plurality would also have to be both similar and dissimilar amongst one another? This, however, would be impossible – for neither would it be possible for the dissimilar to be similar, nor for the similar to be dissimilar?[102] Don't you mean it so? ~ Exactly so, replied Zeno. ~ And thus, since it is impossible that the similar could be dissimilar or the dissimilar similar, so it's impossible that plurality would be. For if plurality were to be it would encounter this impossibility. Is not this, what your books want to say, nothing other than despite the generally held beliefs that you assert the contrary, namely that the

---

[101] "Einst" – This entire paragraph is in the subjunctive tense giving a somewhat mythic *once upon a time* quality; unfortunately English does not support both varieties of subjunctive, lacking subjunctive-I: the sense of narration of what someone else has said. Socrates' appearance as a youth and novice also adds to this mythic quality.

[102] See *Protagoras* 331a–332a (pp. 132–133) for an introduction into the difficulty as regards the similarity and dissimilarity of righteousness and piety. That the *Parmenides* picks up precisely from this point where the *Protagoras* found a major impasse, this supports Schleiermacher's contention of their proximity and relatedness. Indeed, the impasse in *Protagoras* is only to be fully understood if one faces the yawning abyss of self-reference.

many do not exist? and hereby you hold each of your books as a proof so that you mean to have given so many proofs as you have written books? Do you mean this so, or have I not grasped it aright? *[128a]* ~ In no way, replied Zeno, rather you have understood it totally aright: this is the whole intent of my writing. ~ Then I might mention, Socrates continued on, that Zeno wishes not merely for the rest to be bound to you in friendship, Parmenides, but likewise by means of this, his manuscript. For to a certain extent he writes the same as you, only by turning it around he attempts to pull a fast one on us as if he were proving something other. For you in your poems say: *the Whole is One*, and for this you have presented proofs that are entirely good and competent. Now too, Zeno says that it is not plural and he likewise lays down grounds of proof that are many and powerful. Now this, that the one asserts, it would be one, and the other, it would not be many, and each of you discoursing with the appearance as if neither one of you had anything to do with the other, although it must indeed be approximately the same, this is over all of our heads how subtly you have carried it out. ~ Yes, Socrates, replied Zeno, though even yet you also haven't fully grasped inwardly the actual relation of this manuscript, despite that as regards the   *[c]* contents you're on the scent like a Spartan hound and you remain right on the trail. Singularly, first off you have quite missed the point that it is not at all so important that, although nothing more than what you have stated is there, there is no desire to make a mystery of it and keep it from the people, as if we wanted to accomplish something grand. Rather, what you say about the script is simply accidental; for actually my writing is meant to be a support for the proposition of Parmenides against those who make out to ridicule him – as if, were being one, then many sorts of ludicrousness that contradict him himself would come out of this proposition. This manuscript, thus, disputes against those who assert that being is plural and gives them tit for tat and then some, insofar as it seeks to make clear that there are far greater absurdities[103] consequent to the proposition that being is plural than there are to the proposition that being is one, assuming that you follow the arguments properly. Thus, it was out of such a contentious spirit that I wrote this in my youth, and once it was written somebody pilfered it from me. Then, I was at odds even with myself, seeking counsel – whether or not I should *[e]* 'publish' my writings. Hence, in that respect you deceive yourself, o Socrates, insofar as you believe that this manuscript was not written

---

[103] Human truth appears to be defined as that which entails the least amount of absurdity; see *Gorgias* 527a–end (pp. 351–352), or *Theaetetus* 200de (p. 443).

out of youthful contention but think it a veneration that becomes a
more ripened age. Otherwise, as I already said, you have not done
badly at all in your presentation. ~ Good, I accept that, said Socrates,
and I believe that it correlates just as you say. But tell me this: do
you not stipulate that there exists in and of itself a   *<3.~129a]*
concept of similarity and likewise another one the opposite of this
which is dissimilarity? And that on these two, you, I and everything
else that we call plurality take part? And whatever takes similarity
on itself becomes similar, even thereby and insofar as it takes on
similarity? but that which takes on dissimilarity becomes dissimilar?
and what takes on both becomes both? If, however, everything
partakes in both of these opposing concepts and really through this
capacity of having-in-itself of both is similar or dissimilar amongst
one another – what, then, is even so amazing in this? For indeed, if
someone were to show that similarity itself were to be dissimilar or
dissimilarity similar, that would be, I think, a wonder. But if he
shows, as above, that that which has both in itself also is predicated
by both, so I fancy, o Zeno, that this is not at all contrary to reason.
Likewise, if someone shows that everything is one because it has unity
in itself and that the same again is many because it contains a
multitude in itself; but should he show that the actual one itself is
many or, again, that plurality itself is one: this shall certainly amaze
me. And quite the same as regards everything else: if someone   *[c]*
shows that the categories and concepts themselves are predicated by
these contradictory qualities,[104] that would be something worthy of
wonder; however, if someone is able to show of me that I am one and
many, what's to wonder about? in that, indeed, he need only say – if
first he wants to show me as a plurality – that one side of me is my
left, the other my right[105]; one side my front, the other my back; as
also my top and bottom in the same way: for thus, I think, I have
plurality 'upon' myself. But if hereafter as a one, he will say that of
the seven of us here I am one person and so have unity in myself
as well, so that he would quite correctly have shown both. If, now,
someone undertakes to exhibit that things like stones and wood,[106]
and such as this – that these have both unity and plurality, so then,
we want to say that he would have shown us things as one and as
many, but not that one is many, nor many one; and he hasn't brought

---

[104] *Beschaffenheiten*, literally 'creatednesses'; compare to Meno 71b (p. 463). Wherever in
this dialogue the *qualities* of the one are mentioned the underlying German has the verb
beschaffen as a base; in and after section 22, 157b, *beschaffen* is also translated as
constitute/constitution. See also *Protagoras* 330cd (p. 132).
[105] *Phaedrus* introduces dialectics as a study of: 'left-handed' and 'right-handed' love.
[106] Compare to *Gorgias* 468a (p. 283); *Theaetetus* 156e (p. 379); *Sophist* 246b (p. 550).

forward anything wondrous at all, rather we are all happy to admit as much. If however someone, as I only just said, beginning first by separating out the concepts themselves: similarity and dissimilarity, plurality and unity, movement and rest – and all of this type – and then he shows that also these themselves can be mixed amongst one another and separated from one another, that,[107] o Zeno, said he, would overwhelm me with immense joy. I believe that the former was gone through here most astutely; far more, however, as I said, would I enjoy it if, in a like manner, someone might be able to elucidate this same difficulty just as it 'is transposed' *{verflochten}* in the concepts themselves in multifarious ways; and just as you have gone through all of this on the visible things, if you might also be able to demonstrate 'even so' on that which becomes grasped by the understanding.

<4.~130a]

In that Socrates spoke as he did, Pythodorus said, he himself believed that Parmenides and Zeno would really be put out by what he had said – but, as it turned out, they had taken pains to follow along most attentively to his speech and they often looked at one another with smiles, as if they themselves were very pleased with Socrates. Which, indeed, once he finished Parmenides expressed, saying: How greatly, o Socrates, do you deserve to become renowned due to your zealousness for indagations. And speak, do you yourself separate so – as you say – the concepts by themselves as something separate, and that in which they are taken up also as separate? And do you yourself fancy similarity to be outside of the former similarity that we have 'upon' ourselves, and so also the one and the many and everything that you have just heard Zeno mention? ~ So I fancy it, said Socrates. ~ And also with the following, a concept of justice in itself, and of beauty and goodness and of everything that is of this type? ~ Yes, he replied. ~ And how now? Also a concept of man, separate from us and from everyone who is as we are? Such a concept in itself of man, or of fire, or water? ~ As regards these, replied Socrates, I have often times been in doubt, o Parmenides, whether one should assert the same as with the previous or something other. ~ And what about such things, o Socrates, that would come out as utterly ludicrous – like hair, crap, filth and whatever else really is trivial[108] and despicable: are you in doubt as to whether one should assert that for each of these there *[d]*

---

[107] This is precisely what is shown in the *Sophist* 242b through 257b!

[108] "geringfügig" – very small. Largeness and smallness are repeating refrains in Plato, see also: *Parmenides* 164d–165e; *Protagoras* 329a, 356b; *Charmides* 173d; *Theaetetus* 145d, 152d, 165d, 208e; *Sophist* 227b, 234bc, 235e; *Phaedrus* 261b; and – most importantly: *The Republic* 368d: justice writ large in the state, small in the soul; and let's not forget that Socrates' handwriting is very small and just adequate for his own deciphering.

exists an especial concept that is separate from these things that we
have at hand? or whether we should not assert this? ~ In no way,
said Socrates, rather these things are only as we see them and to
believe that there is yet a concept of them that exists separately,
really, this may well be far too amazing. Indeed, from time to time I
am somewhat unsettled – why, then, shouldn't all things correlate in
the same manner. Then, however, when I come to stand here, I flee
in fear of sinking into a bottomless inanity in which I perish; but
when I return again to the previous objects of which we admitted just
awhile ago that, indeed, there do exist[109] concepts, so I occupy myself
with these and am quite happy attending to them. ~ You are yet
young, Socrates, replied Parmenides, and philosophy has yet to get a
grasp upon you as I believe it is going to do when you will no longer
look down upon these things as trivial. Now, however, you are yet
influenced by mankind's common opinions due to your youth. So tell
me this: do you believe, as you say, that there exist   <5.~131a]
certain concepts in which these other things partake and that through
this they acquire their names – so that that which partakes in
similarity becomes similar, what partakes in being big, 'bigness,' and
what yet in goodness and justice becomes just and good? ~ Quite,
said Socrates. ~ Then what partakes in these concepts must either
partake in the whole concept or in just a part of it? Or is there yet
some other possibility outside of these two by which something may
be partaken in? ~ How could that well be possible?[110] countered
Socrates. ~ Do you fancy it so, then, that the entire concept is in
each particular instance of the many, although it is one? or how? ~
What, o Parmenides, asked Socrates, what should hinder it from
being therein? ~ Being one and the same it should simultaneously
find itself in many disparate beings and, thus, even apart from itself
it itself should be? ~ Why not, said Socrates, when one and the same
day is simultaneously everywhere and is, nonetheless, in no way
separate from itself, so too the previous concept would be in all things
simultaneously. ~ Very charming, o Socrates, said Parmenides, do
you place one thing as itself in many places simultaneously – as if in
throwing a sail and covering up many people you would like to say,
the one would be a whole over the many. Or do you not believe that
this, approximately, is what you said? ~ Perhaps. ~ Now, would *[c]*

---

[109] "geben" – German has a lower order way of predicating being by saying that *'it gives'* –
having little recourse I translate this generally with *exists* though this should not be confused
with the higher order state of essential being , *Wesen,* that is translated both as existence and
essence.

[110] "Wie sollte es wohl?" – When this rhetorical answer shows up, as it often does in Plato's
dialogues, it's time for the reader to put on his thinking cap.

that sail be wholly over each, or rather more accurately over each individual a different part of the same? ~ Indeed, just a part. ~ Divisible, then, o Socrates, are the concepts themselves and that which has them in itself would have only a part in itself and no longer is the whole concept in each thing, but just a part of the concept. ~ So it seems, at least. ~ Shall this, then, be what you want, said he, that the one concept for us really shall be split up and shall it, then, still be one? ~ In no way. ~ For look a little further, said Parmenides, if you want to split up the concept bigness and then each of the many big things through one of bigness' own smaller pieces of bigness should be big – isn't this obviously unreasonable? ~ Really, very, said he. ~ And how, if each received a small part of equality then should it, because it has something that is smaller than   [131d] the concept of equality, even thereby be equal to something else? ~ Impossible. ~ But one of us may have a piece of smallness, so shall the concept of smallness itself be bigger than this, this which is only one part of it. Smallness itself shall, accordingly, be bigger; that to which the piece which was taken away was given would become smaller, not bigger as it was before. ~ This really cannot be, said he. ~ In what way then, o Socrates, do you suggest that the other things should take up the concepts since they can do so neither in part nor wholly? ~ By Zeus, said Socrates, it doesn't appear to me at all easy to set this to rights. ~ How about this? What, now, do you think of the following? ~ What's that? ~ I believe that the underlying   [a] reason why you take the position that each concept in itself would be one is this: if, namely, you say that many sorts of things appear to you to be big, so perhaps there appears to you to be one and the same form {*Gestalt*} or idea when you look at all of them wherefore you then believe, 'bigness' is one. ~ Totally right, he said. ~ Now, how about bigness itself and the other big things, if you review all of these together in your mind doesn't there appear to you one 'bigity'[111] by which it is necessary that all of these appear as big? ~ I see what you mean, quite. ~ Yet a different concept of bigness, thus, makes its appearance before you apart from the prior initial bigness and those things which partook therein, and yet again over all of these together *yet another* whereby all of these are big, and thus your unitary concept becomes not one but, rather, an unlimited multitudinous. ~ But, o Parmenides, said Socrates, what if each of these   <6.~132b] concepts is only a thought for which it is only befitting that it be nowhere else other than in our minds {*in den Seelen*}. For so, indeed, each would be 'of-one' and it wouldn't happen to them as was said

---

[111] Rhymes with quiddity, and certainly qualifies as "a different concept of bigness."

earlier. ~ How now, replied Parmenides, each of these thoughts
would be one, but a thought of naught? ~ Impossible. ~ Then, of
something? ~ Yes. ~ Which is, or which is not? ~ Which is. ~
Isn't it true, of a certain something that is known, which is even the
former thought that we noticed found itself in all of the previous
things as one definite form or idea? ~ Yes. ~ And shouldn't this be
the concept that is so conceived as being one, being always the same
in everything? ~ That, again, appears as necessary. ~ But then
further, said Parmenides, if you assert that all the other things have
the concepts in themselves, doesn't this have to mean that you believe
that either each consists out of thought, and thus they are all
thinking, or you believe that they are thoughts and yet are not
thinking? ~ Even that too, said Socrates, that doesn't make any
sense. Rather, o Parmenides, it actually seems to me to correlate so,
namely, these concepts subsist as archetypes {*Urbilder*}   *[132d]*
within nature and all the other things, then, approximate
{*gleichen[are-likened]*} them and are their reflections {*Nachbilder*};
and that the partaking of the concepts in these other things is nothing
other than that these have become reflected[112] in them. ~ If, now,
said Parmenides, something has become a reflection of a concept, is it
possible that the concept is *not* similar to that wherein it has become
reflected insofar as the latter has been made similar to it? ~ No,
that's not possible. ~ And is it not very necessary that the similar
must have taken up one and the same concept as that to which it is
similar? ~ That's necessary. ~ But that through the partaking of
which in itself similar things are similar, isn't that even the concept?
~ Indeed, in all ways. ~ Thus, it is not possible that something be
similar to a concept nor a concept to something other, otherwise
there will always appear another concept above the first and,   *[133a]*
when this is again similar, still another, and this reappearance of a
new concept would never stop if the concept should be similar to that
which is partaking in it. ~ That is very correct. ~ Thus, not by
similarity do the other things partake in concepts, rather we must
seek for some other way through which they can partake in them. ~
That's how matters stand. ~ Now do you see, o Socrates, said
Parmenides, how great the difficulty is when one clarifies that
concepts exist in and of themselves? ~ Yes, very much. ~ Only
know it, nonetheless, said he continuing on, that, to say it straight-
out, you still have not even touched upon how great the perplexity is
if you would want to set up a concept separately for 'each and every'

---

[112] Compare to *Theaetetus* 144bc (p. 362) – "the oil," and 194b (p. 433) – "the wax"; and
also *Sophist* 236a–237 (pp. 538–539): replica {*Ebenbild*} and deceitful imagery {*Trugbild*}.

every time. ~ How is that? asked Socrates. ~ Amongst the many other perplexities, said Parmenides, the greatest is this: that if someone wants to assert that it would be predicated of these concepts that there is no possibility of having any cognizance of them were they to be so constituted as we said that they would have to be, so it would be impossible to prove to him, he who says this, that he is wrong – unless this doubter already is much practiced[113] and quite gifted, and also willingly ready to take pleasure in following many long, tedious and farfetched clarifications brought forward by him, he who would lead the proof; otherwise it would be impossible to persuade him about this, he who wants to assert that the concepts would be unknowable. ~ How do you come to this, o Parmenides?   *[133c]* asked Socrates. ~ Because I believe, Socrates, that you as well as everyone else who stipulates that for every single thing there exists an essence for itself shall also admit, firstly, that not a single such is to be found here amongst us? ~ How otherwise would it be in itself, said Socrates. ~ Quite right,[114] said Parmenides. Thus, those ideas that are as they are only in contra-relation to each other and have their essence in itself only in such relation to each other and not in any relation to their reflections as they present themselves in us, or however else one may contend regarding that by the partaking of which in ourselves we shall be named 'this' and 'that.' That which is present by us is to the like-named former as such again only in connection to one another of itself and not to the concepts, and it is for itself and again not for the former that also are so named. ~ How do you mean this? asked Socrates. ~ So, said Parmenides, that if one of us is the other's lord or servant, so he is not the lord in itself, that which denominates lord, and not his servant; nor also the servant in itself, that which denominates servant; lord is the lord; rather *as men* these are both for one another. Lordship itself, however, is what it is as from servitude itself, and likewise is servitude itself servitude for lordship itself. Whatever is by us does not get its potency in relation to the former, nor do the former from us; rather, as I said, under itself and for itself is the former and ours likewise for itself.   *<7.~134a]* Or don't you understand what I mean? ~ Very well, said Socrates, do I understand it. ~ Hence, he continued on, also the knowledge in itself of what knowledge is would be the knowledge of this in itself,

---

[113] The *Parmenides* is such a practice.

[114] Actually, *Quite Wrong* – which accounts for Parmenides' parody which follows. Moreover, I'd fancy that this is the closest Plato ever comes to saying, albeit obliquely: *cogito ergo sum.* On the other hand – the entire *Parmenides* is, as it were, **a** *cogito sum.* On the other hand, if we are just fleeting shadows, then quite right; i.e.: the truth may fall somewhere in between.

what truth is? ~ Quite. ~ And every particular bit of knowledge in itself would likewise only be knowledge of the objects in themselves. Or not? ~ Well, yes. ~ But the knowledge that we have, must it not be in relation to our truth? and so every bit of our knowledge would necessarily only be of particular objects around us? ~ That's *[134b]* necessary. ~ However, we neither have the concepts in themselves, as you admit, nor is it possible that we might ever meet up with them. ~ In no way. ~ It follows that from the concept in itself of knowledge the categories themselves become known, what each is? ~ Yes. ~ Which we, howsoever, don't have. ~ No, indeed not. ~ Thus, we ourselves will never recognize a concept in itself, as such knowledge is not given to us. ~ It appears not. ~ Uncognizable for us, then, is beauty itself, what it is, and so too goodness and everything of which we have notions as being ideas for themselves. ~ So it seems, unfortunately. ~ But, now, look at this which, yet, is even more exasperating. ~ At what? ~ Will you or will you not admit that if there exists a category of knowledge in itself, this type would have to be far more exact than the knowledge that is by us, and so too with beauty and everything else in the same way? ~ Yes. ~ If this category of knowledge in itself is to be possessed by anything other, so you wouldn't want that anyone else other than God would have this most consummate Knowledge? ~ Naturally. ~ Shall now such *[d]* a God, himself possessing Knowledge itself, be capable, on the other hand, to have cognizance of that which is by us? ~ But, why not? ~ Because, said Parmenides, we did agree, o Socrates, that neither the former concepts have any potency *{Vermögen}* in connection to what is present around us, nor is that which is present around us related to the former; rather, each from the other is separate [being] for itself. ~ Indeed, we did so agree. ~ If, then, this most exact Lordship is present with God and thereby He has the most exact Cognition, so this same Lordship over the former shall never Lord over us, nor will this Supreme Knowledge be cognizant of us or of anything that is around us. Rather, quite the same way as our lordship in no wise lords over the former, nor can we recognize anything of the divine with our cognition, so too and for the very same reason the Gods are not *our* Lords, nor as Gods do they know aught of human things. ~ But, said he, is this not an all too wondrous speech if one steals away divinity's omniscience! ~ But nonetheless, o Socrates, said Parmenides, this and yet much more must follow validly   *[135a]* from these concepts if these ideas of things should be and anyone stipulates the former concept as 'in itself.' So that whosoever hears this must become thoughtful and take contentious issue that such things would exist at all, or if so, that they would have to be completely beyond the cognition of human nature. And whoever says this must not only believe to have said something aright, rather – as we even just said – great are the difficulties in convincing anyone other, and very well-gifted must he be, he who is to be able to conceive this and grasp it, that such a category of particulars exists and an essence in itself; and yet more admirable and the greatest marksman is he: he who discovers these things and is able to lay it all out properly, segregating one thing from the other and, so, is able to teach others. ~ This, o Parmenides, I concede to you, said Socrates, for what you say is wholly in accord with my sensibilities. ~ All the same, o Socrates, said Parmenides, if on the other side someone will not give in that there do exist concepts of that which is – even because he looks over all that we have just said and more of a similar bent – and he will not postulate definite concepts for every particularity, so he shall have nowhere toward which he may turn his understanding if he disallows ideas for all that is, ideas that remain always the same, and so he totally overthrows the capacity for investigating [through discourse and dialectics,] which consequence it appears that you, quite admirably, have foreseen. ~ Totally right, said Socrates. ~ What, then, are you going to do with   *<8.~135cd]* respect to philosophy? whither will you turn yourself if you should be incapable of achieving cognition regarding these things? ~ I don't believe that I can foresee this aright, just now. ~ All too early, said Parmenides, before you have done the proper exercises, o Socrates, do you take on the task to determine what beauty is, and the just and the good, and so too with every other concept. And just recently did I notice this as I heard you conversing with Aristotle. Beautiful, indeed, and godly, know it, is the inclination that drives you to these indagations. But stretch yourself first yet better and exercise yourself with that which has been held for useless and by the great majority is named blather, [all of this twaddle about pure knowing,] and do so whilst you are still young: for if not, indeed, truth will escape you. ~ But what, o Parmenides, is the way and means of exercising oneself? ~ The same, o Socrates, that even now you have heard from Zeno. Thereby I was very much pleased with you when you said to him that you would not allow that the investigations should be limited to just the sensible things and in relation to such, but rather also in relation to that which one eminently grasps with one's understanding and holds to as concepts – and to which and in the greatest degree every-one does ascribe definitive being.[115] ~ It appeared to me, added Socrates, not to be difficult by the former method to show of things

---

[115] "dem jeder ein bestimmtes Sein am meisten zuschreibt." – only in *Akademie-Verlag.*

that they are both similar and dissimilar, and that just about everything that one wants can be predicated. ~ And rightly so, said
Parmenides. Beyond that, however, you still have to do this: that not
only do you postulate being in your indagations and see what results
from this stipulation, rather also you must lay down as a basis that
the same wouldn't be, if you want to exercise yourself even *[136a]*
better. ~ How do you mean that? asked Socrates. ~ For instance,
said Parmenides, to the stipulation that Zeno followed, if plurality is,
what must then be the consequences for plurality itself in itself and in
relation to the one, and also for the one itself and in its relation to the
many; and even thus you also have to investigate if plurality is not,
what then are the results for the one as well as for plurality, each in
itself and in relation to the other. Just so, if you stipulate regarding
whether similarity exists or doesn't exist, you then look to see what
the consequences are for each of these stipulations, as well for that
itself which was stipulated and also for everything other as a totality,
both in itself and in relation, the one to the other. The same applies
to dissimilarity, and to movement and rest, and to coming-into-being
and passing-away, and even to being itself and non-being. And, with
one word, whatever foundation you might postulate, taking it as being
and as non-being or as whatever else, and from here you must look at
what results each time for that itself which was postulated and for
each other particular that you will take up, as well for the majority as
also for everything as a totality, even so. And, then too, what results
for the remaining, in itself and in relation to each particular that you
choose to examine, you might now have started from the proposition
that something is or that it is not – if, then, you desire that these
exercises reach their consummation: that your vision may pierce
through [illusion] right down to the foundation of truth.[116] ~ An
unending occupation, o Parmenides, is what you have described, said
Socrates, and I still do not properly understand it. Why don't you
yourself go through it once, stipulating something or other, so that I
might the better grasp your meaning. ~ A great work, o Socrates,
said he, will you lay upon me, and in my years. ~ But what about *[d]*
you, then, o Zeno, said Socrates, why won't you take something up? ~
Thereupon Zeno answered with a smile: We want to request him
himself, Parmenides; for that is no trifling matter – what he says – or
do you yourself not see what a work it is to which you encourage him?
If, now, there were more of us, it would do us no good to request it of
him: for of no avail is it to converse such things before many, even
less with a man of his years. For only the fewest know that only so, by

---

[116] "wenn du vollkommen geübt auch die Wahrheit gründlich durchschauen willst."

going through and wandering around the whole expanse, thus alone is it possible to really achieve proper insight hitting upon truth. Thus, o Parmenides, I unite myself with Socrates and his request, that after so long a time I might hear you once again. As Zeno said this Antiphon related that Pythodorus himself, as he told him, and also Aristotle and the others, they all entreated Parmenides that he might indeed give them an example of what he meant and that nothing other than this would do. ~ To this Parmenides said: <9.~137a] I must well obey, although it shall go, I believe, as with Ibycus' steed that still a valiant {wacker[117]}, indeed, but aged charger, cognizant of that before which it was standing, the battle of the chariots, it shuttered and even therefore Ibycus gave comparison to himself saying that he too was being compelled against his will and already so aged yet once more to ride upon the track of love.[118]   So I also feel as I think about that before which I am standing, not little fear: how well should I at such an age be able to swim through such a great and difficult sea of indagations.   All the same, for I must satisfy your wishes and particularly as Zeno, too, is in one accord on this – and we are, assuredly, amongst ourselves. Whence, then, *whence* should we begin? and what is it that we want to lay down first? Are you willing, as this arduous game should yet be played out once again, that I begin from myself and from my stipulation by which I lay down the foundation of the one itself: if it is and if it is not – what, then, must result? ~ By all means, do that, said Zeno. ~ But who, said Parmenides, who will answer me? not the youngest? For he would be the least likely to be smart-alecky and would certainly answer what he means,[119] and at the same time his answers would provide me with a resting point. ~ I am ready to answer you, o Parmenides, said Aristotle – for it is me you mean when you mean the youngest. Ask away and do not be concerned about the respondent, I shall willingly answer. ~

<10.~137c]

---

[117] "wacker" likewise is the adjective bestowed twice upon Theaetetus; *Theaetetus* 151d/e, and again in *Sophist* 239b. Note: "wacker" was first encountered just before section 4 at 130a – "most astutely" – (p. 211); note too – other translations use the word "manfully."

[118] Note again a threefold analogy: Parmenides to Ibycus to Ibycus' steed. Nor should we forget that this is Cephalus remembering Antiphon's remembrance of Pythodorus' recollection of his own presence. Incidentally, this is the only spot in *Parmenides* where Plato somewhat quotes from another poet, something which he regularly does in his other dialogues. Ibycus is also mentioned in *Phaedrus* at 242d (p. 27).

[119] Saying what you think is a cardinal rule for Socratic discourse, see footnote #146 (p. 314).

Tallyho, said Parmenides, if one is, then indeed, it cannot well be that one is many? ~ How should that well be! ~ Neither is there permitted to be parts of the same, nor is it itself permitted to be whole. ~ How's that? ~ A part is always, indeed, part of a whole? ~ Yes. ~ And how about a whole? wouldn't that be whole which isn't missing any parts? ~ Quite. ~ In both cases the one shall be made up from parts, if either it be whole or if it is parts? ~ Necessarily. ~ In both cases, then, the one would be many and not one. ~ Right. ~ It should not be many, however, but one. ~ So it should. ~ Neither, then, is it possible that the one be whole nor may it have parts, if it should be one? ~ No, indeed not. ~ If, then, there are really to be no parts, so it has neither beginning nor end nor middle. For the likes as these would already, indeed, be parts of the same. ~ Right. ~ Certainly beginning and end are the boundaries of each and every. ~ How else? ~ Unbounded, then, is the one, if it has neither beginning nor end? ~ Unbounded. ~ Thus too, without form {*Gestalt*} for it can have neither roundness nor straightness in itself. ~ How's that? ~ Roundness is even that which has ends standing equidistant from the middle. ~ Yes. ~ Straight is that, however, whose middle lies right between both ends. ~ So it is. ~ Thus, if it should be that the one would have parts and were to be many, then it might have either a straight or a rounded form. ~ Quite. ~ Thus, it is neither straight nor rounded if, indeed, it doesn't even have parts. ~ Right. ~ *[138a]* Further, if these are its qualities, so it is not possible for it to be anywhere. For neither can it be in an other, nor can it be in itself. ~ But, how's that? ~ Were it to be in an other then it would have to be surrounded with the other all around it and it would be touching the other in manifold ways in many places. But for the one, that which is without parts and has nothing of roundness in itself, it is not possible that it shall be encircled by something touching up against it in many places. ~ Impossible. ~ Then again, if it is to be in itself, it would itself have to encompass itself – and yet being nothing other than itself – if, then, indeed, it should be in itself. For that something might be in something that does not surround it, this is impossible. ~ Indeed, impossible. ~ Thus, something other would be surrounding and, then again, something other would be the surrounded. *[138b]* For as a whole the selfsame cannot both suffer and do. And, accordingly, the one would no longer be one but two. ~ Indeed, not one. ~ Thus, the one is absolutely nowhere if it subsists neither in itself nor in an other. ~ No, it isn't. ~ Take a look, if it correlates so, whether it is well-nigh possible for it to endure or to change. ~ *<11.]* But, why not? ~ Because if it changes then either it moves itself or it alters itself. For these are the only ways of changing. ~ Yes. ~

Should the one alter itself, so it would be impossible for it to still be one. ~ Impossible. ~ Thus, it doesn't change by way of alteration. ~ Obviously not. ~ But, maybe through movement? ~ Maybe. ~ Singularly, if the one were itself to move, so either it would have to spin around in the selfsame place or it would have to switch from one place to another. ~ Necessarily. ~ But, isn't it true, if it spun itself around it would have to rest on its center and have other parts that themselves moved around the center? That to which neither middle nor parts belong, in what way should such ever spin itself around the center? ~ In no way. ~ Should it switch places, so   *[d]* it would come in every other time into some other place and move itself thus? ~ If, indeed, it should be moving. ~ That it should be in something has already been shown to us to be impossible for the one. ~ Yes. ~ Is there not anything yet more impossible than that it come into something? ~ I'm not following you, how so? ~ If something is to be arriving somewhere, then isn't it necessary partly that it not yet be there, since it is supposed to be just arriving, and partly also that it not wholly be outside of the selfsame, since it, indeed, is already arriving. ~ That's necessary. ~ If, then, this can be possible for something, so only for that which has parts. For of such can some of it be in something and the other parts simultaneously be outside of the selfsame; that which has no parts is not in a position to be in any way simultaneously either inside or outside of something else. ~ That's right. ~ That which neither has parts nor is whole, can there be anything yet more impossible than that such should enter into some place, since it can enter in neither partly nor wholly? ~ *[139a]* Obviously. ~ Neither, then, can it switch places by leaving one place and entering into another, nor can it change either by spinning in the selfsame place or through alteration. ~ It appears not. ~ For every type of change, then, the one is immobile. ~ Immobile. ~ But we also assert that it is impossible for it to be in something. ~ We assert that. ~ Thus, it shall never remain in any particular place. ~ How's that? ~ Because it would even have to be in that where it should remain. ~ That's true. ~ But it can subsist neither in itself nor in something other. ~ No, indeed not. ~ Never, then, can the one remain anywhere. ~ It appears not. ~ But what never remains anywhere, this has no rest and does not endure. ~ No, not possible. ~ The one, then, as it seems, neither endures nor changes. ~ Indeed not, as we have seen. ~ But further, it does not become the same *{einerlei}*, neither to its own self nor with an other; but yet again neither could it be that it differs either from its own self or from an other. ~ How's that? ~ Were it to be different from its own self, so it would be different from the one, and thus, not be one. ~ True. ~

Furthermore, if it were to be the same as an other, thus it   *[139c]*
would be the former but would no longer be itself. So that in this way
it would no longer be what it is, one, rather [it would be] an other
than one. ~ No, indeed. ~ Thus, the same as an other or different
from its own self, it shall not be. ~ No. ~ However, it also does not
become different from an other so long as it is one. For it is not at all
suitable for the one to be different from anything at all, rather alone
the different suits being-different and nothing other. ~ Right. ~
Insofar, then, as it is one, it shall not be different. Or do you believe
[it might]? ~ No, not at all. ~ If, however, not in-so-far then also
not in-as-much as it it itself is; and if not in-as-much as it it itself is,
then utterly not itself. If it, thus, itself is in no way different, then it's
also not different from something. ~ Right. ~ But it would also not
become the same as itself. ~ Why not? ~ The nature of the one is
not identical to that of being the same. ~ Come again? ~ Because
not if something should become the same as something does it also
become one. ~ But, what then? ~ What has become the same as the
many, that, necessarily, has become many and not one. ~ That's
true. ~ Rather, only if the one and the same were not at all different
from each other, then it would be necessary that if something had
become the same then it would also always have to have become   *[e]*
one, and when one then the same. ~ Quite. ~ Thus, if the one shall
itself come to be the same as itself it shall not be one with itself – and
so it shall in being one also not be one. ~ But that's quite impossible.
~ Then, it is also impossible for the one to be either different from
an other or the same as itself. ~ Impossible. ~ Thus the one,
accordingly, would indeed be different or the same neither with itself
nor with an other. ~ No, indeed not. ~ It shall also be neither
similar nor dissimilar, neither with itself nor with an other. ~ How's
that? ~ Because that to which some sort of sameness is predicated
is similar. ~ Yes. ~ Sameness has shown itself by its nature to
be apart from the one. ~ It was so shown. ~ If something other
were predicated of the one outside of being one, so more would be
predicated of the one than being one; this, however, is impossible. ~
Yes. ~ Thus, never can the same be a predicate of the one, neither
with an other nor with itself. ~ Obviously not. ~ Thus also, it cannot
be similar, neither to an other nor to it itself. ~ It appears not. ~
Just as little is it a predicate of the one that it be different: for also
thus the one would be predicated as being more than one. ~ Indeed,
more. ~ Now, whatever is predicated as [being] something different
either from itself or from an other, that would have to be   *[140b]*
dissimilar to itself or to the other – if, then, that which has the
predicate of sameness is similar. ~ Right. ~ The one, then, as it

appears, which in no wise is predicated as being something different, is also in no way dissimilar, neither to it itself nor to an other. ~ No, quite. ~ Thus, the one would not be such: neither similar nor dissimilar, neither to itself nor to an other. ~ Obviously not. ~ But, [being] of such qualities, it shall also be neither equal nor unequal, neither to itself nor to an other. ~ How's that? ~ To be equal it shall have to be of the same mass as that to which it is equal. ~ Yes. ~ *[c]* To be larger or smaller it would be necessary that in relation to [various] things of equal mass that it have more mass than the smaller and less mass than the greater. ~ Yes. ~ But in relation to things of unequal mass must it not be of less mass than some and of greater mass than the others. ~ How else? ~ But isn't it impossible that that to which sameness is not at all predicated, could such ever be the same in mass, or the same in anything else? ~ Impossible. ~ Equal is it, thus, neither to itself nor to an other, as it is not of the same mass? ~ No, as it has shown itself. ~ Should it, however, be of less mass or of more, then it would have to be of so much mass, of so many parts and, thus, it again would be not one but 'of so many' as it had mass. ~ Right. ~ But is it just of one mass, so it would be equal to such a mass. But this has shown itself to be impossible that it would be able to be equal to anything. ~ So it was shown. ~ In that it has neither one mass in itself, nor many, nor few, nor utterly any sameness – it shall be equal neither to it itself nor to an other, and just as little be larger or smaller as it itself or an other. ~ In every way, it correlates so. ~ And how? do you fancy that the *<12.~140e]* one would be able to be older or younger or yet as having the same age as anything? ~ But, why not? ~ Because, that it might be the same in age to itself or to something other, it would have to have an equality in time or be itself capable of partaking in similarity, which it even, as we have said, does not have in itself, neither equality nor similarity. ~ Indeed, so we said. ~ But also that it wouldn't have in itself any dissimilarity nor any inequality, this we also said. ~ Quite. ~ How, then, how shall it be possible that it be older or younger than anything else, or even of the same age, since it correlates so? ~ In no way. ~ So, accordingly, the one is neither older nor younger nor of the same age, neither to itself nor to something other. ~ Obviously not. ~ Thus, is it allowable, then, that the one be in time at all – if it has these qualities? Or isn't it necessary that what is in time always becomes older than itself? ~ That's necessary. ~ And what is older is even always only older to something younger? ~ What else? ~ What, then, becomes older than itself, that too becomes simultaneously younger than itself – if, then, it should even have something to which it becomes older. ~ How do you mean this? ~

Thus: one thing is not permitted to become different from the other by first becoming that from which it already is different; rather, from that which is already different, from this it is different, from that from which it has become, from this it did become, from that to which it will become, to this it will be becoming; but whence it ever becomes different, from this it has not yet become different and it shall also not first become so and also isn't so as of yet, rather it becomes even so and is not otherwise. ~ Naturally, indeed. ~ But now, what *[c]* is older is in differentiation from that which is younger, and from nothing other. ~ So it is. ~ Thus, what becomes older than itself, this necessarily at the same time also becomes younger than itself. ~ So it seems. ~ Nonetheless, it must have neither more time in becoming itself nor also less, rather in equal time with itself it becomes, is, has become and will become. ~ That's all quite necessary. ~ Then it is also necessary, as it seems, that everything that is in time and belongs intrinsically to it has the same age as itself and simultaneously is also becoming older as well as younger than itself. ~ That's the way it looks. ~ But the one has nothing from all of these qualities in itself? ~ Nothing. ~ Thus, it also has no time in itself and is not in time. ~ Indeed not, as our conversation has shown. ~ How now? Was and became and has become, do these not point to that which has itself been at some past time? ~ *[141e]* Indeed. ~ And shall be and will have become and shall be becoming – these all at an approaching future. ~ Yes. ~ And is and becomes, at the now present? ~ Without a doubt. ~ If, then, the one in no wise has any sort of time in itself: thus it has never become nor was it becoming nor has it ever been; nor has it now become nor is it becoming nor is it; nor shall it in the future have become nor be becoming nor shall it be. ~ Absolutely right. ~ Is there, then, any other way besides these that something is able to have being? ~ There's none.[120] ~ Then, the one has no modus of being? ~ No, not as it looks. ~ In no way, then, is the one. ~ No, as it has shown itself. ~ It is, thus, also not possible that the one is. For as such it would even have to be and have being in itself. Rather, as it seems, the one is neither one nor is it – if a person is allowed to believe in such a speech. ~ That's about it. ~ However, of that which is not, is it possible for such non-being to have something? – or for someone to have something of it? ~ How should we? ~ Thus, there is also no word for it, no clarification of it, nor also any type of knowledge, [sense] perception or notionality. ~ Obviously not. ~ Thus, it shall

---

[120] This is one of Aristotle's big mistakes, as pointed out by Mitchell Miller's excellent: *Plato's Parmenides – The Conversion of the Soul*, 1986 – Princeton University Press.

not be named, nor clarified, nor do we have any notion of it, nor any cognition, nor is anything else that might pertain to it to be perceived.[121] ~ It appears not. ~ Is it, then, well-nigh possible that this is the way that the one correlates? ~ Most probably not, not as I would fancy it. ~ Do you want, then, that we return once more to the beginning and our stipulation and go through it once again observing whether something shall present itself differently? ~ I want to, very much so. ~   <13.~142b]

All right, if one is – this, indeed, is what we say – what, then, shall follow this; and no matter what these consequences may be, these we must acknowledge. Isn't this true? ~ Yes. ~ Then look once more at the beginning. If one is, is it then possible that indeed it is, but that in itself it has no being? ~ No, not possible. ~ Thus, there would indeed be the being of the one as well, and not just being being the same as the one: for otherwise the former would not be its being and it, the one, would not have being in itself, rather it would be quite the same to say: *one is* and *one one*. But this is not our stipulation, if one one, what then follows, rather if one is. Isn't it so? ~ Indeed. ~ So, accordingly, the is means something different from the one? ~ Necessarily. ~ Shall, then, something other possibly be meant than that one has being in itself, if anyone should say, putting it all together: One is? ~ This, indeed. ~ Once more, then, let us say – if one is – what shall follow out of this. Watch closely, whether this stipulation necessarily shows the one as something that has parts? ~ But, how's that? ~ So. If we speak of the 'is' of the one which is *[d]* and of the 'one' of the being which is one, it is, however, not the selfsame, being and one, rather *of* the selfsame, even of that which we stipulated, of the one which is – is it, then, not necessarily the whole one which is, and shall not one and being be parts hereof? ~ Necessarily. ~ Do we want, then, to name each of these parts only as a part, or don't we have to call each part, part of a whole? ~ Of the whole. ~ Thus a whole is, when one is, and it has parts. ~ Quite. ~ How now? shall perhaps either of these two parts of the one which is, one and being, ever let go: either the one to be a part of being or the being to be a part of one? ~ That shall not happen. ~ Thus, once again each of these parts holds on tight, both to one as well as to being. And so each part comes-to-be again having at least both of these parts. And thus, always in the same way, whichever part is set always holds on to both parts. For one is latched onto being and being onto one so that, necessarily, what always becomes 'of-two'

---

[121] These are the same "ways of knowing" explored in *Theaetetus.*

never is one. ~ Indeed, every which way. ~ Is not, then,   *[143a]*
in this manner the one which is endless in multitude? ~ So, at least,
it seems. ~ Look as well at this. ~ What? ~ We have said that the
one has being intrinsically because it is. ~ Yes. ~ And therefore the
one which is has appeared to us as many? ~ So it is. ~ How now? –
the one itself to which we ascribed being, should we take this into
our mind alone and for itself without that which it, as we said,
has intrinsically, shall it at least for us appear as one, or likewise
again in itself intrinsically[122] as many? ~ As one, I at least believe. ~
Let us see then. Is it not necessary that the being of the same is
something other and it itself also something other as, indeed, one is
not being, rather as one only has being intrinsically? ~ Necessarily.
~ Should, then, the one be something other and being something
other: so it is neither due to the power {*vermöge*} of the oneness of
one that one is different from being, nor is it due to the power of
being that being is different from one, rather, it is due to the power of
difference and otherness that they are different from one another.
~ Quite. ~ So that the different is the same neither with the one nor
with being? ~ How could it be? ~ How now, if we remove   *[c]*
from these any way that you want: being and difference, or being and
one, or one and difference – have we not in every instance removed
what we may rightfully name both? ~ But, how's that? ~ So. Being
can be said. ~ Yes. ~ And then afterwards, one also can be said? ~
This too. ~ Is not, then, each of these spoken of separately? ~ Yes.
~ But if I say being and one – are not, then, both spoken. ~ Indeed.
~ So too, if I say being and difference, or difference and one, so too I
certainly say both every time. ~ Yes. ~ What justifiably is named
both, can that indeed be both but not two? ~ Impossible. ~ What
was two, must not each for itself be one? ~ There's no way around
that. ~ As these, then, are always together two, so also must each be
one for itself. ~ Obviously. ~ If, however, each of these is one and
we would augment any of the combinations by some other one, would
not the total necessarily be three? ~ Yes. ~ And is not three uneven
and two even? ~ How else? ~ And how? – if two exists must there
not also exist duplicity; and if three, triplicity? – for, indeed, in two
lies twice one, and in three thrice one? ~ Necessarily. ~ But if two
and twice are wouldn't there also necessarily be twice two? –   *[e]*
and if three and thrice then also necessarily thrice three? ~ How
else? ~ And how? if there is three and twice and also two and thrice,

---

[122] "oder auch so an sich selbst als Vieles" – unfortunately, English doesn't have the same
fluidity in showing self-reference in two different ways; later – 157c, "an sich" is rendered as
"implicitly."

then isn't also necessary twice three and thrice two? ~ Very much so. ~ Then too, there is evenness an even number of times and oddness an odd number of times, and evenness an odd number and oddness an even number. ~ So it is. ~ If, then, this correlates so, do you think that there might be any number yet remaining that doesn't necessarily exist? ~ None, certainly. ~ Then, if one is, so too, by necessity, is number? ~ Necessarily. ~ And if number is, so is the many and an unending multitude of being? – or shall number not be limitless in multitude and have being intrinsically? ~ Indeed, certainly. ~ If, then, each number has being intrinsically, so too must each individual part of number have being intrinsically. ~ Yes. ~ Thus, under everything which is as many, being is   <14.~144b] divided up and abandons nothing of everything that is, neither the smallest nor the largest? Or isn't it unreasonable to even pose such a question? – for how might it well be possible that being would abandon something that is? ~ In no way. ~ It is split up amongst the smallest and the largest and upon each and every type of being and it is partitioned more than anything else and so there exist innumerable pieces of being? ~ That's the way it correlates. ~ Being has more parts than everything [else]? ~ Indeed, more. ~ How now? – does there exist from amongst all of them something that, though it would be a part of being, but [still it would be] not a part? ~ How would something like this be possible? ~ Rather, if a part is, then, by necessity, so long as it is, it is one; naught can it not possibly be. ~ No, not possible. ~ Oneness is an attribute of each individual part of being and it abandons neither the smallest nor the largest nor yet any other one. ~ So it is. ~ Is the one able, now,   [144d] to be in many places simultaneously and yet be whole?   Look sharp. ~ I am looking and I see that this is not possible. ~ Split up then, if not whole.   For otherwise there is no way that it can subsist simultaneously in all parts of being that are split asunder. ~ Yes. ~ That which is split up into parts is necessarily so many as there are parts. ~ Necessarily. ~ Thus, we did not speak correctly as we even said that just being would be separated into more parts than everything else, for it is no more split up than is the one, rather, equally, as it appears, as is the one; for neither does being abandon the one nor does the one abandon being, rather these two become always and in all places with everything equally. ~ So, obviously, it has shown itself, all around. ~ Thus also is the one, even when cut apart from being, itself many and unbounded multitude. ~ Obviously. ~ Not only, then, is the one which is many, rather also the one itself separated from being is necessarily many.   <15.~145a] ~ Quite. ~ Furthermore, since parts are parts of a whole: thus the one is limited in relation to the whole. Or shall the parts not be encompassed within the whole? ~ Necessarily. ~ And that which encompasses is the limit? ~ How should it not be so! ~ The one, therefore, is one and many, whole and parts, limited and unlimited multitude. ~ Obviously. ~ Not also, when indeed limited, then having borders as well. ~ Necessarily. ~ And how, if it is a whole shall it not have a beginning, a middle and an end? Or is it possible that something would be a whole without these three? And should something lack any one of these, shall such still be able to be a whole? ~ It shall not be able. ~ Thus too, a beginning – as it seems – and a middle and an end belong to the one. ~ It has these. ~ But the middle stands equidistant from the borders, otherwise it wouldn't be the middle. ~ Indeed, no. ~ Thus some unique form, as it seems, belongs to the one which has these qualities, be it now either straight or crooked or a mixture of both? ~ A shape it must have. ~ And shall it not, when it so correlates, be in itself and in an other? ~ How so? ~ Amongst the parts is not each and every in the whole and none of them outside of the whole? ~ Right. ~ And all of the parts shall be encompassed by the whole? ~ Yes. ~ Further, are not all the parts the one, and neither more nor less than these as a totality? *[c]* ~ Indeed, not. ~ And now, is not the whole one as well? ~ How shouldn't it be. ~ If, then, all of the parts are in the whole, but the parts as well as the whole itself are one, and all shall be encompassed by the whole, so shall the one be encompassed within the one and, thus, the one would already be in itself. ~ Obviously. ~ But the whole is still, nonetheless, not in the parts, neither in all nor in a few. For if in all, then too, necessarily, in each one. For not being in any given one, so it would no longer be possible that it be in all of them together; and if this one belongs to them as a totality but the whole, affirmatively, is not in it – how could it yet be in all of them? ~ There's no way. ~ And further, also not in a few of the parts. For if the whole were to be in a few then more would be in less, which is not possible. ~ No, not possible, indeed. ~ If, then, the whole is neither in some of them, nor in one of them, nor in all of them, must it not be either in something other or be quite simply nowhere? ~ That's necessary. ~ And if it were nowhere it would be naught, but being the whole it must be and, since it is not in itself, it is in the other. ~ Quite. ~ Insofar, then, that the one is a whole it is in the other; insofar, however, as it is in all of the parts, it is in itself. And in this wise it is necessary that the one be both in itself as well as in an other. ~ Necessarily. ~ But if the one has these qualities must it not also be in motion as well as at rest? ~ How so? ~ Indeed, it is at rest insofar as it is itself in itself. For in that it is within the one and does not go outside of it, it is in the selfsame, itself. ~ Indeed, so it is. ~ What is always within the selfsame, that must always be at rest. ~ Quite. ~ But, how now? – what always is in an other, must that not in contradistinction be never in the selfsame? – and if it is never in the selfsame, also never be at rest? – and if not at rest, then be in movement? ~ So it is. ~ Thus must the one, since it is always as well as in itself also in an other, likewise always be in motion as *[146b]* well as at rest. ~ Obviously. ~ Further, must it not be the same as itself as well as different from itself, and likewise with the other be the same as well as different, if all of the previous is properly predicated? ~ How's that? ~ Everything relates to each and all thus: either it is the same or different; or, should it be neither the same nor different: it must be a part of something to which the relationship holds, or also for this as its part, a whole. ~ Obviously. ~ Is, then, the one its own part? ~ Nope. ~ And even so little is it its own – as being of a part the whole – in that, so too, it would correlate as a piece of itself. ~ Impossible too, indeed. ~ Is then, perhaps, the one different from the one? ~ That doesn't follow. ~ Then, it's also not different from itself? ~ No, indeed not. ~ If, now, it is neither different from itself nor itself a whole or part of itself, must it not be with itself as the same? ~ That's necessary. ~ And how? – what is itself apart from itself which in the selfsame remains itself with itself,[123] doesn't this have to be different from itself insofar as it should, indeed, be apart from itself? ~ At least, I'd fancy this to be so. ~ But so has the one revealed itself to us, being itself in itself and at the same time in an other. ~ So, indeed, did it show itself. ~ Thus, it would be different, as it seems, in so far the one from itself. ~ It seems. ~ *<16.~146d]* How now? If something is different from something else, shall it not be different to a different being? ~ Necessarily. ~ And isn't it true, everything that is not one is different from one, and the one from the not-one? ~ How else? ~ The one, then, would be different from the other as a totality. ~ Different. ~ Look a bit further: sameness itself and difference, are these not to one another in opposition? ~ How else? ~ Is it possible, then, that sameness can ever be in difference or difference be in sameness? ~ That cannot be. ~ If, then, difference can never be in sameness: then nothing exists in which difference can be for any amount of time. For however long it should be in something, so, during this time difference would be in that which is the same. Isn't it so? ~ So it is. ~ As it is never in the same, so the

---

[123] " – Und wie? was anderwärts ist als es selbst, das in sich selbst bleibende, muß das nicht notwendig verschieden von sich selbst sein, indem es doch anderwärts sein soll?" – the dialectic of self-conscious consciousness.

different shall also never be in any something. ~ Right. ~ Thus, it shall never be – neither in the one nor in the not-one? ~ No, indeed not. ~ Thus, not due to the power of difference is it possible that the one is different from the not-one, nor the not-one from the one. ~ Indeed not. ~ Nor also due to the power of their own selves is it that they differ from each other as neither partakes in any way in *[147a]* difference. ~ How could they? ~ If, then, neither is different from the other due to the power of its own self, nor is either different due to the power of difference, so does this not escape them in all ways, that they be different from one another? ~ It escapes them. ~ But further, the one still has no community with everything not-one. For otherwise it would not be not-one but, rather, to a certain extent one. ~ True. ~ Thus too, the not-one is not number. For as such the not-one would not be wholly and totally not-one if it would have number. ~ No, indeed not. ~ And how, is the not-one possibly a part of the one? – or would not the not-one thus have community with the one? ~ It would. ~ If, then, the one wholly and totally is and the other(s) is/are[124] not-one, so the one cannot be a part of the not-one, nor also the whole for the former as its part; and again even so impossible is it that the not-one might be a part of the one nor the whole with the one being a part. ~ No, indeed not. ~ But we said that of two things that are related neither as parts nor as a whole and likewise not different from one another, that such shall be with one another the same. ~ We said that. ~ Do we want, then, that we also say that the one which itself so correlates to the not-one is the same as it? ~ We want to say it. ~ Thus, it seems that the one is different from the other and from itself and also the same as the former and as itself. ~ That does seem to have come to light from this demonstration. ~   *[147c]* Is it, perhaps, also similar and dissimilar with itself as well as with the other as a totality? ~ Perhaps. ~ Since it was shown, indeed, as different from the other as a totality, so the other is also well different from the one? ~ How else? ~ Thus, it is different from all the other as all the other is different from it – and neither more nor less. ~ Naturally. ~ But if neither more nor less, then equally. ~ Yes. ~ Hence, insofar as the one is predicated as being different from all other than itself, and likewise all other from the one equally, in this wise the same is predicated of both, the one with all the other and all the other with the one. ~ How do you mean that? ~ So: with each word you do, indeed, name something? ~ I, certainly. ~ How now? can you say the same word more than once or only one time? ~ The

---

[124] Once number is removed from 'the other,' it should be no surprise that grammer becomes difficult!

former. ~ Is it possible, now, that if you speak out a word one time you then point out that for which the word is; if, however, more than once, then not? Or, isn't it so that however often you speak it out you also always necessarily say the same thing? ~ Indeed. ~ Well now, different is a word for something? ~ Indeed. ~ Then, if you   *[e]* speak it, be it once or more than once, so it happens not in relation to something else and you're not pointing out something other with it, but even the former, that for which it is the word. ~ Necessarily. ~ In that, now, we say that all the other is different from the one and the one is different from all other, so indeed we say different twice but we use the expression, nonetheless, not for some other concept but, rather, always for that wherefore it is the word. ~ Indeed. ~ Insofar, then, as the one is different from all other and all other from the one, so the same is predicated, namely the difference, and it belongs to the one as well as to all the other; and that to which the same is predicated, that is similar. Isn't this true? ~ Yes. ~ Insofar, then, that the one is predicated as being different from all the other, even to the same extent would all and each be similar to all and each. For indeed, everything is different from everything else. ~ So it seems. ~ But the similar, indeed, was the exact opposite to the dissimilar? ~ Yes. ~ And likewise the same to the different? ~ These also. ~ But this too was shown, that even the one was the same as all the other. ~ That was shown. ~ And yet, this is the exact opposite   *<17.~ 148b]* quality, to be the same as all the other and to be different from all the other? ~ Well, indeed. ~ Insofar as it was different it showed itself as being similar. ~ Yes. ~ Insofar as it is the same it becomes dissimilar by the [very] power of the quality that is in opposition to the former and which made it similar. And it was even the difference that made them similar. ~ Yes. ~ Thus, dissimilarity brings about sameness, or sameness is not opposed to their being different. ~ So it seems. ~ Similar and dissimilar the one shall be to all other: insofar as it is different, then similar; insofar as it is the same, then dissimilar. ~ It does, indeed, seem to have such a relation with all this. ~ But this one as well. ~ Which? ~ That insofar as sameness is predicated of the one then no otherliness is predicated, and insofar as no otherliness is predicated so it is not dissimilar; and insofar as it is not dissimilar, to that extent it is similar. Likewise, insofar as the other is predicated of the one it is different, and as something different also dissimilar. ~ Rightly said. ~ Hence, as the same as all the other and also because it is different, from both standpoints and in each the one would be similar as well as dissimilar to all other. *[d]* ~ Quite. ~ In the same wise also with itself, as it did, indeed, show itself as being with itself both different and the same, so it must appear from both standpoints and from each as similar and as dissimilar. ~ Necessarily. ~ But what about the issue of touching? whether the one touches upon itself and the other or doesn't, what is this relationship? – observe this! ~ I'm observing. ~ Namely, the one did indeed show itself as being in itself as a whole. ~ Right. ~ But in the other as well? ~ Yes. ~ Insofar as it is in the other it touches the other; as far as it itself is in itself it shall indeed be held back from touching the other but touches upon itself, in that it is in itself. ~ Obviously. ~ In this wise the one touches upon itself and the other. ~ It touches. ~ But how so? Must not everything that touches upon something else lay directly next to it taking up the place next to the one in which that lies which is to be touched? ~ That's necessary. ~ Thus too, if the one should touch up against itself, it must lay directly against itself taking up the bordering place to that in which it itself is. ~ It must do so, indeed. ~ Were the one two, so it could very well do such and be at two places simultaneously. *[149a]* As long as it is but one shall it not be able to do so? ~ No, indeed not. ~ Thus, it is for the one the same impossibility: to be two and to itself touch upon itself. ~ The same. ~ But even as little shall it touch the other. ~ How so? ~ Because, indeed, we did say that that which would touch upon must be separate and lie directly next to that which is touched and no third thing may come in between them. ~ Right. ~ There must be at least two if there should be any contact. ~ Certainly. ~ If, however, there is added a third to the two that are bordering: then they are three and so the touching is twofold. ~ Yes. ~ And so with each addition an additional touching shall be added on, and it follows that the touchings are always one less than the number of things. For no matter how many more touchings are added to two things that touched so that their number would surpass it, by just as many does each add on to the number of things and so the things surpass all of these touchings. For each time there is added one to the number of things and one touching to the touchings. *[c]* ~ Right.[125] ~ However many in number there are things, as many less one are always their touchings. ~ Right. ~ And if only one is there and two are not present, then no touching exists. ~ How could it? ~ And isn't it so, we said that the other than one would neither be one nor does it have one in itself, as it is other than one. ~ No, indeed not. ~ Thus, there is also no number in the other as one is not therein. ~ How could it be? ~ Thus, the other is neither one, nor two, nor does it have a name of any other number. ~ No. ~ The one

---

[125] Aristotles' command of numeric permutations is rather limited – unless these "things" are to be understood like a deck of cards.

is alone and no two is there. ~ Obviously not. ~ Then, there is no touching if two are not there. ~ Indeed not. ~ Neither, then, does the one touch upon the other nor does the other upon the one, if there is no touching whatsoever. ~ No, indeed not. ~ In this wise, then, shall – after all of this – the one touch itself and the other as well as also not touch. ~ So it seems. ~ Is it, perhaps, also <18.~149e] equal and unequal to itself and to the other? ~ How so? ~ If the one would be either bigger or smaller than the other or, then again, the other bigger than the one, or smaller – so it would not be for the one by it being one nor for the other that it be other than the one that they would be bigger or smaller in relation to one another, that is, through this, their essence, rather, if besides that which they are each of them would also have equality so that they would be equal one to the other, and should the latter have largeness and the former smallness or if the one were to be big and the other small, no matter to which of the two concepts largeness should be an attribute, it would then be larger, and to which smallness it would be smaller? ~ Necessarily. ~ But indeed, there exist two such concepts, largeness and smallness: for if they don't exist, thus, it wouldn't be possible for them to be opposed to one another and to subsist in that which is. ~ How could they? ~ If, then, smallness subsists in the one, then it must subsist *[150a]* either in the whole or in one of its parts. ~ Necessarily. ~ How now, if it should reside in the whole, would it not, then, either be ubiquitous with the one spread out throughout, or else it would be encompassing? ~ Obviously. ~ And would smallness, then, if it should be ubiquitous with the one, be equal to the one? – but should it encompass it then it would be larger? ~ How else? ~ Is it then possible that smallness can be larger than something or even equal and wouldn't it thus be doing somebody else's job, equality's or that of largeness, and not its own? ~ Not possible. ~ In the whole of the one, then, smallness cannot be; but if it should be, then it is just in a part. ~ Yes. ~ But not in a whole part as then the same problem resurfaces as above for the whole of the one: it would be either equal to or larger than the part in which it would find itself. ~ Necessarily. ~ Thus, in nothing that exists is it possible for smallness to be – as it may be neither in a part nor in a whole; and there shall be nothing that is small excepting smallness itself. ~ It seems not. ~ So largeness, too, shall have nothing to be in: for otherwise there would have to exist an other yet larger being besides largeness itself, *[c]* namely that in which largeness would subsist, and this although for the former there exists nothing smaller over which it would have to predominate if, then, it should be large; but this is impossible since smallness doesn't subsist anywhere. ~ Right. ~ But largeness itself is, indeed, only larger than smallness itself, not of something other; and smallness itself is only smaller than largeness itself, and nothing other. ~ No, indeed not. ~ Thus, the other is also neither larger nor smaller than the one in that it has neither largeness nor smallness in itself. Nor too do both of these themselves have their own   *[150d]* character of predominating or being predominated over for the one, but just for one another. Even so little, now, is it possible that the one is larger or smaller than either of these or than the other as, utterly, it has neither largeness nor smallness in itself. ~ Obviously, as you say. ~ If the one is neither larger nor smaller than the other, so then it is necessary that it neither predominates over the other nor is it predominated over? ~ That's necessary. ~ Now then, that which neither predominates nor is predominated over, this is equalized and, if equalized, then equal. ~ How else. ~ Therefore the one must also correlate so with itself, as it has neither largeness nor smallness in itself, that, namely, it neither predominates over itself nor is it predominated over by itself but is equalized with itself and also shall be equal to itself. ~ Quite. ~ The one, then, would be equal to itself and to the other. ~ Obviously. ~ But further, as it is itself in itself: so it must be outside of itself being all around and as self-encompassing be larger than its own self, but encompassed by itself, smaller; and so again the one is larger and also smaller than its own self. ~ So it is. ~ Is it not also necessary that nothing exists   *[151a]* outside of the one and the other altogether? ~ How could it! ~ But, then too, everything that is would, indeed, be somewhere? ~ Yes. ~ Must not that which is somewhere be in something larger in that it itself is smaller?   For how else could one be in an other? ~ There's no other way. ~ Since, now, nothing exists besides the other altogether and the one, and as these must yet be in something: must they not necessarily be in one another, the one in the other and the other in the one, or else be nowhere? ~ I see what you mean. ~ Insofar, then, as the one is in the other would not the other as surrounding be larger than the one and the one as surrounded would be smaller than the other. But insofar as the other is in the one would not also the one, in the same way, be larger than the other and the other smaller than the one. ~ So it seems. ~ The one itself is, thus, equal to itself and larger and smaller than itself, as well as equal to and larger and smaller than the other. ~ Obviously. ~ And then, certainly, if equal to and smaller and larger, it is also of equal   *[c]* mass and of more and less than its own self and than the other; and as it is with mass so too with parts. ~ How else. ~ But being of equal mass and also being more and less than its own self and the other, is it not also numerically more and less than its own self and than the other, and also equal to its own self and to the other from the same vantage. ~ How so? ~ As that which is larger, as such it carries more mass as well – and of so much mass, so many parts. And even so with the smaller, and likewise with being equal. ~ Right. ~ Thus, if it is to be larger and smaller than itself and also equal to itself, so too it is of equal mass and of more and of less mass than its own self? – and as with mass, so too with parts? ~ How else. ~ If, then, it is of so many parts as its own self, so it is equal to itself in quantity. And if of less, it too is less; if of more, than numerically more than it itself. ~ Obviously. ~ And shall not the one itself over against the other correlate even thus? – insofar it is shown as larger it is also more numerically, but insofar as it is smaller also less; and insofar it is equal to it in size it would be equal to the other in quantity? ~ That's necessary. ~ Then accordingly, as it seems, the one is yet again equal to and more and less than both itself and the other altogether in number. ~ So it is. ~ Whether now, perhaps, the one in <*19.~151e]* itself partakes in time and is and becomes younger and older than itself and than the other, and again, neither older nor younger than itself or than the other – if it partakes in time in itself? ~ How's that? ~ Being must be a predicate of the one, if the one is. ~ Yes. ~ But is being perchance anything other than taking part in existence in the present time, just as having had existence is the was and the shall be is existence in the future? ~ So it is. ~ It has, then, a partaking in time if on being. ~ Quite. ~ But yet, in that time moves on? ~ Yes. ~ And it becomes, accordingly, always older than itself if it moves in time? ~ Necessarily. ~ Let us not forget that that which is older always becomes older than that which is becoming younger? ~ We remember that. ~ Thus, if the one becomes older than itself, then it must become older to itself as it itself becomes younger. ~ That's necessary. ~ Then it becomes both older and younger than itself in this wise. ~ Yes. ~ But it is older – isn't this true – as it becomes in the now of time between the was and the shall be? For it is not at all possible, indeed, that it might move forward from the before to the after jumping over the now? ~ No, indeed not. ~ But doesn't it hold on inwardly with its becoming-older as it meets up with the now *[c]* and doesn't become then but, rather, is already older? For in moving forward it never would have been grasped by the now. Namely, that which is moving forward is so correlated that it touches upon both, the now and the subsequent, abandoning the now and grasping at the subsequent, becoming between these two, the now and the after. ~ Right. ~ But if it is necessary that not all of the becoming should bypass the now: so it is also necessary that it would hold on as it is inwardly with its becoming and, so, it is simultaneously that in the grasp of which it becomes. ~ I see what you mean. ~ Therefore the one also, as it meets upon the now in its becoming older, holds inwardly upon its becoming and, even so, is older. ~ Indeed. ~ Thus, as that which became older, as this it also is older? But it became older than its own self? ~ Yes. ~ It is, however, as the elder older than what is younger? ~ It is. ~ Younger than its self too, is, then, the one as it became older meeting upon the now. ~ That's necessary. ~ The now, however, is an attribute of the one   *[152e]* throughout its whole being. For it is always now, if it is. ~ How could it be otherwise? ~ Always, then, is as well as becomes the one older and younger than its self. ~ So it seems. ~ But shall it be or become in more time than it itself, or in an equal amount? ~ In an equal amount. ~ But certainly that which is or becomes in an equal amount of time is also the same age? ~ How else? ~ That which has the same age, such is neither older nor younger. ~ No, indeed not. ~ Thus the one, as it is and becomes with its own self in an equal amount of time, is and becomes neither younger nor older than its own self. ~ No, I doubt it. ~ But how? Perhaps than the other? ~ I haven't got a clue. ~ But, then too, you do know that the other than one – if indeed it is the other as a totality and not [just] an other – *are* different and, thus, as not singular must be more than one. For if there were just a different, so it would be one, but being the different, so they are more than one and are, thus, multitudinous. ~ So they are. ~ As they are a multitude, as such they have a larger number than the one. ~ How else? ~ And how now? shall we say that as for numbers that the larger come first and have been sooner, or the fewer? ~ The fewer. ~ The fewest then [comes] first: this, however, is the one? Right? ~ Yes. ~ The one, then, becomes first of everything that is numeric. But the other altogether is also numeric, as they are plural and not singular. ~ Yes, plural. ~ Having become first it is, I believe, also earlier, and the other later. But that which becomes later is younger than that which became earlier; and in this manner the other as a totality would be younger than the one, and the one would be older than the other. ~ So it would. ~   *<20.~153c]* How about this? – could it well-nigh be that the one has become in opposition to its own nature, or is this impossible? ~ Impossible. ~ But still, the one has shown itself as having parts; and if parts, then too a beginning, a middle and an end. ~ Yes. ~ But does not everything firstly become with a beginning, as well the one as every other? and then after the beginning all the other as well, all up to the end? ~ How else? ~ But still, we would like to say that this other is all a part of the whole and of the one and that it shall become one and whole only at the time of its end? ~ We would like to say that. ~

But the end, I believe, happens last, and first simultaneously with this does the one fulfill its nature. And so, if it be necessary that the one shall become in accordance to its nature, then it must become even later than the other of its own nature. ~ I see. ~ Thus, the one is younger than the other and the other older than the one. ~ Now, indeed, it appears once again, even so. ~ But how? the beginning or any other part of the one or of something else, no matter what, which is just a part and not [multiple] parts, must this not be one if it is a part? ~ That's necessary. ~ Thus, simultaneously with the first becomings the one became, and likewise with the second? and it does not abandon all the other becomings no matter what might follow *[e]* whatever until finally arriving at the last it has become a whole one, having abandoned neither middle, nor end, nor beginning, nor yet anything other in the process of becoming. ~ Right. ~ With all the other, then, the one retains its same age: so that if the one should not become contrary to its own nature then it cannot have become earlier nor later than the other as a totality but, rather, simultaneously. And so, in this wise, the one is neither older nor younger than the other as a totality, nor also is this older or younger than the one; but in the previous wise it was both older and younger and even likewise all the other correlated to it. ~ Quite. ~ So, accordingly, it is and has become. But how do things stand with the shall be, whether it also shall be older and younger than the other all together and the other than it – and, then again, also neither younger nor older. Does, perhaps, the same relationship hold as with being, so too with becoming, or is it something other? ~ I haven't got a clue. ~ But at least so much can be stated, that if one thing is older than *[154b]* some other it cannot become older still than it has first become in difference of age; and even so the younger cannot become still younger. For if something equal be added to the unequal, be it time or whatever else, the result is always that the same difference remains, namely the one with which they started. ~ There's no way around that. ~ Then, in no way is it possible that a being can ever become older or younger than any other as it remains always with the same difference in age; rather it is and has become older and the other younger, but it shall not become so. ~ Right. ~ Thus too, the one which is shall never become older or younger than the other which is. ~ Indeed not. ~ But look as to whether in this respect they shall become older and younger over against each other. ~ In what respect? ~ In the respect that the one has shown itself as older than all other and the other than the one. ~ But, how? ~ If the one is older than all the other: so it has become for a greater amount *[d]* of time than the other? ~ Yes. ~ Look a little further: if we add the same amount of time to a greater and a lesser amount shall then the greater be different from the lesser by an equal part or by a smaller part? ~ By a smaller. ~ Then, shall not the one, even as it was different from the other in age, also still be different; but too, in that it has increased by the same age shall it not always be different from the other by a lesser part than it was before. Or not? ~ Yes. ~ And what is proportionately less different from something other than it was before, that indeed became younger than before in relation to that to which it before was older? ~ Younger. ~ If the one becomes younger doesn't all other become older over against the one than previously? ~ Indeed. ~ That which was younger in becoming becomes older over against that which became earlier which is older. But never is it older but, rather, it only always becomes older than the elder; the elder increases in 'youthliness,' the younger in aging. Even so, *[a]* again, the elder becomes younger than the younger does. For as they both advance in opposition to that in which they are contrary: so they become as well the contrary from one another, the younger namely older than the elder and the elder younger than the youthful; but never can they arrive at being what they are becoming. For if they would be what they're becoming then they would no longer become but would be it. But now they become older and younger in opposition to one another. Namely, the one becomes younger than all the other because it showed itself as being the elder and having become earlier. And all the other as a totality becomes older than the one because it was later in becoming. But, and for the same reason, the other have the same relationship to the one as it did also appear as older than it and as having become earlier. ~ So it was shown. ~ Insofar, then, that utterly nothing at all becomes older or younger than any other due to the ever same numeric difference of one to the other: in this wise shall neither the one become older or younger than all other, nor shall the other become older or younger than the one. But in the respect that the earlier differs from that which *[155c]* has become later always by a different portion of itself, and as well the later from the earlier: in this wise shall all the other over against the one and the one over against all other become younger as well as older. ~ Indeed. ~ Consequently and in full accord with all the foregoing, the one is and shall become older as well as younger than itself and than the other as a totality; and it is and shall become also neither older nor younger than itself or all other. ~ So it is, in all ways. ~ But then, as the one exists in time and becomes older and younger must it not also necessarily have a previous and a subsequent and a now, as it does exist in time? ~ Necessarily. ~ Thus the one was and is and shall be, and it became and is becoming and shall become. ~ How else? ~ Well, it would be able to have something and one might have something of it, and has had and will have. ~ Indeed. ~ Thus too, there exists knowledge of it and notions of it and perception, as we have now indeed brought up all of this in relation to the same. ~ And totally right do you assert it. ~ Thus too, there exists a word for it and a clarification, and it shall be named and clarified and absolutely whatever is in any manner of all other, that too is of the one. ~ Indeed, in all ways, this is the way it correlates. ~

<21.~155e]

Good, let us also yet go through this – as a third: the one, if it is as we have carried it through, must it not be necessary – since it is one and many and also neither one nor many and therewith having community with time, insofar as it is one by necessity intrinsically have being at one time and, insofar as it is not, likewise also it does not intrinsically have being at one time? ~ That's necessary. ~ And shall it, perhaps, when it has being, even then be able not to have being? Or, when it is deprived of being, be able even then to have it? ~ Not possible. ~ In another time, thus, it has it, and in another it does not have being. For only in this way is it possible for something intrinsically to have and also not to have the same. ~ Right. ~ Hence, there exists also such a time wherein it takes on being and also such a time wherein it lets go of being. Or how should it be possible for the one, in that now it has such and then again it doesn't have the same – if, then, it does not also at some time grab hold and let loose? ~ In no way. ~ And taking on being, do you not name that becoming? ~ I name it so. ~ And letting go of being, do you not name that passing away? ~ Quite. ~ The one, then, as it appears, since it grabs hold of being and lets loose, also becomes and passes away. ~ Necessarily. ~ Since it is now one and many, and becoming and passing away, shall not, if it becomes one, its being many pass away; if, however, it becomes many, its being one passes away? *[b]* ~ Indeed. ~ And in that it becomes one and many shall it not, then, be separated and mixed? ~ Necessarily. ~ And in that it becomes dissimilar and similar must it not also proceed through likeness and difference? ~ Yes. ~ And if larger and smaller and equal must it not also grow and diminish and remain as equal. ~ So it is. ~ And if it is to stand still from being in motion and go over from stillness into motion: so, it must not, indeed, be so itself at one time? ~ How could it? ~ That the previously resting comes to be in motion and the previously moving comes to be at rest, this cannot possibly happen at once without transition. ~ Indeed, how? ~ On the other hand, there exists no one time in which something could simultaneously be neither in motion nor at rest. ~ That surely doesn't exist. ~ But still, it's not possible that it has transitioned without a transition. ~ No, not believable. ~ When, then, does it transition? – for neither at rest nor in motion can it transition? nor being in time. ~ No, indeed not. ~ Is this, then, perhaps, what is amazing, where it is as it transitions? ~ What's this? ~ The moment.[126] For the momentary seems *[156d]* to indicate something like this, that coming out of which something goes over into one of both. For nothing transits out of rest during the resting nor out of motion during movement but, rather, this amazing entity, the moment, lies in between movement and rest, being outside of all time – and in it and from it the moving transitions to rest and the resting [transitions] to motion. ~ That may well be so. ~ Also the one, then, if it rests and also moves itself, must transition from the one to the other, for only so is it possible to do both. But if it transitions: so it transitions in the moment and in that it transitions it is not in time and is neither moving nor at rest. ~ No, indeed, not. ~ Now, does it, perhaps, correlate even so with the other transitions, if it is to transition from being into passing away, or from non-being into becoming, so that then too each time it is in a certain *[157a]* way between movement and rest? and even then neither is, nor is not, neither becomes nor passes away? ~ Yes, it appears so. ~ Then too, even in this wise, if it is to transition from one to many or from many into one, it is neither one nor many, becomes neither separate nor mixed? and from the similar into the dissimilar or going from the dissimilar into the similar, it is neither similar nor dissimilar, proceeds neither through the state of 'being-something-similar' nor that of 'being-something-dissimilar'; and from the lesser into the greater and going over from being equal into the opposites – it is neither less, nor more, nor equal; neither growing, nor decreasing, nor equalized. ~ So it seems. ~ All of these qualities are predicated of the one, if it is. ~ Certainly. ~   *<22.~157bc]*

But how about the qualities predicated of all the other, if the one is, shouldn't we weigh this into our consideration? ~ We want to. ~ Then, let us say: If the one is, how must all the other outside of the one be constituted? ~ Let's say that. ~ Well, if it is the other outside of one – it is, indeed, not the one, or else it wouldn't be other outside of one. ~ Right. ~ Even so little, however, is the other as a totality wholly bereft of the one but, rather, it has it in a certain way implicitly

---

[126] "Der Augenblick" – literally: "eyes-blink." A most eye-opening German word in that blinking is not something one generally considers as a part of vision – anymore than one considers non-being as being inherent in being. The sudden or instant are other possible translations but I prefer "the moment" as I think that this ties in much better to other dialogues wherein Plato speaks of momentary pleasures, etc.

{*an sich*}. ~ To what extent, then? ~ Because all the other outside of the one is yet made up of parts being other as a totality. For if it didn't have parts, so then, it would be whole and, indeed, would be one. ~ Right. ~ But parts, we assert, exist only in relation to something that is a whole. ~ This is what we assert. ~ But the whole is yet necessarily the one of many – whose parts, even, are the parts. For each part must not be a part of the many but, rather, a part of the whole. ~ But, how's that? ~ If something would be a part of *[157d]* many amongst which it itself would also be present: so it would be as well its own part – which is impossible – as also one of each of the others if, then, it really should be a part of all. For were it not a part of one of them in particular, so it becomes a part of only the rest outside of this one. And so, it becomes not a part of each in turn; if not, however, of each, then also of none under the many. But what is of none of them, to be such of all of them, of which it is none, be it a part or anything else whatsoever, this is impossible. ~ Indeed, I see what you mean. ~ Thus, not of the many or totality is the part part but, rather, just of one idea and of the one, which, out of all in total having become completely one shall be named the whole – of this must the part be part. ~ Quite, indeed. ~ If, then, the other as a totality has parts, so it also must have community with the whole and with the one. ~ Indeed. ~ A consummate whole having parts is, then, by necessity, the other as a totality outside of the one. ~ Necessarily. ~ Furthermore, the same is also valid of each single part. For also each part must necessarily have community with the one. Namely, if each singularity is a part thereof, so indeed, *[158a]* this "to be a singularity" means to be a one, namely, that it is one separate from the rest being for itself – if, otherwise, a singularity. ~ Right. ~ Obviously, then, it is able to implicitly partake in the one even though it is other than the one – or else it wouldn't have the one implicitly but would, rather, itself be the one. But now, being the one itself, outside of the one itself, this is for each other wholly impossible. ~ Impossible. ~ But to have the one implicitly is necessary for the whole and the part. For the former shall be one whole – whose parts are even its parts; but the latter shall each be a singular part of the whole, of which each even is part. ~ So it is. ~ Thus, as different from the one shall that which implicitly has the one have one implicitly. ~ How else? ~ But still, the different from one must still be many. For if the other than the one were to be neither one nor also more than one, so, indeed, it would be even naught. ~ Indeed, nothing. ~ But if more than one is – which has community with the one as part and as whole – are, then, these things that partake implicitly of the one not necessarily themselves unlimited

in multitude? ~ But how? ~ Let's examine it so. Is it not so that at
the time when they take up the one, they take it as such, being as yet
not one and not having one implicitly? ~ That's totally apparent. ~
Then, as a multitude wherein the one is not itself present. ~ *[158c]*
Indeed, as a multitude. ~ How now, if we then take away in thought
the smallest bit that we are able to, would not necessarily also that
which was taken away – since the one is not had even implicitly – be
a multitude and not be one? ~ That's necessary. ~ Let us examine in
this way what is always in and for itself the different nature of the
concept: so there shall be, no matter what we always see thereof,
an unlimited multitude. ~ In all ways, indeed. ~ And so, as each
singular part as part has become one, then it has also become limited
as opposed to the others and to the whole, and the whole as opposed
to the parts. ~ Indeed, apparently. ~ Hence, it is predicated of the
other as a totality outside of the one that from it itself and from the
one, when both enter into community, something other comes-to-be
in it that accomplishes limitation one against the other; its own
nature in itself, however, gives it unlimitedness. ~ I see what you
mean. ~ Hence, the other as a totality apart from the one, as a whole
and also in respect to its parts, is unlimited as well as implicitly   *[e]*
having limitation. ~ Quite. ~ And not also similar as well as
dissimilar amongst one another and in itself? ~ To what extent? ~
To the extent that to everything it is unlimited in accordance to its
own nature, to this extent it is predicated as the same {*einerlei*} as
everything. ~ Quite. ~ But also, to the extent that it partakes in the
limitation of everything, also to this extent it is predicated as the
same. ~ What else? ~ To the extent that it is predicated as limited
and as unlimited, are not qualities predicated of it that are in   *[a]*
opposition to one another? ~ Yes. ~ But opposites are that which
is most dissimilar? ~ How else? ~ Hence, in respect to both
constitutions taken singularly it is similar to itself and amongst one
another; in respect to both constitutions taken together it is in both
ways wholly opposed and dissimilar to the highest degree. ~ That
may well be so. ~ In this wise, then, the other is itself with itself and
amongst one another similar and dissimilar. ~ That it is. ~ Then
too, that it is the same and also different from one another, moving
and at rest, and that all of these opposing qualities belong to the other
than one as a totality, this shall no longer be hard for us to discover
after having already seen that these are predicated of it. ~ Rightly
spoken. ~

<23.~159b]

How now, if we were to leave this as already made obvious and were to examine once more: if one is, does the other outside of the one itself also correlate simultaneously not so, or only so? ~ Let's do that. ~ Going once more from the beginning through: if one is, what must be predicated of the other outside the one? ~ Yes, we want to go through this. ~ Now, is not the one wholly cut off from the other and the other also cut off from the one? ~ But, how's that? ~ Because outside of these there is yet nothing else that exists that would be other than the one and, simultaneously, other than the other outside of the one. For everything is spoken of if one says – the one and the other outside of the one. ~ Indeed, everything. ~ Hence, [159c] there exists nothing more that is different in which the one and the other would be able to be present in community. ~ No, indeed. ~ Thus, never shall the one and the other outside the one be in one and the selfsame. ~ It seems not. ~ Hence, cut off? ~ Yes. ~ Also, that the authentic, true one has no parts – we did say this? ~ How should it? ~ Thus, the one can neither be wholly in the other nor yet be a part thereof – if, then, it is cut off from the other and has no parts at all? ~ How could it? ~ In no way, then, is it possible for the other to even implicitly have the one as neither in part nor as a whole may it possibly be had. ~ It seems not. ~ In no way, then, is the other one, nor does it have any other one in itself. ~ Indeed not. ~ Thus, the other is also not many. For if it were to be many then each one of these would be as a part to a whole. But, now, the other than one is neither one nor many, neither whole nor parts – since it has no possible way of partaking in something of the one, not even implicitly. ~ Right. ~ And, then too, neither two nor three is the other neither itself, nor does it partake in number implicitly – if, then, it is indeed in all ways bereft of the one. ~ So it is. ~ Thus too, similar or [e] dissimilar to the one is the other neither itself nor does it have absolutely any similarity or dissimilarity even implicitly. For if it itself were to be similar or dissimilar or would have amongst itself similarity or dissimilarity, so, indeed, would the other than one have two, one another contradictory concepts internally. ~ I see what you mean. ~ But it would be impossible, indeed, that that might in itself have two which does not even have one in itself. ~ Impossible. ~ Thus too, neither similar nor dissimilar nor both is the other. For if it were to be similar or dissimilar, so, then it would have to have [160a] one of these two concepts internally; would it be both, then both contradictory. But this has shown itself as impossible. ~ Right. ~ Even so, it is neither the same nor different, neither moving nor at rest, neither becoming nor passing away, neither larger nor smaller nor equal, nor may anything of this sort be predicated of it. For if the

other than one could support that something like this was predicated
of it – so, then, it would also have to implicitly have one and two and
three, and even [straight] and odd – and such having in itself has,
however, been shown to be wholly impossible for this which is wholly
bereft of the one in all ways. ~ Quite completely true. ~ In this way,
thus, if the one is, the one is all – and also again not once one, as well
for itself and for the other to an equal extent. ~ Totally proven,
indeed. ~   *<24.~160bc]*

Good! But if, now, the one is not, what should follow, don't we have
to weigh this in our considerations next? ~ Indeed, we must consider
this. ~ But what is actually this stipulation: If one is not? Is it
perchance different from this: If not-one is not? ~ Quite different. ~
Different only? – or is it not much more entirely contrary to say:
if not-one is not, than, if one is not? ~ Entirely contrary. ~ How
now, if someone says: if largeness is not, or, if smallness is not, or
something other of the same sort – so he indicates in each instance
that a different non-being is that which is not? ~ Quite. ~ Thus,
now also he indicates that something different from the other non-
beings is named as that-which-is-not in that he says: if one is not?
And we know what he means? ~ We know it. ~ Firstly, then, he
means something cognizable {*erkennbares*} – and after this also
something different from the other, if he says one, whether he   *[d]*
characterizes it with being or with non-being. For the former from
which it was said, it be not, shall yet nonetheless be recognized as
something? and also as different from the other. Or not? ~ That's
necessary. ~ After this, then, let's say, starting at the beginning: If
one is not, what then must be? Firstly, then, there must be predicated
of it – as it seems – that there exists cognition of it, or else nobody
would even have understood what was said if someone says: if one is
not. ~ True. ~ Thus also, that the other is different from it – or
otherwise the former would not have to have named something
different from the other? ~ Quite. ~ Also a differentiation is   *[e]*
predicated of it, then, next to the recognition. For, indeed, what is
meant is not the differentiation of the other when one says that the
one is different from the other; rather, even the differentiation of the
former, of the one. ~ That's obvious. ~ Thus, the one which is not
partakes in [the concepts of] the former and [of] something and the
from-which and for-which and out-of-which and of what [ever else]
is similar hereto. Or else there neither could be any speech of the
one, nor of the other that is outside of the one; nor too would it have
something or would something be predicated of it and it also couldn't
even be spoken of if it would have no partaking either in something

or in the rest of this type. ~ Right. ~ Thus, indeed, being is not possible for the one, if it is not; but this does not hinder it in many ways of implicitly having, rather, this is yet more necessary – *[161a]* if, then, the former one and not an other is not. For if it's neither the one nor the former but, rather, the speech should be directed upon something other: so it is simply not permissible to speak out something at all.[127] If, however, just the former one and not something else is what underlies as non-being: so it must necessarily stand in relationship with the former and with many others. ~ That's quite certain. ~ Thus too, it shall have dissimilarity over against the other. For the other than the one must, as different, also be of a different sort. ~ Yes. ~ And that which is of a different sort is also of other qualities? ~ Indeed. ~ And that which is of other qualities, shouldn't that be dissimilar? ~ Quite, dissimilar. ~ And, isn't it true, if the other is dissimilar to the one: so is, indeed, a dissimilar to a dissimilar dissimilar? ~ Obviously. ~ Hence, the one also has a dissimilarity by the potency of which the other is dissimilar to it. ~ It seems. ~ If now, it has a dissimilarity with the other, does it not necessarily also have a similarity with itself? ~ How so? ~ If the one would have dissimilarity in itself with the one: so it would not be possible at all to speak about such a thing as one but, rather, already the first stipulation is dealing not with the one but, rather, with an other than one. ~ Well, indeed. ~ But it should not. ~ No, indeed not. ~ So the one must implicitly have in itself a similarity to itself. ~ It must. ~ But just as little is it equal to the other. For would it be equal, so too, it already would be and would be similar to it to the extent of its equality. But both of these are impossible if the one is not. ~ Impossible. ~ But if, now, it is not equal to the other – is, then, the other necessarily also not equal to it? ~ That's necessary. ~ And is not that which is not equal unequal? ~ Yes. ~ And the unequal, isn't it to the unequal unequal? ~ How else? ~ Thus also, an inequality adheres to the one by the potency of which the other as a totality is unequal to it. ~ It adheres to it. ~ But to inequality, *[d]* indeed, belongs largeness and smallness. ~ Indeed. ~ Does such a one, then, have largeness and smallness implicitly. ~ It almost seems so. ~ But largeness and smallness are ever separate from one another? ~ Quite. ~ Thus, there is always something in between them? ~ There is. ~ Now, do you know of something other that would be in between them other than equality? ~ No, rather even that. ~ What has largeness and smallness, that too has equality which presents itself in between both. ~ That's clear. ~ Thus, the

---

[127] Cf: *Theaetetus* 183a–c (pp. 417–418) and *Sophist* 237c–239c (pp. 538–541).

one which is not has equality implicitly, and largeness and smallness.
~ It seems. ~ Yes, also being must somehow be had implicitly. ~
How's that? ~ It must even correlate as we say – for were it not to
correlate so: so too we speak falsely in that we say, the one is not.
But if we say something true, then, obviously, also something that is.
Or isn't this so? ~ Indeed, so. ~ If, then, we assert to say something
true: so we assert necessarily also to speak of something that is. ~
Necessarily. ~ Thus, as it seems, the one which is not is.   *[162a]*
For if it is not that which is not but would rather let up from being to
non-being: so, instantaneously it becomes being which is. ~ In all
ways, indeed. ~ It must somehow be bound up[128] with non-being,
namely the nonbeing-being, if it should not be; in a similar manner as
also being must have the non-being of that which is not so that it,
on its side, most fully is. For only so may as well that which is be
properly as also that which is not be properly not – if to being the
being of that which is adheres and the non-being of that which is not,
whereby it may most fully be; to non-being, however, the non-being
of that which is not's non-being and the being of the being of that
which is not, if this also, that which is not, may most fully not be.[129] ~
Totally right. ~ Hence, since there is predicated to being non-being
and to non-being being: so too there adheres to the one, since it is
not, necessarily a being, namely that of non-being. ~ Necessarily. ~
Also being, thus, shows itself for the one, if it be not. ~ It shows
itself. ~ And even also a non-being, since, indeed, it is not. ~ How
could that be lacking? ~ Now, is it possible, perhaps, that that which
is constituted in some manner may also not be so constituted without
transitioning out of this constitution? ~ No, not possible. ~ *[162c]*
Everything like this that is constituted 'so' and also 'not so' indicates
a transition. ~ How else? ~ But a transition is a change? Or what
do we want to assert? ~ Change. ~ But the one has shown itself as
being and as non-being? ~ Yes. ~ Thus, as 'so' and also as 'not so'
constituted has the one shown itself? ~ It seems. ~ Thus, also as
changing appears the non-being one since, then, it also suffers a

---

[128] "ein Band haben" – binding and bands reminds us of the barrels in *Gorgias*; see also
Sophist – Sections 38–39, 253a (pp. 560–563): the vowels are a *band* that unites the
consonants, just as certain concepts intermix with "all things."

[129] "Es muss also ein Band haben mit dem Nichtsein, nämlich das Nichtseiende-Sein, wenn
es nicht-sein soll; auf ähnliche Art, wie auch das Seinde das Nichtsein des Nichtseienden
haben muss, damit es seinerseits vollständig sei. Denn nur so kann sowohl das Seiende recht
sein, als das Nichtseiende recht nichtsein, wenn dem Seienden das Sein des Seiendseins
eignet und das Nichtsein des Nichtseiendseins, wofern es vollständiglich sein soll: dem
Nichtseienden aber das Nichtsein des Nichtseiend-Nichtseins und das Sein des
Nichtseiendseins, wenn auch dieses, das Nichtseiende, vollständiglich nichtsein soll."

transition from being to non-being. ~ That may well be. ~ But still, if it is nowhere as it's not possible for it to be if it is not: so it's not possible that it moved itself from any place to some other. ~ How could it? ~ Thus, it's not through a change in location that it changes. ~ No, indeed not. ~ Even so little is it possible that it spins itself around in one and the same place, for nowhere does it touch upon the same. For the same is being and that which is not cannot possibly be in anything which is. ~ Impossible, indeed. ~ Thus too, the one which is not is not able to spin itself around in the former, in which it is not. ~ Indeed, no. ~ And even so little is it possible that the one alters itself in itself, neither as being nor as non-being. For then the speech would no longer be about the one, should it have become something other than itself, but would be of an other. ~ Right. ~ If, now, it itself neither becomes different, nor spins around in the same place, nor moves itself from its place – is it possible *[e]* that it yet changes in some other manner? ~ But how? ~ And that which doesn't change is, indeed, necessarily at rest, and what rests endures? ~ Necessarily. ~ Thus, the one which is not, as it seems, endures as well as changes. ~ So it seems. ~ But further, if, now, it changes, must it not be indeed most necessary that it alters itself: for insofar as something changes, even so it no longer correlates as it was correlated but, rather, differently. ~ Right. ~ The changing one, thus, also alters itself. ~ Yes. ~ But that which changes in no way alters itself in no way. ~ No, indeed not. ~ The one which is not alters itself and also does not alter itself. ~ That is clear. ~ And that which is altered, does that not necessarily become something different than before? – and hasn't it passed out of its prior constitution? That which doesn't become altered, however, neither becomes nor passes away? ~ That's necessary. ~ Then too, the one which is not as 'something-which-is-altered' becomes and passes away; but as 'something-which-is-not-altered' neither becomes nor passes away. And, thus, the one which is not becomes and passes away and also becomes as little as it passes away.   *<25.~163c]*

Still once more let us return to the beginning, that we see whether the same shall appear to us as it does now or something other. ~ Yes, let's. ~ Isn't it true that we questioned: If the one is not, what load, then, will it have to bear? ~ Yes. ~ The *is-not*, however, if we say this, does it perhaps mean anything other than an essential absence of being for that about which we say – it is not? ~ Nothing other. ~ If, then, we say that something is not, do we mean with this: somehow it may not be and somehow it may be? Or does the is-not mean quite simply that even that which has no being is in no place and in no manner, and that even implicitly there is no modus of being? ~ Indeed, the simplest of all. ~ Thus, neither is it possible for that which is not to be, nor also in some other manner to have community with being. ~ No, indeed not. ~ And becoming   [d] and passing away, are these, perhaps, something other than, for the former, a grasping and, for the latter, a letting go of being? ~ Nothing other. ~ But that which has absolutely no community with being – such, indeed, is not able either to grasp it nor to let it go? ~ How could it? ~ The one, then, as it is in no manner, cannot possibly either hold on to, or let go of, or grasp being. ~ Well, no. ~ Neither, then, passes away the one which is not, nor does it become – since it has no manner of community with being? ~ No, as was shown. ~ Nor, too, shall it in any way be altered: for then it would become and pass away if this were to be predicated of it. ~ Right. ~ But if it does not alter itself, then, necessarily, it also doesn't well change? ~ Necessarily. ~ Even so little, too, shall we say that that which is nowhere endures. For that which endures needs must as the same as itself be perpetually in something the same. ~ How else? ~ In this manner, accordingly, shall we yet again be able to assert of that-which-is-not that it either endures or changes. ~ Certainly not. ~ Nor also is it possible that something which is adheres to it. For if it implicitly would have something that is, so it would also,   [164a] then, already somehow have being implicitly. ~ Obviously. ~ Neither largeness, then, nor smallness, nor equality does it have implicitly. ~ Indeed, no. ~ Nor too is it able to have similarity or difference, neither with itself nor with the others? ~ No, as it shows itself. ~ And how? – is it possible that the other somehow be for the same if, then, absolutely nothing should be for it? ~ That can't possibly be. ~ Thus, neither similar nor dissimilar to it, neither the same as it nor being different from it is the other. ~ No, indeed not. ~ And how? – is it well-nigh possible that a wherefrom or wherefore, a something or a this or of-that or one-another or for-an-other, or yea or hereafter or now or knowledge or notionality or perception or clarification or naming, or anything other which is, is it well-nigh possible that the like exists for that which is not? ~ They cannot. ~ Thus, in this manner, the one – as it is not – shall itself in no way correlate. ~ Indeed, it seems that it itself correlates in no way. ~

                                              <26.~164bc]

Now, let us say yet again: if the one is not, what then must be predicated of the other as a totality. ~ Let's say this. ~ The other must yet somehow be. For if the other simply was not other, so there wouldn't at all be any speech about the other. ~ So it is. ~ And if we speak of the other, so this other is the different. Or, don't you always

use the word for the same: other and different? ~ I, certainly. ~ But
the different, don't we say, is the different from something different;
thus indeed also, the other an other than an other? ~ Yes. ~ Hence
also for the other, if it should be other, there exists something for
which it is other? ~ Necessarily. ~ But what would this well be?
It is not other than the one, since the one is not. ~ No, indeed not. ~
Thus, amongst themselves. For this is all that remains, or else it
would be other in relation to nothing at all. ~ Right. ~ Taken as a
multitude, then, shall each over against the rest be an other. For it is
not possible to take as one – if, then, a one is not; but rather,   *[d]*
as it seems, each mass is unlimited in multitude and if someone
fancies to separate out the smallest possible bit of all, yet suddenly it
appears, like in a dream, instead of the fancy of being one, as many,
and instead of very small, as entirely big in relation to the further
divisible pieces [that come] out of it. ~ Totally right. ~ As such
masses, hence, the others would be others amongst themselves – if
they, without the one existing, should be other. ~ Indeed, obviously.
~ Thus, there shall be many masses, each appearing as one but not
being it – as, then, one should not at all be. ~ So it is. ~ Also there
shall appear to exist a number for them, if each mass appears as one,
since there are many. ~ Indeed. ~ And a few of these shall be even
[straight], others odd – without truly being so, just seem – if, yet, the
one should not be. ~ Indeed, it is not so. ~ Yes, also the smallest of
all, we say, seems to exist therein; but this itself shows itself once
again as a many and as large in opposition to each of the   *[165a]*
many [in it] which are smaller yet. ~ So it is. ~ Then too, as equal
to these many and to these diminutives shall each and every mass be
envisioned. For it is not possible for them to appear to transition
from the larger into the smaller without first seeming to come into
that which lies in between, and this would even be the appearance
of equality? ~ To all appearance. ~ And shall not each mass appear
as limited by some other one and to be for itself, although it has
neither a beginning, middle, nor end? ~ But how's that? ~ Because
every time, if someone holds firmly onto something in his thought as
if it would be one of these three, still – there always appears another
beginning before this beginning, and after the ending another, further
ending, and in the middle a yet more precise and smaller middle than
the former middle – because it is impossible to grasp and hold fast
{fassen} to any of these as a singularity, for one doesn't exist. ~
Absolutely true. ~ And all of being shall be wholly torn asunder,
I believe, into so many pieces, no matter what anyone grasps at with
his understanding – for it would always be grasped as a mass without
the one. ~ Quite. ~ Now, even such appears to him who sees from

far-off[130] and with dull vision necessarily as one; but he who   *[165c]* examines from nearby and with keen vision, to him each singularity appears as an unlimited multitude – if, then, it has indeed been robbed of the one, which, even, is not. ~ That's absolutely necessary. ~ So, accordingly, each and every other would have to appear as unlimited and limited, as one and as many – if one is not but the other than one well-nigh is. ~ It must be so. ~ Shall they as a totality not also appear as similar and dissimilar? ~ How's that? ~ Like certain paintings that, because they all appear as one to whomever is standing at a distance, so they also seem to be constituted as one and the same, and to be similar. ~ Indeed. ~ To whomever comes closer, though, as many and different and through the appearance of differentiation as different types, and dissimilar from one another. ~ So it is. ~ Hence, also as similar and as dissimilar the masses necessarily appear in themselves and amongst one another. ~ Quite. ~ Thus too, the same and different from one another, touching upon and [being] apart from one another, and moving in all different motions and yet also at rest in every manner, and becoming and passing away and neither of both, and everything like this which would be quite easy for us to go through – so do they appear, if, without the one being, many should be. ~ Absolutely true, indeed. ~   *<27.~165e]*

Yet once more let us returning to the beginning say: If one is not but the other than the one is, what, then, must be. ~ Then, let's say that. ~ All right, the other shall not be one? ~ Indeed, how could it? ~ Hence, also not many. For underneath the being many would every time be also one. For, if none of them is one, so too they are as a totality naught and so cannot possibly be many. ~ Right. ~ Hence, if the one is not in the other: so too this is neither one nor many. ~ No, indeed not. ~ And appears also neither as one nor as many. ~ How's that? ~ Because the other cannot possibly have any   *[166a]* community with any such non-being anywhere or in any way, nor also can there be anything from that which is not with anything of the other, for non-being has, indeed, nothing. ~ Right. ~ Hence too, there is no notion of non-being by the other, nor any seemings thereof, and of that which is not there also shall in no manner be any notions anywhere in the other. ~ No, indeed not. ~ If, then, one is not, so too the other shan't be, nor is there any notionality of it whatsoever – neither as one, nor as many. For to have a notion of many without one, this is not possible. ~ Indeed, impossible. ~ If,

---

[130] See footnote #108, (p. 211).

then, one is not, so too neither is the other – nor shall there be any notions of it, neither as one nor as many. ~ It seems not. ~ Thus too, neither as similar nor dissimilar. ~ No, indeed not. ~ Even so little, now, as the same or as different, as touching or as separate, nor as everything else that we demonstrated in the previous as the seemings, from all of this the other is neither anything nor does it seem to be anything, if the one is not. ~ True. ~ Hence, to put it all together, if one is not so naught is – shall we not say this with all due right? ~ Indeed, with the greatest. ~ <28.~166c]

So, then, let it be said – and also that, as it seems, whether now the one is or is not, it itself and the others, and indeed for each in itself as well as in relation one to the other, everything in all ways is and is not and seems to be as well as does not so seem. ~ Absolutely true.

****

Gorgias

for Diana

Now those who live happily must first avoid doing injustice to others and suffering injustice themselves at the hands of others. Of these two, the former is not very difficult, but what is very difficult is acquiring the power that prevents being done injustice – this cannot be completely achieved unless one becomes completely good. This very same thing applies to a city: if it becomes good it lives a life of peace, but it lives a life of external and internal war if it is evil.

The Laws of Plato [131] – 829a

OVERVIEW:

A. Introduction:
    Arrival *after the party.*   Section 1.

B. Main:
    I.   Socrates and Gorgias: Gorgias' definition of rhetoric and the
         problem of rightfulness.   *Sections: 2 – 15.*
    II. Socrates and Polus: Socrates' definition of rhetoric and the
         consequences thereof: The powerlessness of mere power and
         the futility of doing whatever one wants – if the good would be
         absent.   *Sections 16 – 36.*
    III. Socrates and Callicles: The two paths of human existence and
         their relation to the good and the pleasurable.
                                                   Sections 37 – 61.
    IV. Socrates **alone**: Bringing it all together: Socrates'
         presentation of his view on *the good life.*   *Sections 62 – 82.*

C. Conclusion:
    Final Words.   *Section 83.*

---

[131] *The Laws of Plato*–translated by Thomas Prangle, The University of Chicago Press, 1988.

Gorgias – Sections:

GORGIAS

****

CALLICLES, SOCRATES, CHAEREPHON, GORGIAS, POLUS

<1.~447a]

Calli: To war and to battle, it is said, o Socrates, all things have their right time.

Socr: And are we then, as they put it – "partied out" – in that you're returning so late from the festival?

Calli: And what a first-rate party and festivities! For just a little while ago Gorgias gave us such splendid things to hear.

Socr: But for ourselves, o Callicles, our belatedness is due to Chaerephon who made it necessary that we loitered a long while in the marketplace.

Chaer: That's not a big deal, Socrates, for I can also make it up to you. Gorgias is my friend and he'll speak with us as well, if this be so dear to you – either now or, should you prefer, at some later time.

Calli: How's that, Chaerephon, does Socrates have a desire to hear Gorgias?

Chaer: It's even for this very purpose that we have come here.

Calli: Well then, if you would like to accompany me home, for Gorgias is now staying by me, so he will allow that you hear him.

Socr: That's nice, Callicles. But, do you suppose that he'll want to converse with us? For I should like very much to experience   [c] what this man's art[132] is capable of and what it is that he proffers and teaches. Whatever else he may show us, he might, as you say, do at some other time.

Calli: There's no better way than asking him directly, Socrates. For this too is part of his demonstration, namely he asks of everyone to inquire about anything they wish and promises an answer to any question.

Socr: Very well spoken. Ask him then, Chaerephon.

Chaer: What should I ask him?

Socr: What he is.   [d]

Chaer: How do you mean *that*?

Socr: So, that if he were one who makes shoes then he would certainly answer that he would be a leather-worker. Or don't you understand what I mean?

---

[132] The Greek '*techne*' may be translated as art {*Kunst*}, but also as profession or craft as circumstances warrant. "Redekunst" is variously rendered as speechcraft, rhetoric and as oratory. The fundamental role of speech becomes apparent from: *Theaetetus 190a* (p. 427) and *Sophist 253b–254a* (pp. 561–562) and *259e-263e* (pp. 570–576).

Chaer: I understand and I shall ask him.

 [Entrance into Callicles' home]

Tell me then, Gorgias, is it true what Callicles has stated, that you proffer yourself as able to answer whatever anyone asks?

Gorgias: That is true, Chaerephon. Even now I made just such a claim and I tell you, no one has asked me anything new for many years.   <2.~448a]

Chaer: Certainly then, Gorgias, it is very easy for you to answer.

Gorgias: As regards this, Chaerephon, you may make your own attempt.

Polus: By Zeus, if there's any way, Chaerephon, rather let me answer. For I'd fancy that Gorgias is already rather tired; you know he has just lectured at quite some length.

Chaer: How's that? – Polus, do you mean to be better able to answer than Gorgias?

Polus: Do I need to? – if only good enough for you.   *[b]*

Chaer: Indeed, it's no matter. Thus, since you want, so answer.

Polus: Ask away.

Chaer: I ask then: Were Gorgias to be a master in the same profession as is his brother Herodicus, what name would rightly be given him? Even the same as his brother?

Polus: Indeed.

Chaer: If, then, we were to say that he would be a doctor, would we, thus, express ourselves rightly?

Polus: Yes.

Chaer: Were he, however, like Aristophon, son of Aglaophon, or even with the latter's brother in an identical profession, how then would we rightly name him?

Polus: Obviously – as a painter.   *[c]*

Chaer: But now as he is essentially in that profession which he materially understands, how should he be named if we are to name him aright?

Polus: O Chaerephon, there are many professions amongst mankind which by their skill have been skillfully discovered. For it is by skill that our lives become professionally furthered, but it's by amateurism when things are simply done on a notion. Of all these, now, every person grapples in every profession and in ever a different way; the best, however, go for the best, to which group then Gorgias belongs – as he partakes in that which is the most admirable of them all, a real marksman.   <3.~448d]

Socr: On the mark, indeed, o Gorgias, it appears that Polus is well armed when it comes to speaking; singularly though, what he had promised Chaerephon that he would do, this he did not accomplish.

Gorgias: Say what, Socrates?

Socr: That about which he was questioned, it seems to me he has not in any way answered.

Gorgias: Then you go ahead and ask him, if you want.

Socr: Not if you yourself might want to answer, rather, it would be preferable by far that I might hear you. For already from hearing what Polus has just responded it is clear to me that he has far more at stake in the so-called art of oratory than he does in furthering this conversation.

Polus: But, how's that, Socrates?

Socr: Because you, my friend, as Chaerephon asked you to say in what profession Gorgias would be a master, indeed you praised his profession – as if someone had maligned it – but what it is, this you didn't answer at all.   *[~449a]*

Polus: But didn't I answer that it would be the most admirable?

Socr: Yes, indeed. But then, nobody asked you regarding the worth of Gorgias' art but, rather, just what it would be and how one, then, should rightly name Gorgias. Just as previously, in response to what Chaerephon put before you, you gave him short and good answers, even so say now – what his art is and how we should name him? Or, better yet, Gorgias, you say it yourself: how should we address you, as a master of which art?

Gorgias: Of the art of speaking, Socrates.

Socr: An orator, then, is what we'd have to call you?

Gorgias: And indeed, one *fully* perfected, Socrates, if you want to name me as I fame myself, as Homer has it.

Socr: Indeed, so I will.

Gorgias: So, name me accordingly.

Socr: Didn't we also say that you'd be capable of making others to be even so?   *[b]*

Gorgias: So do I offer my services, and not only here but throughout all of Hellas.

Socr: Would you well like, Gorgias, even as we now are speaking to one another, to bring this matter to a conclusion by question and answer; but the long speeches like the one that Polus began, to save these for some other time? Thus, what you promise, don't let us down, my friend, but may it please you to answer the questions short and direct.

Gorgias: There are, however, a few answers, Socrates, that necessarily require a longer speech to be imparted; however, I shall attempt them in the shortest span. For in this too I fame myself: no one would be able to say the same as I with fewer words.

Socr: This is just what I need, Gorgias. Just so, give me a master-piece in brevity; but the long speeches, leave these for another time.

Gorgias: I shall do so and you will have to admit, never to have heard anyone speak with greater brevity.   *<4.~449d]*

Socr: Well then, as you claim to be a master in speechcraft and also able to make others even so, upon what, then, of all things do such speeches relate? So as, for example, weaving relates to the making of garments – isn't it true?

Gorgias: Yes.

Socr: Or the art of intonation to the poetry of song and verse.

Gorgias: Yes.

Socr: By Hera, Gorgias, I take delight in your answers because you really do answer in the shortest way at all possible.

Gorgias: That's my thought, o Socrates, as befits my promise.

Socr: Well said. Now answer me likewise in regards to speechcraft – upon which of all things does it relate as a field of knowledge?

Gorgias: Upon speeches.   *[e]*

Socr: But essentially which speeches, Gorgias? Perhaps upon those that explain to those who are ill by which mode of living they might regain their health?

Gorgias: No.

Socr: Thus, not upon all speeches is speechcraft related.

Gorgias: Indeed not.

Socr: But yet, it enables capable speaking?

Gorgias: Yes.

Socr: Not also, regarding that about which one speaks, *to judge this rightly*?

Gorgias: How else?   *[450a]*

Socr: And doesn't the health profession just mentioned provide capabilities to rightly judge the sick and how to speak regarding them?

Gorgias: Certainly.

Socr: Then too, the health profession has a relation to speaking?

Gorgias: Yes.

Socr: Namely, upon those things relating to health?

Gorgias: Quite.

Socr: And does not, likewise, the gymnastics profession relate to speeches regarding the good and bad conditions of the body?

Gorgias: Indeed.   *[b]*

Socr: And, certainly too, with regards to all of the remaining professions, o Gorgias, the correlation holds: each has to do with those speeches that are related to the object that each profession has?

Gorgias: Obviously.

Socr: But why don't you also name all the remaining professions speechcraft – as even they too have to do with speeches, just as speechcraft is concerned with speeches?

Gorgias: Because, o Socrates, with the other professions there are certain hand motions and similar operations with which, to say it with one word, the whole science goes; but speechcraft contains nothing of the sort that you might lay your hands upon, rather its whole operation and accomplishment goes through speech. Therefore, I let speechcraft have to do with speeches, explaining quite rightly, just as I asserted. <5.~450c]

Socr: Do I perhaps see how you intend to name it? I will get to the bottom of this yet; just answer me. There are, indeed, many professions, are there not?

Gorgias: Yes.

Socr: Amongst these now, I believe, there are some that have a predominance of activity and which require very little speech, a few too requiring absolutely none at all but which can just as well be accomplished in silence, like painting and construction, and many others. It appears to me that you claim of this sort that they belong not at all to the art of speaking. Is this so, or not?

Gorgias: You have grasped it totally right, Socrates. [d]

Socr: Again, there are others amongst the professions that accomplish everything with speech and have very little or absolutely no need for activity – like counting and calculating, measuring and board games,[133] and many other arts – in some of which speech goes right along with the action and, with many, it bears yet the greater burden so that wholly and absolutely is the accomplishment and its realization composed through speech. Of these latter, I opine, it appears that you believe one to be speechcraft.

Gorgias: Totally right. [e]

Socr: But still you shall want, nonetheless, I think, that none of the others that I mentioned be named speechcraft despite that this, literally, is what you have said: that those arts in which the entire employment consists in speech would be speechcraft. And it is possible that someone would be able to conclusively demonstrate this – if he wished by excessive zeal to turn your words against you: "Hence, Gorgias, mathematics as well you name speechcraft?" But I do not believe that you, be it now the measuring arts or the calculating arts, that you would name these speechcraft?

Gorgias: And totally right are you in your belief, Socrates, and rightly do you understand me full well. <6.~451a]

---

[133] The same arts listed as gifts from the Egyptian god, Theuth, in *Phaedrus* 274d (p. 69).

Socr: Well then, now deliver up to me the final answer to which my questions were leading. For if speechcraft is one of these many arts that predominately make use of speech and there are, however, still others of this same type: so strive yet to say upon what, then, is the activity of these speeches realized that are related to speechcraft? Thus, if someone were to question me regarding any of the professions I just mentioned: "O Socrates, what, pray tell, is the art of counting?" – I would say to him, just as you have: "One of those occupations that are realized through speech," and if he then were to ask me further: "Upon what?" – then I would say: "Upon the even and the odd, how large each would be." And if he should ask again: "And what do you name as the art of calculation?" – I would say to him: "It is likewise one of those arts that are accomplished through speech." And if he questioned further: "Upon what?" – I would then say, even as it is called in the assembly: "All the same as earlier, the art of calculation is just like the lore of counting, only in this does it differ: that this teaching of relationships also examines how the even and the odd relate in size in themselves to themselves and one against the other." And if someone should ask me regarding starlore and about my clarification that this profession is accomplished through speech as well, and he were to say: "But the speeches of starlore, upon what do these relate?" – I would say: "Upon the motion of the stars and of the sun and moon, how they relate in their velocities each to the other."

Gorgias: And your speech would be totally right, Socrates.   *[d]*

Socr: Well then, even so, do this as well yourself, Gorgias! Speechcraft is then one of these arts that accomplishes everything through speaking. Is it so?

Gorgias: So it is.

Socr: Then say it, upon what is it directed. What amongst all things is it, actually, to which these speeches relate and upon which speechcraft serves?

Gorgias: Upon the most important, o Socrates, and amongst all human things the most majestic.[134]   *<7.~451e]*

Socr: But this too, Gorgias, is yet once again questionable and in no way something definite. You, my friend, have heard, I think, the drinking song that is often sung at parties and in which they count off: the best thing is health and the second best beauty and, as for the third, as the poet of this song believes, to be rich without being false.

Gorgias: Indeed, I have heard it. But why do you bring this up? *[a]*

---

[134] See *Theaetetus* footnote #152 (p. 359) – "herrlich."

Socr: Because these masters whom the song praises would now step up, blocking you in your way, the doctor, the gymnast and the businessman; and first the doctor would say: "O Socrates, Gorgias fools you, for it is not his profession that accomplishes man's most important good, rather it is mine." And if I were to ask him: "And who are you that you say this?" – so, then, would be his reply: "A doctor." "How do you mean," I would say, "thus the work of your profession would be the greatest good?" "How could it not be so," he would perhaps say, "this being man's health. What, then, would be a greater good than health for man?" If now, after this, in his turn a master gymnast should step forward and say: "I should be much amazed, Socrates, if Gorgias could show you a greater good from his profession than I from mine!" so I would say to him as well: *"And who then are you, man, and what is your business?"* "I am a gymnast," he would say, "and my occupation is this, that which gives to man's body both beauty and strength." And after this one the businessman would then come forward, as I see it, and, with a most righteous contempt of all the others say: "Now look sharp, Socrates, whether or not there might be shown a yet greater good than *[452c]* riches, be it from Gorgias or from anyone else!" "And how," we would then say to him, "are you able to make man rich?" He answers affirmatively. "As who then?" "As a businessman." "And how? – do you then believe that riches are man's greatest good?" we would say. "How could they not be!" he would answer. "But Gorgias here," we would say, "claims contrary to you that, indeed, it is his art which brings forth a yet greater good than yours." Obviously, he would then ask further: "And what then is this good? Let Gorgias answer." Well then, Gorgias, think it over, if you were to be asked by these professionals as well as by me, and give us your answer, what then is it, that which you claim would be the greatest good for man and of which you are the master?

Gorgias: That which in all actuality is the greatest good, Socrates, and by the power of which man as well gains his freedom and also is able to rule over others,[135] each in his own city.

Socr: What, then, do you mean now with this?

Gorgias: If one is able to persuade others with words, as well in *[e]* the places of law, the judges, as also in the parliament, the senators, and in all public councils, the councilmen, and so on in every assembly where official business is conducted. For if you have this in your power, so the doctor becomes your servant, and the gymnast would likewise be your servant, and of this businessman it will easily

---

[135] See *Meno* 73cd (p. 466).

be shown that he is controlled by others and not on his own, rather by you who understand [how] to speak and can persuade the multitudes.

Socr: Now, Gorgias, does it seem to you that you have   *<8.~453a]*
most precisely clarified for me which art you essentially hold speechcraft to be; and, if I do properly understand you, so you say: speechcraft would be the master of persuasion and the whole of its business and essence streams forth from this. Or do you still have something further to say that speechcraft enables, something beyond this causal effect of persuasion in the soul of those listening.

Gorgias: In no way, Socrates, rather you seem to me to have fully clarified it. For this is its main concern.

Socr: Now hear this, Gorgias. For I, you should know, believe with certainty that if there would be anyone at all who might endeavor *[b]*
by discourse to really research properly that about which we are speaking, I too certainly am such a one, and I believe you are also.

Gorgias: And what then, Socrates?

Socr: I'll say it right away. This becoming persuaded through speechcraft, what this is essentially[136] and in relation to which objects persuasion exists, all of this, you bethink yourself, I even still do not know aright. Indeed, I do well have an inkling, I believe, what it is that you mean and upon what, but, nonetheless, I shall question you yet further, what you mean essentially by this "becoming persuaded through speechcraft" and what, then, are the objects toward which it is directed. But why, then, as verily I do have an inkling, why must I still question you and not simply say it myself? Not for your sake, but rather for the sake of our conversation, so that it may continue and so that that about which we now are speaking, that this may become as clear as is possible. For just consider whether you'd fancy this so, that I am right in continuing to question you. Namely, it's as if I had questioned you: "Which painter is Zeuxis?" and you would have answered: "He who paints paintings" – wouldn't I then have rightfully questioned you further: "But what are these paintings and where?"

Gorgias: Certainly.   *[d]*

Socr: Perhaps for this reason, because there are yet many other painters who paint many other pictures?

Gorgias: Yes.

Socr: But if there were none other than Zeuxis who painted such, then your answer would have been good enough.

Gorgias: How else?

---

[136] "was fur eine die ist," literally "what for one it is," translated "essentially." The concepts of essentiality and oneness are correlated in Plato – *Parmenides* lays the foundation.

Socr: Well then, tell me also about speechcraft, whether you think that speechcraft is alone in effecting persuasion, or are there other arts? I mean namely this: whoever teaches anything, does he not persuade others in that about which he teaches, or not?

Gorgias: Heavens, rather, without a doubt he persuades. *[e]*

Socr: If now, we come back to the same professions as earlier, does not numberlore and don't the mathematicians teach regarding the size of numbers?

Gorgias: Indeed.

Socr: And persuades us, then, as well?

Gorgias: Yes.

Socr: Thus too, mathematics is a master of persuasion?

Gorgias: So it seems.

Socr: And if someone were to question us, "What is this persuasion essentially and upon what?" – so we would probably answer him: "A teaching persuasion of the even and the odd and of how large." *[a]* And with all of the other professions we just enumerated we would be able to show that they too are masters of persuasion and what they are essentially and upon which objects? – or not?

Gorgias: Yes.

Socr: Not alone, then, is speechcraft the master of persuasion?

Gorgias: No, indeed not. *<9.~454]*

Socr: As, now, speechcraft is not alone in bringing forth this work, so it would well be with due right, just as before with the painter, to him, he who speaks like this, to question further: "What is the art of persuasion essentially and upon which objects is speechcraft directed?" Or, do you hold this as not being right, to ask further?

Gorgias: Fine by me. *[b]*

Socr: So answer then, Gorgias, as you also fancy this so.

Gorgias: I say the persuasion mentioned previously, Socrates, which happens in courts of law and by other assemblages of the populace, as I already did say, and in relation to that which is just and unjust.

Socr: I also had an inkling already that this was the persuasion that you meant, Gorgias, and in relation hereto. Only do not be amazed if I should soon once again ask you about something which appears to be obvious – and yet I still naïvely question. For, as I said, in order that this discourse may properly be brought to its conclusion, thus do I so question, not for your sake but, rather, so that we do not become accustomed to let things stand which we only halfway comprehend; rather may you, my friend, fully express in each sentence your viewpoint, just as you desire.

Gorgias: And with full propriety do you do this, as I'd fancy it.

Socr: Then come now, let us also consider this: you say from time to time – one has learned something?

Gorgias: Oh yes.

Socr: Also, one has believed something?

Gorgias: I, certainly.   [d]

Socr: Do these, now, seem to you to be one and the same *{einerlei}*, to have learned and believed? and learned knowledge and belief? – or are they different?

Gorgias: I, o Socrates, opine that they differ.

Socr: And you are quite right in having this opinion. You can recognize the difference in the following. If someone were to ask you whether there was such a thing as a false belief and a true belief? – you would answer affirmatively, I think?

Gorgias: Yes.

Socr: But, how now? – also false knowledge[137] and true knowledge?

Gorgias: In no way.

Socr: Obviously, then, the two are not one and the same.

Gorgias: You are right.   [e]

Socr: And yet, those who know are persuaded as well as those who merely believe.

Gorgias: So it is.

Socr: Do you confer, then, that we should declare two sorts of persuasion: the one that brings about belief without knowledge and the other, however, which brings about knowledge?

Gorgias: Quite.

Socr: Which of these two sorts of persuasion, then, is accomplished by speechcraft in the courts and in other assemblages in relation to the just and the unjust? From the one in which belief arises without knowledge? – or the other in which knowledge arises?

Gorgias: Obviously indeed, Socrates, in which belief.   [a]

Socr: Thus speechcraft, Gorgias, is, as it appears, the master of a belief inducing and not a learned persuasion in relation to the just and unjust?

Gorgias: Yes.

Socr: Thus, the orators are not erudite instructors in the law courts and other assemblages regarding the just and unjust but, rather,

---

[137] The German noun *Erkenntnis*, could equally well be rendered here as knowledge or cognition. Perhaps the best way to reflect on this passage is by observing that the recognition of this difference between belief and *Erkenntnis* is itself both belief and *Erkenntins*. *Theaetetus* and *Meno* are Plato's dialogues that examine the quandaries of cognition and knowing in much greater depth; *Gorgias* is principally concerned with morality – which, one would hope, itself is essentially related to knowledge.

accomplish merely belief. Besides, how could he well instruct such a great throng[138] in such a short time regarding such important things.

Gorgias: It's not probable.   *<10.~455b]*

Socr: Well then, let us review what it is that we are actually saying about speechcraft; for I myself am still unable to really properly understand just what I say. If our city assembles itself in order to elect doctors or for engineers to build ships or for some other sort of tradesmen – is it true, then, that the orator is not permitted to give advice? For it is clear that with each choice the most qualified professional must be chosen. And [is it likewise true] also not give advice when the speech regards the construction of city walls, or to bring the harbor into order, or the catapults – rather, then the master builder. Also not, if the council is to give advice in choosing an army general, or in the positioning of the army *vis-à-vis* the enemy, or yet the capturing of some territory; rather the masters in warcraft would advise in these matters and not the orators. Or what is your   *[c]* opinion, Gorgias, regarding all of this? For as you claim that you are yourself an orator and are also capable of making others masters in [political] oratory, so it is right and proper to ask you about that which concerns your art. Verily, believe me, I now bethink myself as being simultaneously concerned regarding your affairs; for perhaps there are many here present who are of a mind to become your students, as I believe to take notice of quite a few who are, perhaps, shying away from asking you further. Just as now you are asked by me, so bethink yourself that you also would be asked by them: "What, o Gorgias, shall we become if we enter into company with you? – regarding what shall we be enabled to give advice in our city? – only upon the just and the unjust alone, or also regarding those things which Socrates just brought up?" Strive, then, to answer them.   *[e]*

Gorgias: So shall I then attempt, Socrates, and right clearly, to uncover for you the whole power of speechcraft. For you yourself have given this a very good introduction. Namely, you know full well that the catapults and the walls of Athens and also the construction of the harbor, these were all created upon the advice of Themistocles – in part too with Pericles – but not upon the advice of any master builders of whatever sort.

Socr: So it is said, o Gorgias, regarding Themistocles;[139] but Pericles, even I myself heard him when he announced his opinion regarding the middle wall.   *[456a]*

---

[138] "Haufen," literally a heap.

[139] According to Thucydides' history, Themistocles engaged in some elaborate political deceptions in his dealings with the Spartans so as to enable the rapid construction of the

Gorgias: And when the advice of such men is brought to bear, as you have just mentioned, so indeed you do see that the orators are the advisers and that their opinions prevail in such things.

Socr: Even because I am in wonder about all of this, Gorgias, have I questioned so thoroughly already: what indeed is actually the essence of speechcraft. For it seems to me wholly superhuman in size when I examine it.

Gorgias: But *if only* you were to know it all, Socrates,   <11.~456b] how, to say it in one word, speechcraft encompasses in its grasp all of the other powers taken together! The following proof comes to mind that I will give you. Namely, quite often have I gone with my brother or some other doctor to an ill patient who either refused his medicine or wouldn't allow the doctor to cut or burn and, as the doctor wasn't able to persuade him, so I spoke up and simply through my art of speechcraft I was able actually to persuade him. Verily, I do assert, and be it in whichever city you might choose, if an orator and a doctor should arrive and present themselves to some council or whichever assemblage and they were to fight it out through speech, which of the two of them should be elected as doctor: so never once would the doctor even be considered, rather, he who understands speech would always be chosen, if he so desired. And even thus in contention with any other professional the orator would be more persuasive than anyone else and would himself be elected. For there is nothing upon which an orator might be outdone in speech before the populace, and no matter what the area of expertise. The power of this art is truly such and so great. Therefore, o Socrates, one must make use of speechcraft just as with any other martial art. For it is true too   *[d]* of the other martial arts, one need not simply make use of them against all people just because one is good with his fists or in wrestling, or because one has learned so well to use the weapons of combat so that one is stronger than friend or foe, and one need not for this reason strike and shove and kill one's friends. Nor, by Zeus, if someone by visiting the exercise gymnasiums has become an able fighter and hereafter he strikes his father or mother or some other relative or friend, is it allowable that the gymnastics master or the martial artist be persecuted and expelled from the city? For they have imparted their arts so that one might rightfully utilize them against foes and in defense against those who would do one harm, not for assault; and only such as the former turn things upside down   *[457a]*

---

walls around Athens after the Persians were defeated, see Chapt. 7 – *Digression. The Beginnings of Athenian Power, The Peloponnesian War*, translated by Rex Warner, 1954 – The Great Books Foundation, 1966.

and improperly make use of their strength and their art. Thus, not the teachers are evil, nor either is the art itself at fault and therefore evil, but rather those, I believe, who don't rightly practice it. The same is valid also of speechcraft. Able, indeed, is the orator to speak against one and all and regarding anything so that he will receive the most belief before the populace and, to put it briefly, upon *anything* he pleases. But he should not for this reason deprive the doctor of his calling, just because he's well able to accomplish this, nor any other professionals their positions; rather, he should make rightful use of speechcraft just as it is with all the martial arts. And I believe, if someone should become an orator and then exercise the power and craft thus enabled unrighteously: so, I think, you shouldn't hate his teacher and expel him from the city. For it was for rightful usage that the art was transmitted; such a person, however, utilized it in a perverse manner. He, then, who unrightfully practices, he it may be right to hate and to expel, but not his teacher. *<12.~457c]*

Socr: I think, Gorgias, that you also have been present at many conversations and have taken notice of the following, that there are many cases in which there is no way that a meeting of minds will easily ensue such that it will be possible at the time of parting that that whereupon the parties set out to discourse, that this shall be determined together so that each would have learned something from the other one and each contributed in the teaching; rather it's much likelier, if they are at odds with one another and disagree and each blames the other that, perhaps, he does not speak aright or is unclear, so they anger one another and believe that the other is saying whatever it may be out of personal disfavor, because namely he is primarily concerned with looking good and his own vanity, but not about the object being discussed. Verily, some like this finally do part in a most disgraceful manner, cursing one another vehemently and, in that they exchange such things to one another, even the bystanders are sorry that they have been present and that they desired to listen to such people. Now, why do I say this? Because I fancy that you have just said something that is out of line and does not properly follow from what you said earlier regarding speechcraft. I have real trepidation, however, in contradicting you, as you might think that I say it not in my zeal for the matter at hand, that it *[458a]* should be cleared up, but rather against you. But, my friend, if you and I are of one kind then gladly will I scrutinize you; if not, then I would rather let it be. And of what sort of a one am I? Of that sort which gladly is led to the rightful path, if then I say something wrong; but likewise will gladly lead others over – if, then, the other one has said something that is not right; and verily, rather the former than the latter. For a much greater benefit do I hold the former to be – as it is assuredly better that one becomes free of the greatest evil than to free another therefrom. For there is nothing, I think, that for mankind is such an evil as having wrong opinions upon that regarding which we now speak. If, then, you claim to be such a one as I, so let us continue our conversation; but if you fancy that, rather, we should just let it be, so let's leave things well enough alone and break off our conversation.

Gorgias: Indeed, I do claim to be also such a one as you, the way that you portrayed it. But perhaps we should also bethink ourselves of those present. For, my friends, long before you arrived here I lectured these present regarding many things and should we continue our conversation it may easily drag on a very long while. We should also, therefore, bethink ourselves of our audience, that we shouldn't hinder them if they prefer to take up something else.   <13.~458c]

Chaer: The clamor of these men! – you yourselves do well hear, o Gorgias and Socrates, how greatly they desire to hear you if you will continue to speak. And I myself would never wish to be so tied up in the intricacies of my business affairs that I should have to let such illustrious speeches be postponed because something else of greater urgency needed to be accomplished.

Calli: By the gods, Chaerephon, I too, although I have been present at many other lectures and debates, I do not know if *ever* I have been so struck as I am now, so that, as for me, and even if you should continue on for the whole day,[140] my passion shall never diminish.

Socr: On my side, Callicles, there are no obstacles – if only Gorgias is willing.

Gorgias: And how unbecoming that would be, Socrates, if I shouldn't want to; even the more so in that I myself called up to question those present regarding their desires. Thus, if they are so well inclined, then speak and question whatever you will.   *[e]*

Socr: Now hear this, Gorgias, what amazed me about what you have said. For perhaps you have spoken totally rightly and I just wasn't able to grasp it aright. You did say that you could make one an orator if he wants to learn the art from you?

Gorgias: Yes.

Socr: And indeed, regarding everything, so that he might then persuade the populace, although not in a learned fashion, rather just exciting their belief.

Gorgias: Quite.   *[459a]*

---

[140] The conversation began quite late in the evening; and it's not unusual for Plato's dialogues to go on through the night and into the next day, e.g.: *Symposium, Republic*.

Socr: For you even said that in matters of health the orator would find more belief than the doctor.

Gorgias: That I also said; before the multitude, namely.

Socr: And, is it true, this "before the multitude" means before those who do not know? For before doctors he would not receive greater belief than a doctor?

Gorgias: In this you are right.

Socr: If he finds more belief than the doctor, then he finds more belief than the knower?

Gorgias: Indeed.

Socr: Without being a doctor – is it true? [b]

Gorgias: Yes.

Socr: He who is not a doctor is uninformed of that wherein the doctor is informed?

Gorgias: Obviously.

Socr: He who doesn't know finds more belief than he who does know amongst those who do not know – if the orator finds more belief than the doctor? Does this follow, or something other?

Gorgias: This follows here, indeed.

Socr: And the orator and speechcraft relate likewise to all of the [c] other arts in *toto*? The matters themselves they need not know, how such matters relate, rather simply by having found an artful grasp in persuasion so that they may win the appearance by those who do not know to know more than those who do know. <14.~459]

Gorgias: Is that not a great advantage, Socrates, that without having had to learn the other arts but just this single one you are not in the least bit disadvantaged to the masters of all the rest?

Socr: Whether the orator, as it so relates with him, is disadvantaged or not behind all of the rest – we shall consider this later when it serves the matter. Now let us first bethink ourselves regarding this: whether also in respect to the just and the unjust, the beautiful and the ugly, the good and the evil – would the orator have even the [d] same relation to these as he did to health and the objects of the other arts; namely, that he does not know of these matters themselves, what is good or evil, beautiful or ugly, just or unjust; rather is able simply by his art to induce persuasion so that he as one who does not know amongst those who do not know is considered to know more than the knower? Or is it necessary to know this and must he who comes to you already be informed of this, whoever is to learn speechcraft from you? If not shall you, then, the teacher of speechcraft, withhold such learning from the novice because this is not a matter that you cover, rather just bring him to the point that he may also appear to the multitude to know this without knowing it, and to seem to be good

without being good? Or shall you be totally incapable of teaching speechcraft if someone should not already know in all of these what is right? or, how does all of this relate, Gorgias? – by the will of Zeus! – do uncover now, as you said previously, the whole power of speech-craft for me and speak, in what is it constituted?   *[460a]*
Gorgias: It's my opinion, Socrates, that if, by chance, if he shouldn't already know the former then he shall also learn this from me.
Socr: Stop! – for that is admirably said. If you should make one into an orator must he not necessarily know what is just and unjust, be it already beforehand or first after he learns it from you?
Gorgias: Quite.   *[b]*
Socr: How now? He who learns the art of building, is he not a master builder, or not?
Gorgias: Yes.
Socr: And he who learns the art of music, a musician?
Gorgias: Yes.
Socr: And he who learns the lore of healing, a health practitioner? – and so also for all of the remaining [arts and professions] by this same rule, he who has learned something is such a one that this knowledge has made him?
Gorgias: Indeed.
Socr: Thus, by the same relationship, he who has learned the just is just?
Gorgias: In all ways, indeed.
Socr: The just person, assuredly, acts righteously?
Gorgias: Yes.
Socr: Thus, it is necessary that the speechcrafter is just – and that the just person acts righteously?   *[c]*
Gorgias: So it has shown itself, yes.
Socr: And never shall the righteous desire to do anything that is unrighteous?
Gorgias: Naturally.
Socr: But the rhetorician is, in accordance with our speech, necessarily just.
Gorgias: Yes.
Socr: *Never*, then, shall the rhetorician want to do anything unjustly.
Gorgias: No, it doesn't seem that he would.   *<15.~460d]*
Socr: Now, do you remember having said just a little while ago that if a pugilist misuses his art in an ugly manner and does an injustice, one should not lay the guilt on the masters of gymnastics nor expel them from the city? Even so, if an orator uses speechcraft unrighteously one should not lay the guilt upon his teacher nor expel him from the

city, rather, just him who does the unjust deed and utilizes speechcraft unrighteously. Was that said, or not?

Gorgias: It was said.   *[e]*

Socr: But now it has been shown that he, namely the speechcrafter, never does injustice. Or not?

Gorgias: So it was shown.

Socr: Also at the start of our conversation, o Gorgias, even there it was said that speechcraft has to do *not* with the even and the odd, but rather with the just and the unjust. Isn't it so?

Gorgias: Yes.

Socr: Now I, as you said this then, understood you so that speechcraft could never be something unjust as the speeches always deal in righteousness. When soon thereafter, however, you said that the orator might indeed use speechcraft unjustly, so, as I was   *[a]* amazed and was of the opinion that this would be contradictory, I spoke the bit about whether you would consider it a plus to be led over – as I myself do hold it to be one: if so it would be worthwhile to bespeak things further, but if not then it would be better if we just let things be. And now that we have reconsidered it once more – you see it also yourself – that once again it has been established that it would be impossible for an orator to make unrighteous use of speechcraft or desire to do injustice. Now this, how it itself really correlates, to investigate, o Gorgias – by the dog! – this may and shall entail quite a long conversation.   *<16.~461b]*

Polus: How's this, Socrates? Do *you* also actually think so about speechcraft as you now speak? Or do you mean, because Gorgias has shamed himself and not disagreed with you on this, that an orator would also need to know what the just is – and the beautiful and the good? – and that, should someone come to him not knowing this, so he would have to teach him? and so, accordingly, by this admission a contradiction is brought into his speech – upon which *you* take   *[c]* delight, after *you* have led the conversation on to such questions. For who, do you well suppose, who would want to deny that he himself would be uninformed of what is right and, so, wouldn't be able to teach others? But, to lead the conversation on into such things – this is no proper way of behaving.

Socr: Now, most beauteous Polus, even expressly for this do we have our friends and sons, that if we ourselves in our advanced ages should go astray you our youths are ready at hand, and so you right us in our life through word and deed. So too now, as Gorgias and I have   *[d]* gone astray in our conversation, you, my friend, are ready at hand – so do correct us. And really, this would be most befitting of you and is right and proper. And I am ready, if you believe that anything at all of that which was agreed to was not rightfully agreed to, to give it back to you, as you will, if only you observe just one thing.

Polus: And just what do you mean by that?

Socr: The long speeches, o Polus, if only you might hold back on these, of which already before you desired to make use.   *[461e]*

Polus: How's that? – it shouldn't be allowable for me to speak for as long as I wish?

Socr: That would indeed be hard on you, most worthy *{Bester}*, as you have come here to Athens, the seat in all of Hellas where there rules the greatest freedom to speak and you alone should have to do without, even here. But just consider the other possibility: if you should speak with no bounds and will not answer what is questioned, would it not, then again, be very hard on me if I should not be allowed to walk away and not have to listen to you? Thus, if you desire to take it upon yourself to correct the previous proposition: so take back, as I just said, whatever should be dear to you and then, questioning and being questioned in an orderly manner just as both Gorgias and I were, lead me over and allow yourself to be led over. For indeed, you fame yourself also that you understand the selfsame as Gorgias. Or not?

Polus: I do assert it.

Socr: Thus too, you encourage that anyone might ask you whatsoever he might desire and you are one who well understands to answer.

Polus: Quite.   *<17.~462b]*

Socr: Then do so now, whichever of the two you wish: question or answer.

Polus: Good, I will do it. Answer me then, Socrates, as you opine that Gorgias is at a loss when it comes to [defining] speechcraft, what, then, do you opine that it is?

Socr: Are you asking, which art I claim that it would be?

Polus: Even that.

Socr: None at all, as I fancy, o Polus, indeed, to speak the truth to you.

Polus: Rather what, then, would you fancy speechcraft to be?

Socr: That from which the professions proceed – if, then, I properly read your manuscript just recently.   *[c]*

Polus: And what do you mean by that?

Socr: A certain skill is what I mean.

Polus: All right, you fancy that speechcraft would be a skill.

Socr: Yes; if, then, you don't say anything other?

Polus: And a skill in what?

Socr: In the production of a certain pleasure and contentment.

Polus: And wouldn't you fancy, then, that speechcraft is something beautiful – as it enables one to be pleasing to mankind?

Socr: How's this, Polus? – have you then already made sense of what in my opinion speechcraft would be that you now are proceeding to question me as to whether or not I hold it to be something of beauty?

Polus: Did I not already apprehend that it's your opinion that it would be a skill?   [d]

Socr: Could you, perhaps, then, as you place such value on being pleased, please humor me in a small matter?

Polus: Very gladly.

Socr: So question me, then, what art the art of cooking appears to me to be.

Polus: I ask you then, which art is the art of cooking?

Socr: None at all, o Polus.

Polus: But, what then, speak.

Socr: Thus, I say – a skill.

Polus: But what, essentially? – tell me.

Socr: I say, then, in the production of a certain pleasure and contentment, o Polus.   [e]

Polus: Cooking, then, is one and the same as speechcraft?

Socr: In no way, rather just a part of the selfsame endeavor.

Polus: But then, essentially of what?

Socr: If only it would not be unbecoming of me to speak the truth, for I really do have serious apprehension in consideration of Gorgias to say it, that thereby he might believe that I desire to make a mockery of his vocation. At the same time, whether *this* is the   [a] speechcraft with which Gorgias is occupied, I don't really know, for even now it has not as of yet become obvious from our conversation what he rightly means. But what I name speechcraft, this is one part of a matter that in no way belongs under the heading of the beautiful.

Gorgias: But what for one then, Socrates? – just say it and don't worry about sparing me.   <18.~463]

Socr: For me, Gorgias, I fancy it so: that there is a certain pursuit which, indeed, is not of a professional nature but which belongs to an audacious soul, one that knows how to hit its mark and is naturally strong in its handling of men – as a whole I name it sycophancy.[141] [b] Now this pursuit seems to me to have many other parts, one of which being the art of cooking which, indeed, is held to be an art but, as my speech already has stated, is not one but, rather, just an exercise and an acquired skill. As other parts of the same I view speechcraft, the art of make-up [cosmetics] and sophistry: four parts for four objects.

---

[141] Sycophancy is both flattery and parasitism.

If, then, Polus desires to question me further, he may do so. For he
hadn't even as of yet asked me which part I considered speechcraft to
be; rather, without even noticing that I hadn't yet answered this
question he asked further, whether I hold speechcraft to be something of beauty. But I won't answer as to whether I hold it to be
beauteous or unbeauteous unless I first have answered what it is. For
that wouldn't be right, Polus. Thus, if you want to experience which
part of sycophancy I mean speechcraft to be, so ask away.
Polus: Then I do ask it and you answer, which part?   [d]
Socr: Whether you will be well able to understand if I do answer?
Namely, in accord with my clarification, speechcraft is a shadow
image of one part of statecraft.
Polus: How now? – do you say it would be something of beauty, or
lacking beauty?
Socr: Lacking beauty. For I name that which is evil as lacking in
beauty – as, indeed, I am to answer you *as if* you might know what it
is that I mean.
Gorgias: By Zeus, Socrates, I myself do not as of yet understand
what you mean.
Socr: That's quite believable, Gorgias. For I have not yet said   [e]
anything definite. But Polus is, well, rather young and all steamed up.
Gorgias: Then just leave him be and tell me how you mean it,
speechcraft should be a shadow image of one part of statecraft?
Socr: Good, I shall attempt to clear it up, what speechcraft seems
to me to be and, if it should be something different, so Polus may
prove me wrong. You do name something body and soul?
Gorgias: How could I not.   [464a]
Socr: And also you believe that each of these may be in good health?
Gorgias: That too.
Socr: How about this? – also a seeming to be well which is not?
I mean such as this: many have the physical appearance of being in
the pink of condition so that no one would easily notice that they
are not so, unless perchance a doctor or someone who understands
gymnastics.
Gorgias: Totally right.
Socr: This sort of thing exists as regards both body and soul
that results in the body or soul appearing to be well, but actually not
being well.
Gorgias: This exists.   <19.~464b]
Socr: Then, tallyho: if I am able, I will now show you more clearly
what it is that I mean. For these two things I propose two arts and
name the one for the soul to be statecraft; the one for the body,
however, I cannot give only one name, rather the care of the body

likewise falls into two parts: gymnastics as the one and the healing arts as the other. And so too with statecraft, standing over against gymnastics would be legislation and standing across from the healing arts would be jurisprudence. Thus, in both cases each of the subdivisions has some commonality with the other in that they both relate to the same object: the healing arts with gymnastics [for the body], and jurisprudence with legislation [for the soul] – and yet they are still different from one another. Now these four that are to be administered always in reference to the best in the concerns of the body for the former and, for the latter, of the soul, are noticed by sycophancy – I do not say they are fully recognized but that they are sniffed out and met up with – and sycophancy then splits itself up into four parts as well and disguised in the outfit of each part *[d]* pretends to be that in whose disguise it appears; and never even thinking of the best each starts off after what is most pleasing to those lacking in understanding and fools these and so appears to be exceedingly valuable. And so the cooking arts appear in the disguise of the healing arts and sycophancy sets itself up as knowing which foods are best for the body so that, be it before children or even before grown men who might by their lack of understanding just as well be children, a doctor and a cook, should they fight it out for preference, which of the two of them would know more regarding healthy and harmful foods, the doctor or the cook, well, the doctor could just die of hunger! Sycophancy I name this and I do assert that it is something bad, o Polus – for I say this to you – because it tries to hit upon what is pleasing without reference to what is best. But I deny that it would be an art, rather only a skill because it hasn't any insight into what it's practicing and what its own nature is and, thus, does not know how to give an account regarding the *grounds* of each and every; but I cannot name anything "an art" where there is no understanding of the matter. And if you should be of a different opinion, so I'll gladly stand and converse this with you. As a healing art, thus, as I said, comes sycophancy disguising the   *<20.~465b]* cook practitioner; but as a gymnast even in the same manner is the make-up artist disguised, being downright corrupt and deceitful, ignoble and indecent – and who by means of formalities, colors, glitz and fancy clothing deceives people enveloping [the made-up person] in foreign beauty but meanwhile neglecting the authentic well-being that comes to be from the expert gymnast. So as to keep things brief I shall express myself mathematically, for now you shall be able to follow me – that, namely, as the cosmetician is to the gymnast so is cooking to healing or, even more so, as cosmetics is to gymnastics so is sophistry to legislation, and as cooking is to healing so is speechcraft to jurisprudence. As I now say it, so these are essentially different, each from the other; but, because they are also so close to each other, so they become all mixed up with one another and the sophists and the speechcrafters make hay with the same things and don't even themselves know what to do with each other, nor too does anyone else have the slightest idea of what to make of it all. For even if it should it be that the soul did not take precedence over the body, but rather the latter by itself and not by the former would compare cooking to healing and would distinguish between them and, thus, rather the body itself would be able to judge with the yardstick of that which is most pleasing: so it would be able to go a long way along the path of Anaxagoras, dear Polus, for then you are informed of these things, namely, all things would be like one another and all mixed up together and inseparable together would remain health and the healing arts, all mixed up with the cooking arts. Now, what I mean speechcraft to be you have heard, namely the counterpart to the cooking arts – but for the soul as these are for the body. Perhaps I began in a way contrary to common sense in that I didn't want to hear any overly long speeches from you and now I myself have been quite long-winded. It isn't, though, asking a great deal – that you will forgive me. For as I answered briefly you hardly understood me and didn't have a clue as to where to begin with the answers that I gave to you; rather, all this required some explanation. If, now, I too shouldn't know where to begin with your responses then you also might expand on your speech; but if I should know so allow me to make as I will, for this is reasonable. Thus, now too, if you know how to make anything with this answer, so do so.   <21.~466a]

Polus: What do you say, then? Sycophancy is what you fancy speechcraft to be?

Socr: Of sycophancy – I said just one part. Is your memory then failing already at your age, Polus, what will you then do when you become old?

Polus: Does it seem to you, then, that the celebrated orators of our city have been odiously respected as sycophants and as bad people?

Socr: Are you asking me a question, or is this the beginning of a speech?   [b]

Polus: I'm asking.

Socr: Well then, they are not at all respected, I opine.

Polus: How! Not respected? – don't they have the greatest power in the cities?

Socr: No, not if you understand by "having power" that it would be something good for those who are empowered.

Polus: Indeed, this is how I do understand it.

Socr: Then I'd fancy that the orators have the very least amount of power in the cities.

Polus: How! – don't they act like tyrants putting to death [c] whomsoever they want, and rob whatever and expel from the city whomsoever, if they fancy this as being in their best interests?

Socr: *By the dog!* All the same, Polus, I am in doubt with everything that you say, whether you say so yourself and are expressing your own opinion, or whether you're asking me?

Polus: Indeed, I am asking you.

Socr: Well, my dear friend! – then you are asking two things at once.

Polus: How so, two things? [d]

Socr: Didn't you just say something like: the orators would kill whomsoever they want and rob livelihoods and expel from the city – if they fancied this as good?

Polus: I said it. <22.~466]

Socr: Well then, I say to you that these are two questions and I will answer both of them. I assert namely, Polus, that the orators and tyrants actually have the least amount of power in the city because, namely, they do nothing that they want, if I may say it straight-out; though, indeed, they do do that which they fancy as best. [e]

Polus: This truly is having power and being able to accomplish many things.

Socr: No, at least *not* according to Polus.

Polus: *I say no?* – but I just said *yes.*

Socr: No, truly, not you at all – as you even say *yes* that having power and the ability to do much would be something good for him who has such.

Polus: Indeed, I say that.

Socr: Do you mean, then, it would be good if someone should accomplish whatever he fancies as best but who does so without knowledge? And do you name this great capability?

Polus: No, not that. [467a]

Socr: Thus, you need to demonstrate that the orators have knowledge and that speechcraft is an art and not merely sycophancy if you will prove me wrong. But if you leave this standing then when the orators do in the cities whatever they fancy as being good, and also the tyrants, such deeds will possess nothing of the good. And having power should even be something good, as you yourself assert. But accomplishing whatever one fancies without knowledge, this – you do concede – this would be an evil. Or not?

Polus: I concede it.

Socr: How, then, should the orators have power in the state, or also the tyrants, if it has not first become proven to Socrates by Polus that they accomplish what they want?

Polus: Behold, here is a man!   [b]

Socr: I call it a lie that they accomplish what they want. Prove me wrong.

Polus: Did you not even admit that they accomplish what they fancy as being best?

Socr: I still admit so much.

Polus: So, they do accomplish what they want?

Socr: That's a lie.

Polus: Despite that they accomplish what seems to them to be good?

Socr: Yes.

Polus: Stuff and nonsense! You say quite miserable and unwashed things.

Socr: Aye, my precious friend, in that I speak to you in your own fashion do not scold me, rather, if you understand to question me then show me to be wrong; if not then answer yourself.

Polus: I will indeed answer, just to see what it is that you mean.

Socr: Do you think, then, that the people want that: <23.~467c] what they do? – or rather, much more, that for the sake of which they do what they do? As, for example, those who take medicine on doctor's orders, do you think that they want this medicine and to be in pain? or, rather, to regain their health – for the sake of which they take the medicine.

Polus: Obviously, in order to regain their health.

Socr: So too with those who drive commerce on the high seas and others who venture forth on business concerns, is this what they want, what they are doing? For who really wants to be in danger floating upon the high seas in the midst of commerce? Rather the other, I think, for the sake of which they venture out, to become rich, for it is for riches' sake that they go out in the ships.

Polus: Quite.

Socr: Is it, then, not exactly so with everything? If someone does something for the sake of something other, so he doesn't want what he does but, rather, that for the sake of which he does it?

Polus: Yes.   [e]

Socr: Is there now, perhaps, something which would not be either good or bad, or yet in between these two, being neither good nor bad?

Polus: One of these quite necessarily, Socrates.

Socr: And now, don't you say that wisdom is good, and health and riches – and all the rest of this type; bad the opposite of these?

Polus: Quite.   [468a]

Socr: But neither good nor bad would seem to you such things which at some occasions belong with the good and at other times with the bad, and sometimes, too, with neither? – like sitting or walking, running or seafaring; and, then again, such things as *rocks and wood* and others of this sort. Would you mean these to be such? – or do you name something other as being neither good nor evil?

Polus: No, rather these.

Socr: Are, then, these middlings done for the sake of the good, when they are done, or the good for the sake of the middling.

Polus: Indeed, the middling for the sake of the good.   [b]

Socr: In the pursuit of the good, thus we go, if we go, in the opinion that it would be better; and, on the contrary, if we remain standing we do so namely for the same reason, the good. Or not?

Polus: Yes.

Socr: Thus, we kill also, if we kill someone, and drive away and rob livelihoods with the opinion that doing such is better for us, to do this rather than not doing so?

Polus: Indeed.

Socr: For the sake of the good one does all of this, he who does it.

Polus: I admit as much.   <24.~468c]

Socr: Have we not admitted so much that when we do something for the sake of something else it is not really that we want what we do, but the former, for the sake of which we do it?

Polus: Indisputably.

Socr: Thus, it's not that we want to execute a judgment or deport overseas or seize assets just simply in itself, rather only if such would be useful do we want to do so, but if it be harmful to us, then not. For we only want the good, as you assert, that which is neither good nor bad we do not want, nor what is bad. Isn't this true? Do you fancy that I am in the right, Polus, or not? – – Why don't you answer?

Polus: Right.   [d]

Socr: If we are as one and see eye to eye about this, so shall, if someone allows a judgment to be executed or drives someone from their country or robs someone of their livelihood in the opinion that it would be better for him himself, it is, however, in actuality worse for him, he who does this, indeed, he does what he fancies as good – isn't this true?

Polus: Yes.

Socr: But perhaps also what he wants – if then, it is really an evil for him? – – But, why aren't you answering?

Polus: All right, No, it seems to me that he doesn't do what he wants.
                                                                    [e]

Socr: Is it well possible, then, to say that such a person has power in this state if being powerful should be, as you conceded, something good?

Polus: It cannot be said.

Socr: Then, I was in the right when I said that someone could very well accomplish in the city whatever he might fancy but, nonetheless, he would not be powerful nor accomplish what he wants.

Polus: Then you, Socrates, would not wish that you might freely do what you fancy as being good in our city and that this would not be preferable to not being able to do so; and you are not envious if you should see someone who has killed whomever, just as it pleased him, or swiped someone's property, or thrown somebody into jail?

Socr: Do you mean justly or unjustly?

Polus: No matter how he has done it, is it not, in either case, enviable? [469a]

Socr: Speak better, Polus!

Polus: How so?

Socr: One should not well be envious, neither of those who are not to be envied nor of those who suffer, rather pity them.

Polus: But, how's this? – do you mean that this is the way that things stand with those about whom I am speaking?

Socr: How else?

Polus: He, then, who can execute a death sentence on whomever he pleases, such a one, if he kills justly, you fancy to be miserable and worthy of pity?

Socr: No, not that; but also not worthy of envy.

Polus: Did you not even claim that he would be miserable? [b]

Socr: Should he kill unjustly, o friend, and then he would be worthy of pity too; but he who kills justly also is not to be envied.

Polus: Much more, he who must die in an unrighteous manner is pitiable and in misery.

Socr: Less so than he who kills, Polus, and also less so than he who must rightly be put to death.

Polus: How's that, Socrates?

Socr: Because doing unrighteousness is the greatest of all evils.

Polus: So this is the greatest? Suffering unjustly wouldn't be greater?

Socr: In no way.

Polus: Would you want, then, to suffer unrighteousness rather than do injustice? [c]

Socr: Indeed, I would want neither of the two; but if one were to be necessary, to do or to suffer injustice, then I would prefer to suffer injustice rather than do injustice.

Polus: You wouldn't like to be a tyrant then?

Socr: No, if you understand this the same as I.

Polus: I understand this to be just as we said, that one wields power in the state to accomplish whatever one fancies as good: to kill, to expel and to do everything for one's own pleasure.   <25.~469d]

Socr: O most worthy, what I want to say to you now, receive this rightly. If I were to come up to you in the crowded marketplace with a dagger under my sleeve and I were to speak: "O Polus, now I have just attained a wondrous power and dominion, for just as it pleases me that any one of these men that you see here should die immediately: so he shall be dead, anyone, just as it pleases me. And if I should desire that someone's face would have to be punched, so immediately it would be done; and if someone's dress cut to shreds, so it would be cut. So much power do I have in this city." If you, then, should doubt it and I were to show you the dagger, then you would perhaps say to me: "Indeed, in this manner, Socrates, everyone may be powerful. By such means anybody's house could be burned down as it struck your fancy, and the Athenian navy and galleys and all of the ships that belong both to the city and privately. But this does not mean that you have power, to do in this manner whatever one may fancy as being good." Or, what do you opine?

Polus: No, not this way, indeed.

Socr: Are you, then, well able to tell me why you would upbraid such power?   [470a]

Polus: I can.

Socr: Why then? Speak.

Polus: Because, necessarily, whoever proceeds thus to work comes to grief.

Socr: And is suffering punishment not an evil?

Polus: Indeed.

Socr: Thus, you marvel, it has been shown to you yet once again that being powerful only then exists if when one does as he fancies this is simultaneously bound up together with it being to his advantage, *and* that it is good; and just this now, as it seems, is to be powerful; but if not and it is an evil, then such is impotence {*Unvermögen*}. And let us also put this into the balance. Do we not admit that from time to time it is better that we do even as we just put forward, kill people and expel and rob others' possessions, but also from time to time it isn't better?

Polus: Indeed.

Socr: This, then, as it seems, is admitted to not less by you than by me as well.

Polus: Yes.

Socr: But when, do you opine, when should it be better to do so? Speak, what is the characteristic that you firmly establish and set down?

Polus: You, o Socrates, do answer even this.

Socr: I then assert, o Polus, as it be your preference to hear this from me, that should one do so in accordance with what is right it would be better, if unrighteously then for the worse.   *<26.~470c]*

Polus: It's quite an uphill battle with you, Socrates, to lead you over; but shouldn't every child be able to convince you that you are wrong?

Socr: So I would know to give great thanks to the child and also to you, if you should lead me over and free me from my foolishness. Thus, don't let it be a great burden on yourself to actively display such beneficence for your friend, rather, disprove what I say.

Polus: Well then, Socrates, it is not at all necessary to disprove you through ancient history; rather the events that transpired just   *[d]* yesterday and the day before are sufficient to refute you and to demonstrate that many people who do injustice are very happy.

Socr: Just which events, then?

Polus: You do see this Archelaus, Perdiccas' son, who rules over Macedonia?

Socr: At least, I have heard of him.

Polus: What do you fancy, then, that he is happy or miserable?

Socr: I do not know, Polus, for I have never had any commerce with the man.   *[e]*

Polus: How's that? If you would have met him you would be able to ascertain this, but otherwise you are unable on your own to have the insight that he is happy?

Socr: By Zeus, not properly.

Polus: Then obviously, Socrates, you shan't even want to know that the Great King who rules over all of Persia is blessed.

Socr: And totally with right shall I say this. For I don't even know how things stand with his insight and righteousness.

Polus: How? – in this alone is happiness constituted?

Socr: At least this is what I say, Polus. For he who is upright and good, he, I assert, is blessed – be it man or woman; but he who is unrighteous and evil, he is miserable.

Polus: Then in your opinion Archelaus is unhappy!   *[471a]*

Socr: Unless he be upright, friend.

Polus: How could he be other than unrighteous for in no way whatsoever does he deserve the dominions over which he now lords in that he was born of a woman who belonged to Alcetas, Perdiccas' brother, she being just a maidservant. Rightfully, then, he now should be Alcetas' servant and, if he wanted to act justly, then he would wait upon Alcetas and would be, by your speech, blessed in service. Now, however, it is a marvel how unhappy he has become due to his utterly unrighteous deeds in that first he invited over even this person, his master and uncle, as if he wished to pass on the *[b]* authority which Perdiccas had stolen from him, and then he dined him and his son, Alexandros, that would be his own cousin who is also about his same age, and he made them drunk and then threw them both upon a wagon and had them carried off at night and let them be murdered so that no one even knows where it is that they were disposed. And after such unrighteous deeds he didn't even in the least bit notice that he himself had become the most unfortunate and most miserable person, and so little did he rue these atrocities, rather he wanted all the more to become unhappy – and this with his brother, the fully legitimate son of Perdiccas who was just a child *[c]* of seven whom he should have raised and to whom he rightfully would have given the dominion. But much rather than do the right he let the boy be thrown into a puddle and drown, and then he said to the child's mother, Cleopatra, that the boy had chased after a goose and, thus, had fallen in. As a consequence to all of this, as he certainly has acted the least righteously of anyone in all of Macedonia, he is now the most miserable of all the Macedonians and not the happiest; and perhaps there are many Athenians, *you at the head*, who would rather be any other Macedonian than be he, Archelaus.

Socr: Already at the beginning of our conversation, o Polus, *<27.~d]* I praised you as it seemed to me that you have made great progress in oratory, although this at the expense to the art of dialogue [dialectics]. Also now, is it not so, this is to be the speech with which any child shall be enabled to refute me and I am even now, as you opine, refuted by this speech in my contention that whosoever acts unrighteously could not possibly be happy. But – how so, good friend? Do I not admit to everything that you have said? *[471e]*

Polus: You don't want to, but you certainly must think just as I spoke.

Socr: You, blessed one, think to carry even me over through your speaking art just as they imagine to lay out proofs in the halls of justice. For likewise there one party believes to carry over the other if for the assertion that he is presenting he is able to bring forward many and esteemed witnesses, the other party, however, only has one or, perhaps, none at all. But such a proof has utterly no value when the truth is at issue. For indeed, quite often people fall victim *[472a]* to the false testimonies of the many who are esteemed as being right. So also now, in what you say practically everyone shall concur, be they Athenian or foreigner; and if you want to call up witnesses against me, that I am not right, so many will come forward for you if you want: Nicias, the son of Niceratus, along with all of his brothers from whom have come the three-legged stools that stand in a line in Dionysius; and also, if you want, Aristocrates, son of Scellias, who gave the beautiful incense burners that are in the Pythean temple; and, if you want – the entire house of Pericles or any other family you may want to choose of the Athenians. But I all alone will not consent to you. For you haven't proven anything at all to me, rather, just by the setting up of many false witnesses against me you attempt to throw me out of my good [holdings] and the truth. On the other hand, if I should not be able to convince you yourself, *as you are a one*, and make you my witness that you have to concur in that   *[c]* which I say, I will not allow myself to believe that I have presented anything worthy regarding our object. But I believe that you also wouldn't have it any other way, if not I alone deliver evidence for you and that you let all of these others go. There is the one type of proof that you and many others bring forward; but there is also another one that I hold to. Let's stand them up one against the other and pay close attention as to whether they differ from one another, and in what? Is not that regarding which we are now arguing not something small, rather, quite possibly that which to know is most beauteous, but not to know most unbeauteous. For, essentially, it all boils down to this, either one has or one lacks insight into who does and does not have happiness. Thus, right back to that about which we just spoke: you hold it to be possible that a man could be happy who acts unjustly and is unrighteous – if indeed you say this regarding Archelaus, that he should be unrighteous and also happy. Is it true, are we to think that this is your assumption?

Polus: Indeed.   *<28.~472d]*

Socr: But I will make it clear that this is impossible. Regarding this one matter, we are in contention. Good. Should the unrighteous perhaps be happy if he encounters justice and punishment?

Polus: In no way. For in that case he would indeed be the most miserable.

Socr: Rather, if the unrighteous does not encounter justice, then, as per your speech, he shall be happy.   *[e]*

Polus: That is my assertion.

Socr: But it is my opinion, Polus, that whosoever acts unjustly and is unrighteous will in all cases be miserable and, indeed, even more miserable if he does not meet up with justice and does not suffer punishment for his unrighteousness, but less miserable if he does encounter justice and suffers punishment – from the gods and from man.

Polus: Senseless, o Socrates, is your undertaking to assert this.
Socr: Nonetheless, I will make the attempt to bring you also, *[473a]* friend, to this point: that you shall assert the same with me. For I do believe that you shall do so. That about which we are at odds, that would be this. Look at it now yourself. I did say somewhere previously that doing unrighteousness would be worse than suffering unrighteousness?
Polus: Indeed.
Socr: But you, that suffering unrighteousness would be worse?
Polus: Yes.
Socr: And that those who act unrighteously, I asserted, would be unhappy, and in this I was refuted by you.
Polus: Yes, by Zeus.
Socr: At least as you believe, Polus. *[b]*
Polus: And totally right, I'd warrant.
Socr: And, then too, that those acting unrighteously would be happy if they did not suffer punishment.
Polus: Indeed.
Socr: But I assert that even these are the unhappiest, but those who suffer punishment less so. Do you want to disprove this as well.
Polus: This is yet more difficult to disprove than the former.
Socr: Not so, Polus, rather, impossible. For it is impossible that truth might ever be refuted. *[c]*
Polus: How do you mean? If an unrighteous man is captured, that perhaps counter to the laws he has attempted to grab power, and then he undergoes torture and his tongue is cut out and his eyes are burnt out and not just he himself undergoes such great and manifold tortures, rather also he sees his wife and children likewise being punished, and at last he shall be nailed to the cross, or tarred and lit ablaze – he should then be happier than if he had remained undiscovered and had become installed as the tyrant, living on and ruling over the state and accomplishing whatever works he wants, an enviable person and joyously praised by the citizens and all others? This, you opine, should be impossible to disprove? *<29.~473d]*
Socr: Now you're frightening me, brave Polus, and again are not disproving me; before you called up witnesses. But just the same help me a little to remember whether you said, if unrighteously striving after power.
Polus: So I said.
Socr: More happy shall neither of the two of them ever be, neither he who unrighteously takes possession and rules, nor he who suffers punishment. For of two miserable persons it is not possible that either be happy, but more miserable is he who rules and remains *[e]*

undiscovered. Now, what's this, Polus? You're laughing? Is this yet another way of establishing proof when someone says something – to laugh at it and not to refute it?

Polus: Do you then believe, Socrates, that you are not *already* refuted when you assert such things, things to which no one would ever possibly agree? Just ask anyone here!

Socr: O Polus, I am not a statesman. Indeed, in the year when it became my turn to sit in session my tribe had the responsibility of going about and collecting the votes and I made a laughingstock of myself – as I had no idea of how to go about it properly.   *[474a]* So please, do not press me to collect the votes of those here present; rather, if you have no better proof than this, as I have already said this once, so yield now to me that I do things in my way and make an effort to follow the proof as I believe that it must needs be. Namely, I understand to call just one witness for what I shall say, the same one that I always use whenever I speak, and all the others, I let them go, and only from this one is the voice-vote encouraged; but I don't even speak with the others. Do look to it, whether you also will stand up to this way of conversing and answer the questions. Namely, I believe that I and you and all of humanity consider doing an injustice to be worse than suffering an injustice, and not being punished worse than being punished.

Polus: But I believe this neither of myself, nor of any other person whatsoever. Would you, thus, prefer to suffer an injustice over doing one?

Socr: You also, affirmatively, and everyone else.

Polus: Not by a long shot; rather, neither I, nor you, nor anyone else.

Socr: Will you answer me?   *[c]*

Polus: Indeed. For I am right curious to know just what you are going to say now.

Socr: So tell me, then, that you may encounter it, just as if I were starting at the beginning: which of the two, Polus, seems to be worse – doing an injustice or suffering an injustice?

Polus: For me, suffering an injustice.

Socr: But how about this, which of the two would be uglier – to do an injustice or to suffer an injustice? Answer me.

Polus: To do an injustice.   *<30.~474]*

Socr: Hence, also worse, if uglier?

Polus: That, in no way.

Socr: I understand. You don't consider these things to be one and the same, the beautiful and the good; and the bad, the evil and the ugly.

Polus: No, indeed not.   *[d]*

Socr: But, how about this. Everything that is beautiful such as bodies, colors, shapes, harmonies, actions – do you call these beautiful without any relation upon something beauteous? As, for example, beautiful bodies, do you call them beautiful either in relation to their use, that to which each has purpose? – or else in relation to some pleasure, if when being looked upon the onlooker experiences delight. Do you know of anything beyond these that might pertain to the beauty of the body?

Polus: I know nothing. *[e]*

Socr: And do you not even thus call all the others – shapes and colors[142] – either because of some pleasure beautiful, or because of utility, or both of these?

Polus: Certainly.

Socr: And also the harmonies and everything that belongs to the musical arts, even so?

Polus: Yes.

Socr: And certainly too, what is beautiful in the laws and the proper way of doing things is not so without the relation that either it be useful or pleasant, or both of these?

Polus: At least, I'd fancy this so. *[475a]*

Socr: Even so also with the beauty of knowledge?

Polus: Indeed, and it is very beautiful how you clarify all of this now, Socrates, in that you clarify the beautiful in terms of what is pleasurable and good.

Socr: Hence, the ugly inversely through displeasure and evil?

Polus: Necessarily.

Socr: If then, of two beautiful things one should be more beautiful, then this is so either because it surpasses the other in one of the two former ways or in both of them and is more beautiful either in being pleasurable, or in utility, or in both?

Polus: Certainly. *[b]*

Socr: And if of two ugly things one of them should be yet uglier than the other, then this is so because it surpasses the other in displeasure, or in evil – and is, thus, uglier. Or doesn't this follow?

Polus: Yes.

Socr: Good; then what were we just saying about doing an injustice or suffering an injustice? Didn't you say that suffering an injustice would indeed be worse, but doing an injustice uglier?

Polus: I said it.

Socr: Thus, if doing an injustice is uglier than suffering an injustice: so either there is greater displeasure, it being uglier due to an excess

---

[142] Cf: *Theaetetus* – footnote #163 (p. 389).

of displeasure, or because of an excess of evil, or both of these. Doesn't this also necessarily follow?

Polus: How could it not? <31.~475c]

Socr: First, let us see, does doing an injustice surpass suffering an injustice in displeasure? – and do those who act unrighteously have more pain than those who suffer unrighteously?

Polus: In no way, Socrates, but indeed, the latter.

Socr: Thus, it wouldn't surpass in displeasure?

Polus: Well, no.

Socr: Thus, if not in displeasure, then also not in both?

Polus: No, as it was shown.

Socr: Then there only remains the other of the two.

Polus: Yes.

Socr: The evil.

Polus: So it seems.

Socr: But if it surpasses in evil, then doing an injustice would be more evil than suffering an injustice?

Polus: Well, obviously. [d]

Socr: But was it not admitted by the majority, and also by you previously, that doing an injustice is uglier than suffering an injustice?

Polus: Yes.

Socr: Now it has been shown as also being more evil.

Polus: So it appears.

Socr: Would you prefer to choose what is more evil as well as uglier, or that which is less? Don't hold back from answering, o Polus, for nothing bad will happen to you, rather, heartened by this speech open your mouth for the doctor and answer either affirmatively or negatively what I ask.

Polus: – I wouldn't choose it, then, Socrates. [e]

Socr: Perhaps someone else would?

Polus: No, I fancy not, not after this speech.

Socr: I was right, then, that neither I, nor you, nor any other person would prefer to do injustice rather than suffer unjustly, for it is more evil.

Polus: Thus it was shown.

Socr: Do you now see it, Polus, if you compare the one proof over against the other, how they are not in the least bit similar. For you had everyone else's voice-vote except for mine; and for me it is quite sufficient that you alone are now in agreement and are a witness and just pursuing your voice-vote, I let all the others go. So, accordingly, this correlates for us. Next, let us pull into view that regarding [a] which we were in the second place at odds: if someone commits an injustice and suffers punishment – is this the greatest of all evils as you opined, or would it be worse *not* to suffer as I for myself opined? Let us consider it thus. To suffer punishment and to be penalized according to the right for having committed unrighteousness, are these two one and the same?

Polus: Certainly.

Socr: Is it possible that you might say that not everything that is right is also beautiful insofar as it is right? Consider this carefully and then speak.

Polus: Indeed, I fancy it as being so, Socrates. <*32.~476b]*

Socr: Bethink yourself now also regarding this. If someone does something, must there not necessarily also be that which suffers from the doing?

Polus: I'd fancy so, yes.

Socr: And indeed, suffering the same as that which the doing does and in like manner as the doing does? I mean, namely: if someone hits – then, necessarily, something gets hit?

Polus: Necessarily.

Socr: And if that which hits, hits hard or quickly, shall not in the same manner that which gets hit be hit?

Polus: Yes. *[c]*

Socr: Such, then, is the suffering in what got hit as the hitting does to it?

Polus: Certainly.

Socr: Not also, if someone burns, shall not, necessarily, something become burnt?

Polus: How else.

Socr: And if he burns badly or painfully, must not, even thus, that which is burnt becomes burnt just as the burning burns?

Polus: Quite.

Socr: Not also, if someone cuts, the same is valid, namely, something becomes cut?

Polus: Yes.

Socr: And if the cut is large or deep or painful, in all cases shall that which is cut become cut even as the cutting cuts? *[d]*

Polus: Obviously.

Socr: Look closely, whether in general you agree to what I have just said, that in all things – as the doing does, so also the suffering suffers?

Polus: I agree with it.

Socr: Now that you have agreed, is being punished a suffering or a doing?

Polus: Necessarily, o Socrates, a suffering.

Socr: Thus, from an other one which does it?

Polus: How else? From he who punishes.

Socr: And he who punishes justly, punishes righteously?

Polus: Yes.   [e]

Socr: Doing it justly or not?

Polus: Justly.

Socr: Hence, he who was punished, who encountered justice, suffers rightfully?

Polus: Obviously.

Socr: But the just, we agree on this, is also beautiful?

Polus: Indeed.

Socr: Of these, then, the one does something beautiful, but the other, the penalized, suffers it?

Polus: Yes.   <33.~477a]

Socr: But, if beauteous, then good as well – for it is either pleasant or useful?

Polus: Necessarily.

Socr: He suffers the good, then, he who encounters justice?

Polus: So it seems.

Socr: Thus, he attains an advantage?

Polus: Yes.

Socr: Perhaps this advantage, the one of which I have a notion, namely: that his soul shall become better if he is rightfully penalized?

Polus: It seems so, in all probability.

Socr: Thus, from a malignancy of the soul, he who suffers punishment is unburdened?

Polus: Yes.   [b]

Socr: Shall he, perhaps, thus become unburdened of the greatest evil? Just do consider it. If one observes the condition of someone's earning-potential *{Vermögen}*, is there anything other besides poverty that would be bad?

Polus: No, rather poverty.

Socr: And if upon the constitution of the body, wouldn't you call weakness to be bad, and sickness and ugliness and the like?

Polus: Certainly.

Socr: And you do believe that also in the soul there may be malignancy *{Schlechtigkeit}*?

Polus: How should this not be possible?

Socr: Don't you mean with this unrighteousness, deficiencies in one's understanding, cowardice and the like?

Polus: Indeed.   [c]

Socr: Hence, for one's earning-potential, for the body and for the soul, as three separate [examples] you have provided three separate maleficences: poverty, sickness and unrighteousness?

Polus: Yes.

Socr: Which, now, from amongst these maleficences is the ugliest? Is it not unrighteousness and, above all, the malfeasance of the soul?

Polus: By far.

Socr: If then, the ugliest, then also the most evil?

Polus: How's that, Socrates?

Socr: So. In all cases the ugliest is the ugliest because it produces the greatest amount either of displeasure or harm, or both of these, as we previously agreed.

Polus: Totally right.

Socr: And as the ugliest haven't we now accepted with one voice unrighteousness and the whole maleficence of the soul?

Polus: So have we taken them on. [d]

Socr: Thus, it is the ugliest of these, either as the most painful by its excess in torment or by the harm it does or by both of these.

Polus: Necessarily.

Socr: Is now, perhaps, being unrighteous and unrestrained, or being cowardly and lacking understanding more painful than being poor or sick?

Polus: It doesn't seem so to me, not in this way.

Socr: Hence, it has to be through incomparably great harm and amazing evil that the malignancy of the soul surpasses all of the others, being the ugliest of them all – if then, indeed, not due to displeasure as you say. [e]

Polus: Obviously.

Socr: What distinguishes itself by the greatest harm that it causes, this would also, affirmatively, be the greatest evil of them all?

Polus: Yes.

Socr: Unrighteousness, dissipation, wantonness – and whatever else belongs to the malfeasance of the soul – such as these are the greatest amongst all evils?

Polus: So it was shown.

Socr: Which art, now, unburdens from poverty? Isn't it – "being employed"?

Polus: Yes.

Socr: But which from sickness? Isn't it the healing-lore?

Polus: Naturally. <34.~478a]

Socr: But which from malfeasance and unrighteousness? Might you not find it in this manner? – just observe. Whither and to whom do we lead the sick?

Polus: To the doctor, Socrates.

Socr: But whither those who act unjustly and are unrestrained?

Polus: To the judge, you would well mean?

Socr: Is it true, so that he directs them to punishment?

Polus: So I mean it.

Socr: But those who penalize in the right manner, don't they do so with a certain application of justice?

Polus: Obviously.   *[b]*

Socr: Thus, industry frees from poverty, the healing lore from sickness, and the application of justice by punishment – which is jurisprudence – from lack of restraint and unrighteousness?

Polus: So it was shown.

Socr: Which of these would well be the most beauteous?

Polus: Of which do you mean?

Socr: From industry, healing-lore and jurisprudence?

Polus: By far, o Socrates, jurisprudence has precedence.

Socr: Thus, it produces either the most pleasure or the greatest benefit or both, if it is the most beauteous?

Polus: Yes.

Socr: Is it, then, perhaps pleasant that one is administered to by a doctor and do they enjoy it who are so administered?

Polus: I would fancy no, not at all.

Socr: But it is beneficial, all the same. Isn't this true?

Polus: Yes.   *[c]*

Socr: For it frees one from a great evil and so it is well worth it, to put up with the pain and then become healthy.

Polus: How else.

Socr: Is it now so as regards the body, that one is happiest if he has been healed by a doctor, or if he has never even gotten sick?

Polus: Obviously, he who never was sick.

Socr: For that wasn't what happiness would be, as it seems, to become free of evil, rather never from the first to have had any commonality with it.

Polus: So it is.   *[d]*

Socr: And how? – which of the two having an evil suffers more, be it either on their body or soul? – he whom has been administered by the doctor and who has become unburdened of the evil, or he whom was not treated and who still has it?

Polus: It seems to me, he whom has not been treated.

Socr: Now, wasn't being punished being freed from the greatest evil, the badness of the soul?

Polus: That it was.

Socr: For the punishment makes one more mindful and more upright, and its administration is the healing lore for such maleficence.

Polus: Yes.

Socr: The happiest of all is he who has no malignancy in his soul – as this was shown as being the greatest evil.

Polus: Obviously. [e]

Socr: Second best, however, is he whom has been freed from it.

Polus: So it seems.

Socr: But that was he to whom one has given admonitions, and also reprimands and punishment.

Polus: Yes.

Socr: But worst of all is he who lives with unrighteousness and does not become free from it.

Polus: This is how it has turned out.

Socr: And now, isn't this he who by the greatest misdeeds and by exercising the greatest unrighteousness has brought things so far that he neither can be directed to what is right, nor restrained, nor [a] administered punishment, even as you were saying that Archelaus has attained this; and let's not forget *all* of the other tyrants, political orators and power-grabbers?

Polus: So it appears.

Socr: For these, most worthy, have taken things practically so far – just as if someone who was afflicted with the most dreaded disease would not even allow the doctor to treat his malignancies all covering his body, out of fear like a child and not wanting to be cut or burnt, as this does hurt. Or doesn't it also appear so to you?

Polus: Yes, definitely. <35.~479b]

Socr: Because, namely, he is not familiar, as it seems, with what the body really needs in order to be healthy and fit. Something similar now appears with those whom we described, o Polus, those who flee punishment. Namely, the painful side they well see, but as to the healing they are blind and do not know that compared to a sick body how much greater yet is the torment of a sick soul, one that is lazy, unrighteous and incurable. From this it results, as indeed they want in no way to suffer punishment and thus become freed of the greatest evil, that they do everything imaginable and are always concerned about having wealth, and about having friends amongst whom they may find belief for their speeches. If, now, this was right, what we have just previously taken up, Polus, do you well notice what the consequences of this speech are? – or shall we, rather, count them up together?

Polus: If you don't mind.

Socr: It follows, then, that unrighteousness and doing injustice are the greatest evil?

Polus: Obviously.

Socr: And unburdening from this evil was shown to be suffering punishment?

Polus: So it appears.   *[d]*

Socr: But not being punished would be remaining in evil?

Polus: Yes.

Socr: The second evil in terms of size is doing an injustice, but not being punished for unrighteousness is the first and the greatest of all evils.

Polus: So it appears.

Socr: Now, didn't we even argue about this, friend, in that you praised Archelaus as happy, he who did the most grievous injustices and nonetheless had not suffered the least bit of punishment; but, to the contrary, I was of the opinion that, be it Archelaus or whoever else it may be whom is not punished for unrighteousness, that these should be held with the greatest precedence before all of mankind as being miserable, and always those who do injustice as more miserable than those who suffer unjustly, and the unpunished more than the punished. Wasn't this what I asserted?

Polus: Yes.

Socr: And has it not been proven that this was asserted rightfully?

Polus: So it appears.   *<36.~480a]*

Socr: Good. If now, this is true, o Polus, wherein then lies the great usefulness of speechcraft? For in accordance to that to which we have now agreed and which we have taken up, every person should above all take care that he does nothing unrighteous in that, even so, he still will have more than enough evil on himself. Isn't it true?

Polus: Indeed.

Socr: But should either he himself do an injustice or anyone else of those about whom he cares: so he has to take himself freely thither where he might as quickly as is possible receive punishment, racing to the judge just as one rushes off to the doctor so that the disease of unrighteousness never gains a foothold within the soul, devouring the soul itself and, by its assaults, making it incurable. Or what should we say, Polus – if, then, our first contentions shall stand? – is it not certain that just this alone is in one accord with them, but everything else not in accord?

Polus: Indeed, what can we say, Socrates!

Socr: To bring forth defenses for our own unrighteousness or for that of our parents, friends and children, or also in defense of a fatherland acting unrighteously, for these purposes speechcraft is not useful,

o Polus; unless one would be thinking, to the contrary – namely   [c]
to appeal for justice primarily for oneself, but, then too, for one's
relatives and for whomever else of one's friends who may have done
injustice; and not that the injustice be covered up or hidden, rather
to bring it out into the light so that the miscreant suffers punishment
and becomes healthy, and oratory should be used to persuade oneself
and others that one shall not be a coward, rather with eyes shut tight
courageously to place oneself as before the doctor for the cutting and
burning, always hunting after the good and the beauteous and not
concerning oneself about the pain, if one commits unrighteousness
that warrants that one be struck, giving oneself over to the blows, if
prison, then to be locked up, if to monetary fines, then to the bursar,
if to exile, then to flight, but he who merits death, to die; each as the
first to prosecute against himself and against the others to whom he is
close and even for this purpose making use of speechcraft and, by
making the misdeeds known becoming unburdened of the greatest
evil, from unrighteousness. Shall we say this, Polus, or not?

Polus: Indeed senseless, o Socrates, at least so this seems to me;
though with the previous it does, perhaps, fit nicely together.   [e]

Socr: Hence, either the former would have to be given up or this
follows necessarily.

Polus: Yes, this is how it correlates, quite.

Socr: And now, if we also take it up from the opposite vantage: if
somebody should do evil to someone else, be it either to an enemy or
to whomsoever else, just so long as you yourself are not harmed – for
naturally one needs to take care for oneself – but if this miscreant
harms someone else then one would be in all ways active, and also in
speech, trying to accomplish that he not be brought to punishment,
nor led before the magistrate; and if nonetheless he should be so
delivered then turn things around in every way imaginable so that the
miscreant be let off and, indeed, not suffer any punishment; rather, if
a lot of money had been stolen, not to have to return it, rather hold on
to it and use it for oneself and one's friends in unrighteous and
ungodly ways; if, perhaps, his transgressions are worthy of capital
punishment, that he rather not die, if possible never, rather live on an
immortal and as an evildoer, at least so long as it is possible as such.
For this, it seems to me, o Polus, speechcraft may well be useful. But
for him who has utterly no desire to do injustice, I don't fancy it to be
of much use – if, then, it has any utility at all – as, then, in the
previous no one at all demonstrated such.

<37.~481b]

Calli: Tell me, Chaerephon, does Socrates mean this seriously or is he merely jesting?

Chaer: It seems to me, o Callicles, that it is for him exceedingly serious. Still, there is nothing so good as asking him yourself.

Calli: By the gods, that I shall do, too. Tell me, Socrates, should we think that you are having a joke on us or are you serious? For then, if you really are serious and mean this to be true as you said it, so then human life here for us would be turned wholly inside out and, it seems, we would be doing exactly the opposite in all things as we should be doing?

Socr: O Callicles, if human beings, some one way others in another, do not meet up with the same, or rather – before everything else with one something wholly and uniquely personal:[143] so it would not be a light undertaking to sketch out for someone else their predicament. But I say this as I have noticed that both of us, you and I, find   *[d]* ourselves now in a similar situation. Namely, we both are in love, and each of us with two: I with Alcibiades, son of Cleinias, and with philosophy; you with the Athenian people and with the son of Pyrilampes.[144] I have noticed this about you at every juncture, so powerful that you otherwise may be, that whatever your beloved asserts and how he asserts that something correlates, you never are able to contradict him, rather you turn yourself round and round in circles, soon one way, soon another. For if in the assembly you have said something and the Athenian people disagree with you, that it correlates thus or so, so you turn yourself about and speak as they want; and with the son of Pyrilampes, that beautiful youth, it goes even the same with you, namely you are unable to contradict your beloved's decisions and arguments. And if someone wanted to express his wonder at how by each turn you say whatever it be for the sake of your beloveds, saying *really* – how nonsensical all of this is, you might perhaps reply, if you should want to speak the truth, that if someone couldn't put a stop to your beloveds from saying   *[482a]* such things then you also wouldn't be stopped from saying the same. Thus, think about this yourself, as now you have had to hear the same from me and be not in wonder that I tell you this, rather make it that my beloved, *philosophia*, be stopped in saying this. For it is always even *her* contention, dear friend, which you now are hearing and *she*

---

[143] "O Kallikles, wenn nicht dem Menschen, Einigen so, Andern so, dasselbige begegnete, sondern einem etwas ganz eigentümliches vor allen andern: so wäre es nicht leicht, einem Andern seinen Zustand zu bezeichnen."

[144] After the death of Plato's father, Ariston, his mother, Perictione, married Pyrilampes. Pyrilampes had an earlier son, Demos, of whom the conversation here pertains, as well as Plato's half-brother, Ariston.

requires by far less creativity on my part than do all of the other formerly mentioned lovers. For, indeed, this son of Cleinias takes his speeches soon in one direction, then another; but philosophy is always namely as stated. And even she says this about which you now wonder; and you yourself were also present as it was said. Thus, either refute what I have just asserted, that doing unrighteousness without being punished would be the most horrid of all evils; or, if you let this remain standing, *by the dog* – the god of the Egyptians – so with himself shall Callicles never be one voice, o Callicles, rather your intonations shall ring disharmoniously throughout your entire life. And at least I, most worthy friend, am of the opinion that it would be better were my lyre to be out of tune and not in harmony, or a choir that I might have to direct, and that it is preferable to be in disagreement with the majority of mankind who may want to contradict me rather than to be alone with myself in discord and to have to contradict myself.   *<38.~482c]*

Calli: O Socrates, you seem to want to blind us with your speeches like a proper jester mouthing off before the populace, and now you'll make fools of us all with this blather[145]   as the very same thing has happened to Polus as before to Gorgias and about which Polus objected. Namely he said, as you asked Gorgias as to whether someone in coming to him to learn speechcraft who also didn't already understand what the just would be, whether such a one wouldn't also have to be taught this, and so Gorgias was shamed   *[d]* into admitting it, that this too would have to be taught, simply due to mankind's prejudices and that people would become unwilling if this were to be denied, and so by this admission he was forced into the necessity of contradicting himself – and it's even in this that you had your joy. And regarding this, I fancy that he was entirely in the right in that he ridiculed you; but now he himself has in turn met up with just the same. And now I am even once again dissatisfied with Polus, that he allowed you your assertion that doing an injustice would be uglier than suffering an injustice. For precisely by this admission he became entangled in the web of speeches and was brought to silence in that he was ashamed to say what he thought. For in all actuality, Socrates, despite your claim to be searching after truth, you always direct the speech upon such sticky things that are good to bring before the masses, namely upon that which is not beauteous by nature but is well enough by law. For these two are for the most part at odds with one another, nature and law. If, now, someone is shamed

---

[145] "Geschwätz" – *Phaedrus* 260d, 270a; *Lysis* 221d; *Parmenides* 135d; *Theaetetus* 195c; *Sophist* 225d, et cetera.

and lacks the courage to say what he thinks, thus he becomes *[483a]* forced into contradicting himself. This is what you even have right artfully noticed and that with which you jump ahead of others in speech – if someone speaks of what is legal, you undercut them with the question of what is natural, but if of the natural, then with the legal. Thus, right away with doing and suffering injustice, when Polus spoke of what is uglier in a legal sense you followed up the legalities *as if* they were to be so according to nature. For in accordance with nature that is always uglier which is more evil, thus the suffering of injustice, but by law it would be doing injustice. And *really,* this is no predicament *for a man,* that he suffer, rather that of a petty servant for whom it would be better to die than to live as, should he be harmed or cursed, so he is unable to help himself or to give help to anyone else he values. I myself think that those who make the laws, these are the weak and the great throng. In relationship to them-selves and based upon that which is most useful to themselves do they determine the laws and the praiseworthy, what is to be praised, the censurable, what is to be censured; and in order that the more powerful people who would be able to have more be held by fear in check, that these might not prefer to take more than they themselves, and so they say it would be uglier and unrighteous to go out always seeking more and that this is doing injustice if one seeks always to have more than the others. For they themselves, I opine, are quite satisfied if they can hold on to an equal portion, as they are the worse. For this reason this becomes named legally unjust and *<39.~483c]* as ugly, this striving for having *more* than the majority, and they name this doing unrighteousness. Nature herself, however, I think, proves to the contrary that it is right that the more noble should have more than those who are worse, and that the more able should have more than the less able. She demonstrates, moreover, in many ways that this is the proper correlation, as well as is the case by the other animals and also with whole states – and even with the discrepancies between families amongst humanity: that justice is so determined that the better rules the worse and has more. For by what right did Xerxes conduct war against Hellas or his father against the Scythians? – and thousands of other examples of this sort could be displayed. Thus, I opine, they do this in conformity to nature and, by Zeus, also in accordance with law, namely the law of nature; though, indeed, not in accordance with the laws that we make arbitrarily for ourselves and by which the best and most powerful amongst ourselves, from child-hood onward – just as is done in breeding lions, through exhortations to equality and through enchantment – and so too we are forced into servile behavior in that we always have them recite such utter nonsense like this one, that *"all men are created equal"* and that even this would be beauty and righteousness. But if, I think, someone who stands out in his natural abilities becomes a man, so he shakes all of this off, tears himself apart, breaks through and tramples over all of our prescripts, juvenile pretensions and unwritten agreements – all laws contrary to nature; and standing up, obviously as our master, he who was a servant, and in all of this nature's right shines through with abundant clarity. It seems to me that also Pindar implies the same in his ode in which he says: *"The laws of the mortal kings and of the immortal,"* and also, *"carried by nature to us justifying the mightiest by their supremely powerful hand. I display it in the deeds of Heracles, who is not bought"* – approximately so is how it goes, for I do not myself know the ode; but he means that neither bought nor as a gift does Heracles drive away the cattle of Geryanes, that indeed cattle and all other possessions are duly accrued to those who are better and deserve more from those who are worse or less able. This, then, is actually the truth and you will have insight into this when at long last you let go of philosophy and move on to bigger concerns. For philosophy, o Socrates, is quite a splendid matter   *<40.~484c]* when someone pursues it in their youth and in a reasonable manner, but if one remains there longer than is requisite then it overripens and leads such men into spoilage. For no matter how majestically gifted one may be, if one philosophizes beyond all reasonable limits of time, then, necessarily, one must remain inexperienced in all of those concerns in which, most of all, experience matters if one ever wants to become a well-respected and an outstanding person of consequence. For not only do these philosophical types remain inexperienced in the laws of the state and in the proper manner in which people must comport themselves in all types of proceedings, be they of a public or of a personal nature, but also they are likewise inexperienced with all the gratifications and inclinations of one's fellow human beings – and even in man's social and civic comforts! – with all of this they remain unacquainted and are at a total loss. If hereafter they attempt   *[e]* to accomplish some business, be it now for themselves or for the community, so they make fools of themselves – just as, I believe, the statesmen also make fools of themselves if they attend your philosophical symposiums. For in this Euripides' maxim admirably applies: *"For in these each shines brightly pursuing as well admirably onward and happily sacrificing ample time to such occupations wherein one excels easily"*; but in that in which one is bad, this one avoids and denigrates, the other, on the contrary, is praised due to one's own good opinion of oneself – as it is believed that in this way one also may praise oneself. But the most rightful stance, I think, is to allow oneself experience of both. And namely with philosophy, insofar as it serves the liberal education, in *this* the pursuit is truly beauteous and in no way would this accrue against a youth's nobility that he philosophized. But if a fully-grown   *[485b]* man should yet concern himself with philosophy! – Socrates, this becomes a comical matter indeed, and for me philosophy is just like stammering and children's playtime.   Namely, when I see young children who are still of the appropriate age lisping and stammering or playing goofy, so this bemuses me and makes me happy, I find it lovely and a natural occurrence befitting to one's childhood. On the other hand, should I hear a young child enunciating quite clearly and speaking properly, this appears as wrong to me, it pains my ears and seems to me to be something forced. And, still again, if I hear a fully-grown man making goo goo talk and acting like a child, that is obviously ludicrous and unmanly and deserves a good beating. Even in this way is philosophy to be judged. If I meet up with boys or adolescents who go in big for philosophizing I have joy, I find that such pursuits will stand them well and I truly do believe that there is something noble in such interests; but he who does not read any philosophy, I hold him to be ignoble and I believe that never shall he himself aim at something great and beauteous. If, to the contrary, I see an older man still philosophizing and unable to pull himself away, such a man, o Socrates, it seems to me, needs a good beating. For, as I even just said, it always will be discovered with such a person – and no matter how beauteous his natural gifts may be – that he has become unmanly, he flees the interiors of the cities and the official functions where, as the poet has spoken, real men show themselves, and he hides himself withdrawn into some corner with three or four adolescent boys for companions and whispers away the remainder of his life without ever speaking out in a noble, great or capable manner. I for my part, Socrates, do esteem and wish you only good, and now betwixt us it may be about the same as with Zethos and Amphion of Euripides, whom already once I quoted.   For I find it a pleasure that I, like the former to his brother, now speak to you as one brother to another: that you, o Socrates, are neglecting what you should be accomplishing and that your inner qualities which are   *<41.~486a]* naturally so masterful are being totally perverted by such juvenile behavior, that you neither know rightly *how* to speak where justice is at issue, nor seemingly *of what* so that it may be presented in a believable fashion, nor also – when it comes to giving advice to others – do you have the courage to finalize whatever decisions are requisite, rather you *never stop* questioning yourself and anyone else whom you might pull into your muddle! And yet, dear Socrates, but don't become angry with me as I say this in your best interests: doesn't it seem regrettable to be in such a predicament as the one in which you find yourself, a predicament which, I believe, applies to all of those who take philosophy far too far? For if somebody now seized you or any other such as yourself and dragged you to the lockup, claiming that you had broken some law or other, though, verily, you hadn't broken any laws, so you know all too well that you wouldn't have a clue as to where to begin with yourself, rather your head would start to spin and you'd stand there with an open mouth not knowing what you should say. And if, then, you came before the court and, though you also would have just an ordinary, petty person denouncing you: so you should have to die if he should just happen upon the idea of asking for capital punishment. And really, Socrates, how could that be seen as wisdom if a profession "*taketh possession of a most able man, tho' maketh him worse,*" so that neither is he able to help himself and be saved from the greatest danger, nor anyone else, and he is easily robbed of all his possessions by his enemies and obviously is fated to live without honor in his own country? Such a one, to say it crassly, one can punch in the face without punishment. Therefore, good man, do hearken and "*cease in your teachings, practice rather the good sounds of beauteous deeds,*" and that through which you appear wise, "*leave to others now these masterly pursuits,*" should I call it clown-play or blather, "*wherefore your home stands poor, empty and abandoned*" and be not in such a rush to follow those investigating into such trivialities, rather follow those who acquire wealth, fame and much else that is good.   *<42.~486d]*

Socr: If I, perhaps, should have a golden soul, Callicles, do you not believe that most gladly would I happen across one of the best of those sorts of stone upon which they test gold, against which, then, I might hold up my soul – and if that stone could be my witness that my soul would be in good standing, so then I would most certainly know that I might be satisfied and would need no further testing?

Calli: But, just why are you asking me this, Socrates?   *[e]*

Socr: I will tell you right away. I believe, namely, now that I have found you, to have found such a treasure.

Calli: How's that?

Socr: I know with certainty that those opinions of mine to which you agree, these, then, shall certainly be the truth itself. Namely, I think to myself: he who should set up a complete examination of a soul, whether it lives rightly or not, must have three things – all of which you have: insight, good intentions and the courage to give freely. For I do indeed meet up with lots of people who are not in a position to examine me because they are not as wise as you are. Others are indeed wise, but don't desire to tell me the truth – as they don't take to me like you have. And, then again, these two foreigners,   *[487b]* Gorgias and Polus, are really quite wise and have the best intentions toward me, but, perhaps, lack a little in the courage to speak freely, rather they become ashamed all too easily. Or how else could it be that they have been driven so far in their modesty that both of them through their shame have been brought to this juncture that they contradicted themselves in their speeches, and did so before all these people present here, and regarding the most important things. But you have all of this that the others do not have. For you have been sufficiently instructed – as certainly the majority of the Athenians would admit – and with me you have the best intentions. How do I deduce this? I shall tell you. I know, Callicles, that four of you have established under yourselves a fellowship of wisdom, you and Tisander from Aphidna, and Andron, son of Androtion, and Nausicydes of Cholarges. And once I listened in on you as you took counsel regarding to what extent one should give oneself up to the pursuit of knowledge, and I know that the opinion gained the ascendancy amongst you – one should never let philosophy drive one to excess, rather far better is it, you admonished yourselves, to be on the lookout that you don't become more wise than is appropriate, as thereby you could easily end up in catastrophe without even seeing it come upon you. As, now, I just have heard that you give me the selfsame advice as these, your most trusted friends: so this is a sufficient proof that truthfully you mean well by me. But that you understand how to speak out freely and without shaming yourself, you did even say so yourself, and, besides, what you have said also proves this. For these reasons it now correlates obviously thus: if you become as one with me in agreement in our discourse then it shall be deemed sufficiently scrutinized through you and me and it shall never be necessary to scrutinize this any further. For, indeed, otherwise you never would have acquiesced, neither due to deficiency in wisdom, nor due to excess of shame, nor also in an attempt to lie to me would you ever acquiesce. For you are my friend, as you yourself have said so. Certainly, thus, that regarding which we agree as one shall have the highest mark of righteousness. But certainly too, o Callicles, there are no investigations that are yet more beauteous than   *[488a]* these about which you have just delivered your critique of me: how namely a man of consequence needs must be and whither he should strive and how far, as well in his youth as also in his maturity. For if anywhere in my life I should act improperly, so be assured that not purposely have I failed, rather due to my lack in understanding. As, then, you have already made the beginning to put me to rights, do not let up, rather display it for me completely: what this is for which I should strive and in which manner I shall be able to attain it. And if you should find that, indeed, now I have agreed with you about something but that I don't stick to my agreement both in word and deed: so consider me then just a helpless case and don't ever waste your time encouraging me any further – in short, that I am one who is utterly worthless. But, please repeat that again from the beginning onward, how you and Pindar along with you believe that things correlate with those who are righteous in accordance with nature? That he who is more worthy may take away with his might what belongs to the less worthy, and that the better should rule the worse, and the noble should have a good deal more than the commoners? – Is righteousness other than this in accordance to your speech? – or have I messed it up?   *<43.~488c]*

Calli: Even this is what I said then, and I say it also now.

Socr: Do you mean the same when you say *one is better* as when you say *one is worthier*? For when you first said it, I also didn't rightly understand how you meant this. Do you call these more worthy who are stronger and should the weaker hearken to those who are stronger, as I fancied it to be meant when you pointed out that the greater states attacked the lesser in accordance with nature's right because they are, namely, worthier and stronger – by which, then, worthier, stronger and better would be one and the same? Or is it possible that one may be better, but also smaller and weaker? – and worthier though worse? Or should being better and being worthier bespeak the same? Just this, please figure out for me right exactly whether all of this is different or one and the same: being worthier, better and stronger.

Calli: So I tell you quite precisely, it is one and the same.

Socr: Are not the many stronger than the individual by nature in that, most assuredly, they make the laws for the individuals, as you yourself said?

Calli: How else?

Socr: What, then, is legal for the many is likewise so for the stronger?

Calli: Indeed.   *[488e]*

Socr: Thus, for the better as well? – for in accordance to your speech the stronger are by far the better.

Calli: Yes.

Socr: Thus, what is *by law* is beauteous according to nature – as these are even the better?

Calli: I admit it.

Socr: And do not the many establish firmly just this, as you yourself stated earlier: that it is *just* that we have equal [portions] and doing injustice would be uglier than suffering injustice? Is this so or not? And don't let me spring this on you out of the blue that you should become ashamed. Don't the many establish this firmly, or not, that having equality and not more is righteous? But don't keep your answer to yourself, Callicles, so that if you should be in agreement with me I might become firmly assured through you, as now a man who is well positioned to judge such things has stood me by with his voice-vote.

Calli: Yes, the many have firmly established this.

Socr: Hence, not only in accordance to the laws is doing injustice uglier than suffering injustice and having equal [portions] just but, rather, also in accordance to nature. So that you may not have   *[b]* spoken truthfully earlier, nor rightfully accused me when you said that nature and law would be at odds with each other, which you said is something that I already would well know and with which I jumped ahead of others in my speeches in that, if someone meant something by nature I would lead them off to the legalities, but if according to the laws then off upon nature.   <44.~489c]

Calli: This man will never let up, spouting off with such pretentious poppycock. Tell me, Socrates, are you not ashamed to be, and at your age, making the hunt with words, and if someone should fail *by just one word* to proudly hold this up as a great find? Do you then believe that I mean something other with being-better than being-worthier? Have I not always said to you that I establish this as one and the same, worthier and better? Or do you believe that I mean, if a throng of servants gathers together or all types of other people who are distinguished by nothing at all except that, perhaps, that they have physical strength – and these, then, should make claims – *that even such should be law?*

Socr: Good! – most wise Callicles! You mean it so?

Calli: Indeed, so.   *[d]*

Socr: I too had a premonition myself already for awhile that you meant something like this with "being-worthier," and I even questioned you further because I wanted very much to know right exactly how you meant this. For you wouldn't always maintain that two are better than one, nor that your servants are better than you because they are stronger than you. Thus, tell me again, starting at the beginning, what then you really understand by the better, if it's not to be the stronger. And, you marvel, do teach me with soft constraint so that I don't have to hide myself from your courageousness.

Calli: You're joking again, Socrates.   *[e]*

Socr: No, by Zethos, by whose agency you were poking fun at me just a little while ago. But, do come a bit closer and tell me: who are these that are "the better"?

Calli: The more noble is what I mean.

Socr: Do you see it now? – that you yourself are only bringing forth words and not clarification? Don't you want to say to me whether, perhaps, you mean that those with greater insight are better and worthier, or should it be some others? *[490a]*

Calli: Well, yes – I mean just these, by Zeus, in all actuality.

Socr: Thus, very often is one with insight better than ten-thousand who are lacking insight – in accordance with your speech, and the former shall rule, the latter shall be ruled, and the ruler has more than those who are ruled over. For this, I fancy, is what you want to say and it is not I that hunt after words if, then, the one is better than ten-thousand.

Calli: Even this is it as well – what I mean. For this, I think, is nature's justice: that he who is better and has great insight rules and has more than those who are worse. *<45.~490b]*

Socr: Stop right there. Just what is this that you're saying now? If, as it is here, right now, very many of us would be gathered together and we were to have all sorts of food and drink to share in common, but we were of all types amongst ourselves, strong men and weaklings, and one of us would be the most insightful person here because he was a doctor, and would himself be stronger than some, weaker than others – isn't it true, so he would be, as he has greater insight than we do, also better and stronger in this?

Calli: Indeed. *[c]*

Socr: Would he, perhaps, have to be served more food because he is better? – or would it be necessary, as he is the ruler, that he divide everything and, as to the amount that he himself should enjoy and require for his own body, wouldn't he strive not for the most, as he wouldn't want to overstuff himself and suffer harm, rather he would have more than some and less than others; and if, perchance, he were to be the weakest then precisely the least of all, Callicles, despite that he would be the best. Isn't it so, my good man?

Calli: You speak about food and drink and doctors and clowns! But I don't mean anything at all like this. *[d]*

Socr: Didn't you say that he who has the greatest insight would be better? Tell me, yea or nay.

Calli: Yes, I said it.

Socr: But not that he who is better would have to have more?

Calli: Not food and drink!

Socr: I understand. But, perhaps clothes, and he who best under-stands how to weave would also have to have the largest outfit and would be dressed wearing the most, and most beauteously parade about?

Calli: Now what! Clothes?   *[e]*

Socr: But obviously, it has to be so with shoes, and he who is most insightful and the best in this would also have more – and the shoemaker gets the biggest and the most shoes for walking about?

Calli: What a chatterbox you are, Socrates, and now chattering on about shoes!

Socr: Thus, if you don't mean anything of the sort, then perhaps it's this, like a farmer who has great insight regarding agriculture and is quite respected – he would have to have more seeds and as many sorts as possible to use on his farm?

Calli: How you are always bringing up the same, Socrates!   *[491a]*

Socr: And not only that, o Callicles, rather too, note it well, regarding the same matter.

Calli: By the gods, won't you ever let up – always mouthing off about shoes and peas, cooks and doctors! – as if our conversation were to be concerned with such stuff.

Socr: Would you like to say, then, in what the more insightful and better should have *more*, that he have it justly. Or do you want neither to suffer my suggestions nor to say it yourself?

Calli: But I have already said it long ago; firstly who the better ones are, and I don't mean shoemakers nor cooks, rather those who are insightful into the affairs and proceedings of the state and who know how these could best be administered, and not only having insight, rather courageous as well – so that they are in the position to carry out what they have thought up and don't tire of the effort due to any squeamishness in their constitutions.   *<46.~491c]*

Socr: Do you see, most worthy Callicles, how it's not at all the same thing – that of which you accuse me and, inversely, that of which I accuse you? For you make the assertion against me that I always say the same and upbraid me accordingly. But I bring the charge against you, to the contrary, that you never say the same thing regarding the same matter; rather, at first you clarify that the better and worthier were to be the stronger, then again it is these who have the greatest insight, but now you're bringing up something different again in that it shall be certain courageous individuals who you give out as being worthier. But, my good man, do say it once and in all finality, who then should be "the better" and in what?   *[d]*

Calli: But I did already say it, those who have insight into the matters of state and also courage. For it falls upon these to rule the states and even in this is righteousness, that these have more than the others, the rulers than the ruled.

Socr: Also more than they themselves, friend?

Calli: How do you mean this?

Socr: I mean that, indeed, each individual does himself rule over himself. Or is that not at all necessary, to rule oneself – but, rather, just the others?

Calli: How do you mean, he rules himself?

Socr: Nothing at all especially difficult to understand, rather, as the people mean it: to be mindful and have power over oneself, holding in check your desires and appetites – which we all have – and ruling.

Calli: What a good Quaker you are. These simpletons you mean, the mindful ones! *[491e]*

Socr: But, why not? How? – isn't everyone in a position to know that this is not what I mean?

Calli: Yes it is, indeed, Socrates, certainly. For how could it well be that someone is happy and blessed who also would be in the service of somebody else? Rather, just this is beauteous and right by nature which now I shall freely speak out – that he who wants to live right well should let his desires grow to be as great as possible and not hem them in by force; and these, no matter how great they'd be, he should nonetheless be able by his courageousness and insight to satisfy most amply, thus gaining fulfillment for himself wherever his desires may lead. By myself, I opine that the great majority are incapable of this and it is for this reason that they upbraid such men out of their shame, burying their own inadequacies and saying that living life to the full would be disgraceful because, as I already mentioned, *[b]* this way they compel those who have stronger natures to do likewise. And as they are incapable of bringing about the satisfaction of their own desires, so they mimic the praise of mindfulness and of righteousness, and they do this due to their own inadequacies to be real men. But for those who either already are themselves true offspring of kings or who by the power of their own natures were able to establish their own dominions or kingdoms and dynasties, what could be uglier and worse than mindfulness for such men – now that they are well able to enjoy the good fruits and nobody stands in their way – if, then, they were to set up some lord, namely that of the laws of the rabble, their blather and their sense of justice. Or how should they be other than miserable through the beauty of righteousness and mindfulness if, then, they cannot reach out more to their friends than to their enemies, and this despite that they are the lords in their own states! Rather, in accord with truth, o Socrates, which verily you claim to be seeking, it correlates so: royalty, free license and generosity – if only there be reserves – these are the real virtues and blessed, but all the rest are mere ceremonies, unnatural propositions and empty, idle chatterings of the rabble, and all worth nothing.

<47.~492d]

Socr: Not in the least with a coward's heart, o Callicles, do you come out fighting, as a great hero – *and free.* For quite openly you have put on the table what the others indeed think, but they don't want to come out and say it. I beg you, therefore, don't by any means let up, that it shall become apparent how one has to live. And so tell me: the appetites, you say, one shouldn't moderate them forcefully if one is to be as one should be, rather let them grow to be as large as possible and prepare to satisfy them, no matter how – and *this is virtue*?

Calli: That is my assertion.   [e]

Socr: Unrightfully, then, it is said: those without needs would be blessed.

Calli: In this manner stones would be most blessed, and the dead.

Socr: But, still and yet, as you've described it, life is a struggle. I myself, at least, wouldn't be amazed if Euripides might have   [493a] been right where he says: "*Who knows whether our life itself is only death, and being dead first life?*" And perhaps we are in actuality dead. Which is something that I also have heard tell from one of the wise, that now we would be dead and that our bodies would only be graves but that that portion of the soul in which our desires exist would be a constant attracting and repelling, upward and downward, which a stately person, a poet of pictures – one probably of Syracuse or from Italy, playing with the words due to the filling up and the wanting to bind or grasp – he named it a barrel, and those who were unrestrained were excluded, and these excluded ones were so due to that portion of their souls where desires run rampant, even because of this lack of restraint and continuous grasping, that they couldn't gain closure and, like a leaking barrel on which this comparison turns, their insatiable appetites excluded them. And quite completely the opposite to your perspective, o Callicles, this artist displayed that in the realm of the shadows, by which he meant the spirit worlds, these just mentioned excluded ones would be the least blessed, and they would have to transport water to these leaking barrels and for   [c] this, likewise, they only had leaky colanders. But by the colander he understood, as he himself explained it to me, the soul, for the soul of the unrestrained type he compared to a colander, as they would be leaky and couldn't hold fast due to their lack of certainty and forgetfulness. This, now, is to a certain extent amazing; but all the same it makes it quite clear that I would like, if only somehow I could show you, to talk you out of your path and turn you about and instead of an insatiable, unrestrained and free-wheeling life that you choose mindfulness and satisfaction with that which always is close at hand. But, how now? – have I persuaded you and will you alter your assertion so that the moral are happier than the unrestrained, or have I accomplished nothing and no matter how many such poetic pictures I might paint, you still will not alter you opinion?

Calli: The latter is closer to the truth, Socrates.   <48.~493de]

Socr: Well then, let me clarify this with yet another image derived from the very same school as the former. Pay heed – whether you find the comparison of these two modes of living, the mindful and the unrestrained, to be right. Here it's as if two people were to each have many barrels. Those of the one would be rotund and filled to the brim, one with wine, one with honey, one with milk, and many more with many other things; but the wellsprings of all of these goods would be meager and difficult as only with great effort and work would they produce something. The former one would have full barrels and would have directed that nothing more need flow in, indeed, he didn't even consider to think any more about it, rather on this issue he was entirely at peace. But the other would have even the same sources that, indeed, do yield something, but only with much struggle; but his barrels were leaky and rotten and he had to work day and night filling or else put up with hideous suffering. Now, do you want, if this is how the two modes of living correlate, to say nonetheless that the unrestrained would be happier than the ethical? Have I perhaps persuaded you to give in that the ethical life would be better than the unrestrained, or have I not persuaded you?   [494b]

Calli: You have not persuaded me, Socrates. Because for the former who has the full barrels there would not be any more pleasure; rather that would mean, as I said before, to live like a stone if everything is filled up, having neither any pleasure nor any displeasure. Rather it is in this that the pleasant life consists: that lots and lots pour in.

Socr: Then too it is necessary, if lots should pour in, then lots must also pour out – and there must be large openings for the discharge?

Calli: Quite.

Socr: That again would be like living the life of a duck, what you mean, not indeed that of a corpse or stone! But tell me, you do mean it even so like hunger, and if you're hungry, eating?

Calli: Yes.

Socr: And to be thirsty, and if you're thirsty, drinking?

Calli: Also; and even so with all the other desires, and you are able to satisfy them and so win pleasure and live happily.   <49.~494c]

Socr: Good, most worthy Callicles! Just remain right there as you have started and don't spring off to the side due to shame. But, as it appears, I too need not shame myself. And so tell me now, firstly, if someone should itch and need to scratch himself – then, only if he were to be well scraped and thus titillated carry on with his life – whether this is called "living happily"?

Calli: In what bad tastes do you always indulge yourself, Socrates, and obviously using a bad analogy. [d]

Socr: Even therefore was I able to frighten Polus and Gorgias, and I made them look asinine. But don't let yourself be frightened and also do not become ashamed, rather, just answer me.

Calli: Then I say, also he who scratches himself shall live pleasantly.

Socr: Thus, if pleasantly, also happily.

Calli: Indeed.

Socr: If, perhaps, only his scalp itches – or, should I ask you still regarding something else? Look closely, Callicles, what shall you answer if I progress step by step to everything that relates with this. And if this correlation holds so it comes out that indulging in sex with adolescents is not abominable, disgraceful and miserable. Or, shall you actually dare to assert that this too would be a blessing, if only they can have enough of what they want?

Calli: Are you not ashamed – Socrates! – that you bring the conversation to such things? [495a]

Socr: Did I, most worthy, bring it to this or he who asserts without qualification that whoever has cravings – and no matter to what extent – he is blessed who satisfies them and, then, doesn't provide any differentiation as to which desires are good and which bad. But, now too, tell me only once more: do you assert that the pleasant and the good are one and the same, or are there things that feel pleasant but which are not good?

Calli: So that I do not give up my proposition by saying that they would be different, so I say: it is one and the same.

Socr: But, Callicles, you spoil your first speech and you would no longer be in a position to research the truth with me if you should say something other than what you mean.[146]

Calli: This holds true for you also, Socrates. [b]

Socr: Thus, neither I proceed rightly if I do this, nor would you. But, most worthy Callicles, do bethink yourself: this is not the good simply to have pleasure in every way. For from what was just pointed out there follows much ignominy that is quite obvious if it so relates, and even more as well.

Calli: At least as you believe, Socrates.

---

[146] Being true to oneself or speaking what one means, this is a fundamental prerequisite for Socratic discourse, see *Phaedrus* 243e; *Protagoras* 312a5, 319b, 336d or, for *not* speaking what one means, 333c; likewise *Meno* 83d (p. 480) and *Parmenides* 137b (p. 219).

Socr: But you, Callicles, do you in all actuality want to proceed in setting this down?

Calli: I do. <50.~495c]

Socr: Shall we, thus, consider this proposition as if you were serious about it?

Calli: Indeed, quite.

Socr: Well then, if this should be so, then please put the following in order for me. You call something knowledge?

Calli: Yes.

Socr: Didn't you also say that there would be such a thing as courage with knowledge?

Calli: I did.

Socr: And isn't it true, this courage would yet be different from knowledge? and therefore you named them as two?

Calli: Quite.

Socr: And how? – are pleasure and knowledge the same or different?

Calli: Different, of course, you most wise man. [d]

Socr: And also courage would be different from the pleasurable?

Calli: *How else?*

Socr: Well then, let us well hold onto this, that Callicles of Acharnia has said: the pleasurable and the good would be the same, knowledge and courage would be different from one another as well as from the good.[147] But Socrates from Alopece does not agree with this. Or does he agree?

Calli: He does not agree. [e]

Socr: But I believe that Callicles also doesn't, if first he himself rightly takes a good look at it. For do tell me about those who live well and those who live miserably, wouldn't you opine that they find themselves in contrary circumstances?

Calli: Indeed.

Socr: Isn't it then necessary, if they are both in actuality contrary to each other, that it correlates the same as is the correlation between health and sickness? Namely, a person is not both at the same time sick and healthy, and also does not lose health and sickness at the same time.

Calli: How do you mean this?

Socr: Take whichever particularity you want of the body and examine it. A person is sick in his eyes, what is called an inflammation of the eyes. [496a]

Calli: Good.

Socr: So he is not simultaneously healthy with them?

---

[147] The latter part of *Protagoras* is a proof of the identity of knowledge and courage.

Calli: In no way.
Socr: How about if, now, he should lose the inflammation – does he also lose at the same time the health of his eyes and has at the end lost them both simultaneously?
Calli: Wholly and absolutely not.
Socr: It also would be, I think, amazing and senseless. Isn't it so?
Calli: Very much so.   *[496b]*
Socr: Rather, each in turn, I believe, he gets and loses each. Not so?
Calli: Certainly.
Socr: Also, strength and weakness are even so?
Calli: Yes.
Socr: And swiftness and slowness?
Calli: Even so.
Socr: Perhaps, too, the good and blessedness; and the contrary to these, evil and being miserable, a person always gets and loses the one for the other?
Calli: In all ways.
Socr: If, then, we were to find that a person should simultaneously have and lose something: so, obviously, this would not be the good nor the evil. Do we want to agree to this? Bethink yourself right well before you answer.
Calli: Yes, beyond all bounds I will agree with this.   *<51.~496]*
Socr: So let's now return to that to which we formerly agreed. Did you say that being hungry would be pleasant or painful? I mean hunger itself.
Calli: I said painful; but then eating when you're hungry is pleasant.
Socr: I also thought this. But hunger itself, painful?   *[d]*
Calli: I agree.
Socr: And being thirsty as well?
Calli: Very much so.
Socr: Should I ask regarding still more or do you agree that in all cases every need and appetite is painful?
Calli: I agree with this; you needn't ask further.
Socr: Good! Drinking when thirsty, don't you say – this would be pleasant?
Calli: I say it.
Socr: In this what you have said, having thirst means having displeasure.
Calli: Yes.   *[e]*
Socr: But drinking is satisfying this craving and, as such, is pleasure?
Calli: Yes.
Socr: Insofar as one drinks, you say, one has pleasure?
Calli: Certainly.

Socr: But – having thirst?

Calli: That's the way that I mean it.

Socr: Thus, having displeasure?

Calli: Yes.

Socr: Do now take note of what follows from this, as, namely, you have said that he who has displeasure simultaneously has pleasure if you say that the thirsty person drinks? Or perhaps this doesn't happen in the same time and place – in the body or soul, as you like. For regarding this, I think, it makes no difference for us here. Is it so, or not?

Calli: It is so.

Socr: But that he who lives well is able simultaneously to live in misery, this you said would be impossible.

Calli: Indeed, I say it. [497a]

Socr: But that someone who has displeasure might also simultaneously have pleasure, this possibility you have agreed to.

Calli: So it seems.

Socr: Thus, having pleasure is not living well and having displeasure is not living badly. And so the pleasant is different from the good.

Calli: I don't know what you're cobbling together with such cleverness, Socrates.

Socr: You know quite well but you're getting desperate, Callicles. And now back off a bit more from your vacillating so that you see aright what's downstream from this fount of wisdom to which you [b] were leading me. Does not every person's pleasure in drinking cease when he no longer has thirst?

Calli: I don't know what you want.

Gorgias: Thus not, Callicles! – rather do answer so that for the sake of all of us this conversation shall be brought to its conclusion.

Calli: But Socrates is always like this, Gorgias, that he questions on about trivial and unworthy things and, thus, contradicts.

Gorgias: But how is this unfair to you? It's no skin off of your teeth, Callicles; rather you just let Socrates prove things as he wants.

Calli: Then, go ahead and ask me about your small potatoes and your pathetic questions, if Gorgias fancies this as being good. <52.~497c]

Socr: You are blessed, Callicles, that you get initiation into the greater mysteries before the lesser; I would have imagined that this didn't happen. Thus, where were we? – answer where we left off: whether everyone ceases to have thirst and likewise to have pleasure in drinking.

Calli: I agree with it.

Socr: Thus too with hunger – and with all of the other desires, the pleasure ceases simultaneously with the craving.

Calli: So it is.

Socr: Thus, pleasure and displeasure cease simultaneously?

Calli: Yes.   [d]

Socr: But the good and the bad, these do not cease simultaneously – as you already have agreed; but, do you not agree now?

Calli: OK – and what's next?

Socr: That therefore, dear friend, the good is not one and the same as the pleasant, nor evil as the unpleasant, for these cease simultaneously but the former do not, and so, obviously, they are different. How should it be that the pleasant would be the same as the good and the unpleasant as the bad? But, if you prefer, we can also examine it so. For, I think, also in this way you won't get through. Just look. Don't you name those to be good in whom goodness subsists, as also those beautiful in whom beauty subsists?

Calli: I do so.

Socr: And how? – do you name those who are foolish and cowardly good? At least you didn't previously, rather the brave and those who are insightful you named to be so. Or, don't you name these good?

Calli: Quite.

Socr: And how? – haven't you seen a small child lacking in understanding who is quite happy?

Calli: Sure.

Socr: But a grown man who lacks understanding, such a person you haven't seen being satisfied and happy?

Calli: I believe that I have, but wherefore this?

Socr: No reason; just answer.   [498a]

Calli: I have seen such.

Socr: How? – also knowledgeable persons who are satisfied and dissatisfied?

Calli: Sure.

Socr: Which have more pleasure and displeasure, those who have more or those having less reasoning ability?

Calli: I believe they would be about the same.

Socr: That too is enough for me. And have you seen cowards during wartime?

Calli: How could I not.

Socr: If, now, the enemy retreats, who would you suppose are more joyous, the cowards or the courageous?

Calli: I'd fancy that they are both more joyous; if not, still about the same.

Socr: This too is not problematic. The cowards, then, also have joy?

Calli: Indeed, very much so.   [b]

Socr: And the fools too, as it seems.

Calli: Yes.

Socr: But when the enemy returns do the cowards alone suffer displeasure or the courageous as well?

Calli: Both.

Socr: Also equally?

Calli: Perhaps the cowards have more.

Soc: And if they pull away again, don't they also have more pleasure?

Calli: Perhaps.

Socr: Thus, in pleasure and displeasure fools and those having   *[c]* insight, cowards and the courageous, they all share in equally, as you assert, and perhaps the cowards more than the courageous.

Calli: I assert it.

Socr: But yet those having insight and the courageous are good, but the cowards and foolish are bad?

Calli: Yes.

Socr: Equally then, those who are good and those who are bad have pleasure and displeasure?

Calli: I assert this.

Socr: Are now, perhaps, those who are good and those who are bad good and bad in equal amounts, or indeed – those who are bad would be yet more good and bad?

Calli: Really, by Zeus, I don't know what it is that you want.

Socr: Don't you know that you said, the good would be   *<53.~498d]* good because goodness subsists in them, the bad due to badness; the good would be pleasure, the bad displeasure?

Calli: I said that.

Socr: Thus, those who have joy subsist in goodness, which is pleasure, if then they have joy.

Calli: How could it be otherwise.

Socr: Thus, as goodness subsists in them, then they are good, those who are joyful?

Calli: Yes.

Socr: And how? – those who are in pain, do they not subsist in the bad, in displeasure?

Calli: Yes.

Socr: And because of the subsistence of maleficence, you say, are the bad bad. Or don't you still say this?   *[e]*

Calli: As always.

Socr: Good are those who somehow have pleasure, bad those who somehow have pain?

Calli: Indeed.

Socr: Those who have more, more; those having less, less; and those having equal portions, equal?

Calli: Yes.

Socr: But now you also say, those having insight and those who are fools, and the cowards and the courageous – all would have pleasure and displeasure equally, or the cowards still more.

Calli: I say it.

Socr: So let's add it all up together, you and I, what follows from these admissions. For also two or three times, they say, one   *[499a]* is allowed to bring up the beautiful and place it in consideration. Good would be those having insight and courage, didn't we say this, isn't this true?

Calli: Yes.

Socr: Bad the foolish and cowards?

Calli: Indeed.

Socr: But again, good those who have pleasure?

Calli: Yes.

Socr: And bad those who have pain?

Calli: Necessarily.

Socr: Pained and happy, you say, are those who are good and those who are bad in the same way, perhaps those who are bad yet more so?

Calli: Yes.

Socr: Thus, those who are bad even as those who are good become good and bad, or the bad yet even more good? Doesn't this follow and also what was said formerly, if someone asserts that the good and the pleasant would be the same? Is this not necessarily so, Callicles?

Calli: Already for some time, Socrates, I have been   <54.~499b] listening to you as I was agreeing with everything that you said and I have noticed that if anyone exposes himself to you, and even if it's just for fun, you become overjoyed – just like a child. Thus, do you really believe that I or any other person would opine that some pleasures wouldn't be better and others worse?

Socr: Oh! Oh! Callicles! – look how badly you've been treating me and playing with me like a child! At one time you're saying, the matter at hand relates thus and so, then again differently, and so you're sneaking around behind my back. And yet, I began in trusting that you wouldn't purposefully mislead me as you did assert that you wanted the best for me; but now I've been lied to and must, as the old proverb goes, take what I can get and make the most possible from that which you've given me. It is, then, as it appears and as you now have admitted, thus: some pleasures are good, others bad.

Calli: Yes.   *[d]*

Socr: Are, then, those which are useful good, but bad those which harm?

Calli: Indeed.

Socr: And useful are those pleasures that, indeed, accomplish good; harmful those having harmful effects?

Calli: I would say that as well.

Socr: Do you perhaps mean it thus? As it is in relation to the body and with the pleasures of eating and drinking, that of these some bring about health or strength or any other consummation of the body – and these are good; but those which do the opposite, bad?

Calli: Indeed.   *[e]*

Socr: Is it not also even so with displeasures, that some lead to health, others to corruption?

Calli: How else.

Socr: Thus, pleasures and displeasures that are good, these are the ones that must be chosen, and these are also the ones that should be done?

Calli: Indeed.

Socr: But not those that are bad?

Calli: Obviously.   *[500a]*

Socr: For it is for the sake of the good that everything should be done, so we two believe, Polus and I, if you still remember this. Do you perhaps believe this and join our side that all activities should aim for the good and that for its sake everything else should be done, but nothing is good for the sake of something other? Do you want to step up beside us as the third?

Calli: I want to.

Socr: For the sake of the good, then, one should do everything else – and likewise do what is pleasurable, but not for the sake of pleasure is anything good.

Calli: Indeed.

Socr: Is it now every man's business to pick and choose from amongst the pleasures, which are good and which bad, or does it require that someone understanding the art chooses in each case?

Calli: Someone understanding the art.   *<55.~500b]*

Socr: Let us now remember what it was that I said to Polus and Gorgias. Namely, I said that there were practices some of which would only go as far as inducing pleasure and accomplishing this alone, but not knowing the better or worse, but others that did have knowledge of the good and bad; and thus I established underneath the former, those which strive for pleasure in regards to the body, the skill of cooking, not an art, but that which likewise strives for the good to be an art, namely that of doctoring. And now, *by Zeus* – the god of friendship – o Callicles, don't play around with me any more and answer me not contrary to your own opinion but do attempt   *[c]* that you hit the mark; nor should you think that I am joking with you in what I shall say. For you do see that we are now ourselves conversing upon such things which certainly every person who has just a modicum of intelligence will admit that nothing could be more serious – as this has to do with how each should live – whether *either* he lives in accordance with that toward which you encouraged me, that, as befits a man, I might forge on before the populace and by the practice of speechcraft govern the state in the same way as currently it even is being governed by the likes of you, *or* whether he should   *[d]* hold to the latter *modus vivendi* and so live life in accordance with philosophy, which well differs from the former. Perhaps it would be best now, just as I attempted to do previously, that we divide things up and only after making the divisions and once we would be in agreement regarding these – that these are the two modes of living – only then take into consideration wherein they differ and in accordance to which one would have to live. Perhaps, though, you don't as of yet know what it is that I mean?

Calli: Not rightly.

Socr: Then I will say it to you clearer still. After we are in agreement, you and I, that there is the good as well as the pleasurable, and that the pleasurable would differ from the good, and that for each one of these there is a striving and a practice toward achieving possession, a hunting for pleasure, then, and one for the good. – Right away, though, do you agree with this, or do you deny it.

Calli: I agree with it.   *<56.~500e]*

Socr: Then tallyho – also regarding that which I said to Polus and Gorgias, make it clear to me whether you fancy that I was in the right. I said, namely, that cooking wouldn't seem to me to be an art but, rather, would just be an exercise or skill, but the healing art well is an art, as I opined, since it would have investigated into the nature of that wherein its care lies and because it can provide *grounds* for what is done and accountability for each particular; the former, however, is solely concerned with pleasure and upon this all of its care is lavished, obviously proceeding with a total lack of professionalism without first having researched into the nature of pleasure, nor into its grounds, in that wholly without reason – if I may speak it straight out –   *[b]* and not at all with calculation but, rather, merely by practice and skillfulness remembering just this: what tends to occur and even by which means the pleasurable is created and brought forth. Now, firstly take this into consideration, whether you believe that this does have grounds for being said and that there actually are such preoccupations with the soul, one according to art that delivers care for the *best* of the soul, others which neglecting this are only thinking upon the pleasures of the soul and to what extent they could be aroused; but upon the issue of which pleasures are better, which worse, neither paying any heed nor utterly with any other concern besides simply being pleasing, pleasant and pleasurable – despite whether it would be for better or for worse. Now for me, o Callicles, I fancy such to be the case and I, at least, do say that this latter sort would be sycophancy in relation to body as well as to the soul – and to everything else that someone might well desire to do without forethought as regards to what is better and what worse. But you, do you set up and proclaim this same opinion as we have, or do you contradict it?

Calli: Not I, rather I give in that this conversation may be finished and so that I shall have fulfilled Gorgias' request.

Socr: Should such things, now, be for one soul but not for two or more?   *[d]*

Calli: No, rather also for two, or for many.

Socr: Thus, also for many and before the great throng one may excite the passions without bethinking oneself regarding what is best?

Calli: I believe it, very well.   *<57.~501de]*

Socr: Now, are you well able to say which are the occupations that do this? Or rather, if you prefer, let me ask which of these seem to belong, for these answer affirmatively, but if not, of these answer in the negative. First, let us examine the art of playing on the flute. Does this seem to you to be such a one, Callicles, which is merely seeking our enjoyment and bethinks itself upon nothing else?

Calli: I'd fancy it so.

Socr: Not too, all the similar ones taken as a whole, like playing on the lyre and all the artful musical contests?

Calli: Yes.

Socr: And how about the performances of the choir and dithyrambic poetry, do these seem also to you to be such? Or would you opine that Cinesias, son of Meles, thinks in the least bit regarding how he shall recite something so that the listeners shall become better? – or rather, only upon how to excite the most pleasure before the great throng?

Calli: The latter, it is well clear enough, namely in regards to Cinesias.   *[502a]*

Socr: Now, and his father, Meles? – do you believe that he took the best into consideration in his lyre concerts? – or he didn't even consider what is most pleasant for he agonized his listeners with his singing refrains. But do just consider it, doesn't it seem to you that playing upon the lyre as a whole and the dithyrambic arts of poetry, that these have only been discovered for our enjoyment?

Calli: It appears so to me.   *[b]*

Socr: And all of the magnificent and awe inspiring works of the tragic poets upon which so many have expended such prodigious labor? Do you opine that their purpose and great effort is simply aimed at exciting their audience's pleasure, or that they would also persevere in their intentions either by withholding material from their speeches despite how pleasing and enjoyable it should be, if namely it should exert an ignoble influence; or that they would present what runs contrary to the tastes and will of their public, if namely such material might be of a beneficial nature; and that they would have the audacity to say such in song and in verse whether the audience is enthralled or even if they seem put upon? Which of these two possibilities seems to you to undergird the artistry of the tragic poets?
Calli: Well, it's quite obvious, Socrates, that they are more concerned with exciting pleasure and in being pleasing to their audience.   *[c]*
Socr: But this, o Callicles, we have even just said, this would be sycophancy.
Calli: Indeed.
Socr: Well then, if one removes from the previous all reference to poesie and song, and also tonalities and rhythm, shall not what remains be speech?
Calli: Necessarily.
Socr: And shall not such speeches be delivered before the great throngs of the populace?
Calli: Indeed.
Socr: Thus, the dramatic art is likewise a working up of the masses?
Calli: So it appears.   *[d]*
Socr: And, isn't it true, as speechcraft it does its work upon the masses. Or doesn't it seem to you that the poets are exercising speechcraft in their dramas up on the stage?
Calli: Well, indeed.
Socr: Now, thus, we have come upon and discovered speechcraft which is directed upon the populace consisting of children and also women and men, servants and free-holders, and with it we are not very content for we say: it would be sycophancy.
Calli: Indeed.   *<58.~502e]*
Socr: But how about those orators who appeared before the Athenian populace? – or before any of the free assemblies of men in Hellas? – what then, of these? Does it, perhaps, seem to you that these orators always speak what is best and with an eye on this, that the citizens shall be made to be better as much as possible by their speeches? – or do these proceed on the assumption that they say pleasing and pleasant things to the citizens and so mold them to their own advantage but neglect thereby the common weal and, handling the

populace like one handles children in that they search for ways to gratify them, but whether they would be made better or worse, for this they're not in the least bit concerned.   *[503a]*

Calli: This is no longer so easily discerned in all generality; for there are some who in what they say do say it in true consideration for the citizens, but then there are also others as you say.

Socr: This is well enough for me. For even though this also is divided: so the one is part sycophancy and a bad influence on the populace; but the other part would be something beauteous – that the souls of the populace would be bettered and to strive always to carry through that only the best is spoken, whether it should be the more pleasing or the more displeasing for those listening. But, certainly, you've never seen such speechcraft? Or, if you are able to identify one such from amongst the orators – why, then, why haven't you also named him for me, who it may well be?

Calli: Yes, by Zeus, I know of none that I might name, at least from amongst the current set.

Socr: How? – perhaps you know one to be named from the past, someone under whose influence it could be said that the Athenian populace has become better after formerly having been worse? – for I don't know who this is?

Calli: How? – haven't you heard what an outstanding man   *[c]* Themistocles was, and also Cimon, Miltiades and, then too, Pericles – he who only passed away recently and whom you yourself have heard speak?

Socr: Yes, Callicles, namely, if what you formerly opined is the right virtue, that appetites are to be satisfied, one's own and those of others; but, if it's not to be this, but rather what we were compelled to take on in the latter portion of our conversation, namely that only those appetites should be satisfied that make mankind better if they be fulfilled, but those that worsened mankind's lot, these not, and that for this there should be an art which is requisite – are you then well able to say that any of these men would have been such?

Calli: I don't know anymore what I should say.   *<59.~503d]*

Socr: If only you investigate this uprighteously you shall, assuredly, find the truth. But let us, in all leisure, let us take a look and observe whether any of these orators was such. Isn't it true, an upright individual who says what he says in reference to the best wouldn't merely speak with empty phrases like the blowing of the wind, rather he would have his eyes set on *something definite* that would clearly be in view – just as it is with all of the other artisans: each focuses his vision on his own particular work and doesn't make stabs on a   *[e]* moment's inclination to lay something new upon his work, rather each works with his materials so that his work acquires a certain, definite form. Just as if you were to observe a painter or a master builder or a ship's carpenter, and all of the other workers, whomever you want, so each of them brings whatever it may be that he uses to work in definite places and constrains each part to be conjoined with the other in a measured way until the whole work is completed with aesthetic orderliness and displaying beauty in its presentation. So it is with these artisans and also with each of the others of whom we spoke previously, those who care for the body, the physicians and gymnasts, these do indeed bring the body into good order and comeliness. Do we accept that this is how it correlates, or not?

Calli: That may well be so.

Socr: A household, then, in which order and comeliness is met up with would be consummate, but one in which disorder reigns, this would be malefic?

Calli: I admit it.

Socr: Even thus with a ship?

Calli: Yes.   [504b]

Socr: And we say the same of our body?

Calli: Indeed.

Socr: But, how about the soul? – would it be consummate if disorder should be met up with, or does it likewise require order and decency?

Calli: It follows necessarily from the previous that the same applies here.

Socr: How does one name that which is composed of order and comeliness in the body?

Calli: You'd be meaning health and strength.

Socr: That's what I mean. But how now? – what is built up from the order and decency within the soul? – do attempt also to give this a name just as you found one for the previous and spoke it out.

Calli: Why don't you say it yourself, Socrates?

Socr: If you should prefer it, I shall indeed say it. But only if you believe that I speak rightly give me your voice-vote; but if not, then prove me wrong and don't allow yourself to be misled. I opine, then, that the order for the body is named the rules of proper hygiene, by which it comes to be healthy and every other virtue of the body is brought into being. Is this so, or not?

Calli: It is so.   <60.~504d]

Socr: But the orderliness and precepts for the soul's development are justice and law, and by the application of these it becomes righteous and decent – and even this is righteousness and mindfulness. Do you affirm this, or not?

Calli: So be it.

Socr: With his view upon this, then, the former orator who brings forth righteousness in aesthetic proportions will order all of the speeches that he delivers for the sake of the soul – and also his activities: that what is to be fostered, this he shall promote, and what is to be denied and removed, this he shall prohibit; and always *[e]* focused on his meaningful intent: how might righteousness enter the souls of his compatriots and how shall injustice be overcome and removed, and so also how to foster every virtue and abolish every vice. Do you come over and concur in this? – or not?

Calli: I concur.

Socr: For what good would it do to give to a sick and shattered body many and ever so delightful delicacies to eat, or various drinks, or anything else which from time to time hardly serve any real purpose – and now do so even less, to speak the truth. Is it so, or not?

Calli: It is. *[505a]*

Socr: For I think that there's no use to go on living if the body is in a wretched state, because so, it also leads a wretched life. Or is it not so?

Calli: Yes.

Socr: And, isn't it true, to satisfy his appetites such as eating as much as desired when hungry and drinking as much when thirsty, the physicians generally allow this for those in good health, but the sick are never allowed to satiate themselves as their passions desire. This, too, you also would admit?

Calli: Yes, I do. *[b]*

Socr: And with the soul, most worthy Callicles, is it not even so? – as long as it is malefic due to its unreasonableness and lack of restraint, its unrighteousness and lack of piety, one must hold its appetites in check and disallow it from doing anything other than that whereby it shall be enabled that it becomes better? Do you affirm this, or not?

Calli: I affirm it.

Socr: For this also is for its own well-being, that of the soul itself, the best.

Calli: Yes, quite.

Socr: And holding it back from all of its desires and cravings, this indeed is called restraining and being disciplined.

Calli: Yes.

Socr: Holding in firm discipline, this then is better for the soul than wantonness and lack of restraint – as, indeed, you opined earlier. *[c]*

Calli: I don't know what it is that you are proposing, Socrates! Please ask someone else.

Socr: This man will not allow himself the pleasure which is even being encouraged by this conversation, that namely he hold himself in check and discipline himself.

Calli: And also nothing whatsoever of anything that you say concerns me at all, rather I have answered you up to now only in deference to Gorgias.

Socr: Good! What are we going to do now? – break off the speech in the middle?

Calli: That you may know better yourself.

Socr: Don't they say, indeed, that it wouldn't be right to break off halfway through even in the telling of a fairy tale, but, rather, that it also should have its head attached so that it doesn't wander about headless. So now, answer me yet what still remains so that our conversation may get its head.   <61.~505d]

Calli: How insistent you are, Socrates! If you were to do as I bid then you would allow that this speech be dropped, or you would speak with one of the others.

Socr: Who of the others would well want to? So that we don't just leave the speech in an incomplete state.

[... silence ...]

Calli: Aren't you able to bring it to an end by yourself, whether it should be that you would now speak in just one contextual flow, or be it that you would answer yourself?   *[e]*

Socr: As also happened by Epicharmus, and now to me, that that which previously was bespoken by two men, I alone suffice. In any event, perhaps it may well be the supreme challenge that one continue on in this wise. But, all the same, if we are indeed to make do, so I think that all of us must use all of our powers in striving to experience what is true in the matter about which we are speaking, and what false; for it is good for all of us as a community that this be brought to light. I will, thus, go through with it, as I believe that it correlates. But if it seems to any one of you that I concurred   *[506a]* with myself when I should not have done so: so you have to step in between and disprove it. For not that I would know it, do I say what I say, rather I seek it commonly with you and in your presence; so that if someone seems to say anything that would contradict me, I shall start off by accepting the objection. But I say all of this now only for the case that you all fancy it to be good that I might bring this speech to its conclusion; should you not want this, so we'll let it be and take leave from one another.

Gorgias: I for my part think not, that we take leave of one another, rather that you follow through with the conversation; and I can well see that the others too are even wishing this. For I also would most gladly hear how you navigate alone through what remains.

Socr: Indeed, Gorgias, I would have happily yet bespoken the matter further with our Callicles, that I might have been able to reciprocate for the speech of Zethos with that of Amphion. But as you, o Callicles, don't want to lead this speech with me on to its conclusion: so at least pay heed and point me in the right way, if you opine that I say   *[c]* something that is not right. And if you lead me over, I shall not be angry with you as you were with me, rather as my greatest benefactor shall you stand inscribed upon me.

Calli: So, just speak it by yourself, good man, and bring it to an end.

Socr: Hear then, how I take everything up again from the beginning.

<62.~506]

Is perhaps pleasure and goodness one and the same? ~ Not the same, as Callicles and I have concluded together as one. ~ Is it necessary, then, that pleasant things be done for the sake of the good, or good things for the sake of pleasure? ~ Pleasant things for   *[d]* the sake of the good. ~ But what is pleasant is pleasant through the presence *{Anwesenheit}* of that by which we become enthralled; good, on the other hand, that through the presence of which we become good? ~ Certainly. ~ But we are good – as is everything else which is good – through the presence of some single virtue? ~ For me, at least, I'd fancy this necessary, Callicles. ~ But the virtue of every particular thing, of an instrument as of the body and also of a soul, and of each and every living being, does not find itself by approximation upon the beauteous, rather by order, rightful behavior and through art, even that which is appropriate for each and every. Is this well the case? ~ At least I would reply affirmatively. ~ Thus, by order the virtue of every particular becomes firmly established and brought into existence? ~ I would affirm it. ~ Thus, there is a certain, uniquely individual order that is built up in each and every making each and every good? ~ So I'd fancy it. ~ Thus,   *[507a]* also the soul that has its own uniquely individual order and morality is better than an unordered soul? ~ Necessarily. ~ One that has order and ethics is moral? ~ How else? ~ And the moral is mindful? ~ Necessarily. ~ The mindful soul, then, is the good one? ~ I, at least, know of nothing that might otherwise be said than this; but, dear Callicles, if you know something, so teach it to me.

Calli: Just speak on, my good man.

Socr: To continue, then, I say: If the mindful is the good, so then – that with the contrary constitution is the evil; but this was one lacking reason and unrestrained? ~ Indeed. ~ But the mindful does everywhere what is appropriate in respect to gods and man; for [b] he would not be mindful if he were to be doing the inappropriate? ~ That is necessarily so. ~ If he does appropriate things to man, so he acts justly; and if toward the gods, then piously; and he who acts righteously and piously, he also is necessarily pious and just? ~ So it is. ~ Yes, also courageous, it is well necessary; for it is not an intrinsic characteristic of him who is mindful to search about and to flee when it is not appropriate, rather he seeks and runs toward those happenings, people, pleasures and displeasures toward which he should, and tolerates steadfastly whatever he should. So that, necessarily, o Callicles, the mindful person as he – as we have shown – is also righteous and courageous and pious, shall also be the fully consummate, good person; but the good shall live well and beauteously in all cases and, as he lives, he who lives well, shall also be satisfied and happy; the evil, on the contrary, and the malefic live badly and in misery and wretchedness. And this would be he who in correlation is contrary to the mindful person, he who is not reined in, and whom you praised. So, at least, do I establish this and I assert that so it is true. But if it is true, so it is necessary, <63.~507d] as it seems, that he who wants to be happy will seek and practice mindfulness but flee from dissipation, distancing himself from the latter so far and so rapidly as is possible and so seek before all other things to achieve that he does not require to be disciplined; but if either he requires it himself or one of his friends or relatives requires it, be it an individual or the state, then lay down the punishment and discipline, if he is to be happy. This I fancy as being the target at which one should aim in the conduct of life and that all of one's own and the community's affairs are conducted with these reins: that always righteousness and mindfulness remain present to him, he who wants to become blessed; but not so, that the desires and appetites are allowed to run rampant and one is constantly attempting to satisfy them – a heavy swinging evil – to live the life of a thief. For neither is it so possible to become friends with another person, nor with a god; for he is unable to stand upright in community, and where there is no community there is no friendship. But the wise have asserted, o Callicles, that the heavens and the earth, god [508a] and mankind only remain steadfastly created and are constituted through community, through friendship and appropriate behavior; and through mindfulness and justice – and so they view, therefore, my friend, the cosmos as one ordered whole, not as chaos and unrestraint. But you, as I fancy it, have not taken notice of this, despite that you are so wise, rather somehow you missed it, that the geometrical equality is so capable by gods and man; but you believe that everything comes from having more because you have neglected your geometry lessons.[148]   Well! – either this proposition must be *[b]* disproved, that the happy are blessed through righteousness and mindfulness and the miserable are wretched through maleficence or, if it remains true, one must pay heed to what follows.   Namely, the former shown previously, o Callicles, follows from everything that you asked of me when you asked as to whether I was serious or joking when I said that if anyone has done an unrighteous deed he would have to be accused, be it he accuses himself, his son, or his friend – and for this speechcraft may be used.   And what seemed to you that Polus admitted merely due to asininity, this was, however, true, that namely doing unrighteousness is so much more disgraceful and would also be so much more evil than suffering from unrighteousness; and that he who wants to become a proper orator would necessarily have to be informed of what is right, lawful and just – which again Polus maintained that Gorgias was so asinine to admit. If this so correlates, let us then see how things stand with what you threw up against me, whether it was rightly said or not that I am incapable, be it for my own self or for any of my friends and cohorts, to be of any help and to rescue myself or them from the greatest dangers, that rather I should be a pawn to every man's   *<64.~508d]* power just like the ignoble are whom anyone to whom it should give pleasure, and so also with me, and, to use your own great words from your speech – could punch my face, or steal my belongings, or drive me from my own country, or finally indeed kill me; and to be in such a situation would affirmatively be most disgraceful in your opinion. My opinion, to the contrary, which often enough has been said – though it may still be said one more time – is: I belie, Callicles, that being struck in the face is the most disgraceful thing; and not, even so, if I should be cut, be it my body or my purse, rather any unjustified assault upon me or upon my goods and any cutting – any such is itself both more disgraceful and more evil.   And stealing as well, and leading off into slavery, and breaking in through force and absolutely every other unrighteous deed against me and against what is mine is for he who transgresses both more evil and more disgraceful than it is for me, upon whom the transgression occurs. This, what was so thoroughly shown in the earlier speeches, as I say, remains steadfast and well protected, though it may have a dull ring, being grounded in iron [and forged upon the anvil of pure reason] – as it has now appeared to us and which either you or someone *[509a]* with yet more courageousness either would have to pull apart or it

---

[148] The central part of *Meno* is a geometry lesson!

is not at all possible to do other than as I have done and yet speak rightly on the matter. For I have always remained steadfast to the same *logoi*, that, indeed, I don't know exactly *how* it all is correlated, but of those with whom I have met and discussed these issues, as also now with all of you, nobody has ever been able to assert anything other than this without making themselves appear ludicrous. Therefore I say again that this correlates so. And if it correlates so and the greatest amongst all evils is unrighteousness for he himself who acts unjustly and yet, if it's possible, more evil still than the greatest evil is not being punished for unrighteous deeds: what sort of help would it be possible that a person could not be capable of accomplishing himself that thereby in truth he doesn't become ridiculous. Is it not those that straight-away deflect the greatest evils from striking us? It is totally necessary, indeed, that the most despicable thing is not being able to accomplish just this help for oneself and for one's friends and compatriots, but next to this that against the second worst evil, and thirdly what goes against the third greatest; and so on in respect to the characteristic magnitude of every evil it is also beauteous to be able to accomplish help against each and despicable not to be able to do so. Does it correlate otherwise, or so, Callicles?

Calli: Not otherwise.   *<65.~509cd]*

Socr: Of the two of them, doing and suffering an injustice, the greater evil is, we say, doing an injustice, the smaller, suffering an injustice. What, now, would someone have to bring into being in order to enjoy these advantages – the one, not doing an injustice, the other, not suffering an injustice? Is it a capability or a willing? I opine, namely, thus: if one wants to avoid injustice shall one already thereby not suffer injustice? – or shall one only then if one has acquired some capability not to suffer injustice also actually not suffer injustice?

Calli: That is really quite obvious, if one acquires a capability.

Socr: And how is it now with doing an injustice? – is it perhaps   *[e]* sufficient if one simply does not want to do injustice – so that, then too, one shall do no injustice; or would there have to be an acquired capability and an art because, if one does not learn this and practice it one should still, indeed, do injustice? Why don't you at least answer me this one, Callicles! Do you believe that Polus and I were brought into this by a true necessity or not, that we admitted in our earlier conversation that nobody would purposefully and willfully do injustice, rather all who do injustice would do so contrary to what they want and against their wills?   *[510a]*

Calli: That too may be as you say, Socrates, if only you will bring this speech to an end.

Socr: Thus here also, as it appears, there has to be the acquisition of some capacity and of an art so that one doesn't do injustice?

Calli: Yea, sure.

Socr: Now, which art would this be through which one achieves that one suffers absolutely no injustice, or so little as possible? Look closely, whether you think about this even so as I. Namely, I think so. Either one would have to himself be the ruler of the state, be it according to law or by brute force, or one would have to be a friend to the ruling power.

Calli: Do you see, Socrates, how ready I am to sing you praise if you bring up something that's right! It seems to me that what you say is very rightly said. *<66.~510b]*

Socr: Put this, then, in the balance too – whether it seems well spoken. Namely, I would fancy that to be a friend of any someone most likely would be he, of whom the elders and the wise say: similar to similar. Is this also your opinion?

Calli: Mine also.

Socr: If, then, a coarse and uneducated person rules somewhere by his own power, shall not such a tyrant, if somewhere in this state there should be a far better person than he himself is, shall he not fear him and not be able to truly be his friend with his whole soul?

Calli: So it is. *[c]*

Socr: But also even so little, if someone were to be worse by far, with him also not. For such a one would despise the tyrant and would prove to be incapable of such attentions as one gives to one's friends.

Calli: That too is true.

Socr: There just remains the one possibility left as the rightful friend for such a person, he who would be of like mind, who praised and condemned the same things and yet let himself be ruled and would want to be subservient beneath the one having power. Such a person would then be most capable in such a state and nobody shall harm him without themselves being punished. Is this the way things are?

Calli: Yes.

Socr: If, then, one of the younger generation should want to consider by what means he best would be enabled to achieve the greatest power, that no one would do any harm to him, so this would be, as it seems, the best path for him: that right from his youth on he would become accustomed to love and to hate just as his lord and ruler does, and so to strive in every way that he might become as similar to him as possible. Isn't it so?

Calli: Yes.

Socr: And for him this shall become accomplished in the city, that he shall not be harmed and, as you say, is able to do many things? *[e]*

Calli: Quite.

Socr: But also, perhaps, this – that he himself does not act unrighteously? – or, failing this test dramatically, if then he should be similar to an unrighteous power monger and wants side by side with him to accomplish many things?   Rather, I think to the contrary, his whole orientation and *modus operandi* shall proceed in the direction that he is just as capable of doing as much injustice as is at all possible, and yet, not be punished. Isn't it true?

Calli: Obviously.   *[511a]*

Socr: Thus, indeed, he carries the greatest evil on himself, namely, due to this imitation of his lord and for the sake of this power he has shattered and perverted his soul?

Calli: I don't know how, Socrates, you manage on every occasion to turn and to twist your speeches, always making the lowest into the highest. Or don't you know that this imitator shall kill the other who refuses to imitate and take everything from him that he possesses?

Socr: I know it, my good Callicles, if then I'm not deaf, as I have   *[b]* already heard it from you and Polus more than once, and also from almost everyone else in the city. But you hear me as well; he shall indeed kill him, if he wants, but he shall do so as an evildoer upon a benefactor and against a pillar of righteousness.

Calli: Now, isn't this really most outrageous?

Socr: Not for the man of reason, as our speech indicated. Or shall every man only care about this, that he live as long as possible and only labor with those arts and professions that always save us from danger – as you do with your speechcraft which I, to act in accordance with your recommendation, should take up and work with as such may be of great help for me before the courts?   *<67.~511c]*

Calli: And it is certain, by Zeus, that I advised you very well.

Socr: But, how so, most worthy?   Do you also hold the art of swimming in high esteem as something grand and admirable?

Calli: Verily, I do not.

Socr: But it too saves men from death if they should find themselves in such circumstances in which the art is required. And now,   *[d]* if you fancy this to be trivial, then I shall name you one grander still – the art of seafaring – which not only can save a person's life, rather also his body and possessions at the same time if he should be in the most dire circumstances, just as you with your speechcraft. And this art holds itself in a modest, square-dealing and disengaged manner and doesn't have any great pretensions in its conduct, as if it accomplished something out of the ordinary. Rather, once it fulfills its task, the same as your legal defense, so it only wants – if, say, it has fortunately rescued someone from Aegina and helped bring him here, I believe, just two silver pieces in recompense; but if from Egypt or from the Pontus, then for this good deed after having brought someone with wife, children and livelihood safely into harbor, at the most two gold pieces suffice; and he himself who possesses this art and has accomplished everything disembarks from the ship and walks up and down the shore next to his boat with a deferential air. He knows, namely, so I think, to calculate that he is not conscious as regards which of the ship's company he actually has supported in a useful way, that there be an advantage in that he didn't allow that they drown, and to which perhaps a disservice, as then he well knows that they have disembarked from his craft in no better a   *[512a]* state than when they came aboard, neither in respect to their bodies nor to their souls. He calculates, thus, that indeed it is impossible if someone who suffers under serious and incurable bodily maladies didn't drown, such a one is indeed in misery in that he has not found death and, thus, utterly no advantage was created through his agency; but if someone who is afflicted with serious and incurable maladies of the soul, which is of so much greater value than is the body, that it might be good for him to live on and that he has created an advantage for him if, whether it be from the oceans, from the courts or from whatever else that he has rescued him, rather he knows that for such a wretched person as this it is in no way better to live because, necessarily, he has only a malefic existence. Therefore it is not to be maintained that the sea captain does grand things,   *<68.~512b]* whether it be true that he preserves lives. And even so little would the master builder for war, you marvel, he who takes care of all of the fortifications, although he is from time to time no less a helper than the major general, not even to speak about sea captains and all of the other ones, for sometimes he even rescues entire cities! Wouldn't you opine that he would be, most assuredly, on an equal footing with your professional administrators? And indeed, Callicles, if he should desire to speak as you do and make the most of the matter, he would really be able to rattle you with his speeches and admonitions, that all of you would have to become master builders and that everything else is naught. He'd have enough to say! But, all the same, you have no respect for him nor for his profession, indeed, as if uttering a curse you call him a mere handyman, and neither would you let any of your daughters marry his son nor take his daughter for your own. And yet, in accord to that by which you praise your profession, by what right can you show so little respect for him and for all of the others whom I mentioned? I know, you'll say that you would be *better* and are of a more noble lineage. But, singularly, if the better be not what I have named, rather if even this should be virtue that one preserves oneself and one's possessions, however it may be done, so your disrespect shall prove to be ludicrous against the fortifiers of the cities, the physicians and all of the other professions whose reasoned purpose is for preservation. Thus, most worthy, take a look whether or not the noble and good is not something quite different from preservation and being well maintained – and whether he who truly is a man, *[e]* just this, only to live and for so long as is even possible, that this would have to be set aside and not at all merely hanging on to life, rather leaving this in the hands of god and accepting the belief of the women that, indeed, no one escapes his fate, and looking just to what is closest: upon which manner he best may live during the time that is granted him, whether he really should emulate the ruling powers wherever he may live and, thus, also in your case, whether you should seek to become similar to the Athenians as much as possible if, then, you want to be enamored here and to be capable of doing many things in our great city. Look closely at this, whether it really is to your advantage and mine – so that it doesn't happen to us as it is said by the Thessalians who desire to bring down the moon, and that we would have to pay for this with the most lovely thing that we possess, just to be able to accomplish much in the city. But if you believe that there be anyone at all who can deliver to you such an art that would make you capable of doing many things and accomplishing   *[b]* much in the city despite that you yourself are dissimilar to its constitution, and all the same whether you be better or worse: so you have been badly advised, o Callicles, as I fancy it. For not only would you have to be an imitator, rather already by nature of a similar mold if, then, you will achieve something of any order in friendship with the Athenians; and so also truly in the friendship with that fair youth.[149]   He who makes you right similar to these, he makes you, as you desire to be a statesman, to be *such* a statesman and orator. For when you speak in accordance to the way others opine it, so these others delight in hearing it, but what is foreign, this goes against the grain – if, then, you don't opine otherwise, noble friend. Do you have something to say contrary to this, Callicles?   *<69.~513cd]*

Calli: I don't know quite how it is, Socrates, but what you say seems to a certain extent admirable; but then, it is yet with me as with the majority, I don't particularly believe you.

Socr: The double love that you hedge within your soul, o Callicles, to the Athenians and to your beloved, stands in my way; but perhaps if we take this into consideration more often and if we manage to speak better, you shall become convinced. Thus, do remember we said that

---

[149] The youth is Demos, son on Pyrilampes.

there would be two methods in the handling of each, the body and the soul, the first of which proceeds according to what is most pleasurable, but the other with a vision as to what is best and not merely pleasing, rather handling with steadfast determination. Was it not this by which we separated the one from the other?

Calli: Quite.

Socr: And the one that is only concerned with what is pleasurable, this was ignoble and essentially nothing other than sycophancy. Isn't it true?

Calli: So be it, however you want.   *[e]*

Socr: But the other, if we seek with all of our powers to do the best with what we touch and handle, be it now body or soul?

Calli: So it was.

Socr: Should we, then, make bold in our handling of the city and the citizens in order to make them better so much as is possible? For without this, as we found out earlier, it would be useless to   *[514a]* bestow any other beneficial deeds – if the mindset of these is not directed to what is good and beauteous, neither for those who should succeed to great holdings in property, nor for those gaining lordship over others, or to any other capability whatsoever. Do we say that this is how it correlates?

Calli: Sure, if you prefer it.

Socr: Now, if you and I were to be entering into public service, o Callicles, and speaking with one another about the affairs of state, perhaps concerned about major construction projects: with the   *[b]* building of the walls, shipbuilding or the construction of important temples – would we not initially have to investigate and insure, firstly, whether we well understood or didn't understand the matter itself, the art of building, and from whom we would have learnt it? – would we have to do this or not?

Calli: Well, indeed.

Socr: And, secondly, the following would be good also, namely whether we had ever at least been leaders accomplished in some sort of building project, be it just for domestic purposes – whether for ourselves or for our friends – and whether this turned out well or badly. And if the results of this investigation demonstrate that we have admirable and renowned teachers and that we played leading roles in accomplishing the construction of numerous beauteous structures and also that we have erected many all alone after having separated ourselves from these teachers, so it would be most appropriate, as reasonable people under such circumstances, that we should also make bold with the public works. But if we couldn't point to any teachers, nor to any buildings, or perhaps to many buildings but all of them of negligible value, then, indeed, it would certainly be unreasonable to attempt to take on large-scale, public projects and to be encouraging one another in this. Do we want to say that this is rightly spoken, or not?

Calli: Indeed.   <70.~514de]

Socr: And is it not the same with everything else, if we wanted to talk each other into taking over the public business of the doctors, that we were capable of the discipline, wouldn't we first put each other to the test, I you and you me, let's see, by god, Socrates himself, what is the condition of his own health? – or whether, perhaps, someone has been freed by him from illness, be it a servant or freeman? – and with even this same method I also would examine you; and should we discover that we never had made anyone to be healthier, neither a foreigner nor a local, neither man nor woman, by Zeus, Callicles, wouldn't it be ludicrous if then people could be so utterly foolish, before they first had proven their capabilities alone for themselves and many actually proceeding thus, willy-nilly, but many also who rightly lead and further their own arts doing good and being sufficiently practiced, similar to the case of the potter who, the proverb has it, now starts off to make barrels, and as well he himself making bold in the furthering of the public business as also in urging others on, that they do likewise? Do you fancy that this demonstrates a lack in reason, to act thus?

Calli: I, well, yes.   [515a]

Socr: But now, most worthy man, as you yourself even have begun to push on into the matters of state and public business and as you urge me on and berate me because I myself have no such drive, don't we want to test each other: well then, has Callicles perhaps already made some citizen better? – is there someone who previously was bad, perhaps unrighteous, unrestrained or unreasonable who has become good and righteous through Callicles' intervention, be it foreigner or local, freeman or servant? Speak, if someone should test you on this point, Callicles, what shall you say? whom shall you claim was made better through having been in your company? Do bethink yourself what you shall reply if, indeed, you have such an accomplishment to demonstrate from the time when you lived for yourself before you made bold to push on into the affairs of state?

Calli: You want always to be in the right, Socrates.   <71.~515bc]

Socr: In no way do I ask simply for being in the right, rather in truth that I may experience how it is that you opine that the state would have to be administered; whether you think, perhaps, that there is something else on which your care should be lavished now that you have taken up the public affairs, something other than that we citizens shall always be made better? Or have we not already often admitted that this is what the public administrators have to accomplish? Are we one in this admission, or not? Answer. – – We have admitted it; I'll answer for you. If, thus, it is this that the righteous person would have to seek to accomplish, so put your mind to this question and tell me once again your opinion regarding the former orators, those whom you brought up earlier, whether you still believe that they were good statesmen, Pericles and Cimon, and Miltiades and Themistocles? [d]

Calli: I do still believe it.

Socr: If, then, they were good statesmen: so indeed each obviously made the citizens to be better from having been worse. Did they do this, or not?

Calli: They did it.

Socr: Thus, when Pericles first began to speak before the populace the Athenians were worse than when he spoke on his last occasion?

Calli: Perhaps.

Socr: But not *perhaps*, most worthy Callicles, rather it follows by necessity from what we admitted above – provided, then, that he was a good statesman.

Calli: And what else? [515e]

Socr: This is what else, just tell me whether it's the general opinion that the Athenians were made better through Pericles – or, to the contrary, that they were corrupted by him. For to this effect at least I have already heard it, that Pericles has brought the Athenians to this, that they be lazy, cowardly, idle-gossiping and money-grubbing people, in that first he lowered them into being paid lackeys.

Calli: You hear this from those with cauliflower ears, o Socrates.

Socr: But *this* I have not merely heard tell, rather we both of us have precise knowledge regarding it, you and I – that, indeed, Pericles stood at first with a good reputation and calling, and that the Athenians were not knowledgeable of any blemishes on him, nor were there any disgraceful accusations against him, that is – when the Athenians were yet worse – but after they had become good and noble, near the end of Pericles' life, then they recognized his under-handedness and roguery and almost went so far as to punish him with his life, obviously, indeed, as a most dangerous man.

Calli: Now? – was perhaps, therefore, Pericles bad? <72.~516ab]

Socr: At least such an overseer of asses, horses and oxen would be deemed bad who would have received them in no such state that they would kick, butt and bite, but who would have allowed them to become so unruly that now they do all of these. Or don't you fancy that every such overseer is a bad overseer – who, whatever manner of living creature he looks after, would get them tame and makes them wilder than when he first received them. Would you fancy this bad, or not?

Calli: Yes, OK, so that I just answer with good will.

Socr: Then also have the good will to answer me this, whether man also belongs to the animal kingdom or not?

Calli: How could he not?

Socr: And Pericles was a ruler over men?

Calli: Yes.

Socr: How then? – shouldn't they, in accord with what we just established, shouldn't they have become more righteous underneath him having been less righteous – if, then, he ruled them as a righteous statesman?

Calli: Indeed. [c]

Socr: Now the righteous are tame, at least according to Homer. But, what do you say? Not also the same?

Calli: Yes.

Socr: And yet he did make them wilder than how he at first found them to be, and indeed, even against his very own self – which he would have wanted least of all.

Calli: Do you want that I say that you are in the right?

Socr: If you fancy that I would be right.

Calli: Then, so be it!

Socr: If, thus, wilder – than also less righteous and worse?

Calli: Verily. [d]

Socr: Thus, Pericles wasn't a good statesman, in accord with this speech.

Calli: No, *as you* – indeed – have asserted.

Socr: By Zeus, *you too*, in accord with what you've admitted to me. But, moving right along, tell me yet regarding Cimon, didn't even those in whose best interests Cimon was engaged, didn't they expel him from the city so that they wouldn't even have to hear his voice for ten long years? – and didn't they even do the same thing to Themistocles and, worse yet, totally banished him from ever returning? But Miltiades – the Victor at the battle of Marathon – hadn't they already decided to throw him into a ditch to rot, and had it not been for the Prytany, well, he would've found an early grave. But then, how could it be that if all of these orators were such admirable persons, as you maintained, how could've things come to such a pass with them? At least this isn't known to be the case with a good charioteer, that at the beginning he shouldn't fall under the wagon's wheels, but then, after he has handled the horses for a long time and thereby also become much more skilled at leading the team, then he falls off. Such things as this don't occur, neither by charioteer nor by any other professional occupation. Or, how do you opine?

Calli: No, indeed not. [517a]

Socr: So our earlier speeches were, as it appears, totally right, that we know of no one who would have been a capable statesman in this city. You do admit, there are none such amongst the present set, though with the earlier set you opine that there are, and then it's even these whom you hold up. But of these it has just been shown that they are just the same as the present bunch. So that, if these were orators, either they didn't understand the true art of speechcraft, for then they never would have succumbed so low, nor also the sycophantic.

Calli: But there is still so much lacking, Socrates, that <73.~517b] you can't really compare the present set to those of the past in their accomplishments, choose whomever you want.

Socr: Do marvel, o Callicles, for then I'm not scolding these men insofar as they were servants of the state, rather by far they seem to me to have been more industrious in their service than are the present ones, and also more capable in creating for the state the results for which it craved. But to turn its cravings around and not to be led astray by them, rather by persuasive dialogue and through their might to lead them onward to that through which the citizens could have been made better, in this, that I speak my intent plainly, the former were no better than the latter – and this is the only [c] business of the righteous and good statesman. Merely building ships, walls, catapults, and many things such as these, in this I gladly concur with you that the former were by far stronger than the current. But we make ourselves ludicrous in our speeches, both you and I. For during the entire time since we began to speak with one another we still have not yet stopped ourselves from always coming back to the same thing and not knowing what it is that we mean. Namely, I think that you have admitted and have shared the insight often enough that there really is a twofold occupation, with the body and with the soul, of which the one is merely servile – in that one is well positioned in getting food if one hungers, if thirsting then drink, if cold then blankets, clothes, shoes and everything else to which the pleasures of the body relate. And I have well bethought myself regarding the matter in that I explain it to you through these pictures so that you may grasp what I mean more easily. He who knows how to procure these things as a fisherman, businessman or manufacturer of such things; as a cook, baker, weaver, shoemaker or tanner – it's no wonder that he fancies himself the caretaker of the body, and also the others, those namely who don't know that outside of all of these things there is an art, the art of healing namely and gymnastics, which

in truth is the caretaker of the body and in relation to which it is meet
and proper that it rules over all of the former arts and puts them into
its own service, namely because it knows what is acceptable   *[518a]*
and what corrupts of the food and drink for the consummation of the
body, but all of the others know nothing of this. It is for this reason
that all of the others rank as underlings, servants and ignoble in their
ministrations upon the body, but these, the healing arts and
gymnastics, rightfully are the lords over all of these others. That now
I also opine that even the same takes place likewise in relation to the
soul, I fancy that you have understood this right well on numerous
occasions and have admitted as much – as if you really would know
what it is that I mean – but then, soon thereafter you come back and
assert that there would indeed have been quite capable and admirable
statesmen amongst us and, when I ask which ones, you set up before
me such people who would totally have even this correlation to
statesmen as if, then, in response to a question regarding gymnastics
you might reply: what excellent men we have had to take care of our
bodies, or yet currently have, and in wanting to answer with complete
sincerity say: Thearion the baker and Mithaecus who has written an
excellent treatise on Sicilean cuisine, and Sarambus the bartender,
that these would have been most admirable tenders to the body, for
the one delivers fantastic bread, the other one spices,   *<74.~518c]*
and the third wine. Perhaps you would then have become unwilling if
I would have said to you – "My dear man, you understand nothing
regarding the tending to the body for you only name servile people
who only work for the cravings and who understand nothing about
what is good and beauteous regarding this, those who, if it so
happens, readily fill up and fatten human bodies and who even are
praised for this, yet they corrupt the meat on our bones." But the
people in their ignorance don't place the blame upon these from
whom they were so well served, that these would have been the root
cause of their current illnesses and of the loss in the robustness which
once they enjoyed, rather only those who are currently round about
them and who now give them advice as, namely, the prior excesses in
satiation have slowly caught up to them with their attendant illnesses
because they were tended to in total disregard of their health, and so
they blame the latter ones and scold them, heaping evil upon them if
they are able to, but they praise these earlier ones who really   *[e]*
bear the blame for the current evil. Now, totally the same do you also
go to work, Callicles, and heap praise upon men who provided service
in even this manner with everything for which the populace had
cravings – and to excess – and of whom it is now stated that they
have raised our city to its greatness; but that it really was merely all

puffed up and has internal fractures due to the *modus operandi* of these elder statesmen, this nobody notices. For without thinking about mindfulness and righteousness they have engorged   *[519a]* the state upon their harbors and shipyards, their walls and import duties, and all such farces. When, now, the rightful eruption of this sickness shall become manifest, so they shall accuse the current advisers – but not Themistocles, nor Pericles and Cimon, those who are the original sources of the evil, these they still will praise and glorify; and perhaps they'll accuse you, if you're not careful, and also my friend, Alcibiades – if, then, you not only lose that which has been recently attained but also the old accomplishments, although, indeed, it is not you who are the real causes of this evil but, perhaps, just accomplices. There is yet something else that is quite unreasonable that I have seen coming to pass and which I hear from these elder statesmen. If, namely, the city incriminates against any one of these individuals as having done injustice, then I hear them muttering and yammering as if they had to tolerate something dreadful and horrendous; namely after they had proven to be such exemplary benefactors, now they should be so mercilessly and unrighteously brought low, as they say it. But all of this is simply false. For no   *[c]* leader of a state could ever unrighteously be brought down as evil by the very state which he has led! Namely, it is quite the same thing with the statesman as it is with those who give themselves out as sophists. For also these sophists, who are otherwise so remarkably wise, they too commit something quite lacking in reason. Despite that they claim to be teachers of virtue they often lament and accuse their students, that these have done them injustice in that they withhold payment and otherwise haven't proven to be grateful to them, despite that, indeed, they have received good. And what could be more senseless than such a speech, that these students who through them shall have become good and righteous and from whom all unrighteousness has been removed and replaced by the flower of righteousness, that even these should do injustice by the capacity of that which they no longer even have? Wouldn't you fancy that as senseless? – my friend. You have forced me, Callicles, to deliver quite a sermon because you didn't want to answer my questions.

Calli: Aren't you able to just keep quiet, Socrates, if nobody wants to answer?   *<75.~519e]*

Socr: It seems that I can't. At least, right now I opine that I have spoken at great length since you didn't want to answer me. But, good man, speak, as you hold me dear, wouldn't you fancy it unreasonable if someone claims to have made someone else to be good – and yet also accuses him at the same time that, although he has been made good and is now in actuality good, nonetheless, he also is bad?

Calli: I would well fancy it so.

Socr: And don't you even hear this complaint from those who fame themselves as educators of virtue for man? [520a]

Calli: Well, indeed. But what would you have me say of people who are totally worthless?

Socr: And what will you say now regarding those who claim that they have provided service for the state and also have taken care that it should become as good as is possible and that, nonetheless, it just so happens they also accuse the state of being so marvelously bad? Do you opine that these are somehow better than the former? Quite the same, worthy Callicles, are the sophists and the orators or, at least, they are very closely related, as I said also to Polus; although you opine from not being informed of this that the one, the orators, would indeed be something beauteous and it's only the other ones that you detest. But in accordance to truth sophistry is to the same extent more beauteous than speechcraft as legislation is more beauteous than jurisprudence and gymnastics more beauteous than the healing arts. And precisely for the men of the people and for the sophists, I believe, it is not warranted that they lament about that of which they have themselves contributed to the making, and what they have espoused, as if this treats them badly, or they also have to lament themselves at the same time, that they have proven to be useless, even they who yet fame themselves as being so useful. Is it not so? [c]

Calli: Indeed.

Socr: And it is precisely for them, as is self-evident, that it would be most appropriate that the services that they are able to provide be provided without monetary recompense – if, then, I was in the right earlier. For he who has been furthered in some matter by somebody else, perhaps he who has been made a faster runner by a gymnast, well, maybe he can run off with his "thank you" when the gymnast sets him free and they are at odds as regards payment, and so he also takes his money along with himself. For it is not through the capacity of moving slowly, I believe, this is not what makes men exercise injustice, rather it is by unrighteousness. Isn't it true? [d]

Calli: Sure.

Socr: Thus, if someone should take even this away from somebody, unrighteousness, so he is not at all allowed to be anxious that injustice would be done to him; rather he alone can make the wager of providing his services without any preconditions, only he, namely, who actually is able to make others good. Isn't it so?

Calli: I admit it.

Socr: Therefore also, as it appears, it is not at all disgraceful that one gives one's advice in return for money in other things, for instance in matters of the building arts and all of the other professions.

Calli: So it seems.   <*76.~520e]*

Socr: But as regards our obligation: by what manner someone could well become as good as is possible and so regulate either his own domestic well-being or his state for the good, in this it shall be looked on as abominable if someone should withhold in speaking his mind and giving out advice unless he would be given payment. Isn't it true?

Calli: Yes.   *[521a]*

Socr: And, obviously, even this is the fundamental reason that amongst all of the services that are performed only this one alone motivates the person who receives it with the like desire that he, in turn, wants to help others. So that this itself is quite a good indicator of who has proven himself to be a good servant – he too receives good service – but he who has not, he will not. Is this actually how it correlates?

Calli: Yes.

Socr: Then, to which of the two manners of handling the state do you embolden me, do voice your determination for me. To the one that wants to strive in making the Athenians become better, as is done by the physicians; or to the other such that one would have to go about being in service of that which is pleasing to the populace? Tell me with uprighteousness, Callicles! – for it is meet and proper, since you freely displayed your courageousness toward me even from the beginning onward, that you remain steadfast in this and say to me what your opinion is. Thus, speak now clearly and directly to the point.

Calli: Then, I say to you, you should serve the people.

Socr: Thus, to become a sycophant, o noble man, you embolden me to this?   *[b]*

Calli: Unless you prefer to be called a Mysier,[150] Socrates. For if you don't even want to do ...

Socr: Just don't say what already you have said often enough: That someone shall kill me, whomever it pleases, so that I shan't have to say again: Yes, indeed, but as a malefactor would do against someone good; and also don't tell me that someone will take whatever I have so that I don't have to respond: Yes, but once he takes it he won't know how to use it, rather just as it is unrighteously taken so too it will be

---

[150] A resident of the ancient country, Mysia, a country on the fringe, next to Phrygia. Also mentioned in *Theaetetus* 209b.

unrighteously used and, if unrighteously, then badly, and, if badly, then also to his own harm.   <77.~521c]

Calli: It seems to me, Socrates, as if you really believe that nothing like this could ever happen to you, as if you lived far off such paths and there is no possibility that the first miserable and totally malicious person who comes along wouldn't drag you before the courts.

Socr: In that case, Callicles, it would be totally reasonable for me to believe that in this society anything might well happen to anyone, however it came to be. But this I also know, that if, indeed, I must come before the courts and should be in such danger as you say I am, so it shall be a bad person who has invited me thither – for no good one would inveigh against an innocent person – and I shouldn't   [d] much wonder at all if, then, I would have to die. Should I tell you why it is that I expect as much.

Calli: Oh, what the hell, finish it.

Socr: I believe that I along with just a few other Athenians, that I don't say that I'd be all alone, belabor myself with true statesmanship; and I am quite alone in furthering the matters of state at this time. As now, I don't speak to them in my oratory with a pleasing manner directed at their good feelings but, rather, with a view to the best – which is not at all pleasant – and as I refuse to concern myself with these majestic things to which you encourage me: thus, I shall   [e] not know what to bring forward for my defense before the courts and it will come to pass with me just as I said whilst speaking with Polus, namely, I shall be tried as would a doctor amongst children who was accused by the cook. For just bethink yourself, how would such a person want to defend himself if he is trapped into such a position and someone accuses him saying: "Dear children, this person has thrust upon you quite a few evils and even the youngest amongst you are not spared his corrupt and frightening deeds so that you have no idea whither you might turn for help – what with his cutting and burning, his starvation and sweating, his bitter drinks and   [a] instructions that you should hunger and suffer thirst; not at all the way in which I always have served you with so many sweets." Now, what do you think a doctor might well say if he were to be placed in such a ticklish spot? Or, should he then speak out the truth and say: "Dear children, I did all of that for the sake of your health"; what, would you well opine, what would be the cries raised by such judges? – can you hear their mighty din?

Calli: I just about can.

Socr: Wouldn't you believe, then, that he would be in the greatest quandary?

Calli: Indeed. *<78.~522b]*

Socr: Even so, I know it all too well, would be my case were I to be brought before the magistrates. For there is nothing pleasant that I should have ready at hand to bring forward and which alone they would see as restitution and good deed – though I have no jealousy of those who can create such things, nor any for those for whom such defenses are created. And if someone says: "I corrupt the youth so that they have no idea as to how they might help themselves," or says: "I abuse the elders by my bitter speeches regarding their private affairs and also the official ones," so, I would neither be able to speak the truth, namely, that I speak with right and so do everything, *[c]* namely, as the best amongst ye, ye judges; nor is there yet some other possibility, so that it is most probable that I will have to suffer whatever may come.

Calli: Can you, then, believe it – that this be good for a person that he finds himself in such a pickle within his own state and is incapable of helping himself?

Socr: If only the following be not missing, which you have often enough admitted: that he has succored himself never to have spoken or done injustice, neither against men nor against the gods. For this is, as we ourselves often have been one in admitting, the most important help that each of us can only himself accomplish. If, now, someone were able to lead me over that I would have been incapable in this, to help myself and to succor others, then I would be ashamed of myself, whether many, or a few, or just one person should do so; and if I should have to die because of this incapacity, that would make me sick. But if it would be due to a deficiency in sycophantic speechcrafting and this necessitates that I die: then you would well see, I know it for a certainty, how lightly I should bear death. *[e]* For death itself does not frighten anyone who isn't otherwise quite and totally without reason and unmanly; but unrighteousness is fearful for man. For to come into the underworld with a soul that is full of many trespasses is amongst all evils the most dreadful. If you want, I shall set it all out and explain to you how this actually correlates.

Calli: It is good, as you now have finished with the former, so now top it off with this at the end.

Socr: So hear it, then, as they tend to say, a most beauteous speech that you may well hold to be a fairy tale, as I believe you think, but I as the truth. For as fully true do I say to you what I shall say.

<79.~523a]

As then, Homer told it – Zeus, Poseidon and Pluto divided up the reign that they had inherited from their father. Now, the following law held sway for man from ye here under Cronos' reign, and it also still stands currently by the gods, that whosoever of mankind leads a righteous and pious life, he shall arrive after his death on the blessed isles and lives on there apart from evil in consummate blessedness; but he who is unrighteous and godless, he arrives in a prison for discipline and punishment that they call Tartarus. Regarding this, already under the reign of Cronos and also yet later during Zeus' reign, the living would judge the living and they sat in session on the day on which someone would die. For this reason they judged the matters poorly. Therefore, Pluto and the overseer of the blessed islands went before Zeus and told him how it was that on both sides undeserving men and women had been sent. And Zeus spoke: I will put a stop to this. For now, indeed, there are bad judgments because, said he, those who are brought in for discovery come all covered by their clothes and are thus judged, for they are judged whilst living. Now many, he said, who have a malefic soul are yet draped in beauteous bodies and shielded by relatives and encased by riches and, so, during the proceedings they bring forth witnesses who testify that they have lived righteously. In part the judges become deafened by these, in part they are themselves veiled – as indeed their souls   *[d]* are also hidden beneath their eyes, ears and their entire body. Now, all of this gets in the way, their own coverings and those of whom they judge. Thus firstly, he spoke, this must be stopped, that they preknow of their death before it happens – for now they have foreknowledge of this. And this is also spoken of by Prometheus and that he should alter it. Furthermore, henceforth they shall be judged in uncovered nakedness. Namely, only after their death are they to be judged. And the judges also shall be naked and be dead, so that they view with naked soul the naked soul of each and every – and suddenly, just as soon as each should die and is removed from all relations and shall have left all ornaments upon the earth; and so shall the judgment prove righteous. All of this I already anticipated before your arrival here, and I named my sons to be the judges, two from Asia, Minos and Rhadamanthus, and one from Europe, Aeacus. Thus these, just as soon as they shall have died, shall sit in judgment in the meadow where the three paths cross and the two ways lead on – the one toward the isles of the blessed, but the other toward Tartarus. And, verily, those from Asia shall be judged by Rhadamanthus; and those from Europe by Aeacus. But to Minos I transfer the main authority, that he may have the final decision if something should be too doubtful for these other two, so that the judgment – by which path humans shall follow – that this shall be totally just.

<80.~524b]

This, o Callicles, I hold as I have heard it, reliably for true and I would respectfully deem that the following can be inferred. Death, as I fancy it, is nothing more than the separation of two things, one from the other, of soul and body. After the two are parted from one another each of them nonetheless has practically the same qualities that it had whilst the person lived. Indeed, the body has its own unique nature and everything in which it has become practiced and all that it has run up against, all of this is quite apparent. As, for instance, if someone either by nature or through their mode of living or through both of these, if someone should have a tall body, so too his corpse is tall once he is dead; and if he were to be fat, so too his corpse is fat; and so on with all the rest; if he liked to wear his hair long, so too his corpse wears long hair. Then again, if he were to be a prison inmate and had scars and markings on his body from beatings, cuts and other wounds, so too one would find all the same markings on his corpse. And if one should have broken or misshapen limbs during one's life, so this too would be evident after death; with one word, *[d]* just as the body existed and was handled during one's lifetime and whatever was done to it, so all of this shows up likewise, at least for the greater part, for some time after one's death. The same thing, I fancy, would also pertain to the soul, o Callicles. Everything is visible on the soul once it has laid the body aside, as well that which belongs to it from its own nature as also all the alterations that result from man's endeavors regarding this and that – all of which have worked upon the soul. When it now approaches before the judge, indeed those from Asia before Rhadamanthus, so Rhadamanthus places each before himself and examines each of the souls without so much as knowing whose soul that it may be, rather quite often, if he has before him the Great King or some other noble lord or prince, so he discovers nothing healthy upon such souls, rather they are all covered with lash markings by their utterly callous perjuries and unrighteousness and, however it may be that every sort of behavior places its own stamp upon the soul, so he finds everything contorted through lies and overbearing pride, and there is nothing straight nor proper because such a soul grew up without truth, rather in all sorts of violent misdeeds and unmanly weakness, overbearing foolhardiness and a total lack of restraint in one's actions, and all of this shows on the soul that, thus, is full of misrelations and ugliness. Once he takes a look at such a one, so he sends it right off bereft of all honor toward the gates of hell where it shall have to endure whatever it has coming. This becomes apparent to everyone who *<81.~525b]* has fallen into punishment and who is being punished in a rightful manner by someone else – that either he shall himself become a

better person and is, thus, gaining an advantage, or that he serves as an example to others, that they may see his sufferings and all that he suffers and so become better out of fear, lest the same should befall them. But the first set whose punishment suffices that they receive real advantage from having undergone punishment, be it from man or from the gods, these are those whose transgressions are of such a nature that they may still be healed. Nonetheless, these achieve this advantage only through pain and torment – not only here but likewise in the nether world – for in no other way is it possible that one becomes free of unrighteousness. But for those who have taken things to extremes in their transgressions and who can no longer be healed, these are simply left as examples for the others and they themselves gain no advantage, as they are beyond help. Still, these are useful to others who see that their transgressions have led to such unspeakable agonies and torments, the frightful evil of eternal damnation set up for all to see in Hades as an example to those who have a tendency toward mischief – that they be forewarned.   *[d]*
Of these, I maintain, Archelaus shall also be such an example, if what Polus has said should be true, and whoever else should be a power monger like him. And I also presume that the greater majority of these examples are taken from the ranks of tyrants and of kings and princes, and from those who manage and control the affairs of state. For it is even such as these that are enabled due to their great power also to commit the greatest crimes and incurable transgressions. And Homer also testifies to this fact for his poetry tells us of kings and princes who are verified as suffering the eternal torments in the realm of the shades, Tantalus and Sisyphus and Tityus. But of the other less consequential, small malefactors like Thersites, who also was evil, no one has written verses that such small-fry undergo the awesome punishments in store for those who are beyond healing. For these have not had enough power that they could become such; and therefore Thersites was more fortunate than were those having such power. Rather, it is amongst the mighty, o Callicles, that the most evil of mankind are to be found. Though indeed, nothing stands in the way that an upright man mightn't also become powerful and it is verily a most joyous event when this does occur. For it is hard, o Callicles, and most worthy of praise that when one has the power to commit great injustices one nonetheless lives righteously – and of these there are only a few such examples. But still, they do exist, not only here but also in other lands, and there also shall be such people in the future, admirable men and women of virtue who rule in all to which they have been entrusted with righteousness.   *<82.~526b]*
And of this sort there is even one especially famed amongst others of

Hellas, Aristides, son of Lysimachos. But the great majority of the powerful, o noble Callicles, become evil. And what I said earlier, when Rhadamanthus encounters such a one in his purview, so he has utterly no other knowledge beyond this, not who he is, nor even whether a man or woman or from what lineage, rather just this, that he is evil; and without more ado he quickly dispatches him right off on his way to Tartarus with the designation as to whether he deems him capable of being healed or not capable of being healed – which then determines what sufferings are meet and proper, [526c] those that he shall endure when he arrives thither. But if, from time to time, he should happen upon the other soul, one that has lived a hallowed life of sanctity and of truth, someone who has lived withdrawn or howsoever else it may be, but especially I mean, o Callicles, one who is a lover of wisdom, he who has accomplished his own and who doesn't have much drive for the external trappings, so he rejoices for such a soul and sends it off to the blessed isles. And, thus too, with Aeacus. And both of these rule with a rod in hand. Only Minos, whose foresight leads onward, sits all alone and holding a golden scepter, as Homer's Odysseus fames himself in having seen him: *"adorned with a golden scepter and ruling the dead."* I, for my part, Callicles, have let myself be convinced through these *logoi* and I strive only in this: how I shall be able to present myself before judgment with the healthiest soul possible. Thus, what other people consider as being honorable, I gladly abstain from this and attempt the hunt after truth in all actuality, just as well as I am able, and to be the best in living as also, when the time to die approaches, in death; and in this I encourage all of the rest of mankind too, as well as I am able. And so I for my part also encourage you to this mode of life and to this ultimate contest, one outranking all others known to man – and I place before you the malediction of what is in store for you should you not be capable of giving succor for yourself – that when you come to stand before the judge and the sentence becomes manifest, looming before your soul and of which I just spoke; that it rather is you who stands with an open mouth and experiences a dizzy spell when you approach the bench and the judge, the son of Aegina, and he sizes you up, just as I here am helpless, and perhaps [527a] there might be someone there who gives you a punch in the face and berates you, fulminating against you in every manner. Now, perhaps you consider that this is just a fairy tale such as those that mothers give to their children and you respect it not in the least bit. And, indeed, it wouldn't be anything especial that this be met by your disdain – if only we somehow could arrive at something that proved to be better and more truthful. But now you three, you who are

nowadays the wisest amongst the people of Hellas, have affirmatively seen that you have been incompetent in demonstrating that there is some other mode by which one might live better – other than this one that also retains its reliability in the afterworld; rather, amongst all of the many speeches that have been disproved, this one alone remains standing: that one must avoid doing injustice more so than suffering from injustice and that before everything else one must strive not merely to appear to be good, rather that one is good, not only in one's particular life but in the public realm as well. But if someone should become malefic in any respect whatsoever, that he, then, should be disciplined, and that this stands as the second best possibility after that of being righteous – that one becomes righteous through punishment and thus satisfies the requirements of justice. And that one flees from all sycophancy, as well in respect to oneself as also in respect to others, be they many or just a few; and that only in this manner must one make use of speechcraft, always for what is right, and so too with all of our other capacities.   <83.~527d]
So pay heed to what I say and follow me thither, whither in arriving you shall certainly be blessed, both in life and in death – as our conversation has promised; and if someone despises you and curses you as lacking understanding, let it be and, indeed, by Zeus, let him be even if he should punch you in the face, that too may be added on, for there is naught about which your anger should be riled up if only you are in actuality noble, that you can hit the mark and you exercise in virtue. And only after first doing this and having practiced this in community with others do we want, if we should fancy it as being necessary, that we take up the matters of state or go wherever else we fancy our counsel as being beneficent, and we shall want to determine this only when we are more able to do so than we are at present. For it would be shameful of us if now in our present state, as it has become apparent that we are, if we were to brag about big issues as if we were something when we are continually incapable of being of one mind even with ourselves regarding the same subject matter, which, indeed, is the most important matter of all – so utter and complete is our incompetence. Let us then use this speech as our guide, what now has become clear to us and which shows us that this is indeed the best way of living: to exercise righteousness and all of the other virtues, thus to live and to die. This path, then, is the one that we want to follow and we call upon all others, that they do likewise; but not that other path in which you placed your trust and to which you encouraged me, for that way, o Callicles, is worthless.

****

Theaetetus

In heartfelt appreciation

Lucy Kunz

"What action, then, is good whilst reading? And what is it that makes a man a good reader? Obviously, if he learns from it."

Protagoras – *345a*

- - - -

' "Sungo," he said, "listen painstakingly, and I will tell you what I have a strong conviction about." I did as he said, for I thought he might tell me something hopeful about myself. "The career of our specie," he said, "is evidence that one imagination after another grows literal. Not dreams. Not mere dreams. I say not mere dreams because they have a way of growing actual. At school in Malindi I read all of Bulfinch. And I say not mere dream. No. Birds flew, harpies flew, angels flew, Daedalus and son flew. And see here, it is no longer dreaming and story, for literally there is flying. You flew here, into Africa. All human accomplishment has this same origin, identically. Imagination is a force in nature. Is this not enough to make a person full of ecstasy? Imagination, imagination, imagination! It converts into actual. It sustains, it alters, it redeems! You see," he said, "I sit here in Africa and devote myself to this in personal fashion, to my best ability, I am convinced. What homo sapiens imagines, he may slowly convert himself to. Oh Henderson, how glad I am that you are here! I have longed for somebody to discuss with. A companion mind. You are a godsend for me." '

Henderson, The Rain King, **Saul Bellow** [151]

---

[151] p. 244 (end of Chapt. 18);   The Viking Press, New York, 1958

Theaetetus – Sections:

Theaetetus

****

EUCLID, TERPSION

<1.~142a]

Euclid: Have you only just arrived here [in Megara], o Terpsion, or did you leave the countryside already a while ago?

Terpsion: I've been here already for quite some time and, then too, I was searching for you in the marketplace and was somewhat amazed that I wasn't able to find you there.

Euclid: That's because I wasn't even here in the city.

Terpsion: But then, where were you?

Euclid: In that I had gone down to the harbor, I met up with Theaetetus who had been brought in from the siege of Corinth to Athens.

Terpsion: Dead or alive? *[b]*

Euclid: Alive, but just barely. He was suffering terribly from a number of wounds that he had [received in the battle]; but his suffering from the malady was even more dire, the disease that has the entire army in its grasp.[152]

Terpsion: You wouldn't be meaning dysentery?

Euclid: Indeed, even this.

Terpsion: What a man is now in danger!

Euclid: Very true, one who is noble and most capable, o Terpsion! And just now I overheard a few who were praising him highly in regard to his conduct in the bloody engagement.

Terpsion: That's quite believable; rather, it would be much more amazing if he hadn't have proven himself. All the same, how does it happen that he's not convalescing here in Megara? *[c]*

Euclid: He's hurrying homeward. For I pleaded with him more than enough and gave him my advice [that he should remain here] – alone, he wouldn't hear of it. And so I went along with him and, then, as I was returning hither, I marvelled as I thought about Socrates and how, amongst all of the others, he also prophesied aright regarding Theaetetus. I believe that this must have been shortly before his own death as it was then that he first became acquainted with him. Theaetetus, then, was just reaching manhood and, so, after having been together with him and cultivating discourse Socrates expressed to me his great joy regarding Theaetetus' nature. As I had come to

---

[152] *"herrscht"* – Related to *herrlich* (translated consistently as majestic) – both have *Herr*: Lord/Sir as their root. In that knowing is the 'ruling' virtue for Plato, this bears mention; see likewise – *Sophist* 230de (p. 529). Note, *Phaedo* is the dialogue that enters into the relation between thought, philosophy and death most intimately.

Athens at that time, so he told me of the conversation that they   *[d]*
had just had, a conversation that well deserves to be heard; and so
too, he said that it wouldn't be possible that Theaetetus shouldn't
achieve distinction if only he reaches his full maturity.

Terpsion: And totally true was his speech, as it seems. All the same,
are you well able to tell me – what then, essentially, were the contents
of this conversation?   *[~143a]*

Euclid: By Zeus, certainly, at least, not so verbally. But right away at
that time I made notes regarding what had been said when I returned
home, and thereafter I reflected upon these in my leisure on
numerous occasions and, thus, I wrote it all out. And then too, every
time I came to Athens I questioned Socrates regarding whatever I
couldn't set to rights and remember properly; and so I brought things
into their proper order so that practically the whole conversation is
written down.

Terpsion: Quite right. I also have already heard from you regarding
this and have been meaning to ask you that you share it with me, but
[till now] it never came to pass. Alone, what hinders us from going
through it all? In any event it's also paramount that I take things easy
now – since I myself have only just come back from an outing in the
countryside.   *[b]*

Euclid: I too could use the rest since I've only just returned from
accompanying Theaetetus as far as Erineum. So let's go now, and in
that we take care to rest our limbs together the [slave] boy might read
it to us.

Terpsion: Well spoken.

   [Entrance into Euclid's home.]

Euclid: This here, then, Terpsion, is the book. But I've composed
the speech in such a format *{Gestalt}* – not as if Socrates were to be
relating the conversation to me as, indeed, he did relate it, but
rather so, as if he actually were speaking to those whom he named as
his interlocutors.   But those he named were the geometrician
{Meßkünstler}, Theodorus, and Theaetetus. And then, so that this
written composition isn't burdened unduly by constant references *[c]*
to who said what, as when Socrates was telling me the conversation
he spoke: "Then I said" and "To this I replied," and of the other
person answering: "He admitted as much" or "To this he didn't want
to agree" – therefore I wrote it down as if it were the immediate
dialogue of Socrates, leaving off all these other things.

Terpsion: Not bad at all, Euclid.

Euclid: So take up the book, boy, and read.

SOCRATES, THEODORUS, THEAETETUS

<2.~143d]

Socr: If it were to be that I especially concerned myself about your countrymen, the residents of Cyrene, o Theodorus, so I would question you regarding them and how matters stand over there: whether there might be a few amongst the youths there who are directing their labors and taking pains in the study of arithmetic *{die Größenlehre}* or into some other field of intellectual inquiry. But now, as my love falls more on the Athenians than to these others and as I hedge an especial desire to know who amongst our youth shall in all probability become most renowned – that, thus, this is an area in which I do desire to do my research – so it is that I've inquired of others, namely of those around whom I have seen our youth happily congregating. And about you, too, I have noticed quite a few congregating, just as you well deserve for so many reasons and   *[e]* particularly due to your knowledge of geometry. If, then, you have met up with such a one, someone deserving special mention, so I wish that you might let me know just who this might be.

Theo: Quite, Socrates, there's nothing holding me back from gladly telling you what you are wanting to hear – the one youngster whom I have discovered amongst *the sons of the Athenians.* For if, perhaps, if he were to be a *beaut* – so then I too might be fearful of telling you about him in that someone might come to the opinion that I hedged some sentimental attachment toward him. But now, and don't get mad at me, he's not in the least bit beautiful, rather he's just like you with an upturned nose and protruding eyes, only he doesn't have these traits to the same degree as you. Brazen, thus, is my speech – and so, know it: that amongst everyone with whom I ever have been acquainted, and I've already had very many congregating around me, still, I have never met up with anyone whose worthiness so amazed me on account of their nature. For that someone who comprehends matters quickly, those matters regarding which the others comprehend only with difficulty, and then to be distinguished equally by an even-tempered disposition and, beyond all this, to have more persistence than the others, such a person I didn't believe to exist and, indeed, I haven't met anyone else of whom the same could be said. Rather, those who have keen minds, are quick-witted and whose memories are good, such as these tend as well to be quick-tempered and are easily driven this way and that, like a ship lacking the   *[b]* proper ballast and, then too, their natures make them rather fervent instead of their having persistence. But then, those who are of a more even-tempered keel, these show themselves to a certain extent to be slow learners and, indeed, as being very forgetful. But he of whom I speak advances so easily and confidently to success in acquiring knowledge *{Kenntnissen}* of all subjects and works through every investigation, and all the while with such a calm composure and even disposition – just as oil spreads itself evenly and quietly over a pool of water – that it's quite astounding how he manages at such a young age to come to grips in such a manner and with so many things.

Socr: Your report couldn't be any more excellent! But to which family amongst the Athenians can this youth belong?   *[~144c]*

Theo: Indeed, I've heard the name – but for now it has slipped my mind. Singularly, he's amongst those who even now are approaching us, the middle boy. For then, he and his friends have just anointed themselves outside of the gymnasium here and now it seems that being finished with putting on the oil, so they're coming this way to see us. Thus, take a look, whether or not you recognize him.

Socr: Indeed, I do: that is Euphronius' son whose deme is Sunium; a man, friend, who himself even fit your description and, then too, he was greatly respected and left quite a large inheritance *{Vermögen}*. But, the name of the boy, this I don't know.   *[d]*

Theo: His name is Theaetetus. In the meanwhile his guardians have quickly run through the inheritance so that very little of it remains. But, all the same, in respect to money his attitude, again, is quite noble, so that this too is a matter of wonder.

Socr: Now your praise of the boy is majestic! So, do call him over, that he might sit down here with us.

Theo: I shall do so. *Theaetetus*, come over here, to Socrates.

Socr: Indeed, by all means, Theaetetus, so that I might take a look at myself and view the essential characteristics of my own face. For then, Theodorus has told me that yours resembles my own. Be that as it may, if it were to be so that both of us would have lyres and Theodorus would have said that they were tuned to the same key, *[e]* would we believe him right away regarding this? – or wouldn't we first investigate as to whether Theodorus was informed regarding musical tones, that he would be able to make such an assertion?

Theae: We would investigate into this.

Socr: Hence, if we should discover that he was such a person, then we'd believe him; but if not and he was bereft of this art, then we would remain unconvinced?

Theae: That's right.

Socr: But now, at least it's my opinion that should we want to be certain as regards the similarity of our facial characteristics so we'd have to take a look into whether Theodorus is a portrait painter and, thus, is able to make an assertion regarding such matters.   *[145a]*

Theae: It seems so to me.

Socr: Well now, is Theodorus a painter?
Theae: No, not that I know.
Socr: Nor a geometer?
Theae: Indeed, Socrates, by all means he is.
Socr: Perhaps as well someone who is well informed of astronomy, mathematics and harmonics – and everything else which goes along with such erudite pursuits?
Theae: I think so.
Socr: Thus, if he says that we resemble one another in some bodily characteristic – and whether this would be said in praise or derision – so, it doesn't really mean all that much?
Theae: No, perhaps not.   *[b]*
Socr: But, how now? – if he were to praise one of us in our soul in respect to virtue and wisdom, wouldn't it be incumbent, on the one hand, that he who heard such praise, that he be ready to take a good look at the person who was praised and, on the other hand, that this person be ready to display himself?
Theae: In all ways, o Socrates.   *<3.~145]*
Socr: So, accordingly, it falls upon you that you display yourself, but for me that I take a good look at you. For you need only know this: that although Theodorus has praised many of his students to me, never once has he praised any of them to such an extent as he just praised you.
Theae: That would be majestic, Socrates. Only do look out, perhaps he's only speaking in jest.   *[c]*
Socr: But Theodorus isn't that type. Hence, don't take his admission back beneath this excuse, that he'd only be speaking in jest – so that he shan't be forced into submitting his evidence in accordance to protocol – for then, certainly no one would accuse *him* of bearing false witness. That rather you remain reconciled with your earlier admission, this is preferable.
Theae: I shall well have to do so, since you opine it.
Socr: So tell me, then, have you learned something of geometry from Theodorus?
Theae: Oh, sure.   *[d]*
Socr: And also regarding starlore, harmonics and making calculations? [153]
Theae: At least, I've been making efforts to do so.

---

[153] The "knowledge arts" are spoken of in *Phaedrus* as a gift of the god, Theuth, who delievered: "numbers and calculation, then also the measuring arts and starlore; furthermore board games and dice throwing and, then, the letters of the alphabet." 274d (p. 69).

Socr: I too, o youth, have been taking pains to learn from this teacher and from others as well – those in whom I have trust that they have some understanding. But, all the same, despite that for the rest I'm quite up in my knowledge regarding these things, still, I have doubts regarding a small matter regarding which I'd like to investigate together with you and these others.[154] So tell me, then, isn't that called learning when one becomes better informed regarding whatever it is that one learns?

Theae: How else?

Socr: And those who are informed, I believe, are informed by knowledge?

Theae: Yes.

Socr: And this is nothing other than cognition *{Erkenntnis}* – [or having recognized whatever it may be]?

Theae: What's this?   *[145e]*

Socr: Knowledge. Or, isn't it so: that one is cognizant of that whereof one is informed?

Theae: How else [could it be]?

Socr: Hence, this is 'one and the same' *{einerlei}* – knowledge and cognition? [155]

Theae: Yes.

Socr: This is even that regarding which I'm in such a quandary, what I'm not able by myself to explain adequately and to put upon a solid foundation, knowledge – what actually might this well be itself. Shouldn't we be able to determine this? What do you two say?   *[a]* Who of us wants to go first? But if he should fail – and so too each time whoever it may be who fails – he, just as the youngsters call it when they're playing ball together, he should sit down as the donkey. But whoever doesn't fail but proves victorious and carries the day, he shall be our king and dictate to us what our tasks in learning shall be, whatever he might want. – – But, why are you both so quiet? – I'm not becoming overbearing due to my passion for speeches, Theodorus, in that I've brought things to this juncture, that such a

---

[154] Compare with *Protagoras* 328e (p. 130) – " a small matter," and footnote #108 (p. 211).

[155] In German – *Wissen und Erkenntnis*; in Greek – *sofia* and *episteme*. What, I would assert, is being pointed to is the faculty of knowing vs. concrete instantiations of knowledge. I might point out that these are not 'one and the same' – although they are essentially related. The different words for knowledge: acquaintance *kennen;* recognition and cognition *erkennen;* to know *wissen;* wisdom *Weißheit* – are a constant challenge for the translator. In general I've settled on *cognition* for *Erkenntnis*, although there are instances where nothing short of *knowledge* fits the bill. It may be remarked that this is a continuum and the precise demarcation of the limits of these words differs in English, German and Greek – where (I would presume) Greek has the most overlap and English the least.

conversation might come to be amongst us and that we relate as friends one to the other and, so, become better acquainted?

Theo: In no way, Socrates, that this would be overly   *[~146b]* burdensome. Rather, you just ask one of these youngsters here, that he might answer your questions, for I'm not at all used to speaking in this manner and for me to become accustomed to it, for this I'm already too old and no longer have the time. But these are well able to do so and it would only be for their own good and serve them well for their future unfolding. For when one is young, it is true, one can develop in all ways. So don't let up a bit from Theaetetus, rather, just as you began with him so do continue on with your questioning.

Socr: You do hear, Theaetetus, what Theodorus has said, that in which you won't want to disappoint him, isn't it so. And, then too, it wouldn't be becoming for a youngster that when a wise man encourages him to accomplish some task, that he wouldn't be obedient to his wishes.

– And so tell me, then, direct and brazen: what do you think that knowledge is?

Theae: I'll have to answer you, Socrates, since indeed, you both have requested it of me. For, in any event, even if I should fail, you'll set things right.

Socr: Quite, in as far as this lies in our power.   *<4.~146d]*

Theae: I believe then, that, on the one side, all of the matters that one is capable of learning from Theodorus are parts of knowledge, namely geometry and all the others that you have named, and then too, on the other side, cobbling shoes and all the professional arts of the other handworkers, all of these seem to me to be nothing other than knowledge.

Socr: Most generous and full of presents, dear one, do you when asked about one thing come with all sorts of things and a multitude instead of just something simple.

Theae: How's that? – what do you mean with this, Socrates?

Socr: Perhaps nothing, but what I'm opining, this I will clarify for you. When you say cobbling shoes, do you mean with this anything else other than the knowledge of how one goes about making shoes?

Theae: Nothing other.   *[e]*

Socr: And when you say carpentry, do you mean anything other than that knowledge, how one works with wood and the manufacture of wooden objects?

Theae: That too is true.

Socr: In both instances, then, you determine *of what* knowledge exists?

Theae: Yes.

Socr: But I wasn't asking you about this, regarding of what matters knowledge might exist, nor too, how many such there might be. For we were asking not with the intent of counting them all up, but rather that we get a grasp on knowledge itself, what it well might be. Or, am I saying nothing?

Theae: Indeed, you're totally right. *[~147a]*

Socr: Weigh this into your considerations as well. If someone were to ask us about something that is quite commonplace *{gemein}* [and of a low order], perhaps regarding clay,¹⁵⁶ what would clay be? – and then we were to answer him that there would be clay for potters and clay for puppet-makers and clay for the artisans who lay out tile, wouldn't we make ourselves absurd?

Theae: Well, perhaps.

Socr: In the first instance, namely, because we would believe that the questioner would be able to gain an understanding of the matter due to our answer – if then, we were to say, as it was again, clay; and whether or not we were to add on to this, be it the clay of the *[b]* puppet-maker or whichever handworker you'd like. Or, do you believe that someone might understand some particular pointing-out of a thing, someone who doesn't know what that thing is?

Theae: No, not at all.

Socr: So too, then, he wouldn't have any understanding about shoes, he who doesn't at all understand what knowledge is.

Theae: No, indeed not.

Socr: And, then too, what the art of shoe cobbling is, or any other art? – he wouldn't understand this, he who doesn't know what knowledge is?

Theae: No, indeed not.

Socr: Hence, it would be a comical and an absurd answer if after being asked, what knowledge is, one were to answer by naming some particular arts. For then, he'd be answering by means of knowledge of something without having been asked regarding this. *[c]*

Theae: So it seems.

Socr: For, then too, since he's able to answer straightforwardly and concisely, nonetheless he describes a never-ending path. Thus, as it was with the question about clay, he could have answered in a non-round-about manner and simply say that clay would be earth mixed up with a moist substance and, then, for whom clay might be useful, all of this he'd leave off. *<5.~147]*

---

¹⁵⁶ As Schleiermacher maintains: there is nothing in Plato which isn't full of meaning – so here too, as clay is that which *binds* things together. Note too the play with "gemein" – *Parmenides* 130c–130e.

Theae: Now, o Socrates, it appears as an easy question. You may well be asking in a similar manner, just as it recently happened in   *[d]* our lessons; namely with me and your namesake, this [boy] Socrates.
Socr: To what, then, are you referring?
Theae: Regarding the sides of square areas Theodorus was drawing on the blackboard and showing us something – in that he proved to us that the squares containing an area of three square feet and five square feet, that the sides of such squares have a length which is incommensurate with the unit of one foot. And so he went through each and every one up to the square having seventeen square feet – and by this one he stopped and held back, reflecting inwardly. Then, something came to us – as the number of square areas seemed to be infinitely many, we wanted to make the attempt to bring them all together into one through which we'd be able to demonstrate all of them.   *[e]*
Socr: And, were you able to discover something?
Theae: At least, I think so; but just take a look and see what you think.
Socr: Tell me.
Theae: We separated all the numbers as a totality into two parts. Those which are able to be generated *{entstehen* [come-to-be]*}* when you multiply the same by the same, these we named square numbers and even-sided and we likened them to the shape of a square.
Socr: Very good.   *[~148a]*
Theae: The others that lie in between these, to which three and five belong and every number which is incapable of being generated by multiplying some number by itself, those, rather, that are generated by multiplying a larger number by one which is smaller or a smaller number by one which is larger, those in short that are always encompassed by a larger and a smaller side, these we named oblong numbers – likening them to the oblong shapes that represent them.
Socr: On the mark. But, what's next?
Theae: All of the lines, now, which build up a square area in the plane and are of like measurement, these we named lengths; but those having unequal measures, these we named powers *{Kräfte}* – because, namely, they can't themselves be measured in a   *[b]* commensurate way as the others are; though, indeed, the areas in the plane that they have the power of generating are measurable. Something similar obtains as well with the three-dimensional numbers [solids].
Socr: Right in the bull's-eye, you boys! Now, certainly, Theodorus shall never be punished for failing in that he delivers false testimony.

Theae: But still, Socrates, I'm not able to give you such an answer in reply to your question about knowledge, one like this one that I've provided regarding lengths and powers, although you – at least, as it seems to me – you are seeking for something similar, so that, indeed, Theodorus seems perhaps to have failed us in getting this right.   *[c]*

Socr: How's that? – if he had praised you as a runner and would have said that he'd never encountered a youth who could run so fast, and then you should be beaten in a race by someone who was a fully-trained professional, and one of the fastest, would you then believe that his praise of you would thereby be one whit the less right?

Theae: No, not that.

Socr: And do you, then, believe that knowledge, just so as I mean to be speaking of it, do you believe that discovering what this is, that this would be something trivial; but isn't it rather so that this belongs as being one of the most arduous tasks?

Theae: By Zeus, amongst the most difficult of all, I believe.

Socr: Then for your own sake be of a good spirit and do believe it, that Theodorus is well right in this. And so make the effort, just as you do with the other things, so particularly as regards knowledge, that you find out how to clarify knowledge, what it actually is.   *[~d]*

Theae: In as much as this depends upon my making the effort, it well shall come to light.

Socr: So come now, as then you've already made a very good presentation, so make an attempt that you use this earlier account of the sides of squares as a blueprint, that you imitate this and just as with these, and no matter how many of them there may be, so you've brought them all together underneath one concept and, so too, do the same for the multitude of things about which there is knowledge, that you describe them all with one clarification.   *<6.~148e]*

Theae: Only you should know, Socrates, that I've often made the attempt to do just this and to find this out, since I had heard this question that you were asking circulating around. But, I'm yet incapable of persuading myself that I've sufficiently thought things through; nor too, I haven't heard anyone else clarify this matter so as you are exacting. But, all the same, I can't help myself: that I'm unable to stop from continually pondering over this.

Socr: You are having birthing pains, dear Theaetetus, because you're not empty, rather you're going about with this weighing upon you.

Theae: I don't know what you're talking about, but I told you what my experience is.

Socr: Thus, you ludicrous boy, you've probably never heard tell   *[a]* that I'm the son of a midwife, one who was quite famed and handled matters in her own way.

Theae: Indeed, I have already heard as much.

Socr: And perhaps, this as well, that I also practice this same art – have you heard this too?

Theae: No, this I haven't heard at all.

Socr: Well then, know it – this is how matters stand. But don't go off blabbing this to the others for nobody else knows this about me, friend, that I possess this art. And as now the people don't know about this, so too they don't say anything about this matter – but then, they do say that I'm the most amazing character of all men and that I lead everybody else into doubt and perplexity. Certainly you've heard this about me?

Theae: From all different sides. [149b]

Socr: Shall I tell you the underlying reason for this?

Theae: Please do.

Socr: If you'll just carefully consider everything about midwives, how everything relates with them, then it shall be easier for you to take note of what it is that I'm getting at. For then, you have noticed that there is no one who delivers babies so long as she herself might become pregnant and carry a child to term, rather, only those who are no longer capable of giving birth are midwives.

Theae: Indeed, so it is.

Socr: This should – as I've heard tell – stem from Artemis, because she, she who was herself incapable of bearing children, she [c] nonetheless did partake in helping others in giving birth. Now, indeed, she wasn't able to bestow this art of midwifery upon those who always were barren because human nature is too weak that it might achieve an art of those things in which it has no experience. But still, she was well able to bestow this gift upon those who no longer bear children due to their age, so that even by this similarity with Artemis herself, by this such a distinction, thus, is made manifest.

Theae: That seems plausible.

Socr: And isn't this also plausible and necessary: whether or not someone is pregnant – this is something that midwives are better at recognizing than the others.

Theae: Very much so.

Socr: And it's also true that the midwives are capable of arousing labor pains through the means of medicinal compounds and by [d] magical incantations and, then, if they should want to they can also cause these pangs to abate; and then too, they are able to help those give birth who have great difficulties in delivery or, not to forget, if these have decided against carrying the child to term and to be rid of it, they are able to abort it provided that the infant is still extremely small.

Theae: So it is.

Socr: Have you also taken notice of this regarding the midwives: that they are also the most adept matchmakers in their under-standing of the fundamentals of how one differentiates as regards which women would have to bind themselves to which men so that their offspring shall be most consummate, this being the goal.

Theae: This is something about which I didn't have any idea. *[~e]*

Socr: Well then, know it: that in this their knowledge is yet greater than as regards how one goes about cutting off the umbilical cord. And just reflect upon this. Do you believe that as regards the tending to the fruit, if this were contrasted with the harvesting of the crops of the earth and, then again, that insight as regards which soil should be trusted for the best cultivation of each and every seedling and plant, do you believe that this belongs to one and the same profession, or to different arts?

Theae: No, rather this all belongs to one art.

Socr: But with the women, do you believe that the underlying issue is different and, thus, that the harvesting would belong to yet another profession?

Theae: That, at least, doesn't seem probable. *[150a]*

Socr: Quite improbable and, thus, it's rather so that only due to the improper and inartistic methods of bringing men and women together which has acquired the [despicable] name, pandering – it's only due to this that the midwives have given up in their free practice of the same, because, namely, they are noble and are fearful that they might fall into suspicion in the one area due to problems in the other. For, in all actuality, it falls only to those who are true mid-wives, to these and these alone, that the proper manner of marriage is upheld.

Theae: Obviously. *[~b]*

Socr: So much can be said about midwifery in itself, though this only approximates what I'm alluding to in my playful way. For then, with these women it does *not* happen that for the greatest part they, indeed, are bringing forth genuine *{ächte* [157]*}* children and from time to time also monstrosities and that the two would be difficult to distinguish. For if this were to be the case, so certainly then, the most beauteous and greatest art of midwives would be the distinguishing of what is right and what isn't. Or, don't you believe me?

---

[157] Compare to *Phaedrus* 276a (p. 71).

Theae: Indeed, I believe it. <7.~150]

Socr: Regarding my art of midwifery, now, everything that I said would be valid just as with the above, but it differs in these respects – that, namely, it helps men in giving birth and not women and, moreover, its burden is the tending for pregnant souls, not bodies. But the greatest thing about our art is this: that it is in a position *[c]* to test and to prove as to whether the soul of the youth is headed in the direction of giving birth to something that is misshapen and false, or whether it's structurally sound and genuine. And, it's true, also as regards the following the same applies to me as well as to the midwives, that I don't myself give birth to wisdom – and it is this about which so many people have badgered me, that, indeed, my specialty is asking questions but that I don't myself give any answers because I wouldn't have anything clever to say – and in this they are quite right. But the underlying cause of this is as follows: God requires of me that I accomplish this help in birthing, but He prohibits me from bringing forth anything of my own. Hence, I am not myself somehow wise in any manner and I don't have anything of this sort to display, something born from out of my own soul. *[d]* But those who congregate about me, indeed, at first they show themselves in part as being quite unteachable, but thereafter, if they hold out for a longer duration, then all those whom God allows make astoundingly rapid progress, as it seems not only to themselves but likewise to others; and this, obviously, without their ever having learned anything from me, rather simply from out of themselves they discover much that is beauteous, and they hold on to it firmly; and all the while it is God and I who accomplish this midwifery. This is brought to light by the following. There have been many who didn't recognize this and who gave the credit for their progress just to themselves, and so they became disdainful of my company – or be it that they let others persuade them that they should split off from me earlier than was right. Then, after such separation, and in part due to the bad influence of the society they kept, they only experienced miscarriages and, then too, they managed to lose all of their earlier offspring due to their neglect and also due to the greater respect that they bestowed upon their more recent misshapen and inauthentic offspring, more than they paid to their genuine births, those that they had had as they were yet in my company. But finally it advanced to the point that neither did they understand themselves, nor yet could anyone else make any sense of them – and one such as this was Aristides, Lysimachus' son; and then, there were many *[151a]* others as well. If, then, they should again return to me and solicit my company, and it's a wonder what they don't stoop to that they might be allowed to return, well, the divine sign tends often enough to contravene and keeps me from having any more contact with quite a few of these, but then, others find acceptance and these take matters up again. And with those who walk the path alongside of me, these have experiences that are similar to expectant mothers – that, namely, they experience torments and don't want to be left alone and be it day or night; and, indeed, they're even yet far more trouble than the former. And my art is able to quiet these torments just as it also may arouse them. Thus, this is how matters stand with these [my adherents]. But from time to time, o Theaetetus, when a few of these no longer appear as being pregnant, such of whom I know that they are no longer in need of my attentions, so it's my business that I freely and willfully parcel these out to others – and may God vouchsafe my judgment, I decide as best as I am able as regards to whom I might send them, whose society would prove to be most advantageous for them – and, indeed, quite a few I've sent to Prodicus. But then, many others I've sent to other wise men or to others, to people who are inspired by divine agency. Now, I have told you all of this in such *[c]* detail, most worthy, because I have a premonition that you too are carrying something – just as you yourself admitted – that, namely, you are having birthing pangs. So put yourself underneath my care as I am a midwife's son and am myself also informed regarding these matters and, so, whatever it may be that I should ask you, make every effort to answer my queries, just as well as you are able. And if during the investigation I discover that something that you have said should be a monstrosity, some aberration which is not genuine and, thus, I take it away from you and throw it away as refuse, so don't allow yourself to become upset as the women tend to do should their first pregnancy end badly. For already there have been many, my virtuous Theaetetus, who have broken out in anger when I've removed some farce and, indeed, they would have liked to have bitten me; and they don't want to believe it, that I do so in their better interest – and also because they're yet far from having the insight that there is no God who is not favorably disposed toward humanity and that I do as I do not because I want evil, that, rather, it is forbidden for me to act in any other way, that I might allow falsity to masquerade as being valid or that I would allow the truth to be struck down.   *<8.~151d2]*

– Thus, make the attempt once more, beginning at the beginning, o Theaetetus, that you say what knowledge is. But that you're incapable of doing this, never say this. For in that God wants this and in that you are valiant *{wacker}*, you shall well be able to do so.

Theae: Indeed, Socrates, if you speak to me in such a way it would be shameful of me were I not in every wise to answer you courageously and to say just what I have. Thus, it seems to me that whoever *[e]* knows something, he perceives what he knows, and so, as it appears now to me: knowledge is nothing other than perception.

Socr: Good and valiant, youth. So one must make oneself clear, whoever clarifies something. Tallyho, let's you and me take a good look at this together, whether it's a proper baby or just an empty shell full of hot air. Perception, you say, this is knowledge?

Theae: Yes.   *[~152a]*

Socr: And it seems that you haven't done poorly at all in your clarification regarding knowledge, that rather you've given the same answer as Protagoras – only that he expressed himself in a different way in his pronouncements. Namely, he said that: *"Man is the measure of all things, of those that are, how they are; of those that are not, how they are not."* You have read this, haven't you?

Theae: On many occasions I have read it.

Socr: And, isn't it true, he meant this so: that as each and every thing appears to me, such too is it for me; and as it appears to you, such, as well, is it for you. For you as well as I – each of us is a man?

Theae: That's what he meant, there's no arguing about this.   *[b]*

Socr: And, indeed, it's most probable that a man who is so wise doesn't speak foolishness. Let's follow along after him. Shall not from time to time, in that the same wind is blowing, shall not the one of us be chilled, but not the other? – or one of us a little bit, the other very much so?

Theae: Yes, quite.

Socr: And should we in this instance say that the wind in and of itself is cold, or isn't cold? Or shouldn't we believe Protagoras, that the wind is colder for the one of us who's chilled but not for the one who isn't?

Theae: So, this is how it would well have to be.

Socr: And so, indeed, the wind appears to each and every as one of both.

Theae: Indeed.

Socr: And this appearing is even this, perception.

Theae: So it is.   *[c]*

Socr: Appearance, thus, and perception are the same in consideration of warmth and everything that is similar to this. For just as each of us perceives, so too it appears for each one of us to be.

Theae: Apparently.

Socr: Perception, thus, is always of that which is *{des Seienden}* and is not deceptive – if, then, it affirmatively is knowledge.

Theae: So it seems.

Socr: Now, perhaps – by the graces – Protagoras was quite excessive in his wisdom and, so, he indicated the matter to us but darkly and through a great deal of fog, but he spoke to his students in secret [158] and put things aright.

Theae: But, how so? – Socrates, how do you mean this?   [d]

Socr: I shall tell you. This isn't a bad speech at all, that, namely, nothing at all is something definite in and of itself and that, therefore, you're not able to predicate of anything rightfully whatever attribute it may be; that, much rather, if you call something big,[159] still, it shall also display itself as being small; and if heavy, also light; and so in an equal manner regarding everything, that there is nothing that is either one having-been {*Ein gewesenes*} nor too of some particular quality {*irgend wie beschaffen*}; that rather through movement and change and mixing everything amongst one another only becomes – about which we say that it is – in that we don't   [e] designate it properly; for never really 'is' anything at all, rather everything only always becomes. And regarding this it may well be that the entire line of wise men, excepting Parmenides, are unified: Protagoras as well as Heraclitus and Empedocles and, then as well regarding the poets, the representatives of both manners of poetry, Epicharmus for the comic and Homer representing the tragic, for when Homer says that he views Oceanus as the father and Tethys the mother, so he's indicating that everything has sprung out of flux and from movement. Or, doesn't it seem to you that this is what he was meaning?

Theae: Quite, to me also.   <9.~153a]

Socr: Who, now – who would well be allowed to argue something against such an army? – and with Homer standing at its head! – who might do so without making himself ludicrous?

Theae: It isn't an easy matter, o Socrates.

Socr: Certainly not, Theaetetus. And, on top of all of this, there also are other sufficient proofs for this assertion, that, namely, in all instances what seems to be and all becoming, these are caused by movement, but that non-being and destruction are caused by rest. For then, once again, it is warmth and fire that generate the other things and hold them in order, and they themselves are generated by revolution and by rubbing together, but these are movements. Or, aren't these the ways by which fire comes to be?

Theae: Indeed, they are.   [b]

---

[158] Compare to *Protagoras* 342c – the secret gatherings of the sophists (p. 145).

[159] *Parmenides* – see footnote #108, 130d (p. 211).

Socr: Furthermore, all species of living being spring up into life as well from even such causes as these.

Theae: How else?

Socr: And, how now? – the entire condition of the body, shall it not degenerate through inactivity and rest, but isn't it best maintained through physical exercise and movement?

Theae: Yes.

Socr: And it's even so with the condition of the soul, doesn't it tend to acquire knowledge through learning and by mental exertion, these being sorts of movement, and thus it gets a firm grasp and becomes better; but then, through inactivity that shows itself as   *[153c]* thoughtlessness and lethargy, through these things not only doesn't it learn anything, rather too it forgets what it already has learned.

Theae: Absolutely.

Socr: Movement, thus, is what is good for both body and soul; and the opposite is the contrary to this?

Theae: So it seems.

Socr: And should I yet bring up the matter of dead calms, doldrums and of everything that is similar to this, how in all of these cases stillness has the effect of stagnation and destruction, but that the opposite encourages steadfastness. And, even beyond all of this, as the final stone upon this edifice of proof: that when Homer speaks of *the golden chain* he understands under this nothing other than the sun and, thus, he's pointing out that so long as the entire heavens are in motion and the sun revolves, just so long too shall everything remain well with the gods and with mankind; but if ever this should come to a standstill, so, then too everything would cease-to-be and be undermined and, as they say, the lowest would become raised up as the highest?   *<10.~153]*

Theae: For me, Socrates, it seems that this is what he is indicating, just as you say.

Socr: Thus, think about the matter, most worthy, so: first, in relation to the eyes and what you call the color white – that this itself isn't something particular outside of your eyes, nor too in your eyes;   *[e]* and, then too, that you don't determine it to be in any particular place – for, if you were to do so then it would have to be somewhere and persist and, so, it wouldn't simply become in its coming-to-be.

Theae: But, how's this?

Socr: Just following the proposition that was stated above – that nothing is in and of itself one determinate – and it shall become clear to us that black and white and each and every other color is generated by the convergence and striking together of the eyes with those movements which belong to them;[160] and that which on every occasion we call color, neither shall this be that which impacts, *[a]* nor that which is impacted, but rather a particular coming-to-be between each of these. Or, would you like to assert that every color, just as it appears to you, even thus shall it appear to a dog? or to any other animal?

Theae: By Zeus, I wouldn't want to make *that* assertion.

Socr: But how? – does anything at all appear to some other person exactly even so as it does to you? Are you right certain about this? or much rather of the contrary, that things don't even appear to you yourself as being the same, since you never are totally related in an identical way.

Theae: I'd fancy the latter sooner than the former. *[154b]*

Socr: Hence, if what you are measuring or touching would be large or red or warm, so then it couldn't be through this, that it would meet up with an other, through this it wouldn't become something other in that it hasn't itself been altered at all. But if, once again, that which was measuring or touching would be one of each of these, so it wouldn't be able – if it should come upon some other object or something else would meet up with the former ones, in that all along nothing would come up against it itself – all the same it couldn't become an other. For then, friend, it would be required of us that we would have to give in and console ourselves to asserting things that are amazing and ludicrous, just as Protagoras and everyone else who wants to assert the same as he would contend against us.

Theae: But, how's that? – and essentially what things do you mean?

Socr: Just take a small example and you shall know everything *[c]* that I mean. Six beans, if you hold four up against them, shall be more than the four, namely, half as many more, but if compared to twelve, then less, namely, half as many; and one is not allowed even once to suffer that anything else shall be asserted. Or, would you like to suffer it?

Theae: Me? – No, not in any way.

Socr: How now, if Protagoras or anyone else asked you: Is it well possible, Theaetetus, that something became larger or greater in some other manner than that it has grown? – what shall you answer?

Theae: If I, o Socrates, should answer this question alone in *[d]* respect to what seems to me as being right, then I shall say – this isn't possible; but if, then, in respect to what you have just said, so, in order to protect myself from saying something that is contradictory, I might well answer that, indeed, it would be possible.

---

[160] Compare to *Meno* 76cd – Gorgias' and Empedocles' theory of color (p. 470).

Socr: Very good, friend, by Hera, and totally divine. Nonetheless, as it seems to me, if you answer that it would be possible then with you it would be similar as one reads in Euripedes: that the tongue, indeed, wouldn't be caught in a contradiction but, then again, the soul would.

Theae: Totally true.

Socr: If, then, we were to rank amongst those men who are mighty in their wisdom, you and I, with those, namely, who have carried through the proofs of *the all* within their souls, so now it would be the case that simply as a matter of passing the time we'd attempt to outdo one another and, so, in a sophistic manner we'd start to battle with one another and each of us would jump ahead of the other with his own speech. But now, as we're only common folk, so we'll want first that we take a good look at the matter in itself, how it may well be constituted, that which we're asserting – whether it's in harmony and in agreement with itself or, perhaps, not in the least bit.   *<11.~154e3]*

Theae: I, for myself, would prefer the latter method in all cases.

Socr: And certainly, so too do I. Since this is how things correlate, are we well able to do anything else other than with utmost composure and being amply at leisure, that thus we investigate   *[a]* once more into this matter beginning again at the beginning and not becoming in the least bit annoyed, that rather we stand up to the test and prove ourselves – what, indeed, are all of these appearances actually for us, of which, now, we firstly shall investigate, at least as I believe, and shall say that never shall anything at all become either more or less, neither in mass nor in number, so long as it is equal to itself. Isn't it so?

Theae: Yes.

Socr: Secondly, as well – that that to which nothing has either been added or taken away, such shall neither grow nor diminish, that rather it shall always remain equal.

Theae: That's totally apparent.   *[b]*

Socr: Not also, thirdly – that, namely, whatever was not formerly, that it's impossible for this to be later without having have become and be becoming?

Theae: So it seems, indeed.

Socr: Now these three assertions are struggling with one another in our souls when we speak as we did earlier in respect to the beans – or if we should assert that I, I who have a definite size and in that I have neither grown nor suffered any diminution within the span of a year, that now, indeed, I'm larger than you who are younger, but hereafter smaller – since, indeed, I haven't lost anything at all in my mass but only due to the circumstance that you've grown. For then, I am afterwards what I wasn't earlier on without having become it.

For without becoming it's impossible to have become and since I haven't lost anything in mass, I shall never have become smaller. And with thousands upon thousands of other matters the correlation holds – if we want to allow that this be valid. You're following me, aren't you, Theaetetus? – at least, it seems to me that you're not lacking experience in these things.

Theae: Truly – by the gods – Socrates, I'm astounded most uncommonly, how, indeed – *how* all of this may well be; and sometimes if I focus properly on all of this I end up by getting terribly dizzy.

Socr: Theodorus, o dear one {*du Lieber*}, has judged your   *[d]* nature totally aright. For even this is the condition of someone who is a friend of wisdom, astonishment; and truly – there doesn't exist any other wellspring of philosophy other than this, and whoever it was who said that Iris would be the daughter of Thaumas, this person seems to have struck the proper chord in his delineation. But, do you already have an inward grasp on these things according to which, as we have said, Protagoras asserts: how it is possible that this actually correlates – or, are you still not quite there yet?

Theae: I'm still lacking a bit, I'd warrant.

Socr: Well then, you'll be grateful to me if I should help you in sniffing out the right meaning, what is concealed in the opinions of this man or, I should say, of all of these many men who are so renowned.   *<12.~155e]*

Theae: How could I be anything else other than grateful – and indeed, very grateful!

Socr: But do look about and take heed, that no one who's uninitiated should be listening in. But then, these are those who won't believe that anything at all would have being unless it should be that they might right heartily grasp it in both of their hands; but of process and of becoming and of everything else that is invisible, such [matters] as these they absolutely won't allow as valid and qualify such as being.

Theae: These are really obstinate and unmanageable people, Socrates, of whom you are speaking.   *[156a]*

Socr: Quite, my child – and the proper adjective would be crass. Much worthier, however, are these others whose secrets I should like to share with you. But as to the beginning upon which everything else depends and of which we spoke earlier, with all of them the beginning is this: that everything is in motion and outside of motion there is nothing at all; but of motion there are two sorts each of which is infinite numerically, but that one of these has its essential being in producing effects {*Wirken*} and the other in suffering {*Leiden*}; and, then, from out of the meeting up and the rubbing together of these two sorts, the one with the other, generations *{Erzeugnisse}* come to be whose number likewise is infinite but which are always produced as twins simultaneously, as the perceptible and as perception – since the latter always steps forward simultaneously and is connubial   *[b]* with what is perceptible. Now, perceptibles come to us with names like these: sight, hearing, smell, warmth and chill; also pleasure and displeasure are their names; desire too, and abhorrence; and then, there are yet many others, unnamed and beyond all reckoning and, then too, also a very good number that do have names. The sorts of perceptibles are always one on one with their connubials: for the many varieties of sight, the varieties of color; and likewise for hearing the many sounds; and so too for the rest of perception the remaining many sorts of perceptibles. Now, what does this narration tell us, Theaetetus, in relation, namely, to what was spoken of earlier? – have you taken notice of it?

Theae: Not yet totally, o Socrates.   *[156~cd]*

Socr: So do watch attentively, whether somehow we manage to get to the end of it. Namely, this teaching says the following: that all of this, just as we have said, is itself in movement. But in this movement there is found speediness and slowness. Now, that portion is slow which has its motion in the same place and in relation to what is nearby, and such generates in this manner. Such is that which is slow and so is its generation. But that which is speedy has its motion in relation with the distant and is so generated; and that which is so generated is speedy, for it moves quickly through space and in such moving out, in this consists the nature of its motion. If, now, an eye encounters such an other with which it is commensurate and [so, the color] red is generated along with its twin sister, perception – neither of which would have become generated had either of them   *[e]* encountered something else – then *becomes*, in that both of them are in motion, namely sight [as the motion] on the side of the eye but redness [as the motion] on the side of the object that generates color and, so, on the one side the eye becomes filled up with its sight-perception and right away it sees and, thus, it becomes not [simply] sight-perception but, rather, a seeing eye; and on the other side that which cogenerates the color shall become filled with redness and, again, this has not become red but rather a red something – whether now it would be a red stone or a piece of wood,[161] or be it whatever else you may have encountered, which, now, is colored by this color. And it's even so with all of the rest, what is hard or warm and all of these others that are understood in the very same manner: that,

---

[161] See footnote #106, *Parmenides,* (p. 210).

namely, in and of itself every "it" is nothing, just as we said   [a]
earlier on, but that, rather, in the colliding together of the one with
the other everything becomes in all sorts of manners by the power of
movement. For, then too, that that which produces effects would be
something and, then again, that that which suffers also something,
this doesn't allow itself to be noticed firmly and reliably as a one –
for neither is something producing effects before it encounters that
which suffers, nor too is something else suffering effects before it
encounters something that works upon it; and it's also true that that
which becomes a producer when it encounters the one which suffers
displays itself, should it happen to encounter some other, as   [157b]
a sufferer. So that as a consequence to all of the above, just as we
spoke at the beginning, nothing is in and of itself a definite, rather
only always becomes for some other; but being has to be shoved out
despite the fact that still, even yet, we are quite often forced in
manifold ways into making use of it, due to our habituation and our
ineptness, and we aren't even allowed – in accordance to these wise
men – to admit of *something,* nor *essence,* nor *mine,* nor *yours,* nor
the former, nor of any other determination {*Bezeichnung* [pointing-
out]} which stands firm, rather, in accordance to nature one would
only be able to speak of that-which-becomes and of effects produced,
of transitioning states of passing and changing – so that, if someone
puts forth in his speech the proposition that something persists, well,
such a person is easily made to rue the moment. Thus, it is necessary
that we speak of each and every particularity as well as of those
[things] that are composed out of many – by which compositions   [c]
we say human being and stone and each and every other animal and
their species. Do you find this as being to your liking, Theaetetus, and
would you find it pleasurable that you might relish this awhile longer?
Theae: I don't really know for sure, Socrates. For then, I can't really
tell if you're just tempting me with this as a test and leading me on,
or whether you say this as your own opinion.
Socr: Have you then forgotten, dear one, that I for my part don't
know anything at all about things such as these and, so too, I don't
bring up anything as being my own; that, rather, I'm totally and
utterly barren in matters such as these. But I'm accomplishing my
task in helping you to give birth and it is for this reason that I'm
placing before you all these delicacies of wisdom, so that eventually
we'll finally bring your own opinion into the light of day. And   [d]
once this is brought out into the daylight, then right away I'll perform
my examination as to whether it shows itself as a healthy birth or
if it's merely a vaporous puff of air. Hence, do retain your patient
composure and be of good spirit – and, so, answer me with brazen

courageousness – what *do you fancy* as regards that about which I am questioning you.

Theae: So, what was your question?   <13.~157de]

Socr: Clarify for me once again whether this seems right to you that utterly nothing is but, rather, there only should become – the good, the beautiful and all the rest about which we already have been elaborating.

Theae: Indeed, it does appear to me as I listen to you explicate the matter so thoroughly that it's all most amazingly well grounded and that it would have to be so conceived, just as you have laid it out, placing one matter beside the other.   *[e]*

Socr: So then, we don't want to leave anything out that yet remains alongside the rest. But there still remains the matter of dreams and diseases and, particularly, one might make mention of insanity – and, then too, let's not forget about mistaken hearing or sight, and all of the other errors and deceptions that are part and parcel of sense perception. For then, you do well know what I'm getting to, that all of this has the looks about it as if by these instances that this   *[158a]* proposition could unanimously become disproved, the proposition that, just now, we were considering, and that in every manner our perceptions would be false in these instances and that there would be a great deal lacking in this proposition according to which: "what appears to each of us, the same also would be" – that, rather, and quite to the contrary, nothing of that which appears would be.

Theae: Totally right, o Socrates.

Socr: What remains that one might say to get out of this difficulty, youth, for those who say that perception is knowledge and that whatever appears to each and every, that such also would be for whomever to whom it appears?

Theae: I'm lacking in courage to admit it, Socrates, that I don't know what I might say – for then, you just berated me a little while ago when I said this. And still, all the same, I'm really not in the least bit capable of arguing the point with you, that those who are insane or those dreaming, that these don't have false notions if, then, the   *[b]* former believe that they are gods and the latter that they have wings and are flying[162] about in their dreams.

Socr: And have you also taken note of this other stumbling block against this proposition, and in particular as regards waking and sleeping?

Theae: But, which one?

---

[162] Cf: *Sophist* 263ab: "*Strng:* The Theaetetus with whom I'm now speaking – flies." (p. 575); and, at the end of this dialogue, at 201e (p. 445) – Socrates' dream.

Socr: The one, I opine, that you have often enough heard, namely, if someone raises the question as regards what characteristic might one possibly give should someone question you, even here and now: whether we are now sleeping and if all of our notions are only dreams, or if we're awake and so conversing with each other?   *[158c]*

Theae: And truly, Socrates, it is very difficult [to know] what characteristic should be given that would prove it. For in both cases the exact same thing follows. For then, even what we've just said, we're able just as well to be speaking this in a dream and, then too, if we opine to be having a conversation in our dreams, so it's totally amazing how similar this is to the former.

Socr: Hence, you see how easy it is to argue – if, then, it's even *[d]* possible to argue about this: what sleeping is and what's being awake. And since the time that we're asleep is about equal to the time that we're awake, and since in each of these states the soul asserts that what is present in its notions in every wise is true: so we assert throughout an equal amount of time – on the one side, the one, then again, even so, that the other really is; and in both instances we persist with equal firmness in our opinion.

Theae: Quite.

Socr: And does the same correlation hold with sickness and with insanity, are these even so? – up to the amount of time, that this isn't the same?

Theae: You're totally right.

Socr: And how? – should the truth be determined by the length or the brevity of the time?

Theae: That would be ludicrous, really, and in so many ways!   *[e]*

Socr: Do you have something else that is of a greater surety, something with which you're able to demonstrate which of these notions is true?

Theae: I'd fancy not.   *<14.~158]*

Socr: So then, hear from me what these people would have to say about this, these who assert that what each of us has as notions, such would also be true for whomever it is that has such. But they would question us, as I believe, thusly. That which is totally and utterly different from some other, o Theaetetus, is such able to have some sort of capability that is one and the same as the former? – and we're not to presume that that about which the question relates is yet in one respect the same as the former and, thus, only in another respect different, rather, only that it is totally different.

Theae: Well, it's not at all possible that the one is one and the same as the other – whether it would be, now, as a capability or as whatever else – if, then, it is totally and utterly different.   *[~159a2]*

Socr: Doesn't one also have to admit that such, necessarily, is dissimilar?

Theae: It seems so, at least to me.

Socr: If, then, it should happen that something becomes similar or dissimilar – be it now to itself or to something other – shall we not, if it becomes similar, say that it's the same; but if dissimilar that it has become different?

Theae: That's necessary.

Socr: And didn't we say earlier on that there exist all sorts of effect producers, their number being beyond all reckoning; and sufferers also?

Theae: We said it.

Socr: And, then too, that one with another and afterwards again mixing with an [other] other – that such shall not generate one and the same in both instances?

Theae: Quite. [b]

Socr: So let's say then, regarding you and me and everything else in this same manner: Socrates when he's ill and Socrates when healthy, should we name the latter as being similar to the former, or dissimilar?

Theae: Do you mean as a whole, Socrates when ill, to the whole, the healthy Socrates?

Socr: Totally right, you understand me – that's how I mean it.

Theae: Then, dissimilar.

Socr: Also, maybe, different in the same manner as being dissimilar?

Theae: Necessarily. [c]

Socr: And likewise as well if sleeping, and everything else that we've just brought up, shall you assert and name it just so?

Theae: I, certainly.

Socr: Shall not, then, every effect producer in accordance to its nature, if it meets up and strikes upon the healthy Socrates, shall it not have to do with a different Socrates; and if upon the sick Socrates, then again with a different one?

Theae: How could it be otherwise! *{Wie sollte es nicht!}*

Socr: And what becomes generated by us in both instances is different: I as the sufferer and the former, that which produces the effects?

Theae: How else?

Socr: Now, if I drink a glass of wine when I'm healthy so it appears to me as lovely and sweet?

Theae: Oh, yes. [d]

Socr: Namely, in this instance and in accordance to what we stipulated earlier the effect producer and the sufferer [striking together] generate perception and sweetness, both simultaneously hovering. And, indeed, the perception that is on the side of the sufferer has made the tongue into that which perceives; but sweetness which is hovering round and about on the side of the wine, this has made the wine for the healthy tongue that it is sweet – and thus is its appearance?

Theae: This, indeed, is what we had agreed upon as one earlier.

Socr: But if the wine should meet up with the sick Socrates, doesn't it strike in truth against not the same [but a different Socrates] – since it has come up against that which is dissimilar to the former?

Theae: Yes.   *[159e]*

Socr: Hence, something different is generated once again with such a Socrates and the drinking of the wine. Upon the tongue, namely, a bitter perception; but with the wine the becoming and hovering about of bitterness – which makes the wine not into bitterness per se, but into a bitterness; and makes me not a perceiver per se but, rather, into a perceiver of bitterness.

Theae: That's totally apparent.

Socr: Hence, I too shall not ever become an other for so long as I am perceiving, for only some other perception of something different makes the perceiver to something different and other; and, then too the former, that which works upon me, shall never – once it strikes up against something other – generate the same and become even such [as it does with me]. For with an other it has to generate something different and become different itself.

Theae: So it is.   *[160ab]*

Socr: But even so little shall I become *for myself* such a one, nor shall the former become such a one for itself.

Theae: No, naturally not.

Socr: Thus, it is as well necessary for me, if I shall be a perceiver, that I become such *of something* – for, indeed, a perceiver but not a perceiver of something, to become such is not at all possible; and then too the former must also – if it is to be sweet or bitter or whatever else is like this – it is necessary that it becomes such for someone. For to be sweet, but not to be sweet for somebody, this isn't possible.

Theae: Quite, it has to be as you say.

Socr: Thus, I believe, the lone possibly remains left for us: that we are or become only for each other; however it may be that we want to say it – as being or as becoming – since, indeed, our being is knotted together by necessity; though neither with some other one nor too with our own selves. Hence, it only remains that it be knotted together for us amongst one another. So that should, now, anybody name this being: he would have to tell us that it would be for something or of something or else in relationship to something; or, then too, if he names it becoming, the same applies. But that whatever either might be or become in and of itself of some equal amount – this he is not allowed to assert for himself, nor, should anyone else assert as much, is he allowed to accept it; just as this speech, what we just went through, demonstrates. *[c]*

Theae: So it is, Socrates, indeed.

Socr: Thus, isn't it true: if something that makes me into something is just for me and not for anyone else, so too, I perceive it, nobody else does?

Theae: How else could it be?

Socr: My perception, thus, is true for me – for then, it would be of my being in any given instance. Hence, I am the judge – just as Protagoras has stated – as well of that which is for me, how it is, and likewise of that which is not for me, how it isn't.

Theae: So it seems. *<15.~160d]*

Socr: Hence, how should I, since I'm not deceitful nor do I ever fail, how should I also not know in my notions of that which is or becomes – what I perceive.

Theae: There's not any other way permissible that one might think about this.

Socr: Right on the mark and most excellently have you spoken: that knowledge is nothing other than perception; and everything has come together into one: that according to Homer and Heraclitus and their whole lineage: Everything is in flux and in movement like a river; and, according to Protagoras – he who was so wise – that *Man is the measure of all things*; and now, in accordance to Theaetetus, if this is how it all correlates then perception shall be knowledge. Isn't it true, o Theaetetus? – do we say that, indeed, this is your little baby and just newly born that I have delivered? – or, what do you opine?

Theae: It's necessarily so, o Socrates. *[160e3]*

Socr: Finally, then, and despite a fair amount of difficulties, we've managed to carry this conception through to delivery – whatever, now, this birth may turn out authentically to be. After the birth, though, truly: we have to carry it about in the circuit, taking up as our research that we investigate further into this, what has been born, whether, perhaps, contrary to what we thought we knew, whether it may *not* prove itself as being worthy that we shall bring it up, that rather it may just be an empty shell of air. Or, do you believe that in all cases your child should be brought up and never set out as rubbish? Or, shall you be able to bear it if you see that it fails this test and you won't become overly distressed if somebody takes away your child, even though it's your first born? *[161a2]*

Theo: He shall bear it well, our Theaetetus, o Socrates, for he's not in the least bit obstinate. Thus, *by the gods!* – tell us, whether or not this correlates so.

Socr: Apparently, Theodorus, you have had a great deal of pleasure in listening in on our conversation and it's very good of you that you believe that I would simply be a treasury of such assertions and that I might simply reach in without any effort and pull one out and say, again, that this correlates so, or doesn't. But the way that the *[b]* conversation proceeds in all actuality, this you haven't noticed as of yet – that, namely, none of these assertions is given out by me but, rather, always only by the person who is conversing with me; and that I don't know anything more than this small bit, namely, how one takes a good grasp upon the speech of the other, wiser interlocutor, and that the speech be handled properly. And so too do I attempt now, that I do the same with him, but not that I myself say anything.

Theo: Thanks for the correction, Socrates, and just do as you say.

Socr: But do you know, Theodorus, what amazes me about your friend, Protagoras?

Theo: And what would that be?   <16.~161c]

Socr: The rest of what he said, all of this I found to be quite to my liking – that what seems for each of us, this also is for whomever. It's only as regards the beginning of his speech that I'm left wondering, that he didn't right away start off in his wisdom that the measure of all things is a pig or a monkey, or what have you from amongst all the sentient beings having sense perception, those that could be named as being less endowed with reason – in that, had he begun thusly he would have begun in a proper, high-minded fashion looking askance down upon us in his speech in that he shows us, indeed, that although we may marvel upon him like upon a god due to his wisdom, yet he wouldn't have any better insight than a half-grown frog, not even *[d]* to mention whomever you might choose, anyone other from amongst all the rest of mankind. Or, what shall we say, Theodorus? For if the truth for each and every should be the notions that each has in accordance to his own perception, and if no one is better able to judge any one else's situation and viewpoint, nor is anyone more capable than anyone else in drawing someone else's notions into a nuanced consideration, whether or not they would be true or false; that, rather, as we already have said, and almost to excess, that each for himself has only his own notions and that all of this is right and true – *well*, how should it be the case, o friend, that just Protagoras is wise and that he shall be chosen as a teacher above all the others and, indeed, his tuition is really quite steep; but then, we, to the contrary, we don't know as much as he does so that we all have to take *[e]* lessons from him and need to attend his school, though, all the same, every man is the measure of his own wisdom? – and how shouldn't we believe that Protagoras isn't just making a great joke at our expense and it's all only brought forward by him in jest? Whatever else one really might contend in regards to myself and my art of midwifery, I don't even intend to make so much as a peep regarding all of this, how much laughter we've set ourselves up for. But then, I believe that it shall be even the same as well in regards to this whole business of scientific review and intellectual debate. For then, that the one and the other shall dispute amongst themselves as regards the notions and opinions that they each hold and that they might place these up for examination and then seek to disprove them – if, now, it be so that *all of them* are right: can you imagine anything so boring and downright infantile if, then, this wisdom of Protagoras really is true and if he wouldn't just be making a joke at our expense and speaking from out of the hidden depths and sanctity of his book.

Theo: The man, o Socrates, is my friend – just as you stated earlier. Therefore, I wouldn't like either to contradict him through my admissions, nor too would I like to speak with you in a way that contradicts my own opinions. Hence, why don't you take Theaetetus up again [as your interlocutor]; he seemed to me to be following you very attentively earlier. *[162b]*

Socr: And you, Theodorus, were it to be the case that you found yourself amongst the Lacedaimonians, there at their training camps, and you saw that they were all exercising in the nude and, beyond this, that amongst them there would be some human specimens who were far from being in tiptop shape, wouldn't you rather fit in amongst them by removing your own clothing and, so, display for them your own figure?

Theo: And why is it that you don't opine, quite to the contrary, that I wouldn't prefer to remain [just as I am, an exception] if only they should allow it and let themselves be talked into permitting me this? Just as I also hope now to talk you into what I desire, that you allow me just to look on and, since I'm not particularly so agile any more, that I don't need to be drawn into this place of exercise; that rather you might prefer to wrestle with someone who is younger and still has that sweetness which is so characteristic of youth.

Socr: If you're so adamant about this being right, Theodorus, so too, it's all the same to me, as they tend to say. Hence, I'll have to turn myself back once more to the wise Theaetetus. *<17.~162c]*

– Tell me then, Theaetetus, firstly as regards to what we just went through, whether you too are amazed that suddenly it was shown that you wouldn't be any worse off than anyone else amongst mankind in respect to wisdom, or also, for that matter, amongst the gods? Or, do you believe that Protagoras' measure has less validity amongst the gods than it does amongst mankind?

Theae: By Zeus – not at all, and what you've just asked me causes me to wonder, indeed, even more. For then, what we were elaborating upon earlier and wherefore it was that they say – *what appears to each, that too would be for him to whom it appears* – I found that this would be said most admirably and is right on the mark; but now, to the contrary, it has quickly done an about-face.   *[~d2]*

Socr: You are still quite young, my child, and therefore you're quicker to respect and get caught up by such cunning speeches – as you give them entry. For were Protagoras here or some other spokesman for him, so he would say to all of this: You all are really outstanding, children and old men alike, that you sit here together and lead one another about and are beguiled and ensnared by these speeches in that you bring the gods into matters from which I entirely exclude them, both in my speech and my writings – whether they are or are not – and all of the rest of it which, indeed, would make such an impression upon the great multitudes if they should hear it; and so on matters like these you converse as if it would be something so utterly horrendous if each and every person wouldn't be any better off in respect to wisdom than any animal. Proofs, however, and the rules and necessity of logic, of these there isn't even a single solitary example! – rather, you satisfy yourselves in that you remain just with the appearances and with that-which-seems-to-be; matters, indeed, that neither Theodorus nor any other geometer would even so much as consider using in his professional work, or, if he did do so, then his results would be totally and utterly worthless. So do reflect upon this, you and Theodorus, whether now in the consideration of such important things you all want to give applause to such speeches, these speeches that consist in and are assembled out of rhetorical chicanery and the mere semblances of truth.   *[~163a]*

Theae: That this would be acceptable, Socrates, neither you nor we would want to state as much.

Socr: Thus, in some other manner, as it seems, we would have to examine this matter – just as you and Theodorus assert.

Theae: Quite right, in some other manner.

Socr: Let's take a look at this matter, then, in the following manner – whether knowledge and perception are one and the same – for this was the issue that our entire speech was aimed at resolving and it was for this purpose that we touched upon so many sorts of amazement. Isn't it true?

Theae: Quite. [b]

Socr: Should we be one in admitting this, that what we perceive through sight or through hearing, that all of this also is immediately understood? For example: when some foreigners are speaking in a language that we don't understand, would we deny that we even hear them when they are speaking? – or should we say that not only do we hear them but also that we understand what they are saying? And likewise, if we're still unacquainted with the letters of the alphabet and yet we direct our vision upon some writing, should we assert that we don't see the letters? – or that we also understand them, if indeed, we are looking at them? [c]

Theae: We shall assert to understand the same that's upon them that we see and hear; namely, as regards the latter, that we see their form and color and are cognizant of these;[163] but of the former that we hear high and low and know these; but as regards what is taught by the language teachers and by the professional translators, these [matters] are neither perceived through sight and hearing – nor, thus, are they understood.

Socr: Admirable and on the mark, Theaetetus! – and it wouldn't be right that I argue this point with you so that your courage grows. But examine this other matter that is coming our way and see to it, how do we want to fend it off. <18.~163d]

Theae: What's that?

Socr: This. Should someone ask us as to whether it would be possible that in that once someone has attained knowledge of something and he is yet retaining this knowledge in his memory and hasn't lost it, then, when he's remembering it – shall he nevertheless *not* be cognizant of what he is remembering? But, take note – I've gotten a little bit ahead of myself as I really only wanted to ask you whether someone, whatever it may be that he's experienced, in that he remembers it, yet – he doesn't know?

Theae: And how might that be, Socrates? This would be a wonder, what you're asking me about?

Socr: But then, am I mistaken? Do watch attentively! Didn't you say that sight would be perceiving and every vision a perception?

Theae: So I say. [e]

Socr: He who has seen something, he has acquired cognition and knows what he saw – this accords with our current proposition?

Theae: Yes.

---

[163] Can it be merely coincidental that "form and color" are mentioned just as in *Meno* at 74b–77a (pp. 467–471) and *Cratylus* 430a–433a! And as regards "replica", see *Sophist* 235e (p. 536); and likewise "letters" being a *Leitmotiv* for Plato's epistemological reflections.

Socr: How now? Don't you admit that there's memory?

Theae: Oh, sure.

Socr: Of nothing, or of something?

Theae: Of something, that goes without saying.

Socr: Good, of that which someone has experienced and perceived, of something from this?

Theae: What else [could it be]?

Socr: And what someone has seen, from time to time he remembers it?

Theae: Certainly, he remembers.

Socr: Even if he has his eyes shut? – or would it be that as soon as he closes his eyes he forgets?

Theae: That would be really exasperating, o Socrates, to assert such a thing. *[164a]*

Socr: And yet, all the same, we have to do so – if, then, we want to save our earlier proposition, if not, so it's *adios* with him.

Theae: I too, by Zeus, am noticing something along these lines, but I don't really have a good grasp upon the whole of it in its precise details. So tell me, how so?

Socr: Thus. He who sees, we say, acquires knowledge of that which he sees. For vision and perception and knowledge – all of these, we have admitted, are one and the same.

Theae: Well, sure.

Socr: He, then, who has seen whatever and has acquired knowledge of what he saw, he remembers this, indeed, even if he should shut his eyes, though he doesn't see it then. Isn't it so?

Theae: You're totally right. *[b]*

Socr: But this – he doesn't see it – means as much as he doesn't know it, if it should be that he sees means as much as he knows.

Theae: That's right.

Socr: It follows, then, that for whomever, he who has acquired knowledge, in that he remembers it, nonetheless he doesn't know it because he doesn't see it; even that of which we said earlier that this would be a wonder should it occur.

Theae: That's completely right.

Socr: Something that is impossible seems to follow if someone says that knowledge and perception are the same.

Theae: So it seems.

Socr: One would have to say, therefore, that each of these is something other.

Theae: That's the way it will have to be. *[c]*

Socr: What then is knowledge? It seems that we have once again to begin over from the start with our clarification.

– Singularly, Theaetetus, what is it that we are about to do?
Theae: Say what?
Socr: I'm having the premonition that we're about to behave like those pranky roosters do – and even before we've made the conquest we're jumping off to the side and crowing our victory cry.
Theae: But, how so?
Socr: It's just as if we only would be concerned with discovering a contradiction and we seem just to be following the words and setting up a contradictory assertion and, then, when by such means as these the proposition is refuted, so we're quite satisfied with ourselves; and though, indeed, we claim that we're not artful fencers but, rather, that we are lovers of wisdom, nonetheless, we do exactly the same as these powerful men.   *[d]*
Theae: I'm still unable to understand a bit about what you're saying.
Socr: Then I shall undertake to make this clear to you, what it is that I have noticed about this matter. We were asking ourselves whether it might well be so that if someone had experienced something and then he is remembering this, what he experienced, he still nonetheless wouldn't know it; and then after we had shown that whoever has seen something and, then, he closes his eyes and now he remembers what he saw, so we demonstrated that he remembers it but no longer knows it; but, then, this is impossible and so the whole matter is lost – the proposition of Protagoras as well as what you have proposed regarding knowledge and perception, that both of these are one and the same.
Theae: Obviously.   *[e]*
Socr: But it wouldn't be lost, I believe, dear one, if only the father of this teaching was still living; that rather he would arrive on the scene and provide assistance and succor for his teaching, and do this in manifold ways. But now, as these teachings have been left destitute, so it is that we're mistreating them; and on top of this not even the custodians to whom Protagoras delivered up these speeches – one of whom being Theodorus here – no one wants to come to their aid. Rather, as it seems, we are all alone in providing help and giving succor to these teachings since they've been left simply hanging.
Theo: Not I, o Socrates, rather much more is it Callias, son of Hipponicus, who is the custodian and defender of these teachings of Protagoras. But I've taken sanctuary, so quickly as I could,   *[~165a]* into my studies of geometry and, so, I've rescued myself from the perils of pure thought. All the same, I shall be most grateful to you if you would take up his cause.
Socr: Well spoken, Theodorus. So take a good look at how it is that I go about this task of giving succor. Namely, someone would have

to admit yet even more outrageous things than those that were mentioned earlier – if, then, he doesn't pay the most precise attention to the words, much more than we tend to do when affirming or denying something. Shall I tell you how so? – or shall I direct my speech upon Theaetetus?

Theo: Both of us together, Socrates. But the younger one of us shall answer you – for if he should fail, this won't look so bad for him as it would for me.   *<19.~165b]*

Socr: So then, right away I'll bring up the most powerful question. But that, I believe, would be such a one as this: Is it well-nigh possible that the same person who knows something, is it possible that simultaneously he both knows what he knows and also that he doesn't know it?

Theo: What shall we answer to this one, Theaetetus?

Theae: I for my part hold that this is impossible.

Socr: By no means – if, namely, you say that seeing would be knowing. For what, then, shall you do with the ensnaring question if you should encounter some relentless adversary who would cover up one of your eyes and then asks you as to whether you would see his coat despite that your eye is covered up?   *[c]*

Theae: I would say to him, indeed, not with the one of them, but that I do with the other.

Socr: Hence, simultaneously you do both, see and also do not see it.

Theae: In a certain way, sure.

Socr: It's utterly of no concern to me, he then says, as regards the manner, the ways and means, and I haven't asked you in regard to this at all – but just, rather, whether what you know you also do not know? But now it has been demonstrated that you see what you also do not see. And then, earlier you admitted and saw eye to eye with me on this, that seeing is knowing and that not seeing is not knowing. So now, you add it all up yourself and make your calculation, what results from out of all this.   *[d]*

Theae: I've already added it up and there results the opposite from what I was stipulating.

Socr: And it has the appearance, you amazing boy, that if you were to encounter more arguments that were like this one – if then, moreover, someone would question you as to whether it may be possible that one could know something keenly and also roughly, or know it when close-by but not be able to recognize the same from a greater distance,[164] and then too, loudly and quietly – and thousands of things like these that someone who belonged to the light infantry,

---

[164] See (as always) footnote #108, p. 211.

a soldier of speeches, would lay into your backside and, once you have proposed that knowledge and perception are the same, so he wouldn't let up from contradicting you in regard to hearing and smelling, *et cetera* – and by all of these types of perception and not ever giving you a moment's rest but always intensifying his attacks until finally you'd become so amazed by his wisdom, which you'd wish that he might share with you, that you'd be all tied up in knots and at his mercy; and thus he would get you into his power and custody from which, then, he'd only release you for so and so much tuition, however much you might be able to arrange for your payments. What, then, would Protagoras have for a speech to give succor to someone in such a pickle? – you may well be asking yourself? Shouldn't we make the attempt to present the counter-argument?
Theae: By all means. *<20.~166a]*
Socr: Well, all of this, namely, what we already said earlier in standing up for him and, then, he would – I believe – come right up to us and somewhat contemptuously looking down upon us say:

[Protag's Spirit]: This venerable Socrates, because a mere child has been frightened out of his wits when he was questioned as to whether the same person wouldn't be able to recognize the same matter that he remembers – and out of fright he denies this because he's not even able to see what's in front of him – and so he's made a mockery out of a man of my standing due to this speech. But the truth of the matter, you overly bold Socrates, correlates thus. If with your questions you are investigating into something that pertains to me, and he who is questioned should answer you just as I would have answered you and then he is led into a contradiction and is, thus, shown to be in error – well then, indeed, I too am brought into a contradictory error. But if he answers you with something other than what I would have said, then this occurs just to him, he who answered you, and to him alone. Hence, in that I merely start off with what lies close-by: *[166b]* Do you believe that anyone shall admit this, that the memory of something that has happened to someone subsists in one's memory just like the occurrence of the event itself, despite that the event is no longer occurring? Not by a long shot! Or, that someone shall have any misgivings in admitting that it is possible both to know and not to know the same matter? Or if, indeed, he should be wary of making such an assertion, that he shall ever admit that what has transitioned out of some condition is yet the same as it was before it transitioned? Or, much rather, that utterly there would even be a "this" *[166c]* and not, much rather, "these," and indeed, countless multitudes of becomings so long as there yet exist transitioning states – if then, one

should indeed pay heed and be on guard that someone is not just making hunt upon the words of the other.   Much more, you simpletons: go yet more courageously forward upon the tracks of what I'm actually asserting if, then, you are able to, and prove me wrong in this, that not each one of us has his own unique perceptions that come to be for each of us; or if this, then, would indeed be so, that nonetheless that what appears to each shall not become for him alone – or if you should say "be," then be alone for him to whom it appears. But if you go on about pigs and monkeys, so then, not only do you yourselves act like swine, rather also you convince others who pay heed to what you say that they also might comport themselves in such a manner against my writings, and in this you're handling matters in an ugly fashion. For indeed, I do assert that perceptions correlate even so as I have written about them: that, namely, each one of us is the measure of what is and what is not, but that, nonetheless, the one of us is infinitely better at this than the other – and, indeed, even because for the one of us things appear and are so, for another, though, otherwise. And I'm very far from asserting that there isn't wisdom or that wise men wouldn't exist; rather, it's even these whom I call wise, namely those who are able to effect a transformation so that for those to whom malignancy and evil is and appears, that this be transformed into good, that the good be and that it appears. But now, don't just grasp again at the mere words of my speech, rather first take up in the following more clearly what I'm meaning. Namely, you only need to recollect the example that was spoken of previously, that for him who is ill the wine that he relishes is and appears as bitter, but for him who is healthy it is and appears as the opposite to this. Now, one shouldn't make the case that either of them is wiser than the other and this isn't even possible;   *[167a]* and, then too, one isn't allowed to complain as if the one who is ill would be lacking understanding because his notion of the wine is such and that the healthy man is wise because his notion would be something other – but, all the same, it is good and one has to effect a transformation for the former because this other constitution is the better one. And, even thus, this is how matters also relate as regards instruction, that one effects a transformation from a given constitution to some other one. Now, physicians bring about their transformations by the aid of medicinal compounds, but sophists through their speeches. And never is it so that anyone brings another who has false notions to having notions that are true. For then, it is neither possible to have any notions of that which is not [non-being], nor utterly of anything other than what each and every one of us generates, and this is always true. Rather, it is only so that for him whose soul capabilities are in a worse constitution – and, thus, his manner of having notions relate in a manner that corresponds to this – one is able to effect a change for the better, so that his perceptions and notions become different from what they were; and it is this which a few people due to their being misinformed call truth, but I only call some notions as being better than others, truer, on the contrary, I don't call anything at all. And amongst the wise, my dear Socrates, I have no intentions of including frogs or tadpoles, rather in relation to the bodies of animals I'm of the understanding that *[c]* physicians would qualify; and in connection to plants, agronomists. For I believe that these may bring about the effect of transforming plants that, perhaps, are ailing and have bad perceptions, to the state of being healthy, that they have a better constitution, one that is healthier and truer – just as wise and good speakers likewise make it so that states which appear as being corrupt might be transformed into being and appearing righteous. For what appears to any state as beauteous and just, that also is so for as long as it is clarified as being thus; but those having wisdom make matters so that instead of the previous corruption now only wholesome salvation is and appears. And just this is the manner of the sophist who understands to educate all of those who allow themselves to be given such instruction and, indeed, these sophists are wise and do well deserve that they *[167d]* receive every monetary remuneration and the greatest amount of tuition from those who receive such instruction. And thus, both matters are valid – that a few of us are wiser than others and, still, that nobody has any notions that are false; and you too, whether you prefer this as desirable or not, you'll have to let this please you, that you too are a measure. For it is just by this that my teaching retains its stature – and, now, you may make whatever objections against this speech, just as you please – if, then, you have anything new that you'd like to bring up against it so that you oppose this speech with one of your own; or you might prefer to challenge it by asking questions, this too is fine by me. For that also is not a matter which a man of understanding need shy away from, rather that in all ways men are ready and able to rally to the attack. Only do observe this one thing: don't be deceptive with your questions. This would display, indeed, the greatest deficiency of reason if one should say that he is most preoccupied with investigating into virtue, and yet he proves himself as being nothing other than deceitful in his line of questioning. And deceit in this matter would be if someone doesn't wholly separate both of these, the one from the other – for then, it's one thing if someone only desires to argue and would compose all of his speeches accordingly, but it's something else again if he really wants to investigate into these matters – and in the latter case, indeed, he still may not ever let up from his jesting and that he allows his subtle cleverness to soar two levels above the grasp of his interlocutor but, all the same, he's quite serious when the proper investigation is broached and he places his interlocutor in the right and proper stance and only displays those errors to him by which he has misled himself, or be it due to the errors of his former companions, those   *[168a]* with whom he used to congregate. If you make your case in this wise, o Socrates, then those who thus converse with you shall place the fault of their confusion and their lack of certainty squarely upon their own shoulders and not accuse you – and they shall follow after you and love you, hating themselves and fleeing from their former selves into philosophy so that they might become different and no longer remain the same old people that they used to be. But insofar as you, like most of the others, do the contrary to this, so too you shall experience the opposite result and those who congregate about you, instead of becoming philosophers, shall be made into archenemies of this matter as they grow older. But if you will follow my lead, so then, you shall not become an adversary nor seek out occasions to argue, that rather calmly and with an even keel and a steady heart you will give yourself over to the real investigations into just how it is that we mean this when we assert that everything is in flux and that the notions that each and every one of us has, so too *is it* for him, the individual just as well as the state. And starting out from here you then follow through as to whether knowledge and perception are one and the same or whether they would be different; but not as you did earlier on, simply and rather nakedly from out of the common   *[c]* use of words and what they indicate, that with which the people traipse about, and just as it comes to them – and thereby they set themselves up for multifarious states of confusion, each one with the other. *[Exit spirit.]*

Socr: This, o Theodorus, I bring in aid of your friend and to provide succor for his speech to the best of my limited abilities, a little of my scant stock; but if only he were still alive then you may be certain that he would have been far more spectacular in his own defense.

Theo: Surely you jest, Socrates, for you stood up for my friend with a right youthful courageousness.   *<21.~168d]*

Socr: Well spoken, friend. But tell me this, did you pay close attention to the point that Protagoras was just making, that in regards to which he was prefacing his objections: that we, in that we are directing our speech upon a child, so we're making use of the fear that this boy experiences against him in our argument? And didn't he name this as being a malicious joke and that he wanted, just as he himself handled his speech – *that man is the measure of all things* – in a very deep, profound and well grounded manner, that we too should seriously comport ourselves likewise with this, his speech?

Theo: How could I help but notice this?

Socr: How now? – so what's your advice in this matter, do we follow him?

Theo: Very much so.   *[~e]*

Socr: But then, you do see – these are all adolescent boys congregating here around us, except for you. Should we follow Protagoras' suggestion, so we have to question and give answers to one another, that we seriously place his proposition up upon the scale of our more mature reasoning and give it due consideration so that at least he won't be able to make this objection, that we've merely been playing with children in our investigation of his proposition.

Theo: How's that? Shouldn't Theaetetus be better able than many others who sport long beards, shouldn't he be better at following the ins and outs of this proof than many?   *[~a]*

Socr: But, indeed, not better than you, o Theodorus. Thus, don't allow yourself to think that I would have to come to your friend's aid and have given succor to his speech in every wise, but that you don't need to stand up for him at all. Rather, come here, best of men, and walk a little ways by my side, only so far until we come to see whether you should be the measure for geometric demonstrations or whether everyone is just as good as you and each is able to satisfy himself in the questions of astronomy and all the rest, those matters wherein you have the reputation of being foremost in your excellence.

Theo: Truly, Socrates, it isn't an easy matter when one takes a seat next to you, that there's just no way to avoid having to enter into discourse with you, though I much rather would have preferred to shoot by you and was hoping that you might have allowed me this much consideration, that I wouldn't have to join in disrobing and that you wouldn't have forced this upon me as the Lacedaimonians do. But now, it seems to me that you resemble Sciron even more than the Spartans. For the Lacedaimonians command one either to disrobe or to keep a good distance, but you seem to direct matters more in the manner of Antaios who, once someone arrives before him, so like him you don't let up your grasp from him until you've forced him into disrobing and arguing matters with you through speech.   *[~169b]*

Socr: Most admirable and on the mark, o Theodorus, do you describe my illness by means of this analogy of yours. Only I'm even more valiant than he. For then, there have been many occasions when a speaker the likes of Heracles or Theseus, these who are so mighty in rhetoric, many such have come before me and expertly ripped me to shreds; but, all the same, I still haven't let up a bit from my quest – so powerful is the love that has me in its grasp and it drives me to these exercises in combat. And so, don't you be a spoilsport, rather enter into this conversation for our mutual benefit.

Theo: All right, I'll not remain contrary any longer. Lead me *whither thou willst*; in every wise I shall have to bear up to my fate, whatever the webs of logic you intend to ensnare me with, that I be contradicted. But, all the same, not one step further than you have just indicated shall I be able to give myself over to you.

Socr: So far also shall suffice. And do pay heed to this for me, that we don't once again end up wandering off into an infantile mode of discourse, that someone once again might be able to fault us with this should we do so.   *<22.~169d]*

Theo: At least I shall make every attempt, as best as I'm able.

Socr: So now, let's resume with even this same matter with which we started off earlier and let's see as to whether we were right or if we acted improperly as matters became difficult and we berated this proposition that he had clarified so – that each and every one of us all by himself is sufficiently able to have the insight, since Protagoras admitted as much, that a few people would be superior and have this distinction: that they determine what is better and what worse and, therefore, these people also would be wise. Wasn't it so?

Theo: Yes.

Socr: If, now, he himself were here present and would have admitted this to us, that we hadn't merely attributed this admission to him ourselves in that, per force, we are representing his views, were this the case, as I say, then it wouldn't be necessary for us that once again we begin all over from the start, that this might be rock solid. But now, perhaps, somebody might assert that we wouldn't be qualified and have this in our power, that we admit something in his stead. Therefore it would be better for us if we go through this matter once more with greater precision. For then, it's no small matter as regards the difference this makes, whether matters correlate thus or otherwise.

Theo: You're right.

Socr: Let us, therefore, look nowhere else, that rather even from out of his proposition itself and in the shortest possible way, that we deduce the admission for this.

Theo: But, how?   *[170a]*

Socr: So. The notions that each of us has – this, indeed, is what Protagoras says – such also is for him, he who has these?

Theo: Quite, this is what he says.

Socr: Hence, Protagoras, are we expressing the notions of one man or, much rather, of all men in that we say that there is no one, no matter who, nobody exists who doesn't hold himself as being wiser in a few things than the others; but that in other matters that others are wiser than he himself; and that in those matters which are most dire, when out upon the field of battle, in sickness and when venturing out upon the high seas and in the greatest calamity, in all such circumstances as these, so they all turn to those individuals who rule and lead them – just as if these men were gods and it's just through them that they hope for their salvation; and these leaders are differentiated from all the rest in nothing other than through their knowing. And our human life is replete with countless examples, people who are seeking teachers and seeking out those who offer up their expertise – be it that they are out seeking for themselves or for others, children or animals, that they might be trained so that they would perform appropriately – and, so too, there are many such who believe that they are in a position to teach others and that they have something to offer. And in all of these instances what can we possibly say other than that all of humanity itself believes that wisdom exists, and also lack of understanding?

Theo: Nothing other.

Socr: And don't they hold wisdom as having the correct insights, but lack of understanding as having false notions?   [c]

Theo: What else [could they be]?

Socr: What then, o Protagoras, what should we do for making a start with this proposition? Should we say that all men always have the right notions? – or, from time to time the right ones but sometimes false ones? For then, there results in either case that men don't always have the right notions but, rather, have notions that go either way. For just bethink yourself, o Theodorus, whether there might be anyone from those who hold Protagoras' view – or if you yourself want to assert this: that nobody believes that there wouldn't be some others who are deficient in their understanding? – and that these wouldn't have false notions?

Theo: Really, Socrates, that would be unbelievable.   [d]

Socr: But, still and yet, this proposition finds itself in such a dire strait, the proposition that states that *Man is the measure of all things.*

Theo: But, how's that?

Socr: If you, all by yourself, if you have come to a judgment regarding something and then you inform me of your notion: so, in accordance to the prior assertion, this is indeed your truth; but doesn't it remain with us, we who are other than you, that we are free and also stand as judges who judge your judgment – or have we decided that you always have the correct notions? – and shall it not much rather be so that in the former instance there will be countless multitudes who argue against you, that their notions are contrary to yours and they believe that your opinions are false, and so too is your judgment?

Theo: Very much so, by Zeus, o Socrates: countless multitudes and, as Homer says – those engaging in commerce throughout the whole world!   *[170e]*

Socr: How now? Do you want that we should say that, indeed, you yourself have the right notions but that the former multitudes are wrong?

Theo: So it seems, at least in accordance with the former proposition, it would have to be so.

Socr: But how do matters stand with Protagoras himself? Shall he not have to make this admission, that if he himself didn't believe that *Man is the measure,* nor do the people believe in this – as then, [in accord to what we've said above] these don't believe it – so that, then, this wisdom would be for no one, the wisdom that he has written? And if he himself believes in it but, then, the people don't belicve in it with him: so then, firstly you do know that the wisdom would more likely not be so than be so insofar as more have contrary notions than those whose notions are so?   *[~171a2]*

Theo: Quite, since the weight of the particular notions shall be balanced one way or the other insofar as they are or aren't.

Socr: Accordingly, this is what is most beauteous about the matter. To a certain extent Protagoras admits as much, that the opinions of those whose opinions are contrary to his regarding this, his opinion, by the power of which they hold that he's in error – that *this* is true – in that, assuredly, he asserts that everyone has notions of being.

Theo: Quite.   *[b]*

Socr: So then, he admits as much, that his own notion is false – if he admits that the opinion of these others is true, these who hold the opinion that he is in error.

Theo: Necessarily.

Socr: But the others don't admit this of themselves, that they are in error?

Theo: Utterly and absolutely not.

Socr: But, then too, he also admits the validity of this notion, that it would be right, in accordance with what he has written.

Theo: So it appears.

Socr: From everyone, therefore, and starting with Protagoras, it shall be a matter of contention, or, much rather, for him a matter of admission – if then, he admits it to him, he who asserts the contrary of that which he asserts, that his notions are correct – for then, *[c]* Protagoras himself gives in and makes allowance that neither a dog nor the first best man is a measure, not even of a single matter about which he hasn't been taught. Isn't it so?

Theo: So it is.

Socr: If this, then, shall be a matter of contention for everyone, so it wouldn't be true for anyone, this truth of Protagoras, neither for anyone else other than him, nor too, even for him himself.

Theo: Beyond all measure, o Socrates, haven't we taken things too far in running my friend this way and that?

Socr: But, dear one, it's yet uncertain as to whether, perhaps, we haven't also run right by the truth of the matter. For then, one should believe that Protagoras, being so much older than we are is likewise so much wiser than we are – and if only now he might be able to work his way toward us, that just his head and neck would become visible, so it's very probable that he would mete out harsh punishment, and not only to me, since I've been talking through my hat, but likewise to you, that you would have allowed me so much latitude; and then, he'd dive down again and be off. Be this as it may, I think that we'll just have to do what we can to satisfy ourselves, that we only say what it is that seems right to us in each and every instance. And so too now. Is it possible for us to say anything else other than that each of us, and no matter who it may be, each would have to admit this: that the one is wiser than the other? – and, so too, one knows less?

Theo: At least to me, I'd fancy this as being so.   <23.~171e]

Socr: And, perhaps, this as well – that the proposition shall fare the best just as we developed it in that we came to the aid of Protagoras, that, indeed, there are many matters that are just as they appear to each and every – namely, warmth and dryness, the sweet and everything else that belongs to this sort. But then, if he is to give in that for a few things one should be better than another, so it would be most likely that he'd want to do this in relation and with his eye set to those things that are healthy and unhealthy – that not every woman or child or animal would be in a position that he or she might heal himself or herself through his or her own knowledge of what is healthy, that rather in this, if anywhere at all, the one would be better than the other.

Theo: So, at least, it seems to me.   [172a]

Socr: And likewise – also in things pertaining to the state and all of the civic affairs: the beauteous and the malefic, the just and the unjust, the pious and the impious – whatever a state grasps as its opinion in regards to these things, and then it sets them down firmly as being so in accordance to law, that too would now be so for each and every in truth, and for things such as these no individual is a bit wiser than anyone else, nor is any state better in these matters than any other. But in establishing and setting this other matter down, how any state might best comport itself or what might be unbearable, here – if anywhere at all – it shall have to be admitted once again that the advice of the one counciler is to be differentiated from the advice of the other, and likewise the opinions of one state from those of some other state, namely – in respect to truth – and, so, in no manner is it to be permitted that someone dares to assert that what a state sets down as being beneficial for itself, that this also shall become beneficial in every manner. But as regards those other things that we mentioned earlier – righteousness and unrighteousness, piety and god-forsakenness – do you want to assert that there would be something of this sort that already has one determinate quality in accordance to nature? or rather, that those notions that are shared and come to be held in common, that such shall be true for the time and for so long as these notions persist. And, indeed, there are so many people who, even if they don't subscribe totally to Protagoras' teachings, still they share these latter notions with him as being a part of their wisdom. – – But, o Theodorus, we're always going from one investigation into the arms of another, and from a smaller one into a larger one.   *[172c]*

Theo: Isn't it so that we have ample leisure time?

Socr: Yes, so it seems. Therefore, you majestic man, I have often enough bethought myself and do so as well now, how natural it is that this happens, that those of us who spend a great amount of time in the pursuit of knowledge – if then, our type should ever have to come and appear in the halls of justice, so they make themselves ludicrous in their speeches.

Theo: How do you mean?

Socr: It seems to me that the others who spend their time from their youth onward pursuing their studies in law school and doing whatever it may be in places that share similarities with such institutions, that in comparison to these those of us who are brought up in an environment in which the pursuit of the liberal arts and of the pure noetic sciences is foremost, well, it seems to me that the former are brought up as vassals in comparison to free men.   *[d]*

Theo: But, to what extent?

Socr: To the extent that, as you yourself have just said it, the latter are never lacking in having ample amounts of leisure time and, so, their investigations are set up accordingly, just as even now with us we've already entered into our third digression, just as the one follows so naturally upon the heels of the other, like knots in a kite-string; and, so too, if the next one that proffers itself is more to our liking than that which already lies before us... and, then too, it's of no particular concern to us, those who just love to speculate, how long or how short our speeches may be – if only we strike up against what's right. But then, the others are always speaking in a pinch in that they're being driven to this by some deadline, for then the water that is flowing from the court clock makes sure that they hurry up and it doesn't even allow of them that they might broach the topics that, most of all, they'd love to speak about, or that they might find the time to enter into a thorough investigation of any matters like these; but, rather, it's so that their opponent is standing right there and he is forcing them that they get with the program and stick to protocol, and particularly to *these* points which simply have to be addressed, and beyond these limits they aren't even permitted to speak, not one word. And then too, let us not forget, their speeches are always in relation and connected to some other vassal whose level they share and, then, their speech is directed up to some master of justice or lord who is seated there before them and who is holding the rods of power in his hands [or is it their paychecks]. And, then too, the disputation is never merely regarding this or that, rather it's always about *the matter*, and indeed, often enough the matter is one of life and death. So, accordingly, through all of these circumstances they have *[173a]* indeed become quite sharp in their focus and they have been whittled down to a keen edge and, then too, they understand very well how they might most aptly speak in an obsequious manner and flatter their lords – as also, it goes without saying, how to arrange things in the performance of their duties so that they leave no stones unturned in being of service to their masters. But, all the same, their souls have shrunk and are all twisted. For then, their subservience from youth onward has taken away a great deal from their growth upward upon the free path which leads straight toward essence; and in that they have found themselves forced into the performance of crooked and shabby things, so their souls that were yet tender became all mixed up and in the greatest danger due to this concern about things regarding which it would be unable to carry through and still remain true to itself, as these things *do* injure that which is true and righteous – and so they are drawn into the lie and into mutual injustice, and turning toward such their souls became all bent out of shape and crippled, and nothing healthy remains for such souls as they pass from adolescence into manhood despite that they may well believe that they have become so wise and powerful. Such, now, is their constitution, Theodorus. Do you want that we also describe those who belong to our group? – or shall we let this matter be and return once more back to our earlier conversation so that we don't overly extend the freedom and lack of constraint that we touched upon a bit earlier?   *[c]*

Theo: In no way, Socrates, rather I'd very much like it if you would continue on and give your description of these others. For you were very much in the right when you remarked upon this, that in that we belong to this other group, so we are not vassals to our speeches but lords who command them, that they should wait upon us – when it is that we decide that we'd be through with them, just as it pleases us. For then, there is neither some judge, nor too, as it is with the poets, some audience, nobody sits before us with the authority to command or to punish us.

Socr: So let's do this, since you find this most pleasant and to your liking; and let's speak about those who find themselves at the apex. For then, what could one well say about those who only   *<24.~173d]* occupy themselves with philosophy in a manner that is unworthy. These others, now, from their youths onward, these don't even know the way to the market, nor where the courthouse stands, nor the assembly hall where the assemblymen meet to give advice, nor too where it is that the other institutions of the state convene that they might exercise the powers entrusted to them. The laws and all of the resolutions of the people, be they written or unwritten, these they never see nor do they hear of anything at all that pertains to such matters. Commercial or economic associations and the elections to the positions of leadership within such bodies, as well as the meetings that are called from time to time to discuss and advise the public, all of the festivals including the musical gatherings where the flutists entertain the public – for any and all of these things it wouldn't even occur to them in their dreams that they might pay heed to such matters. Whether, moreover, a few in their community should be of noble lineage, or if it might be that others carry some disgrace in their past heritage, be it on their mother's or upon their father's side, regarding anything like this he has so little conception as he does regarding how many grains of sand there might be in the ocean. And from all of these things he doesn't even once know that he doesn't know it! For then, he holds himself aloof from such matters, but it's not with any intent that thereby he might make a name for himself, rather in all actuality it's even so that it is only his body that finds itself living within the state and existing within it, but his soul has taken flight and contemptuously holds all of this as being mere trivia and naught, that rather taking Pindar's lead in the contemplation of the vastness of all existence and measuring everything upon the earth and in the depths of the seas and, then too, dividing up the stars in the heavens and, so, throughout the totality of everything in nature he investigates into the whole but never stoops down and totally disregards those things which lie nearby.   *[174a]*

Theo: How do you mean this, Socrates?

Socr: Just as it was with Thales, o Theodorus, when in order that he might better view the stars above and with his eyes set upon the heavens, he stepped back and, so, he fell right into a ditch. Then a charming but witty Thracian maid is said to have ridiculed him, that indeed, he might be striving to experience what would be in the heavens but that that which lay right in front of him and underneath his own feet, this remains unknown to him. And with even this same ridicule, now, people still are striking out against all of them, those of us who live absorbed in philosophical speculation. For, in all actuality, such a one doesn't have any idea about those closest to him and whoever it may be that's living next door, and not only *not knowing* what his neighbor's job and status is but, rather, also hardly knowing whether he be man or some other creature. But then, what the essential nature of man may be and regarding that which most accords with man's nature and status and differentiates humans from all others as regards what a human being does and suffers – this he investigates most painstakingly in his research and through all of his indagations. You do understand me, Theodorus, don't you? *[~c]*

Theo: Very well do I understand you, and what you say is very true.

Socr: Therefore, o friend, it's also so that if such a person has some business that he needs to transact with whomever it may be, or if it be some matter of public concern – as I was saying earlier – if, perhaps, he needs to come before the court of justice or wherever else it may be and, as it were, it's a matter of dealing with some issue that lies right underfoot and things upon which the eyes of everyone else are focused, and then it should become necessary that he speak out and say something, well, so he immediately arouses peals of laughter – and not merely from the Thracians but from everyone else who is present, in that due to his inexperience in lowering himself to such practical realities, so he succumbs to all sorts of anxiety and is totally at a loss and, then, his excessive ineptness is the cause for an immediate consensus of opinion that he's really a hopeless case. For then, when it comes to situations that require that he should abuse those who are beneath him, so he doesn't know how he's to attack anyone at all – in that he's never had an evil word or known anything bad in respect to anyone – as nothing of the sort has ever been the least of his concerns. And, now, because he's at a loss in asserting himself, so he's become comical. And, on the other hand, when it's time to act in an obsequious manner, that one praises his lordship or that one rises to one's feet upon their entrance, so again he makes it exceedingly obvious that he hasn't got a clue – for now it's he who's laughing, and not merely quietly to himself but in plain sight of everyone! – and, thus, he's regarded as nothing short of inane. For when it happens that he hears of some king or tyrant being lauded to high heaven, or that *"the court will now rise,"* so this seems utterly absurd to him, it's as if he were hearing praise given to some herdsman who tends to the sheep, or pigs or goats – and just because this person is most adept at milking them for all that they're worth – only, then too, he believes that the former is guarding over and   *[e]* milking a more unruly and nastier animal than are these latter ones and that due to a deficiency in leisure time, this leaves the one herder as well as the next totally derelict in matters of true ethics and the finer points of higher learning, that each of these is forced to remain inside the enclosures and the confines of the walls that surround his herd, just like the shepherd whose sheep graze high up in the mountains. But if it should be that he hears of the thousands of exotic cultures that exist in other parts of the world, or about those who rule over massive empires – as if these might be matters of phenomenal interest – so it seems to him as if he were hearing mention of some great triviality in that, after all, he's quite accustomed to set his sights over the whole of our earthly sphere. And, then too, if they should start off running on about   *[175a]* their glorious ancestry, so this seems to him to be as well a rather myopic vision and the paltry praise of those who make a lot from so little, that due to their deficiency in knowledge they are incapable of setting their perspective on the greater whole, nor too that they might calculate that each and every has had grandfathers and great-great-grandfathers that stretch back into countless thousands – amongst whom there have been rich and poor, kings and slaves, barbaric foreigners and Hellenes alike – and no one's heritage is a whit better than anyone else's! But then, to trace a family tree back perhaps twenty-five generations and to make a big deal out of such a small matter, that one might believe oneself a descendent of Heracles, son of Amphitryon, well, this impresses him as being the most absurd of trivialities and he can only laugh that, then, tracing things forward the twenty-sixth generation shall be just another one such, whoever happens to land in bed with whomever else, and the fiftieth just as well, regarding whom they don't even pretend to be able to calculate and, thus, he pops the over-inflated balloon of their pompous souls and their idiotic pride in such matters of ancestry. Due, as I say, to everything like this, now, such a one is the sport of ridicule to the masses – and also in that he displays his pride in matters that exceed their comprehension, as it seems to them; but then he's clueless and doesn't know anything at all regarding those matters that lie right underneath his feet, and that he hasn't a bit of advice about any of the particularities about which the others are so concerned.

Theo: It's exactly so, it happens precisely so as you have laid it out, Socrates.   *<25.~175c]*

Socr: But if he draws anyone up to himself, dear one, and if one wants to ascend with him from the question – Whether it be that I'm doing you an injustice or you one to me? – to an investigation regarding justice and injustice themselves, what each of these is and what differentiates each of them from the other and from all the rest, or from "Blessed is the king who possesses much gold" to the question regarding royalty itself and in what it is that human blessedness and misery fundamentally consist and what are the ways that such may be predicated of human nature, that the one may be achieved and the other avoided – just as soon as it's one of these things that is to be investigated through discourse, then should such a small-spirited, sharpshooter and disputant of the right enter into discourse, well, now it's he who experiences a dizzy spell in that he finds himself in such a rarefied atmosphere – so far above his accustomed environs – and he experiences trepidation and *Angst* having nowhere to turn to for help and, being no better than some foreign vassal is in his command of the language, indeed, he doesn't excite the laughter of the Thracian maid, nor too of anyone else who likewise is uninstructed, for then, these don't even notice it; but he does for all of those who haven't been raised as serfs, those of us, rather, whose upbringing has proceeded in a manner that is the polar opposite to these others. This now, o Theodorus, is how matters stand with each of these two sorts, the one which has truly been brought up in freedom with ample leisure time whom you call a philosopher and who may be allowed to appear as a simpleton without any need for reprisal and who, indeed, proves to be worthless when it comes to performing the obsequious duties of a vassal – as, it is true, he doesn't even understand how one goes about tying the knot in one's bundle that is to be carried upon one's shoulder, or how to prepare a savory meal, or how to speak in words most flattering; but then, the others do very much know how to perform all of these mundane tasks with great speed and dexterity but, then again, they don't even understand how it is that one comports oneself and how to fasten one's cloak as a free man and, then too, even less do they grasp what's needed to strike the right notes in their speech –   *[~176a]* that one worthily praises the true Life of the blessed gods and mankind.

Theo: If you, o Socrates, might convince everyone as you have convinced me of what you are saying: so there would be more peace and less evil amongst mankind.

Socr: Evil, o Theodorus, shall not possibly be eradicated, for then, there needs must always exist something that stands opposite to the good; nor too might it be that evil stems from the gods. But underlying the nature of mortal existence and in these environs it has its pull in accordance with the necessity just mentioned. For this reason also, one has to strive to flee from here and go thither as quickly as is possible. The way thither is assimilation with God so far as possible and such assimilation consists in this – that one is righteous and pious with insight. Singularly, most worthy, it's not at all easy to make this clear that the root cause of this, that one should flee from the malefic and strive after virtue, the root cause of this, I say, is not at all how most people contend that you should seek the one and not the other – so that, as they will tell you, that you might seem to be good, not bad. For all of this is nothing other than, as they say, the chatter of old women or the cluck of the hen. But the truth of *[176c]* this matter we want to put forth as follows. God is never in any wise unrighteous, rather in the highest degree fully and completely righteous and, so, nothing is more similar to Him as is that person amongst us who, likewise, is most righteous. And it is in orientation toward this in which the true mastery of man is expressed, as also his nullity and unmanliness. For then, knowing this is true wisdom and true virtue, but being deficient in such knowledge is manifest foolishness and maleficence. But everything else that is held up as mastery and as insight is, if it comes on display in relation to the administration of civil society, only something of a low order, but if in the arts, then it's something which is fettered and inferior. Whoever, then, speaks or acts in an unrighteous or impious manner, for him it would be better by far if no one would condone such speech or such behavior, that his mastery in being such is essentially only a matter of deceit. For then, they make sport of any reproach and believe only to hear that they are not the fools, useless deadweights of the earth, that rather they would be the real men as these would have to be, those who are privileged and are so successful in matters of statecraft. All the same, one has to speak out this truth to them, that all the more are they fools in that they don't believe that they would be such. For they are unacquainted with that regarding which, least of all, one should be unacquainted: the punishment of unrighteousness; not, namely, what they hold as being such, corporeal punishment and death – of which quite often they remained spared when committing their atrocities – but, rather, that punishment from which it is impossible to run away. [176e]

Theo: Which one, then, would you be meaning?

Socr: Two images, o friend, are set up in the world: the divine image of greatest beatitude and the ungodly which is misery – but they don't see this, that this is how it correlates, and so, due to their foolishness and due to this immense depravity in their understanding, they, without even themselves being aware of it, they become similar to the latter image for the sake of their unrighteous actions, but ever less similar to the former. And it is due to this that they suffer punishment in that they lead lives that are fitting to that to which they have become similar. If, now, we say to them that unless they let up from pursuing such mastery then after their lives have ended that place which has been cleansed of all evil will not grant them entry, that rather they shall always lead lives here abouts that are similar to what they themselves have become – as evil living within evil – so they hear this as do the wise and overly clever people do when spoken to by poor fools.

Theo: You're absolutely right, Socrates. [177b]

Socr: I know it, friend. But one thing does make an impression on them: that if they do stand up and enter into conversation about these things regarding which they have so much reproach and if it should be that they really are courageous enough and hold out long enough, and that they don't flee but prove themselves to be the men who they claim to be, well then, my good man, this all ends in a most wondrous manner, that they themselves no longer are pleased about what they have been saying and that their speechcraft ends up like a balloon which has been popped, and they themselves – they appear as children.

– But, enough of this, since we've only entered into this digression by the way; let's stand back from this for otherwise it may be that due the constant flood of new matters our earlier discussion shall be totally washed away. But, as I say, let's return now to the earlier considerations, if you think this appropriate. <26.~177c2]

Theo: For me, o Socrates, the current topic is one that is not any less pleasant to hear, particularly for a man of my years, as it's easier for me to follow. However, if it's your pleasure that we return to the earlier matters, then let's do so.

Socr: Isn't this the point that we were discussing in our earlier conversation in that we were saying that those who took fluctuating being as their position and that that which in each and every instance appears, to him for whomever this appears, that such really would be;

and that for these in regard to everything else, and so too pre-
eminently regarding the just, that these assert that what a state takes
and sets down as being its position, that such would *actually* be right
for it, the state that sets this down, so long as the state allows it to
stand; but then, in respect to that which pertains to the good, indeed,
no one from amongst them would be so courageous that he might
understand to assert that also that which a state sets up as being
useful, just because such is held up as being so, that this also really
would be useful for the state for so long as the state allows that such
be valid. Unless, of course, he only would be speaking from the mere
words and that, really, in relation to what we are meaning, this would
only be done as a jest. Isn't this true?

Theo: Indeed.   [e]

Socr: So, let's not be speaking merely from the word but, rather, of
the matter beneath these names that, thus, shall be drawn into view,
so that we consider it.

Theo: Indeed, let's not.

Socr: But that which the state names as such, every state also seeks
to strike this when it gives out its legislation and makes laws – and,
so, all the laws are directed toward this end, insofar as the state is
able to do so and knows what it's about, that these laws be as useful
for itself as is possible. Or, is the state looking upon something else
when it's making its laws?

Theo: Certainly not.   [178a]

Socr: And now, does it achieve this in each and every instance? –
or doesn't each fall quite short and fail in many respects?

Theo: I believe that they also fail.

Socr: And even the more so – most particularly from this vantage –
everyone would certainly admit the same if one were to pose this
question in relation to the entire class, that which falls beneath the
rubric of usefulness. Namely, in all instances this always relates to
the future time. For then, if we make laws, so we do so because they
should prove useful in the times to come – and this, indeed, is rightly
named by us, the future.

Theo: Indeed.   [b]

Socr: Come, then, and let's ask Protagoras or anyone else who asserts
the same thing as he does, and let's question them. Man is the
measure of all things, as you say, o Protagoras, of what is white or
heavy or light, in short of all things without exception that are of this
type. For then, he has the characterization of them within himself
in that he holds them to be such as he meets up against in that he has
the right notions for himself as to how they are. Isn't it so?

Theo: Yes, completely.   [~c]

Socr: Now, should we also say, o Protagoras, that he has as well the characterization of that which *shall be* in himself, and that what each and every person believes that it shall be for him, that such shall actually also come to be for him, he who believes such? Just as, for instance, how it shall be warm, if someone who is uninformed of medicine believes that he shall become feverish and that such warmth shall come to be for him; but someone else, say a physician, believes the opposite – should we say, then, that the future shall unfold in accordance to one of these two opinions, or perhaps, shall it be in accordance with both of them? – and shall he be neither warm nor feverish for the physician but for himself be both of these?

Theo: But really, that would be quite absurd.

Socr: So, I believe that as regards the future sweetness or dryness of the taste of some wine the opinion of the wine grower is what determines the question and not the opinion of the professional musician? [d]

Theo: How else!

Socr: And even so little is it well possible that regarding what shall ring out harmonically as good or awful, even so little is it possible that a master gymnast has a more accurate notion of this than the musician, even if it be regarding what he, the gymnast, shall be hearing later on.

Theo: No, not at all.

Socr: And so too, if a meal is being prepared, then the judgment of that person who is to be served shall be of lesser validity than the judgment of the cook as regards the pleasures of taste that are expected. For then, in regards to pleasure – what for each and every is or has been, regarding this we don't want that once again we stir up the flames of dispute, but, rather, only regarding this, what shall appear and shall be in the future for each and every, whether here too each of us is himself the best judge or whether it is you, Protagoras, who shall best be able to make the speech that is to be presented before the court so that it shall be believed – and in regard to each of us – and, so too, your notions shall be better than anyone else's, those who are not informed about such matters?

Theo: Hey now, Socrates, with this matter you're well on to something, for it was even in this that he promised to have pre-eminence in being better than anyone else. [~179a]

Socr: Quite right, my dear man. Or else, certainly, nobody would have paid so much money for his discourses if, then, he wouldn't have convinced them that in regard to what shall be and shall seem to be in the future, that neither a soothsayer nor anyone else is better able to judge such matters than he is.

Theo: Totally true.

Socr: And doesn't the legislation of laws and of that which is useful, don't these also have to do with the future? – and doesn't everyone, indeed, have to admit this, that the laws which a state decrees often fail in delivering what is most advantageous?

Theo: Certainly.

Socr: Thus, with utmost decisiveness we're able to say to your teacher that he necessarily has to admit this: that one is wiser *[b]* than the other and only such a one is the measure; but that I – in that I don't even pretend to know – by no means and in no way is it possible that I'm to be forced into being a measure as, indeed, even the speech that was spoken by his spirit would have forced this upon me, and whether I'd like it or not, that I be one.

Theo: In this spot, o Socrates, it seems to me that his proposition is best ensnared – as, then too, it's also ensnared when it allows that the opinions of those are valid, those who quite obviously don't want to hold to his propositions, that these would be true.   *[179c]*

Socr: Yet in many other spots, o Theodorus, is it possible that such a proposition shall become ensnared, that every notion that each of us has should be true. But, as to what touches upon the immediate presence of each and every, out of which the perceptions and notions that are connected and related to these come to be: so it is yet more difficult to make this manifest, that these shouldn't be true. Or, much rather, I'm saying nothing – and, perhaps, these are totally irrefutable and, so, those who assert that these would be without deceit and that they would be parts of knowledge, well, perhaps these might just be saying what's right and, then too, our Theaetetus wasn't all that far from being right on the mark when he set down his hypothesis that perception and knowledge would be the same. We have to venture further down this road – just as the defense of Protagoras' teaching directed us – and we have to rap soundly upon this door in that once again we take a good look at this hovering and fluctuating existence, whether it rings out harmonically as a whole, or if it should shatter. The disputation regarding this, verily, has already been always nothing trivial and not a subject for only a few.

Theo: Verily indeed, in no wise is this trivial, and pre-eminently in Ionia these issues have had a very broad base. For then, the friends of Heraclitus are most able leaders of the constituents, those who defend this proposition.   *<27.~179e]*

Socr: Even the more so, dear Theodorus, is it necessary for us that we step back and starting over from the beginning take another good look at this, how it is that they really delineate this proposition.

Theo: Quite, Socrates. Only, what it is that these Heracliteans or, as you say, those following Homer and what relates to the teachings that are even more ancient – like those from Ephesus – in as much as all of these constituents give themselves out as being "in the know" and informed of such matters, well, letting oneself enter into a serious conversation with these, this doesn't proceed any better than if one wanted to make an attempt to converse with wild animals   *[~180a]* that have become all riled up with barbs – for then, they are unable to remain standing still for even a single moment but, just as matters are proclaimed in their writings, so too, they run on like a river so that to grasp at anything and get a good grip *on hand or foot* by any of their propositions or some question relating thereto – that in a calm and composed manner one poses questions and receives answers from any of them in an orderly format, anything like this is less likely to be expected from them than nothing. Really! – not even nothing is already saying too much, so little calmness is inherent in these people. Rather, if you ask one of them regarding whatever it may be, so they pull forth from out of their sheath of arrows some riddles, anecdotes or snappy aphorisms and shoot these forth into the air and, then, if once more you ask for clarification regarding how any of these were meant, well then, you shall find yourself being struck by another pithy word construction that is similar to the former ones but now comes with a totally new twist as regards its wording. But to get to the end of anything at all, this you shall never be able to accomplish, not with any one of them; nor too do they themselves with each other. Rather, most precisely do they observe their tenet, that nothing remains at rest, and neither in their speeches nor in their own souls in that, as it seems to me, they take care that this itself might be something that persists and against everything else they prove their might in their disputations and are utterly at odds with persistence, scattering any vestiges of the same to the four winds.
Socr: Perhaps, Theodorus, you have only seen these men when they're engaged in war but haven't been amongst them when they are at peace, for then, they're not even your friends. But I believe that such matters are calmly discussed when they share these with their students, those whom they seek to make similar to themselves.
Theo: What students, indeed! – you amazing man! With   *[~180c]* these there is no one who becomes a student of anyone else, rather they sprout from out of themselves, each and every one of them enthused all on his own, and each of them holds the other as being naught. Thus, from these you shan't, as already I wanted to tell you, you shan't get a single question answered, neither of their own good will nor even through force; rather it's totally left up to us, as if we

had received this as our assignment that we do a report on them, so that we draw them into view and weigh them in our considerations. *Socr:* Your memory regarding this is very right. Now, isn't   *[~d]* our assignment so, firstly in regard to these men of yore, those who through the help of poetry managed to keep the greatest portion of their teachings well concealed, and isn't it their conception that the root cause of *the All* is Oceanus and Tethys, that these would be rivers, and that nothing stands fast and firm; but next, in respect to the sages of a more recent vintage, these men who are wiser still and who don't mind displaying everything in total openness so that even the shoemakers might hear their wisdom and learn it and, so, that these finally give up in their foolish ways of believing that a few matters would be permanent from amongst 'that which is' and only other things are in flux; that rather they learn this from them and that they praise them for opening up their eyes to this: that [absolutely] everything is in flux. But I almost would have forgotten, o Theodorus, that others again assert the polar opposite to all of this – that, namely, *the Unmovable* is the right name of the whole, and whatever else Melissus and Parmenides assert in contradiction to all of these others, that *the All is One* and that it exists in itself – as extension doesn't pertain to it, that there is nowhere within which it would be capable of moving itself. What now, dear one, what should we begin with as regards all of these? For then, without even noticing it we've drifted right smack into the midst between these two camps and if we don't manage to come up with some way of helping ourselves out of this, so we'll have to pay the penalty and suffer punishment, just like those who play tug-of-war in the exercise field by the gymnasium and find themselves caught up by the rope that is being pulled by *[181a]* opposing teams in opposite directions. Hence, I think that first off we want to draw close to these in our considerations, those against whom we originally ran up, these contenders of flux, and should it become apparent that they are saying something that is well founded, so then we'll want to give them our help and pull on their side, and that we'd also want to make efforts to escape from the others. But then, if these others – those who hold fast on to the whole – if these seem to be asserting something that is closer to what's right, so, on the contrary, we want to flee over to their side and shy away from the former ones, those who also move the immovable. But then, if it comes to light and is shown that neither side brings forth anything that's really apt – so then, it would really be absurd if we, in that we're just totally average folks, that we'd say something right and so have disparaging views to these primeval sources, to men whose stature in wisdom is so high. Take a look at this, Theodorus, whether you think it advisable that we place ourselves into the midst of such great danger.

Theo: In no way, o Socrates, would it now be bearable if we didn't want to bring this out, to what extent both sides may well be right.

Socr: Thus, there's no way around it, we just have to investigate into this – since you've become so headstrong about it.   *<28.~181c3]*

But the beginning of the investigation has to be made, as it seems to me, with movement – what, indeed, the former ones really understand beneath this [concept] when they say that "everything is in flux" and in motion. Namely, I mean to say this, whether it be that they understand one manner of motion, or, as it seems to me, two. But not only to me should this seem to be so, rather you too should likewise take part in this so that both of us may suffer whatever it may be that strikes up against this. And so, tell me: do you call that movement if something swaps places with something else, or else if it spins around in the same place? [165]

Theo: I name this so.   *[d]*

Socr: This, then, is the one manner. But if, then, something indeed remains at the same place, but if it ages, or if it becomes black in that formerly it was white, or hard in that it was formerly soft, or suffers under any other alteration – doesn't this deserve to be called another manner of motion?

Theo: It seems so to me.

Socr: It's not possibly otherwise. These two manners of movement, thus, are what I'm meaning, alteration and changing places.

Theo: And in this you're doing what's totally right.

Socr: Now, once this separation is made, so let's enter into discourse with them, those who assert that the all is in flux, and ask them: Do you say that everything moves itself in both of these manners, both by changing places as well as by being altered, or that a few things in both manners, others only in one manner?   *[e]*

Theo: By Zeus, I don't know what to say, but I believe that they shall assert – in both manners.

Socr: At least if they don't, o friend, then it would have to be that both movement and stasis appear to them, and then it wouldn't be any more correct to say that everything is in flux than it would be to say that everything is at rest.

Theo: What you're saying is entirely true.

---

[165] *Parmenides* 138b (pp. 220–221).

Socr: Since, now, everything is in motion and immobility should be something that is never encountered in anything at all, so everything has to always in each and every motion be itself in motion.   *[182a]*
Theo: That's necessary.
Socr: And pull this too up into consideration from them and place it on the balance. Didn't we say that the coming to be of warmth or of redness or whatever else you'd like, didn't we approximately clarify this in such a manner, that each of these would be in motion during [the act of] perception between that which produces effects and that which suffers, and that that which suffers shall then be a perceiver, not a perception, and that that which produces effects shall be a "so-qualified," but not a quality. But quality, this, perhaps, is an amazing word to you and you don't understand it when it's expressed in such a general way. So then, hear it when it's expressed in particular [instantiations]. Namely, that which produces effects shall neither be warmth nor redness, but rather a warm or a red something, and so on for all the rest. For then, you do remember from before that we said that nothing is in and of itself one determinate, thus too, neither an effect producer nor a sufferer, but that rather only through the meeting up and encountering of both of them, perception and the perceptible, and by generation, only so shall the one be a so-qualified and the other a perceiver.
Theo: I remember that, how could I forget it.   *[c]*
Socr: All the rest we want to set aside, whether they mean it to be so or otherwise; and just this one issue, the reason why we're speaking of this now, just hold on tight to this – in that we ask them: Everything is itself in motion and in flux, as you say – isn't this true?
Theo: Yes.
Socr: And, indeed, in both manners of motion that we have differentiated in that it swaps places and alters itself?
Theo: How else? Since, affirmatively, it itself should fully be in motion.
Socr: If, now – if it only changed its place but didn't alter itself, then, indeed, we would yet be able to say *what*, then, actually in changing its place is in flux. Or, how should we say this?
Theo: Just so.   *[d]*
Socr: But since also this doesn't even persist, that the flowing red flows, that rather likewise it is changing so that also of even this redness there exists a flux and a transition to some other color so that in this manner it shall not be discovered as persisting, is it well possible now that anyone might name something as a certain [knowable{*gewisse*}] color so that it would be named correctly?

Theo: How should one do so, o Socrates, and even so little as regards everything else that is similar – since, affirmatively, everything is slipping away from between the speaker's fingers as being constantly in flux.

Socr: And what shall we say in regards to perception, whichever manner it might ever be that you want, whether it be seeing or hearing, that there might be persistence in sight or in hearing?   *[e]*

Theo: We're not allowed to do so because, verily, everything is in flux.

Socr: One is no more allowed, thus, and isn't any more right in that one names something as seeing than as not-seeing, and so too with every other perception – since, affirmatively, everything moves itself in all ways.

Theo: No, indeed not.

Socr: But now perception is knowledge, as the two of us have said, Theaetetus and I.

Theo: So it was.

Socr: Hence, when we were questioned as to what knowledge would be, we have answered through something that is no more or has no greater actuality in being knowledge than it does in not being knowledge.

Theo: This seems to be how matters have progressed for you. *[183a]*

Socr: This is really majestic, how matters have arranged themselves in the making fast of our answer – since we were seeking to show that everything would be in flux so that even through this the former answer would seem to be right. For now it has become apparent, as it seems, that if everything is in flux then *any* answer that one might have handy – one says now it correlates so or otherwise – is equally right or, much more, becomes right, so that we don't pretend to have any notion, that this too has some persistence in that we speak it.

Theo: What you say is totally right.

Socr: Regardless of this, Theodorus, that I've said So and Not-so. For, then too, one's not allowed to speak this "So" because the So itself is not in flux; nor too, "Not-so" – for that too isn't any movement. That rather those who assert this proposition would have to introduce some other language for it because up till now there doesn't exist any words for their assumption – unless, perhaps, it be *that in no way*; so it may be to their liking that this most readily is spoken to, expressed totally without any determination.   *[~c]*

Theo: Indeed, this would be the style of speech that best befits them.

Socr: Thus, o Theodorus, on the one hand we may now be done with your friend – and we haven't at all relented or given in to him that *Each should be the measure of all things* – if, then, anyone at all is to be wise and have understanding; and, on the other hand, we shan't admit this either – that knowledge is perception – namely, in accordance to the teaching of the flux of all things. It would have to be that Theaetetus here might have something else to say.

Theo: Spoken most admirably, Socrates, and right to the point. For then, in that this has been brought to its conclusion, so too it must be the case that you're finished pursuing the conversation with me in accordance, namely, with our contract which stipulated as its terminus the point when Protagoras' proposition would have reached its conclusion.

Theae: But not any sooner, however, o Theodorus, than <29.~183d] when Socrates also shall have walked you through the proposition of the others, those who assert to the contrary – that the whole is at rest – just as you two set out to do.

Theo: Still so young, Theaetetus, and already teaching your elders that they act unrighteously and overstep the bounds of their contracts? No, rather that you prepare yourself, just how it may be that you intend to answer Socrates' questions.

Theae: If he should want me to. What I would have loved most, however, would be to hear you two, just as I indicated.

Theo: That's called forcing the horsemen into the plains when one draws Socrates into conversation. You just ask away and you'll well experience the answer.

Socr: All the same, as I'd fancy it, o Theodorus, I shan't be able to comply with Theaetetus and do as he bids.   *[e]*

Theo: But, why not do his bidding?

Socr: Melissus, indeed, and the others who say that *the Whole is One and Immovable*, I shy away from these, that we don't make ourselves silly in our scrutinizing them. However, my shyness in regards to them is far less than the timidity I experience when approaching the lone Parmenides. For Parmenides, as Homer puts it: *"I hold in noble esteem and dread him as well."* For then, when I was still but a youth I entered into community with the man as he, already then, was of an age most venerable – and he revealed to me a depth of mind and spirit that is most rare and majestic. I'm fearful, therefore, that in part we won't understand what he says and in part that we'll be left even further behind in getting to the meaning that lurks behind his doctrines and, what's even more, that that which already we have been tracking after so assiduously, namely in regards to knowledge – what it is – that this will remain unfinished and unresolved because of all of these questions that come streaming toward us if, then, one wants to give heed to all of this, not even to mention the multitude that rises up before us and completely blocks our view [166] – all of that, namely, which we just touched up against; and if we only wanted to consider such an investigation in passing, so this matter would suffer impropriety; but then, if this is followed up in a sufficient manner that reaches into these murky depths, so then, the matter regarding knowledge shall be pushed off into the background. Both, indeed, are not permitted to be; rather we have to make the attempt and follow through in our resolve that we make every effort to relieve Theaetetus of his burden, this pregnancy of his as regards knowledge, that we help him through our art and profession of midwifery in   *[184b]* delivering him of his child.

Theo: Tallyho, if you fancy this good, we'll have to do it, just so.

Socr: So weigh and consider also this other issue, o Theaetetus, how this relates to the former matters about which we conversed. – Perception would be knowledge, this is what you answered earlier, isn't it true?

Theae: Yes.

Socr: If, now, someone were to ask you: "But with what does a human being see white and black?" and "With what does he hear the high and low?" – you would say, I believe, with eyes and ears.

Theae: I, certainly.   *[c]*

Socr: Taking words at face value and not delving into all the minutiae and dissecting out all manners of overly subtle distinctions, this for the most part is not at all acting in an unrefined or vulgar manner, rather the opposite to this is more likely to be acting in a servile and unfree way – only, from time to time it is, nonetheless, quite necessary. So too, it's also necessary now that we attack the answer that you have just supplied – to what extent that it is not right. For take a good look at this yourself, which answer is more correct – whether that with which we see are our eyes, or are they that *through* which we see? And do we hear with our ears, or through them?

Theae: "Through which," I'd fancy, is better than "with which."   *[d]*

Socr: It would also be most vexing, my child, if all of these sorts of perception would all lie next to one another within us, as if we were wooden horses and as if they didn't all run together into some one – you may call it mind, soul or whatever else you ever may like to name it – with which, then, and through the functionality of all of these others, these which I might call the instruments through which we perceive whatever it may be that is perceivable.

Theae: That is why I fancied that through which is better than with which.

---

[166] The "monster wave" of non-being, see *Sophist* 264d (p. 577).

Socr: But why is it that I lead you so precisely to this, whether it be so that with one and the same within us and, now, through the eyes we perceive black and white, and through the other organs other　*[e]* perceptions are taken up and whether, if you were asked, whether you would base all of these perceptions upon the physical body? But, it might be better that I let you answer this yourself, that you clarify this matter yourself rather than allowing myself so much latitude in going into all of this for you. So tell me, then, that through which you perceive warmth and hardness and softness and sweetness, don't you place all of this as belonging to the body? – or to something other?

Theae: To nothing other.

Socr: Shall you also want to admit as much, that that through the power of which you perceive any of these, that it's not possible that you perceive the same through some other one of them? –　*[185a]* that what you perceive through sight you're incapable of perceiving through hearing, and what you perceive through hearing you're incapable of perceiving through sight?

Theae: How should I not want to admit as much?

Socr: But then, if it should be that you think something about both, so it's not possible that you do so through either the one of these instruments nor through the other one, that is – through either of the two of these through which you perceive?

Theae: No, indeed not.

Socr: Now, regarding sound and color, don't you think, first of all, of the two of these – that they both are?　*[b]*

Theae: I think so.

Socr: And not also, that each of them is different from the other but that each is of one and the same sort as itself?

Theae: Indeed.

Socr: And that both together are two, but each of them one?

Theae: This too.

Socr: And aren't you also in a position to investigate into this, whether it may be that they are similar or dissimilar to one another?

Theae: Perhaps.

Socr: Now, all of this, through what do you think all of this about them? For neither through vision nor through hearing is it possible for you that you might grasp at that which they share in common. And this too is yet another proof of what we are saying. Namely, if it were to be possible to investigate as to whether they both might be salty, so you do know what you would say as to with what you　*[c]* would investigate into this – and, obviously, it wouldn't be either with your vision nor with your hearing but, rather, with something else.

Theae: What else might it be other than the capability given through the tongue.

Socr: Totally right. Through what means, then, is it that that capability works through which the commonality of all things – as well as these things that were just discussed – through what, I say, is this commonality revealed; that with which you speak out regarding their being and non-being, in pursuit of which I even just now questioned you. For all of this, essentially what instrument do you want to postulate by means of which our perceiver perceives each of these?

Theae: You mean their being and non-being, their similarity and *[d]* dissimilarity, unity and difference; furthermore whether they are one or some other number. Obviously you conceive beneath this also the question in regard to even and odd and whatever else it is that relates hereto – by the means of or through which part of the body, namely, do we perceive all of this with the soul.

Socr: Totally on the mark, o Theaetetus, you are following me – for this is just what I'm questioning you about.

Theae: But, by Zeus, Socrates, I wouldn't know what I might say except that it seems to me that there wouldn't exist such a particular instrument at all for this or that – but, rather, it seems to me that the soul investigates the commonality of all things just through itself.

Socr: You are a beauty, Theaetetus, and not at all as Theodorus told me, ugly; for he who speaks so beauteously, he is beautiful and good. But besides this, that this was beauteously spoken, you also have bestowed a great favor upon me in that you have helped me rise above a great deal of discourse if this also shall be apparent to you – that a few things are investigated by the soul itself through its own self, but other matters through the various instruments of the body. For it is even this that I myself was meaning and of which I wished that you also might like to be meaning.

Theae: Very much, indeed, do I intuit this.   *<30.~186a]*

Socr: To which of the two of them do you account being? For then, this, indeed, is what stands first and foremost amongst them all?

Theae: To those [matters] that the soul attends upon alone through its own self.

Socr: And the same may also well be said of similarity and dissimilarity, of being 'one and the same' and being different?

Theae: Yes.

Socr: And how about the beauteous and the malefic, good and evil?

Theae: Also of these, most particularly, I'd fancy that the soul investigates into the correlation of these with one another in that on

its own and through itself it sets the past and the present in relation
to what shall be in the future.   *[b]*
Socr: Then, *tallyho* – shall not the soul perceive the hardness of what
is hard and the softness of what is soft through means of touch?
Theae: Yes.
Socr: But the being of both of these, what they are and the opposition
they have one to the other, and the reality of this opposition,
regarding this, thus, our souls attempt to make judgments alone in
themselves through observation and by comparison.
Theae: By all means.
Socr: And isn't it true, to perceive the former, whatever it may be as
regards the impressions that come through the body to arrive at   *[c]*
the soul, this is given to man and animal by nature already as soon
as they are born. Singularly, the final judgments regarding these,
as to their being and their usefulness, this, if it is achieved at all,
this is only achieved with difficulty and with time and through much
exertion and by having instruction – so is this achieved, I say, and
only achieved by those who do achieve it thus?
Theae: Quite; so it is.
Socr: Is it possible that the former reaches as far as the true essence
of something – if, then, it doesn't even reach as far as its being?
Theae: Impossible.
Socr: But if one hasn't reached as far as the true essence of
something, is it possible that one might have knowledge of it?
Theae: Indeed, Socrates, how might one do so?   *[d]*
Socr: In the former impressions, thus, there isn't any knowledge;
but there may well be knowledge in the judgments of them. For then,
to reach as far as to being and true essence, this is – as it seems – only
possible through these judgments, but is not possible through the
former.
Theae: Apparently.
Socr: Do you want, now, that you name the former and the latter as
the same? – since they both display such great differences?
Theae: That doesn't seem warranted.
Socr: What name do you place upon the former ones, seeing and
hearing and smell and being chilled or being warm?
Theae: I name this perceiving. How else?   *[186e]*
Socr: All together, thus, you name this perception.
Theae: Naturally.
Socr: Of which, then, as we have said – such is not conferred upon
it, that it reaches as far as true essence, since it doesn't even make it
as far as being?
Theae: No, not conferred.

Socr: Thus too, not to knowledge?
Theae: No, that doesn't follow.
Socr: In no wise, therefore, o Theaetetus, would perception be the same as knowledge.
Theae: It seems not; much rather it has become totally clear that knowledge is something other than perception. *[187a]*
Socr: But we didn't begin our conversation for this reason, in order that we discover what knowledge wouldn't be, but rather that we discover what it is. All the same, we have gotten so far along that we don't want to be seeking after it underneath perception but, rather, beneath the name that bespeaks the leadership of soul, if it occupies itself for itself with that which is.
Theae: This, o Socrates, shall, I believe, be named notionality *{das Vorstellen*[167]*}*.
Socr: You're totally right that you believe this, dear one, *<31.~187b]* and now once again take a look from the beginning, after we've rubbed out all of the previous, whether now you see more since you've managed to fight your way this far forward and tell me still one more time: what may knowledge well be?
Theae: To say that it would be all notionality, o Socrates, is impossible – in that there also exist false notions. But it may well be that having the right notions is knowledge and, so, this is what I want to say in answer to you. For then, if it should not seem to be so as we proceed further along, then we want to do just as we're doing now and make an attempt that we say something other than this.
Socr: That's right, Theaetetus; and so it is that one has to speak out somewhat more courageously than you were speaking initially – *[c]* as then you were just a bit too conscientious in giving answers. But if we make this our motto, so then, one or the other of these two will happen to us: that either we shall find what we are seeking or we won't believe so much that we know what we don't in any way know. And this too, this wouldn't be a bad bargain and isn't something to be spurned. But how was it now, and what was it you were meaning? Of the two sorts of notions that we may have, one of which is true and the other one false, you clarify that the true one shall be knowledge?
Theae: I do so; for this, now, is what I intuit.
Socr: Should we once again retrace our steps further as regards notionality?
Theae: Only tell me – what do you mean? *[~d]*

---

[167] Compare with *Meno* 85c (p. 483), 97b (p. 497); *Vorstellen* is consistently translated as having notions, hence "notionality"; compare as well *Parmenides* 134c, 142a, 155d, 166b.

Socr: This disturbs me even now, as well as having disturbed me already quite often previously – that I'm so greatly at a loss and anxious, and not only with myself but likewise before others – that, namely, I know not what to say as to what, indeed, is this happenstance within us and how does it come to be?

Theae: But, which one?

Socr: That anyone has false notions. And, so too, even now I reflect upon this dubiously – whether we leave it at this or whether we take this up into consideration, and do so in some other manner than the one that we employed just previously.

Theae: Why not, Socrates, if this seems to you to be necessary in the least little bit. For then, it wasn't poorly done at all, what you and Theodorus discussed previously as regards having ample leisure time, that there's nothing at all that constrains us or has us in a pinch in such things as these.   *[~e]*

Socr: You're totally right in that you remind me of this. Perhaps this wouldn't be so bad at all, that we take up the spoor and follow after it one more time. For then, it is better that one completes a very small bit and does it well rather than doing a great deal in an insufficient manner.

Theae: Quite.

Socr: How now? – what is it that we say, really? Do we assert that any notion at all would ever actually be false? – and that the one of us has false notions but the other one has correct ones so that this correlates so by nature?

Theae: Indeed, this is what we assert.   *[188a]*

Socr: Now, doesn't this happen to be the case in respect to all things and with any and all particularities, that either we know it or that we don't know it? For then, right now let's leave these other matters, learning and forgetting, which happen in between knowing and not-knowing, let's leave these lying off to the side because, for now anyway, they don't at all belong to the matter.

Theae: Then, indeed, Socrates, nothing else remains left over from the former matter other than that one either knows about it or one doesn't.

Socr: Isn't it necessary, then, that whoever has a notion: either he has a notion of something that he knows or of something that he doesn't know?

Theae: That's necessary.

Socr: But that someone who knows something also doesn't know the same, or that someone who doesn't know knows – this, indeed, is impossible.   *[b]*

Theae: How couldn't it be impossible. *{Wie sollte es nicht.}* [168]

Socr: Hence, he who has a false notion of something that he knows – he probably believes that it isn't this but, rather, something else about which he also knows – and so, knowing about both of these, nonetheless, he doesn't recognize either of them?

Theae: But, assuredly, that's not possible.

Socr: Or maybe then it's so: that that about which he doesn't know, this he holds as being something else about which, likewise, he doesn't know; and that is as much as saying that someone who doesn't know Socrates, nor does he know Theaetetus – such a person still would happen upon the idea that Socrates would be Theaetetus or that Theaetetus would be Socrates.

Theae: But, *how* might that ever be? [188c]

Socr: But, all the same, nobody shall believe that that about which he knows would be something about which he doesn't know; nor too, on the other side, that that about which he doesn't know, that such would be something about which he does know.

Theae: Now, *that* would really be a wonder.

Socr: How may it be, then, that anyone might ever have a notion that is false? For outside of these possibilities, indeed, there aren't any other notions that we might have since, then, regarding everything we either know or don't know – and in all of these it seems to be impossible that, somehow, one might have false notions.

Theae: Very true. [~d]

Socr: Don't we want, perhaps, that preferably we reflect upon this, what we're going after, in such a manner: that we don't aim at knowing or at not-knowing but, rather, upon being or non-being?

Theae: How do you mean this?

Socr: Whether it might not, perhaps, quite simply be so that whoever has notions regarding any matter at all, and these notions are of "what isn't," in every case he has false notions, no matter whatever else might pertain to how this might be arranged in his soul.

Theae: That too, Socrates, has a good look about it.

Socr: But how? What shall we say, Theaetetus, if someone questions us: Is this also possible for anyone at all, what you two are saying? – and can it well be so that someone has notions of non-being, whether such should be in and of something [other] or if it should be in and of itself? To this we shall have to say, as it seems, if such a person

---

[168] As mentioned in *Parmenides* 131a, 137d – this rhetorical answer requires the reader to make especial efforts to think the underlying issues through. Meno's slave's "knowledge" of square areas, obviously, is quite relevant here. Indeed, Schleiermacher places *Meno* between *Theaetetus* and *Sophist* because of this.

doesn't believe what is true in that he does believe something. Or, what do we want to say?   *[e]*

Theae: Just so.

Socr: But does this ever happen as well anywhere else?

Theae: What's that?

Socr: Whether someone sees, but yet, he doesn't see?

Theae: How could he?

Socr: But if, now, he sees something – so he sees something that is actual? – or do you believe that something might ever possibly belong to the not-actual?

Theae: I, no, not at all.

Socr: He who sees something, he sees something actual?

Theae: So it seems.

Socr: And, even so – he who hears, he hears something and something actual?   *[189a]*

Theae: Yes.

Socr: And he who feels, he feels something, and if something, then something actual?

Theae: That too.

Socr: And, so – he who has a notion, shouldn't he have a notion of something?

Theae: Necessarily.

Socr: And he who has a notion of something, is it not of something actual?

Theae: I admit as much.

Socr: He, then, who has a notion of something that isn't, he has a notion of nothing?

Theae: So it seems.

Socr: But he who has a notion of nothing, he certainly shall not have any notion at all?

Theae: Obviously, as we see.   *[~b]*

Socr: So, accordingly, it isn't possible to have any notions of what isn't – neither as of something [other] that is, nor too, in and of itself?

Theae: It seems not.

Socr: Hence, having false notions is something different from having notions of something that isn't?

Theae: Something different, so it seems.

Socr: Thus, neither in this manner nor in the manner in which we conceived this earlier, in neither way do there exist false notions in us?

Theae: No, none indeed.   *<32.~189c]*

Socr: Rather, we want to speak about this approximately so, that this is how it happens.

Theae: How's that?

Socr: As a mixed up notion false notions do take place – if someone swaps something actual in his thoughts with something else that's actual and he says: the former would be the latter. For in such a manner he always has notions of something actual, but one instead of the other, and in that he goes astray from that toward which he was aiming one is able to rightfully say that he has a false notion.

Theae: Now it seems to me that what you have just said is totally right. For then, if someone has a notion that something ugly instead is beautiful, or that something beautiful instead is ugly, then he's had a notion that is actually [truly] false.

Socr: Obviously, Theaetetus, you're gaining altitude in the manner in which you treat me and you've lost all of your trepidation of me.

Theae: But, how's that?

Socr: You don't at all believe, I think, that I shall attack this [d] "actually false" and that I shall question you whether it may well be possible that slow is fast or light heavy, or that any other of two opposing matters, that either shall possibly be able to become the opposite of its own nature, that – in short – anything might be the opposite of itself. All the same, I'll just let this be as it may so that not for nothing shall you have been brazen. But now, you find this pleasing and to your liking, as you say, that having false notions should be having notions that are mixed up?

Theae: For me, yes.

Socr: It is possible, then, in accordance to your opinion, that something might be proposed in thought as being an other and not the former.

Theae: This is so – [and happens] too. [189e]

Socr: If now, someone's soul does this, so, indeed, it necessarily has to think either both or one of these.

Theae: That's necessary.

Socr: Either simultaneously or one after the other.

Theae: Spoken as an artist. {Sehr schön.}

Socr: And thought – do you understand underneath this even the same as I?

Theae: What do you understand underneath this?

Socr: A speech that the soul runs through alone by itself regarding whatever it may be that she wants to investigate. Indeed, only as someone who doesn't know am I able to describe this to you. For this is the way that she hovers before me, that, in as long as she is thinking she does nothing other than converse with herself in that she gives answers to herself, agrees and disagrees. But if she, as she goes [a] along – and, now, be it at a slower or at a faster pace – if she holds firmly onto something as decided and she *persists* in the same assertion and no longer doubts it – this, then, is what we name as her having a notion. Therefore I say that notionality is speech, and that having a notion is a speech spoken, not to anyone else and with one's voice, rather alone to oneself and silently. But you, how about you?

Theae: I, just so.

Socr: If, thus, someone has a notion that the one is the other, so he also says to himself, as it seems, "the one is the other"?

Theae: How else?   *[190b]*

Socr: So do take stock of your memories, whether you have ever said to yourself: the beauteous is indeed most certainly ugly and the unrighteous righteous, or also – what is the sum total of all of this – bethink yourself whether it may well be that you may even have attempted to convince yourself of this: the one, indeed, is certainly the other? – or whether not, rather, and quite completely the opposite to this, it would never once occur to you and not even in your dreams that you might say this to yourself, that, indeed, it's totally certain that the odd would be even, or anything else even remotely similar to this?

Theae: You're right.   *[c]*

Socr: And do you believe that anyone else of sound mind or also, indeed, even a lunatic would have the heart that expressly to himself he says: the ox quite certainly would be a horse, or two is one?

Theae: By Zeus, not I.

Socr: Thus, if speaking alone to oneself is named having notions, so there shall be no one who speaks out both and has notions of both, taking both up within his soul, no one shall ever say or have such a notion, as if the one were to be the other. And, so too, you have to say *adieu* and *bon voyage* to the former word regarding the one and the other, that you let this be gone; for, I say it once again: nobody has any such notions as these, that the ugly would be beautiful or any-thing else that is like this.   *[d]*

Theae: I let it go and I fancy that it's just as you say.

Socr: He who has notions of both, for him it's not possible that he has such a notion, that the one is the other.

Theae: So it seems.

Socr: But he who has a notion of only one of both, but totally and absolutely no notion of the other, he certainly isn't at all able to have such a notion, that the one would be the other.

Theae: You're quite right. For then he'd have to simultaneously take something up that he doesn't at all have as a notion.

Socr: Neither, then, does he who has a notion of both nor he who only has a notion of the one – in neither case is it possible for him *[e]* to mix up his notions – so that whoever wants to clarify that false notions would be notions that have become all mixed up, he hasn't said anything at all. For neither in this manner nor in the manner mentioned previously, neither way does it seem possible that a false notion would be in us.

Theae: It seems not.

Socr: Nonetheless, Theaetetus, if this won't at all display itself to us as being actual, so we will be forced into admitting very many intolerable things.

Theae: Indeed – but what, essentially?   *<33.~191a]*

Socr: I don't want to tell you any more about these things before I first have attempted, and in every manner that is at all possible, that I investigate into this matter. For then, I would myself be ashamed for us if we were to be forced during this, our being anxious and at a total loss, that we would have to give in and make allowance for what I'm meaning. But once we have found it out and have, thus, made ourselves free [from any such repercussions], then we want, in that we ourselves have found safety and security against all of the laughter that shall ensue, only then do we want to speak regarding this in relation to the others, how matters stand with them and what they must undergo. But if we should have to give up every hope then we want, I opine, that we hang our heads in humiliation and give ourselves over to the proposition as if we were seasick wayfarers, that this proposition might walk all over us and do to us whatever it wants. So hear now what, essentially, I still see as an escape for this question.

Theae: Just tell me.

Socr: I will deny it, that we were right when we submitted ourselves to this – that what somebody knows, of this it isn't possible for him to have a notion that it would be something else about which he doesn't know; rather this, indeed, is possible in a certain way.   *[b]*

Theae: Would you, perhaps, be meaning this – what I was suspecting when we dealt with this earlier, that such belonged even here, namely: from time to time I, in that I'm acquainted with Socrates, if I see somebody else from afar, somebody, though, with whom I'm not acquainted, I might believe – there is Socrates – he who, indeed, I know. For in this instance it does happen, just as you say.

Socr: But didn't we back off from this because it then followed that something of which we know, in that we know it, still, simultaneously we also don't know it?

Theae: Quite.   *[~c]*

Socr: Then let's not set matters up in such a fashion, but so. Perhaps this will be granted to us as acceptable and perhaps, too, someone also will be all up in arms against this; singularly, we're now in such a tight pinch that it's necessary that once more we have to turn and double-check each and every speech. Do look sharp, whether I'm saying something. Is it possible that something that previously one didn't know, is it possible later to learn this?

Theae: Indeed, it is.

Socr: Then too, at another occasion, something else; and something else yet again?

Theae: How shouldn't this be possible!

Socr: So place for me now – in that we yet shall have a word – place within our souls a waxen nodule that is able to take up impressions; in the one of us it's larger, in another smaller; in the one of us of a purer quality, by another quite dirty; also harder by some and by others softer; and in a few exactly how it would have to be.   *[d]*

Theae: I've placed it.

Socr: This, we want to say, this would be a gift given to us from the mother of the muse, Mnemosyne,[169] and whatever it may be that we want to remember from what we have seen or heard – or also from what we ourselves have thought – these are pressed into the wax in that we store our perceptions and thoughts just like the engravings made by sealing rings. Whatever, now, is stored by making such an impression, of this we have memory and we know it, namely, so long as its image is present. But if it should become effaced or rubbed out, or if it wasn't even able of being impressed at all, so we forget about the matter and we don't know it?   *[e]*

Theae: This should be so.

Socr: He who knows in this manner and then examines something that he sees or hears, take a look, whether he's able to have a false notion in the following manner.

Theae: In which manner?

Socr: In that for him something that he knows, from time to time he holds this as something that he knows but, from time to time, for something that he doesn't know. For that this is impossible, we weren't right previously in that we didn't give in and make any allowance for this, that it does take place.

Theae: What, then, do you now say about this?   *[192a]*

Socr: So – this is how one has to speak in that right off from the start one determines the matter with greater finesse. Of that which someone knows in that he has its thought-impression in his soul, but if he's not perceiving it, to hold this to be something else which, likewise, he knows having its impression in his soul and which he also isn't perceiving, this is impossible. And, then again, to hold some-

[169] Goddess of Memory – daughter of Uranus and Gaea, mother by Zeus of the Muses.

thing that he knows to be something else that he doesn't know and of which he has no impression in his soul; or likewise that which he doesn't know for something else that he also doesn't know; or, then too, something that he doesn't know for something else that he does know – these, too, are impossible. Furthermore, to hold something that, indeed, he is perceiving to be something else which he also perceives; or something that he's not perceiving to be something else that he's also not perceiving; or, then too, something that he's not perceiving to be something else that he perceives, these also are not possible. And, further still, that that which he knows and perceives, in that simultaneously he has a fitting impression of this perception within his soul, to hold this for something else that he likewise knows and perceives in that he also simultaneously has an impression within his soul that befits this perception, this is, if it may be at all, even more impossible than the former. Furthermore, what he knows and perceives having the right impression, to hold this for something else that he also knows, this, likewise, is impossible; and that which he knows with the same suppositions and he also perceives to hold this for something else that he perceives, this too is impossible. And, once again, that of which he neither knows nor perceives to hold this *[c]* for something else that he doesn't know or perceive; or that which he doesn't know or perceive for something else which he doesn't know; or something that he neither knows nor perceives to be something else that he doesn't perceive. In all of these instances there is an excess of impossibility that anyone should have a false notion. There only remains, if anywhere at all that something like this does happen, the following instances.

Theae: Just tell me, in which ones mightn't this be? – whether, perhaps, I might get a better grasp on the matter, for right now, indeed, I'm not following you at all.

Socr: That he holds what he knows as being something else that he also knows and which he is even perceiving; or also for something that he doesn't know but which he is perceiving, or something that he's perceiving and that he knows for something else that he's also perceiving and that he also knows.   *<34.~192d]*

Theae: Now, alas, I'm lagging a much greater distance behind than previously.

Socr: So hear it yet once more in this manner. I, in that I know of Theodorus and call up my memory of him alone for myself, how he is constituted, and even likewise I do the same of Theaetetus – so I see you both, indeed, from time to time and, then too, I don't see you, I touch you and, then again, I don't? – and likewise even so I hear you both or have some other manner of perception of you both and, then again, I don't have any perceptions of the two of you at all, but still I retain my memory of both of you not one whit the less and I'm acquainted with you both alone by myself?

Theae: So it is, indeed.   [e]

Socr: Take note from what I'm going to say, firstly this – that regarding what somebody already knows, sometimes it's not perceived and sometimes, again, it is.

Theae: Right.

Socr: Isn't one also able, just so, of what one doesn't know – sometimes that one doesn't even perceive it at all and, then again, that one perceives it alone?

Theae: That too correlates, just so.   [~193a]

Socr: So watch carefully, whether now you are better able to follow me.   Socrates is acquainted both with Theodorus and Theaetetus, yet he doesn't see either of the two of them, nor too does any other perception of them come to him – in this instance he shall never have the notion as if Theaetetus would be Theodorus. Am I right, or not?

Theae: Oh sure, totally right.

Socr: This was the first one of them, from what I set up earlier.

Theae: So it was.

Socr: The second one, now, was this: that if I'm acquainted just with the one of you two and I'm not acquainted with the other one, and if I don't perceive either of you, then I'll never be able to happen upon the thought that he whom I know would be he whom I don't know.

Theae: Right.   [b]

Socr: The third one was that if I don't know either one of the two of you, nor do I perceive either of you, likewise I'm not able to believe that the one of you whom I don't know would be the other one of you whom I also don't know. And so make the stipulation that once again you have gone through the whole row in this manner and have heard all of the previous instances in which there's no way that I'm able of having any false notions in respect to you and Theodorus – as well under the supposition that I'm acquainted with both of you as also if I'm not acquainted with either one of you – and, finally, that I'm acquainted with the one but not with the other. And even so, now, with the perceptions, if, now, you are following me.

Theae: Now I am following.   [~c]

Socr: Thus, it only remains left, one has false notions in this instance: if I am acquainted with you as well as with Theodorus and from both of you have impressions like the impression of signet rings in the wax, and then I see both of you from far-off and not distinctly enough and, in that I take pains to match up and to bring together as one each of the two wax imprints with the sight perception that belongs to it, that, as I say, I seek to lead each of these into their previous tracks so that I succeed in recognizing both of you, but then I fail in doing this and just like it is when one puts the wrong shoe on each foot and they both get swapped, so the vision of each is forced into the foreign impress, or one might also say that this fails in a like manner as happens when looking into the mirror and what's on   *[d]* the right is shifted over to the left and vice-versa; then the mixing up of notions comes to be and you end up by having a false notion.

Theae: It's really not at all to be said, Socrates, how very much what you've presented resembles what happens with notionality.

Socr: Even so, furthermore, if I'm acquainted with both but perceive one with whom I am not acquainted, but not the other one – if, namely, my acquaintance of the one doesn't correspond – which, then, is what I was saying earlier when you said that you didn't understand me.

Theae: I didn't understand you.   *[~e]*

Socr: Namely, I said this – that he who is acquainted with the one and also perceives him, and he has a perception of him that befits his cognition – it is certain that he won't ever believe that this one would be someone else whom he also perceives and with whom he's acquainted and of whom, likewise, he has a perception that befits his cognition. This is how it was, isn't it?

Theae: Yes.

Socr: So that there only remains what I just brought forward, this is all that's left so that a false notion might come to be, namely: that he who is acquainted with both of them and he sees them both or has some other sense perception of them, but he doesn't possess the   *[a]* impressions of them that are similar to his perceptions and so, like a bad bowman his shot can miss the target and fails in finding its goal – which, indeed, even accounts for the expression and the name given to this: that one has misconceptions.

Theae: And totally right.   *[~194]*

Socr: Thus too, if only to the one impression the perception is reckoned to it, but not to the other one, and then either the perception that isn't actually present is ascribed to it or a perception is ascribed to it wrongly – in all of these instances it is possible that the soul deceives herself. And, with one word, of that regarding   *[b]* which one doesn't know nor of which one hasn't had any perceptions, regarding such, it seems, misconceptions and false notions do not occur – if, then, we've managed at all to have spoken anything that's reasonable. But in respect to what we know and that of which we do have perceptions, in this realm our notions turn themselves this way and that, sometimes hitting matters aright and sometimes straying off course and striking the wrong targets; if, namely, one shoots straight and true the images {*Abbilder*} meet up with the appropriate archetypes {*Urbilder*} and one is bound up appropriately with the other and, so, one's notions shall be true; but then if they fly askew and are bound in a criss-cross fashion, then one's notions shall be false.

Theae: What you say is right on the mark, Socrates.   [c]

Socr: And once you will have heard me say this, so you too shall say it even the more. Having right notions, indeed, this is something beauteous; but deceiving oneself is something bad?

Theae: How should it be otherwise.

Socr: This comes to be, it is said, due to the following. If the wax in somebody's soul has been laid on thick and he is endowed in a rich and sumptuous manner, and if it has been smoothed out and tended to just as is right and proper, then with such people as these everything that comes to them by way of their perceptions and how these are imprinted within their souls – just as Homer himself indicates this to us when he speaks of singularly marked impressions – since, as I say, these are pure and have sufficient depth, so too they tend to endure and such men as these firstly are quite adept at learning and, then too, their memories are good and, furthermore, they're not at all so liable of getting mixed up by the impressions that are given them through perception, rather their notions are always right. For then, they're also able and have an easy go of it – that they divide up the images that are firmly implanted and are adequately spaced so that these meet up with what belongs to them, what is named as the actual, and such men as these are named wise. Or, don't you also fancy this so?

Theae: Quite, very much so.   [~194e]

Socr: But if, now, somebody's wax tablet is rough – something that the poets who know all things go so far as to praise – or if it's all dirty and isn't made from the pure wax, or, then too, if it's too soft or too hard, well, those who have wax that is too soft, indeed, these are quick learners but, then, they're also quick to forget; but those whose wax is too hard are quite the opposite. But those whose wax is all hairy and rough and those having stones mixed in or earth, or if it is all sullied and grimy, such as these have indistinct impressions as, too, do those whose wax is too hard – for then, the impressions don't go down to a sufficient depth; and the soft ones are likewise unclear for they tend to run and, soon enough, they become quite unrecognizable. And if, beyond all of this, if they also should be short on space and have an insufficient area so that the impressions are pressed right up upon one another, if somebody's little soul happens to be sized a junior, well, their impressions become even less distinct. Thus, these shall be the ones who have false notions, for then, if these see something or hear something or reflect upon some matter, so they are incapable of quickly allocating to each thing what belongs to it, rather they are slow and because they get things wrong, so they mistake what they see or what they hear and make errors in thought and they are constantly making such mistakes and deceiving themselves and, so, such as these are called learning impaired, that they lack understanding, and one says of them that they never quite get things right.

Theae: Beyond all bounds, o Socrates, what you say is on the mark.

Socr: Do we want, then, that we say – there exist within us false *[b]* notions?

Theae: With all of our strength.

Socr: And right ones too?

Theae: Yes, these too.

Socr: Should we, thus, finally believe that we've sufficiently proven the matter – that both types of notions exist with total certainty?

Theae: Its sufficiency is total and complete.

Socr: Now, verily, Theaetetus – this is indeed an awful and highly suspect thing to find in someone: that you're unable to budge him a bit from out of his spot when he's speaking.

Theae: How so? – why are you saying this?   <35.~195c]

Socr: Out of vexation over my incapacity for learning and, in all actuality, my implacable tendency for idle conjecture. For how, otherwise, how should one put a name on this: if someone due to the coarseness of his sensibilities is continuously turning and re-examining his speeches, this way and that, and never lets himself be convinced and, so, can never be brought forward from his previous proposition.

Theae: But, dear Socrates, whatever is the trouble now that you've become so vexed.

Socr: Not only am I vexed, rather also I have trepidation, indeed *Angst*, as to what I should answer now, if someone were to ask me: O Socrates, you've managed to discover the source of having false notions, that they neither are amongst our perceptions nor too do they lie within our thoughts – that, rather, the source lies in *[d]* the binding of the perceptions with the thoughts? I shall answer in the affirmative, I believe, and not without puffing out my chest a little bit, as if we would have discovered something very beauteous.

Theae: To me too, o Socrates, it doesn't seem to be bad at all, what even now we've managed to put on display.

Socr: Isn't it true, Socrates, he then shall say, you mean that of a person about whom we only think, but we don't see him, of him we shall never believe that he would be a horse which, then too, we also don't see it or feel it – that, rather, we only think horse and otherwise don't have any other perception of it?

Theae: And, indeed, rightly so. [e]

Socr: How now, he shall say, the eleven that this person also only thinks, shall he also never be capable of holding this as being twelve, that which he also only thinks? Come now, what do you answer to this one.

Theae: I shall answer that in seeing and feeling one is well able to hold eleven as being twelve; but of those numbers that he has only in thought, of these he wouldn't ever be able to have this notion.

Socr: But, how? Do you well believe that someone, alone [~196a] and by himself, once may have taken up five and seven and examined these – but not that he was examining five men and seven men or something else like this, rather five and seven themselves which earlier we took as being thought-impressions in the waxen nodule previously mentioned – and, then, he would have said of them: It is impossible to have any notion in regards to them that is false. If, thus, these numbers are at one time examined by this person and by that person and each of them speaks to himself and each asks himself – "How many are they together?" – and the one of them gives his opinion that together they make eleven, but the other says twelve... or, shall they all believe it and say this, that they make twelve? [b]

Theae: No, by Zeus, rather many of them shall also believe that they add up to eleven. And if, indeed, someone attempts this, such mental arithmetic, by taking up numbers of much greater magnitude, so he's more likely to deceive himself and to make an error, and I believe, indeed, that you're really speaking about every number.

Socr: In this your belief is totally right. And so reflect upon this, now, whether this circumstance wants to say anything other than this: that such a person holds these twelve themselves that are in the waxen nodule for eleven.

Theae: So, at least, it seems.

Socr: Now, doesn't this come back to the speech spoken just previously? For he who meets up with this, he holds something that he knows for something else which, likewise, he also knows – and we took this as being impossible – and it was just through this that we proved that false notions don't exist so that one wouldn't have to suppose that the same person both knows and, simultaneously, also doesn't know. [196c]

Theae: Totally right.

Socr: We shall have to demonstrate, thus, that having false notions is something other than a mixing up of thoughts and the perceptions that belong to them. For then, if it were to be this, so we wouldn't deceive ourselves and err in our thinking itself. But now, either there doesn't exist false notionality or it is possible that what somebody knows, simultaneously he doesn't know. Which of the two of these, now, do you choose?

Theae: A difficult choice you lay before me, o Socrates! *[~d]*

Socr: But both simultaneously, indeed, our speech, as it seems, doesn't want to allow us the both of them. But really – for then, verily, one does have to wager everything on this: how would it be if we were to be so impudent that we do something that is totally shameless?

Theae: But, how's this?

Socr: If we wanted to say – in what, then, knowledge actually consists.

Theae: And what is this, that it should be so shameless?

Socr: It seems that you neglect to bethink yourself of this, that our whole conversation from the beginning onward has been nothing other than a question about cognition and of knowledge, *as if* we wouldn't know what this is.

Theae: I am bethinking myself of this. *[~e]*

Socr: And, nonetheless, it doesn't seem to you shameless that we, in that we don't even know what cognition is, nonetheless we want to show what knowing is and in what it consists? But, Theaetetus, already for a long time we have not been conducting our conversation in a pure and irreproachable manner, no, not at all. For already a thousand times we've said that we recognize this or that, or that we're acquainted with something or other, or that we know or don't know whatever it ever may be – as if we understood one another regarding what we were saying and, all the while, indeed, we still don't know what cognition is. And, yes, even now once again, we've put this word into service, *understood* and *don't know*, as if this were seemly for us that we might make use of them, although, indeed, cognition of these matters still eludes us.

Theae: But in what manner, then, do you propose that we speak, Socrates, if you withhold usage of these from yourself? *[197a]*

Socr: I, in none whatsoever – since I am as I am; but were I, however, to be fond of contentious squabbles and were I such a person, or if someone like this were also to be present amongst us and, indeed, he would be able to assert that he does withhold usage of such from himself and, so, he'd really put us in our places, and quite soundly. But since, now, we are – as I say – just common, run of the mill folk, what do you say, do you want that I dare say this, in what knowledge consists? – for then, it seems to me that this will lead our conversation very much to the heart of the matter.

Theae: So take the plunge, by Zeus! – and if you can't withhold yourself from speaking these words, well, this should be forgiven you, and forgiven gladly.

Socr: So, have you well heard about this: how it is that they clarify knowing?   <36.~197b]

Theae: Perhaps, all the same, for the moment I can't remember and call this back to mind.

Socr: It is said, namely, that this would be having knowledge.

Theae: Right.

Socr: Now, we want to make a small alteration to this and say – possessing knowledge.

Theae: In what way, then, do you mean that this differs from the previous definition?

Socr: Perhaps this isn't anything at all. But hear what it seems to me to be and let's test it together.

Theae: If only I shall prove myself of being in a position, that I might do so.

Socr: It seems to me, then, that having and possessing are not one and the same. Just like if someone has an outfit – which, having bought it, he now has it in his possession, but he's not wearing it, so, we shall not say that he has it on himself but, rather, only that he possesses it.

Theae: And rightly so.   [~c]

Socr: So, watch attentively – whether it might be possible that one, indeed, possesses knowledge in such a manner, but still, one doesn't have it; that rather it's like one has gone hunting after wild birds, pigeons or be they of whatever type, and that one has these at home in a cage – to the ready – and, so, one holds them. For then, in a certain way we would be able to say that he'd always have them, since he possesses them. Isn't it true?

Theae: Yes.

Socr: But then as well – in another sense – that he doesn't have any of them, but rather that only a power may be predicated of him which he has over them in that he's made them subservient: to be taken and "had" if he finds pleasure in doing so in that he can catch them and, then too, let them go again, whichever ones he may want at any given time, and that he's free to do this just as often as this pleases him.

Theae: So it is.

Socr: How it was earlier on – I don't even know anymore what sort of presumptuous waxen mold it was that we sculpted and readied in our souls – so now let's position in each and every soul a birdcage containing many sorts of birds, some of them keeping themselves to their own large flocks and being separate from the others, others to much smaller groups, and still others that fly about as unique amongst all of them, just as this comes to them.

Theae: I've positioned it. But now, what shall ensue? [e]

Socr: In one's childhood one would have to say that this cage would be empty and instead of birds one has to think of cognitions. Whatever the cognitions, now, that one may have taken possession of and, then, deposited them into this, his 'slammer,' of these one says: "he has learned the matter or found it out" – of which, then, this shall be the cognition, and this is knowing.

Theae: It should be so. [~198a]

Socr: But that he still hunts after and grasps for whichever of these cognitions he wants and that, then, he holds them firmly and, then again, he lets them go again – take a look, now, what name does this have to go by, whether the same as previously, before he took possession of them, or some other one? But you'll be able to see yet more clearly what I'm getting at from the following. You do accept, indeed, that there is such a thing as mathematics, an art of reckoning?

Theae: Yes.

Socr: Think of this as the hunt for all cognition in regards to even and odd numbers.

Theae: I think it, just so.

Socr: By the means of this art, now – so do I mean it – anyone who has such, not only does he have the cognitions of numbers for himself, that he has these in his power, but likewise he can carry [b] them over to others by the means of these very cognitions, whoever it may be who does this.

Theae: Yes.

Socr: And we say – he who gives them over to others, he teaches; and he to whom they are given over, he learns; but he, whoever it may be that has them so that he possesses them in the birdcage mentioned earlier, he knows.

Theae: Very well.

Socr: Now do take notice of the following. He who is a consummate mathematician, doesn't he know all numbers? – for the cognitions of all numbers are in his soul.

Theae: How else? [c]

Socr: Now, doesn't such a one as this, doesn't he still on occasion do calculations of something for himself, either pure counting or also the figuring out of something that has numbers as an essential component?

Theae: How should he not?

Socr: And calculation itself, don't we want, indeed, that we propose this as being nothing other than a searching for the *how-many'st* number some number is.

Theae: It is for this.

Socr: What he already knows, it seems that he's searching for this as someone who doesn't know – since, then, we have indeed made allowance for this, that he knows all numbers. For then, you have heard of such trick questions about which people love to argue?

Theae: Oh, sure.   *<37.~198d]*

Socr: Shall we not, in that we liken this to the possession of pigeons and to the hunt for them, shall we not say that there exists a double-hunt: one before possession that is made for the sake of possessing; but the other for the possessor, if he wants to grasp and have at hand what he has already possessed for a long while. And, even so, anyone is able, likewise, to make present for himself that which he already has learned and has had for a long time as knowledge, that he knew it, in that he reacquaints himself by taking up the matter and grasping it firmly, what, indeed, he has already possessed for a long while, but he hasn't had this knowledge present and at hand in his thoughts.

Theae: Quite right.   *[e]*

Socr: It was this about which I even was questioning you earlier, essentially what words one should use to utter this: if a trained mathematician is going to make some calculation or if someone who is informed about language goes to read something, as someone who knows each of these proceeds in that each of them goes about this in themselves – that they each learn what they already know?

Theae: But, there's no rhyme or reason to this, o Socrates.

Socr: Should we say, then, that he reads or calculates what he doesn't know – after, indeed, we've already accredited the former, the mathematician, with knowing all numbers, and that the latter knows every letter of the alphabet?   *[199a]*

Theae: But then, that too, that assuredly is unreasonable.

Socr: Do you want, then, that we say – and we're not at all concerned about which words we use, wherever it may be that each and every may like to pull his understanding of knowing and learning, just as each finds most appealing *{nach Belieben}* – but, after we've set this down firmly, something other would be possessing knowledge and, then again, something other having knowledge, so we assert that, indeed, it would be impossible that what anyone possesses he also doesn't possess, that this, indeed, *this* doesn't happen to anyone, that what he knows he also doesn't know; but having a false notion about this or about anything else, this indeed is possible in that it would be possible that he would have grasped at *that* knowledge rather than at *this* one – if, in that he's making hunt upon his cognitions and these, then, are flying through one another, so he fails in grabbing the right one and instead of acquiring this one he comes up with that other one if, then, he believes that eleven would be twelve in that he's grasped at the wrong number in making his calculations, just like if he would have grasped the wood dove instead of the pouter, that is the big fat one rather than the smaller one with the puffy cheeks.

Theae: This is allowable, that we presume as much. *[~199bc]*

Socr: But if he grasps the one that he wanted to grab, then he doesn't err and wouldn't deceive himself, rather his notion is of *that which is {being}* and this, then, would be having notions that are true; the former, though, are false; and so the previous matter that we found so vexatious, this no longer is standing in our way? Perhaps you shall find yourself to be in accord to what I've said and stand by me? – or, what shall you do?

Theae: I'm with you.

Socr: So, accordingly, we would be happy about our good fortune – that now we are free of not-knowing what one knows. For then, that we wouldn't possess what we do possess, indeed, this happenstance doesn't occur to us any more, whether it be that someone might make a mistake and deceive himself or not. Singularly, it now seems to me that something that is even more vexing shall happen.

Theae: What's that? *[d]*

Socr: If this mixing-up of notions should be the cause of such misconceptions.

Theae: But, how?

Socr: Firstly, already this – that someone who has knowledge of something and, still and yet, he shouldn't himself recognize it, and indeed, not through a lack of knowing but rather even due to and through his cognitions, and, furthermore, that he has a notion that the one would be the other and that the other would be the one. How mightn't it not be that this goes totally against one's better sensibilities – that insofar as cognitions subsist within the soul, yet the soul doesn't recognize them at all, that rather she should fail in recognizing everything. For in accord to this same relationship nothing would hinder the following [absurdities]: that a deficiency in knowing would make it possible that the soul knows something, and a blindness, that the soul sees – if it really is so that a cognition is able to make it so that the soul doesn't know something. *[e]*

Theae: Perhaps, Socrates, we didn't proceed properly when we took on the supposition of the birds in that we said that all of them would be cognitions. Much rather, we should also have supposed that some of them would be fatuousness and that such as these also fly about within the soul and, so, that he who hunts after these birds: on the one hand he might grasp knowledge and, then again, fatuousness, and, thus, have notions of the same object that by the means of fatuousness are false and by the means of cognitions are right?

Socr: It isn't an easy matter, Theaetetus, not to praise you. Singularly, what you've said just now, do reflect inwardly as you look upon it once more. Let it be, namely, as you say: so shall for him, he who has grasped at fatuousness – as you assert – he shall have a false notion. Isn't this true?   [200a]

Theae: Yes.

Socr: But, indeed, he shan't well believe it, that he's having a false cognition?

Theae: How should he?

Socr: Rather, that he's right; and he shall relate as someone who knows about it, that about which he's deceiving himself and is in error.

Theae: How else?

Socr: He shall believe to have grasped some cognition and have knowledge in his hand, not fatuousness.

Theae: Obviously.   [~b]

Socr: After a long and circuitous path, thus, we find ourselves just where we began, that we are totally at a loss once again. For he who rebukes us buckles over in laughter as he says to us: But how now, you men are really adept sharpshooters – knowing of both, that is having both cognition and fatuity within his soul, he holds the one of which he knows as being the other of which he also knows? – or is it so that he doesn't have knowledge of either of them and yet he has a notion that the one that he doesn't know, that this is of the same type as the other one that, likewise, he also doesn't know? Or, is it so – that he holds matters which he doesn't know as being other matters of which, indeed, he does have knowledge? Or, shall it be so that you two comedians are going to say to me that there exist cognitions both of cognition and of fatuousness that the possessor is going to trap into some other ludicrous birdcage or upon some   [c] wax tablet, and that he knows them if and for as long as he possesses them even if he isn't thinking about the matter and doesn't have it at hand? And so you shall be forced that you run through the same circuit a thousand times[170] without ever winning a thing for all of your labors? What shall we answer to this one, Theaetetus?

Theae: Really, Socrates – *by Zeus* – I don't at all know what one might say to this.

Socr: Doesn't our speech, and totally with right, doesn't it make this indictment and doesn't it show us that we were acting improperly in that first we sought after false notionality rather than seeking after knowledge and that we allowed this latter to get away from us? – and that it's not possible to understand the former unless first one has a sufficient grasp of the latter, what knowledge is?   *<38.~200]*

Theae: Necessarily, Socrates – for now one has to believe what you say.

Socr: What should one say, then, that once again and starting over from the beginning, that we say what knowledge would be? For then, indeed, we don't want to give up?

Theae: Certainly not, if you don't so inform me.

Socr: So speak then, how should we at long last clarify this so that we contradict ourselves so little as is at all possible?   *[e]*

Theae: Just as we attempted to do previously, Socrates; at least I don't know anything else that we might say.

Socr: Which answer would you be meaning?

Theae: That having the right notions is knowledge. For with this we can't miss – that this is the right notion – and whatever comes out from this, all of this proceeds well and beauteously.

Socr: He who would ford a river, o Theaetetus, he says that it shall become apparent all on its own. So too, if we are to proceed thus and follow along in these tracks, so, perhaps, it also shall come to us and be right underfoot, that what we are seeking shows itself. But if we remain at a standstill, so nothing shall become clear.   *[201a]*

Theae: You're right. So let's go on with this and investigate into it.

Socr: Well, this most probably is a quick investigation, for then, there is an entire profession that has already proven the matter to you, that this isn't knowledge.

Theae: How's that, and essentially which profession are you talking about?

Socr: The profession of those who stand foremost amongst the wise, those who are named great speakers and who, perhaps, are the most

---

[170] An infinite regress – made famous as the "third man argument" – *Parmenides* 131d–132b. Rather than interpreting such infinity in a negative fashion, I would submit that it needs to be taken in a positive fashion – and that, moreover: Plato's *Theaetetus* taken as a whole is just this "trap" that was mentioned by the aforementioned critic who "buckles over in laughter."

accomplished constitutional scholars or our most august justices. For then, these convince others in their speech through their art and professionalism, but it's not that they teach, rather in that they bring about the effect that one accepts their notions, just as they want. Or, do you hold these as being so worthy of wonder and such masterful teachers that if it should be that someone, without anyone else being present, someone is purloined of his gold or otherwise has suffered some injustice [say, perhaps, lost a major presidential election], that they would understand during the brief time that it takes   *[201b]* for a small quantity of water to run through the court clock, that, as I say, they would prove in a fundamental manner the true nature and constitution of whatever it may be that has happened?

Theae: In no wise do I believe this, but rather, that they only persuade.

Socr: And persuasion is called nothing other than bringing about the effect that one's notions of something *are aligned* in a certain manner?

Theae: How else?

Socr: If, then, the judges have merely become persuaded as to how this befits the matter in relation to something that only he who himself has seen it – only he is able to 'truly know' *[wissen]* it, but otherwise nobody – so this is granted them: that they judge all alone through hearing and through the power of right notionality, but having judged without knowledge *[Erkenntnis]*, and yet, all the same, the persuasion has been right and proper, *namely*, if they as judges have made a good judgment? [171]

Theae: Quite, that's just how it is.

---

[171] It is an all too common misconception that the study of philosophy is far removed from having any actual repercussions. The bracketed mention above of the contested presidential election of 2000 (*Bush vs. Gore*) should help refute this notion – for if greater clarity of thinking existed in the court and in the nation, then the injustice perpetuated by the seeming relevance of having "universal standards" in recounting (the hanging chad issue) – this would be seen for what it actually was. The nub of this issue is the question of the particular and the universal. In that it is only natural that different counties in the State of Florida may well experience different sorts of malfunctions in their own particular voting equipment, so too the decisions regarding what should qualify as a 'yea' vote or a 'nay' vote are necessarily *only fairly to be decided at the local level*. And this itself is a universal standard! – and the only one that in the actual context makes any sense. Had the justices on our most august court greater clarity on the issues which Plato addresses, world history could well have taken a different course. The lie is an all too tempting morsel for those who have neglected their homework in the classics, that is those whose ability to conceive in abstract terms is all too paltry; or else, what seems equally plausible – that the 'majority' just weren't particularly concerned about justice in this particular ruling... and in this the public seems quite content to let things be, which does not bode well for a land that prides itself not only on liberty, but justice also.

Socr: But, o friend, this would not ever be possible if right notionality and knowledge were to be one and the same – as also the best judge and legal proceeding wouldn't have right notions of something without their also having recognized [whatever actually happened]. But now, it seems, the two are different.

Theae: It occurs to me what I once heard someone say and what had slipped my mind until now – as I've only just remembered it.   *[d]* He said, namely, that right notionality that is bound up with its clarification would be knowledge, but what has no clarification would be outside of the domain of knowledge. And so, that for which no clarification exists, such also wouldn't be knowable and, so too, this is how he named it; but of that for which clarification does exist, this would be knowable.

Socr: Certainly spoken beauteously. But this knowable and not-knowable, tell me, how does he differentiate between them, whether we have heard this in a like manner, you and I.

Theae: I don't know if I shall ever get to the bottom of this, but if someone other were to present the matter, so, I believe – I would well be able to follow.   *<39.~201e]*

Socr: Hear then a dream for the other. I'd fancy, namely, that I've heard something like this from a few – that the first and, likewise, the root components out of which we as well as everything else is composed, these root components don't allow of any clarification but, rather, that one might only point these out, each of them in and of itself, but that one wouldn't be able to say anything else about them: neither that they are, nor that they are not – for then, already being or non-being would be attached to them, but one would not be permitted to add on anything else to them, if, then, one wants to speak of them alone. For this reason one wouldn't be permitted to add on to them: neither *this*, nor *that*, nor *only*; none of this, nor any of many others of the like. For it's even these concepts that run about everywhere all around us, and they become melded on together to everything; but then, always as something different from that to which they would be attached. But the former things would – if it were to be at all possible that one might bring clarity to them and that each of them would have its own unique clarification, so they would be clarified without any of the others. But now, it's not possible that clarification of any one of the first things shall be uttered,   *[b]* for then: there exists nothing for them beyond simply being named, they would have even only a name. But what would be composed from them, the name of such as this, just as it is itself composed and weaved out of many, so likewise being weaved out of many it shall be clarified as such. For the weaving of names is the essence of clarification. Thus, in this manner the root components would be unexplainable and unknowable, but still perceptible; contrarily the knots would be knowable and admit of clarification – and, so, through notionality one may have the right notions of them. If, now, someone would get the right notion about something without having any clarification, so indeed, his soul would have possession of the truth, but still she would lack knowledge. For whoever would be unable to stand up in discourse and give clarification, he would be lacking in knowledge as regards this object. But he who also has clarification, he would have everything within his power and would have collected everything and, so, be consummate in his knowing. – Have you heard this even so, or something other?

Theae: Just so, totally and absolutely.

Socr: And do you also find this to your liking and does it please you that you posit as much, that right notionality with clarification is knowledge?

Theae: Obviously, it's self-evident.   [202d]

Socr: Thus today, in such a manner we have attained what many wise men from time immemorial have grown old in their searching after it, and they have done so without their ever having found it?

Theae: Still, Socrates – it seems to me that you have spoken as an artist and what you say is very beauteous.

Socr: And it also has every likelihood of being so, that matters correlate just so as you say – for what should knowledge be without clarification or if one wouldn't have the right notions? But, all the same, there's just one matter that displeases me as regards what was said.

Theae: What's that?

Socr: Precisely what seems as being most majestic, namely that the root components would have to be unknowable, but then all of the knots are knowable.   [e]

Theae: But, isn't this right?

Socr: One has to examine it. It's not as if we have to thrash this proposition to get to the examples that were taken as the starting point for those who contend this.

Theae: But, [essentially] which examples?

Socr: The root components of speech and their knots. Or, do you believe that he who brought this contention forward, that about which we're now speaking, do you believe that he would have had anything else in view other than this?

Theae: No, rather this.   <40.~203a]

Socr: So – let's test this, then, once more from the beginning – or, much rather, shall we not test ourselves as to whether this is how we learned how to read or not. Tallyho, firstly: do syllables have clarification but the letters don't have any clarification?

Theae: Probably.

Socr: I intuit this as well, completely. If, for example, someone were to ask about the first syllable of Socrates, o Theaetetus, speak: What is "So"? – what do you answer?

Theae: It is "S" and "O".

Socr: And thus, here you have a clarification for this syllable.

Theae: So it is.

Socr: Now, come and tell me, even thus – what's the clarification of the letter "S"? [b]

Theae: And how should one possibly be able to give clarification of the components of components? For, beyond this, "S" is a silent letter, it's only a rustling noise as if someone were to zish between his teeth. And "H" doesn't even have a rustling noise or any other sound, and so too with most of the other letters. So, accordingly, it is very well spoken, indeed, that they are not to be clarified – since even those of them that are most distinct of all, these only have a sound but totally and utterly lack clarification.

Socr: This, friend, we would have brought, thus, into order as regards cognition.

Theae: Yes, we seem to. [c]

Socr: But, how about this: that the component isn't knowable but the knot is? – were we also right in proposing this?

Theae: I'd fancy we were, indeed.

Socr: Very well, then. Do we want to say that a syllable would be two letters, or, if it consists in more than two, the entirety of them? – or would the syllable be an especial something that first comes to be out of the former?

Theae: It would be the entirety, I'd fancy, this is what we shall say.

Socr: So, examine this one time in regards to the previous two, the "S" and the "O". Both make up the first syllable of my name. Now, whoever is acquainted with this syllable and recognizes it, shall he not also be acquainted with and recognize both of these letters?

Theae: How else? [d]

Socr: He's acquainted, thus, with "S" and with "O".

Theae: Yes.

Socr: But, how? Although he cognizes neither of the two of them and despite this lack of knowledge of either one, still he cognizes both of them?

Theae: That, really, would be fantastic and is unreasonable.

Socr: Singularly, if it is necessary that he cognizes each of them in order that he recognizes both of them, so, he who wants to have cognition of the syllables, he already has to have cognition of the letters and, so, this beauteous clarification shall slip through our fingers and disappear.

Theae: And it has done so *post haste*.   [e]

Socr: We weren't alert enough in our watch over it. For then, perhaps we should have said that the syllable would not be the entirety of the letters, that rather it would be an especial class that comes to be from them and, so, it would have its very own form and essence, just for it itself, and thus would be different from the letters.

Theae: Most certainly, it may more likely be the case that this is how matters correlate and not the other way.

Socr: We have to examine this matter like men, that we don't betray such a great and majestic proposition.

Theae: Right.   [204a]

Socr: It would be so, then, as we now say: the knot is one configuration all its own which comes to be from out of the component parts which each and every time are melded together – just like it was with the letters, and so too with everything else.

Theae: Quite.

Socr: Hence, it's not allowable that parts exist?

Theae: But, why not?

Socr: Whatever has parts – the whole of such is also necessarily the entirety of these parts. Or, do you say that the whole would be something different that has come to be on its own from out of these parts but, as I say, it is different from the entirety?

Theae: That's what I want.

Socr: But the entirety as a totality and the whole, do you understand beneath these the same, or each of these would be something other?

Theae: About this I'm not certain. But because you always command me to answer courageously, so I'll gamble on this and be so daring as to say – each is something other.

Socr: A courageous heart, o Theaetetus, is good; but as for as your answer, regarding this we'll have to see.

Theae: We do, indeed.

Socr: So, in accordance to the clarification that you give now – the whole would be different from the entirety as a totality.

Theae: Yes.   <41.~204c]

Socr: But, how about the as a totality and the entirety – are these also different? As if we were to say: one, two, three, four, five, six; and if – twice three or thrice two or three plus two plus one – do we in all of these instances say the same, or in each one something different?

Theae: The same.

Socr: Anything other than six.

Theae: Nothing other.

Socr: In all of these formulas, thus, we have found six as being the entirety?

Theae: Yes.

Socr: And, then again, does it mean nothing to us if we say these as a totality?

Theae: Something necessarily, indeed.

Socr: Something other than six?

Theae: Nothing other.

Socr: Thus, in everything that consists out of number we name the entirety and the 'as a totality' as being the same?   *[d]*

Theae: So it seems.

Socr: Now, furthermore, let's say this. The number of an acre of land and the acre itself is one and the same?

Theae: Yes.

Socr: And, even so, with a square mile?

Theae: Yes.

Socr: And it's even so with the number of an army and the army? – and with all things similar to this in like manner? For then, the number of the entirety is their being as a totality – and, so, it is equally of all of these?

Theae: Yes.

Socr: Now, the number of each, is this something other than the parts of it?   *[e]*

Theae: No, nothing other.

Socr: And what has parts consists in these parts?

Theae: Obviously.

Socr: But it's also been admitted that the parts as a totality are the entirety, if the number as an entirety is the being as an entirety.

Theae: So it is.

Socr: Hence, the whole doesn't consist in the parts? For as such it would be an entirety, if it were to be all the parts together as a totality.

Theae: It seems not.

Socr: But is it possible that a part be what it is other than as a part of a whole?

Theae: From the entirety.   *[205a]*

Socr: Right manfully, o Theaetetus, do you defend yourself. But the entirety, is such not even this, an entirety, if nothing is missing?

Theae: Quite.

Socr: But then, isn't this nothing other than a whole, that from which nothing is missing? – but of that from which something is

missing, such as this is neither a whole nor an entirety and in relation
to both it becomes the same from the same?

Theae: Now it seems to me that the whole and the entirety no longer
differ in anything.

Socr: Now, didn't we say – wherever there are parts, there the
whole and the entirety would be these as a totality?

Theae: Quite.   *[~205b]*

Socr: Furthermore, what I've been meaning to get to – isn't it
necessary for the syllable, if the syllable isn't the letters and, so then,
it also wouldn't have these as its parts; or if it is the same as them,
then too it is knowable in a like manner as these are, these letters?

Theae: So it is.

Socr: And so, as we would have preferred that this didn't follow, so
we proposed that the syllable would be something different than
these?

Theae: Yes.

Socr: But how? – if the letters aren't the parts of the syllable, can
you bring forward something else which would be its parts, something, however, other than these letters?

Theae: In no way, o Socrates! For if I should once admit that the
syllable has component parts, then it would indeed be ludicrous that
I'd let go of the letters and, then, search about for something else.

Socr: Thus, in accord with this speech, Theaetetus, the syllable would
be utterly and completely indivisible essence?   *[c]*

Theae: So it seems.

Socr: Now, recollect yourself as regards this, friend, that it wasn't
that long ago when we were quite pleased and satisfied with ourselves
when we believed it to be right that we said in regards to the first
{dem Ersten} – that out of which everything other would consist –
that no clarification might be given because the former would be just
for itself and wouldn't be a composite; and, indeed, that one couldn't
even add being on to it, nor rightfully say anything about it at all –
nor even *this*; because already all of this would be something other
and foreign to it and, so, due to this underlying cause, now, the first
was beyond cognition and clarification.

Theae: I remember this.   *[d]*

Socr: Does there exist any other root cause for this, other than that
it is something simple and indivisible? – at least I don't see any other.

Theae: None have shown themselves, nor, in all probability, shall
they.

Socr: Hence, the syllable falls beneath the same category as do the
former, if it doesn't have any parts and is one determinate essence.

Theae: In every way.

Socr: Thus, if the syllable, now, is one and the same as the many letters and is itself a whole and these are its parts, so, in a like manner, the syllable would be knowable and have clarification as do the letters, since the parts as a totality have shown themselves as being 'one and the same' as the whole?

Theae: Well, indeed. *[e]*

Socr: But if it is one and indivisible, so just like the letters the syllable also is unknowable and without clarification. For the same root cause shall make both of them be the same.

Theae: I don't know what else we might say.

Socr: Hence, we don't want to hold to those who say: the knot would be cognizable and has clarification but the opposite would apply to the component parts.

Theae: No, indeed not – if we are to follow this, our speech. *[206a]*

Socr: But how? – if someone were to assert the opposite, wouldn't you be more inclined to voice your accord with him in view of everything that you can call back to mind from the time when you learned the alphabet?

Theae: What do you mean?

Socr: That as you were learning you didn't do anything other than that you made the effort that you could differentiate between the letters in sight, and even so also through hearing: that you could differentiate each individual letter for itself so that its position wasn't confused if they were spoken or written.

Theae: That's right, totally. *[~b]*

Socr: And having completely learned as to how one plays the lyre, is this called anything else other than being able to follow every note, to which string it belongs – and as regards this everyone shall admit it, that one can call the notes the root components of the art of music?

Theae: Nothing other.

Socr: If, now, one is permitted to make inference and prove this matter regarding the root components and the knotting together of these from that of which we have experience, so we shall have to say that the cognition of the root components is much more distinct and of much greater efficacy than the knowledge given when these are knotted together as regards the consummate learning of each and every matter. And if someone says that the knots would – by their very nature – be knowable but that the root components wouldn't be, so we want to hold this as being a joke, be it made knowingly or unwittingly.

Theae: Obviously. *<42.~206c]*

Socr: Still, there are yet other proofs that let themselves be brought forward, as I'd fancy it. But, let's not forget the object that lay before us, that we examine it as it relates herewith – what, indeed, it should say when someone proposes that if to right notionality clarification is added on, that this is the most consummate knowledge.

Theae: So, let's examine this.

Socr: Tallyho, in which sense does he well want, really, that this clarification shall have meaning. One of three possibilities, namely, he has to have wanted to say, as it seems to me.

Theae: Of which three?   [d]

Socr: The first would be this – that in general one makes his thoughts clear and distinct through the use of his voice and through the power of words, both nouns and verbs,[172] in that just as it is in a pool of water or in a mirror, that one's notions are reflected – and, so, this is uttered by the out-streaming of words from one's mouth. Or, doesn't this seem to you as being clarification?

Theae: For me, quite.

Socr: And of anyone who does this we say that he clarifies himself as regards something?

Theae: That's what we say.

Socr: But, now, every one of us is in a position to do this – be it slower or more quickly – that he brings out what he means in respect to each and every matter, unless it should be that one is completely deaf or mute. And in this manner everyone, as many who only   [e] have had a right notion, all of these shall also bind up clarification to it and there shan't be a right notion anywhere at all without there also being knowledge.

Theae: Right.

Socr: But don't let us lightly condemn him who has spoken thus, that he's lacking in sensibility and hasn't said anything to us at all – he who has given us this clarification of cognition, that into which, now, we are making our investigation. For then, probably he didn't mean it in this wise but, rather, that whoever is questioned, what any given thing is, so he is able to provide the questioner with an accounting of the component parts of the matter.   [207a]

Theae: How do you mean this, Socrates?

Socr: Just as Hesiod speaks of the wagon and the hundred pieces of wood out of which the wagon consists, these which, indeed, I wouldn't know all of their names and, I believe, you don't either; rather we would be satisfied if we were to be asked: "What a wagon

---

[172] Cf: *Sophist* 262a (p.573) – "Haupt- und Zeitwörter"; that some have lamented Plato's lack of knowledge of grammar, this only testifies to their own lack of insight into ontology. And, if one is to "put things together" – note as well the relation of the answer to the question of "What a wagon is?" to *Sophist* 262c – "Lion, deer, horse."

is?" – if we were to know the answer: "Wheels, axles, platform, seat and steerage."

Theae: Very satisfied.

Socr: This former person, however, would have a hearty laugh over the matter if – should we be asked to give a clarification of your name and we'd answer by supplying him with the syllables – so he'd laugh about this and say that although, indeed, our notions are right   *[b]* and that we have spoken just as we say, still, we're very much wrong in that we imagine ourselves as being informed about speech, as if we possessed the etymologist's clarification for your name, Theaetetus, and had supplied it. But one doesn't speak out in a knowledgeable manner regarding something until and unless one is in a position that along with the right notions one also describes everything in reference to its first – or root – components, just as this was mentioned by us somewhere or other earlier on.

Theae: We did say this previously.   *[~c]*

Socr: So too, we would, indeed, have had the right notions of a wagon; but he who would be able of describing the entire essence of the same in reference to the hundred pieces of wood mentioned previously, he also would have – just because he likewise has these descriptions – the clarification of the right notions, and instead of being merely imagining the notionality he would also have professional understanding and would know matters in relation to the essence of the wagon in that he might go through the whole in reference to its root components.

Theae: Doesn't this, now, seem to you as being good, Socrates?

Socr: Whether it seems so to you, friend, and you take this as being so – that the description of a thing in reference to its individual component parts would be clarification, but that matters would remain unclarified if the description proceeds only to the first level or the larger knots – you tell me if you think this good so that, then, we'll pull this into our considerations.   *[207d]*

Theae: I'm ready to accept it, totally.

Socr: And, perhaps, you also believe that someone would have a clarification of something if this same something sometimes seems to him to belong here, sometimes there; or also if he's ready to first think 'this', and then later to think 'that' in regards to this same thing?

Theae: By Zeus, not I, certainly not.

Socr: And don't you remember that this is what happens and what one meets up with when you or others are just starting off in your learning of the alphabet?   *[~e]*

Theae: Do you mean that we ascribed the same syllable, at one time to one letter and, then again, to some other one; and, then too, we set the same letters on one occasion properly in the syllable where they belong but on some other occasion we set them in the wrong syllable?
Socr: This is precisely what I mean.
Theae: Very well am I able to remember this, by Zeus, and I do not at all believe that he actually would know what he's about, he for whom this correlation holds.
Socr: How now? – if at some such occasion, somebody, in that he would be writing your name, so he believes that a "Th" followed by an "e" has to be written and, so, he actually does start off thus; but then, when wanting to write Theodorus' name he believes he'd have *[a]* to write a "T" followed by an "e" and this, too, is what he actually writes – should one say that he knows the first syllable of your names?
Theae: We've even just admitted this and have seen eye to eye on it – that he, for whomever matters correlate so, that he doesn't yet know.
Socr: Now, does anything hinder this, that matters may proceed in a similar manner when he comes to writing the second or third or fourth syllable?
Theae: None that I would know.
Socr: But shall he not – in such an instance – shall he not have the description of your name in reference to its components and won't he write the name "Theaetetus" with notions that are right, if, then, he writes your name in the proper sequence, everything in order just as it belongs?
Theae: Obviously.
Socr: And he does so without having knowledge? – but in that he has the right notions? *[208b]*
Theae: Yes.
Socr: But yet, he likewise has the clarification along with having the right notions, for then, when writing he affirmatively went through the whole row of component parts, and even this is just what we named as knowledge.
Theae: Right.
Socr: Thus there exists, friend, a clarification that is bound up with the right notionality but one that one isn't yet permitted to name as being knowledge.
Theae: So it seems. *<43.]*
Socr: Thus, only in a dream have we become richer in that we believed to have found the clarification that is most right. Or, should we still withhold our judgment? For perhaps one might not like *[c]* our current understanding of clarification, that rather he take the

one which yet remains from the three meanings postulated earlier – one of which, as we said, he needs must pin his hopes upon: he who describes knowledge as right notionality that is bound up with clarification.

Theae: Totally right, your memory serves you well – for one is yet remaining. The first of them was the likeness of an image of thought produced through one's voice; then the one that even was just described, this was the path to the whole through the component parts. But what do you mean as the third?

Socr: What the majority would say: that one would be able of providing some defining characteristic, something through which whatever is being asked about is differentiated from everything else, all of the other things.

Theae: Essentially, what clarification of any something are you able to give to me in this sense? *[d]*

Socr: As, if you want, that as regards the sun it would suffice for you, I believe, that we propose that it is the brightest object of everything that is in the sky and circles about the earth.

Theae: I'm satisfied, totally.

Socr: But do take pains that you note precisely – why it is that I spoke thus. Namely, just as we were saying, if you grasp that aspect in which something is different from everything else, so, some would assert that you would conceive its clarification. But as long as you would only be striking upon something that it shares in common with other things, so too such a clarification would belong to all of these things that belong to this commonality.

Theae: I understand and I'd fancy that this is very right, that we name this the clarification. *[e]*

Socr: He, then, who along with the right notions of something, now, he who also grasps and conceives that wherein it is different from all the rest, he shall have achieved knowledge of the same, that of which before he only had the notion.

Theae: Indeed, this is what we assert.

Socr: But now, Theaetetus, now that I step up a little closer to what we are saying, I find myself in the position of the art critic who heretofore has only seen paintings from far-off and now, standing close-up, I don't understand the least bit of it. Though so long as I was viewing the matter from far-off, then it seemed that something was being said.

Theae: But, how do you get to this? *[209a]*

Socr: I want to make this clear to you, if only I shall be able to achieve this. Under the supposition that I have a right notion of you, so I only shall be cognizant of you if I grasp with this a clarification;

but insofar as I don't do so, in such an instance, then, I only have a notion.

Theae: Yes.

Socr: But your clarification was to be a pointing-out of that by which you differ.

Theae: So it was.

Socr: When, now, I only was having notions about you, isn't this true? – so I didn't strike up against anything about you in my thoughts by which you would differ from the others?

Theae: It seems not.

Socr: I was only thinking of things that you share in common, those things that you don't have any more of than anyone else.

Theae: That's necessary. [b]

Socr: Then, tallyho, by Zeus – how may it be that I had notions of you more than of anyone else at all? For if we propose that I would have thought to myself: This is the one who is Theaetetus, he who would be a human and would have a nose, mouth and eyes, and so too each of the other limbs – shall this thought, now, make it so that I'm thinking more about Theaetetus than I am about Theodorus, or, as they tend to say, the last of the Mysians?

Theae: How should it? [~c]

Socr: Singularly, if I not only think of you as having eyes and ears, that rather you also have an upturned nose and protruding eyes – shall it not be so that I wouldn't anymore be thinking of you than thinking of myself, and whoever else it may be who shares in such a constitution, someone having these qualities?

Theae: Not a whit more.

Socr: Rather, won't it be so – as I believe – that I shan't any sooner have a notion of Theaetetus than before this upturned nose is itself differentiated from all of the other upturned noses that I also have seen, that a differing characteristic has been impressed and remains behind, and so too in everything else, everything out of which you consist, and insofar as it's all this, so also when I meet up with you tomorrow, it's all of this that I remember, and this shall make it so, that I have the right notions of you.

Theae: Totally right. [d]

Socr: Hence, the right notions of any someone already proceed upon their differences.

Theae: So it seems, quite.

Socr: Adding on clarification to the right notions – what, then, might this be named? For if this is called nothing other than that one has notions of that by which something is differentiated from everything else, so this is nothing but a ludicrous prescript.

Theae: How so?

Socr: Of that of which we already have a right notion insofar as something is different from everything else – of this, now, we should yet take up a right notion of the same insofar as it differs from   *[e]* everything else – and so too everything else wants to go around and around in circles without anything at all moving forward from its spot: doesn't this say something about this prescript. One is able with even more right that one calls this the speech of a blind man, he who calls out to us that, indeed, we might like to take what we already have so that we may experience what we already have in our notions: this is quite an adept adage and really hits the mark most admirably – namely, for someone who has lost his vision.

Theae: But, tell me: what was it that you wanted to bring out earlier with your question?

Socr: That if, on the other side, with the adding on of a clarification one were to mean *insight* into the differences and not merely notionality of the same, then this would really be a majestic spoof about the most beauteous side of the clarification of knowledge – for having insight is the name that is given to this, that one has knowledge? Isn't it true?   *[210a]*

Theae: Yes.

Socr: He, then, who is questioned what knowledge is, he should, as it seems, give the answer: right notionality that is bound up with knowledge of the differences. For then, this would be, now, as we were saying earlier, the adding on of clarification.

Theae: So it seems.

Socr: And indeed, this is simple-minded in every manner, that one says to those, they who are seeking for knowledge, that it would be right notionality bound up with knowledge, all the same as to whether it be knowledge of the differences or of whatever else. Hence, neither in perception, o Theaetetus, nor in right notionality, nor in right notionality that has been bound up with clarification – none of these can be knowledge.   *[b]*

Theae: It seems not.

Socr: Do we yet feel ourselves burdened by some pregnancy, friend, and do we have birthing pangs in matters of knowledge? Or have we delivered you of everything that you were carrying?

Theae: I – by Zeus – I, through your help and succor, indeed: I have spoken out more than I had within me.

Socr: And our art of midwifery has said of all of these, that they only would be vaporous puffs of air and wind-eggs, and not worthy that one raise them.

Theae: In all ways, assuredly.   *<44.~210c]*

Socr: Bethink yourself, now, Theaetetus, that if after all of this you shall once again become pregnant, so if this should happen you shall be better able to carry it due to the capabilities bestowed upon you by the present trials; but then, even if you should remain empty, so too you shall be less troublesome for those around you and you shall be of a milder disposition, that in a more prudent manner you won't believe to know what you don't know. For only to this extent is my art capable and of nothing more, nor too do I understand anything like the others, these great men of the present and of former times, those who are so worthy of marvel. But this artistry of midwifery, this my profession was imparted both to me and to my mother from God – for her, namely, for the succor of the women; but to me so that I may provide help for noble and beauteous youths.   *[210d]*
But now I have to go present myself in the Kings Hall because of the charge that Meletus has brought against me. Tomorrow, though, Theaetetus, we want to meet here with one another once again.

****

Meno

for father

William McCormick Lundberg

"Ursus and Homo were fast friends. Ursus was a man, Homo a wolf. Their dispositions tallied. It was the man who had christened the wolf: probably he had chosen his own name. Having found *Ursus* fit for himself, he had found *Homo* fit for the beast. Man and wolf turned their partnership to account at fairs, at village fetes, at corners of streets where passers-by throng, and out of a need which people feel everywhere to listen to idle gossip and to buy quack medicine."

The Man Who Laughs, Victor Hugo [173]

OVERVIEW:

A. Introduction:

Meno's question: Is virtue teachable?	–	*Section 1.*
Socrates' question: What is virtue itself?	–	*Section 2.*

B. Main:

I.	Meno's first attempts at an answer.	–	*Sections 3–5.*
II.	Further clarification of the question through the examples of shape *{Gestalt}* and color.	–	*Sections 6–9.*
III.	Meno's definition of virtue – as *striving for the good.*	–	*Sections 10–13.*
IV.	*Plato's theory of recollection.*	–	*Sections 14–21.*
V.	Investigation into whether virtue is teachable using the inference method.	–	*Sections 22–25.*
VI.	Doubts as to whether virtue is teachable.	–	*Sections 26–34.*
VII.	Meno's vacillating opinion on virtue.	–	*Sections 35–41.*

C. Conclusion:

Virtue as '*divine dispatch.*'	–	*Section 42.*

---

[173] *The Man Who Laughs* by Victor Hugo, p.1 – Arcadia House, New York, 1950 (Currently not in Print in English, although certainly one of Hugo's greatest literary achievements and, incidentally – mentioned by name in Dostoevsky's *The Possessed* (Part I, Chapt.3 – The Sins of Others, Section 3).

Meno – Sections:

MENO

****

MENO, SOCRATES, MENO'S SLAVE, ANYTUS

<1.~70a]

Meno: Could you please tell me, Socrates, whether virtue would be something that is teachable? – or if it's not taught then is it acquired through practice? – or if neither being acquired by practice nor learned is it rather inborn in man through nature, or does it subsist in man in some other manner?

Socr: O Meno, heretofore the Thessalians were famed amongst all Hellenes and they also amazed others due their skill in horsemanship and by their riches, but now, as it seems to me, also due to their wisdom! – and not the least amongst these are the compatriots of your friend, Aristippus of Larissa. And the blame for this must be attributed to Gorgias. For when he visited your city, he, by his wisdom, won over to adoration not only the foremost amongst the Aleuadaens, to whom also your beloved, Aristippus, belongs, but also the rest of the Thessalians. And so you have become quite accustomed to ask and receive answers without shame and in a noble self-assurance that is, then, to be expected by those who know. *[c]* For Gorgias proffered himself as well to every man of Hellas, whatever each should want to know, just to ask him, and no one went away without an answer. But here abouts, my dear Meno, everything is exactly the opposite; there is veritably a dearth on wisdom come over us as it seems to have completely dried up in our locale having moved on over into yours. At least, if you should want to ask such questions to anybody around here you won't meet up with a single one who wouldn't laugh and say: "O foreigner, you seem to consider me blessed that I should know whether or not virtue is teachable or upon what manner one shall achieve it, but I am so far from knowing whether or not it be teachable that I don't even properly know this, what virtue is at all." Also with myself, Meno, it goes even *<2.~71b]* so: I partake in the poverty of my fellow citizens and rebuke myself severely that I know quite nothing regarding virtue. And of that of which I don't even know what it is, how should I know of any of its particular qualities? [174] Or do you fancy it possible that someone who had never become acquainted with Meno, who he is, that such a

---

[174] "What it is" – is designated in *Phaedrus* as the first question needing to be asked. "Beschaffenheiten" – from the verb *schaffen,* to make or create, is the primary word Schleiermacher uses in reference to this question, what something is – translated here as qualities, but also translated as constitution in *Parmenides* and as "a certain quality" in the *Sophist* 262e – as this relates to a sentence – (p. 574).

person still might know whether he is beauteous or is rich, or also if he is distinguished; or quite the opposite to these? Do you fancy this possible?

Meno: No, indeed not. But is it in all actuality so, Socrates, that *[c]* you don't even know the first thing about what virtue is? – and should I tell my friends back home that you have said as much?

Socr: And not only this, dear friend, but rather also tell them that I have yet to meet up with anyone who does know it, at least, so as I'd fancy it.

Meno: How? – didn't you meet Gorgias when he last visited here?

Socr: Oh, sure.

Meno: Now, didn't it seem to you that he knows this?

Socr: My memory is somewhat faulty, o Meno, so that now at this moment I don't quite know what to say – how things seemed to me then. Alone [by himself], perhaps he does know, and you know what he has said. So do bring me up to speed on this, how he explained it; or, if you prefer, just tell me yourself. For certainly you are of the same opinion as he.

Meno: That I am.

Socr: So let's leave Gorgias be as, in any event, he's not present. But you yourself, Meno, *by the will of the gods*, what do you say that virtue is? Speak and don't withhold this from me, rather tell me so that I may have just told the most blessed lie when it becomes apparent that you know this, and Gorgias too, but I said that never have I met up with anyone who knows. *<3.~71e]*

Meno: That's not in the least bit hard to say, Socrates. Firstly, if you will, the virtue of men, this is easy to say that for men virtue is this: that a man is capable in the administration of the affairs of the *polis* and that in this administration he does good for his friends and harm to his enemies, but also protects himself that never might he meet up with the same. And, if you want the virtue of women, so this too is not hard to describe: that she must be a good and able administrator of the home, keeping everything in good shape, and that she obeys her husband. Yet another would be the virtue of children, be they boys or girls; and again that of the elderly, whether they be freemen or, if you like, slaves. And so there are yet many other virtues *[72a]* so that one can never be in perplexity in wanting to say what virtue is – because for every way of doing things and for each age group there is in every occupation and for each one of us his virtue and, I might add, the same also applies to vice.

Socr: It seems, o Meno, that I am exceptionally fortunate since that in searching for just one virtue I have now met up with an entire swarm of them that have settled down upon you. Singularly, Meno, in that I remain with this picture of a swarm, were I to ask you regarding the nature of bees, what the bee-nature might well be, and you would tell me that there are all sorts and many different   *[b]* kinds of bees, what would you then answer to me if I asked you: "Is it your opinion that they are all bees to the extent that there would be many kinds and all different sorts that are separate each from the other? – or, is it due to this, that they are bees, that they are *not* different, and they only are different in something other, such as in beauty or size or in whatever it may be?" Tell me, what would you answer to this question?

Meno: I'd answer this, that they are not different in as much as they are bees each one from the other.   *[c]*

Socr: And if I were to say further: "Tell me then even this in which they are not different but are all the same, what do you opine that this is?" – so you would certainly know what to answer.

Meno: I would.   *<4.~72]*

Socr: So it is also the same with virtue that, although there are many different kinds and sorts, yet all together they have one and the same certain form *{Gestalt}*175 by the power of which they even are virtues, and it is just upon this that you must direct your gaze if you desire to answer the former question rightly, what virtue actually is. Or, don't you understand what I mean?   *[d]*

Meno: Indeed, I believe that I do understand you; but still I don't yet have so firm a grasp inwardly on that about which you questioned as I want.

Socr: Do you, perhaps, opine this only of virtue, Meno, that there is a different one for men than there is for women, and so too for the rest? – or is it even thus with health and size and strength? Does it seem to you that a man's health is different from a woman's? Or is it in all cases the same concept, if it be health, no matter whether in a man or whomever else it may ever be?   *[e]*

Meno: The same, it seems to me, when we speak of the health of a man or a woman.

Socr: Then too, size or strength? If a woman is strong shall she be so due to the capacity of the same concept and due to the same strength be strong? This "of the same" I mean so: that it makes no difference to the being of strength whether it would be in a man or in a woman. Or, does it seem to you to make a difference?

Meno: No, not to me.   *[73a]*

---

175 "Gestalt" – the same word *{eidos}* will soon reappear as shape – a remarkable coincidence? I doubt it; form or idea is the intellectual counterpart to a material shape – and as color goes with shape, spiritual substance accompanies the idea.

Socr: But for virtue it shall make a difference in the being of virtue whether it should be in a child or an elderly person, in a man or in a woman?

Meno: Somehow this no longer appears, at least to me, to be quite so hard and fast as all the rest about which we just spoke.

Socr: But, how's that? – didn't you say that man's virtue would be in the administration of the *polis*, and that of a woman in the administration of the home?

Meno: Yes.

Socr: Is it now well possible that, be it the *polis* or the home or whatever else, is it to be administered well if this isn't done thoughtfully[176] and righteously.

Meno: Certainly not. [b]

Socr: If, now, they administer thoughtfully and righteously, so indeed, they administer with mindfulness and justice?

Meno: Necessarily.

Socr: Both then require the same if they should be good, woman and man – justice, namely, and mindfulness?

Meno: Obviously.

Socr: And how? a child or an elderly person who would be unrestrained and unrighteous, could they possibly be good?

Meno: Certainly not.

Socr: But they would be good if mindful and righteous?

Meno: Yes. [c]

Socr: All of humanity, then, would be good in one and the same manner. For in that they all partake in themselves on the same, thus they all become good.

Meno: So it seems.

Socr: But certainly they would not be able all to be good in the same way if their virtue were not one and the same?

Meno: No, that doesn't follow. <5.~73]

Socr: Since, then, virtue is one and the same for everyone – so make the attempt now to speak it out and bring back into my memory what Gorgias said that it would be, and you with him?

Meno: What else other than that one is capable of ruling over men – if, then, you are seeking something that goes through everything else.

Socr: Indeed, *that* is what I'm searching for. But is this also the virtue of a child, Meno, and that of a servant, that he be capable of

---

[176] "besonnen" and "Besonnenheit" are translated as thoughtful and mindfulness, prudence is the standard English translation. Note that the German word has *Sonne*, the sun, within it, hence: an enlightened mind and reason are of central importance.

ruling over his lords? And does it seem to you that a servant would yet be someone who rules?

Meno: That's not at all as I would fancy it.

Socr: Indeed, this cannot be at all, most worthy *{Bester}*. For put this also into the balance. You say that someone should be capable of ruling. Shouldn't we right away add this on, namely righteously but not unrighteously?

Meno: I believe so, indeed. For righteousness, o Socrates, is virtue.

Socr: The virtue, o Meno, or a virtue? [73e]

Meno: How do you mean this?

Socr: Just as with anything else. For instance, regarding a circle I would say that it is a shape *{Gestalt}*, but not simply the shape. And for this reason, namely, because there are yet other shapes.

Meno: And you would be totally in the right in saying this – for I too don't name righteousness to be virtue all alone, rather there are yet many others.

Socr: But which ones? – speak. Just as I could name other shapes for you if you were to demand more, so you too name for me some other virtues.

Meno: Courage, then, I fancy would be a virtue – and mindfulness, wisdom and generosity; and there are many others.

Socr: Then, once again, we have encountered the same problem. Namely, we have found many virtues although we searched for one only – though this time in a different way than previously; but the one that is in all of these virtues we are unable to find. <6.~74b]

Meno: I am not as of yet able, Socrates, to find the one virtue which you are seeking in all, just as I could do for the rest of the things.

Socr: But that's only natural. However, I shall make an attempt, if I am able, of bringing us further. For you do have the insight that this correlates so with what we were saying. If someone were to question you regarding what was just brought forward: "What then, Meno, is shape?" and you said: "The circle" and he then said, just as I did: "Is the circle the shape or a shape?" – so you would then assuredly say: "A shape"?

Meno: Indeed.

Socr: And isn't it so, for this reason, because there are yet other shapes? [177] [c]

Meno: Yes.

Socr: And if he questions you further, "Which ones?" – so you would name them?

Meno: I would.

---

[177] Note similarity to *Gorgias* 453d: Speechcraft; Zeuxis and the other painters (p. 266).

Socr: And then again, if he were to question in even the same way about color, what it is, and in response to your answer that white would be color the questioner then asked: "Is white *the* color or a color?" – so you would say: "A color" because there are yet more.
Meno: That's what I would say.
Socr: And if he should then call upon you to name the other colors, so you would name others for him that are no less colors than white.
Meno: Yes.
Socr: And now if he, as I did, if he should come back around with the speech and should say: "We always come upon many, but thus not, rather since you do name the many all together with just one name and since you assert that each of them would be a shape and this despite the fact that they are opposites one to another – what then is this, that which encompasses the circle no less than the straight and which you name shape and assert that circular would be no less   *[e]* a shape than straight?" Or, perhaps it doesn't seem to you to be so?
Meno: Indeed, [it is] quite so.
Socr: If, now, you say so – do you then mean, perhaps, that the circle would be no more circular than straight and that the straight would be no more straight than circular?
Meno: In no way, Socrates.
Socr: But shape, you say, the circle would be no more than the straight, and the one no more than the other?
Meno: Right.   *<7.~75a]*
Socr: Now then, what is this, that to which you attach the name shape? – attempt to describe it.   If, now, you say to him, he who questions you, and be it regarding shape or regarding color: "I don't even understand what it is that you want, my dear man," so he would perhaps be amazed and would say: "Don't you understand that I'm searching for that which is the same in all?" Or would you also not know what to put forth if someone were to question you – what indeed is the same in all, in the circle and the straight and all of the rest which you name shape? Make an attempt to give your answer so that you have an exercise[178] for the answer regarding virtue.   *[~b]*
Meno: No, rather you Socrates, would you please give the answer.
Socr: Shall I do this as a favor to you?
Meno: Indeed.
Socr: And then, you shall want likewise to say to me what I am seeking regarding virtue.

---

[178] It may be useful to reflect on the circumstance that the second part of the *Parmenides* is described by Parmenides as being an exercise, without which one shall never be able to know about beauty, truth and goodness – at 135d (p. 217).

Meno: Quite.
Socr: Then, I will give an answer, for it's well worth it.
Meno: Quite.
Socr: Then tallyho – I shall attempt to say to you what shape is. Watch closely, whether you accept my answer, what it would be. Namely, that should be shape for us, that which alone amongst all other things accompanies color everywhere. Is this sufficient for you, or do you desire it yet differently? I for my part would be quite satisfied if you also would clarify, what virtue is, just so. [c]
Meno: But really, Socrates, this is such a simple answer.[179]
Socr: How do you mean?
Meno: That in accordance to your clarification that that should be shape, what follows color everywhere.
Socr: Good.
Meno: This may be so, but what if someone should deny that he knows what color is, rather, that he would be even so ignorant in this as also regarding shape, what do you opine then as regards having answered? <8.~75d]
Socr: Indeed, what's right, I opine. And if the questioner would be one of those wiseacres, battle-artists and word-quibblers, then I would say to him: "Now I have spoken and if I haven't clarified it rightly then it's your affair to take up the word and disprove what I said." But if it would be that we, as now you and I, if we would want to converse together as friends for the sake of learning, then, indeed, I would have to answer in a softer way and more artistically. This "more artistically" may well mean that one not only answers what's right, rather also only using those characteristics that the questioner likewise purports to understand. And in this manner I shall now make another attempt to clarify it for you. Thus tell me – you [e] name something the end? With this I mean something like a border or what's last, everything like this I take to be the same here. Perhaps Prodicus now would be against this, but you name something as having a border or having an end? – just this is what I mean here and let's not use fuzzy logic.
Meno: Sure, I do name something so and believe I understand what you mean. [76a]
Socr: Surface, too, you name as something; and again, something else as body – just as in geometry.
Meno: Yes, that too.

Socr: From here, then, you shall perhaps understand what I mean by shape. For I say that in all shapes that which borders the bodies, this is actually the shape; so in general I would like to say: shape would be the border of the body.

Meno: And what do you call color, Socrates?   <9.~76b]

Socr: You really like to ask too much, Meno! – such difficult matters you lay upon an old man to answer but won't yourself call back into memory and share with me what it is that Gorgias says virtue would be.

Meno: But once you will have explained this to me, Socrates, then I shall certainly say to you what you want.

Socr: Even if you were draped in veils, o Meno, once you speak anyone would be able to notice that you are beautiful and still have lovers.

Meno: How so?

Socr: Because you always simply command in conversation, just as the former spoiled *beaus* do, those who are always so overbearing, at least so long as they remain young. And perhaps you have   [c] already noticed of me that I have not yet become able to resist beauty. I shall then do as you will it and answer.

Meno: Indeed, do as I will it.

Socr: Is it then in accord with your pleasure that I give an answer to your question in the manner of Gorgias, as this is the way that you shall best be able to follow.

Meno: Quite, this is most pleasing for me. How else?

Socr: Isn't it true, you accept Empedocles'[180] doctrine that there are certain effluences which stream forth from all that is?

Meno: Quite right.

Socr: And paths, in which and through which these effluences travel.

Meno: Indeed.

Socr: And that of these effluences certain ones fit into certain paths, but others are too large or too small?   [d]

Meno: So it is.

Socr: Now, you also name something to be sight?

Meno: Indeed.

Socr: Now from this *"take up what I mean,"* as Pindar says. Namely, color is that effluence from shapes which befits and is apprehended through the pathways of sight.

Meno: That's quite fantastic, Socrates; I fancy that you have penned an excellent answer.

---

[180] Empedocles, early philosopher, orator and doctor, and said to have been Gorgias' teacher.

Socr: Perhaps it was penned in a manner to which you are accustomed. And, beyond this, note too that by analogous reasoning you are able to clarify what sound is, and smell and many other *[e]* things of this type.

Meno: Indeed.

Socr: It is namely quite a dazzling answer, Meno, and therefore you find it to be more pleasing than the one for shape.

Meno: At least for me.

Socr: But not the latter, o son of Alexidemus, as I for myself am quite convinced, but the former is the better one. And you too, I believe, would hold the same to be true if, then, you weren't forced to leave us – as you said yesterday – but would be able to remain here long enough to be initiated [into the Eleusinian mysteries].

Meno: I would gladly remain here, Socrates, if you would tell me many things of the latter sort. *<10.~77a]*

Socr: I should not let myself fail you in this regard due merely to a lack in good will, no more for your sake than for my own, that I might say many such things to you – if only I were more capable of doing so and had more like this to bring forward. As it is, now you come forward and make an attempt to fulfill your promise and so clarify for me in a general way, what virtue is. And do put a stop to this making many out of one, as they say in jest to those who tend to drop and smash things; rather, leave it whole and healthy and so tell me now: what is virtue? I have provided you with adequate examples. *[b]*

Meno: I fancy then, Socrates, virtue to be this, as the poets also say:

> *"to delight oneself in beauty and to be capable of it."*

And I name this to be virtue, that a person in striving for the beautiful is capable of bringing it into being.

Socr: And do you mean with such a person, he who strives after beauty, a contender after the good?

Meno: Yes, in all actuality.

Socr: Perhaps as if there would be some who desire evil and others that desire the good? – and does it seem to you, most worthy, that not everyone desires good? *[c]*

Meno: No, it doesn't seem so to me.

Socr: Rather, some desire evil?

Meno: Yes.

Socr: In the opinion that it would be good, is that what you want to say, or indeed even knowing that it is evil they still desire it?

Meno: Both, I fancy.

Socr: Then you believe, Meno, that someone who is acquainted with evil, that it is evil, still desires it?

Meno: Quite.

Socr: And what do you opine that he desires? – that evil becomes him.

Meno: That it becomes him. For, what else?

Socr: Perhaps in the belief that evil is useful to those who partake in it? – or being well acquainted with evil, knowing that it harms   *[d]* whomever acquires this attribute?

Meno: Some, indeed, that believe that evil is useful, but others as well who have recognized that it is harmful.

Socr: And do you then fancy that those who can recognize evil, that it is evil, they believe that evil is useful?

Meno: I wouldn't fancy *that* to be quite right.

Socr: Obviously, then, the former who don't recognize the evil,   *[e]* they don't desire evil any more as such; rather much more they desire what they hold to be good – but it is even evil – so that those who don't recognize evil but believe rather that it would be good, these obviously desire good. Or, isn't it so?

Meno: Well, yes, they seem to.

Socr: And how about those who desire evil and yet also hold the belief, as you asserted, that evil harms whomsoever, whoever it may be who partakes in it – they do affirmatively recognize that they shall be harmed by it?

Meno: Necessarily.   *[78a]*

Socr: And don't these believe that those who are harmed are in misery insofar as they are harmed?

Meno: That too is necessary.

Socr: And not as well that those who are miserable are in a wretched state?

Meno: Yes, I well believe so.

Socr: Is there, then, anyone at all who wants to be miserable and to be suffering?

Meno: No, I wouldn't fancy that.

Socr: Thus, o Meno, nobody wants evil – as assuredly no one wants that he be such. For what could be called being wretched other than striving after evil and achieving it?

Meno: It seems you are in the right, Socrates, and nobody wants evil.

Socr: Didn't you just say that virtue would be this: to want the good and to be capable of it?   *<11.~78b]*

Meno: I said it.

Socr: If this, now, is said – so then everyone shares in this desire and to this extent no one is any better than anyone else.

Meno: So it seems.

Socr: Rather, it is obvious that if someone is to be better than another, then it would be in relation to his superiority in being able.

Meno: Indeed.

Socr: This, then – as it appears – and in accordance to your speech is virtue: the capacity *{Vermögen}* to bring the good into being.   *[c]*

Meno: In every respect, Socrates, I fancy that it correlates just as you have represented it, precisely in accordance with your notion.

Socr: Let's take a good look at this, whether you are in the right, for perhaps you may be right with this. That one is capable of bringing the good into existence, this, so you say, is virtue.

Meno: I say it.

Socr: But don't you name such things as health and wealth to be good? – I mean with this such things as possessing gold and silver, and also one's good reputation or holding high office for the *polis*. Would you name anything other to be good rather than such as these?

Meno: No, rather such as these are precisely what I'm meaning.   *[d]*

Socr: Good! Being able to procure gold and silver is virtue, as Meno asserts, he who stands in hereditary relations to the comrades of the Great King! And do you amend onto this undertaking, perhaps, this as well: that it is to be done in a righteous and pious manner? – or doesn't this make any difference to you, rather, even if someone creates wealth in an unrighteous manner, you name this nonetheless to be virtue.

Meno: Not at all, Socrates! – rather malfeasance.

Socr: In all ways, thus, as it seems, there must be righteousness or mindfulness or piety by these enterprises, or else some other part of virtue; if not, then such shall not be virtue despite that it brings   *[e]* good things into being.

Meno: How could it well be possible that such be virtue without these!

Socr: But *not* procuring gold and silver when doing so would be unrighteous, be it for oneself or for another, wouldn't this lack in enterprise and deficiency also be virtue?

Meno: Well, obviously.

Socr: Thus, the acquisition of such goods is no more virtue than also their non-acquisition; rather, as it seems, only that which happens with righteousness shall be virtue, but everything else which lacks anything of the sort, this shall be malfeasance.   *<12.~79a]*

Meno: I fancy that this is necessary, just as you say.

Socr: Now, didn't we just maintain a little bit ago that each of these would be a part of virtue – righteousness, mindfulness and all of these?

Meno: Yes.

Socr: Hence, Meno, you are making fun of me?

Meno: How so, Socrates?

Socr: Because, although I just entreated you that you neither smash up nor crumple virtue and although I provided you with examples as to how you should answer, nonetheless without being concerned in the least you now say to me that that would be virtue if someone is able to bring forth good things with righteousness, which – as you yourself maintain – is a part of virtue. [b]

Meno: I assert this.

Socr: Thus, there follows from that which you do admit that everything that someone does, if it is done with a part of virtue, that, then, would be virtue. For righteousness, you say, would be a part of virtue, and also each of the others.

Meno: And what now, what if I do assert this?

Socr: That despite my plea that you clarify the *whole* of virtue for me you are yet far away from telling me what it is, rather you only say that every deed would be virtue if it would be done with a part of virtue – as if you would have already clarified what virtue is as a whole and as if I would already now recognize it when you pull it to pieces. Thus, I fancy that once more it is requisite to start at the beginning with the very same question, o Meno, what is virtue – if, then, every deed in which a part of virtue is found should be virtue. For this is what that person says, he who states that every deed done with righteousness is virtue. Or don't you fancy that the very same question is required once again; rather, perhaps you believe that someone might recognize a part of virtue, what this part is, who doesn't know what virtue is itself?

Meno: I wouldn't think that this might well be possible. [d]

Socr: For you may just remember what I previously put forth as answers in respect to shape and that we rejected such answers – those with which we wanted to answer when we were yet seeking and hadn't yet agreed upon that which was one.

Meno: And it is certain that we were right in rejecting them, o Socrates.

Socr: Thus also, don't you opine, most worthy, so long as the whole virtue, what this is, shall yet be sought after, if you bring its parts into the answer, don't opine that you are able thus to clarify virtue to anyone at all, nor too anything else should you proceed to clarify in this manner; rather the original question shall always return – what then is virtue, of which you speak as you did speak. Or, do you fancy what is said as nothing?

Meno: To me, indeed, I fancy it rightly spoken.

Socr: Answer, then, once more from the beginning – what do you say that virtue is, you and your friend? <13.~80a]

Meno: O Socrates, already I have heard it said of you – and this yet before I ever met you – that you yourself were in disarray and totally confused, and also that you brought others into such confusion. Now too, it appears to me that you are bewitching me and putting something over me, and obviously casting some spell that makes me become totally confused and, if I may joke somewhat about it, I fancy that in shape and also otherwise you are just exactly like that broad sea creature, the stingray. For this too makes every creature that approaches it and has contact with it become paralyzed. And even so, I fancy, you also have done something similar to me and I am in paralysis. For, in actuality, in body and soul I am paralyzed and *[b]* I know nothing to answer to your question, and this despite that on a thousand other occasions I have lectured and given many a speech regarding virtue, and before vast throngs of people, and very good speeches too, as I'd fancy it. But now I don't even know the first thing to say about what virtue is at all! For this reason I fancy it would be wisely done that you never travel far from here, neither by ship nor otherwise. For if you ever were to do the same as a foreigner in some other locality, so perhaps you would be led off as a sorcerer.

Socr: My, aren't you the sly one, Meno, and you just about outwitted me and pulled a fast one.

Meno: How's that, Socrates?

Socr: I know very well why it is that you have portrayed me so. *[c]*

Meno: And why then? What do you opine?

Socr: So that I too might want to portray you once again. I know this to be the case by all the *beauts*, that they are especially pleased to have their portraits done. For this contributes to their fame as the portraits of beauties, I opine, are also beautiful. But I shall not make another picture of you. If your stingray is also paralyzed when it paralyzes others, then I am like it; but if not, then I'm not. For in no manner am I myself somehow in order when it occurs that I bring others into confusion and disarray, rather in all ways I myself am likewise bewildered and, thus, simply pull others into the muddle. So too now, what virtue is, I don't know at all; but you, perhaps you knew beforehand, before you touched me, though now you are quite similar to a know-nothing. All the same, I do want to weigh and investigate this with you, what virtue may well be. <14.~80de]

Meno: And in what manner, Socrates, do you want, then, to search for that about which you know utterly nothing at all – what it is? For by which particulars amongst all of the things that you don't know do you want to lay it out and, thus, search after it? Or, even if you were well able to meet up with it, how shall you be able to recognize that it would be that, that of which you know nothing?

Socr: I understand what you want to say, Meno! Do you see what a battle-ready proposition you are bringing into this? Namely, that it is impossible for a person to be able either to search for what he knows, nor for what he does not know. Because namely: not for that which he knows, for this requires no further seeking; nor for that which he does not know as, then, he also wouldn't even know what he should be looking for.[181]

Meno: Doesn't this appear to you to be a beautiful proposition, Socrates?   *[81a]*

Socr: For me – No, not at all.

Meno: And are you able to tell me – why not?

Socr: Oh, yes! For I have received the answer from men and women who have wisdom in divine matters.

Meno: And what, then, did they say?

Socr: Something that if very True, as I respect it, and beautiful.

Meno: But what? And who were they, those who told you?

Socr: They who spoke it are priests, both men and women, as many as there would be upon whom is laid the task of being able to give a reckoning over that which they administer. Also Pindar speaks   *[b]* of this, as do many other poets whose manner of speaking is sublime. And what they say is as follows – but weigh this well, whether you fancy that they speak truly: namely they say that the soul of man would be immortal in that, indeed, now [at one time] it ends – that which we call death – but now [at another point in time] becomes again; but never does it cease. And it is for this reason that one has to conduct one's life in a most sacred manner. For from those

"whom Persephone had freed from the age-old bonds of suffering, these souls are once again returned to the ruling sun in the ninth year,[182] and from hence proceed the well-famed mighty reigns of Kings and those men who excel profoundly in their wisdom – and henceforth these are extolled as blessed heroes amongst mankind."

---

[181] The conundrum here parallels the problem of knowing and not-knowing in *Theaetetus* 188a–188d (pp. 424–425).

[182] The significance to this *ninth* year may be seen if one considers also Plato's Laws, Book I, 624b. From Th. Prangle's excellent translation: *"Don't you people follow Homer and say that Minos got together with his father* [Zeus] *every ninth year and was guided by his oracles in establishing the laws for your cities?"* Putting these passages together would seem to indicate that the reincarnating soul requires new laws for each reincarnation. Hence, justice is itself balanced relative to the evolution of soul. Consider as well *Phaedrus* 248e–249a.

Now, because the soul is immortal and is reborn many   <*15.~81c2]*
times, and as it has perceived everything, both what is here as well
as in the nether worlds: so there also is nothing that would not have
been brought into its experience, and so there's no reason to be
amazed that the soul is capable not only regarding knowing what
virtue is but everything else likewise, that it recollects all of this,
that which earlier it also has known. For as the whole of nature is
related in and to itself and as the soul has partaken inwardly in the
all, so there is no hindrance that whoever shall be reminded of one
singularity, which reminding is called learning by mankind, that
everything else will be found out, as it were, on its own – if only one
is courageous and doesn't tire of the search. For it follows that
seeking and learning are wholly and absolutely recollection. But in
no way shall man be permitted to follow your former battle-ready
proposition, for it would only weigh us down as a burden and it   *[e]*
is pleasant to the hearing only of those who are soft and weak knee'd;
but the latter account makes us active and spurs on our investigations
in which, with good faith as to its veracity, it yet would give me
pleasure that we investigate this together – what virtue is.
Meno: Yes, Socrates. But, do you really mean this in all simplicity,
that we don't learn, that rather what we call learning is only
recollection? Are you able to teach me regarding this, that this is
how it correlates?
Socr: Even already once I have noted this, Meno, that you are a sly
one; and now too you're asking me whether I'm able to teach   *[82a]*
you this – but I have just made the assertion that there is no such
thing as teaching and learning, rather only recollection, and so you
would right away have me appear to contradict myself.
Meno: No, truly, Socrates, not with this intention did I say it,
rather due to habit. If, then, there is any way that you are able to
demonstrate this to me, that it correlates as you say, please do so.
Socr: Indeed, this is no easy matter; but still I shall make the attempt
as an especial favor[183] for you. Call over one of your servants from the
many that accompany you, whichever one you want, so that I can   *[b]*
demonstrate this for you with him.
Meno: Very gladly. You, boy – come over here.
Socr: He is, then, a Hellene and speaks Greek?
Meno: Very well, we raised him in our own home.
Socr: Pay close attention, how he shall appear to you: whether he's
recollecting something or if he learns it from me.
Meno: I shall do so.   <*16.~82c]*

---

[183] "dir zuliebe," literally for my love of you.

Socr: Tell me then, boy, do you well know that such a figure is a rectangle?

Boy: I know it.

Socr: Is there, then, also such a rectangle in which all four sides are of equal length?

Boy: Indeed.

Socr: And are, then, these two lines that go through the middle, are they also equal in length?

Boy: Yes.

Socr: Such an area may be larger or smaller, not so?

Boy: Indeed.

Socr: If, now, this side were to be two feet in length and the other also two feet, then how many [square] feet are contained within the whole? – Consider it so: if there were two feet here but only one foot here, wouldn't the total area be two square feet?

Boy: Yes.

Socr: As now there are two feet on this side as well, shall not the whole be two times two feet. *[d]*

Boy: So it shall.

Socr: Then, it is twice two feet?

Boy: Yes.

Socr: How many, then, are twice two feet? – you do your reckoning and tell us.

Boy: Four, o Socrates.

Socr: Now, is it possible for there to be another area that would be twice as big as this one but otherwise just the same – in that all sides would be of equal length?

Boy: Sure.

Socr: How many square feet would it have to enclose?

Boy: Eight.

Socr: Good! Now make the attempt to tell me, how large would each side of this square have to be? [184] Namely, this first one is two feet on each side; but how long for the square that's twice as large? *[e]*

Boy: Obviously, Socrates, twice as large.

Socr: Do you well see it, Meno, how I have not taught him anything, rather I simply question him? And now he believes that he knows how long the side would have to be from which the square containing

---

[184] Since the square root of eight is a number that is "incommensurate" with the unit of one foot, it is clear to me that *Meno* belongs very closely together with *Theaetetus*; see the blueprint for knowledge 147d (p. 367) and consider the scholarly consensus given on p. xxii.

an area of eight square feet shall be generated. Or, don't you think that he believes to know it?

Meno: Indeed.

Socr: But does he really know it?

Meno: No, not really.

Socr: Yet he believes that it would arise from one twice as large?

Meno: Yes. <17.~83a]

Socr: Pay close attention as regards how he shall recollect further, how one must proceed in recollection.

Now, boy, tell me – from a side of twice the length, from this you have said that an area of twice the size shall arise? But I mean with this *such a one*, not that one side would be shorter and the other longer, rather all the sides must be of an equal length, just like this one here; but the area should be doubled, thus, eight square feet. Look again closely, whether you still are of the opinion that each side would be twice as long?

Boy: So I mean it.

Socr: Good! This, then, would be twice as long as this one if we extend the line – so.

Boy: Quite.

Socr: And from this one, you believe, the square with eight square feet shall be generated, if we draw all four lines.

Boy: Yes. [b]

Socr: So, let's draw in the other lines. Isn't it so, this would be the square that you would hold as being eight square feet in size?

Boy: Quite.

Socr: And are there not contained within it these four other squares, each of which is four square feet in area?

Boy: Yes.

Socr: How large, then, would it be? – not four times as large?

Boy: Not otherwise.

Socr: Is, now, that which is four times as large two times as large?

Boy: No, by Zeus.

Socr: Rather, how much larger?

Boy: Fourfold.

Socr: From a side of twice the length, then, not a twofold area arises, but one that is fourfold in size? [c]

Boy: You are right.

Socr: For when you multiply four by four you get sixteen. Right?

Boy: Yes.

Socr: But the eight square foot square, from which side does this one arise? – And, isn't it so, from this one arises the fourfold?

Boy: I say that too.

Socr: And the four square foot square is generated from this one that is half the length?

Boy: Yes.

Socr: Good. But the eight square foot square, wouldn't it be twice as large as this one and half the size of the other one?

Boy: Indeed.

Socr: Wouldn't it have to arise from a line that is shorter than this one and longer than the other? Or not?

Boy: I, at least, think so.   *[d]*

Socr: Excellent! For always you should only answer what you think to be true. And so tell me, isn't this side four feet long and this other one two feet in length?

Boy: Yes.

Socr: Thus, the side of the square that we are searching for would have to be shorter than the four foot length and longer than the two foot length?

Boy: That it would.

Socr: So, then, make an attempt and tell me – how long would it have to be?   *[e]*

Boy: Three feet.

Socr: Good. If it, then, should be three feet – so we take half the distance of this one and add it to the first, thus we have a line of three feet, for the first was two feet and half of the second is an additional one foot; and if we do the same on the other side, so we arrive at the new square, the one that you mean.

Boy: Yes.

Socr: If, now, this new square has three feet on this side and three feet also on this other side: so the area covered by the square would be three times three?

Boy: Obviously.

Socr: Three times three, now – how many is that?

Boy: Nine.

Socr: But how many square feet should the square contain that is twice the size of the one we began with?

Boy: Eight.

Socr: Thus too, not from the square with a three foot side shall an area of eight square feet come into being.

Boy: No, indeed not.

Socr: But from which line? make an attempt to determine this for us *exactly*; and if you don't want to say it in a number, then just show it to us, which line?   <18.~84a]

Boy: But, Socrates, by Zeus – I don't know.

Socr: Do you well see it, Meno, how far he has come in recollection? For at the beginning he also didn't know in any manner which side would be the one for the square containing eight square feet, as too he still doesn't know; alone, he believed back then that he did know and answered right away as one who knows and didn't believe that he would end up in bewilderment. But now he has realized that he is bewildered and, as he doesn't know he also believes that he doesn't know. *[b]*

Meno: You are right.

Socr: Isn't this an improvement of the situation in relation to the matter that he never has known?

Meno: That too, I fancy as being right.

Socr: In that we have brought him into this state of confusion and paralyzed him like a stingray, have we done him any harm?

Meno: I'd fancy not.

Socr: Much more, we have prepared something and set the stage, as it seems, so that he shall be able to discover how it is that the matter truly correlates. For now he may well want to search about as he doesn't know; but before he believed that without any difficulty he might speak before many on numerous occasions and think that he spoke well regarding the doubling of the square, that it would have to have a side of twice the length. *[c]*

Meno: That may well be true.

Socr: Do you now believe that before he would have gone to the effort to seek out and learn that which not knowing he believed to know – before his being convinced that he didn't know it – and so, falling into confusion he began seeking after knowledge?

Meno: No, I fancy not, Socrates.

Socr: Thus, his paralysis has brought him some benefit?

Meno: Yes, I'd fancy.

Socr: Pay close attention, now, what he is able to seek and discover to rid himself of this confusion in that I only question him and never teach. And pay particular attention, whether you ever catch me teaching him something or lecturing, that rather I simply ask him to follow his own thinking. *<19.~84d]*

Tell me, boy, isn't this here our original square which has an area of four square feet? – do you understand?

Boy: Yes.

Socr: And couldn't we add another one just like it on this side?

Boy: Yes.

Socr: And also a third one here that is the same as the first two?

Boy: Yes.

Soc: And can't we also add one here in this empty corner to fill it out.

Boy: Indeed.

Socr: Are these not, then, four equal squares?

Boy: Yes. *[e]*

Socr: How now? How many times greater is this whole from the first square.

Boy: Four times.

Socr: But we are looking for one that is two times as large – or don't you remember that?

Boy: Quite.

Socr: And doesn't this line which cuts through from corner to corner divide each of the squares into two equal parts? *[85a]*

Boy: Yes.

Socr: And wouldn't these four lines all be of equal length and enclose another square?

Boy: Indeed.

Socr: So examine it: how large would this square be?

Boy: I don't understand.[185]

Socr: Doesn't each of these four pieces contain half the area of the square from which it is cut? Or not?

Boy: Yes.

Socr: How many square feet are there in each of these four squares?

Boy: Four.

Socr: And how many in this half?

Boy: Two.

Socr: And four is what relation to two.

Boy: The twofold.

Socr: How big, then, would this central square be?

Boy: Eight square feet. *[b]*

Socr: And from which line is the square generated?

Boy: From this one.

Socr: From the line which cuts across from one corner to the other in the four square foot square.

Boy: Yes.

Socr: This, now, the teachers call the diagonal, so that, if this is called the diagonal then from the diagonal, as you have asserted, a square of twice the area is generated.

Boy: Quite, Socrates. *<20.~85c]*

---

[185] Just as most people don't bother to understand the beauty of speculative philosophy.

Socr: What do you fancy now, Meno? Did the boy have any notions that were not his own in his answers?

Meno: No, just his own.

Socr: And yet just a little while ago he didn't know at all, as we ascertained.

Meno: Totally right.

Socr: But then, these notions were in him. Or not?

Meno: Yes.

Socr: In him who is a know-nothing, then, there are of that which he doesn't know correct notions?

Meno: That shows itself.

Socr: And now these notions are in him and have come alive, as if in a dream.[186] But if someone questions him about this on numerous occasions and in multifarious ways: so you do know that in the end he would know this no less precisely than anyone else knows it.

Meno: Well, it seems so.   *[d2]*

Socr: In that no one teaches him, rather simply by asking questions, he shall know and shall bring the knowledge out just from inside of himself?

Meno: Yes.

Socr: Now this, to grasp at and bring forth knowledge from within oneself, this is called recollection?

Meno: Quite.

Socr: And hasn't, perhaps, he who has such knowledge, as he does have it – hasn't he either acquired it at some earlier time or he has always had it?

Meno: Yes.

Socr: If he has always had this knowledge, so he has always been one who essentially has known *{wissend gewesend}*. But if at one time he has achieved this learning, so at least it wasn't achieved during this lifetime. Or, has someone taught him geometry? For certainly he *[e]* shall proceed with the whole of geometry just as with this one part – and with all of the other sciences as well. Has someone, then, taught him all of this? For you must well know the answer since he was born and raised in your home.

Meno: I know very well; nobody has ever given him such learning.

Socr: But he has these notions, or not?

Meno: Necessarily, as one can well see.   *<21.~86a]*

---

[186] See *Parmenides* 164d (p. 249) for the dream or 134d for precise knowledge; or, for reviewing over and again what one knows, *Gorgias* 513d (p. 336); and, finally – *Theaetetus* 201e (p. 445). If the notions come alive – note that the pigeons in the birdcage are *alive*.

Socr: If, then, he hasn't achieved such in this life and doesn't know from here – so, obviously, he has had it and has learned it in some other time.

Meno: Obviously.

Socr: Wouldn't this, then, be in that time in which he wasn't a person?

Meno: Obviously.

Socr: If then, in the entire time in which a person is or, also, in   *[b]* which a person isn't, right notions should be within him that can be awakened through questioning and become knowledge – must not his soul always be in this condition of having-learned? For, obviously, he is throughout all time either a person or not.

Meno: I see what you mean.

Socr: If, then, from ye and always the truth regarding everything that is subsists within the soul, so that the soul would be immortal – thus, you may be consoled regarding what you don't now know; this means, however, that which you yourself haven't [yet] recollected; to strive after this you are well able and the search is just calling it back to mind.

Meno: It seems to me, Socrates, I don't know quite how, that you are speaking most admirably.

Socr: Also to my own self, it seems so, o Meno. And regarding the rest about this speech, indeed, I wouldn't like fighting about every last bit of it; but that in believing in the necessity for searching after that which we don't know, that by this we become better and manlier and less burdened down than we would be if we were to believe that it would be impossible for man to find that which he doesn't know and that one, thus, would be spared the looking – for this, indeed, I most affirmatively would fight as best as I am able, both in word and in deed.

Meno: This too, I fancy as being rightly said, Socrates.   *<22.~86cd]*

Socr: As we now are of one mind regarding this, that it would be necessary to seek for that which one doesn't as yet know: shall we undertake with each other this search: what is virtue?

Meno: Very gladly. However, Socrates, I would be pleased most of all if we might investigate together regarding what I first questioned you about, if I could hear whether one should strive after virtue as something that is teachable, or whether it would be so that virtue is inborn or comes into being in man and subsists in some other manner.

Socr: If it were to be my choice in the matter, Meno, not just what I might ask of myself but also of you, so we wouldn't investigate into whether or not virtue is teachable until and unless we first had investigated into what virtue itself is. Alone, since you are not desiring in asking this of yourself, so that you remain free,[187] but you do desire to ask this of me and even have asked me, so I shall have to give in and do as you ask. For what else am I to do? Thus, as it *[e]* seems, we should like to investigate how something comes-into-being of which we don't even know what it is. If then, not wholly, allow me to step back a little from what you request of me and let me observe this from an assumption – the question, namely, as to whether virtue is teachable. With this "from an assumption" I mean this – just as the geometry teachers often will make assumptions in that they observe under what conditions something should obtain regarding a question that is put to them as, for instance, whether it would be possible with a certain figure, say, would this circle be able to enclose that triangle – and thereupon the geometry teacher might well say: "I don't know as of yet whether this type would be such a one but as an assumption for this matter I believe that the following that I have at hand would be pertinent: if this triangle should be such a one so that if you draw the circle around its specified baseline and there should yet remain an area of equal size as the one that the circle encompasses, then, I would fancy, something other would follow, and yet again something other follows if this shouldn't be possible. In relation to this assumption, now, I want to tell you how things may be as regards the enclosure of the same by this circle, whether it be impossible or not." So too in relation to virtue, as we don't at all know what it *<23.~87b]* is nor how it is constituted, we want to consider the question as to whether it would be teachable or not by making the following assumption in that we say: if it, then, is actually thus and such which comes to be within the soul, so it shall be capable of being learned or not be so capable? Hence, the first thing is if it would be something wholly other than knowledge – is it possible, then, that it may become a matter of learning or not, or, as we just noted, brought into recollection? For it shall be equally valid to us no matter which word we make use of. Thus, is it then teachable? Or is it, perhaps, clear to everyone that nothing besides knowledge admits of being taught?

Meno: It seems so, at least to me.

Socr: If now, virtue is a knowledge, then, obviously, it is teachable.

Meno: How could it be otherwise?

Socr: Then, with this we are quickly done: if it should be such, so it is teachable; if not, then not?

Meno: Indeed.

---

[187] Or, at least with an appearance of freedom – man's willful ignorance regarding the soul.

Socr: Next, then, as it seems – we need to investigate into whether virtue is knowledge, or whether it would be something that is wholly different from knowledge?

Meno: Quite, we must investigate this next. [d]

Socr: How now, do we say that virtue is good? and doesn't this premise remain for us, that it is good?

Meno: Indeed.

Socr: Hence, if there should yet be anything other that is good that also is totally separate from knowledge, then, perhaps, virtue also might not be knowledge; but if there is nothing at all that is good and that knowledge does not grasp beneath itself, so it would be allowable of us should we suppose that it would be some part of knowledge, this we would suppose quite rightly.

Meno: That may well be.

Socr: But it is quite certain that we are good by the capacity of virtue.

Meno: Yes. [e]

Socr: And, if good, then also useful – for everything that is good is useful. Isn't it so?

Meno: Yes.

Socr: Thus, virtue also is useful? <24.~]

Meno: Necessarily, from what we have been one in admitting.

Socr: Let us then observe – going through the singularities – what sort of things these are that are useful for us. Health, we say, and strength, beauty and riches are indeed examples that are well chosen. These and such as these we would call useful. Isn't it so?

Meno: Yes. [88a]

Socr: But even these very same things, we say, are harmful on occasion. Or, do you assert that this is other than so?

Meno: No, rather even so.

Socr: Thus, bethink yourself: what would have to rule over these things if they are to be useful to us and what when they should be harmful? Isn't it so: if used rightly then they are useful, if wrongly then they cause harm?

Meno: Indeed.

Socr: And also that which exists within the soul, let us observe this. You name something mindfulness, righteousness and courage – and also the power of grasping with one's mind, and having a good memory, and nobility and everything like this?

Meno: Yes, very much indeed. [b]

Socr: Now, observe these: which of these doesn't seem to you to be knowledge but is, rather, other than knowledge – whether such might on occasion prove to be useful and, on occasion, to cause harm? As, for instance, courage – if it is not guided by insight but rather by a certain audacity, is it not so, if someone should be audacious with no good reason, so he suffers the consequences; but if with reason, then it is advantageous?

Meno: Yes.

Socr: And is not mindfulness even so, and being well learned – if one's erudition is reasonable and proceeds within orderly bounds, then it is useful, but without reason then harmful?

Meno: That's quite certain. *[c]*

Socr: Thus too, then, everything all together that the soul takes up and pursues ends, if insight rules, in blessedness; but if ruled by foolishness, then in the opposite?

Meno: So it seems.

Socr: Is virtue, then, something within the soul that has this property of being useful: thus, it would have to be insight because everything else in which the soul partakes is, in and of itself, neither useful nor harmful and only becomes useful and harmful through the addition of insight or foolishness. Hence, as a consequence to all of this, if virtue would be useful it would have to be insight.

Meno: It seems so to me. *<25.~88de]*

Socr: And so too with all of the rest, riches and everything of this sort, of which we stated earlier that on occasion it would be good, on occasion also harmful – shall not, just as it is with reason when it rules over the rest of the soul making that which is in the soul to be useful, but lack of reason causing harm, so once more the soul by its regency and through making a rightful application of these things brings about utility; but if all of this is not done rightfully, then harm?

Meno: Indeed.

Socr: But the reasonable is right and the unreasonable would be the mistaken and the perverse?

Meno: So it is.

Socr: Is it possible, then, to say in general that for the human being everything else, whether it shall become good for him, this depends upon the soul, but for that which is itself within the soul, this depends upon reason? And, in accord with this speech, reason would *[89a]* be the ultimate as regards what is useful. And do we say, virtue would be useful?

Meno: Quite.

Socr: Thus, we say reason would be virtue, either the whole of it or just a part of it.

Meno: What you say, Socrates, seems to me to be well said.

Socr: If this, now, is how it correlates – so those who are good are not so through nature.

Meno: No, I'd fancy not.

Socr: Then, too, if they were this, wouldn't this well be the   *[b]*
situation, namely: if the good were to be so through nature then there
would be some of us who would know how to differentiate these from
amongst the young, who would be such, and then we would segregate
them and place them in a castle sanctuary for safekeeping, placing a
seal upon them and taking even greater care of them than how we
treat gold so that nobody would be able to spoil them, rather, once
they would have reached the proper age, then we would bring them
forth for service for the polis!

Meno: Quite, naturally.

Socr: Now do those, perhaps, who are good – as they are not so
through nature – do they become so by being taught?   *<26.~89c]*

Meno: That, now, would seem to me to as being necessary, Socrates,
and it is also clearly in accord with our assumption: if virtue is
knowledge that it would have to be taught.

Socr: Perhaps, by Zeus! But that we didn't somehow admit this
without right!

Meno: Indeed, it did seem to us as being very rightly said.

Socr: If only that this might not be too little, that it just seemed
right, rather that now too and that hereafter it also has to strike our
fancy – if, then, there should be something healthy about it.

Meno: What now, again? Socrates! What's wrong now that you are
bug-eyed and no longer believe but doubt that virtue is knowledge?

Socr: I shall tell you, Meno. That virtue is teachable if it should be
knowledge, this I do not take back as if it weren't rightly said; but that
it is knowledge – take a close look whether it seems to you that I don't
rightfully have my doubts. Namely, just tell me this – if any subject
matter is teachable, not just virtue but anything at all, wouldn't there
have to be teachers of it, and students?

Meno: I'd well think so.

Socr: And, on the contrary, if there should be neither students   *[e]*
nor teachers – wouldn't it be right to presume, if we were so to
presume, that it also would not be teachable?

Meno: Well, that's most probably right. But, do you fancy that there
wouldn't be any teachers of virtue?

Socr: Quite often have I searched and hunted, whether there would
be any such, and I have done everything possible, and yet I'm unable
to find them despite that I have joined in with many others in
common pursuit and, indeed, especially with those of whom I
believed that *they* would have to have the most experience[188] in this
matter. So, now too, Meno – and at a most opportune moment –

---

[188] *Protagoras* 320c (p. 121); and *Gorgias* 453b (p. 266) and 527b (pp. 351–352).

Anytus sits down with us. Shall we not ask him, that he partake in our investigation. And truly, it is right that we draw him in on this. For firstly he has a father who is rich and who is a man of   [90a] sound understanding, Anthemion – who has become rich not simply by chance or through a gift as was the Theban, Ismenias, to whom just recently has fallen the treasures of Polycrates, but rather, he by his own understanding and by careful tending has earned his riches. And also as regards all of the rest, his father does not have the reputation of being an aloof or self-indulgent member of the polis, all puffed up and full of hate, rather that of a moral and stately gentleman. Moreover, he has raised his son very well and provided him with the best education – as is obvious from the honors that he has received from the Athenians, for they have, you know, chosen him for the highest honors. It is, thus, easy to see that precisely with such a person our investigation should be conducted regarding the teachers of virtue, whether or not there would be any, and just who they are.   <27.~90bc]

So please investigate this with us, Anytus, with me and with your guest and friend, Meno – who then may well be the teachers of this matter? – But weigh this into your consideration: if we would want that Meno here should become an able doctor, off to whom would we send him? Not to the doctors?

Anytus: Indeed.

Socr: And if we wanted that he become a good shoemaker, we'd send him to those who cobble shoes.

Anytus: Yes.

Socr: And even thus for all the rest?

Anytus: Indeed.

Socr: And tell me regarding this as well. We say that we would be doing right in doing this, sending him to the doctors if we wanted that he become a doctor. If we say this, don't we mean that it would   [d] be handled with more understanding to send him off to those who are engaged in this art rather than to those who are not so engaged. And also to those who receive recompense for their service and proffer themselves as teachers for whomever, whoever should want to come and learn? Isn't it true, it is for these reasons we would do well to send him thither?

Anytus: Yes.

Socr: And shall it not be even so with the musicians, the flutists and all the others: that if one wants to make someone into a flutist that he *not* be sent to others flutists who teach this art and are paid for their services, that rather he be sent elsewhere and fall hard upon someone

other for his lessons, someone who neither gives himself out as being
a teacher nor who has any students in this art in which we would like
that he be taught, he whom we have sent thither? Wouldn't you fancy
this to be great folly and show a lack of understanding?   *<28.~91a]*
Anytus: By Zeus, it certainly does to me, and extremely inept as well.
Socr: Well spoken. And now would you be able to confer together
with us and tender your advice for Meno, our dear guest. For Meno,
o Anytus, has been telling me already for quite some time that he has
urgings for the wisdom and virtue by which human beings administer
the affairs of the *polis* and also those of the home – and by which one
also cares for one's parents and relatives and knows how to take up
and discharge friends and compatriots as is worthy of a righteous
individual. Take this into consideration, then, to whom would we do
best to send him for the sake of achieving such virtues? – Or,   *[b]*
isn't it obvious that in accordance with the speech just concluded that
we should send him to those who give themselves out as teachers of
virtue and proffer themselves to any and all of all the people of Hellas,
whoever wants to learn, and they also set a price and take in some
recompense for their service.
Anytus: And just whom do you mean by this, Socrates?
Socr: You too know whom it is that I mean – they are called
sophists.
Anytus: By Heracles, Socrates! – speak better! That no one, neither
relative nor friend nor anyone else who is native to this place, nor yet
any foreigner, nobody should grasp at such madness that he goes
thither to such as these, and go also to his own corruption. For these
are indeed the manifest corrupters and the misfortune of those who
associate themselves with them.   *<29.~91cd]*
Socr: How do you mean this, Anytus? These alone amongst all of
those who proffer themselves as being able to prove good and do
something well, these should be to such an extent different from all of
the rest that not only do they *not* bring to their pupils any advantage
– as do the others to whom one is given over – rather, wholly the
opposite to these they corrupt their pupils and all the same make no
secret of taking in remuneration for their service? I for my part don't
know how I'm to believe you. For I know that all alone as one person
Protagoras has earned more money with his wisdom than Phidias has
made, he who has completed such magnificently beautiful works, and
even if ten other sculptors are thrown in. And it would indeed be a
wonder, what you say, if when the shoe repair shops and the tailors,
those who make the things that they take in to be better, if these are
not able to stay in business for more than a month with it remaining
hidden that the shoes and clothes that they have worked on   *[e]*

should be given back in worse condition than when first brought in – rather these, if they performed so poorly, would have to soon die of hunger; and yet with Protagoras all of Hellas wouldn't even as of yet have noticed that he corrupted his students and sent them back in worse shape than how they were when they first arrived, and he did this for more than forty years! For, as I believe, he was nearly seventy years of age when he died and he practiced his art for forty years. And for this whole time and still up to today people still have not let up in their praise of him. And not only Protagoras, rather there are yet many others, in part some who were older than Protagoras and others who are yet still living. Now, should we say in accordance with your opinion that these have knowingly engaged in subterfuge with their young protégés and have maimed them, or have they done so without even knowing it themselves? And are we to believe that they are so stupid, these who are seen by a few as being the wisest amongst all of mankind? <30.~92b]

Anytus: Not by a long shot, Socrates, would these be the fools, rather only the youths who give them money, and yet even more than these, those who are their followers and who allow that all of this happens. But the stupidest of all would be the cities that allow them to come in instead of driving everyone away, citizen or foreigner, who would allow this to happen.

Socr: Has some sophist, perhaps, done you a wrong, Anytus? Or why is it that you have such anger toward them?

Anytus: No, by Zeus, never have I had anything at all to do with any of them, nor do I allow anyone of my family or associates to have any intercourse with them.

Socr: Then you are wholly and absolutely unacquainted with these men?

Anytus: And I wish also that I remain so.

Socr: But how, then, is it possible, you wonderful man, that [c] you know anything regarding this matter – whether it may have something of good within itself or if it should only be bad? – if, then, you are totally unacquainted with them?

Anytus: It's quite simple. I'm well aware of what sort of people these people are, whether or not I myself have any personal acquaintance with them.

Socr: You are, perhaps, an augur, Anytus? For how, otherwise, you might know anything at all regarding these men from what you have told me, I can't grasp it. Be this as it may, we weren't indeed asking you who they might be who would make Meno to be worse if we sent him thither, these, if you like, these may well be the sophists. [d] Rather, as I stated earlier, name us those – and pay homage to your guest and friend for the sake of your family's connections – to whom he would have to go in this great city in order that he might accomplish something of worth in the virtue that I described earlier.

Anytus: But why haven't you pointed these out to him?

Socr: Those who I hold to be teachers in this I have named; but it turns out that nothing was said, as you assert.

Anytus: In *this* you may well be quite right. [e]

Socr: But now, you on your side should say to Meno – to whom amongst the Athenians he should go. Name just any one name, whomever you want! <31.~92]

Anytus: What need does he have to hear the name of any single person! For if he goes to *any* good and righteous Athenian whom he should meet, there is indeed no one who wouldn't make him to be better than the sophists, if only he will follow him.

Socr: Have, then, these good and righteous men become so on their own without having learned this from anyone? And are they yet able to teach others this, what they have never learned from others? [a]

Anytus: They too, I think, learned this from those who came before – and who, themselves, also were good and righteous. Or, don't you opine that there have always been many righteous men in this city?

Socr: I for my part believe that presently there still are such who are good and capable in the affairs of the community – and that earlier there certainly were not any fewer than there are now. But are they also, perhaps, good and capable in the teaching of their virtue? For it's even this about which we are now conversing; not whether or not there should be such righteous citizens, nor whether there have been such in the past, rather whether virtue is itself something that is capable of being taught – *this* is what we have been investigating [b] for such a long while. And in respect to this investigation we also are researching into this: whether these upright individuals – those who themselves are most to be admired, and be they current or former – whether they would know how to disperse virtue to others, that these might have a share in it, or whether it can't be so dispersed and is not transferable from one person upon another. This is what Meno and I have been asking ourselves now for such a long while. And now, you might weigh this in respect to your own speech. Wouldn't you maintain that Themistocles would have been a most capable individual? <32.~93c]

Anytus: Totally first-rate.

Socr: Thus, also a capable teacher – if ever there was one in his own virtue it would have been he?

Anytus: Indeed, I believe so – if he would have wanted to.

Socr: But are you, perhaps, of the opinion that he didn't want to, that others too might not become good and righteous through him, particularly his own son? Or do you opine that he didn't much care to favor him and that he purposefully withheld in the dispersal of the virtue in which, so admirably, he himself excelled? And haven't *[d]* you heard that Themistocles let his son, Cleophantus, be given instruction in horsemanship and that he was so far ahead and accomplished in his abilities that he might even stand upright from the horse and still be able to shoot with his bow down upon the enemy; and there are yet many other amazing feats of *techne*, and that in whatever anyone might instruct him he was made to be consummate in the arts, at least insofar this depends upon teachers. Or, haven't you heard about this from the old-timers?

Anytus: I have heard it.

Socr: Thus, no one might reproach his son's natural talents – as if they were to have been deficient.

Anytus: Perhaps; you're very probably right in this. *[e]*

Socr: And how now? That Cleophantus, son of Themistocles, would ever have been praised as an accomplished individual and as a man of wisdom just like his father, this you never have heard anyone say, be they young or old.

Anytus: Indeed, I have not.

Socr: Should we then believe it, that indeed he wanted that his son be instructed in the former arts but as for the wisdom that he himself possessed, that he didn't care to make him any better than any of his neighbors – if, then, virtue would be teachable?

Anytus: That doesn't follow, by Zeus. *<33.~94a]*

Socr: But such a teacher of virtue is he, Themistocles, of whom you have actually admitted that he would belong to the most capable of the elder generation! So let's take a good look at another example, Aristides, son of Lysimachus. Or, don't you agree with me that he was a righteous individual?

Anytus: I do, in every respect.

Socr: And did he not let his own son, Lysimachus, be given lessons of the highest caliber amongst the Athenians – whatever possibly could be taught – and do you fancy that he succeeded in making him to be any better than anyone else? For you yourself have had commerce with this person and you can well see what sort of a person he is. And, if you want, consider Pericles – this lordly man, noble and wise – you do know that he raised two sons, Paralus and Xanthippus.

Anytus: I know it.

Socr: And, as you also know, he let these be given instruction in horsemanship that were as good as any, and also in music and gymnastics and in all of the other arts, and these lessons were second-rate to none; but, somehow, he shouldn't have wanted that they become virtuous men? – I'd think rather so, he wanted this very much, but perhaps this cannot be taught! And so that you don't believe that only a few and perhaps just the worst of the Athenians were incapable in this, so do recall to yourself that also even   *[c]* Thucydides likewise had two sons whom he raised, Melesias and Stephanus, and these also were well instructed so that, namely, they became the best wrestlers in all of Athens. For one was given over to Xanthias for training and the other to Eudorus, and these were commonly held to be the most capable trainers of all. Or, don't you remember this?

Anytus: Indeed, quite well – I've heard tell.   *<34.~94d]*

Socr: Isn't it obvious that he certainly wouldn't only have his sons trained in those matters that require monetary outlays but that in those that wouldn't require any such outlays, in the virtue in which he himself excelled, to make them to be virtuous men, that just these lessons somehow would have been withheld by him – if, then, this would have been teachable? But, perhaps Thucydides was just a coarse person and somehow didn't have any friends amongst the Athenians and their allies. But yet, he did come from a great estate and he was very able to accomplish many things in the city and, indeed, in the whole of Hellas, so that – if indeed it were to be teachable, he certainly would have found somebody from amongst the Athenians or the foreigners in order that his sons might become virtuous even if he himself shouldn't have been able to find the time due to his many obligations for the city. But you see, my dear Anytus, virtue may not be something that can be taught.

Anytus: O Socrates – it seems to me that you are far too nonchalant in your disparaging speeches regarding these men. Now, I would like to give to you a piece of good advice, if you'd like to follow my suggestion – that you should *look out for yourself.* For also in other localities it may be an easy thing that one does evil to someone, and this far more readily than good, but here in this city it is astonishingly easy. And I think that you yourself know this.   *<35.~95a]*

  [Exit Anytus]

Socr: O Meno, it seems that Anytus is awfully mad at me. That too doesn't really cause me wonder. For, on the one hand, he believes that I have been making malicious remarks about these individuals, and, on the other hand, he holds himself up as being one of them. If only he ever should have the insight as to what it really means to speak evil of someone then he would cease in his pretensions and anger, but now – he doesn't have a clue. But, you tell me: are there not in your own homeland good and upright men?

Meno: Indeed.

Socr: How now? – do these men give themselves out as being   *[b]* teachers for the young and do they assert that virtue is teachable and that they teach it?

Meno: No, truly – they do not; rather, sometimes you might hear them say that it would be teachable and, again, at other times that it would not be.

Socr: And should we view those to be the educators in this matter, those who themselves are so far from being of one mind!

Meno: No, I'd fancy not.

Socr: Or, how about these sophists who give themselves out as being alone in this – do you fancy that they are the teachers of virtue?

Meno: It's even this, Socrates, that I especially love as being so   *[c]* excellent in respect to Gorgias – that you certainly shall never hear him promise anything of the sort; much to the contrary he's apt to laugh at the others if he hears them making such promises. Only in speech does he opine to be capable of making others mighty.

Socr: Thus, you also don't hold up the sophists as being the teachers?

Meno: I'm not able to say, Socrates. For I am much like the majority in this: sometimes I believe that they are, and at other times I don't believe it.

Socr: And you also know that, indeed, it's not just you and the other statesmen to whom it sometimes seems so, that virtue is teachable, and sometimes not; rather also the poet Theognis, don't you know – he says the same thing.

Meno: In which of his verses?   <36.~95d]

Socr: In those elegies of his in which he says:

So dost thou do well to acquaint thyself in drinking and feasting with these,
and with these be a boon companion – those who are most capable.
For from the good flows[189] much of goodness that you may learn,
But in society with the bad you easily lose the understanding that you bring.

[e]

Do you note it – here he speaks of virtue as something to be learned?

Meno: Obviously.

Socr: Yet, in other passages he distances himself from this and says:

---

[189] Compare with *Symposium* 175de: "It would be a good thing, Agathon, if wisdom were the sort of thing that flows from the fuller of us into the emptier …".

Let understanding root itself firmly within mankind –
Greatness and nobility then accrue

namely to these who have understanding; and

Never more from noble blood shall one fall into malfeasance –
  tho' raised in healthy strictures!
Alone through teaching shall never a bad man be turned around
  back into the folds of goodness.   *[96a]*

Do you see how the very same subject matter is contradicted here?
Meno: That is clear.
Socr: Now, are you able to name for me anything else at all whereby
those who proffer themselves as teachers are not only *not* recognized
by others as being such, rather even they themselves are seen as being
a corrupting influence in just that matter in which it is that they claim
to be the teachers? – and, on the other hand, that those who   *[b]*
themselves are recognized as being good and capable, these say at one
time that it is teachable and, then again, turn around and say that it's
not so? – and can you believe of such people who are in such utter
confusion regarding this matter, that they would be the teachers of it?
Meno: By Zeus – there's something fishy here.   <37.~96]
Socr: If, then, neither the sophists nor those who are themselves
good and upright individuals are to be the teachers of virtue, so,
obviously, there isn't anyone else?
Meno: No, I'd fancy not.
Socr: And, if no teachers then also no students?   *[c]*
Meno: I fancy you're right; it's as you say.
Socr: And regarding this we were of one mind: in that in which there
are neither teachers nor students, such wouldn't be teachable?
Meno: On this we were of one mind.
Socr: And nowhere has it been shown that there are teachers?
Meno: So it is.
Socr: And, if no teachers, no students!
Meno: So it seems.
Socr: Hence, virtue is not teachable.
Meno: It seems that it isn't – if, namely, we have carried out our *[d]*
investigation aright. And so, Socrates, I'm in wonder: whether there
should be any virtuous men at all? – – or what would be the way and
the means whereby they have become so.
Socr: At least, Meno, it's starting to seem that we two, you and I, are
not particularly competent people and that neither Gorgias has given

you proper instruction, nor Prodicus me. Let us then be even more vigilant in taking care of ourselves and research into this further: who then is able to make us better in any manner whatsoever. I say this namely in connection to our prior investigation which has *[e]* more than sufficiently made us to appear ridiculous, that not only alone through this, that knowledge rules, do the affairs of mankind proceed well and righteously – and it is due to this, perhaps, that our insight has failed us as regards the ways and means by which human beings become virtuous.

Meno: How do you mean, Socrates?   <38.~97a]

Socr: Thus: that virtuous men would have to be useful, this, indeed, we admitted rightly, that it couldn't be other than this. Isn't it true?

Meno: Yes.

Socr: And that they shall be useful if they lead us rightly in our proceedings, this too we conferred in and were of one mind?

Meno: Yes.

Socr: But that someone wouldn't be able to lead aright, someone who lacked knowledge, it is in this that we may have gone astray in the premises that we firmly set down?

Meno: How do you mean this with "aright"?

Socr: I shall tell you. If someone knows the way to Larissa or to wherever else it is that one may want to go, if such a person goes in front and leads the others – shall he not lead them well and aright?

Meno: Certainly.   *[b]*

Socr: How now – if someone *merely* should have the right notion about this, which path would be right, without himself ever having gone there or really knowing it, shall not such a person nonetheless lead aright?

Meno: Indeed.

Socr: And for so long as he continues to have the right notion regarding this, what the other one knows, so he shall be none the worse in leading, he who only has the right notion just as the other who knows?

Meno: Indeed, he wouldn't do any worse.

Socr: Notions that are true are, therefore, no worse in leading to right conduct than true insight would be. And it is even this that we overlooked in our earlier investigation regarding virtue and how it would come to be when we said that insight alone would have to lead one to righteous conduct; but having the right notion does this just as well.   *[c]*

Meno: So it seems.

Socr: Notions that are true are, therefore, no less useful than knowledge?

Meno: Except to the extent, o Socrates, that he who has knowledge always hits the mark, but he who has right notions sometimes hits and sometimes misses.   *<39.~97]*

Socr: Say what? He who always has the right notion, he shouldn't always be on target insofar as he represents things aright?

Meno: That's necessary, this has come to light – so that, o Socrates, I am amazed: if this is how it correlates then why should knowledge be so much more greatly prized than having the right notion,   *[d]* indeed, why then would the one be something altogether other than the other?

Socr: Do you know why it is that you are amazed? – or shall I tell you?

Meno: Indeed, tell me.

Socr: Because you have never given proper notice to the artistic works of Daedalus. But, perhaps you don't have any of his works in Thessaly.

Meno: What are you getting at now?

Socr: Because these too, if they haven't been bound properly and tied down, they move about and fly off; but if they are bound then they remain.

Meno: Tell me more?   *[e]*

Socr: Hence, if you happen to be in possession of one of his works that hasn't been bound properly, then it's of no particular value – just like a frenetic busy-body, for it has no lasting value; but one that is properly bound is worth a lot for they are quite beauteous works. But, what am I getting at? At the right notions. For right notions are also beauteous things, at least so long as they stay, and they accomplish much that is good; but they don't tend to hang around very long, rather they fly away out of man's soul so that they aren't really worth much unless one binds them down through well-grounded thought *{durch Beziehung des Grundes}*. And this, Meno my friend, is even the recollection to which we committed ourselves in our preceding discussion. And once the right notions become properly bound they firstly become knowledge and then they also are steadfast. And it is for this reason that knowledge is more highly prized than having the right notions and it is differentiated from the same even by this, by its having been bound.

Meno: By Zeus, Socrates, it has to be something along these lines.

Socr: Be this as it may, for I do not say this as something *<40.~98b]* which I claim to know but, rather, only as something that I suspect. But that having the right notion is something different from having knowledge, this is something that I not only suspect, rather, if there be anything at all that I might assert to know – and there is precious little to which I do lay such a claim – so I would set this down amongst the few matters that I do know.[190]

Meno: And certainly, Socrates, in this you are right.

Socr: And how now? – am I not also right in this, namely – that if having the right notion leads, then it accomplishes the task at hand not a whit more poorly than knowledge?

Meno: That too, I'd fancy as being true. *[98c]*

Socr: Thus, for all of man's activities having the right notions is no worse a guide and no less useful than knowledge would be, nor is such an individual, he who possesses the right notions, any worse a guide than the man who knows.

Meno: So it is.

Socr: And the just, upright leader, this was clear to us, is useful.

Meno: Yes.

Socr: If, then, it's not only by and through their knowledge that men are virtuous and useful for the *polis*, they who are such, but rather also through their having the right notions, and if neither of these subsists in man by nature, neither knowledge nor right notions, *[d]* and also if neither of these is something which one might earn through effort – or, do you think that either of these two would come to be through nature?

Meno: No, I don't.

Socr: If, thus, not by nature, so too, those who are good are not so from nature?

Meno: Indeed, they're not.

Socr: But if not from nature, then we investigated next as to whether virtue would be teachable.

Meno: Yes.

Socr: And if it were to be teachable then virtue would also be insight?

Meno: Indeed.

Socr: And if there were to be teachers then it would be teachable, if not, however, then it would not be teachable? *[e]*

Meno: That's how it was.

Socr: But, singularly, we were of one mind that there wouldn't be any such teachers?

Meno: Right.

Socr: Thus, we were of one mind that it is neither teachable nor insight?

Meno: Indeed.

---

[190] In respect to this, Diotima's speech in the *Symposium* 202a is most instructive: it appears that Diotima's teachings are an essential basis for what Socrates truly knows. I might conjecture that the character, Diotima, is rather intimately bound up with soul.

Socr: But that it would be good, this stands on firm ground?

Meno: Yes.

Socr: And what is useful and good would be that which leads aright?

Meno: Indeed.

Socr: And what leads aright may only be one of these two: having the right notion or knowledge; and the individual who possesses *[a]* these leads aright. For whatever occurs by chance does not happen by human leadership, but that through which a man becomes a great leader for the right, that would only be from one of these two, having a notion that is true and knowledge?

Meno: It seems so to me.   *<41.~99]*

Socr: If virtue is not teachable, so also it no longer is knowledge.

Meno: Obviously not.

Socr: Of the two of them which lead to the good and useful the   *[b]* one has jumped ship and in the civic affairs knowledge would not be in high command.

Meno: No, I'd fancy not.

Socr: Thus, not by their wisdom of any sort nor as wise individuals have these great men been leaders of the *polis*, Themistocles and all the others whom Anytus brought before us earlier. And it's just for this reason that they also were not in a position to make others to be such as they themselves – as they themselves were not such by knowledge.

Meno: It seems most probable that it correlates just as you say, Socrates.

Socr: Thus, if not by knowledge, so having the right notion is the only thing still left over through which politically adept men   *[c]* have administered the *polis* without any relation to true insight, rather just as the oracles and augurs. For these are also able to say much that is true but don't at all know what it is that they say.

Meno: That may well be so.

Socr: Is it not right, Meno, that we call these men divine, they who without any recourse to reason are able to bring about many kinds of greatness through what they say and do?

Meno: Indeed.

Socr: With all due right, then, we would name these men as being divinely inspired, those whom we just mentioned, the oracles   *[d]* and augurs, as well as the poets; and not least of all would the same also be well deserved of being said of the statesmen, that they are divine and inspired, spirited by the breath of God and receptive of His Being – if they through their speeches bring the great affairs to fortunate conclusions without actually knowing anything at all about that of which they speak.

Meno: Well, indeed.

Socr: The women do this as well, Meno, in that they call virtuous individuals divine; and so too is the usage by the Lacedaemonians, if they want to praise someone as being a virtuous individual then they say that 'so and so' is a godlike man.

Meno: And this has shown itself as being said quite rightly, Socrates, although Anytus is awfully mad at you because of your talk.

Socr: That's a small matter. There will come another day, *<42.~99e]* o Meno, and then we want to speak further with him. But if we have gone rightly to work in our whole investigation and have spoken aright: thus virtue does not come to be through nature nor would it be teachable, rather it comes through divine dispatch and thus subsists in those in whom, having no recourse to reason, it subsists. Otherwise he who was politically adept would have to be such a one who would be capable of making others to be such. But if ever there were to be such a person then he might only be described by other mortals as it is stated in Homer that Teiresias exists amongst the dead, that he alone sees truly, *"the others being nothing more than flickering shadows."* For exactly so does this correlate with such a one and the others, as does a shadow to an actual thing[191] – in relation to virtue.

Meno: You speak most admirably, Socrates, as I fancy it.   *[100b]*

Socr: In accordance with this investigation, therefore, o Meno, it seems that virtue subsists in those in whom it abides through divine dispatch. But we shall only then know more regarding the precise details if, before we question in respect to the ways and means that someone succeeds in arriving at virtue, if we first investigate what virtue is in and of itself. But now it is time for me to go elsewhere. In the meantime, you should try to make clear to your host and friend, Anytus, all of that about which, now, you are convinced so that he shall become less harsh in his disposition. For if you do convince him, you shall also prove to be useful to all Athenians.

****

---

[191] Cf: *The Republic, Book VII* and *Sophist* 266bc (p. 579).

Sophist

for *Usha*

Josabeth: *Soothing tyrant, falsely smiling!*
Virtue's foe I ne'er shall fear;
Flatt'ring sounds and looks beguiling
Lose their artful meaning here!

Go, thou vain deceiver, go!
Alike to me a friend or foe!

Joad: *Reviving Judah shall no more*
Detested images adore;
We'll purge with a reforming hand
Idolatry from out the land.

May God, from whom all mercies spring,
Bless the true church, and save the king!

Abner: *Rejoice, O Judah, this triumphant day!*
Let all the goodness of our God display,
Whose mercies to the wond'ring world declare
His chosen people are his chosen care!

Quoted from: George Frideric Handel's **ATHALIA**, *Third Act.*

Sophist – Sections:

Sophist

****

THEODORUS, SOCRATES, ELEATIC STRANGER, THEAETETUS

<1.~216a]

Theo: In accordance with yesterday's agreement,[192] o Socrates, so by placing ourselves here before you we have fulfilled our promise – and what's more, we've brought along with us a foreigner: a man whose roots are in Elea and who is a friend of those who hold to the writings of Parmenides and Zeno – and who, indeed, is someone well steeped in philosophy.

Socr: Should it perhaps be so, Theodorus, that unbeknownst to yourself you had brought along not a stranger but a god – as stated in Homer whose writings tell us that, verily, the gods tend to accompany not only those of us who are steadfast in righteousness and those who experience shame but also that, most particularly, they are to be found amongst our guests: that they come to observe our audaciousness as well as our piety – and perhaps, so too, this man is accompanying you in the very same manner, that he is one of these higher beings come down to observe us in our feeble attempts in speech, and that he might lead us over in the search for our homeland, a transforming god?

Theo: That isn't at all the manner of *this* foreigner, Socrates; rather he's quite modest in his bearing and not at all like those who are so argumentative. Thus, indeed, I wouldn't fancy this man as a god at all, though certainly he is god-like – for then, I would like to name all philosophers as being such.   *[c]*

Socr: And rightly so, my friend. Only it may well be that this breed, in that I speak it out: this breed is not much easier to recognize than is the race of the gods. For then, it is so that they appear in multifarious disguises *{Gestalten}* due to the lack of insight of the others, and these men – and I don't mean those amongst them who simply are pretending to be philosophers but, rather, the true ones who tread amongst us looking askance upon our base lives from their elevated positions – and to a few these philosophers appear as being totally worthless; others though value them above everything else and often take them as being statesmen or, likewise, they are held as being sophists; but, then too, it has also occurred that a few consider them simply as being insane. Now, I should very much like to hear from this stranger, if he wouldn't mind taking this up: what then, indeed, what is held and what is spoken in regards to these in his neck of the woods?

---

[192] *Theaetetus* 210d (p. 458).

Theo: In regards to which "these"?   *[217a]*

Socr: As regards sophists, statesmen and philosophers.

Theo: But really, how do you mean this? And what uncertainty do you have regarding these that you happen upon asking such a question?

Socr: This, namely: whether they hold all of them as being one and the same, or if they distinguish two sorts, or then again if it should be that just as there are three words, so too there would be three types that are distinguished, that for each name numbered there would be one unique concept to which it is bound and knotted?

Theo: Indeed, it seems to me that he wouldn't have any second thoughts about going through this; or what, o Stranger, what shall we say?   *[b]*

Strng: Just so, Theodorus.   For neither do I have any second thoughts nor is it hard to say that, naturally, they hold these as being three sorts.   But then, that each sort individually be precisely determined, what each of them is: this is neither a small matter nor such an easy undertaking.

Theo: That's quite fortuitous, Socrates, that you have grasped at an object that is very much related to the one regarding which we questioned him earlier, before setting off to meet you here. But then he warded off our inquiry in a manner not dissimilar to the one he now employs with you. For he also confessed to us that he had heard sufficiently regarding the matter and also that he still retains what he heard.   *<2.~217c]*

Socr: Thus, o Stranger, don't bashfully reject granting to us the first favor in that we do now beseech as much from you. Rather, simply tell us your preference – whether it would be more pleasant for you to present us with a lecture alone by yourself and, so, go through the speech in one continuous exposition, whatever it may be that you have to present to us; or if you prefer to question – the latter method being the one that I heard Parmenides employ once when being in his presence he led the discourse regarding certain matters of substance, as then I was still but a youth and he already a man venerable in age.

Strng: If there be one, o Socrates, who knows how to answer without becoming annoyed and who follows along as per my lead, this, being easier, is my first preference; but if this shouldn't be the case, then preferably alone.   *[d]*

Socr: Well then, that being so you stand free to choose whomsoever you wish from amongst those present – for we all are ready to follow you.[193] But if you would like my advice on this then you should pick out someone from amongst the youngsters, perhaps Theaetetus here, or whomever of the others might be in accord to your sensibilities.[194]

Strng: O Socrates, I find myself beset by a particular shame, that now, this being just my first occasion visiting here amongst all of you, since it is not a small discourse that I shall carry through, that we just exchange a few words with one another about this or that – but, rather, I shall be leading a rather expansive discourse, one that is full of interrelated topics, and whether it be that I speak it alone or with someone else: it's as if I were to parade myself naked before all of you. For then, the task that you have set before me is in all actuality not so short as one might expect when so questioned, rather it requires quite a lengthy discourse separating the one matter apart from the others. On the other hand, that I would refuse your request and also the request of these others – and particularly after having heard what you have said to me – this, it seems to me, would not be behaving as guests should, nor would it be proper. For then, *[a]* that Theaetetus would be my interlocutor, this is in every way pleasant to me both because of my earlier conversation with him as well as due to your recommendation.

Theae: You shall also, as Socrates has said, give pleasure to all of us, o Stranger, if you would [begin]?

Strng: In this regard it appears that there's nothing left to be said, Theaetetus, and from here on out my speech, as it seems, shall be directed toward you. But if over its long course you find yourself straining and if it should become difficult for you, so don't place the blame for this upon me, rather upon these friends of yours. *[b]*

Theae: Truly, I do hope that I shan't become tired out just yet. But should it be that this does happen to me, well then, we want that you might take up *this* Socrates[195] – he who has the like name as the elder Socrates but whose age is like my own and who is my exercise partner and, thus, he's used to going through many sorts of ordeals with me.

<3.~218c]

---

[193] *Parmenides* 137a – "they all entreated Parmenides that he might indeed give them an example.."

[194] *Parmenides* 135b – Socrates states here that he is in accord with the sensibilities "nach deinem Sinn" of Parmenides; it seems that philosophy requires a *certain* orientation.

[195] The younger Socrates (first mentioned in *Theaetetus* 147d, p. 367) is the interlocutor for the Eleatic Stranger in the next dialogue, *Statesman*.

Strng: Well spoken, and regarding this you may well confer with yourself for advice as our speech progresses. But now it's necessary that you forge ahead in community with me on into our investigation beginning firstly, as I'd fancy it, that we search out the sophist and that our speech brings this to light, what it is that he might be. For as of yet, now, all that we share in common regarding him is his name, but the matter that we attribute to him, our notions regarding him, these may well differ in that each of us may have his own particular notions. But it is always preferable for all things that one comes to an understanding regarding whatever through clarification rather than simply regarding the name without any clarification. But then, the entire class that now we have taken upon ourselves that we search after it, this is no easy matter for us that we grasp it from amongst the others, where it is that the sophist belongs. But then, wherever great undertakings should meet up with success, regarding this everyone has always been of one mind: that such needs to be worked up to and that one exercises oneself first on smaller and easier undertakings *[d]* before moving on to the greatest itself. And so too now, o Theaetetus, at least it's my advice for both of us that since we hold the sophistic type as being rather arduous and hard to catch, that first off we attempt to prove our method on something else that's easier – if then you wouldn't, perhaps, have something else to suggest, some other easier path that we might follow.[196]

Theae: No, I don't have any such.

Strng: Shouldn't we then, perhaps, fetch something that is wholly trivial – and then with this, that we attempt to use it as a blueprint [197] for that which is greater?

Theae: Yes.   *[e]*

Strng: What shall we set before ourselves that is easy to recognize and is a small matter? – something, though, that wouldn't require a clarification that's any shorter than the greater [object]? Perhaps that fisherman called angler, isn't he something familiar to everyone and spending a lot of effort upon him, generally, would be doing something utterly worthless.

Theae: So he is.

Strng: But as a method of proceeding he should, I hope, show us something – and this will befit the [sort of] clarification that we want.

Theae: Indeed, that would be really admirable.   *<4.~219a]*

---

[196] Compare with *Phaedrus* 272c (p. 66). Note too that this dialogue, like the *Parmenides*, is an exercise.

[197] *Vorbild* – compare to *Theaetetus* 148d (p. 368).

Strng: Then tallyho, let's begin with him. Tell me, do we want to stipulate that he is an artist? – or that he'd be lacking in artistry but that some other capability should be predicated of him?
Theae: In no way, indeed, that he would be lacking in artistry.
Strng: But all of the arts may be subsumed beneath two concepts.
Theae: How so?
Strng: Horticulture, namely, and then each and every endeavor that has to do with mortal bodies and, then too, whatever has a connection with things that are put together or formed, all of that which we call manufacturing, and then as well all of the imitative arts: all of these can rightfully be pointed out beneath one name. *[b]*
Theae: How's that, and underneath which one?
Strng: Wherever someone something that previously didn't exist, and he brings whatever it may be into existence, we say that he who brings it forth makes it, but that that which is brought forth has been made.
Theae: That's right.
Strng: All that which we have just mentioned, all this as a whole has its power in this.
Theae: Indeed, it is in this.
Strng: So, accordingly, one would be able to bind all of this together and name it – the art of bringing-forth.
Theae: Verily, so it is. *[c]*
Strng: But, on the other side, all types of learning and that which has to do with knowledge and, moreover, making money and fighting and hunting – since none of these creates anything, that rather dealing with what is present or whatever has already become, in part through words and in part through deeds, these arts have to do with controlling, in part that they attempt to wrest control over these and in part that they resist – and so, therefore, one would best be able to describe this one art that subsumes all of these pieces by naming it the art of acquisition.
Theae: Yes, that would be acceptable.
Strng: If now, all of the arts belong either to acquisition or to bringing-forth, beneath which of them, Theaetetus, do we want to place the angler? *<5.~219d]*
Theae: Obviously, beneath acquisition.
Strng: But doesn't there also exist two classes beneath the art of acquisition: the one being every sort in which there exists good will on both sides of the exchange, be it in the giving of presents as well as in buying and selling, or also in renting; but then all the rest as a totality through every variety of compulsion, and whether it be by

word or by deed, and all of these may be clasped together and named the arts of compulsion.

Theae: That's quite clear from what you've just said.

Strng: And how now? – shouldn't we divide the compulsory once more into two?

Theae: In which manner?

Strng: In that, namely, we stipulate the one part that is obvious and conducted openly as fighting, but that part which is secretive and uses stealth, this as a totality would be underhanded pursuit.   [e]

Theae: Good.

Strng: And, now again, with the pursuing arts, wouldn't it be unreasonable if we didn't likewise divide it into two?

Theae: Tell me, how?

Strng: The one part to be separated as the pursuit after the lifeless, but the other for all of that which is alive.

Theae: Well why not, indeed, since both sorts exist.   [220a]

Strng: How mightn't they not exist! And the pursuit after lifeless objects that extends even to such depths as the various subtypes of the art of diving, and still others of a similar sort that are too minor that they even have a name, all of these we have to leave undisturbed; but that part which is concerned with the living which, now, would be the pursuit of animals, this is named hunting.

Theae: Verily, it is.

Strng: But as regards hunting, wouldn't one rightfully be able to present two sorts? The one of them that is directed upon all of the species of land animals – and this sort has many subtypes that are all divided up by the many names [of the various animals being hunted]: this is the hunt upon land; and then the other that goes after swimming animals, this is the hunt upon the fluid.

Theae: Quite.   [b]

Strng: But as regards the swimming animals we see the feathered breed and another one that lives in the water.

Theae: And, why not?

Strng: And the entire hunt upon the feathered race, indeed, this is called bird hunting?

Theae: Indeed, that's what it is called.

Strng: And the other one that is directed upon that which lives in the water, this, as a totality, is called the fishery?

Theae: Yes.

Strng: How now? Wouldn't we like to also divide this hunt once more into two major parts?

Theae: And which ones?

Strng: Insofar as the one accomplishes its catch alone by the use of enclosures, but the other by wounding the prey.

Theae: How do you mean this? – and how are these two sorts separated?

Strng: The one because everything, whatever it uses, that it surrounds the prey in order to capture it, all of this would have to be called enclosing. *[c]*

Theae: Quite.

Strng: Fish-traps and slings, ground-nets and everything that is like this, should one call all of this anything other than enclosures?

Theae: Nothing other.

Strng: Capturing in nets or, so approximately – this is what we'd name this part of hunting.

Theae: Yes.

Strng: But the part using hooks and harpoons and which happens through wounding, this now we'd have to differentiate from the former and expressing this with one word we would have to call it wound-fishing. Or how, Theaetetus, how could we better name it?

Theae: Let's not get all worked up over the name, for this too is good enough.

Strng: Now, the nocturnal type of wound-fishing which is practiced by the shining of torches, this already is called by those who occupy themselves with it, torch-fishing.[198]

Theae: Indeed.

Strng: But that which is practiced in the daylight, with barbs or hooks on the very end and using harpoons, this, in all generality, this is called hook-fishing.

Theae: That's what it's called. *<6.~220e]*

Strng: Now, that which happens from above to below with this hook-fishing portion of wound-fishing, this shall – due to the fact that this is the technique principally used by the harpooners – this is named harpooning.

Theae: I've heard a few call it that.

Strng: What remains, now – this is only one type.

Theae: Essentially, which one?

Strng: The one that uses a motion that is entirely contrary, and which is practiced with fish-hooks that are not intended to go into

---

[198] Since the Stranger drops all mention of torch-fishing in what follows, we may surmise that this reference is a hint to the reader of what is actually going on, below the surface of this curious dialogue. Note that the dialogue, *The Republic* is framed around the anticipation of a race on horseback where torches are passed amongst the contestants (footnote, p. 200); this may shine some light on Plato's sublimity and the importance in translating *'the unsaid'* just as much as what is said – where what is at issue is *not Greek*, but having a premonition...

just any portion of the prey's body, as it is with the harpooners, rather in each and every occurrence just on the head and in the mouth, and then, that that which is captured being brought in by rod and reel and pulled up to here from below. And how should we say it, Theaetetus, what would this have to be called?   *<7.~221ab]*

Theae: I'd fancy that what we set out before ourselves, that we find it, this now has actually been fully accomplished.

Strng: Now then we are, you and I, as one not only upon the name of that sort of fishing which is angling, rather it is also so that we have achieved sufficient clarification as regards the matter itself. For then, one half of the arts *in toto* were the arts of acquisition, and from this we had the arts of compulsion and, then, from the compulsory there were the arts of underhanded pursuit, and of these pursuing arts next came hunting and of hunting next was fluid hunting and then from the lower section of this, the fisheries, and then of this part the wounding variety and out of the wounding next came hook-fishing and then from this the next one utilized the method of pulling from beneath toward that which is above and thereby hanging the fish from the ensuing wound whereby the deed itself obtains its image and whither is derived the name by which we call it, angling.   *<8.221c]*

Theae: In every way, now, this is sufficiently illuminated.

Strng: Then tallyho, don't we want to employ just this same technique as a blueprint and, just as it is here, shall we not likewise go about in our attempt to discover what the sophist may well be?

Theae: Quite, indeed.

Strng: But the first question, indeed, is this former one: whether the angler should be seen as possessing an art or whether he lacks knowledge and is just an amateur.

Theae: Yes.

Strng: So too, now, Theaetetus – do we want to postulate that the sophist would be bereft of knowledge? or in every way, indeed,   *[d]* as someone who actually is clever?

Theae: In no way as lacking in knowledge – for then, I do under-stand what it is that you're meaning, that he who commands this designation in all ways has to be of the latter type.

Strng: Hence, in any event, we have to postulate that he does possess an art.

Theae: But, essentially which one?

Strng: Is it perhaps, even so – *by the gods* – that unbeknownst to us the one man is related to the other?

Theae: Who with whom?

Strng: The angler with the sophist?

Theae: How so?

Strng: They both seem to me, quite certainly, to be hunters.

Theae: In what sort of hunting do you place the one? For then, we already have spoken sufficiently of the other. *[e]*

Strng: Didn't we divide the totality of hunting into two parts: the one division was for the swimming and the other one for those animals that go upon land?

Theae: Yes.

Strng: And then we went through the one side, the one that was connected with the animals that swim in water; but the hunt upon the land, we left this undivided and only mentioned in passing that it would have many subtypes?

Theae: That's how it was. *[222a]*

Strng: Up until this point the sophist and the angler accompany one another having both set off together from the arts of acquisition.

Theae: At least, they seem to be.

Strng: But then they part company each from the other at this division of pursuing animals, the one of them going off to the oceans, rivers and lakes and contriving ways of catching the animals that are to be found in these places.

Theae: Obviously.

Strng: But the other upon the land and to streams that are totally different, namely to those of riches and of the youth and, if I might express myself so, to the upper pastures, and so that they themselves gain power over the creatures which are to be found present in these environs.

Theae: And just how do you mean that? *[b]*

Strng: In respect to the hunt upon land there exist two major divisions.

Theae: Which two?

Strng: The wild and the tame. *<9.~222]*

Theae: Is there, then, a hunt upon tame animals?

Strng: Assuming then, that human beings are tame! But postulate matters however you please: either that there doesn't exist any tame animals, or that such do indeed exist but that humans would be wild; or, then too, you might name man to be a tame animal but not necessarily believe that there exist contrivances set upon catching him; whatever would be most pleasing for you to assert regarding this, just clarify this for me, if you would.

Theae: Well then, I do hold us as being tame animals, o Stranger, and I also say that there do exist contrivances for catching men. *[c]*

Strng: Of two sorts, we say, then, once again – of two sorts, then, would be the hunt upon the tame.

Theae: But, why do we say this?

Strng: Robbery, the slave trade, tyranny and the entirety of the art of warfare – all of these taken as a whole, we call all of these pursuits to be contrivances based upon power or force.

Theae: Excellent.

Strng: But matters of policy and orations that are directed upon the people, as well as local customs and even familial matters, all of these together taken as one, we want to name all of these as one art: the art of persuasion.

Theae: Right.   [d]

Strng: But of this art of persuasion we'll postulate two classes.

Theae: Which ones?

Strng: The one of them that takes place amongst a few persons, and the other one being public and officially directed upon the populace.

Theae: Indeed, the two types do exist.

Strng: Of the non-official variety, now, there once again is the one part that expects payment, and then the other that brings gifts.

Theae: I don't understand that.

Strng: It seems that you haven't ever taken much notice regarding the contrivances used in the pursuit of lovers.

Theae: How's that?

Strng: How it is that those whom they have captured, they likewise give presents to these.   [e]

Theae: You're totally right about this.

Strng: Hence, this type would be – the art of love.

Theae: Well, yes – that's entirely so.

Strng: But of the sort that expects recompense there exists first off the one type that is always speaking in a loving manner and in all instances it makes use of pleasure as its bait and most always takes nourishment as its only recompense – and this is the one that we, as I believe, in that we call it ingratiating flattery, so we would be joined by everyone in clarifying that this is a rather captivating artistry.

Theae: Well, but how else?   [a]

Strng: But then the other one, the one that promises that it's for the sake of virtue that one enters into his company and into his care and, moreover, which allows that recompense be handed over in cash – wouldn't it properly be recompensed that we name this other art with some other name?

Theae: Quite.

Strng: Well then, with which one? – make the attempt that you say it.

Theae: It's quite clear – for I'd fancy that we have found the sophist. At least I believe that by clarifying him as being this, so I believe to have named him most aptly.   <10.~223b]

Strng: Hence, and in accord with our present speech, o Theaetetus, it would be a portion of pursuing through compulsion of the acquisitive branch of art and, indeed, by means of a stealthy underhanded pursuit upon that land animal which is man, namely gaining monetary recompense by contrivances other than those of the official variety of persuasion, rather a selling for hard cash directed upon and seeming to educate the youth – and most particularly those who are rich and those having promise; it is, I say, this mode of hunting just as our speech has carried matters through to this conclusion: this is named the sophistic art.

Theae: So it is, quite.   *[c]*

Strng: Still, let's also examine the matter thusly. For it's not just a trivial art that we are searching after, that we glean some portion of such, rather it is one, indeed, that is quite multifarious. For, then too, even from out of the aforesaid there results a seeming – as if it wouldn't be *quite* as we now say, but rather some other classification.

Theae: But, how's that?

Strng: Of the acquisitive arts there were, indeed, the two sorts – in that it has the one part, underhanded pursuit, as well as open exchange.

Theae: So it was.

Strng: For exchanging we want once again that we declare two sorts, the one sort being gift-giving and the other being buying and selling, what now goes as market capitalism.

Theae: That should be valid.

Strng: Furthermore, we want to say that commerce likewise may be divided up into two parts.

Theae: How?   *[d]*

Strng: Separating out from one another the exchange that is done by the individual artisan – who himself makes what he sells – from the commerce of those who exchange the work that has been accomplished by strangers.

Theae: Very good.

Strng: But, how now? Of the commerce that exists within any given city, isn't a large portion of this named retail merchandizing?

Theae: Yes.

Strng: But then, that sort of commerce that is carried out between cities, isn't all of this called wholesale?

Theae: Indeed.   *[e]*

Strng: And haven't we, perhaps, noticed this: that the one part of this wholesale traffic is in goods that are intended for the body, goods which either may be eaten or otherwise used for material purposes, and the other part is for the soul, that it buys such in exchange for cash?

Theae: How do you mean this?

Strng: Acquaintance with matters of the soul would be our stumbling block here – for then, we do understand the other matter well enough.

Theae: Yes. [224a]

Strng: The art of music in its entirety – this, then, is what we want to say – in that it is spread about from city to city, what with all the tours being led hither and thither and with all the tickets that are sold, and likewise with all of the fine arts such as painting and, then too, the magic shows and conjuring and so many other things that belong to the soul – in part that we simply take delight in such things and in part, too, due to a serious interest and occupation with such matters, that we take up such things and buy them and sell them and, so, those who traffic with things such as these are rightly named merchants and, indeed, with no less propriety than those other merchants who generally are called by this name, those who deal in grain or in wine.[199]

Theae: You are totally right. [b]

Strng: Don't you also want, then, that whosoever bundles up information and sells it in this city here and some other city over there, exchanging such for hard cash, don't you also want that he be named with this same designation?

Theae: Very much so. <11.~224]

Strng: Now, of this wholesale traffic in commodities that are intended for the soul, one part could rightfully be called theater – but then, the other, although it isn't necessarily any less comical than the previous, one nevertheless, as it is trafficking in knowledge based information, one would have to attach a name to it that is closely allied to this occupation.

Theae: Quite.

Strng: We want, now, that that portion of merchandizing of information that has to do with the other arts be given one name, but the portion that is intimately connected with virtue, we want to give this part a different name. [c]

Theae: How could we do anything else.[200]

---

[199] Compare with *Gorgias* 518c, Thearion and Sarambus (p. 342); and, of course, *Protagoras* 313a (p. 113).

[200] For those who have sufficiently grasped Plato's love of indirect speech, this one sentence says as much or more than many a treatise written on the topic of Plato's attitude toward art.

Strng: The name "art merchandizing" may well be an apt designation for all of the rest; but you make an attempt that you provide us a name for this other part.

Theae: And what other name might one possibly give to this matter without missing the target entirely except for saying that this would even be what we have been seeking, the sophistic breed?

Strng: Nothing other. So come then, let's place all of this together and say: it would be that branch of the acquisitive arts having merchants exchanging commodities and, indeed, merchandizing in goods pertaining to the soul, namely such speeches and such information that relate to virtue just as this part is bought and sold, this artistry now has appeared for the second time, the art of sophistry. *[d]*

Theae: Admirable, right on the mark.

Strng: Thirdly, I also think that if someone were to become totally settled in the city and, in part he would be stocking up his archives with such information and would also, perhaps, be carving up his own pieces and, then, selling these to others with the intention of earning his living from this – so you wouldn't name him with any other name other than the one that was spoken just previously.

Theae: How should I ever do so? *[e]*

Strng: Hence, in every instance, as it seems, you would name this sophistry – as also this branch of the acquisitive arts, that of mercantile exchange, and both as wholesale as well as retail of one's very own {*Selbstverkauf*}, they both qualify just as soon as the objects being exchanged belong to this type, that sales are made in information.

Theae: Necessarily, for wherever the speech leads me, that's where I have to follow.

Strng: Let's also see, then, whether perhaps the next is to be likened in type to the one whom we are following. *<12.~225a]*

Theae: Who's next?

Strng: Indeed, wasn't one part of the acquisitive arts said to be expertise in fighting?

Theae: Quite.

Strng: Now, even-handedness would require that this likewise be split up into two.

Theae: In what manner?

Strng: The one part would be sport and the other, combat.

Theae: Good.

Strng: Then there is that combat called mortal combat which has to do with life and limb – and this sort we'd be allowed, naturally, most aptly that we give it such a name, calling it something along the lines of violent mortal conquest.

Theae: Yes.

Strng: But that in which word contends against word, o Theaetetus, how should one name this other than by calling it disputation.   *[b]*

Theae: Nothing other at all.

Strng: But that which belongs underneath disputation, this once again is twofold.

Theae: To what extent?

Strng: To the extent, namely, that longer speeches go up against longer speeches regarding what is just and unjust and in that the disputation is held in public and official settings, so this is a legal dispute.

Theae: Yes.

Strng: But if it's just a matter of questions and answers being tailored amongst a few persons, aren't we accustomed to naming this as being nothing other than merely a verbal exchange.

Theae: Nothing other.

Strng: Now, those verbal exchanges that occur in our outings and day to day dealings, those, in short, where matters are argued   *[c]* over and this gets jumbled up with that and everything's all mixed up with one another and all of this happening in an inartistic manner – this, indeed, this has to be postulated as one possible variety as, then, the clarification does recognize it as a different type than the others; but then, it neither has of yet received any especial designation nor does it deserve to receive any such from us.

Theae: Certainly not. And beyond this it's so excessively split up into multifarious and small, insignificant pieces.

Strng: But then, those verbal exchanges that do proceed in a manner that is both right and proper, that *they* are conducted in an artistic vein, and those delving into justice and injustice and other things as well – are we not accustomed to naming this sort as being disputatious oratory?

Theae: Well, how else.   *[225d]*

Strng: But such orations in part deplete one's monetary reserves and, in part, they bring money in.

Theae: That's totally certain.

Strng: So let's make an attempt that we determine the relative designations of each, how we'd have to point out what each one is.

Theae: That's necessary.

Strng: It seems to me that that sort of oratorical disputation which happens from the sheer pleasure that is derived from it and which is practiced to the detriment of one's own responsibilities and, moreover, in respect to the exposition itself, that this is from the greater majority of those who happen to be listening heard only with displeasure: in my erstwhile opinion one would only be able to call oratorical disputations of this variety as being nothing other than idle conjecture, the ramblings of loafers.

Theae: Indeed, that's the way they generally are designated.   *[e]*

Strng: But he, on the other hand, he who is really capable and who derives monetary recompense from the disputations that take place amongst a few – why don't you make the attempt from your vantage to give me a name for this type.

Theae: And what should one say without totally missing the target other than that already once again this amazing sophist has now again, and already for the fourth time, once again he has been pulled from out of your hat!

Strng: So then, this wouldn't be anything other than that type of disputatious oratorical art that brings in hard cash through a mere verbal exchange, that is, a sort of combat and an expertise in fighting through argument and, so, this being one part of the art of acquisition just as our speech has put as much up for display, this is sophistry.

Theae: That's totally obvious.   *<13.~226ab]*

Strng: Hence, you do see how rightly it is said that he is a crafty animal – and, as they say, not at all easy to catch with just one hand?

Theae: Well then, we'll have to use both of them.

Strng: That we do – and, indeed, exerting the utmost of our faculties in that we also follow along yet another trail of his. Namely, tell me: there do exist certain expressions that are commonly used by subservient vassals?

Theae: Well indeed, there are plenty of them, but about which one from amongst this plethora are you inquiring.

Strng: I'm meaning such things like straining and sifting, extruding and winnowing.

Theae: How might I ever be in the dark as regards these!

Strng: And beyond these – there's yet raking [or combing] wool and spinning and beating with the shuttle, and yet thousands of similar procedures; and we know, too, that such procedures occur in all of the other trades. Isn't this true?   *[c]*

Theae: Sure, but just what is it that you're driving at and what do you want to make clear to me that you've given to me all of these examples and now have asked me about this?

Strng: Separating out – this, indeed, is what is common to all of these examples.

Theae: Yes.

Strng: And so, in accordance to my way of proceeding, as there is one art for this purpose in all of these things, so let's impart one name for all of it.

Theae: And how are we to name it?

Strng: The art of selection.

Theae: It should be so.

Strng: Now, observe – whether we also are able to distinguish two different types of selection?

Theae: You're proceeding along with this investigation at too fast of a clip for me.   [d]

Strng: Of all of the selections that have been named, the one sort, indeed, is an exclusion of the worse from that which is better, but then the other is a separation of the similar from the similar?

Theae: Now that you have stated as much, so too, this appears to me as well.

Strng: For the one sort, now, I don't know of any name that is customary, but for the former selection that throws out the worse and leaves the better, for this I do know one.

Theae: Tell me, which.

Strng: Each and every selection of this sort shall, insofar as I understand the matter, be named a cleansing by everyone.

Theae: That's right.

Strng: And shouldn't everyone see this as well, that cleansing is twofold?

Theae: Perhaps given a sufficient amount of leisure; at least I don't yet see what you're getting at.   <14.~226e]

Strng: The many sorts of cleansing of the body, all of these should be collected together underneath one name.

Theae: What sorts are these, and which name.

Strng: First off, of that which is living – just as this shall become cleansed internally both from the various gymnastic arts as well as from the healing arts and, then too, it's also cleansed externally [a] which is a rather insignificant thing to say as this is nothing other than the art of bathing. Then too, for bodies that are not alive: such arts like textiles and the entirety of the cleaning and polishing arts, all of these accomplish their small services beneath names that are quite numerous and comical – if then, one desired to give a name to all of them.

Theae: Certainly, and there are quite a few.

Strng: Well indeed, o Theaetetus. Singularly, though, our method of clarification is not one whit the less dependent for its examples upon the arts of bathing and the various accoutrements that belong to such scrubbings than it is upon the accoutrements used for the preparation of various medicinal compounds – and this is so even though the former deliver very minor and the latter very major benefits through the cleansing that is accomplished. For in that its only concern is in the gaining of insight and, therefore, it seeks to discover what is   *[b]* related and what is not related in all of the arts, so it honors them all in equal portions and, accordingly, to the extent of their similarities it doesn't consider any of them as comical in comparison with the others. But as something that is more elevated and worthier, the field marshal, he who brings to expression the art of pursuit upon the battlefield, he is not held as being significantly different from those classmates of yours who are intent upon the game 'capture the flag' – rather, for the most merely that the former tend to be more puffed up and long-winded than the latter. And so too now in regards to what you have questioned me about, which name we should attach to the totality of these procedures through the means of which a body   *[c]* is cleansed, and be it a living body or one that is not alive, it is a matter of complete indifference as to which of these names might well have the best sheen to it, rather the only concern is that all of these matters be held together on the one side, that side which is concerned with the task of cleansing the body, but then on the other side is the purification of the soul. For then, it's even this cleansing of the soul that now is to be distinguished and separated off from all of these others – assuming that we have understood what our method of proceeding wants.

Theae: I have grasped this very well and I do assent to such: that there are two sorts of cleansing – one of which being concerned for the soul and the other one being separate from this and it's concern is for the body.   *<15.~227d]*

Strng: Most excellent. So, hear now what comes next and make the attempt that you likewise divide it in a twofold manner.

Theae: Just as you lead me, so I shall attempt to make the divisions as per your indications.

Strng: Vice is something quite different from virtue in relation to the soul?

Theae: How should they not be!

Strng: And cleansing, indeed, was this: that the other is to be left behind but that wherever there proves to be something that is defective, that this is to be thrown out?

Theae: The matter was as stated.

Strng: And so also in respect to the soul: wherever we meet up with a purge or a casting-off of that which is malefic we shall, if we call this a cleansing, we shall have spoken well.

Theae: Very much so.

Strng: But then, there are two sorts of malfeasance that may be brought forward.

Theae: And what might they be?　　　　　　　　　　　*[228a]*

Strng: The one sort subsists within the soul just as sickness resides within the body, but the other sort is like ugliness.

Theae: I don't understand you.

Strng: Perhaps you don't consider sickness and turmoil as being one and the same?

Theae: To this, too, I don't know what I should say in answer.

Strng: Do you look upon turmoil as being anything other than discord that has come to be through the ruination of what is related in nature?

Theae: No, nothing other.　　　　　　　　　　　　　　*[b]*

Strng: And ugliness, no matter where it may ever occur, is this anything other than an aberrant instance of unproportionality?

Theae: In no way is it anything other than this.

Strng: How now, haven't we taken notice of this: that within the soul judgment is in strife with the lower desires, the aesthetic faculty with the passions and that reason is confounded by melancholy – and that all of this finds itself to be at odds in those human beings who are particularly inept?

Theae: Very much so, certainly.

Strng: And all of these matters are related to one another within the soul?

Theae: How shouldn't they be.

Strng: If, therefore, we name the depravity of the soul as being turmoil and sickness, so then, don't we express ourselves rightly?

Theae: Totally right, certainly.　　　　　　　　　　　*[c]*

Strng: But, how now? – if something that is predicated as [essentially] in motion[201] and if this something is attempting to reach a goal that it has set for itself – but, then, despite its every attempt it passes it by and misses [the target][202] – should we say that this happens due to their being well proportioned to one another, or is it due to their not being well proportioned?

Theae: Obviously, it is due to the latter.

---

[201] *Phaedrus* 245c (p. 31); *Charmides* 169a (p. 190) and *The Laws* – Book X: 892a–897e.

[202] *Theaetetus* 189b–e (pp. 426–427), etc. – mixed up notions.

Strng: But we do know that each and every soul always errs only contrary to its intent and against its free will?

Theae: Very much so, indeed.

Strng: Falling into error, indeed, this is nothing other than setting out after the truth but, then, passing by the insight and thinking about something else.   *[d]*

Theae: Unquestionably.

Strng: Hence, a soul that lacks understanding, this is one that is postulated as being ugly and one that is lacking in proportionality.

Theae: So it seems.

Strng: There exists, then, as has been shown, these two types of malfeasance within the soul, the one sort that, more commonly, is called depravity – this, obviously, is a sickness within the soul.

Theae: Yes.

Strng: The other is called a lack of understanding; but then, that this too would only be a malfeasance of the soul, this is something that they don't want to admit.

Theae: Obviously, one has to give in and admit as much, that   *[e]* which earlier on when you first stated it I didn't believe you – that, indeed, there do exist these two sorts of malfeasance within the soul and that cowardice, wantonness and injustice, all of these are to be held as being diseases within us; but the pervasive and multifarious appearances of a lack of understanding are to be postulated as ugliness.

Strng: But then, for the body doesn't there exist for the two conditions likewise two particular arts?   *<16.~229a]*

Theae: Which ones?

Strng: For ugliness there's gymnastics, and for sickness there are the healing arts.

Theae: Obviously.

Strng: So too, amongst all of the arts there is well one that is best suited for tending upon the ills of arrogance, injustice and cowardice – and this is the constraining art that administers justice.[203]

Theae: That seems to be true, at least per human judgment.

Strng: But, how now? – what about one art for the totality of non-understanding, would it be possible to name any other that is more correct than the art of instruction?

Theae: None other.   *[b]*

Strng: Well then! – what should we say: whether there is only one type of instruction, or more than one? – and primarily two having the greatest importance, do weigh this in your considerations.

---

[203] Cf: *Gorgias* 477a (p. 294).

Theae: I am weighing it.

Strng: And I'm thinking, thus we shall find what we're seeking most expeditiously.

Theae: How?

Strng: If we examine non-understanding [ignorance]: whether this itself has a split right down the middle. For if this is twofold, so, obviously, instruction shall likewise have to have two parts, one for each type of ignorance.

Theae: How's that? – is that which we are seeking, is this, perhaps, already becoming evident to you.

Strng: I believe to see one very large and meaningful type of   [c] ignorance that is separate from all of the rest and it holds the balance upon which all of the others are weighed.

Theae: And essentially – which type would this be?

Strng: If one believes to know what one doesn't know – it is from out of this that everything else may well come to be whereby one's soul succumbs and fails to achieve.

Theae: Right.

Strng: And this type of ignorance, I think, this alone is named foolishness.

Theae: Indeed.

Strng: Now, how is it that we should name that part of instruction which liberates us from this?   [d]

Theae: At least as I think, o stranger, all of the rest is only instruction in the sense of the handworker but that this, at least here amongst us, this shall be named education in an authentic sense.

Strng: Also as well by all of the Hellenic peoples, o Theaetetus. But it still remains for us that we look closer at this and see whether, now, already everything is divided up so far as is possible or whether there yet exists some division that deserves to be named.

Theae: Well then, let us do so.

Strng: It seems to me that this too is divisible.

Theae: How so?   <17.~229e]

Strng: It seems that the one path of instruction through speech is rougher, but then the other path is much smoother.

Theae: And which should each of these paths be?

Strng: The one that has been passed down already for generations just as fathers have tended to rear their sons and many yet continue to do so: that if their offspring should fail in something, so in part they encourage them to do better using rather heavy-handed tactics and, in part too, they speak to them using gentle words and softly – but the whole of this is most aptly to be named admonition.   [a2]

Theae: I understand.

Strng: But the other path – since, then, it seems to many who believe that they have thoroughly considered this matter, that, namely, all foolishness would be involuntary and that there is nobody at all who would want to learn something about which he already believes that he has a firm grasp of it and, moreover, that despite a great deal of work the path of admonition still doesn't bring one very far.

Theae: As regards *this* their belief is most probably totally right. *[b]*

Strng: And so it is that they've set off to eradicate this opinion in a different manner entirely.

Theae: But, which manner would this be?

Strng: They cross-examine them as regards that about which someone believes that what he says is right, someone who yet, nonetheless, doesn't say anything at all. And so, it's by means of this interrogation that they pursue their research and, thus, it's not all that difficult to display the uncertainties of the vacillating opinions which, then, in that they bring these together in their speech – and it's by this very placing together itself that they show that these opinions contradict one another and, indeed, at the same time in respect to the same objects taken in the same relation and in the same sense. The former individuals, now, when they perceive these contradictions, so they become uncertain with themselves and likewise gentler toward the others, and in this manner they are rid of their high-blown and obstinately maintained opinions; and this release is heard with the greatest joy by all of those who witness it and for him upon whom it occurs this is the most reliable [method]. For, dear son, those who cleanse others believe just so as the physicians who tend to the body hold to the same opinion: that the body shall not be capable of deriving any benefit from the sustenance brought to it until someone has first cleared away the hindrances that exist within; and so too is the thought as regards the soul: that the soul will not be capable of deriving any advantages from the understanding imparted to it until by the means of such a testing education into what is right one brings the individual so tested into a state of shame, delivering him from those opinions that block the path of such understanding and displaying this to him in all purity: that he believes only what he really knows but nothing more than this. *[230de]*

Theae: The most admirable, at least, and the quality of soul most conducive to wisdom is this.

Strng: Therefore now, Theaetetus, we likewise have to say this: that this testing education into what is right is the most majestic and most admirable of all cleansings and we would have to hold anyone, whosoever it might be – and even the Great King himself! – that lacking in this such people are to the greatest degree impure and that precisely in that domain where one has to be the cleanest and most beauteous, he who truly is to be blessed, it's precisely there that such an individual is lacking in education and is ugly.

Theae: In all ways.   *<18.~231a]*

Strng: How now, those that practice this art, how should we name them? – for then, I'm fearful of naming these also as sophists.

Theae: How's that?

Strng: So that we don't confer too great of an honor upon them.

Theae: But what you have just said is very much like them – and seems fair enough.

Strng: As also the hound is like the wolf, the wildest and the most tame. But he who is cautious has to exercise the utmost respect for similarities, for then, these tend to be exceedingly dangerous. All the same, they may be just as you say... since it's not so that this disputation shall resolve itself, I think, due to small determinations, if only one takes up a respectful attitude, one that is right and befits the matter.   *[b]*

Theae: No, one should think not.

Strng: Thus, one part of the art of selection is cleansing, and of cleansing one part shall be separated off for the soul, and from this part instruction, and from instruction education, and then from education we said that the testing portion that is directed upon the emptiness of seeming-to-be-wise, this, in accord with the clarification that just now has appeared to us, this is nothing other than that noble and illustrious art of sophistry.

Theae: Indeed, this is what was said; but now already I too am having grave doubts since he has appeared to us in so many different guises: what should one say if one is to be earnest in one's   *[c]* opinions and assertions, what should one say that the sophist truly would be?

Strng: It's only right that you are having second thoughts regarding this. But, then too, for the former, one has to believe that it would already now be totally perplexing for him as well, how he's to attempt to get out of all of this, our so thoroughly researched investigation. For then, that old adage is quite right – *tis no easy task to escape from many*; so now we have to marshal all of our resources and not let up a bit from him.

Theae: Well said.   *<19.~231d]*

Strng: Firstly, let's stand still and rest ourselves and in that we take pause, let's confer with ourselves and tally it all up together: in how many guises is it that the sophist has appeared to us. I believe that, first off, he was found as a well recompensed pursuer of wealthy young men.

Theae: Yes.

Strng: Secondly, he was a wholesale merchant for the soul, primarily dealing in knowledge based information.

Theae: That's right.

Strng: And didn't he also show himself as a retailer in even the same commodities?

Theae: Yes, and fourthly he was affirmatively shown to be a dealer in his very own tid bits.

Strng: Your memory serves you well. And I shall attempt to exhibit him in his fifth guise. It was as a portion of that art having expertise in fighting that he was cordoned off, namely as an artist in combat through verbal dispute. *[e]*

Theae: That he was.

Strng: The sixth, indeed, was rather dubious, however we did give in and make allowance for this in that we said that he cleanses one of those opinions within the soul that stand in the way of acquiring understanding.

Theae: In every manner. *[232a]*

Strng: Now, wouldn't you take note of this: that if one is himself shown as being informed about many things but yet shall still only be named with the name of a single profession, that this couldn't possibly be a healthy notion, that rather, obviously, whoever encounters such in the naming of a single profession, so he who encounters such doesn't know how to go about uncovering that upon which all of the previous understandings are directed – and isn't it for this reason that he comes up with so many names instead of just the one that belongs?

Theae: With this it may well be that this is the relation that actually obtains. *<20.~232b]*

Strng: Thus, not simply due to our laziness should we meet up with such a result, rather first off let's once again take up something that we stated earlier regarding him – for then, there was one [definition] that especially cast a bright light upon him as being foremost in pointing him out to us.

Theae: Which one?

Strng: We did say, didn't we, that he'd be an artist in verbal disputes?

Theae: Yes.

Strng: And didn't we likewise say that he's quite adept at teaching this artistry to others?

Theae: Undoubtedly.

Strng: So let's look into this: in what, then, do such people boast that they make others disputatious in rhetorical speech. But our

investigation shall proceed starting off thus. First off, in respect to
godly things, just as these are hidden from the greater majority,   [c]
don't they position their students that such matters are disputed?
Theae: This has been said about them, indeed.
Strng: And what's apparent upon the earth and in the heavens,
regarding such things as these as well?
Theae: Quite.
Strng: But likewise in social gatherings, if the topic up for discussion
is being or becoming and these are to be discussed in general terms,
we ourselves do well know this, that their arguments are mighty
powerful in contradicting, and also that they make others adept in all
that they themselves have become.
Theae: In all ways.
Strng: And in regards to the laws and all of the affairs of state, don't
they promise to make one disputatious as regards all this?   [d]
Theae: Well, verily; otherwise nobody would ever speak with them,
if I don't say so myself, if they didn't make promises regarding all of
this.
Strng: And, then too, in each and every profession, how one would
have to go about in contradicting the masters of such, this has been
laid out openly and written down for anyone at all who wants to learn
it.
Theae: You'd be meaning the Protagorean pointers on wrestling and
on all the other arts.
Strng: And similar manuals, o marksman, that have been written by
many many others. But now, doesn't this artistry in contradiction
which in general extends as regards to everything, doesn't this
demonstrate a far-reaching aptitude for disputation?
Theae: One can hardly find anything at all that remains untouched.
Strng: But, my child — by the gods! — do you consider that this is
possible? — for perhaps you youngsters have a sharper vision for such
things and we old duffers see matters only vaguely!   [233a]
Theae: But, what's this, and in what is it that you'd be meaning? For
then, I don't yet understand quite what it is that you are questioning
me about.
Strng: Whether it might well be possible that any one person knows
everything.
Theae: Our race, o Stranger, our race would then be blessed.
Strng: How could it ever be possible that someone who himself is
uninformed, how might he ever contradict a person who is in the
know with something and do so in a healthy manner.
Theae: There's no way.

Strng: What then, actually, what is the secret in this piece of sophistic artistry?

Theae: In which piece? [b]

Strng: In which manner are they positioned so that they bring their young protégés to the opinion that they would be the best informed of everyone, and in regards to all things? For, obviously, if they neither contradicted succinctly, nor if the former didn't have the appearance of being contradicted, or even if they did seem to do so but due to all of their disputatiousness they wouldn't be held as being any wiser, well, then they might just wait around, as you yourself said previously: they might simply wait for anyone who would give money to them so that he might become their student.

Theae: It's quite certain, they would wait.

Strng: But now, they do get students?

Theae: Indeed, quite a few.

Strng: Hence, they do seem to be informed about that regarding which they are so disputatious? [c]

Theae: How else!

Strng: But they do so in regards to everything, didn't we say this?

Theae: Yes, indeed.

Strng: They seem to their students to be wise regarding all things.

Theae: Without a doubt.

Strng: But still, without being so, for this has been shown as being impossible.

Theae: And how mightn't it be anything else other than impossible!

Strng: Hence, seeming to be in the know about all things but not being in possession of the truth, so has the sophist shown himself.

Theae: In all ways; and what you've just now said about him seems amongst everything else to be right most of all. <21.~233d]

Strng: Only let us sketch yet another example, one that is even more perspicacious.

Theae: Which one?

Strng: This one. Look to it that you give this your due attention and answer me.

Theae: Just ask away.

Strng: If someone asserts that he neither understands speaking nor does he understand contradicting – but, then, that he's well able to make and bring forth everything all together through one art. [e]

Theae: How do you mean everything?

Strng: Thus, already at the beginning of what I said, you already don't understand us. As it seems, namely, you don't know this "everything all together."

Theae: No, indeed I don't.

Strng: I'm meaning even you and me beneath this everything all together, and outside of us there's also all the plants and all the animals.

Theae: How do you mean that?

Strng: If someone asserts that he wanted to make you and me and everything else that lives and grows.

Theae: What sort of a making should that be, really? You don't   *[a]* mean the agrarians, somehow, for then you did say that he'd also bring forth the animals.

Strng: I say it; and to top it all off yet the oceans and the earth, the heavens and the gods, and everything all together. And once he finishes this in his rapid flourish, so he gives it all away for a tidy little sum.

Theae: You mean this as some sort of joke.

Strng: And how now – if someone says that he would know everything and he wants to teach this to others for a little cash and that he'll do so in short order, shouldn't one hold this as being a joke?

Theae: Well, indeed.

Strng: And are you acquainted with a more artistic and aesthetically becoming manner of joking than that of imitation?

Theae: Certainly not. For then, what you've just said encompasses a gracious plenty, indeed, and you've brought it all together into one category that is in all probability the richest and fullest.   *<22.~234b]*

Strng: In regards to him, he who promises that he is enabled by his very profession that he can make everything, so we do know that it's through the manufacture of images which are like-named to that which is actual, it is by means of his skill in painting that he shall be in a position to deceive young adolescents who are still lacking in the power of reflection, that is when he displays his paintings to them from far away[204] – as if he, and no matter what it is that he wants to make, as if he were to be fully competent of bringing this forth in all actuality.

Theae: Indeed.   *[c]*

Strng: But how now, are we not able to anticipate this: that there wouldn't exist a similar artistry of words through the power of which it likewise is possible that the youth are deceived, those who are yet far removed from the essential truth of things, that these are entranced by the intonations resounding in their ears in that one displays shadow images to them through the power of words and, thus, makes them believe that what is said would be true and that he

---

[204] See *Parmenides* – footnote #108 (p. 211).

who says it would be the wisest person of all, and in regards to all things?

Theae: How should it be that this other sort of artistry wouldn't exist! [d]

Strng: But shall not the greater majority of these, o Theaetetus, those who would previously have heard this but who, after a sufficient amount of time has elapsed and after their having become mature and having met up together in close vicinity to these very things and experienced them directly and, obviously, they shall be forced that they touch these things – shall they not, then, necessarily have to transform all of their previous notions that they entertained earlier so that what then seemed to be small, now it shall be big, and what earlier was difficult, this is now easy; and in regards to everything [e] all of the deceptive word images shall be destroyed – if, then, the things themselves come to visit them in their occupations?

Theae: So far as I'm able to judge this at my young age, certainly. But I believe, too, that I am one who yet stands at a greater distance.

Strng: For this very reason we shall all search out a way, just as we already have been endeavoring to do: that we also bring you so close as is possible, and do this without the undue influences mentioned formerly. But going back to the sophist, tell me this: whether so [a] much is already quite certain, since he is an imitator of what is actual, so he does belong together with the magicians? – or do we still have second thoughts about this and might it be so that as regards everything about which he is so adept in contradicting others, regarding all of this, might he indeed possess knowledge?

Theae: How should we *possibly* entertain this, o stranger? Much rather it is quite certain from what was said that he belongs as one amongst those who tend toward some sort of jesting.

Strng: Thus, we have to set him amongst the imitators, the magicians and the actors?

Theae: How else! <23.~235b]

Strng: Thus, tallyho! – from here on out we're right on his heels and we're not going to let up a bit from this wildman. And, then too, we've practically gotten him all entangled underneath our netting which, truly, in respect to our modus of hunting is nothing other than speech and, as good fortune would have it, this is what we even have thrown over him so that there's no way he'll wiggle out of it.

Theae: Say what?

Strng: That he's not one amongst the breed of conjurers, nor a Houdini?

Theae: Indeed, it seems to me that this too is very much his sort.

Strng: Hence, I propose that right away and without any delay we categorize the parts of the art of imitation – and should the sophist stand his ground right off as we make our divisions, so then we'll catch him just as prescribed by royal decree, and then we'll   *[c]* present our catch to the royal authority; but if, on the other hand, if he tries to hide himself in different portions of this art of imitation, so then we'll likewise categorize any and all portions into which he runs and we'll continue doing so until he's caught. For in no wise should either he or any other breed be allowed to boast of themselves that they've managed to escape from the methodology of those who understand how to handle the particular and the universal.

Theae: Very well spoken, and now this is how we have to make our way.

Strng: So, in accordance with our previous method of dividing, I now believe that I once again see two types of this art of imitation; but into which of the two of them the *Gestalt* that we're seeking is to be found, this is something that I'm not yet in a position to decide.

Theae: Just tell me first off and speak out the division, which two parts are you meaning?

Strng: The one of them that I perceive is the art of reconstruction of that which is even-so. This is actually comprised in this: if someone follows the relations of length, breadth and depth that exist in the archetype, and so too he gives to each and every portion the *color* that befits it – and so he sets to work in imitating, that his replication comes into being.   *[e]*

Theae: But, how's that? – don't all imitators attempt to do this and isn't all imitation even replication?

Strng: At least those don't do so, those who are sculpting or painting some great work. For then, if these wanted to reproduce the true relations of what is beautiful, so you do well know that that which is higher up would be smaller than is right, and that which is lower down would appear to be larger – since the one is seen from a greater distance and the other would be seen from close-up.   *[236a]*

Theae: Quite.

Strng: Don't these artists, then, don't they let the truth be as it may well be and don't they seek out something other than the actual relations that obtain in that they bring the appearance of beauty into their images, that this is what becomes in their works?

Theae: Well, indeed.

Strng: Hence, it's not asking too much that we call the one of them, since it is a likeness, that we name it a replica *{Ebenbild}*?

Theae: Yes.

Strng: And that portion of the art of imitation that is occupied with this is named replication, just as we stated earlier.   *[b]*

Theae: It shall be named so.

Strng: But how about what only seems, because it shall be observed straight on from a given vantage, to be like that which is beautiful but which, if someone were able to observe it precisely, so it wouldn't be similar to that which it seems to be like – as is asserted – how do we want to name this? Shall we not even call this a deceptive image *{Trugbild}* because it seems to be similar but isn't really?

Theae: Undoubtedly.

Strng: And this portion is not to be underestimated in its significance, both for those artists who paint as well as for the entirety of the constructive arts.   *[c]*

Theae: Naturally, how else!

Strng: And that artistry which brings forth a deceptive image rather than a replica, shall we not most appropriately name this the imagery of deceit?

Theae: This is by far the most appropriate.

Strng: These two sorts, now, are what I was meaning earlier on when I said that there would exist the two types of art that construct images, the one being replication and the other being an imagery of deceit.

Theae: Right.

Strng: What I left undecided earlier, in which of the two the sophist belongs, I'm still not yet able to see this determination. But this man is truly puzzling and hard to recognize for, then too, even now   *[d]* he's downright beautifully and slyly slunk off and retreated into a concept that's terribly difficult to research.

Theae: It seems he is.

Strng: Are you affirming this out of your own insight or have you just been pulled along by the force of the wind, as you have become rather accustomed to my tack, that you are so fast in agreeing with me on this?

Theae: How's that, and why are you questioning me about this?

<24.~236e]

Strng: In truth, my good Theaetetus, we have just entered into indagations that are difficult to the extreme. For this appearing and seeming without being, and speaking indeed, but nothing that is true: all of this has always been full of dubiousness and cause for reflection, both earlier on and even now as well. For in what manner one should speak this out, that there actually exists false speech or opinion without already falling into contradiction in every way in one's very statement, this, o Theaetetus, is hard to grasp.   *[a]*

Theae: How so?

Strng: Verily, this speech itself presupposes as a prerequisite: that what isn't [non-being] is. For otherwise, actual falsity would not exist in any manner. But the great Parmenides, o son, sharpened our wits with this whetstone and began doing so already when we were yet children – and continuing on right up to the end in that, be it in free-flowing prose or in his poetic stanzas, he spoke it out. *Never shall you be able to understand,* spoke he, *that that which is not is, rather pull back your inquiring mind from entering upon such a path.* So is his testimony – but, certainly, above all the speech itself has to demonstrate this when it is tested appropriately. So then, first off let's scrutinize this, if you don't have anything against it.

Theae: Only believe me when I say that everything would be pleasant, just as you want and so as the speech would best let itself be presented, so you should go about these indagations and lead me along the same path.   *<25.~237bc]*

Strng: As you say. And so tell me, then – that which has no modus of being, indeed, would this somehow fall within our compass, that we might speak of it.

Theae: But, why not?

Strng: I don't mean this simply to be argumentative or as some sort of joke but, rather, if one of those who is present listening   *[c]* seriously considers this and he should then show us where it is that this word is brought forward, *non-being,* do we believe that he himself knows where he's headed and what he's about that he has to make use of it, and that he might be able to point this out and demonstrate it to others?

Theae: That's a hard question and, if I don't say so myself, for someone such as myself it's downright and totally impossible to answer.

Strng: So much then, indeed, is certain: that non-being cannot possibly be attributed to any something that is?

Theae: How might it ever!

Strng: If then, not to that which is, so too, whoever would attribute it to something, so such an attribution is not right at all.

Theae: How's that?

Strng: This too, indeed, is quite clear to us: that each and every time we would say this word "something," so we say it of something that is? For then, singularly, to speak it out simultaneously naked and removed from all being, this isn't possible. Isn't this true?

Theae: Impossible.

Strng: And don't you also admit this much in hindsight to this: that he who says something, he says at least one something?

Theae: Certainly.

Strng: For then "something," you shall say, is a pointing-out of one; "some" or "a few," on the other hand, are markers for many.

Theae: So it is.

Strng: He, therefore, he who doesn't even once say something, it is totally necessary that he, as it seems, he says totally and absolutely nothing at all. *[e]*

Theae: That's totally necessary, indeed.

Strng: Wouldn't we now, perhaps, wouldn't we not even be allowed to admit a single instance of this, that, indeed, such a person is talking but that he's not saying anything at all – but, rather, wouldn't we even have to deny it, that he's talking: he who starts off in an attempt to speak out non-being?

Theae: Then, indeed, all of the dire difficulties of this matter would quickly come to an end. *<26.~238a]*

Strng: Don't magnanimously congratulate yourself just yet. For then, there is yet one dire difficulty that still remains and, indeed, it's easy to see that it's the first and the greatest – for this strikes at the initial beginning of this matter itself.

Theae: How do you mean this? – speak, and don't hold anything back.

Strng: It is well possible that one being might be predicated of another.

Theae: Without a doubt.

Strng: But do we want likewise that we admit this, that it would be possible that being would be predicated of any something that is not?

Theae: How should we ever!

Strng: All numbers all together, we do, indeed, postulate that they are.

Theae: If then, we are to postulate that anything at all is to be. *[b]*

Strng: So then, we are not permitted: neither that we dare to attribute plurality of number, nor too dare we attribute singularity to non-being.

Theae: Indeed, we wouldn't be acting properly, as it seems, if we were to dare do this in accordance to what was said in our speech.

Strng: How might someone ever be able to articulate non-being and utter this from out of his mouth – or, then too, even be able to conceive and grasp this in his thought?

Theae: Why are you asking me this?

Strng: If we say "beings that are not" – don't we place a plurality of number into what we say? *[c]*

Theae: Indeed.

Strng: And if we say "non-being," then again, this is the singular?

Theae: That's totally certain.

Strng: And yet we do say: it would neither be right nor acceptable that anyone attempts to meld being together with non-being?

Theae: What you say is absolutely true.

Strng: Hence, you do see how totally impossible it is to speak out non-being or to say something about it, or even to think it in and for itself; that, rather, how it is something unthinkable and indescribable and unspeakable and not to be clarified?

Theae: In all ways, indeed.

Strng: But haven't I myself gone somewhat astray and erred a bit when I said that I now wanted to bring forward the greatest difficulty about this matter?

Theae: How so? – is there yet some other difficulty even greater than this?

Strng: How indeed, you marvel, don't you notice this even upon that, what I have only just said, that even for those who are opposed: non-being brings these likewise into dire straits so that even as someone attempts to disprove it, so he too shall be forced that he contradict himself in what he says.

Theae: How do you mean this? – say it to me with greater clarity.

Strng: There's no need at all that someone sees this upon me   *[e]* with greater clarity! For I, I who have made this firm determination: that non-being shall neither be permitted to partake in unity nor in multiplicity – so I used the singular earlier and even now I have again named it as one. For I say, "non-being." Do you notice?

Theae: Yes.

Strng: And then too, just a little while ago I said that it would be unspeakable and indescribable and beyond clarification. Are you following?

Theae: I'm following. How should I not?

Strng: In that I attempt to knot non-being together with being, so I spoke out something that contradicts what I stated earlier.

Theae: Obviously.   *[239a]*

Strng: And at the same time that I was ascribing the former to it, then too, I spoke of non-being in the singular.

Theae: Yes.

Strng: And also when I named it as not to be clarified and indescribable and unspeakable, so I directed my speech upon it as if it were one?

Theae: Obviously.

Strng: But we do assert, he who should speak appropriately has to stay in line with this determination: that it neither is one nor many, nor too may it be named at all – for already then through the mere declaration he would have spoken of it as one.

Theae: Quite. <27.~239b]

Strng: What, now, shall one already have to say about me? For already for some considerable time and now too one would have found me to be in contradiction with this refutation of non-being. For this reason let's cease in this futile searching for the right expression as regards non-being, as I already said earlier; rather come: we want to observe it on you.

Theae: How do you mean?

Strng: Come here valiantly, just as the youth tend to be, and exert yourself as best you're able and, so, do make an attempt that in accordance to the rules that are right and proper that you speak something out about non-being and do so without attributing to it: neither being, nor unity, nor multiplicity of number.

Theae: Great, indeed, and without rhyme would my audaciousness have to be were I to be led into accepting such a challenge knowing full well how poorly you have fared. [c]

Strng: As you will; so then, we want that both of us shall be let off of this hook. But until we meet up with someone who is able to accomplish this, until then we have to concede this: that in an extremely clever fashion the sophist has managed to slip away and escape into a spot that is difficult to the extreme.

Theae: Very much so, as was shown.

Strng: Hence, whenever we assert that he's in possession of an artistry of deceptive imagery, so it's an easy thing for him that he grasps us by our very words and turning them around, using them against us he'll then ask us, if we should name him a maker of images: What, then, in all generality do we mean when we say image? Thus, we have to take a good look, o Theaetetus, what should one give in answer to this young whipper snapper.

Theae: Obviously, we shall lead him to the images that are to be found in water and in mirrors, and, then too, to those that have been painted or formed in some other way, and to all the others of these that do exist. <28.~239e]

Strng: Now one sees this plain and clear, Theaetetus, that you've yet to meet up with a real sophist.

Theae: How so?

Strng: You might think that he'd blink or that he doesn't even have any eyes at all.

Theae: But, how's that?

Strng: If you give him such an answer and try to speak with him about mirrors and sculpted artworks, so he'll have a hearty laugh on you and upon your speech as you are telling him about all of this and he'll look upon you and make a show as if he neither would know anything about water, or mirrors, nor in all generality regarding anything at all having to do with sight – and, so, he shall always simply question you from out of your clarification. *[240a]*

Theae: Only tell me?

Strng: The general principle in all of this, what you, indeed, since you have spoken of many different things – that which you want to point out with one name in that you called all of them images – what, really, in all of this is just one. So now, speak and defend yourself without giving up any ground to this young man.

Theae: What else should we say that an image would be, o Stranger, other than saying that in respect to the truth it's an other such having been made similar.

Strng: An other such that also is true, is this what you mean? – or which way is this "such" pulling? *[b]*

Theae: In no way at all as true but, rather, certainly only as seeming to be so.

Strng: And what are you meaning when you say true? – that which is in all actuality?

Theae: That's what I mean.

Strng: And how now? Beneath that which is not true, the opposite of true.

Theae: What else?

Strng: Hence, as not being – this is how you've clarified the seeming – if then, indeed, you describe it as untrue.

Theae: But it is! – really.

Strng: How? certainly indeed, you don't mean that it truly is?

Theae: No, indeed not. But still, it really is an image.

Strng: Hence, now, is it not real and not being, yet still real in that we name it image?

Theae: Into such an interweaving, indeed, it seems that that which is not is interwoven with that which is, and this is totally lacking in rhyme. *[c]*

Strng: How should it be anything else other than unrhymed? – and now you do see it, don't you: how it's through this quick maneuver and swapping that the many-headed sophist has forced us against our will that we admit this: that that which is not somehow is.

Theae: I see it, only too well.

Strng: And how now, how are we to proceed? What might we finally say as a determination of his artistry so that we shall become as one with ourselves?

Theae: But how's this and what are you worried about that you care to ask me this?

Strng: If we say, now, that he deceives us with false imagery and that his artistry is one of deceit, do we then say that our souls [d] have false notions through the agency of his art? – or what is it that we're saying?

Theae: This, for what else might we say?

Strng: But having false notions is the opposite of having notions of that which is? – or how else might we state it?

Theae: The opposite.

Strng: Hence, you say that having false notions is having notions of that which is not?

Theae: Necessarily.

Strng: Perhaps that non-being isn't, is this the soul's notion, or that that which is not in any manner whatsoever yet somehow still would be? [e]

Theae: Well, indeed: necessarily that that which is not somehow still would be – if, then, someone should be deceived, and be it only to the smallest degree.

Strng: And isn't it also possible that he has this notion: that that which is in every manner wouldn't be at all?

Theae: Yes.

Strng: And that too is false?

Theae: That too. [241a]

Strng: And so then both of these, I believe, are to be held as false speech and both in an equivalent way: the one which says that that which is wouldn't be and the other that says that that which is not would be.

Theae: How mightn't such a speech ever be anything else!!

Strng: Not very easily! – most probably. But this is what the sophist won't admit. And how might anyone who has a healthy sense make allowance for this – if, then, it has already been admitted what was stated earlier: that non-being is unspeakable, indescribable, not to be clarified nor thought – which, then, is what our earlier speech was all about. We do indeed understand, Theaetetus, what it is that he means?

Theae: How should we not understand that he's getting ready to say to us that we are asserting the opposite from the previous testimony if we dare say that falsity should be in our notions and in our speech? For then we would be forced in manifold ways that we knot non-being

together with being and do so after already having stated that this is
of all things the most impossible.   *<29.~241b]*

Strng: Your memory serves you well. But now it's time that we
huddle and come up with some plan: what are we to do with this
sophist. For you do see how all these twists and difficulties easily
come streaming upon us – and numerically they do richly abound – if
we want to set ourselves out upon his trail in that we place him as an
artist in deceit and as a magician.

Theae: Very much so.

Strng: And, then too, we've only taken up a small portion of these
difficulties – since they are, most precisely, never-ending.   *[c]*

Theae: That being the case, it seems that it would not be at all
possible that we shall ever catch the sophist, if this is how this
correlates.

Strng: How's that? – do we want to be softies and call it quits?

Theae: No, I say – that's something we shouldn't do, not so long as
we are yet in a position that we might nab him, and if only in the
smallest degree.

Strng: Shall you then exercise constraint, stepping back a bit and, as
you've just said, be satisfied if somehow we only are able to peel off
just the smallest amount from such a stalwart proposition?

Theae: How should I not be satisfied with this?   *[d]*

Strng: So too, I also now would request yet something else from you.

Theae: What's that?

Strng: That you don't look upon me as one who uses violence against
his own father.

Theae: But, why is it that you say this?

Strng: Because it shall be necessary for us, if we are to defend
ourselves, that we take up the proposition of father Parmenides and
that we test it, and we'll have to strong-arm it: that to a certain extent
non-being is and, then again too, that being somehow is not.

Theae: I see what you mean, that this shall have to be taken up in our
speech and fought through.

Strng: How should anyone not be able to see this, indeed, as they
say: even for a blind man! For if the former is not refuted and   *[e]*
our thesis shall not be admitted, so then, nobody will be positioned in
their life that they might speak of false speeches and of false notions,
be it now of shadows, replicas, imitations or deceitful *Gestalts* themselves, nor also of those arts that are occupied with such as these: no
one will be able to speak of these without making himself ludicrous in
that, necessarily, he contradicts himself at every turn.

Theae: That's true, absolutely.   *[242a]*

Strng: It's for this reason that we have to be daring and that we take the plunge, that we seize at this former proposition; or we'd have to totally leave this matter well enough alone – if, then, we yet had any doubts or second thoughts about this that would hold us back.

Theae: There shouldn't be anything that somehow holds us back from this.

Strng: So then, thirdly, I should like to request yet another small favor from you, a triviality.

Theae: Just tell me.

Strng: Indeed, I even was just saying that I have always been deterred from entering into this refutation and, so too, even now.

Theae: You said that.

Strng: Now, even this is making me apprehensive, what I said: that perhaps I may come forward as being totally wild in that I turn myself about on this very spot, flipping myself over from below to above.[205] For then, it is for your sake that once again we want to renew our testing of this proposition and the refutation – if, then, we are to have any chance of success at all.

Theae: It doesn't seem to me that there's anything improper in your actions, that this might not be right if you move onward to this proof and refutation; therefore – just be brazen and proceed.   *<30.~242]*

Strng: Tallyho, with what shall we begin now, that we dare the wager of making such a risky speech? I'd fancy, child, that this is the path that is totally necessary for us, the one we have to embark upon.

Theae: Which one?

Strng: What we now believe in total certainty that we have it, let's firstly scrutinize this: whether we are in error and whether it's   *[c]* simply due to the complete lack of depth in our thinking that we have admitted this *as if* we had reflected upon it most precisely.

Theae: Just tell me more clearly – what it is that you're meaning.

Strng: From a somewhat elevated stance it seems that Parmenides has been conversing with us, and probably too all of the others who have dared to speak about a division of things in order that they determine of how many sorts and of how many numbers they are.

Theae: Why's that?

Strng: Each one of them seems to have narrated his pet theory to us as if we were children. The one says that being would be of three sorts, from time to time some of it in strife amongst one another and, then too, everything would be re-united in friendship –   *[d]* since then, there exist 'marriage festivities' and 'birthings' and the

---

[205] "mich umwende von unten nach oben" – the phrase recalls the 'anglers' method of nabbing fish which is the same motion: from underneath to above, at 220e (pp. 515–516).

upbringing of what has been generated. Someone else describes
being as twofold: wet and dry or warm and cold, and he brings both
of these together and elaborates upon all of the details. But our
Eleatic folk, starting with Xenophon and going back even further,
these lecture us and their historical rendering is so: it's as if what
we name "the all," as if this would only be one. But then, later on
certain Ionic and Sicilian muses have remarked that it would be an
improvement and more certain if one were to say, putting both of
these pet theories together, that being would be many as well as one
and that everything is held together by attraction and repulsion. For
even in separating being also always is getting mixed, thus say the
more hard-nosed muses, but then the softer ones let up a bit from this
saying that it shouldn't always have to be thus, and so they say that
each takes it turn: that from time to time the whole is one, united by
Aphrodite, and then too, that it is many having been excited   *[243a]*
into animosity with one part set against the other and that this is due
to strife. Whether, now, in all of this any one of them has spoken
something that is true or not, this is hard to judge – and it's also
outrageous and rather irreverent of us that we'd dare to make any
objections at all against these men whose fame in antiquity is so lofty;
but still, I am able to assert this much, indeed, without incurring any
danger that I might be stepping out of bounds.
Theae: What's that?
Strng: That to a very great extent they have cast their gaze above us,
the others, and have treated us as very small fish indeed. For then,
without even asking us whether we happen to be following them   *[b]*
in their speech or if we've been left behind, so each of them brings his
own work to its completion.
Theae: But, how do you mean this?
Strng: If any one of them speaks out and asserts that it would be or
has become or shall be many or two or one, and a mixture of warmth
with cold, or taking up any divisions and unifications from wherever
it even may be, do you understand, Theaetetus – by the gods – and
have you ever understood anything of what it is that they mean? At
least for myself when I was younger I did believe that I understood
this which has become so hard for us that we understand it now:
non-being; for whenever anyone spoke of non-being I believed that I
understood what he said most precisely. But now you do see, don't
you, into what dire straits we've ventured.
Theae: That I do.   *[c]*
Strng: But perhaps we'll meet up with the same, and not one whit
the less, when we turn our intellect [soul] upon being: that we have
only believed that there wouldn't be any dire difficulties with being –

and that we would understand whatever anyone said about it, though not about the former, although in respect to both the correlation is absolutely equivalent *{ganz gleich verhalten}*.

Theae: Perhaps.

Strng: And as regards all of the rest of what I mentioned just earlier, shouldn't the same likewise be valid?

Theae: Quite. <31.~243d]

Strng: Now, the multivariousness of all the rest, we want to pull all of this into our conversation as a follow-up – if and when you opine that you are ready for it; but right now we have to scrutinize the greatest and the most pivotal issue.

Theae: What are you meaning? – or, obviously, you want that firstly we shall make headway into our investigation of being: how they who speak about being, indeed, what it is that they actually mean to place before us?

Strng: In the right spot, o Theaetetus, you have grasped it. I mean, namely, that this is the method that we have to turn to: that we question them as if they themselves were to be present here. Tallyho, all of you who say that *the all* would be warmth or cold, or any two others like this, what is it now that you're actually saying and speaking out about these two when you state that both and each of them would be? What should we be thinking underneath this, *[e]* that which you call being. Should we postulate it as a third that is outside of the former two and so postulate the whole as three and no longer as two in accordance to what you say? For then, if you name one of the two of these being, so then you no longer say that both of them are in an equal way – and, so, in both ways only one would be and not two.

Theae: Totally right.

Strng: But you all want that both, indeed, are named being.

Theae: Perhaps.

Strng: But, my dears,[206] do we want then to say with this that so too you also would be saying with total clarity that the two are one.

Theae: That's right, absolutely. *[244a]*

Strng: Now, since we haven't got a clue, so then do make your presentation of this plain and clear: what, indeed, what do you want to signify when you say: being *{Seindes}*. For then, it's quite obvious that you've already known this for quite some time but although, indeed, we previously believed that we knew it, well right now, as I already said: we haven't got a clue. So do teach us this first off so that we don't simply imagine that we are understanding what you are

---

[206] "ihr Lieben" – reminiscent of *Protagoras* 353c.

saying when what we have encountered is entirely the opposite. If we were to speak thusly, child, and when we expect and exact as much from these, as well as from all of the others who say that the all would be more than one, shall we be committing a great injustice?

Theae: Certainly not, none at all.   <32.~244bc]

Strng: How now? – shouldn't we perhaps likewise pursue our investigation with those who present *the all* as being one, shouldn't we research this also to the full extent of our capabilities: what it is that they well are saying about being, about that which is?

Theae: Without a doubt.

Strng: They may well answer us this, then. You all say that it would be only one? – "That's what we say," this is their answer. Isn't it so?

Theae: Yes.

Strng: And how, you name being, something?

Theae: Yes.   [c]

Strng: The same as one? – and do you make use of two names for the same? – or how?

Theae: What should they now answer to this, o Stranger?

Strng: Obviously, o Theaetetus, given the former supposition it isn't at all easy to answer the question just posed, nor many other questions that are similar.

Theae: How's that?

Strng: To admit that there exist two names if someone has postulated nothing more than one, this is ludicrous.

Theae: How should it not be ludicrous!   [d]

Strng: And, verily, that anybody would let themselves be pleased or satisfied if somebody should say that there exists a name that does not, indeed, admit of any clarification at all.

Theae: But, why's that?

Strng: Because were he to postulate that the name is something different from the matter, so, indeed, he names two.

Theae: Yes.

Strng: But if he postulates that the name is one and the same as the matter, so either he shall be forced into saying that it would be the name of nothing, or if he wants to say that it's the name of something, so the outcome of this is that the name is the name of the named and of nothing else other.

Theae: So it is.

Strng: And likewise the one, which then is only of the one one, this too would once again only be a name of one.

Theae: Necessarily.

Strng: And how? – the whole would be different from the one which is – shall they say this, or that it's one and the same?

Theae: How should they ever say anything but the latter, now and always. *[e]*

Strng: If now, it is whole – just as Parmenides likewise says:

Similar from every vantage, the most beauteously rounded sphere, equally extending out from the midpoint: for to be greater over here and lesser over there, this shall never be sanctioned;

and, thus, that which is as such has a middle and ends – and having these it also, necessarily, has parts. Or how?

Theae: So, indeed.

Strng: Singularly, that which has parts is able to partake in *[245a]* unity in relation to the wholeness of its parts and nothing stands in the way that in this manner it would be a whole and an all as well as being one.

Theae: How else?

Strng: But isn't it impossible that this, that to which all of this is postulated, that this would be the one itself?

Theae: How so?

Strng: The true one, indeed, has to be absolutely indivisible – if it shall be taken up in accordance to a clarification that is right.

Theae: Indeed, it has to.

Strng: But such a one that consists of many parts, this is in discord with this clarification. *[b]*

Theae: I understand.

Strng: Now, should that which is, so that it is predicated by this quality of oneness, be one and whole; or should we simply and totally stop saying this, that that which is would be whole?

Theae: That's a difficult choice that you're laying before me.

Strng: Your observation is totally right. Because if that which is only has this quality of being one in a certain way, thus it shows itself, verily, as not being the same as the one, and so, indeed, everything becomes more than one.

Theae: True.

Strng: But if, on the other hand, if that which is is not whole *[c]* – since this only is predicated of it by the former – and also as the whole itself is, so, verily, shall that which is be robbed of its very self.

Theae: Indeed.

Strng: And as a follow-up to this: if it is robbed of its very self, so, verily, shall that which is not be being.

Theae: Quite.

Strng: And, then too, it shall all become more than one if that which is and the whole each receives its own essence separate from the other.

Theae: Yes.

Strng: Over against this, though, if the whole totally and absolutely isn't, so then, not only does that which is encounter what we   [d] named earlier, rather too beyond this, that it isn't, so too it can no longer have become, not even once.

Theae: But, why not?

Strng: That which has become has always become a whole. So that neither being nor becoming are to be presumed if one doesn't postulate the whole underneath that which is.

Theae: In all ways, it seems that this is the correlation.

Strng: But, then too, and utterly – that which isn't a whole is not permitted that it somehow may have size. For if it were to be of some given size, so too, indeed, it is of whatever size it even may be, even so large necessarily as a whole.

Theae: Well, obviously.

Strng: And it shall become evident even so as here, that there are thousands of other insurmountable difficulties laying in wait for him, he who ever says that being would only be two, or only be one.

Theae: This has already been revealed through what has just now come forth, what is apparent from the above. For then, upon each and every difficulty another one is knotted and each brings even greater and more difficult perplexity into the befuddlement that already exists.   <33.~246a]

Strng: Now, those who have entered most precisely into this matter regarding being and non-being, these as a whole we haven't even gone into their positions, indeed, at all. Still, this is already rather enough. But, then too, we shouldn't forget those who clarify matters differently, that we also pull these others into our indagations so that we shall have observed this matter from all sides: that it's not any easier to clarify being than non-being, what it is.

Theae: So, let's then proceed onward to these.

Strng: Between these it seems to me that this is truly a war amongst giants, due to their disunity amongst one another in regards to being.

Theae: How's that?

Strng: The one camp pulls everything down from out of the heavens and out of the invisible, it pulls all of this down upon the earth where they might clutch it in their hands, literally clambering upon it like rocks and oak trees. For then, its upon everything like this that they support themselves and they go on to assert that only this alone would be: that which one can knock up against and what one can   [b] feel, in that they clarify this so: physicality and being are one and the same. But then, if one of the others says that there also would be something that doesn't have a body, so they don't pay any attention to him at all, utterly none, and they won't even hear another word about it.

Theae: Yes, bull-headed people are these about whom you now are speaking – for then, I too have already met up with more than a few like this.

Strng: And its even for this reason that those who argue against these approach the matter most delicately from above to below and, so, from out of the invisible realm they assert that certain thinkable, non-bodily ideas would be true being but that the aforementioned bodies and everything that the former named truth, all of this   *[c]* is shoved aside as being totally trivial, and they ascribe to all of this merely a fleeting becoming rather than being. But between these two camps, o Theaetetus, there has always been an immeasurable battlefield of slaughter raging.

Theae: True.

Strng: Hence, let's exact from both of these sides, one after the other, that they clarify for us the being which each has taken up.

Theae: But, how should we do this?

Strng: From those who postulate that it is in ideas, from these this is easier to do, for then, they are more tame; but then from the others who forcefully pull everything down into the physical, from these it is more difficult, perhaps even downright impossible. But, all the   *[d]* same, I believe, thus is how we'll have to make do.

Theae: How?

Strng: The loveliest resolution would be that we make them better, if only this were possible; but then if this isn't an option, then at least in our speech that we'd require of them that they answer us with greater propriety than they have tended to do heretofore. For then, what is agreed to by those who are better is of greater value than what is agreed to by those who are worse. And verily, we aren't particularly concerned about them, rather we only are searching for the truth.

Theae: Totally right.   *<34.~246e]*

Strng: So then let them, these who have become better, let them give you their answers and you carry these over to us, what it is that they say.

Theae: I shall do it.

Strng: Would they be so kind as to tell us, then, whether they accept this – that there exist mortal creatures? [207]

---

[207] "sterbliches lebendiges" – literally "dying livings."

Theae: How should they ever not admit that!

Strng: And then, whether they agree that such as this would be an ensouled [animated] body?

Theae: Well, that's totally certain.

Strng: That, therefore, they postulate the soul underneath that which is?

Theae: Yes.   *[247a]*

Strng: And how? – don't they accept that the one soul would be righteous, another unrighteous? – and that one would be reasonable, another lacking in reason?

Theae: Without a doubt.

Strng: And don't they also accept that it's through the presence of righteousness that each and every soul becomes righteous, and it's through the opposite that it would become the contrary to this?

Theae: Yes, they also admit this.

Strng: But then, that that which possibly is present and possibly absent, that this would in every way, indeed, be something – this too is something that they well shall say?

Theae: Right, and so they say as much.

Strng: Hence, if righteousness and reason and all of the rest of   *[b]* the virtues and likewise the soul in which all of these subsist, if all of these really are actual, so do they assert, perhaps, that some of all of this would be visible and something that one might grasp, or is it all invisible?

Theae: Well, nothing of all of this is visible.

Strng: But how? – do they say that something from all of this would have a body?

Theae: This is something that they no longer shall be able to answer in one and the same way, rather the soul itself seems to them to possess a body; but as regards righteousness and everything else about which you were inquiring, well in regards to these they shall be ashamed of being so audacious as to say either that some of all of this wouldn't be at all, nor too would they be liable to insist upon this, that all of this would be totally incorporated into a body.   *[c]*

Strng: Obviously, Theaetetus – these men really have become better. For then, there's not one amongst all of these who is of the legitimate sort, the purebred variety of these earth-born clodhoppers, not one who would shy away from saying this, rather they would make it a point and remain insistent upon this: that anything that they are incapable of mashing in between their fingers, anything like this *is not*, totally and absolutely.

Theae: You're right, that's exactly how they think about these things.

Strng: Hence, let's start over again once more with our [d] questioning – for then, if they might want to give in even in ever so small an amount, that that which is includes the non-physical, even this is already quite sufficient. For then, that which simultaneously is suitable *{eignet}* both to this as well as to what is bodily, namely that upon which they are looking in that they say that both of these would be: this, then, is what they would have to declare. Now, perhaps they might become confused or somewhat at a loss for words in doing this and if something like this is encountered, so do observe this: whether it may well be that if we hold it up before them, whether they would accept this and concede as much, that that which is would be something like this.

Theae: What's that? Speak that we might find out right away.

Strng: Thus I say – whatever possesses any sort of capability, [e] this only – and be it now that it makes an effect upon anything other, or then too if it should suffer[208] even to the smallest degree, and even if it would only be once: all of this would actually be. Namely, I'm postulating as a firm clarification for the purpose of the determination of *that which is* that this isn't anything other than capability, power *{Vermögen, Kraft}*.

Theae: Very well; and in that they don't have anything else at hand that might be an improvement upon this [thesis] that they might say, so they do accept it.

Strng: Excellent. For, then too, in what follows something other than this may possibly become evident, both to us as well as to them. Thus for now, anyway, we remain together with them on this, that this is set down firmly as our common starting point.

Theae: It remains. <35.~248a]

Strng: And now let's approach the other ones, the friends of ideas. But you also might convey to us exactly what it is that they say.

Theae: Thus, it should be done.

Strng: Well then, you all take it that being and becoming are separate, each from the other. Isn't this true?

Theae: Yes.

Strng: And then, it is with the body that we would have community with becoming through perception; but it's through thoughts that occur within the soul that we have community with true being, which, as you say, always correlate in the same way; but then becoming always differently.

Theae: Indeed, this is what we say. [248b]

---

[208] "wirken und leiden" – compare to *Theaetetus* 156a; and see footnote# 52, p. 31.

Strng: But then, this having community, my most virtuous friends, what should we say, really, what is it that you actually mean with both of these in that they have community? Is this anything other than that which we spoke about earlier?

Theae: To what are you referring?

Strng: A suffering or producing an effect – which is due to some power and this comes to be from the meeting up and striking together of the one with the other. But perhaps, o Theaetetus, you aren't rightly able to pick up on what they say in answer to this question, though I'm somewhat better positioned to hear it due to my longtime acquaintance with them.

Theae: Then, how is it that they clarify themselves about this?

Strng: They don't give in and make allowance for what we said earlier on to the earth-born combatants in respect to being.   [c]

Theae: But, what was that?

Strng: We postulated this as a sufficient clarification of that which is, didn't we, if anything was characterized as having a capability, and no matter how small this capability might be, that it might suffer or do?

Theae: Yes.

Strng: And this, then, is how they expostulate upon this: that indeed becoming is well suited that it suffers and produces effects, but then as regards being they assert that neither of these capabilities quite fits the bill.

Theae: Now they're talking.

Strng: To which then, all the same, we have to counter that we'd very much appreciate it if we might experience this yet more precisely, [d] whether or not they are one with us on this: that the soul cognizes and that being shall be recognized.

Theae: Indeed, they've got to affirm this, certainly.

Strng: And what about cognition or whatever has become known – do you all name this as a doing or as a suffering, or as both? – or is it so that the one of them is a doing and the other a suffering? – or do you mean to say that neither has any creative interplay with either of these two others? But then, it's quite certain: neither with either, for otherwise they would contradict what they said earlier.

Theae: I understand.

Strng: This namely: that if cognition is a doing then it follows by necessity that what is recognized suffers, that, therefore, in accordance with this clarification of being, whatever becomes   [e] recognized, insofar as it is recognized, so it also shall be moved due to this suffering which, indeed, as we say, can't possibly occur to that which remains at rest.

Theae: Right.

Strng: But how – by Zeus! – how should we allow ourselves to be so easily persuaded and talked into this, that in all actuality movement and life and soul and reason are unsuited to that which truly is? That it neither lives nor thinks but rather is deprived of the glory and sanctity of reason and stands motionless? *[249a]*

Theae: A rather bull-headed assertion, o Stranger, is what we would give in to were we to allow this!

Strng: Or should we affirm that it has reason, but deny that it's living?

Theae: How's that?

Strng: Or should we say that both of these subsist within him and we only want to assert that these would not be present within a soul.

Theae: But, in what other way is there that it might be able to have such as this?

Strng: Thus, we want to say that it has reason and soul and life ... only that although it is alive, still, it just stands there totally motionless?

Theae: All of this seems to me to be totally unreasonable. *[b]*

Strng: That, therefore, there has to be things moved and movement – allowance would have to be made for this, that these are.

Theae: Doubtless.

Strng: For then, verily, it does follow, o Theaetetus, that if everything is unmoved then nobody might possibly have any understanding of anything.

Theae: Yes, obviously.

Strng: Singularly, if once again we were to allow this, that everything shall be moved and everything undergoes alteration, so, likewise through this assertion we also close out the very same [the possibility of knowledge] from that which is.

Theae: How's that?

Strng: These [terms/actualities] – "in like manner" and "even so" and "in the same relation" – would you fancy that these might possibly take place without quiescence? *[c]*

Theae: In no way.

Strng: And do you, perhaps, see this: that barring these knowledge of anything at all couldn't possibly be or come-into-being?

Theae: No it couldn't, not in the least.

Strng: And that there is no one against whom one has to argue more vehemently than someone who scuttles knowledge, insight and understanding off to the side and doing away with these still wants to make an assertion about something.

Theae: You can say that again.

Strng: And thus, the philosopher, he who prizes this in the highest degree, is, as it seems, for this very reason in every way required that he doesn't pay any heed at all: neither to these who propose the all as quiescent – and no matter whether it's postulated as one idea or many – nor too, on the other hand, does he pay any heed to   *[d]* those who would move being through and through; rather just as the children tend to desire things, he too has to have it both ways and, so, of both that which is and of the all he says that it would rest as well as that it moves.

Theae: Absolutely true.   *<36.~249de]*

Strng: How now? Doesn't it look to you as if we, with this clarification of ours, that we would have encompassed being in a right orderly way?

Theae: Quite.

Strng: Oh woe, Theaetetus! – how I see this: that now we shan't understand the least bit of it, nothing more than that there exists no way out by such an investigation!

Theae: But, how so? – and what's wrong that already once again you are at such a loss?   *[e]*

Strng: You, lucky one, don't you share this insight that even now we've fallen into the greatest abyss of reasoning[209] and that we are simply imagining that we've managed to say something?

Theae: I'm still imagining that we have... and how, consciously, anything more should better describe our position, this is what I haven't yet grasped in the least.

Strng: Just examine this more precisely, whether once we've admitted everything as above, whether then we rightly are liable to be asked just so as we ourselves questioned these others earlier, those who said that the all would be warmth or coldness.   *[250a]*

Theae: But – do remind me, just what was the question?

Strng: Gladly. And I want to seek out a way that I do this so, namely, that I ask you just like we questioned the former ones – so that at the same time we might advance a little further.

Theae: Good.

Strng: Very well, then – don't you consider movement and quiescence as totally contrary, one to the other?

Theae: How mightn't I consider them anything other than this?

Strng: But you did, indeed, say that both of them and each of them is? – and each one to an equal extent?

Theae: Indeed, I do say this.   *[b]*

---

[209] Compare with *Parmenides* 130e: "sinking into a bottomless inanity" (p. 212).

Strng: Now, do you mean that both and each of them shall be moved when you give in and make allowance for this, that they are?

Theae: In no way.

Strng: Rather, that they both repose, is this what you want to signify when you state that they are?

Theae: But, how's that?

Strng: Hence, you set that which is as a third within your soul, [as something] that is outside of these other two in that you enclose quiescence and movement, that both are bound up together and it's upon their community within being that you take them up, that both have this attribute, that they are.

Theae: We might very well signify 'that which is' as a third, in all actuality – in that we say that movement and quiescence are.   *[c]*

Strng: Thus, that which is is not movement and quiescence taken together, rather it is different from these.

Theae: It seems so.

Strng: Hence, it's not due to its own nature that that which is shall either move or rest.

Theae: Hardly.

Strng: Whither, then, whither should someone turn his thoughts: he who wants to firmly set something down about this, that he do so with clarity?

Theae: Well, *where indeed?*

Strng: There's nowhere that's easily [accessible], I think. For then, if something doesn't move, how should it not be at rest? – or that which isn't resting in any manner, how should it not be in motion? But then, that which is or being has shown itself, now, as outside of both – is this, now, is this well possible?

Theae: Certainly, this is the least possible of all.

Strng: But, 'tis well that we have to recollect ourselves upon this.

Theae: What's that?

Strng: That earlier on when we were questioning about non-being: *where* one would have to bring this word forward, so we also were trapped and caught up in total perplexity. Don't you remember this?

Theae: How shouldn't I remember it?   *[250e]*

Strng: And are we in any less perplexity as regards being?

Theae: For me, o Stranger, we seem to be in even greater perplexity – if this is possible.

Strng: Thus, this lies here undetermined. But now, since being and non-being proceed into this perplexity – and do so in portions that are totally equal, so there is yet hope that if only the one of them is displayed to us – and be it, now, darker or more distinctly – so too the other shall show itself even so; and if we shouldn't see either of them, well, we at least want to bring the clarification of them both further along, and that we do so in a manner that is most respectable, insofar as we are able.

Theae: Excellent.

Strng: So clarify this, then: in what manner, indeed, do we name – in each and every instance – the one and the same matter with many names?

Theae: But, how [do you mean this] and what [do you mean by this]? – give me an example.   *<37.~251ab]*

Strng: Indeed, we say all sorts of things about a person in that we denominate him as being 'this' and 'that': that we attribute to him color and form and size, and then too, mistakes and virtues; and in all of these instances and hundreds of thousands of other ones we don't only say that he's a person, rather too that he would be good, and we give him innumerable other qualifications – and even so too is the correlation with everything else, all the other things, that we postulate that each of them is one and still, all the same, we say many particulars about it and clarify it through many sorts of words and, likewise, using many sorts of denominations.

Theae: What you say is true.

Strng: In doing this, I think, we've prepared quite a meal, now, for adolescents and hard-headed elders. For then, verily, this is so easy to grasp and lies right under one's hand – that it would be impossible for many to be one or one many[210] – and it gives them joy that they're not going to suffer such things, that someone names a   [c] person as good, that rather the good is good and a person is a person. You've certainly often met up with such deep thinkers, I think, Theaetetus, those who place a lot of significance in this sort of thinking, older people who due to their impoverished mental acuity are in wonder about matters like these or, then too, they themselves opine that they've discovered some amazing wisdom in this.

Theae: Quite.

Strng: Thus, that we turn ourselves to all of them, whoever has ever lectured us anything at all as regards being, so to these as well as to the rest of them, those with whom we already have been   [d] conversing, don't we yet have to bespeak the following with them as a questioning probe.

Theae: What's that?

---

[210] *Parmenides* 129b – "Likewise, if someone shows that everything is one because it has unity in itself and that the same again is many because it contains a multitude in itself; but should he show that the actual one itself is many or, again, that plurality itself is one: this shall certainly amaze me."

Strng: Whether it's so? – that we neither [are allowed to] knot being on to quiescence and movement, nor utterly any one together with an other, that rather we'd want to postulate in our speech that all are unmixable and none capable of partaking with any other? Or whether we do bring all together into one, that they all are capable of having community amongst themselves? Or finally, indeed, that a few are capable but others are not? Which of these choices, o Theaetetus, which shall we say that they favor?   *[e]*

Theae: I don't know what they would answer to this. Why not take up each possibility in turn and see what follows from each one of them?

Strng: Well said. Thus, first off let's postulate, if you want, that they say that nothing has any such capability of entering into community with anything toward any something. In this instance movement and quiescence shall in no manner ever have any partaking upon being.

Theae: No, indeed they won't.   *[252a]*

Strng: And how? – shall either of them well be able to be – if, then, they wouldn't at all have any community with being?

Theae: Neither shall be.

Strng: Suddenly, then, everything is caught up in discord through this assumption, as it seems, and no matter whether it's by those who contend that the all moves or, then too, if it's those who place it as one and who take up this position that the correlation would be in ideas that always correlate to being in an equal way. For then, all of them do indeed knot being in: the one side saying that it would actually be in motion and the other side says that it would actually be at rest.

Theae: Indeed, that's obvious.

Strng: And even so do these, those who at one time place the all together and at another time they separate it, and no matter,   *[b]*
now, whether it's the one and the infinite [emanates from] out of the one, or if it would be so that the all be separated into a finite number of components and is composed from all of these placed together – and however they might like that this be taken, that this happens in turn or has always been happening. In each and every instance they all, indeed, are saying nothing if this mixing doesn't exist.

Theae: Right.

Strng: And, further – those who won't suffer this, that any something be predicated with a name of an other through partaking in community, these would themselves have to be punished by the utmost ludicrousness of their very speech itself.

Theae: How's that?   *[c]*

Strng: They are forced, indeed, and quite at every turn as regards everything, that they make use of *being,* and also *without* and the *other* and thousands of sorts of others that they are quite incapable of repressing, that such wouldn't be knotted up within their own speech and, therefore, they don't even require that someone else steps forward to contradict them or prove them wrong, rather, as the saying goes, they bring their own opponent and flip-side from home and he's muttering the opposite from within whenever they open their mouths, just like Eurycles' jester – and, so, he tags along with them wherever they go.

Theae: Your similitude is most apt and true!   *[d]*

Strng: But how now? – what if we allow everything to have a capability of binding up together amongst one another?

Theae: Even I am able to refute this.

Strng: How's that? Because movement itself would then in every manner be at rest and, likewise, quiescence itself would be in motion if both of these were to meet up together and, indeed, this is impossible on all grounds that movement rests and resting moves itself.

Theae: Doubtless.

Strng: Thus, there remains for us the third alone.

Theae: Yes.   *<38.~252e]*

Strng: But one of these is indeed necessary, that either everything or nothing or a few, indeed, but not others might possibly be mixed?

Theae: That's totally certain.

Strng: And two are found to be impossible.

Theae: Yes.

Strng: Hence, everyone who wants to answer aright has to take up what remains from the three.

Theae: Obviously.

Strng: If now, a few themselves understand this but others don't, so this proceeds along accordingly almost as it is with the letters of   *[a]* the alphabet. For here too a few don't allow of themselves that they be placed together amongst one another, though others are well able to be unified.

Theae: Here you're on firm ground.

Strng: But the vowels proceed eminently in front of all of the rest and like a band they intertwine throughout all of them so that without one of these it is also impossible for the rest, that one binds up to an other.

Theae: Totally impossible.

Strng: Now, does everybody know which is able to enter into community with which? Or does this belong to an art if one wants to make the right connections?

Theae: An art.

Strng: Essentially, which one?

Theae: Speechcraft. [253b]

Strng: And isn't it even so in regards to the high and the low tones? – that he who possesses this artistry has insight into this: which of the tones it's allowable to mix amongst the others and which ones are not to be mixed; and such a person is a musician, but he who lacks this understanding, he wouldn't be musically adept?

Theae: Even so.

Strng: And by each and every other art and [even with] inartistic methods of proceeding – we shall find other similarities.

Theae: Doubtless.

Strng: Now, since we have conceded this, that the concepts likewise correlate with one another in an equivalent manner in the design of their intermixing, wouldn't someone also have to proceed thus with his speech, if he knows what he's about and arranges it according to science, wouldn't he have to direct it thusly, he who wants to display this aright, namely: which concepts agree with one another harmoniously and which ones do not support such intermixing? – and, then too, whether there do exist such concepts that generally [c] hold all of them together and that these are positioned such that they intermix amongst themselves? – and, not to forget, in respect to the divisions – whether other concepts are the root cause of divisiveness throughout?

Theae: How mightn't there not be a science required for all of this and perhaps, indeed, the greatest one of all! <39.~253]

Strng: And how, Theaetetus, how should we name it? – or are we, by Zeus, and without even noticing it, are we stumbling in upon the knowledge of free men? – and may it well be that in seeking out the sophist, so, first off, we've managed to discover the philosopher?

Theae: How do you mean?

Strng: The separation into classes, that one neither holds the [d] same concept as being some other, nor some other concept as being the same, don't we want to say that this would belong to the science of dialectics?

Theae: We do.

Strng: He, then, who understands what belongs and he who proceeds along accordingly, he shall note precisely how one idea expands out through the many particulars that are divided on all sides, each one from the other, and that many ideas which being different from one another are outwardly encompassed by the one; and, then too, that one through and through is knotted only with one from amongst the many; and finally, that many are totally set apart from one another. This, then, is called knowing to differentiate *[e]* by type to what extent 'each and every' *{jedes}* is capable of entering into community and to what extent each is not so capable.

Theae: By all means, certainly.

Strng: But then, the occupation with dialectics, I do hope that you shan't bestow this upon anyone else other than the pure, those who philosophize inspired simply by what's right?

Theae: How else! – it shouldn't well be that this accords with anyone other.

Strng: In this locality here abouts we shall, thus, now as well as later on when we go seeking after him, it's here that the philosopher shall be found – though, indeed, it's hard to recognize him exactly, only this difficulty is of quite a different variety than that which belongs to the sophist and what pertains to him.   *[254a2]*

Theae: How's that?

Strng: The one who is fleeing into the darkness of non-being with which he's become most adept through his inartistic practices, this one is hard to recognize due to the darkness of the waters in which he resides. Isn't this true?

Theae: It seems so.

Strng: The philosopher, quite to the contrary, he who is continuously preoccupied in the methodologies of ordered reasoning as regards the idea of being, he too is by no stretch of the imagination easy to perceive, and this is due to the brightness of his environs. For then, the spiritual eyes of the greater majority are simply incapable of beholding the divine for any extended period.

Theae: This too, no less than your earlier remark, is quite revealing – that this is how matters correlate.

Strng: The latter one, we shall examine him yet more precisely later on when this suits our pleasure;[211] but, obviously, it's not allowable that we let up now from our present pursuit of the sophist – not, at least, until we've perceived him to a sufficient degree.

Theae: Well said.   *<40.~254bc]*

Strng: Since, now, we are as one in our admission of this, that a few concepts want to partake in community with one another, others do not, a few just a small amount, others more, and then there are others

---

[211] Schleiermacher contends that Plato's *Symposium* is this examination – or, more precisely: that the *Symposium* is an examination of the philosopher *in life* and the *Phaedo* an examination of the philosopher *in death.*

too that are not hindered from having community with all: so now let us pick up from where we left off in our speech earlier by further remarking that we don't want to examine this upon all concepts – so that we don't fall into a state of confusion due the vast multitude – that rather we do so upon just a few pre-eminent ones, those having the greatest importance, that first off we'll examine what each one is and then how each correlates in respect to its capability for partaking in community with the others, and that we do this for the following reason, namely, that even if we're not yet capable of grasping being and non-being with complete clarity at least we won't be totally lacking, that indeed we do have a clarification to show insofar as this is given to us through the style of our current investigation and that it would perhaps be possible to a degree that we proceed along with this without incurring any damaging repercussions – in that when we *[d]* speak of non-being, that it actually would be non-being.

Theae: Indeed, this is what we have to do.

Strng: The most important concepts from the ones that we were going through earlier are, indeed – being itself, and quiescence and movement?

Theae: By far.

Strng: And the two of them, we say, indeed: the two are totally at odds *{unvereinbar}* with one another and not unifiable.

Theae: Fully.

Strng: But being may be unified with both? For then, indeed, they both are?

Theae: How mightn't they not be!

Strng: Thus, that would be three.

Theae: Indeed.

Strng: Of which, then, each is different from the other two but the same as itself?

Theae: So it is.   *[e]*

Strng: But what is it that we've said just now – the same and the different? Aren't these themselves yet two more that are different from the other three but necessarily always getting mixed up together with them? – and wouldn't we have to direct our attentiveness upon the five of them and not just upon the three? – or have we merely pointed at one of these previous concepts with these, the same and the different, without even knowing it?

Theae: Perhaps.   *[255a]*

Strng: But movement and quiescence, indeed, are certainly neither sameness nor difference.

Theae: How so?

Strng: What we attribute in common both to movement and quiescence, that couldn't possibly itself be one or the other of these two?

Theae: Why not?

Strng: Movement, then, shall be at rest and quiescence, on the other side, would be in motion. For since in either instance, whichever one of these two you might choose, so it would have to be a valid substitute for both, thus the other one would be required that it metamorphoses into that which is contrary to its nature because, verily, it would have a partaking in this, its contrary.   *[b]*

Theae: Indeed, that's obvious.

Strng: But now, both do indeed partake in sameness and difference.

Theae: Yes.

Strng: Hence, we don't want to say that movement would somehow be the same or that it would be the different, nor too would quiescence.

Theae: No, indeed not.

Strng: But perhaps being and sameness are for us to be thought of as one?

Theae: Perhaps.

Strng: But if being and sameness don't mean different [things /concepts], so, then again, in that we say that movement and quiescence both are, so we would put these out as the same, as being.

Theae: Singularly, that is quite impossible.   *[c]*

Strng: Then it's also impossible that sameness and being are one.

Theae: Well-nigh.

Strng: Hence, as a fourth concept to the former threesome we'd have to postulate sameness.

Theae: Quite.

Strng: And how? – should we postulate difference as a fifth? – or should one think, perhaps, difference and being as two names for one concept?

Theae: That may well be.

Strng: Singularly, I think that you shall admit that as regards being – some shall always be named [as being such] in and for itself, but some only in relation upon something other.

Theae: How might I do anything else!

Strng: And the different always only in relation upon an other. Isn't this true?   *[d]*

Theae: So it is.

Strng: But it wouldn't possibly be so if being and difference were not far removed from one another; rather if difference likewise would have portions of both types just as being does, so too there would also exist different things whose difference wouldn't be related upon anything other. But now, this obviously is what does come to fore, that indeed whatever is different is this, what it is, necessarily in relation upon some other being.

Theae: It correlates just as you say.

Strng: As a fifth, thus, we'd have to specify the nature of difference underneath the concepts that we have chosen. [e]

Theae: Yes.

Strng: And we'd have to say that difference goes throughout all of them in that each and every individual is different from the rest, and not due to its nature but, rather, due to its sharing in the idea of difference.

Theae: That's obvious, quite. <41.~255]

Strng: Let us assert this about the five in that we repeat the particulars.

Theae: But, what's that?

Strng: Firstly, that movement is totally and downright different from quiescence. Or, how did we say?

Theae: Just so.

Strng: Hence, it's not quiescence.

Theae: In no way.

Strng: But it is, indeed, due to its sharing in being. [256a]

Theae: It is.

Strng: But, then too, movement is also different from sameness.

Theae: Well-nigh.

Strng: Thus, it is not sameness.

Theae: No, indeed not.

Strng: But still, it was indeed the same to a certain extent because, verily, everything has a portion of this.

Theae: Certainly.

Strng: That, therefore, movement would be the same and also wouldn't be the same, one has to acknowledge this and not be [b] difficult about it. For then, when we say that it is the same and not the same, indeed, we don't mean this in an equivalent manner; rather if the same, so we say this due to its partaking in sameness, but if not the same then due to its commonality with difference through which quite apart from sameness it doesn't become the former but, rather, something different – so that once more it rightly shall not be named as the same.

Theae: Quite.

Strng: So if somehow movement itself also would have a portion of quiescence or standing still – this wouldn't be astounding that movement be named as standing still.

Theae: Totally right, since we did indeed admit this, that a few concepts want to intermix with one another but others don't.

Strng: As regards this, then, we proceeded along with the proof already earlier than our current consideration since we displayed that this would have to be so, quite naturally.   *[c]*

Theae: Quite.

Strng: And once again we said that movement is different from difference, just as it is also other than sameness and quiescence.

Theae: That's all necessary.

Strng: Not [being the] different it is still to a certain extent also different – according to the former speech.

Theae: Right.

Strng: Now, how shall we proceed further? – should we say that movement is different from the other three but deny that it's different from the fourth... since we have, indeed, already conceded this, that there would be five upon which and about which we wanted to   *[d]* pursue our investigation.

Theae: How should we do this? – for then, it's impossible that we might specify a smaller number than the one that has been shown.

Strng: Without any trepidation, thus, we want to speak this out and fight for it, that movement would be different from being.

Theae: Without the least little bit of trepidation.

Strng: Hence, this is totally clear that movement is not essentially being, though it still 'is' to the extent that it has a portion of being.

Theae: Yes, this is totally clear.

Strng: Thus non-being, verily, necessarily is – as well in regards to movement as also in relation to all of the other concepts. For this is valid of them all: that the nature of difference which makes them   *[e]* different from being, so it makes each of them that each is not – and we are able to rightly name all of them all together as "not being" in this manner to an equivalent extent, and also, once again, as being – and say that each would be because it has a portion of being.

Theae: It may well be so.

Strng: On each concept, thus, there is much being, but much, indeed an innumerable amount, which is not.

Theae: So it seems.   *[257a]*

Strng: Doesn't one also have to say of being itself that it is different from the rest?

Theae: That's necessary.

Strng: Thus also being is not – to the extent that the rest is. For in that it isn't the latter, it itself is one but the innumerable many which are the rest, it isn't.

Theae: So, well-nigh, this is well the correlation.

Strng: Thus, there also are no difficulties here for one to make a big fuss over – if, indeed, the concepts naturally tend toward having community, one with the other. But if anyone doesn't want to admit this, so he shall persuade us and talk us out of our earlier conclusions, and then he might talk us out of the latter ones.

Theae: What you say accords with the firm decrees of righteousness.

Strng: Now, let's also observe this. *[b]*

Theae: What's that?

Strng: If we say non-being, so we don't mean, as it seems, something that is contrary to being, rather only something different.

Theae: How's that?

Strng: Just like when we name something as not big, do you opine that we signify the small any more than what is middling?

Theae: In no way.

Strng: Hence, we don't want to admit this, that if a negation shall be used that then the opposite shall be signified, rather only so much: that the preceding "not" (or un-) signifies something different than the words that come after it, or much rather, than the things that are signified by the words that come after it.

Theae: By all means, indeed. *<42.~257c]*

Strng: And further, let's also bethink ourselves whether *this* likewise seems to you to be so.

Theae: But, what's this?

Strng: The essence of what is different seems to me to be even so split up into pieces as is knowledge.

Theae: How's that?

Strng: The latter too is, indeed, only one – but each part which relates to some other object becomes cut off and each is given its own name – and it's for this reason that there exist so many arts and sciences. *[d]*

Theae: You're totally right.

Strng: Now, don't the parts of what is different also proceed even so, although this too is one?

Theae: Perhaps, but tell me how and to what extent?

Strng: One part of what is different is all of that which, indeed, is set over against the beautiful.

Theae: Yes.

Strng: Is this, now, without a name or designation, or does it have one?

Theae: It has one. For then, that which in every instance we name unbeautiful, this is different from nothing other than from the nature of the beautiful.

Strng: Very well, so tell me then, what this is.

Theae: But, what's that?   *[e]*
Strng: Is it through this, that we've brought whatever it might be
beneath a classification of being, is it through this that an other one
that is set against it, here the unbeautiful, through this that it has
come to be?
Theae: So, indeed.
Strng: Thus, an opposition in being against something other is, as it
seems, the unbeautiful.
Theae: Totally right.
Strng: In accord with this clarification does the beautiful belong
more underneath [the classification of] being and the unbeautiful
less?
Theae: Not at all.
Strng: Even so, thus, one has to say that what is not large is just as
much as that which itself is large.   *[258a]*
Theae: Yes, one just as well as the other.
Strng: So too, that which isn't right is to be postulated as equivalent
to what is right in this respect, that the one is no less than the other.
Theae: Without a doubt.
Strng: And the same shall be said about all of the rest – if, indeed,
the nature of that which is different, or difference, has shown itself
beneath being. For if difference is, so necessarily the parts of
difference are not to be postulated as being any less.
Theae: How mightn't they not be so?
Strng: Hence, the opposite from one part of difference and   *[b]*
being also is – if these shall be placed over against one another – and
no less, if one is permitted to say it, being no less than being itself is;
and in no way do we mean this as a contrary, rather only so much as
being something different than being.
Theae: That's totally certain.
Strng: Now, how should we name them?
Theae: Obviously, verily, non-being is even this – and this is what we
were seeking on account of the sophist.
Strng: Do matters stand, thus, as you said: that neither takes
precedence in being? – and one is already permitted to say as much
and say it whole-heartedly, that there's no arguing about this, that
non-being has its own nature and essence – and just as the large was
large and the beautiful beautiful, and just as that which isn't large *[c]*
and that which isn't beautiful is not large and not beautiful, even so
too non-being was and is not being and counts along with all the rest
as a concept beneath the many that are? Or do we yet have any
doubts or second thoughts that go against this, o Theaetetus?
Theae: Nope, none at all.   *<43.~258]*

Strng: And do you also well know this: that we've gone beyond Parmenides' prohibition and have strayed essentially from his path?
Theae: How so?
Strng: Beyond what he prohibited us that we investigate into such, we have ventured forward beyond this in our indagations and we have put it up on display.
Theae: How's that? [d]
Strng: He said, indeed: *Not capable art thou, verily, to understand that non-being is; Rather from such a way hold back your inquisitive mind –* ?
Theae: That's what he said, quite.
Strng: But we haven't merely shown that non-being is, rather too – we've exhibited the concept beneath which non-being belongs. For then, after we showed that difference is and that it is portioned out amongst everything that is, one against the other, so we dared to make the wager of saying that of those which stand over against each being, that even this in truth would be non-being. [e]
Theae: And in every instance, I believe, we have clarified matters aright, fully and completely.
Strng: Thus, don't let anybody paraphrase us as if we would have displayed non-being as the contrary of that which is and had then dared to assert that it would be. For from a contrariness of being, verily, already for a long while we have given notice and taken leave from this in our investigation – whether such is or is not and whether it might be clarified or if it's totally and downright beyond any [259a] clarification. But what we have now described that non-being would be, one either has to prove us wrong in a persuasive manner – that what we said isn't right – or so long as he is incapable of doing this, so he too says just as we say: that the concepts intermix amongst one another. And since being and difference proceed throughout everything and also through one another, so now the different shall, in that it partakes of a portion of being, so indeed it is due to this capability [given to it] by this portion that difference is, but it is not the former, that upon which it partakes, rather as a different; but as different from being, verily, it is obviously entirely and necessarily non-being. And, once again, in that being has a portion of difference, so it is verily different from all of the other classifications and in that it is different from all of these all together, so it's not any one from each and every one of them, nor of all of these others all together, rather [it is] only itself. So that yet, once again, being too is not thousands and tens-of-thousands of sorts – this is entirely non-contested – and so too all of the others as individuals and all taken up

together *is* in downright manifold ways, and *is not* in downright manifold ways.

Theae: True.

Strng: And if someone doesn't want to believe all of these contradictions, so he should look sharp and then lecture us with something that is better than what we have presented; but if   [c] god only knows what amazing things he's managed to think through and cobble together in his mind, and if he finds his joy in this, that he pulls the speech first in the one direction and then in some other one, so then he's taken hardships up upon himself that aren't particularly worth the bother, just as our present speech bespeaks. For then, this is neither majestic nor particularly hard to discover; but the former is even so hard and simultaneously beautiful.

Theae: What's that?

Strng: What was clarified earlier, namely, allowing this – that as much as is possible one ventures into testing out all of the particulars of what was said: if one postulates that that which is different in a certain sense also again may be postulated as the same, and what is the same as different – in that sense and in that relation in which he says it, that one of both of these is postulated. But then, that one asserts of the same without any qualification as to how, that this would be different, and that the different would be the same, that the big is small and the similar dissimilar, and that one finds joy if only one is always able to bring contradiction into one's speech, in part this isn't truly an investigation at all and in part, certainly, it's a very adolescent one that indicates that someone has only first begun to feel his way amongst these things.

Theae: Well, that's totally obvious.   <44.~259e]

Strng: But then too, most virtuous Theaetetus, that one wants merely that everything be torn apart, this too doesn't qualify anyone else either as having any particular aptitude – but least of all in respect to philosophy – showing much rather only that one has been forsaken by the muses.

Theae: How's that?

Strng: Because this is the ultimate insult and obliteration of all speech, that each and every be separated out from all the rest. For then, verily, it's only through a contrasting interweaving of the concepts that a speech is able to come to be.

Theae: Quite.

Strng: Now, reflect upon this: how precisely at the right   [260a] *moment of time* we now have argued against such as these and have required of them that they fess up and admit this, that the one mixes with the other.

Theae: In what relation, then?

Strng: Because, indeed, speech also is one of the actual classifications. For then, if we were to be robbed of speech we likewise would be robbed of philosophy, that which is greatest; but, then too, we still have to unify ourselves now regarding this also, what a speech is. If we were to want that speech is totally shut out, that it shouldn't partake in being at all, so we wouldn't be capable of speaking another word. But we would be shutting it out if we were to give in and allow this, that there wouldn't exist any strands that knot, that naught is connected with naught. *[b]*

Theae: Well, you're totally right about this; but why it is that we'd now have to clarify speech, this is something that I haven't understood as of yet.

Strng: Perhaps if you'd want to follow me a bit further, so you shall easily be able to grasp it.

Theae: But, how's that?

Strng: Non-being has shown itself, indeed, as one of the concepts that is dispersed throughout all of being.

Theae: That's right.

Strng: Now, let us look next at this, whether it well may be bound up with notionality and with speech?

Theae: But why?

Strng: If it is not bound up with these, so, necessarily, everything is true; but if it is bound to these, so false notions and false speech do come into being. For having notions of non-being and speaking these out, that is how falsity is able to enter into our thought and into our speech.

Theae: Quite.

Strng: And if falsity and error are, so too is deception.

Theae: Yes.

Strng: And if deception is, then too, certainly, everything is full of shadowy figures and images and deceitful appearances.

Theae: How mightn't it be anything other? *[260d]*

Strng: And the sophist, we said, he would have taken flight into this realm, but at the same time he totally denied that error would exist at all. For then, non-being can neither be thought nor spoken. Because on being non-being wouldn't have any partaking.

Theae: That's how it was.

Strng: But now, indeed, it has been shown that it would have a portion of being. So that he might not want to argue with us anymore from this side but might well say that only a few sorts would partake in non-being, others wouldn't – and then that speech and notionality would belong to those that didn't, so that he still doesn't let up from arguing that image-making and the artistry of deceit (where we say that he'd be at home) *these are not* – says he – because, namely, notionality and speech don't have any commonality with non-being, for then, error doesn't exist as soon as such commonality is denied. It's for this reason that now, first off, we'd have to properly and   *[e2]* thoroughly pursue our research into speech, opinion and notionality, what this is, so that if it becomes evident that we also perceive their commonality with that which is not and, then, if we do perceive this so we point out error as it is and so, having shown this, right away we'll securely bind the sophist up within it – but, then, if he manages to work his way out of this, well, then we'll have to let him be on this count and go about seeking for him beneath some other classification.

Theae: Obviously, o Stranger, what was said at the beginning about the sophist is quite true: that this breed is one that is hard to catch. For then, one does see this, how like a chameleon he's always changing his color at every juncture and how there's no end to his ploys: that for every weedbed within which he hides himself, still, he's always ready with another, which then, necessarily, we have to overcome it as well if we are ever to approach him himself. For now, hardly have we managed to break through the difficulties of non-being, what he threw up before us as if it wouldn't be, so already he's come up with something else that blocks our way, and so now we have to display this, that falsity exists in speech and in notionality, and after this perhaps there will be yet something else, and then something else yet again, and it seems that we'll never get to the end of it.   *[261b3]*

Strng: One's good courage must never waver, o Theaetetus, even though progress is always only to be obtained with small steps. For then, he who already loses his courage in such an instance as this, what shall he do in other cases, those in which nothing at all is accomplished, or when he may even well have to beat a retreat? There's more here than meets the eye, as the saying goes, and Troy wasn't taken either on the first day, nor without many travails. But now, my virtuous Theaetetus, if only that which you say shall fortuitously find its terminus, then for sure we shall have scaled the strongest of the walls and the others shall all be easier and of a lesser height.

Theae: That's a good word.   *<45.~261cd]*

Strng: Thus, as I was saying – let's now take up speech and notionality so that thereby we'll be that much more able to calculate without being deceived – whether they extend as far as non-being or whether both are true in all ways and neither of them is ever false.

Theae: Right.

Strng: Then tallyho: just as earlier on when we clarified   *[d]* ourselves about the concepts and letters, even so too let's observe the words – because in this manner what we are now seeking shall most probably show itself.

Theae: In respect to what, actually, should we be attentive as regards words?

Strng: Whether all of them may be melded together, one to the other, or none of them, or that a few want this but others do not.

Theae: But that's obvious: a few want to and others don't.

Strng: You're opining this perhaps so: that those that also inform you about something when they are spoken out one after the other, these may be melded together; but those which don't mean anything when they are placed together, melding these together doesn't   *[e]* work out.

Theae: How do you mean this, really?

Strng: So as I believed that you yourself would have thought it as you agreed with me. There exists for us, namely, a twofold manner in which we express information about being through our voices.

Theae: How's that?

Strng: The one of them is naming or using substantiatives, the other is action words.

Theae: Describe them both for me.   *[262a]*

Strng: Expressing information that is directed on activities, these we name action words, or verbs.

Theae: Yes.

Strng: But the tokens which speech places along beside what these former activities accomplish, these are the substantiatives.

Theae: Indeed, that's obvious.

Strng: And isn't this true – from substantiatives alone that are spoken out one after the other, from these a speech or even a sentence never comes into being; and even so little too from action words that shall be spoken without any substantiatives?

Theae: I didn't understand that.

Strng: Thus, you obviously had something else in mind when *[b]* you agreed with me just a bit ago. For it's even this that I wanted to say, that from these, just so, one after the other, no speech shall come into being.

Theae: How so?

Strng: Something like – go, run, sleep; and so too with the other action words that signify other activities; and even if one would say them all one after another, still, one wouldn't bring about a speech, nothing would come from this.

Theae: And really – how should one do so!

Strng: And it's even so, once again, if one shall say: Lion, deer, horse – and whatever else for denominations, that which tends to be named for accomplishing activities, also from this list one never shall be able to make a speech. For neither in this way nor in the former manner is it possible that that which is spoken out portrays: neither an activity, nor an absence of activity; neither the essence of that which is, nor the essence of that which is not – at least not until someone mixes the action words together with the substantiatives. But that's when they get melded and right away with their first nuptials a speech or a sentence comes to be; and this may well be the first and the smallest one of them all.

Theae: Just how do you mean this?

Strng: If someone says: "Man learns" – so you'd probably name this as the shortest and simplest sentence.

Theae: I do.   [d]

Strng: For then, it's through this that he informs and makes something evident – whether it be about something that is or becomes or has become or shall become; and he doesn't only name this or that but determines something as well in that he binds up the substantiatives with the action words. And this is also the reason why we can say that he's speaking and not simply naming, and then too, this is why we've bestown this entangling or knotting-together with the name: speech.

Theae: Right.   <46.~262e]

Strng: Just as the things in part are melded together and in part they are not, so too with the tokens through the medium of the voice, in part these are not melded, but those that are construct a speech.

Theae: So it is, in all ways.

Strng: Still, there's yet a wee bit more.

Theae: What's that?

Strng: That a speech, if it is, necessarily has to be a speech about something – for it's impossible for it to be about nothing.

Theae: So it is.

Strng: And it also has to be of a certain quality *{Beschaffenheit}*.

Theae: Undoubtedly.

Strng: Now, let's become quite attentive upon ourselves.

Theae: We want to do so.

Strng: I'd like to deliver a speech to you in that I bind up some subject matter with an activity through the use of substantiatives and action words, but that about which the speech pertains, this is what you should say to me.

Theae: Fine, I'll do it – as well as I'm able.   [263a]

Strng: Theaetetus is sitting. – That's not such a long speech?

Theae: No, rather very moderate.

Strng: Now, it's up to you to clarify what it is about and what it describes.

Theae: Well, obviously, it's about myself and concerns me.

Strng: Now, once more, how about this one.

Theae: Which one [essentially]? *{Was für eine?}*

Strng: The Theaetetus with whom I'm now speaking – flies.

Theae: This one too, nobody would well say anything else other than that it speaks about myself and concerns me.

Strng: And each and every speech, this is what we say, each one has some quality?

Theae: Yes. [b]

Strng: Thus, how shall we say that each of these would be qualified?

Theae: The one, indeed, is false; the other, true.

Strng: And the true one says, indeed, the actual about you, that it is?

Theae: Yes.

Strng: And the false one, something different from the actual?

Theae: Yes.

Strng: Hence, that which is not actual and what isn't, this is what it speaks out as being?

Theae: Well-nigh.

Strng: Namely being, only it's different from that which is as this relates to you. For in relation to each and every we said that there exists much that is and also much that is not.

Theae: Well obviously, indeed.

Strng: The last speech, now, which I spoke out about you was, [c] in accord with our earlier determination as regards what a speech is – first of all, as is totally necessary, one of the shortest possible.

Theae: So, at least, we did see eye to eye on this.

Strng: Then it did speak, indeed, about something.

Theae: Certainly.

Strng: And if it wasn't about you, then, certainly, it wasn't about anyone else other than you.

Theae: No, indeed.

Strng: And if it spoke of nothing, so it wouldn't have been a speech at all, totally and absolutely. For then, we have pointed this out, that this would be entirely impossible for a speech, what it is, that it should be a speech about nothing.

Theae: That's right, fully.

Strng: Shall you, thus, speak out and compose a speech from [d] the different as if it were the same, and from non-being as if it were to be being – so, such a speech, one that comes to be through the placing of action words together with the substantiatives, such shall actually and truly be a false speech.

Theae: Absolutely true.   *<47.~263]*

Strng: And how do matters stand with thoughts, opinion or notionality and with perception? – isn't it also quite clear that all of these occur as true and false within our souls.

Theae: How's that?

Strng: You'll probably see this more easily if, first off, you define and set this firmly down – what they are and how each of them differs from the rest.   *[e]*

Theae: Just go on, tell me.

Strng: Well then, thoughts and speech are the same – only the internal speech of the soul with itself, that which proceeds by itself without vocalization, this by us has become named thought.

Theae: Right.

Strng: But the expression of the former through the agency of sound issuing forth from one's mouth, this is called speech.

Theae: True.

Strng: And in speaking, indeed we know this, the following occurs.

Theae: What's that?

Strng: Affirming and denying.[212]

Theae: We know that.   *[264a]*

Strng: Now, if this occurs silently as thoughts resting within the soul, do you perhaps know of anything other to name this other than opinion.

Theae: But, how else?

Strng: But how about if something like this occurs not alone from the inside but, rather, that it is predicated by the agency of perception? – shall it be possible that there is another manner of naming this other than calling it perceiving?

Theae: No, nothing other.

Strng: Since, now, speech may possibly be true and possibly false, and as regards the rest thought has displayed itself as the internal speech of the soul with itself, and having notions or having an opinion is the consummation of thinking – and then, that which we name appearance is the unification of sense impressions with opinion, so it shall be necessary that also in regards to these sense impressions, since they all are related to speech, that from time to time a few are false.

Theae: How mightn't they not be?

---

[212] Cf. Euclid's characterization of the dialogue *Theaetetus* 143bc (p. 360); "go, run, sleep."

Strng: Now, do you see this – that false notionality and speech, these weren't such a difficult thing to find out and put on display as we feared when we expected that we might be embarking on a never-ending project and that we'd be grasping at straws when we went seeking after these?

Theae: I see it.   *<48.~264c]*

Strng: So let's not lose heart as regards the rest, rather after having seen how speech, notionality, opinion and perception have shown themselves, so let's also remember our earlier divisions.

Theae: Yes – but which ones?

Strng: We separated within image making the two sorts: the art of replication and the imagery of deceit.

Theae: Yes.

Strng: And as regards the sophist we said that we were perplexed: in which of these two he should be placed.

Theae: So it was.

Strng: And during this time of perplexity when we were at such a loss, that's when we were drenched by this monster wave that blackened our horizon entirely, this proposition which is the end-all argument, that there doesn't exist any mirroring, nor images, nor any deceiving appearances whatsoever – since there never exists falsity, no where and no how.   *[d]*

Theae: Rightly said.

Strng: But, now that false speech and notionality have shown themselves as being actual, so too the following takes place: that there exist reconstructions of that which is – and, so, from out of this correlation the artistry of deceit likewise comes to be.

Theae: Yes, this does take place.

Strng: And it is even right here that the sophist belongs, this was already determined earlier on?

Theae: Yes.

Strng: So let's take this up once more and make the attempt that we divide the classification which is lying before us into two, and that we proceed along always upon the right side – the side in which the sophist finds himself, holding himself firmly within that with which he communes – until we have separated him out from everything else that he shares with the others so that finally his own unique   *[a]* nature is all that remains left and, thus, pre-eminently we shall display this for ourselves, but, then too, likewise for those whose nature tends toward such a methodology, that these might relate to what it is that we're doing, [that we didn't go fishing for nothing.]

Theae: Right.

Strng: Way back, then, we started off with the separation of all of the arts into two: the arts of bringing forth and the arts of acquisition.
Theae: Yes.
Strng: And back then the sophist appeared to us as a pursuer, a verbal combatant and, then too, as someone involved in commerce – and there were a few other such arts, all of which belong beneath the arts of acquisition.
Theae: Quite.
Strng: Since, now, the art of image making has taken him in, so first off we'd have to divide the art of bringing forth into two. For then, image making, indeed, is bringing something forth, namely images – this is what we say – but not the images of the things themselves. Isn't this true?
Theae: In all ways.
Strng: Firstly, then, there should be two parts of bringing forth.
Theae: Essentially, which ones?
Strng: One that is divine, and one human.
Theae: I still don't understand this.   <49.~265]
Strng: Bringing forth – this, indeed, is what we said – if we recollect ourselves as to where our speech began: each and every power that is the cause that that which earlier on was not, that this becomes – such is creation.
Theae: I remember.
Strng: Now, all mortal creatures and all of the plants that grow up upon the earth sprouting out from seeds and from various roots, and, then too, all of the material bodies in whatever form they might   [c] be – liquid, solid or gas – should we say that all of this has become through anything other than God's divine creation, since previously it didn't have any being? – or should we fall back upon using the vulgar doctrines and such a mode of speaking?
Theae: To what do you refer?
Strng: That we say that nature generates all of this due to the power of some cause that is active without thought? Or is it with reason and divinely emanating from God's knowledge and foresight?
Theae: Indeed, I myself have often turned myself this way and that, perhaps due to my youth, from one of these notions to the other... but now, as I'm looking at you and as I suspect that you believe that this comes to be through divine agency, so I'll also take up this same position.
Strng: Very good, o Theaetetus, and certainly if I were to hold you as being someone who might think otherwise in the future, so then we would take this up right away in our speech, that I might bring you to agree as one with me on this through compelling proofs. But since I

can perceive this already in your nature, that it is one that   *[e]*
already without any such persuasion tends in this direction all on its
own – thither where you confess as being drawn – so I'll leave this be,
for it would only be wasting our time. So then, I set this down as our
firm postulation: what mankind ascribes to nature, all of this has
been brought forth through divine agency and is God's work of art;
but what arises out of this through man's agency, this is humanly
created; and so, in accord to this clarification there exists two sorts of
the art of bringing forth, the one human and the other divine.
Theae: Right.
Strng: Now, make an incision of these once more and cut the two
right down the middle.
Theae: How's that?
Strng: As if previously you had cut the entirety of the art of   *[266a]*
bringing forth from West to East, and now you make your incision
from North to South.
Theae: Verily, so be it.
Strng: Thus, all together four parts of the same come to be through
this: two human that are by us and two godly spheres that are divine.
Theae: Yes.
Strng: From this aforementioned fourfold division the first member
of each of the previous parts is the real portion of creation, but both
of the remaining parts could most aptly be called the imaginative, and
in this manner the entire art of bringing forth is once again separated
into two parts.   *<50.~266b]*
Theae: Just tell me again – how each of these actually would be.
Strng: We and the other animals and that which underlies
everything that grows, fire and water and whatever belongs here – we
are, as we know, all together God's creation, and each and every itself
has been brought forth. Or how?
Theae: Nothing other.
Strng: Every bit of this, now, is accompanied by images that are not
the matters themselves, but these also have come to be through divine
arrangement.
Theae: What, essentially?
Strng: That which appears in dreams and also what we call the
natural illusions of our waking state – like the shadows that flicker
through all of the dark places despite the bright sunlight, and seeing
double if the reflections produced by the striking of some unique   *[c]*
rays of light come together in a strange way being reflected upon
shiny or smooth surfaces, all of this results in images being produced,
something that contradicts the usual perspective, the way that the
senses normally perceive things.

Theae: These, then, would be the twofold workings of divine creation, the matters themselves and the images that accompany them.

Strng: And our own arts, shall we not say that the house itself is brought into existence by the various building professions – but, then, that the art of draftsmanship brings forth yet another [the blueprint] which is equivalent and may be compared to a human dream that has been accomplished for those who are awake.

Theae: That's totally certain. *[d]*

Strng: And shall we not also present in all the others two sorts, that our art of bringing forth creates works in a twofold manner: the one being the matter itself through its real creation and, then, the image through imitation.

Theae: Now I understand this better and likewise postulate the two types of bringing forth in this twofold manner: the one division being that between the divine and the human, and then the other being this division between the matters themselves and this other one through which something comes to be which is similar. *<51.~266e]*

Strng: From the art of image making, now, we want to recollect ourselves upon this, that the one sort occupied itself with replications, but the other should be occupied with this imagery of deceit – if then, namely, that which is false actually is to be false and would have been shown as being so by its very nature.

Theae: So it was.

Strng: But now it has been shown why we even have tallied these two sorts – and that we have done so without any strife or controversy.

Theae: Yes. *[267a]*

Strng: In the imagery of deceit, now, we'll once again make a division into two.

Theae: How's that?

Strng: The one of them uses tools but in the other, whoever commits himself to this, so he makes a tool out of himself.

Theae: How do you mean this?

Strng: I mean that if someone would make his own voice seem to be exactly like yours or if he should disguise himself so as to appear as being you, such a disguising of one's body, so this portion of the imagery of deceit is usually called impersonating.

Theae: Yes.

Strng: We want, then, to separate this off from the whole and name it the art of impersonation, and that we put aside all of the rest *[b]* – so that we make ourselves comfortable and just deal with this portion, and that we'll leave all the rest for somebody else, that he gather it all together into one and predicate it with whatever name is apt.

Theae: Fine, so this part is split off and the other parts are relinquished.

Strng: But this part too, o Theaetetus, it's worthwhile that we also look upon it as twofold. Watch closely, why this is so.

Theae: Just tell me.

Strng: Those who are impersonating do this in part in that they recognize what it is that they are imitating, and in part without any such recognition. And, essentially, what could possibly make a greater difference that one might postulate than that between awareness and ignorance?

Theae: None, certainly.

Strng: The example used previously, now, this was the impersonation that is done knowingly. For then, only he who is able to recognize you and your Gestalt, only he can impersonate you.

Theae: Doubtless. [c]

Strng: But how about the Gestalt of righteousness and, utterly, of the entirety of virtue? Doesn't there exist, indeed, very many who actually are not aware of this, what it is, that rather they just have an approximate notion; but then, all the same, they do take particular pains that they comport themselves as if this subsisted within themselves so that they appear to be virtuous in that, as much as they are able, they impersonate this, and do so both in their actions as well as in their speech?

Theae: Very many, indeed.

Strng: And do, perhaps, all of these fail in this, that they seem to be righteous – since, indeed, by no means are they? – or isn't it rather totally the opposite?

Theae: Totally and absolutely.

Strng: These impersonators, thus, shall have to be clarified as being different than the others, from those who knowingly impersonate, as these lack this knowledge.

Theae: Yes. <52.~267d]

Strng: Thus, from where does one appropriate for each of these a name that is apt? – or isn't it obvious that this is hard to find because in respect to the divisions of this classification into types our forefathers had an ancient, unconscious foundation {Grund} so that nobody would even attempt to make such a division – and it's because of this that I can't easily come up with a name for this. All the same, even if it should be rather impudent and audacious of me to say it, we'd want for the sake of the differentiation that we call the former, those who operate on a mere notion, this we shall call a conceited impersonation; but then, if it is done with cognition, this, then, we'd call it an informed impersonation.

Theae: So be it.

Strng: Thus, it's with the former that we would be concerned. For the sophist didn't fall beneath the rubric of those who know but he was amongst the pretenders.

Theae: Very much so.

Strng: The conceited impersonator, thus, let's examine him like an iron bar – whether he's all of a piece or if there's yet some telltale trace that shows itself, that he's been forged and struck together from out of two elements.

Theae: Yes, we want to do this.

Strng: And these can be shown right visibly. The one, namely, is noble and really believes that he does know that of which   *[268a]* he only has a notion. But the behavior of the other one – because he turns himself so excessively in his speeches, first this way and then that way – shows that he himself is motivated by an extreme suspiciousness and by a malicious guile, that he too doesn't know what he wants to put on airs before the others, as if he would know it.

Theae: Certainly, there exist some of both these types, just as you describe them.

Strng: Do we want, then, that we postulate the one sort as the simple-minded impersonator, but the other as one who has lost himself and is out of sorts.

Theae: That fits the bill.

Strng: And does there only exist one sort of this type, or two?

Theae: Well, what do you see?

Strng: I see it already and it appears to me, indeed, as being two: the one who does so openly and likes to lose himself in long-winded speeches before the populace; but then the other who goes about amongst small groups and in pithy sentences he forces those who converse with him, that they contradict themselves.

Theae: What you say is absolutely right.

Strng: Who do we want to demonstrate that he would be, this long-winded one? The statesman or the crowd-pleaser?

Theae: The crowd-pleaser.

Strng: And how do we want that we name the other: as a wise man or a sophist?

Theae: Well, it's impossible to call him wise – since we stipulated *[c]* that he's bereft of knowledge; but since he's an impersonator of the wise so he'd have to retain something from this in his designation and now I do understand this very well that we'd have to designate this type just as formerly indicated: that he is in all ways the true and the legitimate sophist.

Strng: Do we now want, like before, that we bind his name up in a secure knit and intertwine all of this from start to finish?

Theae: In all ways.

Strng: Hence, as an imitator in that art which brings one into contradiction and within the impersonating portion of conceitedness that through a deceitful manner in the constructive arts, and certainly not of divine origin, rather as all-too-human, and pretending to have expertise in myriads of artistic and professional matters through the conjuring up of wondrous speeches [right out of the thin air] – so have we separated him out: and whoever describes his genealogy and blood-line in accordance to such a methodology as is found here, he shall, as it seems, speak with the greatest propriety.

Theae: In all ways, certainly.

****

Printed in the United States
27078LVS00001B/121

9 781418 449766